WARRIOR

WARRIOR

Donald E. McQuinn

A Del Rey Book
Ballantine Books · New York

A Del Rey Book
Published by Ballantine Books

Copyright © 1990 by Donald E. McQuinn
Map copyright © 1990 by Random House, Inc.

Library of Congress Catalog Card Number: 89-92606

ISBN: 0-345-36504-6

Manufactured in the United States of America

First Edition: November 1990

10 9 8 7 6 5 4 3 2 1

To the best of us—Tim, Conn, and Mark,
with love.

WARRIOR

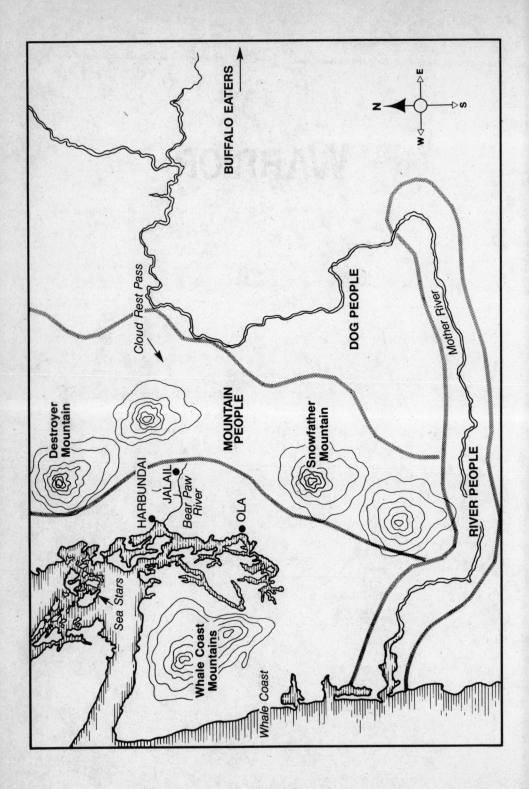

PROLOGUE

The sleeping child stirred fitfully, one small hand reaching out from under the fur blanket as if she would hold off the things scratching, scuffling, whispering across the darkness.

Little by little the sounds grew louder, and at every gradual increase they seemed to spread, so that by the time she was fully awake, it was impossible for her to say exactly where any came from. For several long, heart-thudding moments, she listened.

Even the steady breathing of her parents on their bed against the opposite wall of the hut failed to comfort her, and the assorted sniffs and sighs of her four brothers and sisters were useless.

She'd had bad dreams before. When she cried out, everyone was angry. She bit her lip and told herself she had to be brave.

But this was no dream. The things outside—by now she was certain there was more than one—were real. The four walls that had always been her warm, safe, home-place suddenly seemed flimsy and vulnerable. Something huge and terrible stalked them, crouching to leap and rip them apart.

The image broke her nerve. She called her mother. Instead of a concerned mumble, reassuring in its waking drowsiness, coarse shouts answered from outside. Her mother was up and scrambling across to the children before her father could reach the door. Even as she was being lifted out of bed, the girl watched him, excited and very afraid, but aware. She knew he was reaching outside for the axe he kept by the chopping block.

The light of flames from a burning thatch roof played across his bare back.

Then he was coming back, shouting, holding the axe in front of him with one hand. The other hung at an angle, moving in pained jerks, the way flying ducks flopped out of the sky when a hunter's throwing stick hit them.

Two men lunged at him with swords. One carried a torch. The light flickered across his horrible painted face. He shrieked and stumbled away as her father swung his axe. The other plunged his sword into her father.

She saw no more for a while after that, because her mother dropped her, and it hurt. She cried then. When she pushed herself to a kneeling position and opened her eyes again, her mother was lying down, making a sound she'd

never heard before. Worse than that was the wet stain on her chest that grew
and grew. The girl knew it was blood, because she'd seen many animals
killed. It had never occurred to her that the same thing could happen to her
mother. The shock of the idea stopped her tears.

A hand reached for her, and she jerked away with the instinctive quickness
of a cat. Before the hand could come at her again, she was between the
blood-spattered legs and out the door. A loud shout followed her, but not
the man. Then she heard the screams of her brothers and sisters.

Sick with fear, she knew only that she had to be with her family.

She ran back into the hut and threw herself at the man's legs from behind.
As she did, she saw the rest of the children on the floor. They neither moved
nor cried. Something deep within her told her they never would. Her father
groaned. Her mother strained to get up.

She bit the man as hard as she could.

He yelled and grabbed her arm and heaved her high in the air, all the way
up, level with his terrifying, painted scowl. Looking into his eyes, the only
thing she saw was her own face, reflected so small she looked like a bug.
When he raised his sword, it gleamed terribly, red and steel together in the
firelight of the burning hut.

Another man came in, roaring, and grabbed the sword at the handle. The
swordsman lowered her.

She thought he was going to give her back to her mother, and as soon as
her feet touched the pounded earth of the floor, she tried to go to her. The
man's grip was unbreakable.

Her mother rose on one elbow, the other hand clawing the air in the effort
to reach her child. She called her name, and then fell back.

The girl was very disappointed by that, and angered, because she was
trying as hard as she could to get away from the awful, awful man, and her
mother wasn't helping. She started to cry again.

And then her mother tried to speak once more. She failed. Instead, she
made a sound that pierced the girl with a spike of ice. It was a different thing,
a hoarse sigh that knew no other breath would follow.

The child intuitively knew what the sound was. She stretched her own
mouth until it hurt and she screamed and screamed, and nothing came.

Rough, hard hands dragged her outside. The whole village was aflame,
making the night into day. Unresisting, the girl was jerked off her feet once
more, tumbled into a basket strapped to the side of a mule. There were three
other children in the basket with her, wild, hysterical with despair. The girl
was numb, almost unaware of them. Nor was she troubled, then, by the
coarse weave of the basket, so open that tiny arms and legs slipped through
the gaps to chafe on the rough slats. She barely noticed as someone stuffed

in yet another child and lashed down the top on their cell.

A whip cracked. The mule humped and started forward. The girl looked back at the burning village. All the huts were on fire, collapsing, fountaining sparks high in the air to be swallowed by smoke and darkness.

She couldn't tell which one was hers.

BOOK I

Escape to Challenge

CHAPTER 1

A silver blade of dawn slit the gray cloud mass to create a horizon. Gan shivered, pressing his body flatter against the graveled hilltop. The searching light seemed to bring on greater cold, as if it helped the wind find gaps in his furs to sneak through and dull his mind.

The thought brought on a quick thrill of increased awareness.

Nightwatchers held the camp in their hands. It was a sacred trust.

Some resented the loneliness and discomfort of Nightwatch. He was used to being alone. Long ago, he'd convinced himself it gave him time to think, to observe. More than that, he secretly relished the responsibility and the skin-prickling sense of danger when he thought of the hostile world waiting for his smallest mistake.

The first curve of the rising sun bloodied the new day, and Gan lifted his torso to make the Three-sign in the prescribed manner of his clan, right hand first touching his forehead, then to left and right of his heart. Silently, he mouthed the required words. "I greet you, the One Who Is Two, and the Father, One in All."

He inched back from the crest, still prone. One hand carried his bow, the other assured the belt-slung sword made no noise. Once downhill, he lowered the weapons, stood up, and peeled off the fur jacket and trousers. He stretched luxuriously.

He was tall, fair-haired, lean rather than slender, with long muscles stretched across heavy bones. It was a youthful body at the edge of powerful manhood. Drawing the sword from its wooden scabbard, he began a series of limbering movements. The weapon was called a murdat. It was two feet long, including the grip with its hand-protecting metal shield. The blade widened gradually from the tip along its length like an elongated spear head, ending with a dramatic flare at the butt. It slashed or stabbed with equal deadliness.

Lost in contemplation, he was caught unaware by the sound of another presence approaching the hillcrest from the far side. Instantly, he charged.

A shaggy, brindled gray hound peered down at him, fangs bared in what could have been laughter. Yellow eyes gleamed. "Raggar!" Gan lowered the blade, chagrined. "You surprised me, boy."

The huge dog listened impassively, red tongue lolling. Gan realized it was alone. "Where are the others? Is someone coming?"

Raggar shifted his weight from one foreleg to the other, impatient. Gan hurriedly replaced his outer clothing and fell in behind the animal. They moved at a trot, the only sound the whisper of the winter-struck grass that came to the dog's shoulder and the top of Gan's thighs. A few patches of snow gleamed in shaded hollows. Sullen clouds warned winter could still strike. Nevertheless, tender green shoots struggled for sunlight, tinting the rolling land with an eager glow.

Raggar slowed, testing the air, then struck off to the right.

Gan fitted an arrow to his bow and followed, bent forward until he was not much taller than his dog. From a distance, anyone seeing his furs move through the growth could easily mistake him for one of the fearless great bears that prowled the grasslands.

They finished the climb to the top of a knoll in a crawl, side by side. A tan dog almost as large as Raggar lay there. It acknowledged them with a quick look, then resumed watching a hooded, cloaked figure on horseback in the distance.

"Good girl, Rissa," Gan said, patting her head. The heavy tail thumped once.

The horse was small, ill-favored. It picked its way along in nervous twitch-es. Gan sneered. The Horse Chief would never tolerate such an animal.

From under his blouse Gan drew a silver whistle on a leather thong and put it between his teeth. When the rider was within fifteen yards, he rose, bow and arrow in hand. The rider reined in sharply. The horse reared, snorting and rolling its eyes. The whistle's silent commands sent Raggar and Rissa running to positions at the front and flanks of the intruder. Two more dogs appeared in the distance, running flat out. They stopped at a discreet range to bar retreat.

The rider was very good. Even while fighting to control his mount, he swung in the saddle to mark the approach of the other two dogs. Once he had his horse under control, he advanced to greet Gan with both hands over his head, forefingers and thumbs forming a circle in the sun picture of peace. A heavy ring and gold bracelet glinted boldly.

When the rider was a few feet away, Gan whistled again. The dogs moved closer. "Who are you?" he demanded.

The rider threw back the hood. Shining black shoulder-length hair cas-caded free to frame the fine-boned features of the most beautiful woman he'd ever seen. He caught his breath while eyes the color of summer's hottest sky sought his, challenging. Her voice was husky. She said, "I am a War Healer. I am a Rose Priestess and my name is Sylah. I seek the camp of the Dog People."

Her haughty pride reminded him he was staring like a dolt. He straightened. "We have our own Healers. And we are not at war, so need no others. Why should we welcome you?"

The Rose Priestess smiled. Despite her beauty, it was not a completely pleasant expression. "Because Dog People never turn away a hungry traveler. Because I have news and gossip to entertain your Elders, who would discipline a young Nightwatcher who sent me away unheard. But mostly because I bring a message from the place you call the Enemy Mountains."

The bow jerked threateningly. "From the Devils!"

Her smile had been disturbing, like ice stilling a singing stream, but hearing the wildness of her laughter was worse. She said, "I come with their warning." Suddenly she gestured at Gan's weapon. "Put that away. You know I'm not to be harmed. Every hand in every tribe that prays to the One in All will be at your throat." She waited, imperious, until he quivered the arrow, then went on. "I come from the kingdom of Ola on a mission for Church and my king. On the way, I have lived with the Mountain People, those you call Devils. The summer will bring them down from the mountains."

She paused to swallow, and when she spoke again she was pale. "War is coming to you, as never before. The Devils mean to destroy you, to kill all who resist and carry those who survive back to the mountains for their amusement. Your living will curse your dead for their good fortune even as they watch the coyotes and magpies fight over the bodies."

CHAPTER 2

The soft noises of the cave slipped through the darkness, hinting at secrets they wished to share. There were lights, as well, hundreds of them in rows, emerald dots of a cold smoldering.

One blinked. For a few seconds it was as if it had never been, and then it came on for a brief while and went out again.

It flickered spasmodically, with no rhythm, no pattern, but in the complete blackness of the place there was a desperate, struggling quality to its efforts.

Then it was gone.

Another sound entered the easy constancy of the other noises. The new one was no louder, although it seemed so because it overrode everything else. High-pitched, its two notes exactly an octave apart, it called.

In that place that knew no time, the sound went on monotonously until, abruptly, it stilled.

Something different came to life in the blackness, something that hissed and moved with careful stealth. Its progress was marked by occasional grating, as even its measured course discovered litter to crush. More, it carried a single, dull red light that cast about continually, seeking. It stopped at the place where the green light had been. Clicks and hard, gnashing noises marked invisible activity. The hissing resumed. The thing retreated, cautious as before.

A smell lingered behind it, a weight on the air rather than a definable substance. It was a thing that touched deeper than senses.

A man who breathed there would have known what it was. He would have felt his skin tighten, would have braced mind and body against the ice-chill that clutched his spine. He would have fled with his knowledge.

Death walked that place.

CHAPTER 3

Gan and Rose Priestess Sylah breasted Tiger Rocks Plateau two miles from camp, and he called a halt. She turned from her position a few paces ahead to watch as he called Rissa. The dog loped through the tall grass. Diamond glints of frost sprayed around her, starred her coat. Gan tugged her ear, smiling, then took some string from a belt pouch and secured it to her collar, leaving one end hanging longer than the other. He tied two knots in the longer one and a single, more complex knot at the end of the shorter. Finished, he ordered, "The Watch tent. Rissa, go!"

The Priestess turned a questioning half smile on him, and Gan was certain he saw a touch of warmth behind the unwavering superiority. Unreasonably, it made him feel shy. His tongue stumbled over his explanation. "Rissa's got pups. That's why I sent her ahead."

"You sent the string message report so they can prepare to welcome me? How long before we arrive? Where can I wash and prepare?"

Gan's face warmed. "I said I bring a prisoner."

"Prisoner?" Her quick aggressive posture alerted the dogs. She failed to notice them crouch. The horse did, however, and jittered as she added, "When I speak to your Chiefs—" She broke off, heeling the horse forward. "I told you I'm a War Healer. I'll enjoy watching you apologize."

"Then know me; Gan Moondark, son of Col, a Nightwatcher of the North Clan."

"Col Moondark? War Chief?"

"Yes." Gan resisted asking what more she knew of his father. He wanted to speak of Col Moondark's many honors, and those of all the North Clan, because this was a most irritating woman who badly needed educating. He clenched his jaws, remembering his father's constant admonition to trade on no reputation but his own.

He wished he had one.

White, even teeth worried at the woman's lower lip. When she swiveled back to the front, her cape made an audible swish. The touchy little horse hopped into a trot. Raggar growled at the quick move, and the horse shied. The Priestess wrestled it under control, determinedly giving no sign of concern. Raggar looked to Gan, who hid a reluctant admiration for her as he hand-signaled the dogs to bracket her in a moving square.

Jogging at her side, he felt her stare. He looked up into hard blue eyes studying him with the routine condescension of one who rides toward one on foot. She said, "You have no mount. Don't they trust you with one of the Dog People's fabled horses?"

Gan ran easily. It was a soft pace, as natural to him as walking, and he could have gone much faster for a full day. He said, "Horses draw tigers and the young wolves." He gestured behind him, checking their back trail as a matter of course.

There was movement two hills away, something furtive. Calling to the Priestess to stop, Gan whistled at the dogs. A male nearly Raggar's size trotted forward, tail wagging. Gan pointed. "Kammar, search," he said.

Obediently, Kammar ambled back the way they'd come. Responding to the silent whistle, he angled off to his right. Within seconds he was hidden by the brush. Gan drew an arrow from his quiver.

The Priestess said, "You hunt? You have a visitor to escort!"

He continued to watch the distance. "I'm not hunting, and you're a prisoner, not a visitor." He motioned for the woman to come with him to the tumble of huge rocks that gave the place its name. Hidden among them, he made her dismount and sit before he took up a watching position.

She scoffed. "There's no one back there, and if there is, what do you think you can do about it?"

"Find out who they are, first."

"A wildcow. An antelope. If it's people, it's wandering Peddlers. Are the Dog People so weak they fear tribeless scum?"

He waited until the back of his neck no longer burned. "We survive because we're watchful."

Kammar barked in the distance. The other dogs, lying in the grass, were on their feet instantly.

The sound confirmed his fears. He'd committed a grave error by assuming the woman rode alone, and compounded it by carelessly allowing whoever followed her to trail him. His dilemma was simply stated: run or fight. Even if he released his fastest dog, it would only weaken his team. A large party could override him and still strike before the tribe was prepared. He decided quickly. Boldness would have to answer for the mistake.

He gestured. "Raggar. Scar. Flanks." He looked to the woman. "Kammar's coming in. He's excited. Stay hidden. If you really are a War Healer, you're holy, so you have nothing to fear. I don't want the people coming to see you and start looking for me."

Kammar appeared in the draw below them, running hard. He stopped in front of Gan, then looked back over his shoulder and growled.

Gan tested his bow.

"Don't be a fool." The Priestess confronted him, scathing. "If it's a raiding party, they'll kill you."

"Your confidence inspires. Stay where you are."

He ran to a minor spur leading off the plateau. It gave a clear view of all slopes leading to their nearly flat locale, as well as the surrounding draws. He kept Kammar nearby, sending the tan female, Scar, to the far side of the high ground and Raggar to hide in the brush lining the creek in the valley.

A cock pheasant flushed hysterically around the bend of the draw on Scar's side. Whoever came was avoiding the most likely route, probably extra cautious because of Kammar's earlier bark. When the first horseman appeared, Gan's stomach twisted.

The Devil warrior's death paint leaped across space at him; stark white face, huge black circles for eyes. Simulated trails of blood ran from a red-painted maw to the chin.

Four of them rode in diamond formation, rigged for combat in padded leather trousers and the woven willow and buffalo-hide armor jackets they called barmals. The horses wore hard leather skirts to deflect arrows as well as protect against attacking dogs. Each warrior had a short recurved bow dangling from the pommel horn. A sheathed extra-long sword, the deadly sodal, was lashed to the horseman's peg fixed to the rear of each saddle.

Gan despised the peg. By hooking a leg around it, or catching it with a heel, a man rode on the side of his horse, shielding himself with the animal's body.

It was a discouragingly effective technique, but a thing of no honor.

He crouched, heartbeats jarring his bones. They passed him on their way up the hill. The formation closed up as the lead man crested the top. It was the tactical error Gan had hoped for, bunching them nicely. He rose from the grass behind them, no more than ten yards from the drag man, as the rear member of the diamond was called.

"Don't move!" he bellowed, praying it would keep his voice from cracking. It did, and the four froze. He said, "Point man! Face down on the ground, hands on head." Stiffly, the man dismounted. He was large, wide across the shoulders. The black expanse of the barmal across his back seemed as big to Gan as a ceremonial feast kettle.

"Right flanker," Gan said. "You next. *Don't turn!*" He had no desire for them to know exactly where he stood or that he was young and alone. As a precaution, he sidled to his left.

And saved his life.

An arrow sizzled past his right shoulder and thumped into the ground. The sound of it was still in his ears when screams and growls erupted from the other hill as Raggar savaged the man who shot at his master.

Seeing the drag man leap in his stirrups, Gan released his first arrow without pause. He was amazed that there was a part of his mind still calm enough to note the delicate flick of the bright feathers when the shaft passed through the rider's neck.

The flanker riding on the left turned as Gan's second arrow punched through his right bicep and into his rib cage. He spurred his horse convulsively, and the animal bolted, throwing him off in a whirling arc.

The right flanker leaped onto his mount, turning its side to Gan, leg over the horseman's peg. With his sodal, he held off Scar while the point man scrambled to his feet and swung back aboard his own horse. Again and again Scar launched herself at them, only to be turned aside by the leather skirt. When the huge point man's horse stumbled, she leaped instantly, her forequarters stretching across the saddle. Fangs ripped at the man's restraining leg. Slashing her, he yelled and fell free. She dropped in a sprawl, great jaws clashing as she snapped at the air in agony.

Kammar closed like a thunderbolt just as it appeared the man might regain his mount yet again. Instead, he took the dog's full charge in the chest, sprawling backward.

The last mounted man rode to help. Gan's desperate arrow skipped harmlessly off the leather skirt, and he cried out involuntarily as the sodal glittered out in front of the galloping animal like a searching steel tongue.

They both underestimated the strength of the largest rider. Somehow he managed to get his hands under Kammar's forelegs at the shoulder and heave. The dog flew through the air, and the man sat upright. He was just in time to catch his companion's blade in his chest. The rider jerked it away, but it was far too late.

The wounded man got to his feet so quickly it was as though nothing had happened. Unbelieving eyes stared at his ripped, bloody barmal. He fell as if arguing with his dying, first to one knee, then to both, and finally sprawled on his face.

Kammar gathered himself to go after the last rider, and from the corner of his eye Gan saw Raggar headed the same way. The smaller male wasn't moving well, so when the distant rider shouted, Gan whistled the dogs to a halt.

"A talk!" the man called.

Gan whistled again, and the dogs dropped out of sight in the grass. He breathed deeply. "Say what you want."

The man held out his sodal, the blade on the palms of his hands in the nonaggression gesture of his people. He looked much smaller now. Still, he bristled with malice as he rode closer. His voice was in keeping with the look of him, hard and tight.

"I am Fox Eleven, a Manhunter of the Mountain People. I'll recognize your track when I see it again, boy."

"I am Gan. I know you, Fox."

"I know you, Gan. I mean to take you. I'll wear the hides of your dogs."

"So your friends thought. My dogs will eat your guts."

Fox spat before replacing his sodal and galloping away.

Priestess Sylah hurried up while Gan stood watching him go. "You're not injured?"

"No. I don't think so. It happened so fast—"

"It's not over. You have an enemy. I lived among them, and I know Fox means what he said."

Gan swallowed. It was no time to have his voice reveal the screech of fear echoing in his head. He drew his shortknife from its sheath, then knelt and severed the first joint of the drag man's little finger. He was on his way to the point man when the woman spoke. "A warrior's body is his tribute to his tribe. I was told Dog People mutilate the dead. I called it a lie."

"We take one finger joint, the smallest, as trophy, and only from those who die by our hand." He paused. "This is the one Fox Eleven killed. I'm not sure I should claim him."

She made a harsh sound and turned away. Defensively, Gan said, "It's as proper as claiming the dogs' kills. And before you choke on your concern for these Devils, think back on what you saw when you lived with them. We don't hunt for heads. We don't make musical instruments from men's bones, either. One finger, for trophy; no more."

"A fine distinction."

"Fine enough. I have to find the other man hereabouts, then Raggar's kill. Come."

She swirled her cape around her. "I wish to refresh myself at the stream before we enter your camp."

"When I'm done. You're still my prisoner."

Chin raised, eyes flashing, she said, "I give my word to make no escape."

"Accepted."

"There! How easily tricked you are."

"I'm taking my first bones from men who thought so, Priestess."

"First? I thought—" She checked, then was almost apologetic. "You seemed so sure."

He was glad his back was to her. He looked at Scar's body and the Devils, their death paint smeared, flies already jostling at the edges of blood spills darkening in the sun. He heard himself say, "There were several bad guesses this morning." He listened to her leave before getting on with his work.

When he returned from the other hill, she was just straightening beside the stream in the draw. Respecting her privacy, he drew away, and so it was that she approached from behind him and he failed to see her. Otherwise, she would never have caught him sitting with Scar's head cradled in his lap. Sylah noted the empty waterskin on the ground. He'd washed Scar clean. She could have been resting, enjoying his gentle stroking of her wiry coat. Tears streaked his cheeks.

By the same token, when she silently backed away, he failed to see her tight-lipped blend of sympathy and pain. Neither did he catch the force of will that quickly erased all expression, leaving flat inscrutability in its place. He never heard her whisper, "Fox, you bloodthirsty idiot, you could have ruined *everything*. I hope you live long enough for me to see you pay for it."

CHAPTER 4

Kammar, released with another string message, alerted everyone. Gan and the Priestess were still a mile from the camp when they were intercepted by the first boys galloping out to them. The youngsters whooped and showed off their most daring horsemanship, their brightly colored finery brave in the early sunshine. The horses pranced exuberantly. Snorting, high-stepping, they reveled in their strength as clearly as the boys.

Sylah was intrigued by their equipment. Gan was glad to explain. The saddles were lightweight affairs, clearly designed for mounted fighting, although they were equally effective for working herds. They featured swelling projections on the forward edge that reminded her of mumps. He said they were to protect the upper legs as well as offer a purchase in hard turns. A leather loop hanging from each projection was there so a warrior could hang on and trot alongside. The horse lent speed to the runner without having to carry his weight. Gan went on to point out that each saddle also came with a rear-mounted leather bag. Today they were empty and rolled up. When needed, they could carry enough equipment to sustain an individual for weeks; every male of twelve years and older was required to maintain a kit in his tent that included everything from a complete change of clothes to a needle and thread. It was always ready.

She remarked—critically, Gan thought—on the smaller murdats and bows the boys carried. He solemnly assured her that Dog warriors came in all sizes and ages, enjoying her sniff of disapproval.

Gan called to one of the first arrivals, telling him of the fallen Scar and the prospect of Devil horses to be captured. The boy sobered immediately and yelled to others. A group of ten pounded hard toward Tiger Rocks.

A second group of riders approached more slowly. They remained distant, silent, yet clearly transmitted hostility across the intervening prairie.

Bitterly, Gan watched them. For a little while he'd allowed himself to think his accomplishment in destroying a raiding party might change things. It was not to be.

Worse, there was more involved than his feelings. He chanced a sidelong glance at Sylah and drew himself erect. If he made it a point to never let

18

the tribe know his aloneness troubled him, he'd certainly never let a stranger see it. Still, the worst part of the unfriendly reception from the adults was that the Priestess was quickly going to see even more of the antagonisms tearing the tribe apart.

She couldn't have picked a worse time to come. Few people dared step on Dog lands in the best of circumstances. Not even Church had sent anyone in his lifetime. There were occasional Messengers. And Peddlers.

No one interfered with Church because her missionaries and Healers were holy, their lives inviolate. Messengers were the responsibility of all. Anyone who even interfered with one of them condemned his tribe. All other tribes and nations were required to attack on sight those who interfered until proper amends had been made.

They brought word of peace as well as war, news of disease prevention or warning of plague, and all the other information that linked men. Accordingly, all were required to protect them. Many times Gan had thought they were the only non-Dog people he could envy. Traveling when and where they wanted, they saw everything. The only unsavory aspect of their calling was a common belief that they sensed every threat in the air. It seemed that whenever there was trouble, they were present, ready to perform their function. Still, Gan had noted that they were frequently available when there was tranquillity; he believed their reputation as harbingers of disaster was exaggerated.

Peddlers only survived because they were necessary. He almost smiled, comparing the elegant, haughty Priestess to those homeless wanderers, with their slippery, fawning dealing.

Stealing another glance at her, he decided she was beautiful even when she was displeased.

She'd managed a complete change of clothes from the small bag lashed to her saddle. The raised hood of her cloak presently shrouded darting eyes alight with excitement. Gan watched her as they approached the edge of the plateau. He always looked forward to his first sight of the camp, and today was a special opportunity to share the moment. Despite the troubling presence of their escort, he slowed to enjoy it. He gestured with a sweeping arm. "The main camp of my people."

She gave a small exclamation of pleasure. Nestled in a lush valley, tents spread from hillside to hillside in concentric circles. The center featured a large mound in its own starkly cleared round. There was some sort of construction on top. When he saw her curious stare, he directed her attention far away, to the limit of the valley, where steam billowed from hot springs. He told her their tribal medicine insisted that cleanliness fought unseens. He confessed he didn't know exactly what they were, but he knew they made the sick weaker and sometimes caused the smallest wounds to infect and bring death.

For a moment she burned at the presumptuousness of it; he dared lecture a War Healer of the Iris Abbey. Once she saw his naive earnestness, she smiled inwardly, letting him go on. In fact, later, when he grinned mischievously and suggested that the primary reason for the Elders' decision to site the camp there was a desire to soak their old bones in that hot water all winter, she joined him in laughter.

In a distant draw to the left he pointed out the rough shelters of the Dog Chief's wards in their neat rows, trainers at work. Closer to the springs were the corrals where the Horse Chief oversaw the breeding and training of the animals in his charge.

She'd already seen the dogs in action. She knew of the horses; her abbess had been insistent that she treat both with the greatest respect. Gan said the horse was as important to his people as water, adding flatly that any three ordinary mounted warriors were fools to engage a Dog Nightwatch man on his trained war-horse with his four-dog team beside him.

Vivid memories of the fight at Tiger Rocks convinced her the boast was probably true.

Beyond here, he went on, were outlying settlements, miniatures of this one. There were six to the south, four more several days' ride to the east.

She reveled in the valley, emblazoned by the tents of the tribe, jewel-bright against the pastels of early spring. Dusty green sage emphasized the sharper greens and reds of the cloth. Sky-blue was repeated occasionally, intensified elsewhere to sapphire or turquoise. Splashes of yellow and orange presaged summer, when the round-shouldered hills would concentrate the sun's heat, turning the campground into an oven.

The people would be gone by then, she knew, off to the cool foothills of Snowfather Mountain.

She also knew the hundreds of rounded tents were made of blankets, the pride of the Dog women. Her abbess had subtly made her understand that the abbey would be pleased to discover the secrets of that cloth. All that was certain was that they were cotton. What wasn't known was how they were treated with the women's secret compound of beeswax and plant extracts that made them waterproof while retaining a high degree of pliability.

Gan broke into her thoughts, telling her that in winter the tents were double-hung with woolen interior blankets to retain heat. One identified families by the symbol pennon on the twelve-foot post in front of every dwelling or by the repetitions of the symbol in the blankets. In Moondark's case that was a red circle with a yellow winged vee across the top third. Family history was chronicled in other blanket designs.

He broke off his narrative abruptly at the sight of his father leaving their many-blanket tent, riding toward the edge of the camp on his finest horse.

The riders who'd paralleled Gan and Sylah broke away, riding to join the community, and it was when they arrived and dismounted to mingle with the larger group that the factionalism within the tribe crystallized. The mass of people seemed to seethe. Sharp lines cracked open to isolate a group taking shape immediately behind Col Moondark and the twelve Elders. Even at Gan's distance the latter managed to give the impression that they were close to his father but not with him.

Just as he led the Priestess onto the level floor of the valley, he saw his South Clan uncle, Faldar Yan, with the usual picked group of warriors around him. They jostled to the front row within shouting range of Col.

The Priestess dismounted to walk next to Gan and Raggar. She murmured questions he ignored in the hope she'd stop. Finally, out of patience, he snapped at her. "This is a formal matter between warriors. No chattering female *prisoner* is part of it."

A silence followed that sent small needles of apprehension prickling across his shoulder blades. When she spoke, however, there was throaty quality in her voice that sounded almost like amusement. "I didn't think you had any more surprises for me. I was mistaken. I'd never have believed your mouth is even larger than your heart. Maybe not quite so large as that stiff-legged brute beside you, but close enough."

"Brute? Raggar? He's anhyo now, a war dog who's killed. He'll be honored the rest of his life."

Their exchange ended there, as the War Chief raised his hand in greeting and they stopped in front of him. Gan surreptitiously extended a hand to touch Raggar. The dog leaned against his leg, as if reassuring his master.

Col Moondark looked older than his fifty winters. Silver hair ruffled in the wind. His face was lined and furrowed as if in imitation of the landscape he'd roamed and fought over throughout his life. Battle had marked him fiercely. A welted scar trailed from his right temple across his forehead, down across his left eye, and ended at the pronounced ridge of his cheekbone. A puckered knot of tissue on his neck spoke of a slingstone wound. Gan remembered the tribe singing the death prayer over him on that occasion, and yet again for an arrow wound now hidden under his black-and-white cowhide vest.

He wore plain deerskin trousers. His only decorative touch was a single earring. It dangled from his pierced right ear, a jade cabochon set on a leaf-thin bar of hammered gold a half-inch wide and two inches long.

Gan related the events of the morning, keeping the tale as flat and unemotional as possible. When he heard himself becoming excited, he steadied himself by remembering he'd never heard a measure of pride or warmth in his father's acknowledgment of any of his son's accomplishments.

Why should this occasion be any different?

When he stopped talking, Col looked to the woman. "I know you, Rose Priestess Sylah. You are well?"

"I know you, War Chief Col. I am unharmed, thanks to your son."

He said, "These are dangerous times. You are welcome among us, Rose Priestess," then added to Gan, "We will all mourn Scar."

"Hold, Col. I want to speak to our visitor."

Faldar Yan forged past the Elders to stand beside Col, who stared straight ahead, ignoring his brother.

Smiling broadly, Faldar introduced himself, then asked bluntly, "Why did the Devils follow you?"

She had watched him ease forward, and she'd decided he looked like a thick-witted badger. In the same moment, she warned herself to beware; the body was stubby and heavy, but the eyes said the mind was nimble as a weasel. "I know you, Faldar Yan. They were my escort, under orders to turn back last night. I think they hoped to surprise you—"

His deep voice cut across her answer. "And would have succeeded, but for good luck." He turned to the crowd. "You heard?" he shouted. "What more proof do you want? Now Devils respect us so little they risk the wrath of their own leaders to attack us. And why? Because they think the mighty Dog People—we, who once prided ourselves that we ruled wherever we rode—have grown weak and cowardly."

Goaded beyond endurance, Gan took a half step forward. Faldar Yan saw it from the corner of his eye and whirled to meet him, his expression suddenly wary. Gan said, "Would 'cowardly' be aimed at me, Uncle?"

The older man smiled, the falsity of it like grease on his chin. "Of course not." He faced the crowd. "Gan's courage is beyond question, as is the courage of all our young men. What we have lost is the will to use that courage, the ambition to remain strong."

Col backed his horse, forcing Faldar to move hastily. He said, "And the Priestess is losing needed sleep." To her, he added, "We'll talk further when you're rested."

A low, angry rumble continued to well from the crowd, punctuated by several shouts repeating the demand for respect.

Faldar accepted having his speech shut off with the easy satisfaction of a man who knows his point's been made. He went on amicably. "The Rose Priestess can't be an unescorted guest in your widower's den, Col. I've given orders for a tent to be put up for her. Immediately next to yours, of course." To Sylah he added, "My daughter Neela will be your companion. Wait here, please, and she'll join you." He turned, his followers closing her off with their backs.

Col smiled at her as a small boy stepped forward to take charge of her horse. "Faldar's my half brother. Same father, different mothers. He wants to be War Chief. He sends his daughter to be your companion and his ear. Moving her into a tent so close to mine demonstrates his willingness to make her hostage to tribal peace." A sudden frown darkened his face, and Sylah instinctively tensed, but when he spoke, his irritation wasn't for her. He added, "Please don't think of her as a spy. She's an obedient daughter—nothing less, nor more."

Indignantly, Gan said, "You said hostage? You'd never harm her!"

"Many in the tribe think I would. Learn from him. Whether a thing is true or not is unimportant. What is *believed* is reality." He touched his brow in salute to Sylah before turning away.

"Your father impresses." She spoke calmly enough, but Gan caught the nervous fumbling as she unfastened her cloak's hood string. When it fell back to clearly reveal her, a sigh of appreciation moved through the crowd.

The man who stepped forward ignored her completely. Broad-shouldered, deep-chested, he was a shade shorter than Gan. His clothing was even plainer than the War Chief's. Leather trousers and vest were unadorned. He wore a plain snakeskin-handled murdat in a wooden scabbard secured with brass nails. Two things distinguished him—a carriage that bespoke complete confidence, and a tattoo on the right cheek of his cragged features, a solid black one-inch square.

He advanced on Gan, embracing the younger, slighter figure. He lifted him off the ground, squeezing hard enough to pop out veins on his arms. Gan's eyes bulged, as well.

"Good work!" he shouted, then lowered Gan and delivered a comradely blow to his shoulder that staggered him. "Four Devils! They'll be singing songs about you. Women'll be after you like trout after cheese."

Gan shot a look at the Priestess and blushed just as the newcomer jerked his sword arm up in invitation for the crowd to cheer. Embarrassingly weak applause sputtered in response. Meanwhile, he spoke from the side of his mouth. "You let five horsemen ride up behind you. I should break your skull."

Sylah's whisper was outraged. "This man fought off a war party. He lost a dog he loved."

The man's smile turned brittle. "Couldn't leave her on the prairie for the tigers, could you? *Don't frown.* Look brave and modest. We want everyone to leave thinking good thoughts about you. You heard Faldar already using this mess to make trouble for your father."

Then he turned to Sylah. "I know you, Rose Priestess Sylah. I'm Clas na Bale, fighting instructor for the tribe."

"Instructor in bad manners, too, I'm sure."

"Me? Bad manners? You nearly got him killed." He waved at the crowd, smiling. People sidled off.

"You insufferable—"

"Don't waste your breath. I've been called names that'd make you sick with envy. You are a guest, though, so I'll explain that a Nightwatcher's first responsibility is to warn the camp. A South Watch man failed in my grandfather's father's time. We lost over a hundred dead to raiders. Seventeen women of bearing age were carried off."

" 'Bearing age.' Otherwise they wouldn't be important, is that it?"

"This isn't Ola. Our women don't have to hide in a church to live like people."

She blanched, and Gan interrupted. "Our guest isn't trying to make an argument." Even as he corrected Clas, he wondered what women ever saw in his friend. They seemed to battle with him as often as not, but they constantly sought him out for the privilege.

A new voice calling Sylah's name was perfectly timed to nip the unpleasantness. A beautiful girl, fair and bright in a blue cotton skirt, blouse, and wearing beaded hightop boots, hurried toward them. "I know you, Rose Priestess Sylah. I'm Neela, child of Faldar Yan. I'm to accompany you until you're at ease among us."

Grudgingly, Gan conceded there was no better choice. Neela's father was a man to despise, as were his six sons. She was a single flower among rocks. She'd started perfectly with the Priestess, too. One indicated esteem for a guest with a greeting that ignored all others. Normally, Neela took special pains to acknowledge himself and Clas. He'd long since recognized it as her way of compensating for the antagonisms dividing the tribe.

He hung back on the walk to his tent, letting the women get acquainted. It gave him an opportunity to watch the people they passed. There were many unpleasant expressions aimed at the Priestess. More were for himself. That was no great shock, but it did surprise him to realize he was worried about it. He was resigned to the fact that the vast majority of the tribe saw him as a misfit, the motherless son of a War Chief who opposed war. They knew his father wanted him to be the next War Chief. The elders despised him for his parentage and what they saw as his presumption to a rank that had to be the people's choice. The younger people hated him because of his father's efforts to keep the tribe at peace and because Gan had learned—

painfully—how to best any of them with weapons or barehanded.

Now, however, he was surprised to discover the events of the morning had added disturbing emotions to his reactions. His blood felt hot in his veins. At the first crude remark aimed at either himself or the Priestess, he'd be honor bound to react. He almost feared the seething anticipation, and yet something in him still thrilled at the gut-wrenching exhilaration of the earlier battle.

When the bad moment came, it was the sort of scene he'd feared. Three boys, not yet old enough to own weapons, dashed out from between tents and openly jeered at him. The boldest laughingly made good-bye waving motions in the way Dog warriors scorned a beaten enemy. It was a gross insult, and Gan stopped in his tracks, hand dropping to his murdat instinctively. Embarrassed, he let it fall free. The boys, having gotten what they sought, were already running away, screaming childish triumph.

Gan looked beyond where they'd come from and saw what he expected. Another warrior, older, watched with a smirk. He averted it a shade too late, but held his ground with nervous defiance as Gan approached him. Gan was careful to stop just out of murdat range, the warrior's way of showing no attack was planned. Seeing that, the other's smirk partially surfaced again. It disappeared when Gan asked, "What kind of man encourages his youngest brother to torment a man he won't face himself?"

Angrily, the man denied it. Gan put on a surprised expression. "I didn't accuse. I asked. Would you say that would be a weak, dishonorable thing to do?"

The man growled something about having no time for useless chatter and having to meet some friends. He bore down on the last word in a final small-minded swipe. Gan could only hope he'd spun away too soon to see how telling his remark had been. He also hoped the Priestess missed the symbols on the man's jacket that identified him, shamefully, as from Gan's own North Clan.

He rejoined the Priestess and Neela. They were both still nervous from the tension of the incident, but tactful enough to resume their walk without mentioning it.

Visibly anxious to get back to their own South Clan territory, Faldar's men were just finishing the tent as they approached.

So far the tribe had managed to keep knowledge of its dissension confined to its own people. That could no longer be. The Priestess was sure to speak of what she'd seen.

Other tribes, other nations, would all turn to watch, alert for any flaw. As far back as the tribe's tale-tellers could go, clear to the beginning, that was the way of things. Strong fed on weak.

When they entered the tent, Gan's speculations stopped, his attention riveted on the plump woman waiting for them. Downward-pulling lines at the corners of her mouth, and tight, restless eyes gave her an aura of ingrained disappointment. She said, "I know you, Priestess Sylah. I am Kolee, Healer to my people. The War Chief wishes me to speak to you." Her voice caught at the ears. It always made Gan think of nettle leaves, so ordinary on the surface, with a surprising, vicious sting hidden on their undersides.

Sylah made a small bow. "I know you, Kolee. I greet you as a sister."

"I am not Church."

Laughing, Sylah reached as if to touch her. The gesture fell short at Kolee's expression. Glossing over the rebuff, Sylah continued easily. "I know. We're sisters in our aims, nevertheless. You know my training is wounds and injuries. What is your discipline?"

Kolee colored. "We're simple people. I know some herbs, some treatments."

There was a flicker of movement in her earth-brown eyes, so quick Sylah almost missed it, yet it gave her the feeling there was much secret knowledge hidden in this deceptive woman. The hair on her neck stirred. She forced a smile. "What are we to talk about?"

Gan was startled by the power he heard under Sylah's civility. This was his first experience with a contest of feminine wills, and the quiet dynamics fascinated him. Nevertheless, he made a reluctant move to leave.

Sylah shook her head. "Wait, Gan. There are things I may not understand. I'll be more comfortable with someone to advise me if a question arises."

Neela excused herself with what he thought was unseemly haste. He followed the two women to the sleeping room, sitting stiffly on the cushions in the corner Kolee indicated.

The room was small and dark, double-blanketed to assure privacy. A pair of oil lamps cast wavering puddles of ineffectual light. When the two women settled on their cushions, facing each other, Gan had the uncomfortable feeling that, where the darkness obscured the Rose Priestess, it welcomed Kolee.

Kolee said, "The Dog People demand strong leadership. Col Moondark has avoided war and raids, except in retaliation, for ten years. Young men who've never tasted battle are eager to measure themselves. In addition, we've seen two terrible winters. Our herds suffered. The farming tribes make us pay more for wheat and cotton, and foraging has been lean for our women. Peddlers bleed us. Now you come, unannounced, unrequested. Many think you come to spy out weaknesses for Ola. As a child I was sent to Ola to learn of healing, you know. I learned we must protect our right to our own ways."

Sylah said, "There are many religions. Church challenges none."

"Ola is no friend to anyone. And Church works to undercut all other beliefs; everyone knows it."

Kolee's open scoffing embarrassed Gan, but it had no apparent effect on the Priestess. Calmly she answered, "Sister, I bring a message from my king for your leaders. It's my duty. Church sends me only to bring what I know to others."

For a long moment Kolee sat as if unhearing, and Gan saw that her focus had wandered. When she spoke, she was contemplative. "We who weren't Olans had to live in the Violet Abbey, but were kept away from any secrets of Church or Abbey because we were savages." Her eyes, hot with remembrance, swung back to Sylah. "Four years, proud Rose Priestess. Watched. Distrusted. I stayed and struggled to learn because my people needed whatever I could acquire. Church gave me nothing. Now you travel all this far, at great risk, bringing us your wisdom."

"My abbess and my king ordered it."

Kolee made a sound in her throat and twisted on the cushions. Then she started on her questions about Sylah's qualifications and intentions. Gan squirmed at her harshness. It seemed hours before she finally rose, favoring stiffened muscles. "I'll ask them to let you stay among us until I learn all you can teach. No longer."

She shuffled through the exit slit in the fabric wall. The breath of her passage disturbed the oil lamps' flames, creating fitful, roiling shadows on the swaying cloth.

The Priestess' attention remained fixed on the exit. Gan was caught unawares, still staring when she turned quickly. Her eyes pulled at him. "Can I trust you?"

He had to push the single word through an uncooperative throat. "Yes."

Her smile seemed to drain his strength even as it made him feel he would dare anything to deserve it. Then he was beside her, back in the main room of the tent with only the vaguest recollection of walking there. Neela was there. She looked at him quizzically before saying, "Our fathers were called to a meeting with the Elders. Col says you're to rest as long as you like, Priestess."

"My friends call me Sylah."

Neela smiled and repeated the name. She turned to leave with Gan, but Sylah stopped them, speaking to Gan. "I don't know if it's proper for a stranger to speak of Scar. Please forgive me if it's not. She was truly noble."

Gan looked at the floor carpet. Stiffly, he said, "She was true. She'd be proud to hear one such as you praise her."

He was certain he'd offended her when her face swiftly formed into the mask that blocked out the world. Yet it was she who shivered and swirled from the room.

CHAPTER 5

A vast expectancy flooded the living rock. Beast sounds crept from the cave walls, deep, resonant groans, the dissatisfaction of a creature powerful enough to challenge mountains and rivers.

The ranked multitudes of green lights had dwindled dramatically. Great gaps yawned in the formation. The remainder trembled, individually at first, then in unison, pulsing in tempo at the bidding of the urgent sound. Along their length they acquired a mathematical precision, each vibrating at precisely the same rate, creating a glittering arc across the impenetrable blackness. No longer dots, they were transformed to scribed lines.

Suddenly there was another sound, a rending crack the cave had never known. Dust exploded from surfaces that had never moved before. Pieces of ceiling plunged to the floor.

The sympathetic strum of the lights burst apart in fragments. Some expired with crisp, tinkling notes. Others merely died. All movement slowed.

Stopped.

A vast number of lights had disappeared.

The plaintive octave-spanning call erupted in dozens, filled the cave's renewed silence with a manic choir of asynchronous high-low, high-low bleating.

The sibilant thing that listened for the notes responded, but the sheer weight of activity seemed to daze it, overwhelm it with opportunity. It reeled across the darkness, single eye spearing in all directions. Soon it was standing in one place, hissing balefully, the eye fixed in insensate rage.

More lights went out.

The cave moved in gentle settling. The rock sighed softly.

A new thing came to the cave, a smell of heat. And new lights.

Tiny white lights.

Warmth.

CHAPTER 6

As soon as the overlapping fold of the sleeping room softwall exit closed behind Neela's departure, Sylah collapsed on the mat. She sprawled, staring up at the sky-blue ceiling liner. Its ornate foreground pattern of twining vines and brilliant birds mirrored the complexity of her thoughts.

She'd believed herself too excited to be tired. But the talk with Kolee had been more draining than anything she'd expected. The harder she tried to focus, the more her mind skittered off to something else. And her legs ached. Was that a cramp pulling at her shoulders? Irritably, she turned, first on one side, then the other.

The Healer wasn't the problem, nor Gan's fight, and not simple weariness.

These were *good* people: Gan, Neela—so young, so vibrant; Col, worried about his tribe; Clas—that blunt, abrupt man, oddly interesting.

She shook her head, unaware of the movement.

Faldar Yan. Not good at all. Yet what she had to do might destroy Col and put Faldar in his place.

Could there never be good without a countering evil?

The muscles in her shoulder seized.

She must rest, restore mind, body, purpose.

The Apocalypse Testament says: In the past is the future. All we do, all we can become, must be learned from what has gone before.

Chanting softly, she descended into the trance of concentration. One by one she took control of the rhythms and tensions of her body and reorganized the harsh clangor of stress into flowing harmony. When it was time, she freed her mind to flee to the safe haven she had created in her imagination, where her thoughts ran ice-smooth and fire-bright. Her inner eye watched the still grove of massive trees take form. Shafts of sunlight angled through their ageless patience to center her in green-gold luminosity.

Twice strong. Twice-proven.

Church had its plans for her. King Altanar, as well.

No one knew her heart. Her plans.

A breeze stroked the tent. The inner softwalls, suspended from networked truss lines attached to the outer blankets, danced sibilant arcs across the

29

coarse ground carpet as the structure breathed. The noise should have intruded on her; instead, her mind drew it closer, transformed the alien sound to that of distant drums and the metallic clash of chings, the throwing circles used as hand chimes in the war dances of Ola.

The present dissolved.

Memory.

The crowded King's Hall was huge. The pillars to the roof were tree trunks carved in the likeness of men standing on other men's shoulders. They were three high, and her head barely reached the middle of the chest of the bottom figure.

The raised throne altar was so far from the main entry she had difficulty making out the person lounging there. Twin ranks of firepits, ten feet square, each with gleaming copper hood and chimney, defined the avenue down the center of the room. Smaller firepits stood between the larger ones and the somber stone walls. Smoke escaped despite the pit hoods, so the cavernous interior swam with a hazed, ruddy glow that changed the most commonplace objects into mocking fantasies. The red, shifting muddle conjured flickering, half-glimpsed images of blood and burning.

To escape threatening panic, she studied that which was solid and identifiable. There were probably three hundred nobles present. Carefully controlled anger sharpened their staring faces. The very thought of an unescorted woman in the throne room galled them almost unendurably.

She looked about, careful that no sudden movement of her hood betrayed her inspection. There was a handful of wives and concubines present. Immediately on eye contact, all sent her exaggerated expressions of respect, some going so far as to curtsy.

They knew their role.

The woman who wasn't Church earned her way into the King's Hall by hanging onto her man with an unending show of infantile dependence. No matter how intelligent or diligent she might be, her only avenue of accomplishment was through the man who owned her. The most successful of them hid implacable ferocity behind a simpering smile.

Sylah consciously straightened her posture, reminding herself that men needed the skills of the Healers. Even so, she thought ruefully, they had their ways of keeping a foot on the needed neck. Women were allowed no distinguishing titles of rank, save within Church, and those were chosen to reflect beauty and delicacy. Rose Priestess. Lily Priestess. Iris Abbess. Violet Abbess.

Except one: War Healer. As though they healed the madness of it, rather than merely cleaning up the wreckage left behind.

Titles invented by men, granted by men, perpetuated by women who had no other choice.

Within the shielding confines of her hood she permitted herself a grimace.

There was no time remembered when women were treated as human beings. Some bolder sisters hinted that women were practically the equals of men during the time of the giants. Such illusions filled her with more pity than irritation. In the first place, talk of the giants was always discouraged. All the evidence proved they were indescribably evil and destructive. Whatever flame of hope their "equality" kindled among living women burned out quickly at their first sight of a godkill or story of a radpad and the horrible deaths they caused in the past.

Women were, and always had been, property. They were status symbols, measured by the number and quality of children they bore. Despairing women had created Church sometime in the unknown past. It was their sanctuary, and with tiny, agonized steps, they had generated a form of moral authority that was still spreading from society to society.

She wondered how much truth was buried in the jumble of legends, lies, and deductions Church called history.

The suborder of Healers spearheaded the search for influence, but behind everything was the shadow form of the Teachers.

They had lived in the days of First Church, which tripped herself with the declaration that her Teachers were on the brink of a new world. When Church demanded equality for her women as the price for a better life in this world as well as the next, the men who ruled called it revolt. Missionaries died; abbeys were burned. The most grievous loss was the Teachers. Secretive even at their peak, they were rooted out mercilessly and exterminated, their very existence a forbidden subject. Their sin of having tried to drag humanity through a mysterious Door lived on.

From the Purge grew present Church, crippled, harried, but indomitable.

The usher chose that moment to beckon. Awkwardly, she jerked her feet to movement, her mental wanderings swallowed by a frightening, inspiring awareness that there was no turning back.

Heat from the crackling firepits buffeted her. Smoke clogged her throat. At the plain board of the audience bench she knelt quickly, bowing her head. Even the wood intrigued her, its bright gloss testimony to thousands of supplicants' knees.

Curiosity overcame inhibition. She peeked at the King through her lashes. A narrow face and pronounced nose called to mind a rapacious sea gull. His skin was pale, blushed by the firelight. He wore loose sea-green trousers and matching blouse of beautifully woven wool. Jeweled rings winked from every finger. A golden chain around his neck held a massive diamond at his breast, the famed Badge.

He held her paper as if it could soil his fingers. "You petition assignment as a War Healer missionary?"

"Yes, King."

A smile crawled onto his face. "That's all? No thrilling tales of faith and revelation? How refreshing. But expected. I've heard of you. Some say you should burn."

This was the cat's play she'd been warned to expect. Any sign of fear or weakness would only bring out sharper claws. She said, "Anyone may petition the King."

"Stand up." When she didn't move quickly enough, he shouted. "Stand!"

His eyes probed with blunt admiration, and she was glad for her heavy robe. He said, "One of Church's brightest young leaders; my whispers say ambitious. Beautiful, as well. Are you sworn?"

The coarsely casual assessment swept away her discretion. She lifted her chin, a rebuke already forming on her tongue, when she saw the eager gleam in his eye. She coughed, found a safe answer direct from her catechism. "I am sworn to Mother, the Healer."

He looked away sourly. "Women's drivel." Then, quickly, pointing up his first two fingers to the east in the male sign that asks the blessing of the One Who Is Two, he said, "I acknowledge Church's goodness, of course. Nevertheless, I'm told you're dangerous."

She forgot herself, extended a hand toward him as she pointed to the paper. At the scrape of a guard's sword being drawn she dropped the hand quickly. "I ask only to serve Altanar and the kingdom of Ola."

His earlier smile returned. Her self-assurance had been building bit by bit, but now it shriveled at the hint of madness in his unblinking amusement. The stories shared in the darkness of the Chosen nunneries came back, such as the one about witches who read the brains of sleepers and slipped back to their masters before dawn.

Too casually, he asked, "How old were you when you became Chosen? Where were you taken?"

Altanar was far too shrewd to be so transparent. He knew something. *What?*

Her concentration shattered.

Why does he ask about that, of all things?

Chosens were spoils of war, female children too young for slave chores, but not ugly enough or sickly enough or badly injured enough to warrant elimination. By law, Church took all she wanted. By moral necessity, she

took as many as she could. Conquest fed Church and simultaneously burdened her, all with the same orphaned scraps. The children found refuge,
only to be bound in iron discipline. But they lived.

The one inviolable requirement was that they have no concept of other
identity.

Words thickened on her tongue, "My only memories are Church. I was
given to Mother by the King, who is my only father."

Altanar walked swiftly to the bottom of the throne-altar steps. "There is
another reason for your mission."

Behind her the crowd was out of earshot, but their experience of Altanar's
moods alerted an animal awareness in them. They quieted with the diminish-
ing sound of rain moving away. Her chest tightened against a racing heart.

How could he know?

She couldn't keep the tremor from her voice. "Not so, King. No."

Someone giggled. It's shrillness tingled on the back of her neck.

"Come." He spun away. She had to hurry to keep pace, paralleling his
course along the front of the throne altar. The crowd's babble followed them
to a hallway leading out of the room, then the hollow boom of a thick door
behind them shut the noise out. Altanar entered the first side room. A guard
shut that door, as well, leaving them in a windowless box.

After the feverish gloom of the hall, the brightly lit room was a relief, as
was the crisp cedar scent of the beeswax candles. Even as her senses registered those facts, Sylah saw her abbess, regally erect in her green and blue
robes, behind a small table at the opposite end of the room. She acknowledged Sylah with a nod. No expression altered the calm of the aged, lined,
face. Sylah wanted to run to her, embrace her, but the elderly woman's
steadiness held her in place, buoyed her courage.

The Abbess was big-boned, amply fleshed. Lively brown eyes contradicted
iron-gray hair and bent, arthritic hands. A stiff finger constantly stroked the
bracelet on her left wrist. Massively wrought of fine gold, it featured the irises
of her abbey. A dragonfly hovered beside the flowers. Only the most suspicious mind would have suggested the stylized insect resembled the forbidden
cross.

A movement to her left drew Sylah's attention, and only then did she
discover the other woman in the room. She sat in an ornate chair against
the farthest wall, and she was so small that the tiny feet peeking out from
under her robes dangled inches above the floor. There was a strange, resistant
quality about her; her pale face, fully revealed by the candlelight, resisted the
warmth of the flame, denying age as well as feeling.

Sylah knew her well. She was Priestess Lanta of the Violet Abbey. She
possessed the Sight.

Altanar broke the silence, speaking to Sylah. "You will report to me about the Dog People."

He was about to say more, but the Abbess interrupted with the assurance of accustomed authority. "Iris Abbey missionaries do not spy." She sent a look of dismissal at Priestess Lanta before adding, "Church forbids."

Altanar said, "A bald lie, Abbess. Church spies on everyone." He faced Sylah. His grin sent a chill dancing up and down her arms. She folded them, hands inside voluminous sleeves as he said, "You aren't being sent as a spy. You'll do whatever War Healer work is necessary. In addition, you'll simply ask questions and send the answers back to me. Along with any observations you make."

The Abbess leaned forward, her twisted fingers drawn into pained fists. "That's not spying? What is it?"

"Observation." Hard lines of anger at the corners of his mouth belied the flippant answer.

"No." The Abbess shook her head. "Church forbids. And if she were discovered, who knows what a warrior tribe would do to her? I withdraw her petition."

Altanar's laughter was a mirthless gust. Sylah stiffened, and the Abbess warned her with a glance. To Altanar she said, "We cannot be forced to go where we don't wish to go, King. It is the way."

"She asked. You recommended. I approve. All that remains is to assure she serves me as loyally as she serves you."

Sylah looked over to the small figure still perched on her chair. Her hood was drawn over her head now, as if she'd withdrawn from everything around her. The posture symbolized Lanta's life. Whispers branded her as one who used her powers for her Violet Abbey, for the King, even for her own ends. Sylah had always discounted the talk, had even tried to befriend her. Once, she thought she had. For one awesome moment her deep, dark eyes had looked into her own with such agonized longing she almost cried out. Then, instantly, the gaze had turned as hard and impenetrable as twin mirrors.

They had not spoken since.

A movement disturbed her thoughts, and before she had fully collected herself, the King had his hands on her shoulders. She flinched, and he shot a look—of triumph, contempt?—at the glaring Abbess and laughed harshly before speaking. "Don't flatter yourself, virgin. You think I'd bring this old witch down on my head out of some passing lust for the likes of you? No fear. Go speak to Priestess Lanta."

The Abbess said, "No!" She rose slowly, wincing at grating joints that robbed her of grace. "You must not use Church women to persecute other Church women. You are near blasphemy."

He blanched, but snapped at Lanta to proceed. Silently, still hooded, the small Priestess gestured for Sylah to follow her to a small table with its own oil lamp. She lit the woven cotton wick, creating a squat triangular flame so still that it seemed almost an illusion.

Sylah settled onto a stool opposite the Seer. In a way, she felt sorry for her. They make us all tools, she thought, to use or destroy. She was surprised to realize she was smiling across the table.

Lanta extended a hand. Sylah was too startled to react, but the Abbess was there immediately, arm around her shoulders, shouting at Altanar. "Unspeakable! No Seeing can be done flesh to flesh. Church forbids!"

Sylah said, "We know we do the right thing. There can be no fear in that."

The Abbess stepped away, visibly shaken. A serene determination filled Sylah. She recognized it as complementary to her earlier feeling of commitment. If Lanta exposed her secret, the King would find a way to have her killed.

She almost laughed. She had made a decision. Instead of apprehension, she was filled with a wild sense of freedom; no one would ever take her self away from her again.

Her grip so hot and dry it canceled the faint prickle of the lamp's flame, Lanta's hand trembled as she accepted Sylah's above the table center.

Sylah's heartbeat quickened and stubbornly refused to slow. Worse, a queer, high note sang in her ears.

Lanta's grasp tightened spasmodically. She threw back her head, spoke with startling resonance.

"One from Church finds the savage child to serve Ola's desire; Harbundai falls. Ola gratefully embraces the savage who fights to open the door to Ola's future."

She stopped, jerked to her feet, her eyes clenched shut. She choked violently, one hand clutching her throat while the other flailed for support. Her pale face glowed with a cold, bluish cast. Instantly, Sylah lowered her to the floor and provided the Healer's kiss. The irony of the situation rang in her ears with the rhythm of her breathing as she pushed her own life into the small, inert body. What had Lanta seen?

She was in her hands.

Soon Lanta gagged, and Sylah recoiled as she next inhaled, shuddering. The Abbess produced a small bottle and passed it under her nose; the pungent ammonia set Lanta coughing, and when that passed, they helped her back to her seat. The Abbess told her it was Sylah who ministered to her. Lanta made her thanks without looking up.

Altanar wasted no time with niceties. "How dare you speak of Harbundai?

You were told to discover if these two have a secret reason for this mission. Traitor!"

Lanta cowered. "My abbess explained to you, King—I have no control. The words burn across darkness. I repeat what I see."

He smashed the tabletop with his fist. "You give me riddles! Is Iris Abbey true to me?"

Sylah's tongue was a wad of dry cotton.

Lanta's tiny fingers worried themselves into a wriggling mass. She said, "What I saw, I spoke. There was nothing written of treachery. Harbundai falls," she repeated, almost pleading.

He twisted away, striding to the door. With his hand on the massive iron handle, he scanned them with narrowed eyes. "You will proceed, acting for me, Rose Priestess Sylah."

They waited until his footsteps faded away.

Lanta's nervous quickness brought her to the door first, as Sylah tended to the Abbess. She opened it, bobbing in and out, birdlike. As Sylah reached her, Lanta strained upward, hoarsely confidential. "The guard is gone. Oh, please; I beg forgiveness. The King threatened . . . I told him what I saw. Truth. But there was a *voice*. You have to know."

The Abbess seized her hands. "Bless you, sister."

Lanta continued, with obvious difficulty. "The voice said, 'Sylah will reap blessings for Church and herself. She will gain what is sought.' " She swallowed, composed herself. "It said, 'Sister, say this to her: Sylah must lose what she holds most dear.' "

The yearning Sylah had seen in Lanta's face once before reappeared and was gone, quick and delicate as a shadow cast by moonlight. Without another word, she was away, the tiny feet pattering like raindrops down the hall.

Sylah followed the Abbess blindly.

Rose Priestess, the King said. *Rose Priestess Sylah.*

They were at the abbey, walking up the stairs to the Abbess' rooms, when she spoke, clearly attempting to draw Sylah out of herself and bring some lightness to events. The Abbess did it with the easy humor of one who knows respect and is comfortable extending it to others. "So you're a Rose Priestess. Privileged to wear the embroidered red rose on your cloak, free to travel anywhere in Ola without permission from the local sheriff. We've already taught you to read and write, but now you can even learn a foreign language—if you can afford lessons. You can buy and sell commodities; sorry, won't let you control a company or own land. Would you like to own a slave? No fear. One, male only, under the age of puberty, of course, and you really don't mind that he can be freed any time at the discretion of an all-male panel—which may or may not compensate you for his value—do you? Certainly not, you loyal *woman*, you. However, enough of new prestige and power. What next? Iris Abbess?"

"Never." It was too quick, too blunt.

"Do you still resent us so, child? Have you never forgiven?"

"I remember nothing, so have nothing to forgive."

The Abbess sighed.

Sylah knelt in front of her, gently cradled one of the tortured older hands between her own. "I'm glad I came to you. I have a mother."

The Abbess brushed her aside with a bluster of false impatience. She busied herself lighting charcoal under a pan of water and measuring an herb she called osh into a porcelain pot. She chuckled as she explained the crushed leaves were a gift from a Nion ship's captain, something he refused to bring the King.

In unspoken agreement, they used the time waiting for the water to boil to marshal thoughts. When the water was ready, she poured it over the osh, stirring it gently with a silver and ivory rod. They exchanged anticipatory smiles at the intense aroma before she poured the liquid into translucent turquoise-blue cups the size of chicken eggs. Sylah did as the Abbess, inhaling the steam, barely dampening her lips with the rare fluid.

"You're an amazing person, Sylah. Lanta saw nothing of our plan. And you knew she wouldn't. How did you know?"

"It was just a feeling." Sylah lied. It wasn't the first, and came easily because of it. She could hardly explain to the Abbess that the touch of freedom meant so much to her that it overrode the fear of Altanar's vengeance. She didn't really understand it herself. Nor did she understand everything Lanta had said. She asked, "What did she say about me losing something?"

The Abbess gestured carelessly. "No matter. The important thing is that she didn't discover that we mean to keep the Dog People out of the imminent war with Harbundai. Our secret is safe."

Sylah ached with the temptation to confess, to share.

Dear Abbess. Heart of my heart. My secret lives!

Before morning prayer was the only time she allowed herself to remember. Once each day she unleashed the raw images. Leaping flames. Obscure figures. A child who had a name that was not Sylah tried vainly to shriek her terror.

Her mother's death sound was a life-saving last gift. It shocked the child to speechlessness, and by the time she recovered enough to allow responses to the cowled women who owned her, she'd heard other Chosens speak of home, of parents. They disappeared.

Sylah understood the sequence. But she continued to remember.

The Abbess misinterpreted her protégé's expression. "Do not be too eager, my child. Your well-being is more important than success." Saying it aloud broke some internal structure. Her years settled on her all at once, forcing her shoulders into a wearied slump. Her voice grew querulous. "If only we could support you. I dare not even give you the names of the contacts in Harbundai."

"They'll find me." A sudden, intriguing new thought flashed across her mind. Lanta mentioned a door. Could it be the one, the Door of the Teachers? Feigning anxious innocence, she put the question to the Abbess.

She dismissed it with a smile. "That old tale. Ignore Lanta; concentrate on what you must do. Remember, the contact signal in Harbundai is three red roses." She grimaced. "How thoughtful of our king to promote you accordingly. If he knew—"

"We've been too careful."

"Never think so. I wish—" There was a hesitation, and then the bent fingers holding the cup seemed to grow confused, and she dropped her cup. Steaming osh splashed the polished floor. The porcelain sprayed away in tiny, chiming splinters.

"Now look what I've done! All the way across the Great Sea, and a clumsy old woman wastes it making a mess."

Sylah mopped up with a handkerchief. "You're tired, Abbess. I'm going."

The Abbess agreed reluctantly. She embraced Sylah, then stepped back and held her at arm's length, treasuring her. She said, "Those who share the secret of your courage will pray for your success. Mother Church will welcome your triumphant return."

At the head of the stairs leading to the ground floor, Sylah paused, hand on the banister.

Four of us—the King, the Abbess, Lanta, and me—in that one room, she thought. Not really parts of the same puzzle at all, but four separate puzzles interlocked at one point.

I'm the center, because I'll bring him down. I'll be more than vengeance. I'll rise until no one will be able to humble me or humiliate me.

I will not be a *thing*.

I cannot be a man, with that iron strength.

I am a woman. I will be the fire to consume any iron.

CHAPTER 7

Overlapping scales of blue-gray stone gave the brooding dome at the center of the Dog People's camp a reptilian look. A full hundred feet across, it was as high at its peak as the surrounding family pennons snapping in the breeze. The very earth around it isolated it and warned of inviolability; it was scraped clean of the least blade of grass or random stone. Two narrow paths led to a pair of rectangular holes in the ground at opposite sides of the dome. Carved steps led downward in each. The southern pit was the entrance to the underground building. The northern side was the exit. They symbolized the legend of northward migration.

Centered on the dome's crest were twin barrel-shaped drums, as tall as a man at their ends. They were mounted parallel to each other in timber cradles, suspended from thick leather straps. Two men, bare from the waist up and carrying clubs in both hands, strode purposefully up the dome's side to the drums. Taking position facing in opposite directions, each paused in dramatic deliberation, then struck a furious, thundering beat.

At the first sound, Sylah flung back the softwall, rushing into the room where a startled Neela scrambled to her feet at her appearance.

"What is that?" Sylah hugged herself, pulling her sleeping gown around her protectively. Neela was already fully dressed.

By then the rumble was slowed to a once-a-second tempo. Smaller drums took up the cadence. Realization washed across Neela's apprehension; she giggled before answering. "The Elders' drums. We call them vozun. The smaller ones just starting to talk are pala. The vozun speak to the tribe. The pala are for the clans and families. Today they call a meeting in Earth Heart. You must've seen its roof from Tiger Rocks."

Reassured, a little embarrassed, Sylah retreated to her room to dress. After offering a hasty morning prayer and splashing through an almost sinfully brief ritual wash-up, she returned to the main room. Neela produced two decorated pottery cups from a cleverly woven willow-wand cabinet. Twisting the wooden spigot of a rough clay jar, she filled them with a tan herb tea. She said it contained rose hips for strength, chamomile for calmness, and

39

a bit of mint for flavor. The first sip was astringent, with a hint of bitter aftertaste, but remarkably refreshing.

"I can't remember ever sleeping so long," Sylah said. "Such a long day; Kolee's questions and the hours with your father and Col last night, talking about the message from the Mountain People. And my mission, of course. And that terrible fight—Gan, and poor Scar." She shook her head. "Tell me what else I should know of your drums."

Neela grew serious. "The pala drums are only music. The vozun and war drummers put their souls into their instruments. It's very dangerous. While they play, the soul is between this world and the next. They call for the attention and help of the One in All. If a war drummer is killed in battle, the Elders have to pray the soul back, so the drummer can pass safely into the next world. A vozun drummer can only make his own way. Today they call a meeting—the War Chief, the Elders, Chiefs of the family clans, the Dog Chief, and the Horse Chief."

Sylah elected to avoid the religious aspect of the drums. It was outside Church doctrine, and she didn't want any more clash than necessary. She asked, "Each family has its own Chief?"

Golden braids flashed as Neela shook her head, and Sylah realized she'd failed to see exactly how pretty the girl was and how beautiful she would become when her womanhood was fully realized. Ignoring so primary a consideration was dangerously lax.

"Kin are joined in clans; each clan has a Chief and elects three Elders. They govern the tribe, along with the War Chief, the Dog Chief, and the Horse Chief. The clans are named for their place in defense—North, South, East, or West." Taking a piece of charcoal from the firepit, she drew a circle on the back of a hide, then divided it into quadrants. "Round is the perfect form. Sun and moon are round, the seasons an unending circle. The tribe defends a circle, clans defend directions. Each clan provides young men for Nightwatch."

"Where does that man Clas fit in this?"

"Clas supervises all war training. He commands Nightwatch. They're our best fighters. He's the best warrior of all. He was born to South Clan."

Sylah hid a smile at her naive pride, and was somewhat surprised when Neela continued, "North warriors are the boldest. Except for Clas, of course. Most War Chiefs come from that clan. South men are usually organizers and thinkers."

"You haven't mentioned the women."

Neela laughed, a clear, infectious amusement. "Every woman thinks her clan's best. They say easterners are sunrise, bright and cheerful. Westerners are dusk; mysterious, sometimes dangerous. North women are blunt and

forceful. South women are shrewd and demanding. Maybe a little bit tricky."
Her grin turned mischievous.

"Aha. Well, I'll have to watch you, won't I? What of Kolee?"

The girl was quick enough to hear the edge to the question. "She's South,
too." An impulsive hand shot forward, rested on Sylah's. "Don't be angry
with her. She only means to protect us."

"So do I. She should see that." She got up swiftly. "It's still light. Can
we walk?"

"I have a better idea." Smiling, merrily conspiratorial, she refused to say
more.

A sudden, searing flash of irrational anger almost made Sylah shout at her,
warn her that she should understand that people who spoke pleasantly could
be far more dangerous than enemies with sodals in death paint.

A memory from her stay with the Mountain People came to mind. An
older warrior, scarred and lame, sneered at the Dog People. "We'll wipe
them out, sooner or later. They fight well, but their thoughts are soft." He
laughed past broken teeth. "Warriors won't name their horses because they
think it's bad luck. We don't worry about an animal's luck. When it outlives
its strength, we kill it and eat it."

At first she'd been repelled by the callousness. Then, with gnawing persistence, something in her mind asked if she really believed she could pursue
her personal goals without a similar attitude. Just by reporting to Altanar,
she'd be abusing trust. But unless she did, her own future had no chance.

They stepped out of the tent directly onto one of the two main streets
that cut the camp into quarters. Neela's horse was tethered to the family
pennon post. There was a second horse there, far better than the one Sylah
rode into camp, and the girl presented it as a gift from her father, grinning
happily at her pleased surprise.

"My horse is Sunflyer," she said. It was only conversation, but for Sylah
the naming brought back the unsettling memory of the Mountain warrior's
laughter. The girl prattled on. "I've always called yours Copper, but you can
call her whatever you want."

"Copper she is," Sylah said. "I'm very impressed. I mean, a horse—so
expensive a gift."

Neela waited for her to mount, then led the way. "The tribe owns thousands of horses. Everyone has at least five, even children who have to be lifted
up to ride. Our law says there has to be a horse tethered outside every family
tent for every person over five years old—unless the horse is being ridden,
of course. It's so we can't be surprised without them." She made a face,
pointing at Sylah's boots. "You won't need spurs anymore. We never use
them."

"I should think you'd be called the Horse People. The only dogs I've seen are Gan's."

The dogs were companions, Neela explained, bred to hunt and fight beside Nightwatch men. They were dangerously protective of their masters, and barred from the camp except when their presence was necessary. Horses were trading capital, although it was forbidden to sell a war-horse. Dogs were never sold.

Sylah soon realized their ride wasn't as aimless as Neela pretended. They were moving deeper and deeper into her South quarter.

The change in the people was apparent. Neela was liked in the North quarter; people smiled and waved freely. In her home district the feeling was different, and Sylah had difficulty defining it until she remembered seeing one of Altanar's sons ride through a fair. Those greetings carried warmth, too. And a hint of fear. Not for the actual person—the son was something like eighth in line for the throne, and utterly without influence—but for the fact that this was someone with access to vast authority.

The small observation was an insight more powerful than words. The people acknowledged Neela as a princess. That could only mean they saw her father as a king.

She wondered how soon they intended to make that a truth. And how they'd do it.

Preoccupied, she was caught short when Neela reined to a stop in front of a particularly large tent. Its entire front was thrown open to garner the last of the day's light and as much fresh air as possible. A short distance to the side stood an elongated furnace about five feet high, its fires generating a steady bass rumble. More striking than the noise, the clay wall sealing the front end portrayed a snarling face. A ceramic plug filled the mouth opening, and a smaller one blocked a smaller hole in the face's eye. As they watched, a compact, muscular man clad only in leather shorts yanked the smaller plug to inspect the fiery interior. Looking up, he saw the riders and grinned. When the plug was replaced, he stepped outside to greet his visitors. Away from the sweltering heat, the cold air struck clouds of steam from his sweating body. Hands on hips, he said, "I know you, Rose Priestess Sylah. My name is Saband Guyd, first smith of the Dog People, and South Clan member. Welcome to my version of the Land Under."

It was a bold jest, using Church's name for the place of afterlife punishment, comparing it to the fire and noise of his work.

She liked him for it. "I know you, Saband Guyd. Are you so terrible that you deserve that world alive *and* dead?"

His laughter bellowed. "Come in, Priestess. And you, little Neela—I never see you anymore. Your brothers are here frequently."

"You used to make necklaces and jewelry. Now it's just war things. Why would I come here?"

A muscle in his jaw twitched, but he remained jovial. "To brighten our day. Maybe I'd even find time to make a copper bracelet for you." He turned to Sylah. "What can I show you, Priestess? Here we still work in stone, as well as use the most modern tools." He stepped to a machine and patted it fondly. "As good as any in Ola. A lathe, for arrow shafts. Every one exactly like every other. We can put on a point of flint, obsidian, bronze, steel—not just iron, but good steel. You know anything of my art?"

"I know that repairing damage done by your wicked toys forces me to use *my* art."

He burlesqued a huge wince, staggered, clutched his chest. "I wish my blades had an edge like your tongue."

She laughed with him, but quickly grew serious. "Do you have trouble finding metal? I heard they found a very large godkill in Ola recently, and it's mining out well. Do you dig godkill sites, too?"

"We have. We don't like it. Some of them were radzones, and we don't know which ones. We prefer honest ore. In the olden times radzones and unseens were so feared that Dog law said anyone who so much as touched something of giant-make was to be executed. We're modern now, though, and not so fearful. Still, a man never knows what went into the giants' metal. When I use ore, I know what I'll get."

"This is where you treat the ore?" Sylah asked.

He smiled. "No. This is where I make my steel. Iron is melted outside the camp. There are rituals, special prayers—from the earliest times." An almost imperceptible change swept over him. The intensity was too great to escape her, yet was swift and vague as cloud shadow. His voice and his small gesture toward the furnace were perfectly casual as he continued, "Nothing goes in the door without being properly prepared and tested. You understand."

Her skin crawled. She knew—and he did, too—that the knowledge of iron and steel dated back to the Teachers. It was why smiths were a breed apart. Their forge was their altar, and Church ignored them, saying she'd despaired of controlling them generations ago.

Part of her yearned to duel with him, challenge him to say more. Years of weighing every word had bred a caution that was part of her, however. "Can you tell me about your steel?"

He nodded. "I mix bits of iron with wood chips and secret earths in heavy clay pots. We seal them, then heat them until the iron becomes liquid. After it's allowed to cool, I break the pots and make weapons from the steel inside. *My* steel." He took a brightly new murdat from a scabbard and buried the point in the log butt holding his anvil. Slowly, steadily, he bent the weapon almost double. When he released it, it sprang back. With a smug look he ran it down his arm, piling up shaved hair in a neat little windrow.

A demanding, careless voice interrupted. It filled the tent. "I know you, Rose Priestess Sylah. I've been looking for you." She turned to see Faldar Yan enter. He and Saband exchanged formal greetings. When the smith turned away, Faldar advanced to stand beside her. "Walk with me, Priestess; there are things to be said for your ears only." She let him take her elbow and guide her to the horses. He handed her reins up to Neela, and Sylah noted wryly there was no need for him to instruct her to take them and lead Copper back the way they'd come.

When Neela was gone, Sylah noticed the two young men. The taller was a full head above his companion, yet something in their stances made Sylah feel the shorter was the authoritative one. Even when he assumed a subordinate position, walking slightly behind as the two of them came toward herself and Faldar, she had the impression he was playing a role.

"My eldest son, Bay." Faldar proudly indicated the larger youth. He was about Gan's age, she decided, but where Gan was supple, this man suggested rocklike solidity. She remembered one of the Abbess' remarks; some Dog men bragged that they'd rather break than bend. It was a humorous turn of phrase then. Staring up at Bay, it lost any hint of comedy.

His companion, Likat, was gaudy, a dandy. The right half of his head was shaved. A large spider was drawn in red on the bare skin. The hair to the left of the center line was long. Sleekly oiled, it was plaited in long braids and studded with bits of glass and glossy stones. She'd noticed some of the younger warriors affected the style, as opposed to the close-cropped majority. Bright feathers, cleverly sewn into flowers, sprouted on his vest, which was already ornately decorated with a running line that snaked into silhouettes of animals and birds.

She chafed under the distraction of Faldar's prattle about his eldest son's qualities of leadership, and other doting trivia. Likat demanded attention. Something about his studied indifference to the conversation made her suspicious, so she was watching him when his gaze swung to Neela's back. She would have sworn he tensed like a stalking leopard.

Faldar directed both young men to follow and assure his talk with Sylah wasn't disturbed. This time it was Bay who noticed Likat's hot stare after his sister. He grinned, bending forward to whisper in his friend's ear. Startled, Likat's first reaction was to turn bright red, but he said nothing, recovering quickly to produce an answering leer.

A breathy roar from behind startled her, and she twisted to see Saband opening the furnace's blazing mouth while a boy pumped furiously on a bellows. Saband looked directly at her. The fiery glow leaping from the hole painted his face and bared teeth red. She was sure he was going to speak, but he merely waved and turned away.

The insistent strength of Faldar's hand on her arm turned her. As they walked, he spoke with elaborate carelessness. "Did your king tell you of our negotiations? Of his efforts to enlist us in his attack on Harbundai?"

The shock of it made her stumble, nearly lose her balance. Altanar had led her to believe there was no contact with these people. Was there no truth anywhere? How could she deal with this surprise? She must have time to think. Faldar was watching, vastly amused. Her words sounded strangled to her own ears. "Church is no part of such things!"

They continued walking. Faces smiled at her from doorways, from passersby. Logic told her the expressions were friendly. Her emotions twisted them into smirks.

In the silence, memory of the Abbess' words rang in her ear. *We must protect Harbundai. The Queen Mother is struggling to save Church, to protect women. You will be forgiven any crime, any act, but you must keep the Dog People out of that war!*

Faldar ushered her into his tent, where she obediently took a seat on the cushions indicated. He sprawled comfortably in front of her. Bay and Likat took up positions at the door. Coming out of her mental fog, she noticed that Bay posed just outside, letting everyone know he was guarding the important things being discussed in his home. Likat squatted inside, arms folded across the tops of his knees, chin resting there. The position hid his eyes, yet she caught glimpses of their shine, and knew he was peering up at her through his lashes. As much as she disliked meeting his predator's stare, she preferred that to this shadowy observation.

"Church has made no move to cooperate with my tribe for two generations," Faldar said. "Now, when we're involved in a power struggle, and I'm conducting secret negotiations with your king, Church suddenly honors us with our own War Healer. Don't insult me by denying that you spy for Church or Altanar. Probably both. Tell your leaders this: Church can work among us so long as she doesn't interfere with me in any way. I'll control the tribe by the time we reach our summer camp. We can attack Harbundai any time after that, but it's Altanar's responsibility to provide us a cleared pass through the Enemy Mountains."

He nodded, indicating she had permission to speak. In spite of all that had gone before, that small condescension infuriated her beyond everything else. Her voice rose to defiance. "I will not be used this way! I am a War Healer, not to be harmed!"

Complacent, Faldar waved away her protest. "Harm you? Priestess, I've shared my secrets openly, put myself in grave danger. Not that you'd consider informing on me." His eyes flicked toward the watching Likat, and he winked suggestively before continuing. "Just as I'd never inform on you, of course, because we all know that not even Church can shield a spy." He rose ponderously, fixing her with a cold gaze before leaving. "You *will* be used, you know. Accept it and profit, or suffer needlessly."

It took a moment for her to get her breath back. When she got up to leave, Bay was gone, leaving Likat as the sole guard. He looked up, wearing a sleepy smile, forcing her to push past him to get out. As she reached to fling back the exit flap, he clamped a hand on her ankle. Reflexively, she kicked at it. He was on his feet before she could move, spinning her across the room, backing her against a pole. She struggled for a moment, then realized he was laughing at her, enjoying the unequal struggle. She stopped, composed herself. "This is a mistake," she said. "Let me go. Now. Before there's trouble."

He leaned into her with the weight of his body. "You're the one who should worry about trouble, Priestess." His face was practically touching hers. He lowered his gaze to where the rise of her breast pressed against him, then slowly rolled his chest from side to side. "You're going to be here for a long time," he said. "Faldar can be very harsh with people. You need someone to speak for you. To protect you."

She glared, disdainful. "You disgust. If Church hears—"

"I spit on your Church." The cruel mockery disappeared. A look she knew too well was on him. She had feared being murdered once. Now she did again.

He was raising her skirt. She gasped and twisted at the touch of his flesh on hers. He grabbed her throat, crushing a rising cry before it could escape. In seconds she was drowning in a red-black mist that stole her vision, her strength.

Somewhere, far away, a voice called. It wasn't for her, but she strained to answer, desperate for help. A sharp pain under her left breast snapped her eyes open. Likat's face hovered over hers, slick-shining under greasy sweat.

She tried once more to cry out.

The pain in her breast came again, much sharper. She looked down to see him holding a shortknife there, its point out of sight in the material. He moved his hand, and the pain became a burning coal. He clapped the other hand over her mouth.

"Not a word." He was closer now, the words rank with his breath. "Say anything, and I swear I'll kill you. Tell me you understand!"

She nodded, managed something that sounded like yes. He watched her for another second, speculating. His lips twisted, and he gave the shortknife one final jab, keeping her quiet with the other hand. "We'll talk again. That's to help you remember," he snarled.

A wash of light flooded the room. A dismayed Neela cried, "What happened?" and then Sylah was lifting her head.

Likat answered. "She fainted. There's been too much travel, too much to learn. It just overcame her. She says she's all right. Aren't you, Priestess?"

Sylah nodded. Her view wandered past Neela. Bay's attention was directed at his sister. He seemed to resent the girl's concern. Oddly, when he finally did look at Likat, his face was a careful blank. Likat met it with an easy smile.

They all helped Sylah to her feet. She clutched her collar to cover any bruises on her throat. Her whole left breast throbbed, the pain radiating from the wound like heat from a flame. A trickle of blood inched down her side. By wrapping her cloak around herself, she assured that no one saw anything. Unsteady, she let them support her through the exit. Outside free, she threw off Likat's hand with a violence that nearly tumbled her.

Her step was firm by the time she and Neela reached their tent. She let the girl make tea and fuss over her for a few minutes, then pleaded the need to be alone to rest.

The sight of her violated flesh filled her with revulsion, not for the ugly little wound, but because it made her feel, all over again, the degradation and shame he'd caused her during the episode.

When she was finished treating herself, she rummaged through her equipment until she found a small leather bag. Opening it, she sniffed at the contents. The fragments of dried leaves and bark gave off a mustiness that conjured images of darkness and unseen things that scuttled. Properly steeped, as a tea, the blended materials induced a hypnosis that opened a victim's mind, turning it into a receptacle for commands, a powerless thing as soft as blossoms. A heavy touch, however, made the brain a permanent playground for madness.

Several herb-witches had died very unpleasantly before Altanar's torturers found the one who revealed the ingredients.

Only Sylah, ministering to the poor creature's last breaths, heard her repeat herself as she slipped into her next life.

She held out the sack, crooning. "We'll make them pay, my little friend. Let's see how anxious Faldar Yan is to send his savages against Harbundai when I've taken his precious daughter there as hostage."

CHAPTER 8

In the existence of the cave, it was less than a moment after the crescendo of destruction created by the earthquake and the sudden onset of new lights and heat before a new sound filled its spaces. In the terms of man, it was almost a full day. The sound was a whir of gentle competence, as though machines of compassion worked at their tasks. Another of man's day periods passed before there was yet another sound. The mewing complaint begged to be heard.

When it stopped, the reborn silence pulsed with significance.

The lights grew brighter gently, never exceeding a dim, dusklike quality.

Wreckage was strewn wildly throughout the area, which now stood revealed as an altered natural site, with man-made side rooms and a floor of level concrete. Hundreds of large glass and metal objects with the ominous ballistic lines of missiles lay on the floor, some crushed under fallen boulders, most trailing snapped wires and tubes. Once arranged in two neat opposed rows, each shape on its own low, wheeled table, they were now in terrible disarray.

A large machine with flexible arms and clawlike grips for hands lay on its side in what had been the aisle between the rows. A metal snake of a nose extended from its front, drooping to the floor, the red bulb at its end now lifeless.

More noise started in the cave, a whine similar to the first sounds. Groans came from one of the shapes, one marked by a small, steady white light.

In the distance another noise started, a high-speed humming. Lurching out of a room cut into the rock wall of the main cave, a dusty little machine about three feet square thrust itself importantly into the mangle of shapes and rocks, fat wheels spinning. It jammed solidly against the mess within a foot of its exit. The tires continued to rotate. In a while they gave off curling wisps of smoke that drifted gently in the direction of the groan, which rose again.

A shape that still remained on its wheeled carriage trembled, thereby identifying the source of the cries. A horizontal line appeared on its side, as if the thing would open like an elongated clamshell. The top seemed almost

48

to rise, then was still. A few moments later it visibly lifted, only to fall once more.

Some yards distant a second shape did exactly the same thing. Far away, yet another made more complaining sounds.

Whirring even more impatiently, the square machine seemed ready to explode in sheer frustration.

With a loud clatter the top of the first shape flung completely open.

The ceiling lights glowed more brightly yet.

The tires of the square vehicle blew out.

One of the white lights flickered. Died. The melancholy octave-spanning signal started, and for a moment the red light of the clawed machine glinted. A dull click told of an electric motor inside its dented body refusing to function.

Something moved in the shape with the raised lid.

Inch by agonized inch a man wearing denim shorts and a tee-shirt of heavy mesh fought to rise to a sitting position. The face was young, the body muscular. Stone-faced, he waged a gray, gasping struggle. A pulse chugged in his throat. Occasionally he made a sound. It was the weak, kittenish cry of the previous silence. Only the unmistakable agony of it kept it from being ludicrous.

There was a shelf next to him in the shape. It was lined with things that looked like small pumps, miniature distilling devices or purification equipment, all whizzing and clicking busily. Clear tubes led from each device to the man, and their liquids flowed into him through large, shining needles. A network of insulated wires spiderwebbed his body, each ending at a metal disk on his bare flesh. They were all gathered together as a larger cable that disappeared through a hole in the shape, to reappear as a sort of umbilical cord leading to the side room.

Upright from the waist, he worked to disengage himself from the tubes. He was still expressionless, and he moved with such infinite slowness he might have been uninvolved in the process. White flesh puckered and gripped the needles as he pulled them free. Trickles of blood marked their going. When the electrodes at the ends of the wires were lifted from their points of contact, his muscles writhed.

He never changed expression.

The blank face lied. His eyes were glitteringly alive.

They boiled with fear.

When the last connection was gone, a desperate lunge tumbled him out of the confining shape. He collapsed in an untidy pile on the floor. Unable even to crawl, he slithered like a reptile toward the square machine.

He passed out three times covering the ten feet to where the wheel rims busily gouged into the cement. During one of his unconscious periods another shape door lifted. No one appeared, however, and the white light flickered menacingly several times. Another voice rose from another location. That white light remained stable.

On reaching the square machine, the man continued to move with the same sluggishness, searching out the clasps that held the top down, then opening it. Spent, he sagged, panting, then clawed his way up until he could reach inside. A stainless-steel water bottle lay there, and he cried as he fumbled it open. He drank greedily, almost retching, then rested.

Minutes later, visibly stronger, he pulled wires free until the machine's wheels stopped spinning. Then he found the food pellets. They were small, not much larger than peas, but it took several tries to get one in his mouth. That accomplished, he discovered he couldn't chew. Rolling the thing around softened it, mixed it with water residue and saliva. He had as much trouble swallowing as chewing, and the resultant mess streamed down his chin. He wiped it off and tried again. He got three more pellets down, actually chewing the last one.

He slept.

He knew he was stronger as soon as he woke. When he tried to stand, though, it was as if there were no bones in his body, so he contented himself with more snakelike wriggling, this time shoving the water bottle ahead of him and clutching a handful of food pellets in each hand. He headed for the shape with the open door.

Another man looked up at him, his only sign of life a rapid blinking of his eyes.

The free man recognized in the other the terror he'd felt earlier. He dribbled water on the pale lips, forced part of a pellet past them.

Forming the words was excruciating. He said, "Hear me? Hear?"

The eyes blinked several times.

"Conway." He repeated it, "Conway." His voice sounded like no one he'd ever heard. "You eat." He slumped to the floor, drained. A rattling crash announced that someone else lived. He moved that way, found the strength to go over some rock instead of detouring around it. He popped another pellet in his mouth, chewing it with such sober concentration as he scuffled along that he realized how ridiculous he must look, and he felt his face move in what he could only guess was a smile.

Conway managed to give water and food to four more people, but when he attempted to reach another, he fainted again. When he woke, that white light was gone.

He beat his fist on one of the fallen shapes. It was precariously balanced on a piece of dislodged rock, and Conway's blows toppled it. The already loosened door sprang open. A woman's body fell out, arms and legs flailing as if attacking him, long blond hair shrouding his face. He screamed and kicked himself back, slamming painfully against another shape. This one fell with a great crashing of glass.

Behind him a voice called, wordless, frightened. He worked his way around, breathless as much from shock as exertion. A woman was attempting to escape as he had. He remembered feeding pellets to a woman. Perhaps two? More? His mind brought up flashes, nothing coherent.

She was dressed in a more modest sleeveless jacket in place of the mesh tee-shirt the men wore. The denim shorts were identical. Angry marks indicated where she'd taken out the sustaining needles. She gestured at her mouth, and he made his way to her with food and water.

Instead of forcing herself directly out of the cabinet, she worked at a series of isometric exercises, pushing against her own strength. Something like joy flooded him as he watched the color changes in her limbs and features. When she did crawl over the side, he helped her, and she made the transition in surprisingly good style.

"Conway," he said. "Matthew Conway."

She tried to speak, dribbled, and turned away with an uncoordinated jerk that made her sway.

"No worry," he said. "Me, too."

He showed her the food machine, and when the next voice sounded, they both went to it.

Within a few hours they were each tending three other people, none of whom showed either the strength or inclination to separate from their pump-driven support system. The woman was able to speak by then, and she introduced herself to Conway as best she could. "Nancy Yoshimura. Electronics tech."

He tapped his chest. "Traffic manager."

That was when they acknowledged the masses of shapes, hundreds of them, stretching down the length of the cave as far as the eye could see. Even as they watched, small white lights were winking off. The emergency call had choked to silence without their notice. When she looked back at him, her eyes were blurred with tears, but when she started toward the latest shape to open, she cried out and fell clutching legs knotted in cramps. Together, they massaged until the muscles relaxed. It was as much effort as either could manage. They fell asleep where they lay.

Nancy woke first, screaming. Conway spun around, grabbing her shoulders, shaking her. She continued until he shouted her name. She quieted then, and a drink of water ended the outburst.

"I didn't know where I was," she said, "and then I opened my eyes and saw all the crèches, and I knew." Her eyes flew wide. "My God, I'm *talking*! Normally!"

He nodded, afraid to try himself, despite the earlier shout. He worked his mouth, then blurted "How do I sound?" almost as one word.

"Great. Oh, God—wonderful. How do you feel? I think I'm stronger. I know I am." She added emphasis by getting her feet under her and rising, using the food machine for support. He followed her lead. Swaying, holding on, they grinned at each other. Then, almost simultaneously, their gaze swept the scene around them. Conway spoke first. "It's a disaster. We have to try to save the others."

"I lost one last night. I didn't want to tell you."

"What went wrong? They said there'd be attendants."

"They warned us. Everyone went in with their eyes open."

He grimaced, dropped the subject. "Can you deal with these here? I'll get something to carry food pellets and water and go as far as I can."

"Is there a radio? You know, so we can talk?" She shivered. "I don't want to be alone."

"Then help me out of this box." The voice frightened a yelp out of Yoshimura. Moving with more certainty now, they hurried to look in at the man who'd spoken. He was older than they, with close-cropped hair showing the first flecks of gray. Pale blue eyes watched their faces, revealing nothing. He spoke again, and although it was still rasping, there was no mistaking the purposeful manner. "I got rid of the needles, but I can't seem to coordinate. The electrostimulator's working on my muscles; I can feel it. I've been lying here practicing talking and trying to move, and then I heard you. Be something if the only thing working is my mouth, wouldn't it? I think I'm okay. You're Conway. Gave me water and food. It's hazy, but I remember thinking something was wrong. How're the others?"

Conway handed him a food pellet. The man took it with stiff fingers, but he managed to feed himself and take a drink. Then he said, "I'm Burl Falconer. Colonel, U.S. Army. You didn't answer me. What's wrong?"

Nancy said, "Maybe if you sat up, Colonel?"

He glanced at her shrewdly before he extended a hand. Upright from the waist, he looked around him and blinked. "Catastrophe. Worse than I feared."

Conway said, "I'm going to see what the rest of the cave looks like."

Falconer nodded. "Hurry. They said we had to have attention within forty-eight hours after the thaw starts. I— Wait a minute. You're not attendants. Who helped you, Conway?"

"Nobody. I got out."

"So. It can be done, then. Never mind. See what you can learn. What's your name, young woman?"

"Nancy Yoshimura."

"Well, Yoshimura, help me out of this thing and I'll help you while Conway scouts."

It was several hours before Conway returned. When he did, he made no effort to disguise his anger at the sight of Falconer working on the clawed machine. The red bulb at the end of its tubular nose was glowing again, and it was on its wheels. Another man pulled his hand out of the motor compartment as Conway walked up. Conway ignored him.

"What's the matter with you?" he demanded. "We've got lives to save. Leave the machines alone!"

"I'm working to save lives. So is Leclerc. Louis Leclerc, Matt Conway; Conway, Leclerc. Louis is a chemist. Matt's a traffic manager."

The small, dark man, looking up with quick eyes that seemed to memorize all of Conway's features in one quick glance, grunted and went back to his efforts.

Conway turned to Yoshimura. "How could you let him do this? You're losing people every minute! It's even worse at the far end—the rocks broke open hundreds—" He choked, shook his head. "Maybe twenty of us. Out of over a thousand."

Falconer worked his way upright. "And we'll die if we don't get rid of the bodies." Conway blanched, and Falconer's words drilled at him. "There are no attendants, Conway. They left for a reason. It wasn't the earthquake, or they'd be here now. Whatever's outside, we certainly won't be strong enough to deal with it for a few days. In the meantime, we're trapped with over a thousand decomposing bodies. Help us dispose of them, or we join them. Take your pick."

He shook his head. "I can't. It's too . . ." He failed to find the word.

"Then stop whining at me," Falconer said. "I mean to survive this, and your delicacy's getting in the way."

"I saved you! I wasn't too delicate for that, was I?"

"And I'm grateful. Thank you. Now, I've got work to do. Excuse me." He knelt to speak to Leclerc. "How's it look?"

In answer, the man connected a wire to a terminal. The electric motor hummed easily. Immediately, the tube-mounted eye was alive, seeking. Leclerc touched a switch and it went out.

"Useless," he said, pointing at the lights mounted on wands above the places where the crèches had rested. "See, each of our cryogenic crèches has three lights. Green, for a correctly running system. When the life-suspension failed for any reason, this machine was alerted sonically, and it sought the automatic red light, disposing of the contents."

"My God." Conway reached to support himself with a hand on the wall. "Contents. My God."

"The dear departed, if you prefer," Falconer said sardonically. "We have to find out where it put us, and quickly."

Conway's jaw set. "We can take our chances outside. Whatever's there is better than this."

"Don't be foolish." Yoshimura joined them. Conway was startled by how haggard she appeared. He also noted that she avoided looking at the machine. She went on, "I entered the cry facility here the same day the first missiles hit. They lectured us hard about the nuclear winter, about the radiation dangers, about the probable pestilence. Our responsibility is to survive, to help put together what's left outside this cave. The Colonel's right—the attendants abandoned us for a reason. What if this damage is the result of a nuclear strike, and not an earthquake? What if the nuclear winter's still going on out there? Or high levels of radioactivity? We save no one if we don't save ourselves."

"I'll work to bring the living up to strength," Conway said. "The mechanics can deal with their machines and the dead." He stormed away, not looking back. Yoshimura made a helpless gesture at Falconer and Leclerc. The smaller man remained expressionless, but Falconer nodded understanding. "He'll be all right. We all will." He turned to Leclerc. "Let's get on with it."

Leclerc fiddled with the machine's works. Thin wires, like antennae, extended from its front. They played across a crèche, sensing devices, relaying information to some sort of internal computer. The machine paused, digesting the data, then moved to sever the single cable that was the crèche's electrical umbilical cord. Another move, and the claws were directly opposite two recessed handles in the metal shape. Slowly, as if aware of the solemnity of its task, it hoisted its burden and proceeded down the aisle.

Falconer moved to follow. Unsure joints and muscles gave him a burlesque clockwork action of his own. The small smile he turned on Yoshimura was pained. He said, "My first job in the rebuilding of my country—disposing of its dead."

Leclerc stopped the machine while he cleared a rock from the path. Yoshimura moved quickly to touch Falconer's arm. "It has to be done. You're doing the right thing. It'll be over soon, and things'll be better when we get out of here."

He covered her hand with his for a moment before bending to help Leclerc. Over his shoulder he said, "That's the courage we'll need."

CHAPTER 9

The eleven other survivors sat in a rough semicircle in front of Falconer. All wore new trousers and jackets in blotched camouflage pattern, making it difficult to differentiate the six women from the five men at a quick glance. An open doorway behind Falconer led to a huge underground warehouse. Remains of shelves and crates jutted infrequently from under tons of fallen rock. The group's hushed conversation reverberated eerily down the crèche-littered reaches of the cave. Physical actions and voices were essentially normal as bodies adjusted to movement.

Falconer jerked a thumb at the scene over his shoulder. "That warehouse held the material that was supposed to bring us up to speed in the reconstruction effort. There's plenty of food for those of us who survived the earthquake, but hardly any equipment. Weapons in abundance. Lots of clothing. That's it."

Leclerc spoke up. "Explain about the air lock."

Falconer nodded. "That's a funny thing. When we followed the disposal machine"—Conway made a noise, which Falconer ignored—"we discovered it loaded the crèches into the evacuation chute we were all briefed about, the one leading to the underground river. We were expected to use the chute to get rid of waste while we lived here and built up our strength, remember? Anyhow, they altered it while we were frozen. It's equipped with an air lock now, big enough to handle four crèches at a time. A valving system used to prevent untreated air from leaking in when the lock's operated. It's broken, too. The good news is that the valve's jammed open, and the pumps are pulling in fresh air from outside. We found a portable radiation detector that works; we can guarantee the air in here's clean in that respect. We're pretty sure we still have a slightly positive air pressure, too."

"Does the Colonel think it's safe to go out?" It was the single black in the group, a tall, slim woman. Conway knew her only to shake hands and exchange names. Her general appearance first made him think of a model. She had the sweeping cheekbones and a challenging sensuality in her curiously tilted eyes. Her manner and carriage changed his guess to military. Her use of the third person in her question convinced him.

Falconer answered her. "The fresh air only compounds our dilemma, Tate. We know all incoming air was to be treated as long as the NBC equipment detected identifiable nuclear, biological, or chemical hazards. Unfortunately, except for the rad detector, we've lost contact with all outside sensors. We're totally isolated."

A short, heavy man said, "Then why'd they activate the thaw process?"

"We don't know, uh, Harris; right, Steven Harris. Sorry. I'm still getting the names right. Anyhow, Ivan Karoli here is a communications technician, and he's been working our radio. We've got power, and he's sure we're transmitting. He says we're not raising anyone, and no one's trying to raise us."

Harris faced Karoli, who was a burly man, tall. He had to look up to ask, "Have you tried any frequencies except the one we were assigned?"

Karoli shrugged. "Everything I can reach. I have to wonder if they're not still firing high-altitude nukes, screwing up electrical equipment with electromagnetic surge."

"Quite likely." The new contributor was another woman. Graying black hair drawn back in a severe bun failed to detract from a soft, olive complexion and luminous eyes. "For those of you I haven't met, I'm Margaret Mazzoli. Everybody just call me Madge, please. Communications is my specialty." She smiled at Karoli. "Organization, not technical maintenance." Then, businesslike again, "Our war games indicated a need for long periods of radio silence, as well as prearranged irregular schedules of activity. I suggest we confine ourselves to listening. If this structural damage came from a nuclear weapon, we shouldn't be advertising our exact location. Or our existence, for that matter."

"She's right." Harris wheezed excitement. "Someone activated the automatics that thawed us. They obviously did it with a radio signal when they realized what damage the earthquake—or bomb—did here."

"I don't think so, Harris." Conway fiddled with his collar, nervous under the pressure of the group's anxious attention. "If they wanted to revive us, they'd have sent attendants."

Another man interrupted in a calm, reasonable voice. "I'm sure they did send attendants, and that something happened to them." He smiled easily, and Conway was startled to realize he couldn't remember similar behavior from anyone else. It was to be expected in his case, though; Pastor John Jones was a negotiations specialist, famous for ending several hostage-taking incidents favorably. He went on, "They wouldn't just push a button and bring us out to face this." He waved in the general direction of the destroyed crèches. His eyes remained fixed on Conway.

Falconer said, "They told us they'd keep attendants here, Pastor. They didn't. They turned us over to machines."

Conway said, "I believe the answer's in that air pump. If you were going to leave a cryogenic preservation center tended by equipment, instead of people, you'd want positive protective measures. I think they set up a zero humidity situation under pressure."

"Why not a vacuum?"

"Because if a minor leak develops in a vacuum, you either physically patch it or the vacuum fails. In a positive system, a minor leak acts as its own entry denial. Obviously, a big enough break defeats the pump. I suspect the earthquake triggered the thaw machinery without knocking out the pressure maintenance system at the same time."

Harris said, "You're saying we almost all died because a sensor got banged around?"

"It doesn't matter." Falconer's tone warned him. "None of this matters. We're going outside."

He moved toward a steel door nearly a hundred yards away. It was round, mounted in a polished steel frame that filled the dimensions of the tunnel. A series of four spoked wheels mounted on the circular slab of the door itself controlled extended metal arms that led to worm-geared locking bolts. The latter disappeared into the frame and penetrated beyond and into the rock itself. When closed, it was a seal. Conway remembered the general description from the supposedly calming small talk when they prepared him for cryogenic suspension. He'd thought at the time the thing looked like the door on a bank vault, and had taken an inexplicable dislike to it.

Leclerc picked up the radiation detector and followed Falconer.

Before they'd gone more than a few steps, Yoshimura said, "You're forgetting biological and chemical agents, Colonel. Shouldn't we at least go through the supply warehouse and try to find test equipment?"

He turned a taut grin on her. "I wish I could forget them. We've already got outside air coming in here, and no way of knowing if it's treated. If it's not . . ." He turned up his palms. Then he added, "Our major problem is right here; we're trapped with over a thousand bodies. I originally hoped we could dispose of them, but there are simply too many, and the passageway too obstructed. We've got to get out before—" Mazzoli's quick intake of breath stopped him. He looked at her horrified expression, coughed, and let the sentence go unfinished.

The Pastor said, "We can't simply walk off and leave our companions, Colonel. You're a professional soldier, and I realize spiritual matters aren't your highest priority, but I feel we should at least try to provide them a burial with proper services. I mean no offense."

Falconer paused, and something in his manner caused Conway to tense, but the answer came with a softness and consideration that was a surprise. "None taken, Pastor. Later, though, please. The living, then the dead."

The Pastor nodded, resigned to the logic, and the group continued toward the door. Conway bumped shoulders with Yoshimura, drawing his attention to the way they were all unconsciously closing ranks, moving closer to each other. Twelve strong, their faces all reflecting awareness that they advanced on an unknown world, they picked their way through the rubble.

When they reached the door, they formed into work parties of three without instruction, each team taking a locking wheel as their project. None opened easily. As the first was forced, it cracked loudly, followed immediately by a shrill, startling squeal as the locking bolt backed out of its hole. A spontaneous cheer erupted from the other teams. The Pastor took a small victory bow, and the others attacked their wheels with greater spirit. Two more came free exactly as the first, and were greeted with similar applause.

Conway, Yoshimura, and a large woman named Bernhardt strained at the fourth. The veins bulging in their necks were soon bright with sweat. Karoli and Falconer tapped the women on the shoulder and took their places.

Grudgingly, with no sudden crack, but with an angry, grinding sound, the bolt gave ground. From the corner of his eye, Conway caught Falconer's frown, and followed the Colonel's troubled gaze to the point of his concern. A deep scratch marred the extracted metal rod, pointing at the hole in the wall like an accusing finger. Conway noticed a thin, hissing sound. He twisted his head about, trying to locate the source.

It was at or near the place where the bolt was coming out. He shut his mind to the implications.

The appearance of the end of the bolt touched off a wild cheer that trailed off to contemplative silence as the full impact of its significance overruled the plain fact of accomplishment.

Conway tore his eyes away from the juncture of door and frame, anxious to avoid unnecessary alarm for his companions. Looking around, he saw a continuous shift of emotions ranging from happiness to worry, from confidence to fear.

"Well," he said, "let's find out what's going on outside."

The Pastor put a hand on his shoulder and said, "You gave me food and water in the crèche when I thought I was going to die. Whatever we find when we open the door, I thank you for what you did. I hope we're heading into a world of peace."

"Amen," Karoli said, and everyone was busy shaking hands. There was some surreptitious brushing at eyes.

Falconer said, "Let's all push together. We have to share this, all of us."

Laughing, joking, the twelve moved to positions like children playing a game. Conway maneuvered to have the end position, nearest the insistent hiss that plagued his mind more than his hearing. He thought he caught a sharp glance from Falconer, but when he tried to verify it, the other man was lowering his shoulder to the door.

At the Colonel's command, they heaved in unison.

Nothing happened.

Falconer laughed. "I knew this'd happen. It looks like a Navy door, it works like a Navy door. We'll have to push harder. All together, when I say go. Okay, go!"

Again there was no perceptible effect, nor was there any joking. Instead, a soft murmur of concern, like the wind of a distant storm, moved through the group.

Conway was certain the hiss had changed.

He called Falconer to his side, pointing at the line of the juncture. "Air's getting out through the seal. That's why the lock was jammed tight and it's why the door won't open. It's jammed."

"Jammed?" Harris rushed up. His face was blotched red, his breathing ragged. "How can it be jammed? It's unlocked!"

"The earthquake," Conway said. "The frame's twisted. Not enough to see."

"Impossible! It weighs tons, it's machined to a perfect fit. Any bend would show."

"You can hear the air going through it. When we pushed, it got louder. It's there."

Leclerc gestured Falconer out of the way as he produced matches and a handkerchief. He lit the cloth, then snuffed the flame against the cement floor. The resulting smoke from the smoldering material sped for the line of the door and disappeared.

Falconer said, "Let's try pushing some more."

Desperation echoed in the grunting efforts. Falconer was the first to stop, standing back, thoughtful, inspecting the remorseless steel face. The concentrated efforts to push the door open degenerated to frustrated rage. They kicked, cursed, beat the cold, mocking metal until their hands were swollen. One by one, exhausted, they fell away or slumped to the ground where they stood. The last was Mazzoli. She remained upright, back against the surface, one hand on a wheel as though that delicate weight might find a way to free them. To no one in particular, she said, "We're trapped. We can't get out."

"We're not dead yet," Falconer said.

The woman named Tate laughed harshly.

CHAPTER 10

The group shared a half-dozen camp stoves. The blue light of alcohol flames wavered under military field cooking pots full of simmering stews. Empty dehydrated-food packets identified military rations.

The closest pods were disposed of, creating a cleared area that extended several yards past the large side room housing the control panels and machinery for running the site. Conway looked at the blinking lights and dials, cursing their superiority, the cold technical efficiency that so far refused to admit them to any level of control. The only one to make any headway toward understanding what any of it did was Leclerc, and all he'd identified was the air circulation system. Nevertheless, they enjoyed the major blessing of unfailing electrical power. Leclerc was certain some of the instrumentation referred to a nuclear power source, but confessed his lack of specific knowledge.

More than that beckoned, however. Hopeful, covert eyes glanced continually from the cooking circle toward the door, invariably returning, sadder, to stare into some personal distance.

Stirring his dinner, Falconer said, "I've been thinking about the design of that thing." No one had to ask what he meant. "As I remember, the hinges are on the right side, as we face out."

"They're on the left." It was Harris, arguing with growling surliness. His face looked swollen. It was blotched with red patches.

Tate sneered. "Well, grab the memory expert. Aren't you the one who said it couldn't be stuck?"

He ignored her.

Falconer asked, "Is anyone certain?"

Conway said, "They're on the right."

Harris got to his feet. "You people think you know everything. I've been watching you. You think I'm stupid. You're the stupid ones, dead as the rest of them in their fancy pods. You're not even smart enough to know that." He kicked over his steaming pot and stomped through the door into the warehouse. They sat in abashed silence, listening to him thrashing about, shouting obscenities that echoed as hollow retorts.

Mazzoli busied herself cleaning up the mess of the dinner she'd meant to share with him.

Falconer said, "We've got plastic explosive in the warehouse, and primers. If I can find it in that wreckage, we might be able to blast the door free."

"You'll bring the roof down on us," Karoli scoffed.

"Hor-rors." Tate drew the word into a two-syllable drawl of sarcasm. "We die if we just sit here. We die if he blows us up. Maybe we step outside and get some disease or fill our lungs with nerve gas. Maybe we open up in time for the second nuke to hit us."

"There was no bomb!" Mazzoli rose, twisting a handkerchief in white-knuckled hands. "We'll find people working out there, recovering from the war. They're waiting for us."

"They're dead." Harris stood in the doorway, an apparition. His flat statement drummed in the warehouse behind him. He turned and disappeared again.

Mazzoli began to cry. Yoshimura left Conway's side and hurried to her.

Falconer moved to Conway. He spoke quietly, assuring his words carried no farther. "Tate's right; we have to chance it. Help me persuade the others."

"Me? Make your own arguments, Colonel. You're the leader."

"You saved everyone's lives, you and Yoshimura. We're indebted to you. Because of that, you're credited with position, whether you want it or not. We should present a united front."

"Forget that. If I think you're right, I'll help you. If not, I'll oppose you."

"So be it. Now, what about the door?"

"It happens I agree with Tate. What can we lose?"

"Good." Falconer rose and entered the warehouse.

Conway ate, looking up when Yoshimura returned with Mazzoli. The older woman's nervousness was gone. She wore a strange, too-cheerful smile. She patted Conway's arm. "Don't overdo on this terrible food. I'll fix you something special tomorrow, to celebrate. Everyone's invited."

He caught Yoshimura's expressive silent plea for understanding. To Mazzoli he said, "Sounds great, Marge."

She laughed gaily. "They'll fly us to Seattle first, but then we'll be off to Washington. Did I tell you that lovely Donnacee Tate—isn't that a lovely name?—is a major in the Marines, and she was stationed in the District? Anyhow, we'll all get together our first evening back for one of my special Italian dinners. You must see my garden; the azaleas are wonderful this time of year."

One of the other women was standing on the other side of the cooking circle. She took a step toward Mazzoli. Conway remembered her name: Janet Carter. She was quite small, and intensity crackled around her, even her short, black hair glinting, as if giving off sparks. When she spoke, the quickness of her words and gestures made Conway think of an irritable little bird. She said, "Time of year? We don't even know *what* year."

Her companion, a plump young woman, more motherly in manner than her years would seem to indicate, shushed Carter, clearly embarrassed.

Mazzoli gave no sign she heard. "I turned the house over to my daughter-in-law when I was selected for the cryogenic project. I was one of the very first. My son—" The shine of her eyes dulled to grief. She inhaled deeply before continuing. "My son was stationed in Germany when it started. People were saying they might never use the missiles, but I didn't care, and afterward—afterward, they said they needed people without immediate family." She stopped, as if tripped by a vagrant thought, then went on as if nothing had happened. "At least I know he died. So many people never heard anything. And now we're all looking ahead. We'll have lots to do, and work's the answer, don't you think?"

Conway said, "Certainly. That's what we'll do; build."

"Was there much destruction?" Mazzoli said. "I saw nothing before I joined the project. Was it horrible?" She looked away, blinking furiously. A hand plucked at a loose thread.

"Be glad you didn't see."

"Oh, I am. Did you see the District? The suburbs? My daughter-in-law— Falls Church?"

Conway couldn't tell her the complete truth. He was one of the last to go into the project, and then only because he evaluated his chances of survival as nil, either way. "I only saw the center of D.C. They took me out at night. The chopper to Dulles was sealed."

"Did you see fires? Smoke?"

Conway looked down at his feet. "The nuclear winter was started, Madge. That's all I know, really."

Mazzoli sagged. Yoshimura touched her shoulder. "Walk with me. I'd appreciate some company."

She started, recovered quickly. "The exercise'll be good for me. Janet, will you and Sue come along? Let's clean up here, then go see what we can find in the warehouse. I don't think the Colonel and his friend really know how to look for things, do you? I always had to pack for my men, of course. Helpless, all of them." She was still chattering as Conway watched the foursome collect their eating utensils and move to the washing area in the control room near the disposal shaft.

He was still staring after them when Falconer and Leclerc came back. Falconer took a position on a large boulder. His partner remained on the floor.

"Listen up, everyone!" Although the command voice projected confidence, Conway had the sensation that Falconer was working very hard at control. Still, his effect on the group was galvanic. Closed faces opened to growing excitement. The four women in the wash area hurried out to listen. He held out his hands, showing off khaki packages. A larger number were stacked on the ground beside Leclerc.

Falconer said, "We're going to make it. There's enough Hy-Pex here to turn that miserable door into steel wool. What I intend to do is hit it with what we call shaped charges. That's explosives that direct their force in a primary direction. I'm going to shear off the hinges. The door will fall. We'll walk out."

"It's too dangerous," Carter said.

"There's danger. Look, I want this to be democratic. We'll vote—do we try to get out of here, or do we take our chances that help's coming?"

"Some choice." Karoli was unimpressed. Bernhardt, the woman who'd helped Conway at the door, eased over to stand beside him. "We're a democracy when it's convenient for you to duck sole responsibility. We vote on 'When did you stop beating your wife?' How do you know help's *not* coming?"

Leclerc's thin intensity was like a knife aimed at Karoli. "You're the one supposed to find them. You tell us."

"Why not blast?" Tate rose languidly, putting herself directly in front of Falconer and, more importantly, between Leclerc and Karoli. Conway was certain it was no accident. "Mama used to say, 'Better be hanged for a goat than a sheep.' Go ahead and make magic, Colonel."

Falconer looked to Yoshimura and Mazzoli, then at Conway. "What's everyone else think?"

Yoshimura drew herself to her full five-foot-two. "Go for broke."

Conway nodded silent agreement.

Mazzoli said, "Whatever everyone else wants is fine." A muscle twitched in her cheek.

The Pastor disagreed. "If we're to risk the lives of all, we should wait until we're in extremis. Maybe later; not now."

Karoli and Bernhardt looked at each other. The woman shrugged, and Karoli grinned. "We'll go along," he said.

The quiet women named Sue Anspach and Janet Carter leaned into hushed argument. The small woman pulled away and answered first. "Sue cancels me out. I say we wait."

Anspach said, "I'm sorry, Janet."

Falconer spread his arms, encompassing everyone. Conway realized it was a conciliatory gesture, yet he almost laughed aloud at the irony of a peace-making sign complicated by several pounds of high explosive dangled from one hand and a packet of blasting caps in the other. Falconer said, "That's seven for and two against, with Mazzoli not voting."

Carter said, "What about Harris? Doesn't his vote count?"

Falconer tensed. There was a hint of aggression in his manner. He said, "Leclerc and I didn't mention him because we were afraid someone might think we used what's happened to influence attitudes. There's no nice way to tell you this: Harris hanged himself."

Falconer leaped down from the boulder before the buzz of shocked questions was fully under way. His course took him close to Conway. Quietly, he said, "The group's going to hell faster than I feared. 'Then there were eleven.' And the Mazzoli woman looks odd. You know anything?"

"Withdrawal, rejection—whatever. She's on the edge of fantasy," Conway said.

"Damn. 'Then there were ten.'"

"Wrong, Falconer. We're still eleven. If you're going to play at being leader, spare us your fixation on counting our bodies, won't you?"

Before Conway realized what was happening, he was on his toes, his collar twisted in Falconer's fist, his breathing almost totally cut off. "You sanctimonious snot," Falconer said. "Eighty-six of my men are dead here. Men I picked, trained, men I loved like family. Never speak to me about what my position means, you hear me? Never. I won't warn you again."

Conway saved himself from falling with an outflung hand as Falconer roughly shoved him away. He was massaging his neck when Yoshimura rushed up. "What happened?" she asked. "He's losing his mind!" Her hands fluttered at his chest, afraid to light.

Conway said, "No harm. I said something stupid and he let me know it. Forget it."

Carter sidled closer, confiding. "Military mind." She nodded wisely, beaming a smile as fixed as paintwork. "Arrogant. We don't have to take his crap, you know."

Conway stared at Carter and Yoshimura. What he saw drove him to look at the others. There was something on their faces he'd not seen before. At first it looked like lust. Then he realized it was deeper, more dangerous. Restraints were breaking. They wanted a scapegoat.

He made excuses to get away, and watched Yoshimura resume her conversation with the same three women. She was back in a few minutes, saying, "Janet Carter insists we check on Harris. She's not ready to believe he hanged himself. It should be investigated." Seeing his uncertainty, she added, "You should be the first to wonder, after the way Falconer treated you."

"He didn't 'treat' me. He reacted perfectly normally to a stupid remark."

"My God, you're defending him. You're as brainwashed as one of his tin soldiers."

"I'm not— Yes, I am. I'm defending him, and there's no reason for it. He hasn't *done* anything."

"All of us aren't that sure. Even if we were, we can't leave poor Harris the way he is. We're getting Pastor Jones to come with us and bring him out. It's only right."

Conway said nothing, and Yoshimura flounced away. The four women and the Pastor huddled briefly. The women sent Conway poisonous glares before nervously entering the warehouse area.

Conway walked to where Falconer and Leclerc were busily hacksawing two sections of tubular air duct in equal lengths. Falconer greeted him with, "We can use another pair of hands. It'll give you something else to think about. At least we've got the tools for this job."

"What's the duct for?"

"We pack the plastic inside in the shape of a hollow cone. It has to look like we jammed an ice-cream cone point first in the stuff and pulled it out, you follow? Next, we pile rubble so we can place the charge perpendicular to the door, with the wide end of the cone aimed at where we think the hinges are. If we guess right—if the explosive is properly shaped and just the right distance from the door—when we set it off, all the explosive force is formed into a single pillar of energy. It'll go through this bastard like a hot nail through a butter patty."

"And if we miss the hinges?"

Falconer's grin tightened. "We try again. If the mountain will let us. If we have enough Hy-Pex."

"Listen," Conway said, "there's something you ought to know."

"You mean about the budding mutiny?"

"You knew?"

"Read it in their faces. You know you're being tarred with my brush, just helping here?"

"I said I'd help when I thought you were right. I don't think I have any choice."

Leclerc looked up from where he unwrapped rectangular blocks of cream-yellow explosive. His smile was wolfish. "Poor fool." He went back to his task.

It took longer to properly stack the rock to form a platform for the shaped charges than it did to make them. When they were in place, Falconer inserted the wired blasting caps. He led the way back to the group. Leclerc followed, paying out cable.

The fear and hostility in the air was palpable. Falconer ignored it. Leclerc busied himself with his wires. Yoshimura and her three friends approached Conway as he stood off by himself. Carter opened the conversation.

"We found something we want to talk to you about before anything else happens," she said.

He waited, and Yoshimura held out a briefcaselike object. He took it. "A VDP," he said, opening it to look at the video screen and incorporated disk player. She offered him a disk that looked like a smooth half-dollar.

"What's on it?" he asked.

She shook her head, mute. He read the center label. " 'For Colonel Burl Falconer, United States Army: Redesignated Mission and Reasons There-fore. (In the absence of Colonel Falconer this recording is the property of the senior United States Government official present in the Northwest Cryogenic Reconstruction Unit.)' " He scanned the waiting faces. "You've played it?"

Almost as if rehearsed, Yoshimura said, "We demand that Colonel Fal-coner be present when the rest of us hear it."

"Why? What're you saying?"

Carter said, "It was only a few feet from where—from Harris' body. They'd cut him down. They must've seen this. They already know what it says. They never thought we'd go in and find it."

Falconer shouted to them, unaware of the discussion. "Take cover, folks. We're going to blow."

"Wait!" Yoshimura was shrill, outraged. "Tell us about this vidisk!"

"What?" Puzzled, he walked toward them.

Carter held her ground as the others gave way nervously. She snatched the disk and VDP from Conway, holding them out. The gesture was accusa-tion. "This disk you and Leclerc watched in the warehouse."

He took it, brow wrinkled, reading silently, then still without speaking, he handed the electric cord to Leclerc and slipped the disk into the play slot. The screen lit up. A haunted, shattered face stared at them across a littered, rough desk. A limp American flag drooped on a pole behind him. The man wore a leather jacket, zipped up, despite being obviously indoors. The voice was painfully weary.

"Colonel Falconer. If you ever hear this, my apologies for what I'm doing to you and the rest of your unit. Things have gone badly in the cryogenic program. I've no time to be kind. Bluntly, you're all that's left."

A gasp went up from the listeners, now crowded around.

"We're adapting your facility to avoid the failures that . . . eliminated the others.

"First, I must tell you there will be no attendants. Every available hand is being relocated here to the provisional capital in the Alleghenies. The war's over, Colonel. Everyone lost. We're ending our second year with practically no summer in a world gone mad. National boundaries disappeared long ago; the United States, the Soviet Union simply don't exist. England is an island, nothing more. The continents of South America and Africa are chaos, and Australia is essentially devoid of human life. Asia is a charnel house.

"Between the hammer and anvil of nuclear weapons and chemical warfare, we managed to reduce the human population to remnants. No one knows who initiated the first attacks using species-specific genetically engineered bacteriological vectors, but now they're rampant. Everyone had their secret hoard, and population became everyone's prime target. After the first incurable disease showed up on three continents almost simultaneously, the thrust of the entire global conflict was revenge and extermination.

"Our best estimate of the population east of the Mississippi is somewhat less than one million men, women, and children. Most are desperately ill. All over the world, if conditions are not similar, they're worse.

"Your cave complex has been rendered airtight. A small nuclear generator of the most advanced design is installed at its deepest limit. I'm assured its life span is virtually eternal. We don't expect it to have to last quite that long."

The speaker attempted a smile, and someone among the watchers groaned audibly. The address continued.

"The entire facility is powered by the generator. A primary device will extract nitrogen from the air and create a positive two-atmosphere nondecay environment at essentially zero humidity. Machines have been provided to, uh, maintain the bacteriological integrity of the facility in the event of, uh, crèche failures."

He paused, wiped a hand across his face irritably. His frown remained, and Conway wondered if it ever really left. He went on:

"I apologize for ordering the heartless disposal of our dead this way. There's no alternative. So . . .

"When your monitor system determines that the environment favors your reentry, the pump will introduce fresh air. There are sustenance devices that will attend to the reestablishment of proper organ function and muscular stimulation. You already know your supply status is adequate for months without outside help.

"Colonel, you last saw America's teeming millions forging through the twenty-first century. What I tell you now may sound ludicrous. However, it's true. It is tragedy. Your trained fighting unit of eighty-seven men may be the largest, strongest military organization left in the world.

"The mechanization of the Northwest Cryogenic Unit is complete. We'll need the technical skills of your crèche companions to bring society back up to speed quickly. We still have enough electrical capability for a technology-fueled comeback, even though we're very short on population. We anticipate activating your reentry sequence by radio command in a decade; perhaps a bit more. That's a bit longer than we—or you—anticipated. I'm sorry. Help will be sent you if circumstances permit. You are ordered to conduct military operations as your situation requires until further instructed. If we're still functional, we'll answer your radio signals. Whether we are or not is im-material, as my last orders implied. Your mission goes beyond us here, beyond the members of your unit. You are the senior military man to have a chance of surviving this new Dark Age. I give you your mission in the simplest terms. You will execute it in whatever manner necessary.

"Reestablish the United States. What you cannot do in your lifetime must be charged to those who follow in your footsteps. The nation has fallen. It shall be raised."

In his intensity, the speaker leaned forward, and as he did, a cough ripped from deep in his lungs. He had to grip the desk with both hands before he could continue.

"If you have died, and someone else is watching this message, as President, I charge that person to assume Colonel Falconer's burden."

The screen flashed a printed message identifying the speaker as Mitchell Calderon, Acting President of the United States.

Bernhardt smothered a scream. "I know that name! He signed off on my last agronomy study. He was an Assistant Secretary of Agriculture. What's happening out there?"

"We'll know in a little while." Falconer spoke quietly, taking the detona-tor from Leclerc. "I want you to understand, I knew nothing of the VDP. If I had, there'd have been no vote on what I'm about to do. Believe that. Everyone into the control room."

Carter started to speak, but he silenced her with a glance. Inside the room, he said, "Pastor, if you have any special benedictions for powder monkeys, now's the time."

Jones smiled. "I think a silent prayer from all of us is in order. Will everyone bow heads and join me for one minute?"

He signaled an end with a loud "Amen." The response was subdued.

The explosion was ear-shattering. Cries of alarm turned to shrieks as slabs of rock shook free throughout the complex, adding their crash to the uproar. It was several seconds before the last noises subsided.

Conway staggered to his feet unmindful of trickling blood from a cut behind his ear. Others groaned, forcing themselves upright. He looked them over quickly, saw no major injuries, and stepped out into the tunnel. A heavy glow forced its way through the dust-laden darkness. He shouted hoarsely and broke into a run toward it.

Minutes later they were all pushing aside the fake rock door at the mouth of the tunnel, stumbling out in a crowd that laughed almost uncontrollably even as they choked. The continually working pump blew swirling clouds of dust after them. Rubbing eyes full of tears caused by equal amounts of grime and delight, they cheered and clapped each other's backs.

Anspach spoke first. Confusion dampened the gaiety in her voice. "Did they move us? This looks different."

Conway said, "There were no trees like this." He pointed at a huge fir, easily eight feet in diameter. "And there was a town in our valley."

Falconer stepped away, finding clearer air. He pointed up the slope. "Blast damage. See the places where it melted the rock to glass? They nuked us, blew away our outside monitoring devices."

Conway said, "That explains our isolation." He and the Colonel exchanged looks. Conway said, "If the air coming in isn't radioactive, they hit us a long time ago."

They turned to the trees again. Bernhardt joined them. She was trembling violently. "There were only two forests like this left in the country. And look—there's no damage to these trees. A nuclear explosion that close would've atomized them."

"Who cares about trees?" Karoli was furious. "We're out, and you three act disappointed. Aren't you ever satisfied? Harris told you it was an earthquake and not a bomb. Can't you stand to be wrong about anything?"

A pulse jumped in Falconer's temple. "These trees are at least five hundred years old. They grew here after we went inside."

CHAPTER 11

Smoke rose in funneling whorls from the tents until the breeze from the surrounding hills caught the plumes and bent them into a frayed cloak that shimmered with the warm reds of the setting sun. Nighthawks cried harshly, their stooping dives ending in small thunder. Far to the east, a solitary wolf howled.

Gan saw none of it, heard none of it. He retreated clumsily. His sword arm burned with exhaustion and his knees were like water, hardly able to sustain his weight. A puffed-up jaw ached dully. The point of Clas' wooden training murdat held his eye the way a snake transfixes a bird.

The duel was practice and it was punishment. It had been that way every evening since the skirmish at Tiger Rocks. This time, however, what had started as teacher-pupil had blazed into a struggle at the raw edge of passion. Each man now fought for self-control as well as victory. Gan knew he should lose. A force in him said *win*.

He struck with the last of his strength, shouting at the effort.

If the weapon had been steel, Clas would have been impaled. Even so, only his leather and iron practice armor saved him from serious injury. He grunted and staggered back, signaling an end. Tracing a bright scuff on his stomach plate, he said, "Look at that," barely believing.

Gan sagged against the training tent, relishing the luxury of a deep breath. Clas lit the four torch baskets on poles around the fighting circle. He said, "The opening was there."

Clas walked to the water gourd, poured himself a drink. When the cup was offered to Gan, he murmured polite thanks and sipped, resisting the need to drain it in a gulp. Clas said, "There was no opening. You created one. If we'd been using real murdats, my guts'd be on the ground. How'd you do it? Think."

Gan closed his eyes, visualizing. "Your left foot cheats forward. You lower the right shoulder and strike. The blade comes from my left and angles slightly across, not directly ahead. Your body turns to your left, denying my counterthrust a flat target. I struck as your foot moved."

"You may be the very best. If you continue to think while you fight. If the Elders don't send you on the Honor Journey."

"It's been more than a week. They won't let me stand my watch. They've never asked me again about what happened with the Devil riders."

"They will. Tomorrow."

"They've decided I was wrong. So has my father." His lips thinned to a line. The wooden weapon tapped against his thigh. "Other warriors are insulting me, Clas."

"The Elders aren't against you, they're being deliberate. And hold your temper. If you strike out at someone, you embarrass Nightwatch and your father. And you harm your case."

He jeered his answer. "Me? Embarrass him? Faldar will see that the Elders do that. Anyhow, all he cares about is being War Chief."

"Careful. Col's my friend, remember."

Gan stiffened. "Not mine. Nothing I do pleases him."

"He's spare with praise, I admit. He's actually very proud of you."

"Have you ever heard him say so?"

Clas winced. "Not in exactly those words, but what're words, after all?"

A weak smile partially relaxed Gan's resentment. He said, "Sometimes I wish I really didn't care what he thinks."

"You must. He needs you. I know." He clapped a hand on Gan's shoulder, directing his next words into the night. "Whoever's out there, step up where I can see you."

Following a small sound of surprise, a voice answered, "It's me. I know you, Clas na Bale—it's Neela. We saw you were talking so we—"

"We?"

Rose Priestess Sylah swept into the torchlight circle. Her black garb disappeared against the night, and her face, pale and beautiful, seemed to float toward them. "I know you, Clas; Gan. If we're interrupting, we'll leave."

Gan returned their greeting, then said, "We're finished here."

"Good. We've just come from Faldar Yan's tent."

Gan laughed. "And what new lies did my uncle share with you?"

Neela hissed like a cat. Sylah cut off her angry retort with a hand on her arm. She said, "He spoke of a possible Honor Journey for Gan, but wouldn't explain further. It's dangerous, isn't it?"

Clas said, "It's not certain he'll go."

Gan wanted her to understand. "There are always wrongs the tribe hasn't avenged. A Journeyman seeks out the enemies who committed the wrong. If he succeeds and survives to return, it's a sign the One in All forgives him, and we do, too. Win or lose, though, his honor is restored."

"Ahh, now I understand the stories the Mountain People told of Dogs raging into their camp only to kill and be killed. How many Journeymen return?"

"I remember two. One only came home to die, though."

Her temper flared, but instead of Gan, it was Clas she turned on. "Do you care so little for him? Tell me what I must do to stop this."

"You can do nothing. You cannot speak in Earth Heart, and that's where all decisions will be made."

"How cruel you all are—how unfeeling!"

Neela's sharp interruption startled everyone. Gan was astonished to see unshed tears trembling in her eyes. "That's not so! They'll decide what's best for the honor of the tribe. No one *wants* Gan harmed."

Clas said, "This is pointless. It's improper, as well. Women mustn't know what men say in Earth Heart."

"What men say." Sylah's rough scorn made them all blink.

Gan waited for Clas' explosion, but he merely sighed and said, "Can we speak of something else?"

"If the Dog code of honor allows you more than one subject." Then, with a lightning quick change of mood, she spoke to Gan with a tenderness that was as soothing as her anger was fierce. She leaned closer to smooth back his hair, and almost destroyed his ability to comprehend her words. "You and I started badly. I want to make apology and show you that even in a loss such as yours, there's renewal. Here is Shara."

Unobserved, Neela had stepped outside the circle of light. Now she came back. The lanky pup accompanying her on its leash looked at Gan as if it understood what was taking place.

Speechless, Gan bent to him. The dog licked his new master's face and wiggled happily while being inspected.

Clas said, "He should be outside camp now, Gan, and I want to talk to Priestess Sylah. Will you excuse us, please? Tell your father I'll be at Earth Heart with both of you tomorrow."

Gan turned to leave, but Clas wasn't finished. He said, "I've had no chance to tell you, Neela, but you get prettier every day. Did you charm the Dog Chief into giving you Shara?"

The girl blushed at the bluff flattery. "Oh, no. When Sylah told him why we were there, he took us straight to Shara." She hesitated, then finished in a flustered rush. "And thank you, Clas na Bale."

He laughed. "I first saw you the day your father took me on a bear hunt. It was your fourth birthday. I think we've known each other long enough for you to call me Clas, especially now that you're all grown up."

Neela was away so quickly, Gan had to hurry to catch her. Shara, delighting in companionship, leaped to nudge them both.

When out of earshot, Gan looked over his shoulder at the couple in the torchlit circle. He said, "She's a strange woman. Sometimes, when she doesn't think anyone's watching, she gets a fierce expression, and I think she must hate all of us. She makes me uncomfortable when I'm around her, but—" He paused, then blurted, "She's so beautiful. Do you think she really likes Clas?"

"Clas? Her? Honestly, Gan, you spend too much time alone. She's a War Healer. Clas needs a woman who can make a good home, raise children with him."

"You think so? Good. For him, I mean. Still, War Healers marry." Musing, he added, "He looks at her—I don't know—different." He looked over his shoulder again, missing Neela's growing agitation.

"Clas is only ten years older than I am; I'll be seventeen in two months. She's at least his age."

Gan scoffed. "You're blind."

"I'll just ask her."

"That's rude."

"Not for me; she's teaching me about healing. She says we're sisters." The last was a taunt.

Stung, Gan said, "Important people are supposed to be nice to nobodies. That reminds me—what'd she talk about with your father?"

"Everyone knows your father wants you to be War Chief after him. My father said no one inherits that title, especially not you. He said you've been nothing but a shadow all your life, following Clas or your father. Bay said you don't have a single friend."

"Bay's a bully. So are all your brothers, and the sheep that flock after them. They're the ones with no friends."

Neela's eyes narrowed to slits, and she resumed her walk to the tent with stiff, jerking steps. The tight silence lasted to the entrance, where he attempted amends. "I'm sorry. I shouldn't have said that."

Her answer crackled. "What happened with the Devils proves you're a dreamer. My father says you're proof your father's no leader." She slipped inside.

The words echoed in his ears. He went to his own tent, boiling with helpless fury. As he readied for bed, he imagined the Elders facing him, stern, giving him his Honor Journey task.

He would show them, the Priestess, his father, Neela, *all* of them. Especially Neela.

Why had he thought that? *Neela?* What was she, compared to the others? He fell asleep wondering if he was losing his sense of proportion.

*   *   *

Sylah turned from watching Gan and Neela walk away with the dog. The firelight of the torches emphasized the tattoo on Clas' cheek. He said, "I understand you were conferring with Faldar for quite a while today. Again." The last word was almost an accusation.

Her own resentment caught her off guard, and she answered more sharply than she meant to. "My work is no business of yours."

Dryly, he asked, "Your work? Is he so badly injured? He looks healthy to me."

"Your tribe has only one Healer and no War Healer. We discussed bringing more here from my abbey. Church wants to help you."

"And herself."

"Oh, stop being so suspicious. Ask yourself, how could Kolee manage if a killing sickness struck the tribe?"

He stiffened, and she was sure his hand twitched, ready to make a Three-sign to ward off danger. He said, "We don't speak of such things. You shouldn't."

"Someone has to have the courage and skill to care for the ill." She heard the thin smear of superiority in her voice too late, saw his flare of injured pride. She told herself it was exactly what she should have expected. He was unable to deny his dread of sickness, and unwilling to admit to any fear. Quickly, she rushed on, trying to repair the damage. "More Healers can only benefit you all."

"And we'll need them, if Faldar has his way. He wants war."

She hated him for so bluntly speaking the undeniable truth. Her need to maintain close contact with Faldar outweighed all other considerations, she thought. It was the only way. Having satisfied himself she was a spy for Altanar, Faldar now believed he'd disarmed her by confronting her. He was still secretive about his exact plans, however, and that information would solidly confirm safe haven in Harbundai. That, plus the girl, would be enough.

She thought of what she intended for Neela, and a surge of shame made her deny Clas' declaration. "He doesn't want war. He asks me what I learned among the Mountain People and of the activity in Ola and Harbundai. He understands that the restlessness in the west means your tribe must be prepared."

They argued until the torches were nothing but smoldering remains dripping brief sparks that gleamed for one last beautiful moment before blinking out on the hard-packed earth of the fighting circle.

It was she who called for an end, feigning exasperation in order to get time to deal with her spiraling confusion. She hated her own lies, the deceitful attempt to make him believe—as she must make them all believe—that her sole concern was their well-being.

When he offered to escort her to her quarters, she accepted. He had to stow his equipment, and she waited where she stood. As he strode off, she tasted the lies on her tongue and yearned to call him back.

That was impossible. She steeled her resolve. The only strength she could rely on was hers.

She was alone.

A humorless smile twisted her lips as she recalled how clearly Likat had made her understand that fact. Without his lesson, she might have tried to find a different way to forestall Faldar.

Now she wanted only to succeed. At whatever cost.

After all, Church's goal was the survival of Harbundai, for the hope it offered all women, including those of the Dog People. Even if lives were lost, their sacrifice would be for a great step in the advancement of half the world's population. Surely that was worth her few lies?

Clas was coming back, his figure a shadowy bulk against the pale tent, when a final, stinging question crossed her mind: Would she be so willing and ruthless if she didn't have her own goal?

Who was she, really? A Rose Priestess who schemed for Church in order to better the lives of all her sex? Or the bitter Chosen, determined to gain the mysterious power of the Door and revenge herself?

Did the Door even exist? Could she risk so much on a legend?

He was in front of her by then, the rugged features softened by the faint light from the distant tents. They both hesitated, spoke at once, stopped, then laughed inordinately at the break in their mutual tension. She started again, and he reached to put his index finger to her lips, a surprisingly gentle touch. When he withdrew the hand, she felt shy. Awkward, somehow. He said, "Me first. I'm sorry if I was disagreeable, but I worry that someone will think you're taking sides in our troubles. You'll be disliked by all."

"Even by you?" The question was out before she realized it.

He hesitated. When he continued, his tone was the same, but caution gave the words an untypical smoothness. "Never that. I'm your friend. Not that many would advise you to seek me out." He laughed humorlessly, and when it earned him an arch look, he explained. "You spoke of Faldar's awareness of changes coming. Believe me, there is more than he dreams. This I know. He's persuaded almost all the younger warriors and most of the tribe to believe his foolishness about peace being responsible for our problems. It's important you not get involved, as I said." He paused, and she knew he was planning his next words. "You should also know I'm Col's friend, and Gan's. What happens to them happens to me. Gan's more than an ordinary young man. I want you to know him, and to understand all of us—Col, him, and me."

She asked, "Why? Especially since I have no intention of getting involved in your problems."

There was suppressed excitement and a touch of wonder in his voice. "Tonight I saw something I've expected for a long time." He related the duel and its ending. "He *will* be a leader, and a leader has to have the heart to strike with all his strength when he sees an opening. Gan's never had that, no matter how often others called his name."

"Called his name?"

"Challenged him to fight. It hasn't happened for a while. No one dares. He's had a lonely, difficult growing up, and now he's coming to be a man. Church should help him."

She covered a smile with her hand. He was as subtle as a spear. She wanted to tell him she was already drawn to the boy, but that might lead to an expectation of commitment, or support. That couldn't be. Her own program was all-important. Nothing must interfere. That included the Abbess' mission, of course.

They strolled in silence for a while. Sylah surrendered to the atmosphere of the camp. Voices rose from the tents in a lulling, beelike hum. Occasional laughter cut across the predominant sound, reminding her of the glimmering sparks of the torches. Once, fragments of song drifted past, borne on soft, strummed music. She noted the reactions Clas generated. All children watched his every move with nearly idolatrous awe. Adults greeted him effusively or avoided him. She recognized the behavior and was saddened. There are men who are identified too closely with death.

She returned to the pleasures of their walk. Just as she inhaled deeply and remarked on the savory smells of burning wood and cooking, a woman's voice called out names and announced dinner. A whirl of shouting children raced by, and Sylah and Clas shared more laughter at their carefree happiness.

An innocent thing destroyed it all in seconds. Nearby, someone was boiling water, using the technique called choga, dropping heated rocks into a container. The smell of steaming granite generated a memory picture of Ola, with its precise geometry, where summer's hot stone and brick walls made the narrow streets nothing but elongated, humid, filthy cells. She remembered columns of little girls, two by two, as like as beans in their uniform dresses. They marched with shining faces, singing songs they barely comprehended as if their lives depended on it. Which was small exaggeration for Chosens.

He interrupted her reminiscence, stopping abruptly, taking her hand in his. Automatically, she pulled against his grip. He held her firmly, unbreakably, and yet unthreatening. His gaze sought hers. He said, "I have to go on a scouting patrol tomorrow. A pleasant ride, actually. Come with me. I want to continue our talk. Perhaps there are things you want to say to me. I think I have some idea what it must be like for you here."

She spun away, retreating inside her cloak, needing a respite from his honest, sympathetic eyes. Once she thought him incapable of caring. Now she realized that, for all his terrible skills, there were dreams and desires and vulnerabilities behind that deliberately forbidding visage. She wondered what they might be, wondered if anyone else ever concerned themselves about them.

She turned back to him, reaching to soothe the muscle that worked so furiously under the black tattoo. His skin was remarkably supple against the unyielding bone. The tremor faded under her touch.

A distant movement interrupted her. Against the light of a tent, she saw a party of four Nightwatchers trotting out to their posts. Firelight flicked across their bodies, glinted on weapons. One of the dogs barked excitedly, and a man shouted a command.

She heard voices, saw colors like that once before, far away, long ago. *Screams.*

She jerked her hand back.

He said, "I leave at first light. Will you come?"

"I'll look forward to it." She was proud of the perfect words, smooth and convincing. She ducked past him and through the entry slit, hurrying to fall on her bed.

It was wrong of him to make her ashamed, wrong of him to make her mind wander from its goals.

Those young men, with their deep, confident voices, their intimidating metal trappings.

Yes! He commanded Nightwatch. He knew they'd come and frighten her. He planned it. That was exactly why she was forced to do these unpleasant things—she admitted it: cruel things—that she hated doing. It was all because they all wanted to use her. It was their fault. He was no different.

Her hands hurt. Holding them to the light, she stared at the half-moon gouges her fingernails had etched in her palms. The pain was fading quickly. She blamed it for the rush of hot, needling tears, nevertheless.

CHAPTER 12

Through ingrained habit, Sylah was up early, washed and dressed by the time Clas whispered her name through the softwall.

He had Copper saddled and ready. The animal acted glad to see her, shaking its head and prancing. The rich coat wasn't quite so lustrous in dawn's chill light, she thought, but that only drew attention to the way the long, heavy muscles moved under it. She fed him a piece of dried apple before swinging up onto his back.

They rode south in companionable silence. In plain fact, she didn't want to talk. Sleep had been elusive and fitful the previous night. She'd almost decided not to go with Clas. She'd told herself over and over that her logic and insight had saved her from foolish sympathy for Clas and the other savages. Her own needs far outweighed their problems. Nevertheless, the prospect of leading him on to confide in her made her skin crawl.

The early morning stir of the waking camp was a needed distraction. Roosters crowed indiscriminate challenge from every direction. One shepherded his flock away from the horses' hooves, glaring over a gleaming black-green shoulder until they were well past. A baby cried, eager to be fed. Horses whickered and shuffled in the small brushwood stables that stood behind every tent. Distant cattle and sheep bawled. Few people were up yet. The half-dozen early risers they saw stumbled drowsily on their way to or from the latrines or one of the banks of shower rooms.

It was several minutes until Sylah and Clas cleared the last tents, and a while longer before she smelled the sulfurous fumes of the hot springs. Pointing with his chin, Clas said, "The soaks are just ahead. There's time for you to try it."

She shook her head. "I've nothing to dry off with."

"I brought drying cloths."

"Not this morning, thank you."

They continued around a bend, coming to a series of unroofed rectangular cubicles constructed of light timber frames with hide walls. With a floor space perhaps seven feet by four feet, each had its fourth wall rolled up, revealing the interior. Wooden pipes carried water from the springs to tall wooden tubs designed for seated immersion. The term "soaks" was appropriate, she decided. When she looked at him, he was grinning. He tried to swallow it, failing miserably, and she laughed, too, telling herself she had to behave naturally. And he was amusing, really. In a crude sort of way. He said, "Maybe you'd like to reconsider?"

"I would. And you're an evil-minded man. You knew I'd think there was no shelter, that I'd just be—well—uncovered."

"It was fun to let you think so." He handed her a soft cotton cloth. She glanced past it at a roguish, teasing expression that was yet another totally unexpected facet. She grabbed the cloth and entered a room.

Inserting the tub's plug, she turned the faucet on the pipe. Swirling steam rose to capture the bright sunlight, taking on glowing life. She hung her clothes on pegs jutting from the room's wooden frame. A large clay jar with a dipper puzzled her until she put a hand in the tub and jerked it back. She reduced the pipe's flow and ladled in cold water from the jar.

Sinking into the water, there was a brief sting as the heat touched the healing wound left by Likat's knife. It passed quickly, and she groaned with pleasure, only to start at Clas' worried, "Are you all right?"

She assured him she was, and continued to sink up to her chin, smiling to herself at the paradox of being almost frightened by his presence while taking comfort in his availability.

There was a shelf within easy reach, holding a collection of clay pots and a stiff, coarse brush. She pushed the latter aside, wincing at the thought of it. The pots held oils and herbal infusions, some spicy, some sweet, and one that had a brisk, springtime touch she decided was exactly appropriate. She trickled a generous dollop into her bath and abandoned herself to sheer enjoyment. The perfumed water buoyed her, took away weight, care, and the hard edge of consciousness.

Her head lolling to the side woke her with such a jerk she popped upright, sloshing water out of the tub.

Clas called again, this time through laughter. "Are you practicing diving over there?"

"Never mind. I just moved a little, that's all." He was so close. Not that it was important. After all, she'd dealt with many naked men.

None of them were Clas na Bale. Nor had she been naked, one thickness of cowhide away. And no one else within miles.

She examined the wall. She wondered if he were doing the same thing. It suddenly looked very flimsy.

The water seemed to be growing warmer. She looked down, where the shimmering surface and rising steam gave her body a filmy softness. Only the curve of her breasts was clearly visible, the white swell of them half submerged.

She knew she attracted Clas. There was need as well as want in his sidelong glances. In a different world, it would be interesting to probe the complex man behind the image.

Another face, the loathsomeness of Likat, tried to form. She willed it away.

What was it Neela had said? *Life is a circle.* A person's life circle was only completed by another person.

Her head drooped, bringing the water almost to the lazy smile curving her lips.

Clas' words broke in on her. "Sylah? I have to go."

Getting out, she enjoyed the briskness that nipped at flesh without being able to touch the inner warmth beneath it. Her clothing hoarded the warmth and scent of the bath. She felt snug, immaculately clean, and marvelously refreshed. She was humming when she lifted the wall flap and rejoined him.

They continued south as he explained the reason for his ride. Night-watchers had reported an increase in wolf talk. When she laughed, teasing him about talking animals, he laughed with her. Still, he defended the phrase. She hadn't expected the tribe to take such a thing seriously.

Their conversation drifted casually. When she skirted close to subjects he thought intruded on tribal matters, he simply said so. She thought back to the elaborate, double-edged conversations of Ola and shuddered. Emboldened by his openness, her curiosity gnawing at her, she asked him about the tattoo.

For several long, silent seconds she was certain she'd crushed a growing friendship. The prospect of loss shocked her, left her wondering exactly what she did think of him. Last night she blamed him for her pain. An hour ago she was reassured—yes, gladdened—by his company.

A vein throbbed painfully at her temple. Nothing was the way it was supposed to be.

He was *infuriating*.

He said, "No one asks me that. The tribe knows, of course, but no one ever speaks about it."

She tried to retreat. "If it bothers you—"

He interrupted her. Voice and manner pleaded that she hear and understand. "It was a hunting party. Twelve years ago. Twenty boy-men on our first long hunt. East, in the country of the Buffalo Eaters. I led.

"We found an area with good sign, then searched out the resident band, exchanged greetings and gifts. They were hospitable. It was a trick." Sorrow colored his voice across the years. "They came in the dark. One of our watch lived to give the alarm."

They rode for a long while before he started again. She could almost feel the anguish of his waking that night. He said, "Once they'd lost complete surprise, they lost most of their courage. In the morning they offered to talk. I said no, but the others wanted it. As leader, I went. The Buffalo Eaters said we had to give them half of our horses. I bargained. All the while, they moved warriors closer to our party. When the next attack was launched, they captured me. They made me watch them slaughter my friends."

"How did you escape?"

His hand rose breast high, fingers extended toward the tattoo. He stopped the motion before completing it. "They tied my hands and feet. They slit my cheek and put a metal strip through it, then pulled it out my mouth and nailed it to a long stick. The other end they nailed to a post. It was just long enough so I could kneel."

Something hot burned the back of her throat. She swallowed and asked, "How long—"

"I don't know. Long enough for me to work the rawhide off my wrists. By then they probably thought I was too weak to do anything if I did get free."

In the fleeting moment before his grin forced her to look away, she confirmed what she'd suspected all along. Violence had created him. It sustained him, was required of him. His skills and sense of duty were two jaws of a trap closed on his life. He was no less a prisoner—or product—than she.

He told of silently murdering his way across the camp to the horse corral. Releasing all but one mount for himself, he drove them ahead of him until he was sure he was clear. From that day, he hunted men as others hunted animals.

Pausing, he heaved a great sigh, and Sylah felt it was safe to look into his face once more. He said, "Scars are natural. A perfect square is not, and men are not. Why can't we—" He stopped and shook his head. "Enough. I talk too much."

"I'm sorry I asked."

He looked at her with an intensity almost as strong as before. "Don't be. I'm not. Anyhow, I think you may have a story of your own."

She kept her focus on the horizon. He went on. "None have dared take our children for many years, but we remember raids and slave-takers. We know about Chosens. You're one. There's more to you than you've said."

"You don't know anything about me."

"I will."

She heeled Copper, sending him into a surprised hop that left Clas behind. About the time she convinced herself that she was being foolish, he called to her, pointing. Looking up at the ridge above the wide draw they were following, she saw nothing. When he caught up, she accused him of playing tricks. He laughed quietly, directing her gaze until she saw the wolf. Immediately, she saw another, then two more. She grabbed his arm. In a rough whisper he said, "Quiet! No more talk," and indicated they should move forward.

The wolves disappeared, and then, materializing like dust, there was one paralleling them on the skyline. Noticing Clas looking to the left, Sylah did the same. Another padded down that ridge.

She felt more eyes, knew there was something behind her. Slowly, stiffly, she turned.

There were two more. They alternated between watching the riders and the back trail. Their gaze was steady, unblinking.

Clas took Copper's reins, urging both mounts to a trot. She watched him, the set of his jaw, the stone-gray eyes never still. She almost wished the brutes following them would attack so he could show them who they were dealing with. The wild notion was gone as quickly as it came, but the delicious tingle of it surged in her veins a good deal longer.

Sylah estimated they traveled over three miles before Clas reined in abruptly. Ahead, on the flat top of a prominent hill, a wolf looked down at them. It inspected them for a few moments longer before it finally padded around in a tight circle. Then it marked a bush and retreated out of sight.

Clas led up the hill. On top he rode back and forth, still not speaking. Dismounting, he showed Sylah some broken stems and flattened grass. She frowned. "That means nothing to me. Why did they do that to us?"

He continued to examine the ground. "The wolves? They help us, although they never entirely trust us." He grinned up at her. The image of the panting wolf seemed to blend with his for an instant. "We never hunt them. In hard times, we share from our herds. Sometimes we share in the hunt. This pack's led us to where outsiders have rested."

She shivered. "You should have told me they're friendly."

"They're not. Gan—" He stopped, exactly as he had the previous night when he sensed his words were outrunning caution, then ended, "Gan never has real trouble with them."

She peered about anxiously, moving closer to him. "You mean they *do* attack people?"

"Not those packs that share our land." Then he pointed at the ground. "Four horsemen, two days ago." He squatted, exclaiming over a discarded carrying bag. Woven of cedar bark, it looked like any other to her. When he rose, he said, "Devils," making it a curse.

"I warned you. They're coming."

"From the south?" He shook his head. "Something's wrong. This makes no sense."

On the ride back, he remained deep in thought. She coaxed him into conversation by asking him what stories the Dog People told of their origin. He responded reluctantly, saying he didn't believe there were ever ten thousand members of the tribe at one time, but the legend said that's how many originally lived in the south. A man simply called Leader banded together families and other semiclan groups when people made their way through God's Scourge.

She asked him if their legends were the same as Ola's, and he shrugged, saying everyone he'd ever heard told the same story: All people were originally born from a womb called the Great Burning into a world called the Dark Cold. It was the One in All's way of punishing them for wanting too much, even as they were still being carried by Mother Earth. Those who survived being born were further tested by disease and radpads, where people died of the unseeable radeath. The land of the Dog People's origin was thick with godkills and radpads. Wherever they ran, disease and radeath were there, waiting. They became worse than animals, without even the human necessities of clan and tribal loyalties.

Constant losses and flight from other groups eventually drove them to a small stronghold on the edge of a land called the Dry. That was when the second leader appeared, a stranger accompanied by his pack of great dogs. He was their proven Siah; he brought the message that the tribe must fight its way north. It took several generations for the now-called Dog People to reach this homeland.

Clas' manner changed at that point. His gaze fastened on a point on the horizon. Almost defiantly, he said it was hard for him to believe in the giants who were supposed to have been the forerunners of all people. No one could question they existed. Everyone mined and quarried the places where they built their sacred cities. But that was the point: If they were so strong and wise, why did the legend say they were cursed? How could they disappear? If the so-called cities were sacred, why were most supposed to be lost to all men forever? And if they'd been sacred, why were they desecrated, turned into godkills and radpads, deadly to all for almost a century after the birth and beginning of men? He'd heard that some nations still executed anyone known to have been near either a godkill or radpad.

Muscles bunched in his jaws, and he made a cutting gesture with the edge of his hand. "We still fight constantly. We still suffer plagues. Nothing changes."

Her retort flew from her mouth. "It *can* change. It must." She'd spoken of her own goals, not his history. She wished she could call the words back, and waited for his next question with dread. Rather than that, however, he merely studied her. At last he said, "You may speak more truly than you can imagine." Then, to her amazement, he threw back his head and laughed in peals that echoed from the draws.

Two miles south and east they came to the mouth of a shallow valley leading off the major one they were following. When it opened to her view, Sylah exclaimed in wonder and delight. The meadow that was the valley's floor exploded with flowers, more than she'd ever seen in one place. A small creek cut across the far side, the glitter of the water like shy laughter from behind the shielding brush. It was a moment before Sylah realized that those were the only tall plants in the entire valley. Then her eye was drawn to the far end. An altar dominated the narrow neck. It was a single huge table of black stone mounted on two gray boulders, each the size of a large Dog tent. The flat slab must have weighed tons; she wondered how they'd ever gotten it up there. Clas said, "The altar's our place of burning. The women keep the valley like this."

"It's a lovely place, Clas. I've never seen anything like it."

He looked puzzled, and she went on. "We have cremation places, too, but ours are dull and sad. These flowers, the stream—it's a place for pleasant memories."

He turned away, looking uncomfortable. His words seemed to come with difficulty. "The flowers weren't our way, either. Before her."

"Before her? Who?"

"My wife." The new voice grated like steel on steel. She twisted in the saddle, looking at the clumped rocks beside them. She was just in time to see a scowling Col Moondark whip his horse at her.

Chapter 13

Col's horse reared to a stop less than a yard from Sylah. With its ears flattened to its head and its gnashing teeth bared, it clearly understood its rider's frame of mind and was ready for battle. It champed at its bit as Col held it in check. Copper trembled violently, but held firm.

Clas grinned easily at Col. "Never expected you here," he said.

Col nodded. "I know you, Priestess. I heard he took you riding this morning. Has he told you everything?"

Stung, Clas abandoned any pretense of guest-manners. "Of course not. But I still think we should."

A sudden coldness seized Sylah, sent ice rushing through her body. These men, these ignorant, trusting, men were going to reveal secrets to her, secrets they'd already argued about sharing.

And she had to betray them.

"I won't listen." It was her voice, from a distance. "I don't want to know."

"Please." It was Clas, soothing. "It's to help Gan. The tribe." He looked at Col again. The older man nodded, approving. Clas went on. "There are things—and people—involved. More than us."

The coldness was in her mind, telling her she owed them nothing, owed Church her promise. And without supporting Church, she failed herself. At the same time, she saw the soaring hope in him, heard the unspoken conviction that they had knowledge of special importance.

She took a deep breath and said, "Church serves all." They would hear the true phrase. Only she knew the lie hidden behind it.

When Col dismounted, she was impressed by how slow he was. He moved with the deliberation of a man who trusts his strength and coordination, but acknowledges that the resilience of his youth has faded. The spring blossoms reached to the tops of his mid-calf boots. Sylah joined him at his invitation, and within a few steps they were both wearing a wash of pollen, hers a wide swath on the black robe, his repeated stripes on boots and leather trousers.

He walked as he'd dismounted, with measured steps, and his beginning words were as carefully chosen.

He revealed that his wife was a gift woman. In his younger years he'd led a raid against a river tribe, and was about to put their homes and boats to the torch when they offered her to stop him.

Sylah was shocked and angered. When he added that he'd accepted, despite the fact that owning slaves had been unknown among the Dog People for almost a hundred years at the time, she rejoiced. He deserved to be deceived, and her conscience would be clear.

The woman's name was Murmillanh, and when he pronounced it, it rolled from his tongue like a song of loneliness. In the one word Sylah felt she knew the other woman's soul. Torn from her people, she'd spent the rest of her life among strangers, listening for the softness of the river's passing, yearning to see once more the mysterious dark waters, yet loved as few women dared hope to be. Listening to him describe how her tribal Elders had displayed her, naked save for a girdle that was little more than a belt, she realized he still felt her shame.

A smile finally worked through when he told how furious his warriors were when he refused an alternate prize, a hundred pounds of fine steel. "They wanted that steel," he said. "They didn't understand. One look. She was my woman." He stopped and looked at her, willing her to grasp that instant, so many years ago. Grudgingly, she conceded she was listening to a romance.

The tribe was scandalized when they returned and he announced that she was his wife. It was a lie. He grinned at the admission. "I courted her," he said. "In my own tent, like a tongue-tied boy. For the first month she never even spoke to me. It was almost a year before she finally came to my bed. When she did, she was more than I'd hoped, more than I'd dreamed. The next day she told me two things. I would never hear her say she loved me. Only a free heart can express love, she said, and because I took her body as a bribe, the heart within it had never been free to make a choice. Then she said we would have a son. I was too drunk with pleasure, with happiness, with the possession of her, to truly hear what she said."

Sylah said, "It sounds straightforward to me."

He smiled. "Murmillanh saw things that were yet to be. Not everything; sometimes she knew the numbers of a person's days, but not how they ended. Sometimes she knew exactly how a person left this world, but not when. I've heard her name the sex of children yet to be conceived, and describe the fathers before they'd ever seen the mothers."

He stopped walking then, growing silent. A breeze sighed across the valley floor, rich with the taste of rain. Col said, "She died the night after Gan was born. She held my hand and told me she'd lived as two people in one body, and now she was giving me a son who was the same. She cried. She knew she was dying, and she cried because she was afraid for me. Our son would bring about my death. He would destroy what I created, because he would be destroyer and creator. Then she quoted something. To do with Church, I think. It went something like, 'Birth is how we defeat death, because birth is not the reappearance of the old, which is known, but the creation of a new vision, with new hope.'"

They remained in silence several long minutes, giving Sylah time to quiet a racing heart. The "something" Murmillanh had quoted was from First Church, part of the ancient, forbidden teaching.

Who was this woman? Where could she have heard those words?

A bit later he looked in all directions and even scented the air before speaking, even though they were alone in the featureless meadow. He finished his story. Murmillanh begged him to stand by Gan so long as one still had breath, declaring her son would need protection. His future, she said, would be dangerous and vast, a flame that would devour all that touched it. Or consume Gan himself. She saw two fates, equally likely. If one prevailed, his fame would reach beyond the tribe, beyond the Enemy Mountains, beyond lands as yet unknown to the Dog People. If not that, wild animals would gnaw his forgotten bones. Col said, "Her last words were, 'However my son lives, before he dies he will have opened the door to the future of the cross.' You, of all people, know what happens to women who speak of the cross."

The wind was up by the time he finished, whispering scandal through leaves and stems that tossed in agitated disarray. Thunder sounded suddenly in the distance, a tearing crack that shook the earth and then died with a surly growl. Sylah's pulse was like galloping hoofbeats. Col looked at her with pain scoring deep, dark lines across his face.

"I shared what she said with one person, my friend Clas na Bale. Not even Gan knows. I believe his mother was right about him, although he shows no signs of leadership. Still, when I look at him, I feel I'm watching that second person struggling to be known. The wolves understand there's a power in him." At the sudden lift of her eyebrows, he nodded. "Since he was a baby. Where he is, the wolves are. They watch for him. He hunts with them. They talk on Nightwatch, singing to the moon and each other. Many times I've thought they're the only real friends he has, except for his dogs and Clas."

"Why tell me this? I have nothing to offer you."

Col shook his head. "When the Elders send Gan on the Honor Journey, Clas and I will ride with him. I've thought long and hard about this, and I think the One in All sent you here, intended that you help him. After all, 'the cross' can only mean Church. While he's gone, you convince the tribe that it would be a special sign of religious favor if he comes back. He will. And Church will benefit, as well as himself."

Trying to appear calm, Sylah forced a small laugh, appalled at the scratchiness of it. If Col noticed, he gave no sign. She said, "What purpose does it serve for you both to go with him? I don't understand."

He started to answer, stopping to peer up at the increasingly angry sky. There had been no more thunder, but the first drops of rain were coming down now, and he led her back toward the patient Clas and their horses. On the way, he explained that neither he nor Class would survive long under Faldar Yan's rule, and that leaving the tribe was the only way they could prevent a partisan clash. Then, as close to shyness as he could come, he confessed, "My life, and Gan's, have been built on Murmillanh's prophecy. I withheld love from him because I believe he must kill me, and I want it to cause him as little pain as possible. But I do love him—you must never repeat that—and I'll protect him as I promised. And that's enough for now. Hurry; the rain."

Later he slowed to allow her to come up beside him. She realized he was waiting for an answer to his request for her help. She told him she needed time to think. He made no effort to hide his disappointment, but nodded agreeably enough.

Single file after that, with her between them, they plodded through the rain. A short distance from the camp, Col split off, leaving them to enter as a couple, the way they left. She and Clas continued, still wrapped in their individual silences, until they exchanged good-byes outside her tent. His desire to talk to her was so transparent, she felt guilty pretending not to see it, but she dared not. Not then.

As soon as she was alone in her sleeping room, she stripped off her wet clothes and put on a robe. She warmed quickly, but a persistent shiver continued to plague her. There was a coal-keeper in the firepit, a small jug made of porous unglazed clay, with a lid of the same material. Coals placed in there, with a supply of crumbled wood, would keep alight for days. When she opened it and tried to touch a waxed taper of plaited shavings to the glow, her hand shook without stop. She eventually succeeded in starting a fire in the pit, and even that failed to completely quiet her tremors. Finally she curled up under the quilted blanket on her bed. Then she called on the trance.

As hard as she tried, her body refused to react properly. Instead of slowing, her heartbeat increased, and her skin felt hot and prickly. It occurred to her that it might be wise to abandon the effort while her emotions were so complicated by the events of the day, but she urgently wanted to concentrate on Col's request. She persisted.

The grove failed to appear. Rather, it tried and failed. A sere, blasted view opened in front of her. Fierce, jagged mountains loomed in the distance. A hot wind beat at her with stinging sand.

She hated this place. She fought to come away from the trance, to regain control.

Something pulled her. She was slipping away.

Unable to cry out, she strained to open her eyes. Lanta's voice echoed hollowly, warning. Then she was falling, falling in silent, blind terror.

The trance wouldn't release her.

Deceit.

Time collapsed. She was thrown back to Ola.

The Abbess lay in her bed, the first tint of returning health no more than brush strokes on the drained features. Words husked in her throat like windblown leaves. "The other sisters tell me you ate here, slept on the floor beside me. Over a week."

"In case you woke and needed something."

Her smile was an effort. "I need you. I'm blessed; I found you."

Found. What of those who lost me, and whom I lost?

Sylah's need to tell the older woman what she'd babbled in her sickness clamored within her. Church's deepest secret—the Door—was believed to exist by the oldest, most faithful of her leaders, even though it had been lost for centuries. The forbidden psalms of First Church exalted it. The Abbess' ravings spoke of clandestine committees that debated searching for it.

The bent, delicate bones in her hand were as frail as straw when Sylah patted it, disguising pity as sympathy.

Protector. Owner. If the power of the Door is so strong you fear it, I will have it.

The Abbess had kissed the hand fondling her own. So weary, so near death for so long. She said, "You are the daughter of my heart."

She felt the trance reject her, send her mind spinning back to her like a scorned offering.

An uneasy sleep came quickly. It was rank with terrible dreams, full of unfocused fears that flung her from side to side on the bed until she woke to confront a dark that mocked her with uncaring stillness.

CHAPTER 14

The squat, square form of Faldar Yan watched Sylah and Neela approach. Dressed in coarse gray trousers and a darker gray woolen blouse, he stood in front of his tent, legs spread, feet planted. Copper shook his head back and forth as Sylah guided him closer, as if arguing with her directions. She wanted to compliment him for his good sense.

They exchanged greetings. Sylah felt cheapened by his every glance, and she turned away while he chatted with his daughter. When she gave Copper his head, she was gratified by the way he inched away from the conversation. Soon she was distant enough to be ignored by both father and daughter. For a few moments she let her attention wander, becoming engrossed in some children. They played a game with their bows and blunt arrows, with one of their number elected to roll a disk past their waiting line. Each shot at

the target in turn. A hit drew loud cheers, and the triumphant archer ran
to take his place at the end of the line. From there, the most accurate teased
the less proficient.

A movement at the corner of her vision distracted her. She looked back
to the tent in time to see Bay and Likat stepping out.

Bay smiled in imitation of his father as he acknowledged her. The smaller
man shot her a quick glance that managed to be as threatening as it was slyly
suggestive. Then he dismissed her utterly, mouthing his formal greeting with
his full attention focused on Neela. Despite her hatred of him, Sylah found
her own feelings overridden by concern for Neela, because she saw what
none of them could.

One of the first things a Healer was taught was that the body, through
physical action, could reveal more than speech, and was frequently far more
trustworthy. In Likat's case, Sylah agreed as never before. Anyone unaware
of what he'd tried to do to her would look at him now and swear his attitude
toward Neela was one of utter, honest devotion.

For all his deception, however, he was transparent. Not only did his eyes
burn with a single-minded fire, but the aggressive forward thrust of his torso,
and the curled fingers, almost fisted with tension, revealed the dark, posses-
sive side of his interest. Parted lips bared a white line of teeth, but there was
no hint of smile in the expression.

Sylah was pleased to see Neela sensed something spurious in him. There
was a tightness in the tendons of her neck, and her nostrils flared at each
breath. Her gaze darted to him, then away, never meeting his stare. Unconsciously, she was reassuring herself that he was still outside the "safe circle"
around her. Most disturbing was her suggested undercurrent of confused,
almost helpless fear.

Neela chose that moment to lean back in her saddle, unconsciously increasing her distance from him. What impressed Sylah was that Neela made
no effort to get closer to Faldar or Bay.

That observation drew Sylah's attention to them. There was no need to
listen to Faldar to know he commanded the conversation. His gestures
routinely excluded his son and Likat. When he meant to make a point, his
chin rose appreciably, and when he condescended to address the other men,
there was a definite, albeit slight, swelling of his chest.

At first Sylah attributed the way Bay positioned himself so close to his
friend to coincidence. Then, for no apparent reason, Faldar shifted his own
location so that Neela couldn't talk to him without including Likat. Sickened, Sylah realized Faldar and Bay were selling him. They listened with
comical seriousness to his occasional comments, then hurried to agree. Still,
she was sure she saw uncertainty in Faldar's performance. He was doing his

best to make Neela approve, but he lacked the enthusiasm he tried to display.

Neela was nervous by then, trying to manage a polite departure. Taking the initiative, Sylah reminded Neela that they should be off on their ride.

Likat frowned. "You know Clas claims he found proof of Devil scouts south of here. It's too dangerous on the prairie for two women alone. The tigers and bears are still winter-thin. The wildcows, the buffalo, and the horses are all jumpy. They could stampede any time. Clas is probably wrong about the Devils, but it's just another thing to worry about. You should stay in camp."

Neela directed her answer to Faldar. "We're not going far. I want her to see our weavers and where they work. After that we may ride out to see the herd boys at work, but that's all."

"Be careful," Faldar said, beaming a benevolent smile.

Its effect was lost when Likat demanded, "Which herds? Where will you go?"

As if accused of something, Neela stammered, "The west lands, on the way to summer camp. Why?"

He stroked his jaw. "Worried about you, that's all. The north and south herds are both too far away."

Sylah heeled Copper, sending him off at a walk. Her abrupt ending of the situation drew her a glare from Likat.

She thought of the small leather bag and its hypnotic medicines. Perhaps it wouldn't be needed. What if Neela were anxious to leave her tribe?

They were outside camp, making their way past a flock of sheep. The boy watching them had taken the saddle off his horse and sprawled on its back, his head pillowed on a rolled-up jacket on the horse's rump. They laughed and waved, and the boy waved back, acknowledging his less-than-alert work with an impudent grin.

Sylah watched Neela until she was sure the small incident had helped her relax, then said, "Your brother and Likat seem to be especially close. Is he a relative?"

Shocked distaste flashed across her features. "He's no kin to us. He's important in the tribe, though; before his father died, he built his horse herd up to one of the largest and best. Likat's very wealthy. The rest of my family thinks that's very important."

"Why don't you like him?"

"He makes me uncomfortable. The way he looks at me. And other women. I've seen him look at you, too, when he thought no one was watching. Don't ever trust him."

So, Sylah thought, the babe can instruct the teacher. Did she sense how hard her father and brother were working on her?

Before she could think of a way to lead into the question, Neela was pointing out Weaver Creek. The stream itself was clear and brawling, no more than five feet across, hurrying down a rocky bed between tree-lined banks. On a point where it bent in a long curve, a group of women moved about busily in a grove of cottonwood trees. The leaves were young, still pale with new life, and the bright sun pouring through their screening took on the cast of old gold. The dappled, dancing light lent a festive air to what was actually very efficient activity.

As Sylah and Neela rode closer, the women saw them, some calling welcome. Sylah almost forgot her manners, completely distracted by the force of so much color. Her eyes couldn't rest, racing from point to point. She marveled at the profusion of hues and patterns on the looms.

Spinners were next to weavers. Hanging beside the stream, exposed to the sun, drying hanks of yarn steamed like fragments of a shattered rainbow. Other women poked at fires and stirred simmering dye pots.

There was nothing comparable in Ola. Communal work was common enough, but it was hurried, bound to a quota.

Sylah wanted to rush ahead, to luxuriate in the friendliness and acceptance that flowed so freely among the workers.

Neela took on the role of knowledgeable guide. The yarn was from their own stock—goats, sheep, and llamas—as well as material from wild animals. "We'll use anything," one of the women said, fondling Sylah's long hair and grinning. "With this I'd make you a much finer robe than the one you're wearing."

"Finer, perhaps, but a bit small for modesty, don't you think?" she said. The woman threw back her head and laughed. Some of the remarks that followed brought flames to Neela's cheeks, and Sylah herself was taken aback by the unabashed earthiness. Although she suspected they'd be more reserved if their men were present, she was certain they were too comfortable with themselves for sniggering whispers.

Still red, Neela doggedly resumed her lecture.

Every family had traditional techniques and designs, but all basic schools were shared. Family crests remained exclusive. Nothing was written. Children learned from mothers and aunts.

When Neela got into the technical points of warp and weft and threads per inch, Sylah begged for time to simply enjoy, complimenting everyone on the dazzling array. Laughing at her own runaway enthusiasm, Neela led the way to the dye pots. "We produce any color you can imagine," she said, unconcerned that she was boasting.

A woman looked up, eyebrow cocked in quizzical challenge, and Neela giggled. "Well, Jesha can produce any color, anyhow."

The woman nodded amused satisfaction, and said to Sylah, "Only a few of us have the knowing—what earth will make the color fast, or bring out the brightest hue of the dye. And we're the ones who know how to make the waterproof cloth for the tents."

Sylah answered absently, adjusting to two rather baffling surprises. In the first place, what she'd thought were metal dye pots were actually waterproof baskets. They were using the choga technique, heating with hot rocks. More than that, what Jesha was doing seemed to have nothing whatever to do with color. The hanks of bound yarn floating in the near-boiling water looked merely clean. As she started to ask about that, another woman shouted warning, hurrying toward them with a smoking rock in a pair of tongs. She dumped the rock in the basket, where it sank through the loops of yarn, spitting and growling. Sylah sniffed at the steam and said, "I smell iron."

Jesha beamed and winked. "Good for you. That's part of the secret. The easy part. This is a mordant solution. We'll dye the wool with rhododendron-leaf liquor to turn it brown, and the iron'll make it dark and rich. It'd favor your coloring, actually. The important thing is, we know what to add to keep the color from fading, and we know just how much of the iron stuff to use. No one else knows how to handle it right. Their iron-mordanted wool's always streaky, and it comes apart before you know it."

"You know so much—how long have the Dog People known these things?"

She was watching the hot rock send off bubbles and currents in the water as she asked, and for a few seconds the dull silence failed to register. When she lifted her head, however, there was no escaping the mantle of hostility that had descended around her. Not only Jesha, but Neela and everyone else within hearing stood with the taut bodies and stiff expressions of false nonchalance.

Jesha said, "We're proud of our work. Have you met our smith?"

"Saband Guyd? Yes, I did. I've never seen steel like his. Nor woven goods like yours."

Jesha ignored the compliment. "He used to make many things. For almost a year all he makes are weapons. We hear your king wants alliance with us, to make war against . . ."

She paused, and another woman said, "Harbundai."

Jesha nodded, thanking her, then added, "Wherever that is. We've been asking ourselves why Church sends a missionary at just this time. And why a War Healer, one who treats injuries, rather than sickness?"

Sylah said, "I'm no spy. I came on a mission, and was ordered to bring a message from my king. You know I had no choice."

"Perhaps so. But we don't trust Church and we want no war. We have enough trouble dealing with raids by the Devils, or the Buffalo Eaters, or the River People. Tell your king that whatever Faldar Yan says, the people want only peace."

Stiffly, Sylah said, "I came to teach you new things we've learned."

The burgeoning hostility in Jesha's manner evaporated, replaced by a distinct nervousness. From the corner of her eye, Sylah saw several of the women executing Three-signs, and she noticed that not all of them did it the same way. It hadn't occurred to her that the group was made up of women from all the clans, but the differing style of signing would indicate it. Jesha reached to touch Neela's arm. She said, "What's been said here, and what may be said, is woman's talk. It must be secret. We know you love your father. If you'd rather not hear . . ." She left the sentence hanging.

Neela said, "I stay," and Sylah felt a surge of pride before sternly warning herself that she must remember that Neela was a pawn.

Then Jesha was saying, "You went to the place of burning with Clas na Bale yesterday. Did he speak to you of Murmillanh?"

Surprised, Sylah could only nod.

"Did he tell you we called her witch?"

The blunt question angered Sylah, and she snapped her answer. "She was lonely, taken from her people. She died among strangers. Perhaps she was lucky that she didn't know you better."

Jesha surprised her yet again, smiling sympathy and understanding. "We use the name for many reasons, Priestess. With Murmillanh, it was because she told us of things to come. Be easy—she wasn't hated. Much of her aloneness was her choice. She walled herself off, except for when she had something important to tell us. Sometimes I felt she was more afraid *for* the Dog People than afraid *of* us. But never mind that. It was she who promised us a Teacher would come; a woman, and not from Church. Was she wrong about that? You said you came to teach, and that's a word Dog women use cautiously."

Sylah said, "In Ola we can't use it at all. We have to say 'to make someone know.' I'm sorry to disappoint you. I'm only here to share what I know of injury healing. Only with women. It's the way. Everyone knows. But tell me what else Murmillanh said about a Teacher."

"Nothing more. We believe, though. And hope."

Excitement fluttered in her breast again, a feeling that some unseen force was beckoning to her, offering her one more clue. It was the same as when the smith, Saband Guyd, alluded to a Door.

No. She was being foolish, illogical. Murmillanh had made some accurate guesses about the sex of babies, and entertained dreams of glory for her only child. Now all these superstitious people were eager to accept her grandiose prophecies. How could a gift woman from an obscure fishing tribe know anything of Teachers? It was ludicrous.

But she mentioned a Door. She quoted First Church, spoke of crosses. *Impossible.*

They talked for a few more minutes, but Jesha seemed to sense that Sylah's defenses were up now. She was friendly again, even affable, but it was apparent the conversation was over. Neela led the way out of the grove.

They'd ridden less than a mile, their conversation limited to bird watching and comments on how clear the weather was after the previous day's rain, when Neela reined up sharply, startling Sunflyer into a flurry of outraged crow hops. She stroked his neck in silent apology while she frowned at Sylah. "Are you my friend, truly?" she asked.

Not wanting to appear too anxious, Sylah said, "I'm beginning to think of you as the younger sister I never had. I want to be your friend. But you're the one who has to say I am, Neela. When you don't have to ask, that's when it'll be so."

Neela thought about that for a minute, and Sylah squirmed, waiting, before the girl said, "Then you are. I know I can trust you."

Sylah could only nod, which was just as well, because Neela seemed to realize she'd said a great deal. They rode on.

Lost in thought, it was some time before Sylah noticed they were headed south. A quick look to the mountains on their right confirmed they'd covered a considerable distance. The peak that concerned her most was still easily visible, but now it was to the northwest. Ahead of them the prairie was thick with animals. The wildcows particularly intrigued Sylah. In her own experience, cattle were short-legged barrel-shaped creatures that barely reached her shoulders. These things were nearly half again that tall, their long legs ropy with muscles, their chests deep, tapering up to narrow loins. Rangy, raw-boned, they sported immensely long horns with points as sharp as daggers. Now, in the spring, the bulls were testing each other, and the clash and clatter of duels was incessant. The more dignified buffalo, stockier and much heavier, kept to themselves. Their fights lacked the whirling, slashing grace of the wildcows. The young buffalo slammed into each other with the single-minded determination of falling rock, pushing and grunting until one decided he'd had enough and lumbered off.

In the far distance what looked like a cloud shadow on the earth suddenly split and moved in two directions with unnatural speed. She leaned forward, shielding her eyes against the afternoon sun, and only then realized she was looking at horses, hundreds of them.

Scattered among the wildcows and buffalo, smaller creatures fought their smaller battles, grazed, or dozed fitfully. Sylah counted three different kinds of antelope, coyotes, rabbits, one wildcat, and something flashing across a distant draw that might have been a tiger. When she mentioned the latter, Neela looked nervous, explaining that spring brought the big cats down from the mountains to prey on the herds. They rarely strayed far onto the grasslands, she said, preferring brushy or timbered country, where they usually killed deer and elk. The real danger was the huge, shambling prairie bear. It was far faster than it looked, and it considered people game, just like everything else. Worse, they were fearless, as willing to attack a warrior as a child.

Her own words apparently frightened her a bit, because she pulled her feet out of the stirrups and stood in the saddle, balancing easily as Sunflyer continued to walk along. Nervously, Sylah scolded her. Neela merely laughed. "We do this all the time. It's a lot better view, and Sunflyer doesn't care." She sat back down, flashing a cocky grin, adding, "As long as nothing spooks him, and he doesn't leave me standing in the middle of the air."

Sylah shuddered. "I think you take too many chances. And I don't think we ought to go any farther. Remember, the Devil warriors weren't far from here."

"That was just Likat trying to make us think we need his protection. Anyhow, the Devils won't come after you; you're Church."

The thought of Likat's threat crawled across Sylah's mind. If he had no fear of killing her, were there others? She said, "Let's stop at that bluff by the stream. We can eat, then go back."

"You brought food?"

From her saddle bag Sylah triumphantly raised a cloth sack. With the other hand she produced a rectangular box, opening it with a flourish. Nested inside were two thin wooden plates, with matching cups and utensils. Neela exclaimed at the glowing silver inlay, tracing the intertwined irises of the pattern. Aware of their hunger now, they urged the horses forward, and they were soon at the bluff. The crystalline stream below them twisted the sunlight into everchanging patterns across its rock bed. Beyond it, the land rolled away to the mountains, alight with the spring greens of grass, shrubs, and deciduous trees displaying shy new leaves. Beyond that, ranks of firs and pines rose against the Enemy Mountain slopes in uncountable numbers. The black-green mass of trees was unbroken up to the level where climate and lack of soil conspired to thwart them.

Sylah dug into the sack and brought out cheese, a small piece of smoked ham, and the hearty three-grain bread of the Dog people. There were dried tomatoes, pickles, slices of dried apple and peach, and even a small clay container of pepper oil for spice.

Their conversation was innocuous, as though each was anxious to avoid any subject that might cause discomfort, and yet it had the spontaneity of friendship. Both voiced surprise when Sylah noticed how much the shadows had lengthened. When she started down to the stream to rinse the dishes, Neela insisted it was her chore, as Sylah was the one who'd remembered to bring them.

Sylah argued politely before surrendering.

She watched the younger woman step up into her saddle. Her smile collapsed as soon as Neela was hidden by brush. Wasting no time, she grabbed the box the wooden plates and utensils came in. A quick twist with the blade of a shortknife opened a nearly invisible seam where the sides joined the bottom, revealing twin mirrors, one in the chest's false bottom, the other in the removed outer shell.

Altanar had promised an Olan scouting party would constantly maintain a camp in the foothills directly in front of the peak she'd used as her reference during the ride with Neela. She could only hope they were alert.

Because the sun was already in the west, there was no need to line up one mirror to reflect light to the other. She sighted across the top of one.

When a flash of light answered, she released pent-up breath in a gusting sigh.

A series of long and short flashes identified her. When she finished sending that code, however, she was forced to confront her dilemma. If she signaled all was well with Altanar's plan, she guaranteed Faldar full support; Col Moondark would be the same as dead. If she lied, Altanar would still learn, sooner or later, that Faldar was eager for the alliance.

She pressed her mirror to her bosom as a distant glint demanded response.

It was their own fault, all of them! Faldar meant to destroy Col no matter what she did. Likat's fear of exposure would force him to kill her, if she stayed. Kidnapping Neela from such a nest of liars and murderers was no crime.

And what if Gan died? It would only prove he was fated for the shorter life his mother envisioned.

Too bad. Everyone died, after all.

Clas. Neela.

She seemed to smell the evil mix of drugs in the leather bag, felt something slick and greasy slide across her tongue, down the back of her throat. She gagged.

She brought the box to her face, hating the sight of it. She sent NO AGREE, and as the last letters burned across the miles toward her coconspirators, she remembered Altanar's loving description of what would happen to her if she misled him, accidentally or not. She added the word YET.

CHAPTER 15

The utensil box was together, its secret hidden, when Neela returned. The ride back passed quietly, the concern over territorial wildcows or wandering prairie bears somehow lessened by the prospect of going home, rather than riding out among them. Even the horses were relaxed, shuffling along with lowered ears and easy gait.

The truth, Sylah thought to herself, was that she was in no mood for idle chat. She'd just done something very foolish, and to no purpose. Lying to Altanar solved nothing. She must prevent the alliance at any cost. She'd faced that fact once, even if it was in reaction to the scene in Faldar Yan's tent.

She felt the rage and shame of Likat's hands on her, reminding herself that it could—*would*—happen again, if she failed to protect herself. And Neela. The plan really was for the girl's protection, if one thought about it.

A branch caught at her stirrup. She kicked at it viciously. The pungent smell of sagebrush filled her nose, and she included it in her anger. Stinking stuff. Stinking place.

Admit it, she told herself; you weakened. Tomorrow you send Altanar a true message.

The bribes paid the Mountain People would afford her safe passage with Neela through their territory, even though the heartless scum had refused to provide guides or assistance. Their neutrality would be enough. She'd memorized the landmarks and she had a north-needle secreted in her medical equipment.

Food would be a problem, after the first few days.

Merely acknowledging that difficulty forced her to confront the raw desperation of her plan. Hundreds of miles, with a dazed captive, and the finest horsemen in the world raging on her trail.

The Mountain People anticipated the same thing. They never asked her why she thought she might be running from the Dogs the next time they saw her. They nodded, demanded more gold, and then grinned and whispered among themselves. She'd understood. They hoped she'd lead their enemies into ambush.

The thought hadn't bothered her at the time.

Neela interrupted her thoughts by nervously gesturing for quiet. Bent over, she guided Sunflyer, reading signs visible only to her. Her eyes were in constant motion, flicking up from the ground to search the surrounding area. When the trail led into a small draw, she backed away, taking a roundabout course to high ground overlooking it.

Sylah had no desire to follow the unknown rider—or riders; there was no message on the ground for her. If Neela were concerned, she reasoned, they should race away to tell people. Furthermore, she didn't understand how it was possible for any unknown parties to ride so close to the camp without having been discovered long ago.

When they reached a point near the overlook, Neela signed they should dismount. Crawling, she made her way forward. Sylah scrabbled along with her, feeling more ridiculous every moment.

She found herself peeking down from a point a good thirty feet above a lush bog. Challenging its quiet beauty was the dandified finery of Likat. Even more startling, the plump form of Kolee stumped along beside him. Their horses were hobbled in the distance while they searched the fringe of the bog on foot like oversized, disparate herons.

Kolee found something. She dropped to her knees, cutting at a plant, ignoring the damp earth staining her skirt. Her knife flashed, and she raised a hand as if displaying a trophy. Sylah strained to hear her, but breeze and distance combined to swallow the sound. Likat shared in the excitement of her find.

"What's she got?" Neela whispered.

"I can't tell," Sylah said. "Why is Likat with her?"

"She's probably worried about the Devils."

Sylah looked over her shoulder before asking, "So close to the camp? I can't imagine—"

Neela cut her off. "Or animals. I told you about the bears. She's old; older people are more easily frightened."

The whole thing seemed farfetched to Sylah, but Neela's manner warned her that the matter was closed. Changing the subject, she said, "I wonder what she's looking for? New growth's not very good for medicines. It usually takes a season for a plant to accumulate properties."

"Well, I don't want to be caught spying on them. We're leaving," Neela said, inching away from the edge.

Miffed by Neela's blunt assumption of leadership, Sylah stubbornly held her ground, turning for one last look. Likat was gesturing at Kolee, shaking his head in vehement disagreement. Her response was to bend down, straightening with a hitherto unnoticed bag in her hand. She pushed it at

Likat's face, and he jumped backward so violently he nearly fell, throwing both hands straight in the air. When Kolee laughingly lowered the bag, her words were indistinguishable, but his boiling anger was clear. He stomped past her toward the horses, keeping well clear of the mysterious sack.

Neela's urgent whisper pulled Sylah away. She was pleased when Neela seemed anxious to put as much distance between them and the pair as quickly as possible.

Sylah said, "Do you want to tell me why Kolee would pick Likat, of all people, for her companion?"

She made a face. "Likat's her nephew. My mother says that when his mother died, Kolee made such a fuss, his father finally gave him to her. She never had any children."

"None?" Sylah was shocked. For a healthy woman to have no children was unheard of, save for the celibate few tolerated in Church.

"She and her husband fought, my mother says. He was bitten by a rattlesnake. Mother says he was the only adult she lost to snakebite in two years, and some people were really suspicious. Especially since everyone knew she loved Col Moondark."

Surprises were falling like raindrops. Sylah goggled at her.

"Oh, yes," Neela said, pleased by the reaction she'd caused. "Kolee's husband died while Col was on a raid, the time he brought back Murmillanh. Kolee's hated Col ever since; Murmillanh, too. When Gan was born, she wouldn't help at all." She mumbled the next words, and Sylah had to lean toward her quickly to catch them. "I heard her tell my father it would've been better for the tribe if he'd died then."

They'd come to a clump of thick brush, penetrated only by a narrow game trail, and Neela spurred Sunflyer into the lead. Sylah fell behind. Dodging branches amid the snap and crackle of their passage made conversation impossible.

Her thoughts went to Col's wife, the gift woman. How twisted her life had been! To fall in love with a man she hated, and then to bear a child into the face of more hatred. Worst of all, the hate was so pointless, so misplaced.

Nevertheless, Murmillanh's solitary existence was a strong argument for doubting her prophecies. It wouldn't be too unusual, even for a person of her strength, to create dreams to hide behind.

When the trail widened back onto grassland, they were within view of the camp. Neela seemed to have thought better of her gossip in the interim, because she brushed aside Sylah's attempts to resume the conversation. Instead, she spoke of the celebration scheduled for the evening.

Another surprise, thought Sylah, almost afraid to ask what this one might be.

Neela explained that custom required a feast the night before any man entered Earth Heart to learn if he was required to undertake the Honor Journey. If he was not, the celebration was an acknowledgment of no-longer-questioned integrity. If he was directed to go, however, he went with happy memories of merrymaking.

Sylah was reminded of a parable in the Apocalypse Testament that dealt with the necessity of fighting for the right to worship, a tale that started, "We who are about to die salute you." It was supposed to be an ancient message, dating back to when giants ruled the earth. She always suspected it was just another way of making people who had no choice believe they were doing the right thing.

She remembered Clas' comments about the giants and what they must have been like. That reminded her of the remarkable similarities among all origin tales. Everyone spoke of a leader who'd created a first tribe from the straggling survivors of a terrible catastrophe. Everyone spoke of summers so cold crops failed, of fires that melted rock, of disease that killed in minutes. No one spoke of what brought all those things about, unless one accepted the gospel that the giants schemed with the One in All to change weather and earth to punish man.

The paradox was that the stories had such a common theme, yet almost every day in Ola brought patients or travelers with differing customs, differing cultures. Some, like the Nions from across the Great Sea, even had differing appearances and languages. Still, the origin stories were almost exactly alike.

There had to be a reason.

The bustle of the camp banished all those unanswerable questions. She remarked to Neela she'd heard nothing of the planning for this event, and it looked to be a large one.

"It's supposed to be unplanned. That's so the journeyman can leave, if he has to go, telling himself the celebration 'just happened,' and wasn't meant to send him off with good memories. It's important that he go with a good heart."

At the edge of her vision, Sylah caught her quick glance. Her face wasn't clear enough to read the expression, but her manner was defensive, hands suddenly drawn up, chin tucked in. Whether she admitted it or not, she knew Gan was being put at risk unfairly. Hot coals might not make her say so, but the understanding was in her.

Sylah felt very sorry for her.

They reached the tent a few minutes later, and Neela excused herself to go get better clothes for the evening. Sylah used the time to enjoy a shower and a nap.

Later, they strolled together out to the area set aside for the festivities. They stopped first by the firepits, where youngsters turned whole animals on spits. Others slathered them with sauce. The dripping grease sizzled and spat on the fiery coals, filling the air with the tang of beef, venison, and pork, as well as the aromas of onions, tomatoes, hot peppers, and so many mingled herbs Sylah stopped identifying and resigned herself to some abandoned overeating.

Leaving the fires, they went to where a multiblanket fly suspended from poles provided a pavilion for burdened food tables. Prepared fish of every description filled dozens of wooden platters. Another whole table was made up of various cooked-apple dishes, and another featured dried cherries and peaches in one guise or another. Soups steamed in caldrons. It was too early for fresh vegetables, but huge mounds of tender, new-growth greens glittered further enticement.

They ate from simple, square wooden plates and bowls, using wooden utensils. Neela showed her where they were thrown when one was finished, explaining that they'd be burned to help provide firelight for the dancing that would follow.

The musicians were just tuning up when Sylah made one last trip to the tables. She was amazed to find them practically stripped. A few forlorn drops of soup and some wilted salad remained.

By the firepits young men wearing the distinctive leather and metal gauntlets of the dog trainers were collecting the last bits of meat and the bones for their charges. They used dog carts for hauling. The dogs seemed stockier than Raggar or the others, and she assumed that's why they were used as draft animals. They were still impressive, and she was glad they were securely harnessed to the lead poles. They already regarded the leftovers as theirs, and their dark, luminous eyes watched passersby with warning.

The first piece by the impromptu orchestra started slowly. Even before hearing Neela's whispers or the words to the song, Sylah knew it was about the wanderings of the Dog People before they found this homeland. Stringed instruments and flutes gave the opening theme a soft, haunting quality.

It was the singing that engaged her, however. The voices started quietly, melding with the instruments, then pulled them to greater tempo, fiercer emotions. Men and women harmonized in rich, intricate chords that carried them from sadness and weariness to passion and triumph.

Immediately after that, the pace leaped to a driving, demanding beat. The pala drums of all the clans led the way, and Sylah realized they, too, had individual tones that the drummers wove into a tapestry. The fire was burning high by then, so that when the first warrior leaped from the crowd to the bare earth semicircle, there was plenty of light to gleam from the polished silver buttons of his vest and trousers. His murdat whirled over his head in a shining blur as he leaped and slashed in mock combat. A second man joined him quickly, and then many more. They formed lines, the original freeform activity suddenly disciplined, yet retaining its savage enthusiasm. The men danced with dazzling swiftness, their dexterity with the murdats drawing shouts of appreciation as blades clashed wildly or whipped past partners with no room for error.

When the music stopped, they moved in a group, shouting and laughing, to help themselves at the tubs of beer. They were back quickly, however, most still holding drinking gourds, as a new song began. It was time for the women to perform, and Sylah, despite her protests, was dragged into the circle. Her cloak was given over to waiting hands, and, laughing, Neela and Jesha told her this was the Weaver's Dance. They handed her a pair of sticks for which she couldn't imagine any use, then led her through the first swaying movements. Next came the sharp striking of the sticks together, the sound mimicking the clack-clack of the loom. Shortly, what had seemed impossibly intricate was simple and flowing, and she let the rhythm claim her. The last expression of her normal cautious thinking process was a giddy sort of surprise at being completely immersed in friendship.

She had no way of knowing how the absence of stress softened her features, or how her joyful smile made them glow. Her hair, free of restriction, swept back and forth in undulating swells like a midnight sea.

When they were done, she wandered off with Neela to find a viewing point for the other dances. For a while everything seemed as it should be, but when Sylah was on her way back from retrieving her cloak, she caught the younger woman watching a particular area with a frightening intensity. Following her gaze, she saw Likat and Bay. At that moment Likat shifted his position. Their eyes met. With calculated cruelty, he looked to Neela, then back, before sending her an almost imperceptible smile. The gloating confidence of it made her stomach heave.

A few minutes later Neela pulled Sylah to the outskirts of the crowd. Without any preamble, words tumbling forth in anguished torrents, she described meeting Likat as she left her father's tent. Small drops of sweat touched her temples and outlined her upper lip as she told of almost telling him she'd seen him at the bog with Kolee. Something warned her, though, so she asked where he spent the day, instead.

She turned a face of pure torment to Sylah. "He lied. He said he was far to the south, examining the grazing. He even told me he was with other men,

and what they talked about. Why? We saw him with Kolee. I'm afraid.
What are they doing?"

Affecting a calm she didn't feel, Sylah tried to comfort her. She said, "It's
nothing to worry about, I'm sure. I imagine he's hired Kolee to help him put
together a love potion, or something."

Neela's eyes rounded and she made an erratic Three-sign. "Is that possible? Really?"

It was exactly the response Sylah wanted. She laughed, seeing how her
amusement drained some of Neela's stress. She said, "Please—if a potion
could make people happy, wouldn't we all drink it all the time?"

"You really think that's what they were doing?"

"That, or something equally useless. Don't think of them; let's enjoy the
evening."

Anxious to be convinced, Neela accepted the argument. Sylah wished she
could do the same. Her bitter experience with Likat made her doubt he'd
trifle with anything as subtle as a potion. Force and terror were his methods.

Which underlined the question: What were they planning?

An hour later she was certain she had her answer. She caught Likat and
Bay surreptitiously watching Gan and Clas as they enjoyed the dancers. Likat
whispered to Bay. They exchanged conspiratorial grins and sniggers.

Then, with startling clarity, everything fell into place.

Kolee hated Gan and Col.

Bay, Faldar, and Likat would all benefit if Gan died on the Journey.

Neela was very disturbed by Gan's impending departure, and Likat
wanted her. If he suspected she had any liking for Gan at all, murder would
be his first thought.

That had to be the answer. They were working together to poison Gan.
Not to kill him outright, but to send him on the Journey so weak and
disoriented he'd have no chance whatever. Except that they didn't know that
Col and Clas intended to go with him, if it came to that. How would that
affect their plan?

Another change in the music plucked at her attention. Her mind was
already crackling with the implications of Neela's discovery, and she resisted
the distraction irritably, but finally she looked up. Her breath caught in her
throat at the sight of Gan, alone, dancing a simulated duel. Unlike the other
man who'd danced alone, Gan moved slowly, sinuously, everything he did
exaggerated and multiplied, the moves smoothly confident. She was amazed;
how had she ever thought of him as a boy? Muscles writhed and bunched
under skin ruddied by firelight. Magically, he'd taken his step, gone beyond
childhood to young manhood. The tribe was silent as death, watching what
all knew might be his last expression of life. An aura of power and strength

seemed to shimmer around him, as fearsome—yet as achingly temporal—as the flames of the fire.

He moved to face Neela. Sylah had no idea how she'd gotten to the forefront of the crowd; she was just there, her eyes locked with Gan's.

He stopped his dance and bowed his head. Sylah was moving by the time he raised it, forcing aside the crowd as if moving through reeds. If she'd been more than a yard away, she'd have missed his words to Neela. He said, "I know I'm leaving. We were always friends until I angered you. Please, tell me you won't be angry anymore."

The golden head nodded, and Sylah saw she was too emotional to speak, beyond tears.

Gan smiled and danced away.

He finished soon after. The weaver dancers clattered their sticks together in approval and the rest of the crowd applauded by stamping the ground in rhythm. The drummers took up that beat. Another dancer yelled a war cry, leaping into the firelight.

Across the arena Sylah watched Likat shiver with repressed rage.

You filth, she thought. I can't stop this idiotic Journey, but I can stop your miserable plan. You and your kind—Altanar, Faldar—you can't have everything. Gan may die chasing a fool's glory, but not at the whim of scum like you. I'll stop you myself!

It took her a full minute to realize she meant to do it.

CHAPTER 16

As Sylah made her way toward the tent of Faldar Yan, Copper was fractious, spooking at the flutter of a sparrow or the shout of a child. When she reached forward to scratch one of the nervously flicking ears, he laid them back for a moment, tossing his head as if angered further by her attention.

Calming him steadied her own nerves before she dismounted to call at the front entry. Above her the family pennant hung limp, a red-and-black smear against the clear blue of the sky. She called twice before he appeared. His wife stood behind him, her small features flitting unhappily between smile and frown. The action reminded Sylah of the soft confusion of butterfly flight. When the woman heard the broad friendliness of Faldar's greeting, she immediately nodded and grinned widely before mouthing the same words in a shy twitter that carefully duplicated his every nuance.

He went on, "What can I do for you, Priestess? Did I overlook something at our last meeting?"

Sylah felt muscles loosen. He was in a particularly expansive mood; it might make the difference. She said, "Something happened last night that makes it urgent that I speak to you before the Earth Heart meeting."

Behind her husband the woman gasped. Her hand flew to her mouth as he rounded on her. He caught himself before speaking, and when he faced Sylah again, he managed to mask his anger. Only then did he introduce his wife by name, adding, "Chelo is an old-fashioned woman, not accustomed to hearing women speak of Earth Heart. Excuse her." He turned again, telling her to get them hot mint tea, then gestured Sylah inside to some pillows. They exchanged small talk about the food and music of the previous night while they waited. Sylah realized she'd actually paid little attention to the tent on her previous visit, and this time she took pains to inspect it more carefully. It was far more richly furnished than any other home she'd seen. Faldar had a taste for luxury. The small table in front of her was wonderfully carved, its surface representing a battle between two men and two huge lizards with enormous mouths full of ivory teeth. The men wore large, floppy hats and stood upright in a slim boat that looked dangerously unstable. They plunged spears into the writhing creatures. The whole scene vibrated with captured energy.

Faldar said, "I see you like my little table. The Peddler who brought it here swore there's a place where this sort of hunting goes on. They're all such liars. But the table is yours; I'll have one of my sons bring it to your tent."

She tried to argue, but Chelo swooped in, skirt billowing, cups rattling together on the tray in her haste. Sylah knew that any sign of discord would throw the poor woman into a fit of distraction, so she bowed her head and made her thanks as politely as possible. Chelo was glowing with goodwill as she left.

Faldar was more brusque. "Something concerns you?"

She told him she'd sent a message to Altanar. When he indicated no interest in how she'd managed it, the disquieting thought that he already knew jarred her confidence, but she pressed ahead. Then she told him that the message indicated he wasn't yet ready for an alliance. His face flamed. If he weren't so dangerous, she thought, his disbelief would be comical.

She rushed to explain. "Hear me out. My king wants alliance with a united Dog People. I'm not so blind that I can't see that Col Moondark has much support in the tribe."

"That is not your concern! You lied. About *me.*"

Sweat tickled Sylah's side. "I only created time, that you might take advantage of an opportunity. Why give Altanar the impression of strife where none need exist? Why not destroy Col as completely as Gan? Wouldn't your position be better in dealing with King Altanar if the entire tribe were united behind you?"

"You say I'm not already respected?"

"No, Faldar, but you can be respected *by all.* You can eliminate Col Moondark's last, whining supporters as swiftly as the sun melts away frost."

He liked that image; she saw it in the way he stroked his chin while his measuring eyes tried to gauge the thoughts behind her words. At last he said, "What do you propose?"

"Don't let them send Gan on the Journey." She leaned forward, matching his own sudden aggressive posture, but twisting her lips into what she hoped was a properly conniving smile. "What if he survives? Do you want to see Col's son a hero? But what if he's denied the opportunity? Shame him as a dreamer, an incompetent, unworthy of dying for the new tribe. Show the people how he's to be pitied because he's never been accepted as an equal, how he keeps to himself and never made himself a true Dog Warrior. You show the tribe's new fighting spirit and at the same time display mercy by not sending an unfortunate boy to certain death. The Moondark name will drown in dishonor. Then you can speak of alliance with King Altanar on *your* terms."

Rising with a swiftness that contradicted his bulk, he glowered down at her for long moments while her nerves hummed with suspense. He turned away to pace the tent, grumbling inarticulate arguments with himself as he did. Stopping abruptly, he said, "If you ever presume to think for me again, I'll have you stripped naked and dragged behind a horse to Ola, and Church can have whatever's left. Now you tell Altanar we'll negotiate an alliance. Nothing more. Nothing less."

He gestured her toward a different exit, on the side of the tent, and she moved quickly to escape, backing through the flap. She continued to watch as the material fell back in place, but something moving near the front of the tent caught her eye. She looked that way quickly. There was nothing there. Still, the feeling that she'd seen motion was lodged in her mind. She had to go that way to reach the tent lane, in any case, so she moved warily, telling herself she wasn't just chasing stray breezes.

Rounding the corner, she almost bumped into Chelo coming out the front entry. The twittery woman squawked surprise and jerked away to avoid the collision. Sylah barely caught her as she tripped over a tent rope. Catching her breath, she blurted embarrassed laughter and apologies, explaining she was hurrying out to intercept Sylah; would she please excuse her husband's rudeness?

It was all Sylah could do to forego telling Chelo exactly what sort of rudeness her husband was capable of, but she swallowed the words, smiled sweetly and thanked her.

She was already at her horse when she heard Chelo make a clucking, scolding noise. Sylah looked back, curious, to see her bend swiftly to scoop something from the ground. Their eyes met for the briefest of moments, and then Chelo, still bent almost double, was scurrying back in the tent. In her haste, she neglected to completely hide her discovery in her clenched hand. Sylah saw it clearly. It was a feather, brilliant blue, like the ones sewn into decorative flowers on Likat's vest.

Likat stormed into Kolee's tent. From a different room she shouted, "Who's there? Wait. I'll come."

He ignored the order, plunging through the softwall.

Kolee squatted on the floor, facing away from him. She twisted around in a defensive crouch, hissing like a trapped cat. Her body continued to shield what she was doing. As soon as she recognized Likat, her alarm changed to shrill anger. "You frightened me," she said. "You could have—"

Likat cut her off with a gesture. "The Olan bitch just ruined everything." He stepped around her, pointed at the odd, flat metal pan on its stand over coals. "There's no need for that. Or that." He indicated the cloth bag in the corner. "We have to think of something else."

Kolee scowled and turned back to her work, poking the barely glowing fire. Likat reached for her, thought better of it. "Didn't you hear me?" he demanded.

"I heard. Now I want facts."

"I saw her go into Faldar's tent, so I listened outside."

She blinked in disbelief. "You did *what*? Were you seen?"

"I acted like I was waiting for Bay. Do you want to know what happened or not?" When she sniffed and went back to her task, he repeated the conversation he'd overheard. Kolee kept silent long after he finished, and in exasperation he pressed for a response.

The woman talked softly, almost to herself. "The Priestess is shrewd; she understands that Murmillanh's whelp is unnaturally lucky. It would be like him to survive the Journey. Still, nothing need change. All along we've planned that Bay must challenge Gan. Faldar's decision changes nothing. Bay *will* do it, won't he? Challenge Gan at Earth Heart meeting?"

"I think so."

"Don't think. Do. He must."

Likat sprawled on some cushions on the other side of the pot. "All right, don't get upset. I can make him do it. I'm sure."

"It's the key." She changed the subject. "What about Neela? Have you had her yet, naughty boy? What does Faldar say?"

"She needs some lessons in manners. And no, Faldar hasn't promised her to me yet. Bay's been trying to convince him. You know, things would be a lot easier if we just got rid of Faldar, instead."

"We can't. Not yet. I've told you a thousand times, Likat—one *plans*. By dishonoring the Moondarks, we eliminate all opposition to Faldar. By having Gan kill Bay with a poisoned murdat, we accomplish both of those objectives, and we put you in position to take Bay's place at Faldar's hand."

Likat made a bored grimace, then lay back on the cushions with his eyes closed. He said, "You worry too much. What it all comes down to is that they're stupid, and we're not. That's why we should rule, and why we will."

Kolee knew the tone of voice that meant dismissal. There was much more she wanted to say, but he'd only grow unpleasant if she persisted. She sighed and returned to her task. She dipped a metal spoon in the liquid, noting it was already reduced halfway down the inch-high sides of the pan. She spread the coals; it was important the alcohol and water mixture that drew the poison from the sheets of bark in the pan be evaporated without coming to a boil. Carefully she brought the spoon close and smelled it, pulling back as if burned by the acrid smell. Her nose tingled for a moment. She stared into space, savoring, considering.

The chokecherry bark was from a special growth, one tended by the women of her family for generations. Every year she continued the traditions. In the fall, at the first breath of frost, she went to her grove and denuded the branches, storing the leaves in a composting box in the grove's center. While winter held the land dormant, she trimmed excess growth, keeping the plants to a manageable size and open to full sun and breeze for summer. With spring, just before new growth swelled in buds and twigs, she dug a trench around one tree, a different one each year. The trench was carefully sited no farther from the central trunk than the reach of the branches. In addition, she had an arrangement with most of the women who dried peaches for their families. They saved the pits for her, to be strewn in the trench. Kolee wasn't sure they helped, any more than she was sure the poison from the iris root helped the mixture in the pan, but the peach pits smelled the same as the cherry bark, anyhow. It just seemed like a good idea. The pits were followed by the previous year's leaves, and then both were covered with manure.

In the summer she scoured other chokecherries for the particular variety of boring beetles that her aunt said stimulated the plant to produce its poison in the bark and soft cambium. She called it the blue death. There were years when some of the other kinds of bark-eating insects needed only a few nibbles before tumbling from the trunk to the ground. It gave Kolee a feeling of power she conceded was out of all proportion to the fact when she watched them feebly kick their lives away.

Oddly, the bark was superior for cough and sore throat. Dried and powdered, taken with or without honey, it gave instant relief. The tribe knew she collected it for their benefit.

What Kolee knew, and what brought a contemplative smile now, was the effect of soaking the bark and concentrating the decoction.

A Healer made decisions. Col Moondark's peaceful policies had all but eliminated the need for her to put a wounded warrior out of his misery, but an occasional patient still required a last little push into the next life when his or her injuries were beyond repair. And if the Healer didn't keep the tribal blood pure by gently lifting the hand of the One in All from the deformed or defective newborn, who would undertake the task? She needed only to touch dry residue from her pan to an open wound or the lips; there was a gasp, some frothing, perhaps some brief spasms. So quick, so beneficial for all, and no one the wiser.

Sniffing the air, she frowned. The alcohol was quite strong-smelling now. She sprinkled a handful of ground cedar on the outer rim of the coals. Clouds of pungent smoke safely masked everything else.

Alcohol was forbidden. Church believed distillation was one of its secrets. She thought of Sylah, not aware her lips were moving as she did so: "There are so many things you don't know, mighty Rose Priestess. How I'll enjoy watching your education. Just as your sisters enjoyed watching mine."

She wiped her brow. Her gaze fell on Likat, now breathing heavily in deep sleep. Her frown mellowed to affectionate exasperation.

He was an irritating boy, but who could resist him? Heartbreakingly handsome, clever as a magpie, held back only by a boyish laziness that could drive her nearly mad. And the jealousy of others; that made him almost uncontrollable sometimes. But underneath, sweeter than honey. That was the real Likat, the one who'd promised her she'd ride back into Ola's proud abbey mounted on a white horse, draped in furs, glittering with gold and jewels from head to foot. She believed him. Why not? She'd raised him to think of goals, to understand that men took what they wanted or settled for what was thrown to them.

And their time was coming.

A movement from across the room distracted her. She straightened with a muttered exclamation about her daydreaming. Getting to her feet, she went to where a rough cloth bag acted as if it had taken on a life of its own. Reaching behind a cabinet, she produced a long, hollow rod with a cord through it that formed a loop at one end. The sack was held closed by a knot in its open end, and as soon as she touched it to undo it, the unmistakable whir of a rattlesnake's warning filled the room. Likat was moving away before he woke, not stopping until he was actually backing against the opposite softwall.

Kolee sent him a quick, teasing smile as she used the looped end of the rod to lift the edge of the cloth. Crooning an off-key tune, she touched the moving lump. A huge, triangular head poked out into the light. Coaxing, wheedling, she talked to it. The snake's tongue flickered constantly as it tried to understand what was happening. Suddenly it lunged forward, and with equal quickness she dropped the loop over its head and pulled tight, lifting it off the carpet.

Likat made a strangling noise as the six-foot-long reptile flung itself about in a rattling frenzy. Its sinuous muscularity rocked Kolee in an eccentric dance until it tired. She brought the head close to her face, crooning again, as if she'd kiss its crown. Her hands were confident as she moved for a grip immediately behind the jaws and released the loop. From the cabinet, she drew a wide-mouthed porcelain jar. The snake renewed its efforts to break free, coiling itself around her arm. A small frown rippled Kolee's forehead, but she persisted as calmly as ever. Squeezing the snake's jaw hinge forced its mouth open. She forced the daggerlike fangs into the jar, milking the golden poison from their sacs. The snake continued to rattle furiously as she lowered it back into the sack and retied the knot.

Sweat beaded Likat's face and stained his shirt.

Puffing from her exertions, Kolee said, "When the vozun drums start, come directly here. I'll have a cloth prepared. The bark poison decays in a matter of hours, but the snake venom will last much longer. If the bark doesn't kill him quickly, the venom will still get him, only slower. You need only dampen the blade with the cloth and dust the mixture on it."

Bulging eyes locked on the small bottle of venom, Likat nodded absently. Kolee flew at him, holding it under his nose, pinning him to the wall. "Calm yourself! Nothing must go wrong, nothing must be overlooked. What plans have you made concerning Col and Clas na Bale?"

Twisting away, Likat glared back. "What can they do? Who'll believe—"

"Likat!" Kolee's disappointment slashed at his complacency. "Have you ignored everything I've ever told you? Do you think those two won't know who poisoned the blade? The only murdats allowed in Earth Heart are the sacred dueling weapons, and you're the man who'll inspect Gan's before the fight."

"You're not supposed to know what happens in Earth Heart," he said, sulking.

She sniffed. "I probably know more than those doddering fool Elders. Listen to me; Col and Clas will know they can never prove you and not Gan poisoned the blade. They won't bother to try. They'll race to see which one takes your fingerbone."

Likat swallowed. "You never said anything about this before. Maybe the poison's not a good idea. Gan's sure to kill Bay, anyhow."

"We can't be certain. And we need the poisoned blade. The winner of a duel in Earth Heart is required to ceremonially clean the weapons for the Elders and ask forgiveness after the dead man's been burned. I'll make the Elders see the poison before the burning. Surely you can arrange for warriors to attack Col and Clas, once they hear Gan's broken the honor of the entire tribe? What of Bay's brothers? Get them involved; it would be a great help to you if the Moondarks and Clas cut down a few of that litter. Likat, Likat—you *must* think of these things yourself. What will you do when you're War Chief if I'm gone from your side?"

He straightened, frowning. "Never say that. I depend on you."

She turned away to hide a quick, proud smile. Making her voice gruff, she said, "Well, then, you have to help me. Now go see to the arrangements for after Gan's killed Bay. And be sure you only talk to good friends, people you can trust."

He kissed her on top of the head, then turned and left. She followed quickly, holding the exit open a bare slit so she could peer through and watch him walk away.

How could anyone else lead the Dog People? He was so obviously the man for War Chief. It showed in his every move.

She let the blanket fall closed, walked back to her fire with her fingers to her lips, face drawn in taut concentration. She'd have to learn his plan, of course. Sometimes he didn't think everything through quite properly. And there was the complication of involving someone else in the plot. She hoped there wouldn't be more than one or two knowledgeable helpers. Three at the most. No one who knew the secret of Bay's death could be allowed to live, and fatal accidents to more than three people would be hard to arrange. Someone might even get suspicious, and then . . .

Her eyes went to the flat pan and she rubbed her neck wearily. There was always so much to do.

CHAPTER 17

Gan and Clas fell into step with the solemn rhythm of the vozun drums. Gan was saddened by the prospect of the Journey. He understood the odds against his return. Still, try as he might, he couldn't imagine his own death. That could only mean he was meant to survive, and gloriously.

There was no fear. Clas said a man who didn't know fear didn't understand life. Perhaps that would come later. Right now he felt an excitement that was like walking without touching the ground.

When they arrived at the dome, it was cloaked in an eerie gray-white haze. His pulse quickened at the thought of a magic softness shielding Earth Heart and it's secrets. He broke off the thought, smiling to himself. What an odd, dreamlike notion, and on this, of all days. Anyhow, the haze was only smoke from illumination torches oozing through ventilation gaps under the slates.

They made their way to the steep stairs of the south entrance, following a passage so confined they had to bend past the wall-mounted oil lamps. The tunnel exited onto the floor of an amphitheater. Torch fire, the beating sun, and the body heat of the hundreds of men, crushed down on the graduated rows of benches with smothering oppressiveness.

Gan stopped as if he'd hit a wall. Beyond the normal smells, an eager, feral stink burdened the air.

The warriors had gathered to touch death.

Hackles rose on his neck. Stiff-legged, he joined the North Clan men. They made space for him beside one of the sloped, spokelike ramps leading up from the floor. Clas sat next to him and devoted his full attention to cleaning his fingernails with his shortknife. Gan wished he could be so casual.

Every man present was in his best finery. Polished metal, stones, and glass glittered from every direction. For an instant Gan's mind staggered, as if flickering between two realities, and he saw every pinpoint of light as a seeking eye. The sensation lasted no longer than a blink. In itself, it was disturbing enough, but when he remembered the other fantasy of a few minutes earlier, the realization he'd done such a thing twice left a knot in his stomach.

An increased urgency in the buzz of conversation announced Col's approach. He wore elk skin tanned to the softness of cotton and a flat steel collar for decoration. Trophy bones dangled from it on fine gold chains. Gan knew there were thirty. Col came straight to him, gripping the bare shoulder outside his vest's shoulder strap. The hot dryness of the touch was a shock. Col stared deep into his eyes and said, "Whatever happens, know this: No man ever had a better son than I."

It was revelation, the words he'd dreamed of hearing. They shut out the vozun drums, the crowd, everything. He tried to speak and failed completely. But words piled against each other in his throat. By the time he thought to reach out, to substitute contact for speech, Col was gone, stalking to the Elders' Bench.

Faldar Yan and his sons filed in. Bay came directly behind his father, towering over him. Likat trailed them both like a sly shadow. The Yans' kin set up a wordless chant of greeting. Many members of other clans joined in. Gan looked up and behind at North Clan. None cheered, but many wore expressions more eloquent than cheers.

Faldar singled them out for an especially broad smile.

At the center of the floor Col faced east and made his prescribed Three-sign. There was a sound like misting rain as each warrior did the same in the manner of his own clan. That done, Col turned slowly, ceremoniously greeting each direction.

Gan studied the oblong rings of seated men and the taut, eager expressions. He was reminded of a pack of coyotes trailing a hunting tiger.

In the midst of that thought, he noticed that Likat's attention wasn't fixed on Col or the Elders, either. He was looking directly at him.

There was no time to wonder about it. Col moved to take his seat, and the Elders gave Faldar permission to address the gathering. He spread his feet wide and aimed his words at the younger, more excitable warriors relegated to the higher seats.

At first it was what Gan expected. Faldar decried Col's attempt to groom his son to be War Chief, and so forth. Then, ominously, the tenor of his voice changed to an abnormal softness.

He said, "We're here to discuss sacrificing a youngster, make no mistake. Honor isn't involved. How can there be? What can we expect of a boy who never knew a mother, who grew up in a tent filled with nothing but greed and ambition? Men my age will remember that his mother, like him, refused to befriend anyone. She bragged of knowing things ordinary people—meaning Dog People—cannot know."

A high keening burst across Gan's hearing. He looked away from Faldar, and he was sickened to see his father listening with his eyes closed, so composed he might have been sleeping. He hated him more than Faldar Yan.

He fought anyone who spoke of his mother with less than immense respect. Col's callous unconcern brought back the memory of every insult, every snigger, every bruise and drop of blood her honor had cost him.

Bitter fire seared his throat. A handful of soft words from his father, and Gan had let himself be tricked into believing the man could care like other people.

Louder, demanding noise from the crowd pulled him out of his thoughts. Faldar was pointing at him. "To send this boy on the Journey is to punish him merely for being born. If the Dog People are to be equal to their destiny—and I intend to see that we are—we must be able to show pity as strongly as we seek vengeance. Gan Moondark failed on Nightwatch. No matter that he killed; remember, he struck from behind. More, his responsibility was to warn the tribe. If they'd killed him, they'd have been on us before we knew it."

"All five of them." Gan was mildly surprised to discover he was standing. He felt he was watching himself, hearing an icy voice he barely recognized. Clas stared up at him in disbelief. Gan went on. "I understand how you'd fear such an army, but Nightwatch lives to protect you."

Faldar spun around. "You are forbidden to speak when another is in the center of Earth Heart!"

"A lie has to be killed before it grows too large to deal with. You should know that, Faldar; your son Bay's a walking lie, and look how big he's gotten."

Enraged, Faldar made a step forward, but Likat was after him in one leap, holding him back, calling Bay to help him. Between them, they restrained the older man. As he calmed down, Likat pulled Bay clear, speaking with cupped hand directly at his ear. The larger man gave no sign of hearing, staring hatred at Gan. Likat continued to harangue him as Faldar waved the roaring crowd to silence.

Faldar said, "Reject this boy, I say; unname him as a Dog. Let all other tribes see that when a man loves life more than honor, the Dog People grant him his life."

At the ensuing sullen rumble of disagreement, Faldar's demanding gaze centered on certain individuals. Leaping to their feet, they argued his case for him. Hands began to go up in approval of Faldar's position.

Gan resisted the almost overwhelming urge to strike back, to brand Faldar a liar, but something told him to wait, that this wasn't the end of it. In fact, he felt his earlier exhilarating lightness return.

Likat dropped back to his seat as Bay stepped past his father and addressed the Elders. "My father's mercy is misplaced. Even though Gan's a man of no honor, he insulted my family. I claim blood right."

Once again Faldar seemed ready to explode, but instinctively he looked to the crowd, and for the first time he seemed aware of what Gan had seen all along. The warriors' interest wasn't in justice or tradition. They wanted excitement, and his failure to react to Gan's taunts wasn't sitting well. Speaking past stiff lips, he said, "We'll leave the matter to the warriors. Either we strip Gan of his membership in the tribe and reject him, or he answers for insulting my family."

The vote for a fight shook the tree-trunk rafters and support beams. Gan watched Col rise from his seat and come to stand beside him. At the edge of Gan's vision, Clas moved to join them.

Aside from shortknives, the sacred fighting murdats were the only weapons allowed in Earth Heart. They reposed at the feet of the senior Elder, encased in a box decorated with gold and jewels. After reciting the prayer for reconciliation, with its obligatory three pauses so the antagonists could speak to each other if they wished, he opened it. He turned it so all could see the ancient weapons, with their wooden handles and straight, unflared blades. Then he called for friends of the fighters to come forward for the customary inspection. Clas and Likat volunteered, and Likat produced a folded cloth. He gave it to Clas, who wiped a blade clean and handed it back. Then Likat folded the material over once more and ran the second blade through the fold, first one edge, then the other. He handed it to Clas.

Faldar moved then, brushing the advancing Bay aside like a gnat. "You insulted all of my family," he said, "and that means you'll fight me." He smirked at Col. "I know what you're thinking, but remember the rules; only two may fight. The death of one ends all challenges between those clans for a full year."

Gan saw his father tense momentarily, but his answer was restrained. "Gan will see you've no need to concern yourself with me. Or anyone else. Ever."

Faldar barked laughter, snatching the weapon from a stupefied Likat. Bay made one last attempt to argue with his father and was nearly bowled over for it. Likat scrambled out of his way and retreated to his seat, where he sat bent forward until he was almost in a fetal ball.

An Elder carrying an ornately carved wildcow horn at least three feet long stepped to the center of the arena. The shouting of the crowd died to a murmur and finally to utter silence. The Elder blew a single note. In the confines of the dome the cushioning bodies absorbed the sound and gave it a muted, haunting distance. The hair moved on Gan's neck and arms, and then the Elder spoke in the formalized singsong his office required. "Challenges must be answered. The sacred murdats are issued. There can be no other weapons or shields. Once wakened, the sacred blades must take life before they can be returned to rest. Know all present that victory does not signify right, nor defeat wrong. The duel answers only honor and courage. That is the way."

At the Elder's signal, every head bowed. The prayer for courage was over in seconds.

Clas whispered hoarsely behind Gan, barely audible against the growing sound of the crowd. "He'll rely on his size, try to intimidate you. Tire him. When he slows, kill him."

Facing his father and Clas, Gan said, "Only to save my life."

Veins stood out in Col's throat. Before he could speak, the command "Fight!" came from the Elders' seats.

Gan hefted the weapon. It was lighter, not as well balanced as his own murdat. It consoled him that Faldar was as unaccustomed to his.

He couldn't understand how he'd suddenly become so terribly thirsty. His lips felt dry and cracked when he licked them.

Faldar, his jacket stripped off to reveal a hairy, bulking torso, advanced in a shuffle, knees bent, blade poised for attack or defense.

Gan moved slowly to his left, defending.

The larger man rushed furiously. Gan stepped away, taunting. "Clumsy old man." He managed to smile, adding to the sting.

Faldar charged once more. The fury of it tumbled Gan against the front bench. When Faldar chopped down at him, he rolled under it. Scrambling spectators cursed and trampled each other getting out of the way. Gan's counterstroke at Faldar's ankles would have severed his feet, but he leaped away. Before he could recover and attack again, Gan was upright, ready.

Gan took his eyes from Faldar's weapon long enough to study his face. He saw the older man was chastened by the wasted opportunity. There was more there, as well; there was a respect that carried the first taint of fear. A lunging feint sent Faldar dodging away.

At that first sign of caution, Gan went on the offense. Faldar was forced back, and jeers cascaded from the stalwarts of North Clan.

Bellowing, he gathered his strength and rushed Gan again, his swordplay like axe work. Instead of absorbing their force, Gan deflected them. The clash of metal on metal grew fainter, less frequent. Gan's confidence soared.

He relaxed. And took a thrust into his left shoulder that burned like fire on contact and left him with the amazing sensation that an iron spike was still nailed there.

Bay yelled triumph, "Kill! Kill! Kill!"

The crowd took up the chant.

Faldar penetrated his defense, slashed eagerly. At the last instant Gan flung himself to the ground to his right, rolling. As he rose, Faldar was past him, pivoting, raising the sword to strike again, but it was too late. Gan drove with his entire body, arm extended, aiming at Faldar's unprotected middle.

The thick figure stopped in a lurching, tiptoeing motion. He dropped his weapon, but refused to look down at the sword in his stomach. Gan stepped back, pulled it free, and Faldar opened his mouth as if he would speak or cry out. He managed only a weary sigh, and it seemed to carry away the last energy left him. He went down on his back like a great, felled pine.

Bay's shriek brought Gan around in a crouch, instinctively ready for this new threat. He attempted to avoid the attack, warding off Bay's shortknife with his empty hand, but the sacred blade took blood again, nicking Bay's wrist. By that time Likat and several others were pulling him back to his seat. A ragged chorus of disapproval aimed at Bay was quickly refuted by South Clan, who came to their feet as one, complaining that Gan had struck at an unarmed man.

The wildcow horn restored order, and the senior Elder collected the weapons. All watched in silence while he blessed them and placed them beside the box on the bench, where they would wait for the cleansing rites. There was another rustling Three-sign though the crowd. Only when it quieted would he acknowledge them.

"The fight was fair," he declared. "The challenge is ended. Bay Yan acted rashly, but not dishonorably. Gan Moondark made no attempt to injure. The original question before the Elders was, 'Shall Gan Moondark be sent on the Honor Journey for failure on Nightwatch?' The answer is that he must go. However, the victor of a duel must attend the burning ceremony for the defeated. Gan Moondark will ride to strike the Mountain People's main camp immediately after Faldar Yan's burning and the cleaning of the sacred weapons. It is said. It is the way."

With the cautious tread of strangers, Gan, his father, and Clas moved to the north exit. Gan's knees shook now, and when he stole a glance at his father, he was startled to see a white line of tension at his nostrils and the quick, ceaseless scanning of a man who expects attack. Clas was the calmest, but fully alert. Still, it was he who spat on the ground as soon as they were in the daylight. Bitterly, he said, "Well, Col? If not now, when?"

Col shook his head, jaw set. "It may be time, but I'm not ready. Not yet."

Gan said, "You're talking about me, something I should know."

After a pause, Col said, "Yes. But there's one more thing we have to be certain about. I'll tell you as soon as I can." He looked to Clas. "It has to happen right. You know."

Clas growled. "Yes, I know."

Col struck off toward his tent, leaving Gan and Clas no choice but to follow.

CHAPTER 18

Within minutes of walking from Earth Heart to his own tent, Bay Yan collapsed, clutching the wound on his wrist and moaning. When they had to pry his hand open and the minor cut was seen to be already ugly and discolored with infection, the news struck through every tent like lightning.

Everyone had already remarked on how solicitous and helpful Likat had been on the walk from Earth Heart to the Yan tent, and all hearts went out to him when they saw how distraught he was at his friend's collapse. His reaction paled beside Bay's mother's however. She stepped outside just in time to see her son crumple to the ground and promptly flew into monumental hysterics. It was also agreed by everyone that it was a marvelous stroke of luck that Kolee happened to be visiting the Yan tent at the time. Remarkably, a few minutes' private conversation with Kolee had Likat rebounding from sick depression to confidence that Bay would recover. So great was his assurance that he immediately assumed control of the increasingly hostile and agitated younger warriors. In Bay's name.

Not everyone saw all these activities in the same light.

Sylah felt she'd seen as much anger as distress in Likat's performance. His loud insistence that the Moondark men were somehow responsible for the frighteningly swift degeneration of Bay's flesh had a discordant ring, as well.

There were other factors, as she had explained to the Moondarks and Clas that night. It was late as they talked in her tent, and she was exhausted from working on Bay. His situation was demanding, and Kolee was a complicating, hostile presence, bitterly protesting every contact between him and Sylah. Only Chelo's pleading and Neela's insistence forced the older Healer to tolerate "interference." Kolee's further response to Chelo's attitude was to supply her with a "soothing tonic," which had the woman snoring like a prairie bear within minutes. Sylah said Kolee was still laboring over Bay when she left the tent, and then surprised the three men by adding that she admired Kolee's work. She explained that when she arrived where Bay lay on the ground, Kolee had already cleansed his wound. There was little else for her to do, Sylah went on, so she'd checked his sweat. Gan had boggled at that, and she told him that the smell of sweat could tell her as much as footprints told him. Bay's carried the biting tang associated with men injured in conflict. At her abbey they simply called it battle sweat; it was unmistakable. Then, within a minute or so after they had him carried to his bed, she checked again and discovered a completely different and unknown scent, a pall that made her think of mushrooms. More than that, his heartbeat was weak and rapid.

Sylah admitted that the speed and impact of the change baffled her. Kolee had moved with calm haste, however, keeping Bay warm, immobile, and full of soothing chamomile. It had seemed too ordinary to Sylah, but she said that by the time she left to get some rest, it was clear he wasn't going to die.

His recovery might be a much different story. Privately, she feared the hand would never function properly again.

The two older men had exchanged long, searching looks. Sylah felt the atmosphere of the room shift. Where there had been concern—even worry—now there was relief, as if a course had been decided. When she tried to find out what they were thinking about, they politely and transparently denied any hidden thoughts. She'd gone to bed immediately, too tired to bother being frustrated.

The following morning the Elders declared Faldar had died of violence, his death uncontaminated by disease. Likat continued to try to convince others that the Moondarks were guilty of *something*. Neela pointed out to him that his arguments might change the Elders' minds, and if they decided Faldar's death was tainted, they'd have to send Faldar to the fire without the preparation his status demanded. Likat merely quieted his ranting near the Yan tent.

And he had allies. Sylah saw the knots of warriors as she moved about the camp. There was always at least one man in their midst demanding they condemn the Moondarks.

The entire camp understood that what had been started couldn't end at this point. Not even children were allowed to disturb the cloak of expectation; at the first breakout of shrill laughter, an adult would descend on the guilty one like a hawk on a chick, scolding, shielding, their own faces twisted into the angry concern that children can never truly understand.

After her attempt to stifle Likat, Neela behaved as if dazed. She attached herself to Sylah. If they were separated for more than a few minutes, she returned to grip Sylah's hand in a desperate need for reassurance. She hardly spoke, and when Sylah tried to sympathize, the girl thanked her with stilted formality. A moment later she shook her head and said that wasn't what bothered her most. Still, when Sylah probed further, she'd only muttered about a falling tree knocking down saplings.

That afternoon they ate together in Sylah's tent, trying to ignore the pala drums of South Clan that thumped unending reminder that their leader went to the fire at the next sunrise. The question on everyone's lips was, would Bay be next to him?

On their way back to the Yan tent, a large stone skipped off the road a yard in front of them. It left a scar in the dirt and a flat, ugly sound that seemed to hang in the air long after it had bounced away. Sylah stopped short, looking in the direction from which it came. A group of perhaps a dozen young warriors huddled there, jostling, giggling. One of them whispered something, and the rest laughed coarsely.

Sylah lightly touched Neela's elbow. "Ignore them," she whispered. "Hurry."

Another rock bounced in front of them before they'd traveled three strides. Neela rounded on them. "Don't you dare throw things at us! I know who you are. My brothers will call your names."

The one the others found so amusing spoke for them. "No one would hurt you, Neela. We admired your father. We like your brother. But you shouldn't be walking with that Olan—" He smothered the word, but his friends heard it. They laughed some more.

Sylah said, "I'm on my way to help Bay Yan. Why are you angry with me?"

"You're a spy for the Moondarks."

Another voice rose, "And for Clas. He's just like them."

Something clammy squeezed Sylah's heart. Neela looked at her peculiarly, waiting for her answer.

In that look Sylah felt more challenge than the troublemakers represented. To the warriors she said, "I speak to anyone I choose. That's the way of the Dog People, and I'm a guest of your tribe. Go home. Ask your mothers to teach you manners. Ask your fathers if they show their courage by stoning women."

She continued her walk, Neela proud beside her. For the first time since her father's death, she smiled. It wasn't much, but Sylah cherished it.

Abreast of the next tent, Likat called to them. Neela seemed ready to break away. Yet again she clutched Sylah's hand, careful to keep the contact out of Likat's sight. Gently, Sylah freed herself and moved to stand in front of him. With a bob of her head she indicated the other warriors. She said, "You heard?"

He smiled. "I was curious to see what you'd say. You're bold."

She waited, unamused. He spoke to Neela. "I wanted Sylah to see how much our men need discipline."

Neela said, "Are you the fighting instructor now? Or the War Chief?" Likat took no apparent notice, but Sylah had to repress a wince. Neela's voice was shrill, scratchy; her control was very uncertain.

Likat said, "Your brother will be War Chief."

Neela's lower lip was trembling. "We shouldn't be talking this way. He's too sick."

"No." He let them wait, enjoyed the hoarding of his secret. Then he said, "He spoke to Kolec and Chelo. He asked for you, Neela."

Instantly Neela was running for her home, graceful as an antelope, skirt swirling, golden braids flashing. Likat watched, and once more Sylah saw the way he looked at her. She started to follow her, but he caught her arm. "Bay and Chelo have some things to tell our Neela. They'll want privacy, fortunately, because I've been wanting to speak to you about your position here."

"You have nothing to say about that."

His face hardened around his smile. "Yes I do. As you'll see. First, however, you're very close to Neela."

Sylah nodded.

"Good. She's going to be my wife."

She stared, immobilized. He went on, "Neela's a beautiful thing, but not really interesting, you understand? I'll need someone else to entertain me. When I'm bored, I become irritable. Sometimes I hurt people. As her friend, you wouldn't want her injured. Am I being clear?"

Her words grated. "When Church hears what you said—"

He twisted her arm, made her gasp. "When do you think you'll tell Church your tale? I control the camp now. You're forbidden to leave."

It was like a blow, and she staggered. "You think the Dog warriors will risk their souls for your—your *entertainment*?"

"There's a rumor that you're not really a Priestess. I explained to my men that you won't try to run from us unless you've something to hide. And if someone comes along to vouch for you, why, Church forgives." He let go of her arm, emphasizing her helplessness. "You chose the wrong friends. Learn to live with the new reality and your life will be better for it." He walked away jauntily.

Her heart drummed at her ribs. As soon as she felt able, she hurried to the Yan tent, careless of her steps. She tripped over a guy rope and sprawled flat. Ignoring amused gawkers, she brushed absently at dirt and bits of grass. When she burst through the entry flap without bothering to announce herself, she was at least presentable.

The main room was empty. Heated voices penetrated the softwall, coming from Bay's room. She moved determinedly in that direction, but as she reached for the flap, something made her check.

It was a man's voice she didn't recognize, deep and resonant, one accustomed to authority, but now uncertain. He said, "The wife has taken her daughter away, as you asked. That changes nothing. The sacred murdats have never been seen by a woman. I can't believe your accusation, and that's the only reason you give me for wanting to see them."

Kolee said, "I can prove what I say. Are the weapons in that case?"

Sylah edged away from the flap, trying to imagine where they were standing. She had to steady the hand holding her shortknife by bracing it with the other, but she managed to open a slit about an inch long in the material of the wall. Slowly, she pulled it open, peering in.

The Elder faced her in his ceremonial jacket decorated with ermine tails. A decorative band of mink ran down the outside of each trouser leg. A coyote pelt formed his hat and extended cloaklike down his back. It had polished agate eyes set in silver sockets. They looked back at Sylah, cold with accusation.

Bay lay on his bed, his hand a frightening purple-black, so swollen it looked ready to burst. Nevertheless, the upper arm looked much better, and he was sleeping soundly.

The Elder held up the blades for Kolee's inspection. Even from her clumsy vantage point Sylah could tell they were very old, much more crude than anything Saband would create in his smithy. The Elder's voice trembled as he said the same thing to Kolee, pointing out how the metal surface was marred by hundreds of tiny pits and cracks.

Kolee nodded impatiently, interrupting to say that it was the condition of the blades that made her think of poison in the first place. She added that Bay's reaction reminded her of her own departed husband. As she talked, she examined one blade, then the second, holding it under the Elder's nose. He looked ill as she pointed out the grainy, dustlike smudge on its surface. She forced him to restate that Faldar unmistakably died from the thrust of the weapon; no poison had time to react on him. Then, just as his confusion over that apparent contradiction struck him, she argued that Faldar's body absorbed most of it from that part of the blade; the remaining trace caused Bay's trouble.

He didn't want to believe. "We don't really know there's poison on it. I've heard Likat's accusations against the Moondarks. I know his ambitions for Bay, and I know you support them. Col and Clas are honorable men. You understand I must see proof. What you're suggesting is the worst crime in our history."

Kolee's harsh expression faltered. She blinked, and a surprisingly pink tongue slipped across her lips. Rather than remorse or pity, however, there was a pulse of eagerness in her voice as she bobbed her head and repeated, "Yes, yes, yes." Then, in her aggressive waddle, she went to the opposite slit entry and opened it, giving a low whistle. One of the Yan brothers appeared, carrying a chicken. He handed it over to Kolee, who dismissed him, watching until she was sure he was gone. Still unspeaking, she used the edge near the butt of the suspect blade to make a small cut in the bird's leg. It jerked and squawked, fluttering wildly for a moment before calming. In seconds it was in distress.

When Kolee put it on the carpet, it could barely stand. It stumbled drunkenly, falling and rising. Sylah looked away, her gaze drawn to Kolee. A barely repressed smile twitched the Healer's lips. Sylah had the sickening feeling the woman was somehow proud of what was happening. The Elder demanded she end the bird's misery. She wrung its neck and recalled the boy to carry it off.

Kolee said, "A rattlesnake couldn't have killed it quicker. What more proof could you ask? Who had access to the blades?"

He said stiffly, "Me."

Kolee prodded gently. "Aren't they examined before the fighters use them? It could have been Clas who fouled it, as easily as Gan. But you *saw* Likat wipe it clean."

He nodded soberly. Sylah nearly choked on the urge to shout at the man. Couldn't he see that Kolee had detailed knowledge of the sacred murdats that "no woman had ever seen"? How did she know the weapons were inspected? How could she know who inspected them?

The Elder was so shaken he wasn't thinking. And he was their last chance. Dully, he said, "They must have put the poison on the blade during the prayer."

Sylah pulled back from her eyehole as he returned the blades to their case.

Likat was the poisoner. Of that she was sure. But everyone knew Faldar had accepted the challenge after Bay— Of course! Likat meant for *Bay* to die, not Faldar.

Kolee. She knew. Sylah's mind flashed back to the pair of them, sneaking about near the bog. She gestured at Likat with a sack, and he'd been frightened. She said it: *rattlesnake.*

Kolee was practically babbling. ". . . at the burning tomorrow morning. They'll have to be there, all three of them. My son will confront them then, with the entire tribe to witness. It's Col's fault. Col Moondark. He and his spawn have shamed the people. All these years—now, revenge. For this horrible thing, I mean. The poison."

The Elder watched her warily, but muttered agreement, allowing her to guide him to the other exit. He insisted the information be held secret until the proper moment. The flap was still settling behind him when she clasped her hands under her chin and whirled in a clumsy circle of joy.

Sylah darted for the outside exit, actually had her hand on it when Likat called just outside, identifying himself, asking if Kolee was present. From behind her Kolee shouted for him to come in.

She was trapped.

CHAPTER 19

Sylah dove at Kolee, relying on surprise to bowl over the older woman.

Kolee was more than surprised, she was dumbfounded, but she reacted instinctively, grappling with her attacker. The two of them tumbled into Bay's room, Kolee's short arms around Sylah as tight as she could hold. Likat, after a split second of confusion, ran after them. He arrived just as Sylah broke free, searching wildly for the other exit. He wrapped a forearm under her chin and gripped that fist with his other hand, lifting and squeezing. The tips of her toes barely touched the floor.

Blood roared in her ears, and her eyes seemed to be swelling out of her skull. He was closing down the artery in her neck; how many times had she gently massaged it to ease one of her patients? How often had she been warned never to interfere with its function, because without its continuous feeding of the brain, the entire body stopped? She clawed at his arm, reached for his face, but he merely made a growling sound and lifted harder.

A red mist settled across her vision, blotting out the sight of Kolee, who was dancing about clumsily in her excitement, flapping her arms and making wet-mouthed gobbling noises.

The mist turned gray, then black. The noise in her head stopped.

The next sensation she was aware of was the touch of a hand under her jaw. She tried to think where she was, and couldn't, which was unpleasant, but the hand wasn't hurting her, and she was too tired to pull away. Something warned her that she should be afraid. It was too much trouble. Anyhow, her eyes throbbed; she told herself she'd open them later, when she felt better.

A faraway voice said, "She's alive," and another one answered, "Not for long. She overheard, didn't she?"

"What are you saying, Likat! We can't kill a Priestess!"

Likat. Kolee.

Awareness and remembrance seeped into her brain on waves of pain. She concentrated all her will on hearing and understanding.

"She knows exactly what we did." That was Likat.

Kolee protested. "She only heard what I told Elder Alt. She doesn't know—"

"*They* know. If she tells the Moondarks and Clas what she heard, they'll come for me. You said it yourself. Until you ruined it, we had the perfect way to accuse them. Now we have to do something about her."

"Don't kill her," Kolee pleaded. "Church will name you. Your soul will be taken."

"Our souls, Kolee. Church will make room for you, too, so we have to be clever. An accident, or something."

After a thoughtful silence that stretched Sylah's nerves to breakpoint, Kolee's sly voice rose again. "What if she were part of their plan?"

"What?" Likat's tone questioned her sanity.

"Someone had to prepare the poison. Why not her?"

"She's just going to confess?"

Kolee bubbled with excitement. "We convince everyone she's diseased; no one but me will get near her. We keep her in my tent until after Faldar's ceremony tomorrow morning. When we come back from getting rid of the Moondarks and Clas, we'll 'find' her with a poisoned shortknife beside her. Church will reject her."

Likat spoke musingly. "I've never been convinced she's just a missionary. I think I'll ask her some questions tonight."

"You mustn't. We agreed, you're going out with your Nightwatch friends, just in case something goes wrong. You promised."

"We'll see." It was grudging, and Sylah's palms were suddenly damp. Then he said, "Give her something to make her sick. And what about Bay?"

"Sleeping like a baby. He's recovering well. Except for his hand. It's going to be useless."

Likat's careless grunt disposed of that subject.

Sylah steeled herself for the inescapable. Her stomach rolled dangerously at the thought of having to swallow whatever concoction Kolee was preparing. She heard the Healer—and gritted her teeth at the irony of the title—puttering about. She recognized a series of musical notes like tiny bells as something dropping into a metal pot. Next came pouring water, and the sounds of stirring and crushing.

Likat lifted her head roughly, pulling her jaw open. Feigning unconsciousness, she got the vile mess down. She couldn't identify the taste, but the effect was almost immediate, and she rolled over to be sick.

"Holly berries," Kolee said. "She'll be too weak to blink."

"Holly? More poison?"

"It shouldn't be enough to kill her. Actually, it makes little difference when she goes, does it? We have to hurry, though, so people will see you carrying her and believe she's diseased." Her cheerful malice sent Sylah into another spasm of vomiting. As if dealing with one of her own patients, she noted how her heartbeat had grown erratic, her skin clammy.

As Likat lifted her, she fainted again.

Her consciousness returned as a sharp transition, with a lingering dream sensation of falling from warm comfort into frigid water. The reality was that she was cold and shivering.

She lay on her right side, her hands lashed together behind her back. A cord looped tightly around her neck led to her ankles, pulling them up behind her; when she attempted to straighten her legs, the loop choked her. She hurriedly returned to the bent attitude that avoided strangling.

In addition to her bonds, there was a gag in her mouth. Her stomach warned her not to think of the taste of it.

She opened her eyes the merest slit, peering through her lashes. Across the tent, Kolee sat slumped against a mound of pillows. The dim light of the single candle made it impossible to tell if the other woman's eyes were open or not, and Sylah finally opened her own fully.

Kolee shifted, muttering to herself. Then she began to snore.

Sylah tried again to move. The loop stopped her.

And this was where it all led.

Silent tears slid down against the rough cloth of the gag.

Her mind swept her into the darkest part of her past, dredged up all the worst childhood images. She trembled uncontrollably, remembering being thrown in the basket with other children. The pressure of her bonds was the same terror she'd felt when the shock of capture wore off. She remembered twisting and squirming, sitting on someone, jouncing, being sat on.

And then came the selection.

They took her. Owned her.

Now she was owned again.

And this was where it all ended. The Abbess' schemes. Her own plans.

The Door. I'll never know what it led to.

Cheated. Always. Now for the last time.

More tears came then, searing drops of disappointment as well as sorrow. She swallowed hard, clenched her teeth against the shivering and the sobs.

They'll kill me. They won't defeat me.

The first time she saw the movement, she thought it was a shadow, the wind moving a softwall. When she noticed no other wall was moving, she wanted to cry out for help. The thought that it was probably Likat stopped her. Indeed, she looked anxiously to Kolee, hoping the older woman would wake.

A black presence slipped into the room and was absorbed by a dark corner. It stalked the sleeping Kolee. Silently, swiftly, it grabbed her exactly as Likat had grabbed herself. She twitched in sympathy as the woman's eyes flew wide and she flailed helplessly.

It was over quickly. The black figure lowered her to the floor as a second figure entered and moved directly to herself.

Before it bent over her, she knew it was Clas. He reached to cut the truss line at her neck, bringing his black-painted face only inches from hers. The rush of blood to her head made her giddy. For a moment, she saw the same softness in his expression she'd seen in the women who had made her a Chosen, but then he was slashing the bonds at her wrists and removing her gag, and she was still crying, foolishly, happily, infuriatingly.

He helped her to her feet, quickly scooping her into his arms when she would have fallen. Kolee was already bound and gagged as they passed, and Gan was waiting at the exit flap. As they reached the deserted path between tents, Sylah's breath caught at the sight of three dark shapes rising ahead of them before she recognized Gan's dogs. The animals led the way back to Col's tent.

Inside, they placed her on cushions. Their heavy-handed solicitousness made her smile, which threatened to bring on the maddening tears again, but she pushed them back. She asked for bread and milk, and Clas trotted out, returning with a pitcher, a mug, and a whole loaf. There was a jar of honey, as well.

Between bites and sips she told them what had happened. When she asked why they'd risked contact with someone diseased, Col merely said, "For several reasons." She knew better than to probe, and he reinforced her decision by suggesting she rest for a while.

He turned to Gan. "You still hold to the choice you made earlier?"

"Yes." Pain scored the determined features. "There is no choice. We have to run away."

"Accept disgrace? Abandon the tribe when it needs us most?" Clas' voice accused, but Sylah saw anticipation in his quick lean forward and in the way he cocked his head to the side. She was convinced he was seeking an affirmative answer to questions she'd have sworn were unthinkable. Then something happened that destroyed all her neat logic. Worse, she had to wonder if she knew the least thing about these people. Clas' eyes went to

Col, studying him, registering his solemn approval of Gan's statement. Then he looked back at Gan, and she saw resignation, and—what stunned her—a sort of helpless fury.

Gan answered stubbornly. "We could kill some of Likat's and Bay's friends, maybe even them. That won't prove we *didn't* poison the weapon. We'd end up dead, and others would say the dying branded us guilty. Even worse, there are those who'd believe us and die beside us, for no purpose. Our only chance to prove our innocence is to survive. If our absence hurts the tribe, then the tribe will only be paying for its mistakes."

This time Sylah concentrated on Col. He was actually relieved, smiling openly. And then it struck her, and she realized she'd been a fool. Gan still didn't know of his mother's prophecy. Col was still withholding the information that might influence Gan's course of action. The father knew he must die as part of his son's promised rise, yet he had so much faith in his son's destiny he refused to risk affecting him.

Or to admit his love.

She hated him for being so brave that his courage demanded her complicity.

She sat up, unsteady. Clas moved to help, but she smiled and shook her head. She asked, "How long before the people start moving toward the burning place?"

Col glanced at the water clock. "About four hours. Don't worry, we're already prepared. We've a litter for you, if you're too weak to ride."

"Neela must come with us."

Col stared, taken aback. Gan said, "Why?"

Sylah told them what Likat had said, adding, "You don't know what it is to be property. I won't leave her here."

Gan ran a finger across his lips, thinking. "This is her home, her tribe. She may not want to come. After all, we don't know where we're going."

Sick, weary, Sylah knew she had no strength for argument. She lifted her shoulders in a shrug. "If she decides, so be it. If she stays, I must."

"Stay? Here?" Clas' voice tore at her. She wished she had a choice. He went on, "I won't let you!"

She smiled at him. "That's just it, Clas. You'll never understand. Not being allowed, I mean." He didn't understand. He clamped his jaws tight. She reached for his hand. "Get me into her room. Please."

"Crazy. You can hardly walk," he muttered, already conceding.

Gan said, "What if she gives an alarm?"

"She won't."

Gan made a face, then turned to Clas. "I'll go with you."

The trip to the Yan tent was a nightmare series of impressions as she fought the effects of the poison. She was stronger, and able to support herself, but her feet were wooden and her mind insisted on drifting into other times. At one point she was sure she was talking to the Abbess, and once she was sure Lanta held her hand and was seeing into her thoughts again. She came away from that memory with a sense of falling, and discovered that she had, indeed, stumbled and Clas' grip was all that saved her.

Gan left them huddled in the shadows while he crept to the tent. Neela's room, he knew, was next to Bay's sickroom. If they hadn't moved her. If she didn't scream. *If.*

He crawled on his belly past the suffused light coming through the tent wall, closing his mind against the throbbing of his wounded shoulder. With his murdat he carefully sliced an opening just large enough for him to crawl through. Next, he wrapped his jacket around the blade and poked it through the hole; when no one slashed it, he followed it inside.

The scent of the room, a mix of flowers and spices, told him it was Neela's. Light through the softwall from Bay's room allowed him to see her on her bed, curled up so small he doubted his eyes, at first.

He positioned himself directly in front of her, then lifted a lock of her hair. It was like a mist, delicate in the luminance through the softwall. He followed it with his eyes as he drew it across her cheek, and missed her frightened waking.

She lunged at him with the hand from under her pillow. Only his hundreds of hours of arms practice saved his life. The shortknife whispered past his throat so close he thought he felt its cold edge. Grabbing that hand, he slapped the other over her mouth, but not before she had time to say, "No, Lik—"

"It's me, Gan!" he whispered hoarsely. For a second she continued to press against him. Her heart hammered against his until she pulled back. At a querulous noise from the next room, he started, but she shook her head. With her free hand she mimed someone drinking, and he understood she was indicating that her mother was drugged.

They sat that way, staring at each other, his hand still clasping her wrist, for almost a full minute. When he was satisfied they were undiscovered, he leaned close enough to touch her ear with his lips. "Sylah wants you."

"She's here? Now? Why are you here?"

He let go of the knife hand, and she lowered it back to the pillow. He said, "Is there a place safe for talking?"

She shook her head again, frightened eyes fixed on his, and he suspected her reaction was more a rejection of him than an answer to the question. He went on, "She said she has to talk to you. We're leaving. She won't come unless you do. Clas is outside with her now."

She froze. "Outside? Here?" Without waiting for an answer, she clutched a blanket around herself and gestured for him to follow. They made no sound on the carpet as she led him into the main room. She indicated where he should wait while she looked in on Bay, then rejoined him. She pulled him down closer to her mouth, then said, "My brothers sleep like the dead, and my mother won't hear us. Why is she leaving with you? Is Clas going, too?"

"She'll tell you." He hurried outside. They half carried Sylah in, then left to lie just outside the entry.

Sylah took Neela's hands in hers. "I know about Likat," she said. She took a deep, steadying breath to help her forge ahead. "I was sent here by my abbey to destroy any alliance between your tribe and Ola. My abbess and I decided that the surest way would be to take Faldar Yan's daughter to Harbundai as a hostage."

Her face is so white, Sylah thought. It's as though I'd drained the blood from her. But she must know.

"I have a mixture in my medical kit. It makes a tea that will make you forget what I tell you to forget, do what I tell you to do. It was my last resort to make you come with me. You are expected. You'll be treated well. And I would have influence and power. Nevertheless, I can't betray you. Still, I beg you to do what I want you to do, not for my sake anymore, but for your own. Neither Gan nor Clas nor Col poisoned the murdat. They're waiting for me to leave with them, because it's the only way they can hope to restore their honor. Likat and Kolee made me their prisoner this afternoon because I learned they're the poisoners. I think, in your heart, you've known that all along, and you said nothing because you believed your brother might be involved. I swear to you Bay knew nothing of it. Likat meant for him to die. Is such a man to be your mate?"

Neela almost snarled. "Gan killed my father. He hurt my brother. You only want me for your own purposes. You lied to all of us. How are you different from Likat?"

"I love you."

The girl crumpled. "Don't say that! I want to believe you, and I can't. Not any longer. You know I love you; how can I tell you're not just saying that?"

"Come with me. Quickly."

"No! I belong with my people."

Sylah sighed. "I'll tell Gan and Clas. I stay, too." She started to rise, still weak and awkward, and Neela pulled her back down easily.

"You said Likat and Kolee made you a prisoner. How'd you escape?"

It all seemed so useless. The floor swayed like a willow branch in the breeze. For the merest instant she saw a flash of a girl playing by a streamside, and it took all her strength to avoid closing her eyes to drift off and join her. Dispiritedly, fighting nausea, she told of Likat's plans and how Gan and Clas rescued her from Kolee.

Even as she droned on, her mind examined her own situation. Nothing's changed, she thought; not for me. I tried. I did my best. But when they do it—she couldn't bring herself to think of dawn bringing death—it will be for my reasons. No one owns me anymore.

Neela stood up, pulling her along. She said, "Bay will make the alliance my father wanted. If I can prevent my people going to war by leaving, I must. Your story of staying here when you know you'll be killed doesn't impress me, because I don't believe you. Go tell Gan and Clas I'll be out front as soon as I can."

She ghosted from the room, leaving Sylah alone. She made her way to the entry. Before leaving, she turned to stare at the place where Neela had disappeared into the darkness.

If this was victory, why did she feel such a tearing sense of loss?

CHAPTER 20

The awe in Gan's voice as he described Neela's appearance in their midst brought a thin smile to his father's face. He said, "She was like a deer, on us before we knew it. And with both horses, her own and Sylah's. No one else could have kept them so quiet."

Neela ignored him. She'd closed herself off from all of them since agreeing to join them. She continued to help Sylah pack, stuffing clothes into a leather bag. Gan wished he could say or do something to make her feel better. One look at her would tell anyone she didn't need reassurance, however. Her strength of purpose surprised him. In thinking about it, he remembered that she'd agreed to meet with Sylah only after he told her Clas was escaping with them.

The thought sent a slimy sensation running up his spine that left him feeling soiled. Shocked, he recognized the touch of jealousy. It embarrassed him.

He was pleased when Col indicated they were ready to load the pack-horses. All the equipment for their escape and survival was packed in water-proof soft leather bags. The load-carrying racks were padded to prevent injury to the animals. As a seminomadic people, the Dog People had learned long ago that the pack animals required as much attention as war-horses. When survival depended on mobility, that which couldn't move must be sacrificed. Everyone knew everything they carried was precious, if not irreplaceable.

Moving swiftly and surely in the dark, the men had the bags lashed on the racks in minutes.

The bandage on Gan's shoulder bulged under the tough leather and chain mail of his combat gear. The wound cut down on his ability to lift, but it was a minor consideration, thanks to Sylah's treatment. The strong smell of the valerian root powder she'd sprinkled on it made his nose itch, but the wound was clean. He winced more at the memory of the carelessness that brought it than the actual pain. It had been a good lesson.

He also remembered the touch of her hand, the soothing of her voice as she described the treatment in progress. She'd calmed him, drawn pain from his body, made him secure in her care.

He caught himself watching Clas, and spun away and ducked back inside the tent, making the excuse that he wanted one last inspection for anything forgotten. By the time he returned, the others were already mounted and impatient.

The men wore trousers of the same sort of leather as their jackets, although the trousers sported metal strips sewn along their length, rather than chain mail. The odd-looking objects hanging by woven straps at their left shoulders were called war masks. They were metal hoods, with hinged jaw plates that swung forward to close across the mouth. The plates were perforated to permit speech, and left the eyes and nose unprotected. They hung low enough in front, however, to offer some protection to the throat.

The horses were prepared for fighting with leather and mail armor on heads and flanks. The men's shields were strapped to their saddle pommels; their recurved bows and otterskin arrow quivers hung from the cantle at the back. The superbly trained animals shifted nervously, but quietly. The dogs also sensed the tension, and Raggar patrolled the area in his aggressive posture, head down low and forward. He was literally hunting trouble. Shara and Cho, less belligerent, padded along behind him.

Rising into the saddle, Col gestured them forward.

By the light of a quarter moon and uncountable stars, the small column headed north, away from a life become unlivable into a future already unimaginable.

They cleared the camp without incident, and as the first hint of color touched the horizon, they were well past Tiger Rocks. At that point Col had them dismount.

From a brushy defile Gan watched with the others as a Nightwatcher trudged toward camp with his dogs around him in a tight group. His chest ached at the sight. Until then, everything had been challenging. Now he felt lost, insignificant. His father, Clas, the women—they seemed as helpless and futile as himself. He couldn't take his eyes from the Nightwatcher. Gan wondered if that one, too, inhaled the thick morning air until his lungs ached with the beauty and unbelievable freedom of the new day. Did he taste the sweetness of crushed grasses and sage? Did he imagine the hapless bushes to be enemy warriors, and did he sometimes draw his murdat and duel with them in the half light of going home? Did he dream of saving the Dog People, of leading them to glory?

Raggar whined softly and leaned against his master.

With the Nightwatcher safely past, they turned due west. Instead of mounting, the men trotted beside their mounts, their pace faster, if anything, than the previous rate of march. Sylah finally saw the importance of the strange loop attached to each saddle. The men grasped it, allowing them to use a fraction of the horse's strength to augment their pace.

By unspoken agreement Gan became the point man. The dogs fanned out far ahead of him. Clas settled himself immediately in front of the women, who took responsibility for the packhorses. Col covered the rear.

They continued without incident for approximately an hour before the shouts echoed from behind them. Col was out of sight at the time, on the back slope of a hill, and Gan and Clas mounted quickly, galloping toward him. They were almost to the crest of the hill when he appeared, riding. He gave the arm signal that all was well, but then followed it with another indicating they should continue to move dismounted, but faster. When Gan attempted to ride to him to talk, Col sent a stern signal that meant obey. Col remained on his horse.

The sun was at its high point, and Gan had just reached a plateau with a copse of larger trees and a commanding view, when he heard Col whistle for a stop. Gan called in the dogs as the others made their way up to join him.

In the bustle of getting the horses hidden in the grove, no one noticed Col's appearance as he approached. At Sylah's small sound of alarm, they all looked, and were taken aback. The cragged face was ashen, and the sharp lines of its character were indistinct. The long scar seemed to have concentrated the remaining color in his flesh, and it smoldered across his features. When his horse stopped, he bent forward, then swayed upright to an exaggeratedly stiff pose. That was when Gan noticed the otterskin quiver was open.

By then the blood oozing down the back of his leg and staining the horse's flank was obvious. He swung out of the saddle with the slow grace of one avoiding sudden movement. When Gan hurried forward to offer a hand, he took it without comment, shaking his head at their flood of questions as they tried to make him comfortable.

"It wasn't your dogs' fault, Gan," were his first words, as Neela worked to remove his armor. "There were three. They came from behind, and to the south. From the camp, looking for us. They should have ridden back to tell Likat." He frowned as Sylah came up, flicking water from her fresh-washed hands, preparing to examine the wound, then added, "Now they can't tell him anything. East Clan men; Dog warriors. How can this have happened?"

Sylah was brisk. "It's going to take time for me to get this out. That's a lance point broken off in there."

He smiled grimly. "I remember the incident. There's no use going after it. We both know that."

"I have to try. My credo—"

He interrupted. "Has no place in this situation. I'm dying. You can't stop it. Don't trouble yourself."

"No." Gan heard himself before he realized he'd spoken. "You can't."

Col shook his head. The silver hair that had always seemed so metallic, so helmetlike, was lifeless in limp disarray. He said, "This is the way," and sent a knowing smile at a stone-faced Clas before continuing. "You'll change, the way the animals adapt to the seasons. You'll learn from those you meet. You'll build, son."

"And destroy." It was Clas, and although he kept his eyes on Col, Gan knew the anger in them was for him.

His father sighed, then coughed violently. A startling red froth speckled his lips. He brushed it off on his sleeve, frowning at the stain as if it were a personal affront. He faced Clas. "Now he'll hear. Take the women. And the dogs. Tell them to obey him, son."

For a long moment Gan was unable to move or speak. To commit his dogs to another was a Nightwatcher's last act.

He called the animals to him, speaking too softly for anyone else to hear, pointing at Clas. They immediately trotted to him, Raggar turning for a last look at his master before sitting beside the man. Shara stood behind the larger dog. He acted as if he'd been beaten, his eyes jerking between Clas' face and Gan's. Cho crowded against Raggar, lying down, clearly disturbed. The larger dog ignored her, totally concentrated on Gan. At Col's gesture, the others walked off into the trees. The dogs obeyed Clas.

Sylah hurried to walk beside him. "What did he whisper to them?"

Clas looked miserable. "A secret word the Dog Chief gives the Night-watcher. Every dog has a different one. When the dog hears it, it knows it's to obey whoever the Nightwatcher indicates."

"As simply as that? What if . . . ?" Sylah let the question trail off, her eyes instinctively searching the distance for pursuit as she dismissed what she considered a minor issue in favor of something important. When she felt Clas' silence, she turned back to it. His glare was like a blow.

He said, "Simple, you say? If the Nightwatcher doesn't reclaim them soon enough, some dogs die. Some go mad and have to be killed."

"Then why would Col make him send them off? I don't understand."

He looked troubled. "I'm not sure. Maybe just to be alone with his son. It's the last time."

"Oh. At least Col understands. Poor Raggar! Wish I could touch him, or reassure him somehow."

Neela came to stand beside them as Clas laughed bitterly. He included the whole group with a sweep of his arm. "I wish you could reassure all of us."

Raggar stopped trying to see through the intervening trees. The great head swiveled from Clas to the women, then back to where he'd left his master. He whined. It was a thin, worried sound that grew until it sang as a spine-chilling howl. When Sylah impulsively dropped to her knees beside him and threw her arm around his neck, he trembled violently and quieted. His eyes remained fixed on the distance.

CHAPTER 21

Col pressed against the tree at his back, forcing his torso erect. His legs stretched out flat on the ground. Gan, squatting in front of him, literally felt the will of the man, the refusal to concede that his life was draining away. He gestured for Gan to help him with his waterskin, took a drink, then said, "I was wrong." It wasn't apologetic or rueful. He went on, "Your mother foretold this. I've no time to tell you all of it. Get the whole story from Clas. Listen to me now. I want you to understand her, how strong she was, and how loving. There are things you must hear from me alone. She said you'd be responsible for my death, that we'd be disgraced together. I never thought— No matter. I reasoned no son would want to kill a father who held him at arm's length. It's the sort of thing that takes passion. Yours was taken up by fights with those who understood neither of us."

Gan tried to interrupt, and the older man silenced him with a peremptory nod. "You'll lead your people to a brighter time. Don't worry about having been lonely, or being lonely in the future. A leader must know loneliness. It's the one lesson I taught you I'd take back, if I could. And know this, too: Murmillanh said, 'If you love him, he'll live.' When I'm gone, remember that. I loved you."

Another fit of coughing seized him, harder than before. He reached out to clutch Gan's arm, as if drawing strength from it. When the coughing stopped, he remained bent over, and Gan covered his hand with his own. For several long moments neither moved or spoke, until Gan said, "Is that truly what you and my mother would wish? She said I'm to be this leader? It's what you both hoped for?"

Col nodded.

"No matter the cost?"

That brought the older man's head up. He fixed a steely gaze on Gan, who returned it unflinchingly. All the years of cross-purposes and noncommunication finally confronted the abiding love that had always bound them, and little by little comprehension and understanding mellowed the aged, wounded face and the young, fierce one.

Col said, "At any cost that's worthy."

Gan made a Two-sign and rose. "Then I have my goal."

The older man blinked. "No Three-sign, as prayer?"

"The Two-sign, to ask for protection from the One Who Is Two." He found a weak smile. "One son to another."

Col tried to return the smile, but lost it to another cough. When he recovered, his gaze swept past Gan, out to a view only he could see. Gan thought of the great white-headed eagles, the way their proud eyes claimed the land to its farthest end. Then Col spoke again. "No man has heard me say this. I ask you to forgive me."

Gan's first thought was to protest, to explain that he cared nothing for what had gone before. Then he realized Col would only know that to be true if his request was answered directly. He said, "I forgive. And I love you."

"Thank you." He was as hard and brusque as ever. Rubbing his eyes, he complained of a lack of sleep. Gan heard, but his attention was fixed on the brush at the foot of their knoll. Col looked up to see his son distracted and followed his gaze as best he could. Suddenly, like a conjurer's trick, a wolfpack ten strong appeared, loping up toward them with the distinctive swagger of their kind.

Col nodded. "There's why I had you send the dogs off with Clas," he said. "I had a feeling they'd come now."

Cautiously, as silent as rising water, the pack eased over the edge of the knoll onto the flat plateau. They stopped there, and then the dominant male stalked forward with long-legged grace. First he sniffed the air close to Gan, then clawed the ground in great furrows, sending clods flying. Then he advanced on Col, circling him slowly, inspecting, always with wary eye for Gan. When he'd completed the circuit, he sat down, facing Col. The shining black nose flared as he bent forward and sniffed at his bloody leg. He rose again to all fours and walked to stare up at Gan, who met his gaze for the briefest moment before turning his head to study the distance. The wolf, appreciative of the courtesy, relaxed some of his vigilance. Still, he backed away to rejoin the pack.

As silently as they'd come, they were gone.

Gan went to his father, sitting beside him once again. He said, "I think you always knew Clas was my only friend. He had many duties. When I was most alone, the wolves understood. They let me see into their lives, even when I couldn't be one of them. We aren't friends. We have a bond."

Col said, "I don't understand it, but I don't question it." Wryly, he added, "Your mother taught me that. Now, call the others back."

The dogs raced to him at his first call, clearly overjoyed. Clas searched Gan's face, then Col's, before kneeling down to eye level with the older man. "As long as I live, I'll be by his side, my friend. I swear."

Col's lips moved in what could have been a smile. "Even though Murmillanh's prophecy has killed me?"

"Prophecies don't throw lances, but I admit I was thinking the same thing. Murmillanh has nothing to do with my feeling for Gan. He's my brother. I stand with him because I choose to. A life's a small thing; any force strong enough can claim it any time. A man's choice is his own." He rose, standing beside Gan.

Neela interrupted with a sharp cry, pointing east. Horses spilled down a faraway hillside like dark grains of sand. The dust of their passage was a suggestive smear against an otherwise flawless landscape. Col struggled to his feet and hobbled to his horse to remove the quiver and bow. "I'll meet them here," he said, settling against a tree.

Gan said, "The three of us will make our stand. It'll be a fight the people will sing about forever. Anyhow, even if we make it to Ola, you said yourself King Altanar wants alliance with the tribe for an attack on Harbundai. He'll give us up to keep Bay's support."

Sylah stepped forward. "That's why we must go to Harbundai." Her head involuntarily jerked toward Neela, but she avoided looking at her. Gan realized Sylah was suffering more than she dared admit, yet she was driven to speak. This was confession, not argument. She continued, speaking to Col,

"With her in Harbundai, Bay won't dare attack. What other choice have you?"

Gan spoke first. "What makes you think we can get there?"

Sylah told of a patient, a Peddler, who spoke of secret trails, of little-known passes with names like Tell-No-Other, Midsummer, and Cloud Rest. Defiantly, she said, "I learned them because I meant to use the information. Only later did it become part of the plan to force the Dog People to reject war with Harbundai."

"She meant to kidnap me as hostage," Neela volunteered bitterly, and Clas' jaw dropped open.

Sylah went on. "Church has her own reasons for wanting to keep Altanar's hands off Harbundai. We'll be helped there. Gan's right about King Altanar; he'll give Neela back to the Dog People and the rest of us will die."

Gan said, "With the tribe after us, and Altanar so inhospitable, you tell me our other choice is to travel across the whole of Devil country while they hunt for us. A pretty thought."

Col growled in his chest. "Your first test, that's all. Go, while there's time."

Clas opened his own quiver. "There isn't time. Gan's right. This is as far as we go."

Col lifted his chin, pulled back his shoulders. For the moment he was as sturdy and commanding as ever, the cragged, scarred features implacable. "I am to be obeyed. You are Dog warriors. I am your War Chief. Leave me. Now. I do what I must. So shall you."

In Gan's mind loss fought with love, pain with pride. He looked into his father's eyes, willing him to understand what he could never speak.

Col smiled and nodded.

Gan led the way and never looked back.

The skirmish where Col waited was a brutally brief scar on the deep quiet of the country. A man shouted pained surprise. Dozens of angry, confused voices responded. The volume swelled to a crescendo of indistinguishable noises, and then, suddenly, sickeningly, there was a triumphant South Clan war cry.

Gan flinched as if whipped.

He pressed straight on.

Slowed by the packhorses, they were losing ground steadily to their pursuers and straining for the scant protection of a range of rough foothills when they heard the wolves. A daylight howl was very unusual, and howling so close to galloping warriors was unheard of. Even at their distance Gan could see nervousness disturb the riders, and several horses broke stride to buck and rear. Suddenly, at the rear of the group, one horse, limping badly, simply ran away with its rider, rejecting the bit and all semblance of training. Clas muttered, "A straggler. I suspect Col put an arrow in it." Gan agreed and watched as individual wolves dashed out of cover to further frighten the horse, only to duck out of sight before the warrior could aim properly. His arrows whizzed harmlessly into the brush.

Several of his companions fell back to help him.

Other wolves singled out a different horse, a tired one, and started their game again. This time an even larger number of riders rode at them in pursuit. Arrows liberally sprinkled the scrub, but no wolf yelped.

Gan noted with deep satisfaction that the pursuit was stopping. A few riders were already easing back the way they'd come.

Gan stood in his saddle, murdat in hand. Warriors pointed at him. Scattered jeers drifted up from some, but the mass had a shaken look. They made no move to resume the chase. As Gan waved the murdat in a circle over his head, many surreptitiously executed quick Three-signs. He shouted at them, his voice echoing wildly from the cliffs. "Never forget me. I will remember you."

He dropped into the saddle, and without another word, continued the march west.

After a while he called Clas to his side and asked him to tell him of his mother. He listened so stoically that several times Clas stopped, watching him, and on every occasion Gan quietly asked him to continue. He made no comment, gave no sign of any emotion. When Clas told him there was no more to be said, Gan nodded.

Clas was in a foul mood when he dropped back.

Sylah and Neela attempted to console him, and he responded angrily. "She was a wonderful woman, one of a kind. When I told him the whole story of the prophecy, he just nodded. I told him how she died, and he never even blinked. She said he'd be two men in one. Well, I've seen both. The first is confused and the second one's as empty as a rotten nut."

Neela said, "Hurt doesn't always show, Clas. The worst almost always stays hidden."

When Sylah said softly, "Clas understands," he looked at her sharply, and for the briefest instant she saw embarrassment in him, but then he shook his head and let the anger reclaim him.

Several miles along, the women rode with him when he approached Gan again. His question was aggressive. "If we're going to Harbundai," he said, "why are we pushing so far west into Devil territory? We should be headed north already."

In answer, Gan pointed at the sky. "When that storm breaks, we'll turn. The rain will hide our tracks."

"No one's after us. Your wolves scared them off."

"For now. Likat and Kolee will tell them it's proof I'm evil and have to be destroyed. She'll say some special prayers for them and they'll be back out tomorrow. Better they look for us where we're not going." His smile made Sylah's skin tighten.

Clas fell back, sullen, and Sylah went with him. For a moment she thought Neela would attempt to join them, but she seemed to think better of it, electing to ride by herself for a while. Sylah said, "I mourn Col, too, Clas. But remember, he started his son on a path he believes in. He was a warrior, and he ended as one."

"Fighting his own people. In shame. Because of him." He spat in Gan's direction. "You saw how he left? Never looked back once."

"You promised to be beside him. You must have had your own reason."

The twisted features softened. "I don't want to. But so much has happened—" He shook his head in resigned bewilderment. "I told you before. I see something in him. He's like my younger brother. But sometimes he frightens me."

She burlesqued surprise, trying to inject a bit of lightness into his mood, and he gave her a small, tight smile in return. He said, "I'm not as fearless as you think. Or as I'd like you to believe." Serious again, he went on, "The more I told him of his mother's prophecy, the longer I talked about Col's belief in him, the more he seemed to . . ." He struggled for the right word, slammed his fist against the pommel horn. "He looked like he was falling in love. It was like he'd been looking for something and found it, and it was more than he hoped, you understand? He fell in love with *all* of it, good and bad."

"You don't mean his father's death, as well? You can't say a thing like that, Clas."

"I can." He shook his head again, and she thought of the wildcow bulls, driven by forces they couldn't control; they, too, gored each other in a ritual they were powerless to question. "I know Gan hated to see Col die, but he accepted it as part of his fate. I want to believe he grieves, but I can't understand his way."

There was nothing she could say. She patted his arm and drifted to Neela's side. Sylah's heart sank as she looked at her, saw the blank, dazed look. It took no words to tell her Neela was just beginning to feel the full impact of what had happened to her. She would need care. Sylah looked to Clas. He, too, suffered, but he was the stronger. He'd have to get by with less help.

A tinge of resentment lasted only a moment. There was nothing she could do for either of them yet, anyhow. Gan had promised they wouldn't stop to rest until the dawn of the next day.

She glanced back over her shoulder for perhaps the thousandth time. There were no warriors to be seen, and the wolves had gone quiet long ago.

She looked ahead at Gan's back, so youthfully straight, so graceful in the saddle. How unlike we are, she thought, and a sudden perception came to her with a shock. She actually jerked at the force of it, and Neela stirred from her lethargy. The girl reached to steady Sylah, who thanked her shortly, eager to examine the new concept.

He takes what the world gives and uses it, she thought. Show him ten doors, and he'll pick one without hesitation, and kick it open if it resists. Clas was right; he's in love. He wants to marry fate and sleep with glory. Those smiling whores.

And how do I differ? I must always fight to be in control. The Door's no husband to me, doesn't warm my heart. The need to find it pours through me like a mountain stream, clear and cold.

We're different. We're the same.

Can either of us learn not to be alone?

Her gaze moved to Neela.

She's the weapon I use to control them. A weapon for my own destruction?

Why do I feel that we'll all know glory? And despise it?

CHAPTER 22

Conway got to his feet, ignoring the distant voices from the depths of the cave. He wished he'd brought a coat to stand guard; once the sun got behind the crest of the mountain, the temperature dropped fast. Still, it was better to be where the air was fresh.

It occurred to him he'd never smelled air quite so pure. It had a tang of earth and vegetation that throbbed with vitality.

He wondered if it was a reaction to the atmosphere in the cave. He was sure it had changed, yet he was equally sure he hadn't noticed a difference until after Harris' funeral. Remembering depressed him. It was hard enough to lose one of their number, especially in such a terrible manner, but the argument over final disposition of the body was ugly. Falconer had insisted on using the disposal chute, resisting any effort to inter the man. He cited security, the likelihood of animals digging it up, and Harris' right to be with the others who'd died there. Harsh disagreement almost came to fighting, and although he'd stayed out of it, Conway had the uncomfortable feeling Falconer would have accepted force as merely another way to win his argument. Regardless of those suspicions, there were undeniable wounds that would be a long time healing.

Something moved uphill from his position. He advanced. Stopped. Unarmed, he was no match for wild animals. Or whatever sort of human life might exist in a world reverted to primeval. He took another step forward, craning to look up the slope. A jay screeched at him, a sapphire-blue bird with a black crest. It repeated its cry, opening its mouth so far he could see into the dark throat.

His hand shook as he retreated to his watching position.

There was probably no point in guarding the doorway, he thought, particularly since Falconer's optimistic report of plenty of weapons had proven fatally flawed when it was discovered the ammunition was still buried. In spite of that, he felt the watch was a good idea. It was best to take no chances. A warning of impending danger might do little good, but it eliminated surprise.

He smiled to himself. It'd almost be worth an attack to know someone existed.

Once they'd assured themselves they were in the same cave they'd been sent to for cryogenic suspension, there was no escaping the fact that they'd outlived the world. Further observation of the valley showed heavy forestation where the small community had been, and absolutely no sign of habitation.

The Pastor had prayed for smoke, for the shine of something metallic.

Bernhardt examined the trees and plant life. When she was done, she verified Falconer's off-the-cuff estimate. The trees were at least five centuries old. More than that, however, the forest was different. She found plants of species and size that surprised her, and concluded that there were climatological changes in the area, as well. For some reason, the eastern slope of the Cascade range was getting more moisture. She offered no surmise.

No one really cared. If there was no one to farm, what difference did it make if there was more or less rain than before?

The woman named Tate made the most impressive discovery, great gouges clawed out of a tree. Fresh, just starting to ooze yellow, sticky sap, they had Leclerc scratching his head comically. He claimed wild animals marked territory that way, and took some good-natured ribbing. Everyone knew the few animals allowed to roam free were continuously monitored as mutual protection for them and the people licensed to hike. Bernhardt alone sided with him. She pointed out that centuries must have effected change in the animal population of the forests. Her credentials as an agronomist lent credence to her theory until she sent everyone into gales of laughter by suggesting it would take something as large as a tiger to reach so high.

Still, the episode had its effect. Everyone retreated to the mouth of the cave. That was when Falconer suggested they get serious about unearthing their ammunition and conduct a complete search for anything usable in their warehouse. The response had been immediate; work was under way.

Conway was sure Falconer already had a plan, and equally sure it had to do with exploration. It would be the man's first response. Conway admitted he felt the same. He couldn't accept that they were all that was left. His mind could acknowledge the thought, but not the possibility. When he tried to pin it down, to consider how they should conduct themselves if they were the surviving remnants of humanity, coherent thought slid away from him like wet soap.

The two women who'd paired up so quickly as friends, Anspach and Carter, stepped outside, squinting in the light, even though it was already fading. The evening clouds were tinted bright salmon, and the low ground at the base of the hill had a soft, delicate wash of warm color over the hard green of coniferous forest. Carter held a shielding hand above her eyes. Conway suppressed a smile. She wouldn't take kindly to being considered amusing, but her dark color added to the notion she was practicing to be an Indian. Her eyes adjusted to the light, and she looked away from the view to Conway, then back. She offered no conversation and her stiff back implied she wanted none.

Anspach smiled apology for her, and the two of them walked a few paces toward the trees. The soft duff of the forest floor absorbed their footsteps.

Brush crashed and snapped up the hill above them. Something roared, a thing of gut-twisting ferocity, followed by a bleat of utter helplessness. The women made shrill, frightened noises, too startled to scream. They ran, wild-eyed, for the cave entrance, nearly bowling over Conway, who had to dodge them to get into position to look for the source of the disturbance. In the distance, where a rock outcrop allowed brush to dominate instead of the massive firs, Conway saw greenery thrashing and shaking, but nothing else. Too fascinated to obey the clamor in his mind that urged retreat, he braced himself against one of the massive trees and waited.

Suddenly there was stillness, more frightening than the noise. It carried a finality that sent the hair straight up on the back of his neck. For long seconds the forest was silent, drawing the lowering dusk about itself, anxious for lengthening shadows to hide what had happened. Then there was a rustle, the sound of something massive shifting its weight. A low growl rolled down the hill, a warning and a triumph.

The thing that killed told all that heard to stand away.

Conway vaguely heard the yelping shouts from inside the cave. He bent forward, peering, and came to the terrifying realization that he was looking directly into a snarling, striped face without having been aware of it.

There were no tigers in America.

It leaned toward him, growling again.

He took his hand from the tree, slid a foot tentatively toward the safety of the cave. The tiger drew itself together to spring.

Conway fled, screaming. The others, arriving at the door, were knocked out of the way like straws in a wind. Falconer, gun in hand, covered the babbling, confused group that streamed along behind Conway. They all stopped at the broken vault door, where Falconer took up a firing position beside Conway and shouted for everyone to be quiet.

Conway, still shaking, sat with his back against the metal. He described what he saw, then, "It was the shock. I don't think I'd have run from a bear or a cougar that way."

Falconer glanced at him, and Conway bridled. "It was a tiger. I don't care what you think."

The Colonel rose, gestured with the weapon. "We'll wait for it to leave. At least we've got the ammunition out. Right now, let's get you calmed down, and then I've got some things everyone has to see." He called to Leclerc and the Pastor, telling them to gather up anything that would burn and start a fire at the mouth of the cave.

The rest moved back to the small living area adjacent to the control room. Conway gratefully accepted some medicinal brandy from Yoshimura, and when Tate joked that she got no whiskey when she discovered the cat's claw marks, the laughter was relaxed and genuine. Conway offered her a sip from the small bottle, which she refused with a comedic snub.

While they reviewed the excitement, Conway noticed Falconer stepping into the warehouse. He came out carrying a briefcase and the VDP. He plugged it in before asking for everyone's attention.

"This briefcase is full of vidisks. I found it just when Conway decided to go into his 'mighty hunter' act. I expect the people who decided to leave us here provided some record of what was going on when they sealed the door. I wouldn't want my friends to wake up a few centuries down the road and not know the reason why they'd been shut away. I think—I hope—the disks in here will tell us."

Karoli said, "There doesn't seem to be much to tell, Colonel. They killed off the race. You want to look at pictures of it?"

Falconer set up the small screen so everyone could see it and opened the briefcase. "I'll start with the last date. Might as well get the worst news first."

The screen jiggled. The familiar preliminary muddle of dots and flashes had a quieting effect on the group, Conway noted; his own hands were steady already. He looked at his watch. Fifteen minutes ago he'd stared into the eyes of a kill-excited tiger and run in stark panic. Now he was relaxing, preparing for tiny electronic pictures of a world dead half a millennium, not because he was conditioned to running away from tigers, but because he was conditioned to running to tiny electronic pictures.

The screen showed him a city too burned to do more than smolder. A cold, clinical voice told him it was New Orleans. The picture faded. The earth appeared, a view he recognized as an infrared picture from a satellite. It was splattered with irregular sores. He didn't need the voice to tell him they were fires. Blight trailed from each of them, smoke that blanked out the sun. Where the industrial might of civilization had reared so proudly, there was flame. Around the flame was winter. The voice discussed temperatures, crop failures, unpredictable rains, snows, and droughts.

Movement distracted him, and Conway looked up to see the Pastor and Nancy Yoshimura leading a crying Madge Mazzoli away.

Tate said, "Come on, Colonel, there has to be something else we can watch."

He nodded, flicking off the power. On the second disk the same narrator described the breakdown of society. Conway marveled at the man, pictured him sitting in a studio while the entire world collapsed outside his window. Conway watched images of looters, vigilantes, refugees, and confused, hapless troops arrayed against all of them. The image shifted to churches, packed to overflowing, and meetings being held in fields.

Conway duly noted the ragged jackets and coats on open-air worshipers. The speaker identified the locale as San Francisco and the month as July. He also saw how dank the ground looked. Bernhardt caught his eye. "I think that's how a meadow would look if it got lots of rain and very little sunshine," she said. "Most of the plants are surviving. Nothing's really healthy." She shuddered, and when she looked back to the screen, her features were controlled, as flat and blank as stones.

The voice told of schismatic sects and cults mushrooming everywhere. The camera panned a zoo, then a wild animal farm. Gates and doors hung ajar, glass cage fronts lay in shards. The work of Williamsites, the voice reported, a charismatic cult that contended God was punishing man for abusing the world, and man could only petition for forgiveness by returning to a natural state and freeing all imprisoned creatures.

Leclerc clapped a hand to his forehead. Bernhardt stopped the picture and they all waited expectantly. He said, "I know him! I specialized in protein structure. Williams was a fine scientist, but he became an administrator with the central genetic bank in Maryland. Years ago he got himself declared a church or something, and then he hustled enough funds and believers to set up genetic banks in about every climatological zone that exists. I always thought he was a whacko, you know—preaching Armageddon, and all that. Wow. Anyhow, there were rumors that some of his labs were re-creating extinct species, cloning, doing genetic engineering, and so forth." He nodded at Conway. "I bet you did see a tiger, probably the descendant of one of his lab projects. I'll bet there's a lot of surprises like that out there."

Everyone shifted uncomfortably, glancing toward the door, giving knowing nods to each other.

The machine had finally given them something they could identify with, something that touched their present. Conway had trouble holding back laughter. He knew he must, because he could taste the acid of hysteria in it, a delayed reaction to his experience outside and the unintentional comedy of the video presentation inside. Of all the things that identified them as survivors of the world that had murdered itself, the only thing to touch them in this new place was a misplaced, aberrant wild animal doing the only thing nature meant it to do. And it had threatened to attack him because he had less right to be on the mountain than it did.

Bernhardt started the disk again, and the voice added that Williamsism had acquired new adherents all over the world, since one of their saints was an electronics technician and pirated time on one of the few satellites still working.

That was the last hint of humor in an unrelieved litany of increasing savagery. For an hour the disk detailed the efforts of mankind to destroy itself. In the middle of a detailed discussion of genetically altered diseases beginning to sweep away entire populations in days, shouts erupted in the background. The image wobbled to darkness, and the previously imperturbable voice cracked on the single word, *Gas!*

When the picture came back, a new voice, scratchy and untrained, reported that the United States was withdrawing its forces from all foreign soil as part of a multinational agreement with the Soviets, the Chinese, and the Brazilians to do the same.

Falconer switched off the machine. His face was pale as he walked from the room.

Conway sat, staring at the screen, not caring that the others were leaving.

He didn't know how long he'd been there before he noticed Leclerc standing beside him, watching him. He looked up, waiting. The small man said, "A penny for your thoughts. The way you're concentrating, they ought to be worth at least that."

Nodding at the blank VDP, Conway said, "I was just thinking how much I hate having to look at more of these disks."

Leclerc agreed grimly. Several minutes passed before Conway reached to turn the VDP on again.

For hours they watched news reports, political speeches, morale films. Mealtime came and went. Other members of the group joined them, moved on, returned.

Tate crawled out of her sleeping bag and strolled over. "Anything worth-while? I gave up a couple of hours ago. You guys have too much stamina for me."

"Gluttons for punishment," Conway said, standing. "I can't believe they didn't leave us books, maps, tables of information, or something useful. This," he spun the disk into the briefcase, "is repetitious crap."

She nodded. "That's all I saw. One thing, though; you remember, one of the items from the last days was about air-dropped handheld radio direction finders? They said they were for people stranded in rural areas, so they could find their way to central locations, right? Don't you think if things were that bad, people would've already banded together?"

"I guess so, yeah."

"You know they would. I figure the direction finders were a last-ditch shot, that they'd lost touch with everyone, that the whole works just came apart. I think the people who set up this program died before they could get back to us. Or they knew the nuke hit our hidey-hole and just scrubbed us off the roster." She laughed, an edged sound. Conway couldn't resist a nervous glance her way, and her expression softened. She patted his arm. "Don't worry, I'm not losing it. I was seeing the irony of the sequence. Someone nuked us because we were a healthy, organized cadre, invaluable for recon-struction. Instead of frying us, they assured we'd live, but they messed up the timetable. Then a natural disaster gets everyone except our dozen. And finally, here we are, full of knowledge, outliving all the gas, the germs, probably even the radioactivity. So what? There's nothing to reconstruct."

Pastor Jones had joined them. He said, "Then we'll construct. Surely you're not conceding, you of all people?"

She smiled. "Put money on it, Pastor. I'm a Marine. I can be beat, but I won't be stopped. I'm scared, but I'll handle it."

Jones said, "We all will. We must. A new earth awaits us."

After he'd gone, Conway and Tate listened politely while Leclerc ex-plained that Jones had been entered in the program because of his skill as a social psychologist. He was, Leclerc explained, a specialist in negotiations. When he paused, Conway interrupted. "That's interesting, Louis, but you know that's not what any of us is thinking about. Isn't anyone going to say it?"

Leclerc grinned. "I know what I'm thinking. I don't know about you."

Conway swung his arm, a gesture that took in the VDP, the broken crèches, and the tiny group of survivors. "This is what we did to the old earth. If I was part of the new one, I'd get rid of us any way I could."

The others nodded and laughed with him.

CHAPTER 23

The murmuring conversation of the others brought Conway out of deep sleep slowly, hoisted him toward consciousness with time for soft dreams of other wakings. He remembered the mornings of Antigua, as complex and gentle as lace, tingling with the smell of salt and the touch of heat already spiraling up from the sand. And the bed and breakfast place in Nova Scotia, where the sound of the cows leaving the barn woke one.

Or two.

The good wakings always involved Leona.

He came fully awake, staring at the rough rock overhead, scarred where pieces had shaken free in the earthquake.

Leona was dead these five years plus five hundred. Or whatever time it was.

He hadn't thought about her since waking up here.

Leona's accident was part of the start of things, now that he considered it in perspective. At the time, she was just another number chalked up to some particularly vicious and efficient terrorists. No one considered how the steady increase in the number of murders and bombings and destructions imperceptibly gnawed away the restraints of other men. When the tempers broke, and those who had suffered the losses struck back, the world accepted massive retaliation and holocaust and genocide as localized phenomena.

And for many years that was the way of it.

Leona, and the hundreds like her, were easily relegated to old, minor news when the slaughter escalated to what the politicians and press learned to refer to as "recent significant figures." The aggrieved remembered. Brooded. And their numbers grew.

A world conditioned itself to commit the unimaginable. Everyone saw the fuse sputtering. Everyone refused to believe the bomb would go off.

Leona's accident. He still used those words.

Leona's murder.

As if it made any difference now.

"Conway?" It was Falconer. He was immaculate, creased, shined, ready for inspection.

Conway found an answering smile. "Ah, room service. Good fellow. I'll have orange juice—freshly squeezed, of course—dark toast, scrambled eggs. Fluffy, mind you; the chef knows I won't tolerate runny eggs. And coffee now, please."

Falconer extended a steaming cup. "See? Our every moment is dedicated to your comfort and pleasure. Did I wake you?"

Conway shook his head and reached for the coffee. Strange, he thought, how they used the single word, wake, for becoming conscious in the morning and for their thawed return from the dead.

"You ready to think yet?" Falconer asked.

"I wouldn't want to do calculus. What's on your mind?"

"Survival." The thin mouth continued to smile. The eyes were serious. They rolled meaningfully at the ceiling.

Conway nodded. "You may be right. It could come down on us."

"I've tried to analyze the situation from every point of view, including the defensive quality of this place. There's enough room between where the vault door dropped and the actual entrance for a living space. Of course, we'd have to wall off everything." He gestured without looking back at the wrecked pods. "I think the plain truth is we've got to get out of here, and fast. I'm pretty tough, but even I'm not up for living with that."

"We should be trying to find other people, too."

Quick surprise touched Falconer's face. "What makes you think there are any?"

"Pessimism."

Falconer laughed hard. "Too mean to die, right? Could be. Tell you what, though. If they're out there, they're going to be some tough dudes. And probably hostile."

Pastor Jones was passing by and overheard. He gestured with his plastic coffee cup, until he managed to swallow a mouthful of hard cracker. "I'm sorry, Colonel, but I have to remonstrate. If we look for other men in fear, we must surely create the very hostility you mention."

"I don't mean to antagonize anyone, but I do certainly intend to be wary." The other members of the group drew close, listening, and Falconer's frown darkened. "You saw where we are. It's untamed."

Sue Anspach disagreed. "The survivors would band together, share skills, teach the young civilized behavior. It wouldn't be a world of continuing war."

Her friend Carter agreed. "Anyone who survived what we saw would be finished with war and fighting forever. We'll probably find a small, contemplative agricultural society."

"I hope so. It'll be the first time I've ever fit right in," Bernhardt said, laughing. She looked embarrassed when the others ignored her slight humor. Karoli took her hand, and she smiled shy thanks.

Falconer said, "I hope you're right, too. But let me tell you something about the world of those survivors. Way back in the early 1940s, the Brits detonated some test bombs on an island off their coast. They wanted to see if they could use that technique to disperse anthrax bacilli, see if it'd survive to infect anything. Anthrax kills men as well as sheep, remember. It worked, all right. Over forty years later the soil was still crawling with a thriving culture. The whole island was a deathtrap."

Conway watched their faces as the implications struck them. In his own mind, he pictured a tattered, hungry band of survivors learning to glean a living from a reluctant earth, only to stumble across an area contaminated by demons lurking in the seemingly innocent soil.

Falconer went on. "I suspect I was given a bleaker picture of what to expect than the rest of you. Remember, my job was to be civil control. My men and I were prepared to come out of the crèches and face a worst-case scenario." A sardonic smile briefly cracked his composure, but then he was back to his brisk, contained self. "Anyhow, there's more to it than people dying. To people whose society has crashed down on their heads, the cities would be a magnet, at first. Supplies, possibility of companionship, shelter—"

Leclerc interrupted. "Radioactivity, toxic chemical concentrations, unstable construction, predatory gangs—"

"And an ongoing breeding ground for more disease," Conway added. "Anyplace that was a potential source of civic reconstruction would more and more become associated with death— Worse, with death by disease and radioactivity, two things the survivors wouldn't have any way of detecting. To them it'd be a cosmic judgment."

"Nevertheless, we have to assume they may not be hostile." The depressed expressions around him obviously made Falconer feel the picture was too dark. He seemed to be trying to soften the blow. "I said they'd be tough. I meant we'd have to be very careful in our dealings with them. I expect they'll be primitive."

Tate said, "Stands to reason, Colonel. If you're right, if they were thrown back to simple survival, they'll be in the middle of some very interesting social patterns. *Some* of what went before will have to be part of their present behavior. I mean, if a carpenter survived for any length of time, he'd be sure to teach some kids something about carpentry. And so on."

Joining in, thinking aloud, Conway added, "It'd be like trying to construct a body from just a couple of bones. Different groups would strike out in different directions, each one influenced by whatever prejudices and skills the strongest survivor could bring to bear." He smiled at Carter. "We may even find your thoughtful farmers."

She smiled thinly. "Your analogy about bones is particularly unfortunate. Did you know that one of our leading museums had the wrong skull on a dinosaur skeleton for decades before anyone caught the error?" She turned the smile on Falconer. "Think of this—a skeleton representing hardworking civilians and a bone-solid skull representing military control."

Falconer appeared genuinely amused. "I'll put in a good word for you, Janet." To Conway he said, "There's a lot of salvageable stuff in the warehouse. Tate and Leclerc are helping me inventory. Will you? After you eat?"

Conway agreed. As the three left, he saw the covert revulsion aimed at him by some of the other faces. Everyone still suffered for Harris' madness in one way or another. Some already resisted entering the warehouse with every excuse they could think up.

There was another interesting facet to the way the group reacted, exemplified by the way they separated to go about their business of the morning. Relationships among them were solidifying. Nancy Yoshimura and Madge Mazzoli found what they needed in each other. Mazzoli needed care, Yoshimura needed someone to care for.

Kate Bernhardt and Ivan Karoli were like kids, thrown into an adventure so big they tended to trivialize it. Conway decided there was a solid core to them, however. He knew he'd depend on them, if real trouble came.

Sue Anspach and Janet Carter were intellectual twins, even when they disagreed. They bridled at any suggestion that they might make emotional decisions, yet their every word was filtered through personalized ethics, an awareness of the assumed feelings of others. They'd resist any authority as instinctively as they'd pull back from fire, but their intelligence was beyond question. And necessary.

Falconer, Leclerc, and Tate seemed to be shaping up as a team, one that worked together while recognizing Falconer as the most equal of equals. Their group decisions would be hard to resist.

That left Pastor Jones and Matt Conway as the odd men out. Objectively, Conway decided, it gave him more influence than he wanted, largely because Jones resisted any side in an issue. He could be depended on to point out the moral high ground, which was necessary, but it was quite possible the outside world wouldn't care about ethics. Conway remembered the tiger. It killed and ate. If there were men out there with similar directness, there would be little room for Jones' negotiating skills. The real test of the man would arise if the group needed his strength in a survival situation against other humans. There was already an observable tendency by some to pay less attention to his comments than to those of others. That was a mistake. He was diffident, but he was the most sensitive of all of them. It could prove more valuable than either learning or intellect.

That was conjecture. There were realities, as well. Discussion within the group had already tended to pit the military-oriented three against the more scholastic dogma of Carter and Anspach.

If he agreed with the women on an issue, his vote would cancel the trio's unity. If he sided with Falconer—he smiled to himself, realizing he'd just joined Tate and Leclerc in recognizing Falconer's leadership—his vote was almost too much for the women to surmount, assuming the rest of the group split its vote.

Mixing powder and water in his cup, he prepared his artificial orange juice. Not bad, he told himself, and was shocked to think there probably weren't any oranges within a thousand miles, and certainly no vitamin-enriched, mineral-added, nutritionally balanced crystalline substitutes.

For the second time that morning he found himself studying his companions. This time he closed out thoughts of political maneuvers. He wondered if they had any reasonable hope of survival. The men's physical condition could be described as functional, at best. Thinking back to his stint of guard duty, he remembered being afraid he'd see another man—until he saw the tiger. It disturbed him to realize he'd have wanted to run away in the exact same manner if a man had appeared who looked hostile.

He knew he wasn't a coward. He also knew he wasn't equipped, either by nature or training, to exist in a world where his right to live was a function of his ability to protect himself.

And if the unthinkable had come to pass? If they were the last humans, could the men fulfill the ancient function of protector of the hearth? He remembered reading about some mutineers—the *Bounty*, that was the ship—who ended up killing each other off. Would this group fall into the trap of jealousy and murder?

Depressed, he argued with himself that fighting the elements alone would be enough to keep them too busy to brawl among themselves. In that respect, the women were, if anything, slightly better equipped to withstand climatic hardship, for the simple reason that biology made it so.

There were sure to be other dangers. The vidisk spoke of created diseases that nature never dreamed of. That meant no natural immunity. And what of the possibility of mutant creatures?

In short, for all their advanced knowledge and skills, they were no better suited for the environment outside than the earliest survivors of the war.

Tate interrupted his contemplation. "Finished eating, Matt?"

He didn't want to admit he'd spent the time staring into space, or the reasons his appetite had disappeared. He rose quickly, and she filled him in on their discoveries to that point, adding that weapons instruction was being scheduled. He offered to help, based on his Army Reserve training.

It amused him to see the effect of the information on her. She was probably unaware of it, he thought. Some of her condescension simply evaporated, and a flicker of something that could have been respect passed across her features. They talked more, pleased to discover a mutual interest in history, especially the American Revolution. Such esoterica in their present environment triggered hilarity. They enjoyed the most intimate, relaxed laughter Conway could remember in the group. There was a moment of asperity in her tone when her rank was mentioned, and he was silently amused to learn it was a sensitive issue. The promotion of Major came with the job she was expected to perform postcrèche; actually, her age was proper for a junior Captain. She was quite specific about it, without mentioning any particular numbers. Then they shifted back to the problems at hand. He was embarrassed to see how much more confident she was of her ability to deal with whatever they found. She expected a hostile place.

He'd never thought of himself as a potential soldier, certainly not as an infantryman. But it had come to that. Worse, he'd be expected to sneak around through the forest pretending to be some sort of Ranger. It was ludicrous. For the present, however, it cost nothing to be polite and listen.

She told him there was a large supply of vacuum-packed vitamin and mineral supplement pills, as well as basic equipment for the troops Falconer had expected to employ as a palace guard at the underground headquarters in the Appalachians. Fortunately, she went on, Bernhardt said they were early in the spring season. Heavy winter clothing wasn't included in the stores, and Bernhardt indicated the plants showed signs of heavy snowfall in winter. A hint of a frown touched her brow as she summarized; the plan that sent them into the cryogenic state never anticipated that they might be abandoned entirely. No one had been willing—or able—to accept the utter destruction of the civilization they were meant to help put back on its feet. There was no survival equipment, as such. What they had gave them a running start into whatever world existed outside. The rest of the race was exclusively up to them.

There was grumbling when Falconer announced his determination to investigate the area around them, and something like panic when he made them face up to the fact that they couldn't depend on the cave forever.

It was like watching children consider birth, Conway thought. The womb lacked many things, but it was a place of perfect psychological and physical safety. After all, their bodies were unharmed, despite the earthquake. That had become proof, an article of faith. The cave was *home.* To listen to the almost obsessively blunt soldier describe it as dangerous forced consideration of abandoning the known for the unknown.

It occurred to Conway that Falconer himself probably feared the outside. His appreciation for the man's integrity moved up a few notches.

When Falconer asked for volunteers for the first exploratory trip, there was a chatter of alarm.

To Conway's surprise, Pastor Jones was first to raise his hand. He attached conditions immediately. "I carry no arms. In addition, I insist that you promise I shall be allowed to approach any humans we meet, that you won't initiate hostilities."

Falconer rubbed the back of his neck, eyes fixed on the Pastor, who matched the cool appraisal with his own serenity. Falconer said, "I can't do that, Pastor," and someone made a derisive sound. Falconer's eyes never moved. He went on easily. "If something happens and I don't save you, someone's sure to say I didn't act soon enough. Or acted too soon." He paused, shifted his gaze to Janet Carter's wiry intensity, then away.

Conway had to admire the cleverness of the move. The glance was too quick, too casual, to be seized on, yet it was distinct enough to leave no doubt in anyone's mind that Carter was the target of Falconer's demur. When he continued, he was looking at Jones again. He said, "The only way I take you is if we have a watchdog. If we meet other humans, you'll be allowed to make the first contact. I won't do anything to interfere, even to save your life, until the watchdog directs it. Fair enough?"

"Completely."

"Never!" Carter jerked with outrage. "You're trying to shift the responsibility for his life onto someone else. You can't do that."

"Then I'll decide when to shoot and who to shoot."

For a long moment they faced each other, emotion practically crackling between them. At last she said, "I don't trust you. I'll speak for the Pastor." She turned to him. "I'll try to be as brave as you. I can't let someone kill you, though."

He smiled. "I certainly hope not. Don't worry. It's going to be fine."

Conway volunteered. Soldiering had seemed ridiculous during his conversation with Tate. That was then. This was now, a time to act. It wasn't funny, either.

When Tate stepped forward, Falconer refused her, detailing her to guard
the cave entrance in their absence. Karoli joined them in her stead. Falconer
and Leclerc were already equipped with weapons, and it was a matter of
seconds to hand Conway and Karoli theirs. Everyone but Falconer carried
a pistol and four spherical grenades as well as a blunt, ugly thing that looked
like a rifle welded to the top of a shotgun. Outside, Falconer held the weapon
up to display it.

"Just so we're all together, I'm going to review your primary weapon for
you, show you how to load and fire. We'll be starting intensive classes when
we get back. Officially, this is the 'Weapon, Infantry Personnel, All-Purpose.'
The Army tried to get the troops to pronounce the obvious acronym as
'whip.' They preferred 'wipe,' and that's what it is. Was. Is. The entire
weapon's called a wipe, but when we speak of 'wiping,' we're speaking of
firing the smaller barrel. It uses a twenty-five caliber plastic round. The
plastic strips off within five feet, exposing a steel flechette. That's what does
the damage." He cut open a bullet with his pocketknife. "You'll notice the
round is self-contained; no brass cartridge. Now, see, the flechette's this
thing that looks like a little arrow. The effective aiming range is a hundred
yards. If you shoot at anything farther than that and hit it, put it down to
luck. However, whatever you hit, out to 250 yards, it'll stay hit, believe me.
See, the flechette tumbles when it changes its environment. That is, going
from air through cloth, or hide, or skin, it goes unstable. I'm not going to
get into weights and muzzle velocities and so forth, because we don't need
it. Just understand this—if Conway had shot that tiger in the foot with one
of these, it probably would have shattered the animal's whole foreleg."

He thumbed a catch on the weapon and it swiveled open, revealing the
breech of the shotgunlike lower tube. Falconer had Leclerc pass around
ammunition that looked like oversized bullets. "The thirty-millimeter tube
is called the 'boop.' Has to do with the sound. We're carrying A.P., or
antipersonnel, rounds—the ones with the green stripe—as well as W.P., the
red-striped incendiaries. Max range is three hundred yards. The incendiary
is loaded with white phosphorus, and when it goes off it sprays the stuff out
to fifteen yards. It burns as long as it gets oxygen, which means it'll burn
clear through a man if it lands on him. The A.P. round is essentially like the
hand grenades you were given. Again, it's lethal within fifteen yards."

Karoli said, "What happens if you shoot somebody with a boop round?
I mean, they're closer than fifteen yards, and I let go—what then?"

Falconer smiled. "If you hit him, you blow a thirty-millimeter hole
through him. The round won't arm—theoretically—within fifteen yards of
the muzzle. My advice is, don't test it if you have any chance to use the wipe.
If things are so hot you don't have a choice . . ." His shrug was eloquent.

Conway asked, "What about animals? Will the flechette kill a tiger? Will the antipersonnel round stop one?"

"Don't know. Hit an elephant direct with an A.P. boop, and I guarantee a tranquilized elephant, if not a dead one. Don't stop with one round, though. Shoot till it's down, unmoving, dead. We've got one rule—nothing's as important as our lives. Nothing. We're no good to our friends if we're dead. So we live. At any cost, we live."

There was a clash in his voice that threw Conway's mind back to memories of missile trails and the syrupy stink of decomposition swimming up from cities too radioactive to admit burial crews. He remembered wishing irritably, impatiently, for the smoldering ashes to burst into flame again, that they might purify the clotted air.

He watched as Pastor Jones and Carter clasped hands momentarily. When the Pastor bowed his head and closed his eyes, she withdrew from the contact. It was a gentle move, and although there was a hint of condescension in her smile, her eyes were thoughtful and the freed hands moved once, as if they'd touch him again.

Falconer was saying, "We'll travel single file. I'll go first, because I'm the only one trained in this sort of thing. Pastor, as our designated greeter, you and Carter stay closest to me, about ten feet back. Then you, Leclerc, the same distance behind them. You other two follow him, with Conway bringing up the rear. Check our back trail constantly."

He got to his feet. "We're going down to the valley. If we're going to find anyone, that's where they'll live. Follow me." He led off at a brisk pace.

CHAPTER 24

Conway's vantage point at the tail of the column allowed him to watch the others. There was little brush to obstruct his view, due to the immense trees of the forest. He estimated the lower branches at twenty to thirty feet above the ground. The conical tops were almost totally hidden by overlapping growth. Their shade turned the bright day to something like dusk. It was a peculiar, haunting light of no shadows that shrouded the distance, yet made whatever was close appear magnified. The plated, channeled bark of the huge firs made him think of eons-dead dinosaurs.

He wondered if the trees didn't have similar thoughts about the humans skulking past.

The slope was gentle for the most part, with only an occasional steep bench that forced them to pitch downward from tree trunk to tree trunk. Heavy breathing and scuffling at those times was almost the only thing to break the silence. Once, a bird called harshly, and the entire group crouched before collectively regaining enough composure to continue. No one had spoken since they set out. In fact, whenever one of the faces in front of him appeared in profile as that person scanned to left or right of the route, Conway saw how tightly the jaws were set, how intent the eyes. Conversation was the last thing on those minds.

Ahead of Conway, Karoli was sweating. A small stain darkened the camouflaged material, spreading inexorably as they continued. The dim forest was cool, but the work was hard. Their lack of condition was showing already.

The distance proved deceptive. From the cave it looked like a good walk to the valley floor. Now that they were actually on the way, their goal seemed little closer than when they started. The forest provided only occasional breaks for long-distance viewing. One of the things that cheered Conway was the sight of vast meadows below. He looked forward eagerly to being out of the trees. They made for a runaway sense of claustrophobia.

Another steep drop appeared. They stopped while Falconer negotiated it, then followed singly. Waiting, Conway felt a chill. They were walking a broad ridge, and their progress brought them into the path of a breeze that coursed the valley. It knifed through to his damp underclothes. A second shiver racked his body.

In a while there was a discernible thinning of the trees. There were occasional clumps of brush to avoid, but there was also more light. The sun felt good.

About ten minutes later Pastor Jones jerked to a stop, mouth agape, looking and pointing off to the left. Thirty yards away, another tiger lay on a small rise, indolently stretched out parallel to their line. Carter, watching the ground as she walked, ran into Jones. The animal had been content to merely watch them. The stumbling, staggering movement pricked up its ears. For several hammering heartbeats they formed a tableau, animal and people, and then the cat appeared to levitate to a standing position. Once on its feet, its hindquarters moved away from them in an almost comical dance step, the huge paws daintily crossing over each other. Muscles like hawsers rippled under the thick, striped coat. The action brought it perpendicular to their column, a position that lent itself to a charge.

Jones straightened, inch by inch, and with equal care the tiger sidled backward into a thicket. It melted before their eyes.

"Did you see that?" Leclerc said, his voice squeaking with excitement. "Bigger than any Siberian I ever saw in any zoo!"

They continued to stare at the last trembling leaves marking the cat's disappearance. When Conway turned away, he was looking at Leclerc, and was intrigued to see the man was flushed with an eagerness he'd not seen in him before. It made Conway think again that there was something about Leclerc that hinted this entire experience was less of a shock to him than anyone else. In unguarded moments he gave off an aura of release, as if everything happening was to be absorbed to the fullest. Conway wondered if the mountain men of the 1800s might not have been similar.

Falconer interrupted his speculations, saying, "He might not have looked so big if there were bars or a moat between you. He had some size, though, didn't he?"

"Huge." It was Carter, and she was pale, fists bunched at her sides.

Falconer got them moving again. At first they bunched up, much closer to each other, but quite rapidly they spread apart. Though no more than a few feet, the distance represented confidence. The tiger hadn't overtly threatened them, yet it was a creature of potential peril. They faced it without breaking. The incident changed them from a line to a patrol. They felt better about themselves. And each other.

By the time they reached the final slope to the valley floor, they were positively chatty, whispering observations up and down the line, pointing at new discoveries. The gaps between the trees grew spacious, and then they were on level ground, forcing their way through waist-high dead grass, detouring around thick clumps of alder and willow. They flushed browsing deer, a buck and three does, that bounded away in fluid leaps. For quite some while afterward they gestured and regaled each other with hushed descriptions. The same thing happened, on a lesser scale, when they saw their first rabbit. An hour later, when Falconer announced a lunch break, they were so used to seeing both creatures, the only reference to them was Karoli's complaint that both species had left so many droppings it was hard to find a clean place to sit.

Falconer formed the group in an outward-facing circle, reminding them they still had good reason to be on the alert.

As they drank their orange mix and crunched freeze-dried rations from plastic packets, they became aware of a noise in the distance. It was faint, similar to a wind through leaves, but different. No one quite believed it was real. They checked each other with nervous glances, unwilling to be the first to confess a crack in the newly acquired poise.

Conway tried to analyze it. For some reason he thought of it as abnormal. High-pitched, unsteady, it seemed to grow louder, then weaken, only to come back stronger than ever. Although there was only a slight breeze and the sky was perfectly clear, there was a suggestion of high energy, or speed, in the sound. Even more perplexing, he felt he should know exactly what it was.

At last Carter broke their silence. "That noise—it's disturbing. Doesn't anyone know what it is?"

Falconer got to his feet, checking his weapon. Jones and Carter inched backward on their buttocks to the center of the circle. Conway and Leclerc moved to close around them, fingering triggers, still facing outward.

The sound increased. To the south a pillar of smoke spiraled upward with amazing speed, and Conway wondered how a fire could grow so hot so quickly, especially since the dead grass seemed to hold enough moisture to preclude what appeared to be an almost explosive combustion. Then, inexplicably, it swirled, dove back down toward the ground.

The sound came from the smoke.

"Birds!" Conway remembered a city park at night, under a roost tree. A car accident startled the birds, and they rose in their thousands, fluttering and twittering, before settling down again. This mass was similar, except that their numbers dwarfed anything he could imagine. The huge flock flowed up the valley with amazing velocity, breaking into fragments that leapfrogged each other in shrilling waves. Their course took them directly past the huddled people, whom they ignored entirely, flying close enough to brush them with their wings. They were small creatures, which made their incredible, overwhelming numbers all the more inconceivable and therefore frightening, somehow.

The sound now was a physical thing, not so loud it deafened, but so persistent, so pervasive, it had dimension, a pressure that insinuated it into the body to rasp every nerve. Conway found himself sinking to his knees, swinging his arms, batting at the enclouding mass. They blotted the light. His breath caught in his chest.

Dimly, he heard shrieking, and looked to see Jones on his feet, unseeing eyes rolling wildly in his grotesquely contorted face. He struggled to pull free of Carter's grip. Conway bowled into them, and between them they held the Pastor down.

Almost imperceptibly, over long, agonizing minutes, the noise lessened. Peering out through still-squinting eyes, Conway was shocked by the destruction. Grass was mashed flat. Branches were broken, their leaves knocked to the ground. A lush alder thicket, a spring-green mass of new growth moments earlier, was ripped bare, back to winter's stark tracery.

Cautiously, Carter lifted her head. His eyes locked with hers. They eased away from Jones, who remained facedown, shuddering every time he inhaled. They got to their feet along with the others.

Dozens of birds had been struck by the group. Conway picked one up, examining it. "I don't believe it," he muttered. "English sparrows."

Carter said, "Not surprising, actually. Very adaptive, very aggressive. Interesting."

Jones sat up slowly, looked at the filth on his clothes and was promptly sick. Everyone else swallowed hard.

Falconer said, "There has to be a stream around here somewhere. Let's get moving."

Taking his place in line, an embarrassed Jones apologized, smiling sheepishly. "We all have our phobias, I guess. Mine's birds. They frighten me. This—" He gestured broadly, at a loss for words. Lamely, he finished, "I couldn't handle it. I'm sorry."

Leclerc said, "You haven't seen anything yet, preacher. Wait'll you see how I behave when a spider gets on me. I'll show you what panic's all about."

Jones seemed surprised by the sincere sympathy. After a look of appreciation, he grew studious. Conway assumed he was reevaluating the other man.

It took only a few minutes for them to stumble across their goal. Up front, forcing a passage through particularly thick mixed growth, Falconer gave a surprised grunt and stopped. When they forged up beside him, they saw why. A beautiful, rock-bottomed creek was at their feet. It was quite wide, and their side was a shelf, only ankle deep. They stepped out into it— exclaiming at the coldness—and waded upstream to a convenient grassy bank. Conway and Falconer stood watch as their companions splashed about, shouting like children. Carter waded downstream to the deeper water at the first bend, modestly sinking in up to her shoulders to take off her clothes and scrub them. The men took their turn when she was finished, Falconer and Conway going last.

When their clothes were wrung out, they spread out as individuals. No one strayed more than a few yards from the closest neighbor, however, as they examined whatever took their interest. Conway strolled upstream to the next bend. There was a pool there, carved by the abrupt change in the stream's direction, and what he saw in it made him exclaim aloud. There were fish as long as his arm, sleek creatures suspended in the current. He backed away until he was sure he was clear, then broke into a trot. Falconer looked up from his inspection of the streambank, tensing at Conway's hurried approach.

"This creek's packed with fish," Conway said. "Steelhead, I think. I'm going to cut a sapling and try to spear one."

Falconer grinned, relaxing. "I've got a better way." He called to the others. "Conway and I are going upstream for a minute."

They crept to the pool overhang. Falconer pulled the pin on one of the small hand grenades. Glancing at Conway, he smothered laughter. "I wish you could see your face. You must be a really dedicated sports fisherman."

"I am." Conway made no effort to keep the stiffness out of his voice.

Falconer said, "I promise not to do it often. Can't afford the grenades, for one thing. Anyhow, Matt, remember—no one's been on this stream for centuries. We deserve a treat for dinner today, and I don't think just this once is going to ruin the fishing, do you?"

Conway had to smile. "I guess not. Goes against the grain, though."

Falconer winked. "You'll forgive me when you taste one."

The force of the explosion carried to them as a heavy push to the stomach. Water geysered several feet in the air to fall back with a hissing splash. They rushed to the bank. Fish bellied up to the surface. Others struggled weakly, carried away by the current. Conway hurried downstream to intercept them where the water ran shallower. Shouting to the others, he soon had them scooping at the slippery harvest. They caught a half-dozen, but missed others.

It wasn't until they were all walking ashore that he realized Falconer had been standing watch. They exchanged looks, and Conway nodded shortly to indicate he understood the lesson. Someone was always to be on guard. Always.

A shrill cry stopped them in the midst of cleaning the catch. An eagle, severely majestic in black and white against the turquoise sky, swooped to stab talons into one of the fish beached downstream. It was a trying load, and the bird struggled fiercely to get airborne again. Successful, it screeched triumph, flying directly to a high, naked branch where it fed, looking back at the people on the bank between bites. Full of arrogance, he seemed to be telling them that the meal was his due, payment from interlopers to one of the rightful lords of the country. Falconer caught the feeling, and he gestured at the bird, saying, "Look at the pride of that thing, would you? Any other creature would slink off and bolt its meal under cover. He's wonderful."

Even Jones seemed to be taken by the scene, Conway noted, and he was especially pleased to see Carter paying more than passing attention.

This life was going to be hardest on her, he decided. He realized he was worried about her. She'd shown good instincts in reacting to Jones' panic, so she was more than an intellectual mass of social concerns. He hoped she'd allow herself to direct her mind to the new areas that would need her now. Of the whole group, Carter and Mazzoli appeared to have suffered the greatest loss between the old life and this one.

They had all expected to cooperate in rebuilding the framework of a shattered country. From what little he'd heard, he gathered that Carter had pictured herself shaping its ethic.

Falconer led them on a slightly different route back up the hill. The return was unremarkable. Tate welcomed their approach with a relieved smile that turned to outright glee when they held up the fish. She shouted back into the cave, and everyone tumbled out, bubbling appreciation. Conway, as the experienced fisherman, volunteered to cook.

He'd brought an armload of alder switches with him. Yoshimura helped him rig six things that looked like primitive tennis rackets. Butterflying each fish, he laid it on an alder frame, then lashed it in place with two more switches. Driving the handle into the ground exposed the rich, red flesh to the direct heat of the fire. Within minutes the air was redolent with broiling steelhead.

Leclerc spoke softly to Karoli, and the two of them took up watchful positions at the outer limit of the group, facing the forest. Conway remembered Falconer's look from the riverside. Apparently other people were becoming aware of the necessities of this life, as well. Even though the others laughed and joked, they stayed within a few feet of the mouth of the cave, never going beyond the fire's circle of light. The night imprisoned them.

Similarly, they ate clustered around the entrance. Later, as they watched the fire, conversing softly, Falconer rose to make an announcement. He said, "I found something today we all have to think about. Now that we're well-fed and rested, we've got to have a serious conference." He reached inside one of the voluminous jacket pockets, then held up an object about two inches long between thumb and forefinger.

They all moved to see it. The only one to speak was Tate, and she said, "Well, there it is, folks. We're not alone."

Falconer said, "Whoever else is still alive uses arrowheads like this. We know that now."

Mazzoli said, "Oh, that could be hundreds of years old."

Conway was close enough to see it more clearly. He said, "I'm afraid it proves a great deal, Madge. If Falconer found it on top of the ground, it's probably not old at all."

She took a backward step in unconscious denial. "I've seen lots of arrowheads; you can't tell how old they are just by looking."

Falconer said, "This one was on the bank of the stream. Look, there's still a fragment of the cord left that held it to the shaft."

Yoshimura left her friend's side and advanced on Falconer. She reached out, took the arrowhead from him, and pushed past to examine it more clearly in the firelight. In her smaller hand it looked deadlier, more intimidating. "Oh, God," she said. It was almost a prayer. Her mouth formed a small circle of shock. "It's not stone at all. The green patina . . . It's *bronze.*"

Falconer nodded slowly. "As Tate said, we're not alone. But who are we with?"

CHAPTER 25

The debate about leaving or staying started then. It lasted long into the first night and had continued heatedly the following day. As Conway had anticipated, the character of the group was such that personalities discolored issues from the outset, with the result that no one could truly be said to be interested entirely in facts.

No one harbored any notions that the cave could be made livable. There was a gloss on the air in it already, an oppressiveness that worked in the mind, convinced a person that if they turned quickly enough they might catch a glimpse of something waiting. They still went in and out, hauling out anything that appeared desirable, like antic monkeys loose in a storehouse. Already, a pile of discards grew next to the entrance. The VDP and its disks were there, hauled out by someone who forgot there was no electricity anywhere else. It rested on top of a typewriter. Pastor Jones had wanted to bring it with him, saying it would be necessary for him to prepare his observations and lesson plans when they linked up with other people. Yoshimura, acting in her self-appointed capacity as nurse-mother, gently dissuaded him by pointing out he had no paper and wasn't very likely to get any.

The major argument firmly polarized them in three predictable subgroups; for, against, and unwilling to decide. Minds had lodged there solidly, perfecting arguments and rebuttals.

On the fourth day after the discovery of the arrowhead, there had been no further patrols and the arguments about leaving were becoming so heated there was an unspoken moratorium. Conway noticed it by midmorning and deliberately spent the entire day drifting among his companions, watching and listening carefully. There was a forced comradeship in every look, every phrase, that worried him.

In the dark morning hours of the fifth day, he lay in his sleeping bag, staring at the interwoven branches that made up their ceiling now that they slept outdoors. They kept a small fire burning all night, backed against the uphill side of one of the massive trees. This was Falconer's idea; it was supposed to keep animals at bay without illuminating their camp for any curious human eyes in the valley.

He listened to the even breathing of his companions and watched the multiple coils of smoke dance shyly in the faint light of the flames. They rose sinuously, stroking each other, lingering over each contact, sometimes blending, sometimes separating, finally twisting to invisibility in the night.

The group had grown similarly complex, equally unpredictable. It might also disappear as easily as the smoke.

There was more to worry about than animals, more than arrowheads.

Leclerc was nervous about the reactor. While the others argued about their next move, he never participated except to reiterate his agreement with Falconer. He puttered constantly, checking dials, twisting knobs, reading meters. When asked to be specific, he merely shook his head and mumbled about nothing lasting forever. Yesterday he'd grown increasingly testy, and when approached by Yoshimura, who merely asked sociably how things were going, he snapped at her that he was no nuke tech and wasn't about to go poking around where he could get fried if he made a mistake. If she wanted his best guess, though, he figured the thing was about out of fuel.

Falconer immediately ordered all unnecessary power cut off, which included the positive pressure blowers. Conway was surprised, and not a little disturbed, at how quickly everyone moved to obey. He told himself it was only a reflection of general understanding of the situation.

He wondered if he was simply reacting to Falconer's militarism. Carter made no pretense of her resistance to almost every word the man uttered. She went out of her way to initiate discussions in his hearing that unfavorably compared the effectiveness of military action with her area of expertise, international trade law.

As much as he wanted to be correct in his own decisions, Conway found it almost automatic to question Falconer. The Colonel said he wanted them to equip themselves as best they could and strike out to make contact with whoever they could find.

Conway tended to agree, but he'd refused to commit himself. There were good reasons, he argued with himself, beyond his concern that Falconer was becoming more of a dominant character than a consensus leader.

Their present situation offered everything but progress. A spring nearby would suffice for water. There was game in the valley, and fish. They would learn more about foraging for edible plants. But that was only the base requirement.

An attempt to remain in place was more than a decision, it was a complex statement that left more unsaid than it defined. It acknowledged the creation of a community, with the need for societal rules and behavior norms.

Of all the women, Madge Mazzoli was the only one past child-bearing age. When the arguments for remaining near the cave were being most strongly promoted, she disagreed. Conway noticed that she was the only one who maintained eye contact with any of the men for more than a moment. She had the least to say, but her ability to concentrate on the issue without being snared by the unspoken biological considerations made her the most effective spokesman for moving on.

"We're people from a more advanced world," she'd argued simply. "Whoever's out there, they need us."

"Need what?" Karoli countered angrily. "What have you got to offer people who shoot bows and arrows? You going to tell them about TV? Computers?"

Surprisingly, her eyes sparkled with spirit, a resurgence of the will that had collapsed earlier. "We know about cleanliness. We know about reading and writing. We know some things about first aid, and CPR, and geometry, and chemistry. We're smarter than you think, Mr. Karoli, and it'd be a sin and a shame for us to sit somewhere and pretend the rest of the world doesn't exist."

Falconer applauded, which drew a smile from her. As they watched, the expression lost definition, grew soft and doughy. In growing dismay, they saw her sink back to pleasant impenetrability. Everyone shifted uncomfortably, unsure how they should react to a telling argument presented by someone they all knew was gradually retreating from reality.

In the end, on that first night, with the moon turning the encircling trees into silver-etched ebony columns, they'd carefully laid in a stock of firewood for the watch and gone to bed.

Tonight, as then, Conway was restless.

Crawling out of his sleeping bag as quietly as possible, he made his way to Anspach's post by the fire. She was alert, and heard him coming at some distance. When he complimented her on it, she held out an exaggerated shaking hand and made a face. They chuckled together, the necessity to keep quiet forging an intimacy between them that made Conway feel a bit shy and daring. Anspach's usually quiet face seemed more animated than usual, too, he thought. He asked if she'd like him to take the watch when they finished talking. "No sense in both of us being awake," he said.

She shook her head in a vigorous no. Puzzled, he asked her about it. Her answering laughter was embarrassed, and she gave him a hard look. "You won't laugh at me?"

"Of course not. What's wrong?"

She poked at the fire and pulled her coat tighter, gathering herself. "I'm an academic," she said. "I've never slept anywhere except in a house or hotel in my whole life. In my family, we ate fried chicken with a knife and fork off china, you understand? When my parents died, I lived alone in the same house, with the same behaviors." She got to her feet, looked down at him. The firelight deepened the lines around her mouth, hid her eyes in the sockets. "Janet's as close to a friend as I ever had. She did a grand thing the other day, saving Jones. I want to live up to her, to all of you, but I'm afraid of what's out there. I'm even more afraid I'll do something stupid and get someone hurt. Or find out I'm a coward."

He said, "We all feel exactly the same, Sue."

She shook her head. "You've succeeded in your life. Failed sometimes. I've never done either."

"Fake it, then." She frowned, not trusting his remark, and he went on. "Do what you have to do with enthusiasm. Make the rest of us believe you're not afraid. Who knows—maybe you'll convince yourself."

"Is that what you do? You don't look scared all the time."

"You mean I only look scared part of the time, right?" He laughed openly at her stammering attempt to explain the phrasing, pleased to see her finally surrender to the humor of it and smile. Then he said, "You and Janet aren't great outdoors folks, but you're bright people. Don't cheat us out of that brain power by worrying it to paralysis. Trust yourself; you'll be all right."

"Thanks for saying so, anyhow."

"I'm moving over to that clearing to look at the stars. Want to come along?"

"Would it be all right? The Colonel said this was my post."

"Did he nail you to the ground?" He was sharper than he should have been, which only heightened the irritation generated by her concern for absolute obedience. He spun away.

The night was chilly away from the fire, and they both hunched tighter against the cold. For a while neither spoke. Anspach whispered that the stars were so close it was like looking at them through a telescope. Conway agreed, leaning back against a tree, enjoying the feeling of shared solitude.

A little later he heard a sound from her, as of something catching in her throat. Suspicious, he bent forward to look into her face. There were wet streaks down her cheeks. He said, "Hey, I thought we had things straightened out."

She managed a smile. "I was remembering a painting. It showed the Louvre, destroyed in the revolution. People were using the paintings to build shacks, and burning the frames for firewood. It's all gone—the painting, the Louvre, and all. God. Oh, God. Think of it, Matt—the Statue of Liberty, Westminster Abbey, the Imperial Palace . . . We've lost more than people, more than civilization. The heritage of the race is gone."

It stunned him to realize he hadn't accepted the fact. All the while he'd told himself he was being forthright in his acknowledgment of the hammer-blow truths of their situation. He'd volunteered for the patrol, smirked at Jones' irrational desire to pack his typewriter if they left, laughed to himself at the lack of thought that lugged the VDP and its disks out of the cave. He told himself he'd adapted.

He'd cheated. In the back of his mind was a hoarded fantasy of cities frozen in time. Remnants, possibly decrepit to the point of collapse—he desperately wanted them to be still *there*. In that world, university buildings would continue to harbor knowledge, museums would be protecting and preserving the art and science man had created in his hundreds of thousands of years and his millions upon millions of lives.

Sue's forlorn analysis made him face the truth. If there was even rubble where the cities had towered, the centuries had seen it overgrown, turned into a lair for animals. If today's humanity could even get up nerve enough to approach those sites, they'd come humbled to dust, not as owners, but as garbage pickers.

Perversely, the more he thought about it, the more determined he became to surmount that destruction. What had been could be again, and better. Man could build once more, and perhaps this time make something of man that would last through the ages.

He considered telling Anspach his thoughts. They stuck to the roof of his mouth. Instead he sympathized in a general, conversational manner, then announced he intended to try sleeping again. As soon as she was comfortably placed by the fire, he made his way back to his sleeping bag.

The next thing he knew, Yoshimura was shaking his shoulder, calling him to face the new day. He rolled out eagerly, hurrying to wash up. By the time he was finished shaving—he'd shown the other men how to put a razor edge on the huge hunting knives Falconer's troops were issued, and he grinned at the image of himself maneuvering the oversized blade around his face—he was secure in his mind.

He cornered Falconer. "Listen," he said, tapping the surprised Colonel's chest, "We've got to get out of here, take our chances. I've thought it over. Madge is right; we owe the survivors whatever we can offer. We volunteered for this project with that in mind, and just because the boundaries have been changed doesn't mean we can quit the game."

"You know that's my point. I don't have a choice. You heard the vidisk they left for me."

Conway smiled. "You mean put the U.S. back together? What with, string?"

"If I have to. Those are my orders."

"You can't mean that. Use your head. Look down there, right there in that valley. It used to be home for over thirty thousand people, remember? Orchards, farms, factories. Sidewalks. Electricity. Gasoline. It's *wilderness*. Who cares about artificial political boundaries?"

"Look, you want to improve the minds of whoever's left. Jones wants to teach them they've got souls so he can save them. Carter wants to teach them that the working man is God Almighty and all they have to do is form a good union to prove it. Me, I want to get those artificial political boundaries reestablished so you can all have your rightful place to do your wonderful things. Do what you want. I'll make a nation."

"You're crazy."

"Possibly. I don't think so." He smiled, an expression of self-mockery. "Consider that: a new world. We can define our own terms. We can decide what crazy is."

Conway walked away. When they had their next group discussion, though, he threw in on Falconer's side.

He expected heated reaction, and it came. Yoshimura, in particular, insisted the rigors of a long move would be unacceptable. The unspoken object of her concern, Madge Mazzoli, smiled pleasantly the whole time. Her decline tried Conway's new resolve more than any argument. In the end it was Pastor Jones who proposed they acknowledge that the cave was unlivable. Once that point was cleared up, he suggested they all agree to move until they found a place to settle that all could accept. The compromise was approved.

That done, he led them in a short prayer for those remaining in the cave. The solemnity of mood afterward couldn't stand up to the excitement of preparing to leave.

They chose partners in order to help each other organize equipment. Conway was pleased to team up with Tate. She was quick, good company, and, he was sure, totally dependable. Surprisingly, she'd been the strongest advocate for moving to the valley, but not farther. In thinking about that, he decided it was less a breakup of the Falconer-Leclerc-Tate axis than a tactical decision on her part. She probably saw the valley as defensible and a place that could easily be developed into a sustaining community. Those would be her major concerns. Although chagrined to see Conway come into the balance against her, she was very forbearing when she told him there were no hard feelings.

They spent the day getting ready for departure. Conway held school on their weapons again. Falconer appeared with a new type he'd dug out of the warehouse wreckage. It was a long rifle in a special case. He described it to them during a class break.

"The inside of the case lid is a solar power pack," he said, opening it, revealing a series of black panels connected to each other by small wires. "The piece can be used as an ordinary rifle. Plugged into the electrical source, it's a thinking sniper's weapon." He connected a wire from the rifle stock into an outlet in the case, then flipped the caps off the scope. Pointing into the valley, he said, "I align the scope cross hairs on the target and push this button. The laser gets the range and an LED gives me a digital reading on the lens. Push it again and the piece adjusts for a correct aim. I add wind estimate with this knob beside the laser/ranger button." Displaying a cartridge, he went on, "Thirty caliber. Antique size, but a bust-ass slug. Special powder, blazing muzzle velocity. I can guarantee a one-shot kill out to a thousand yards on a still day. From there out to two thousand the odds change, mostly due to wind uncertainty. Let me see where the first round strikes, though, and I'll bet cash money on the second."

Conway disliked the weapon, with its elegant, superior look. It seemed to want to fire, to flaunt its power. When Falconer extended it for him to handle, he stepped back, shaking his head. Words popped out. "It makes me think of assassinations."

Falconer's frown came slowly, unusually delicate, the expression of someone deciding to overlook a regrettable descent into bad taste. He said no more, repacking the rifle. Conway went back to teaching about the other weapons.

The magnitude of their choice seemed to fall on them simultaneously as they stood looking at their stacked equipment that evening. Falconer had directed an inspection. Everyone must have a helmet and properly adjusted body armor, a full canteen and ammunition. Packs were checked for weapon maintenance kit, rations for ten days, vitamin and mineral supplements, first aid equipment, and three complete changes of clothes. They examined their own gear and each other's. Suddenly, almost in chorus, they agreed to spend the following day, one last day, rehearsing tactical and march formations, fire commands, and trail discipline.

It went quickly, frenetically. Time seemed to leap across itself. The last dinner was a nervous meal, bolted down. Conversation came in snatches, almost entirely devoted to reviewing theoretical situations of defense, attack, or retreat. At darkness there was a last rush of making ready, last-minute unpacking and repacking. They were a long time settling into the sleeping bags. Listening, Conway was sure no one slept.

His eyes flew open at the first spoken word from Falconer, who stood the last watch of the night. For a moment he couldn't make himself believe dawn had slipped up on him.

Breakfast reminded him of a locker room before a game. The laughter was too loud, the conversation too casual and, just before they left, too confident.

Fear coated them like sweat.

CHAPTER 26

The move from the cave was a wrench for everyone. As Falconer and Conway moved among them, checking their equipment, making sure they understood their position in the unit, no one managed to avoid at least one look back. They packed all the discards inside and replaced the false rock cover as best they could, trusting to nature and time to complete their imperfect camouflage. Falconer lectured them one last time—move in teams of two, with one person designated to fire-wipe rounds, one restricted to longer-range use of the boop.

Conway smiled at the comedy of such terms for such deadly weapons. Before the thought was fully formed, he remembered the smoke from ruined suburbs reaching for his helicopter on the ride to Dulles.

After that he tried to concentrate on the move itself. The war he'd seen was over. He hoped they'd find people who had no word for the phenomenon.

Falconer's remark about defining their own terms came to mind as they made their way toward the valley. Leclerc, leading the way with Yoshimura close behind, pointed out the patch of brush where they'd seen the tiger. Conway couldn't hear the hushed commentary, but was willing to bet Leclerc was calling the mound Tiger Place, or something like it. Descriptions like that would be the names of the new world. So much for Washington or Connecticut or Oklahoma. Did the people who made the bronze arrowheads name their territory? Did any of the old names carry over?

They were on the lower shoulder of the slope when Falconer signaled a stop. Self-consciously applying their newly learned doctrine, the teams of two took cover facing outward.

Falconer spoke to Leclerc, then made his way to where Conway knelt beside a tree with Tate. Squatting beside them, he wiped a sweating brow and said, "I'd give my soul for a pair of binoculars."

Tate gestured widely. "Even a map. All I know is directions, and if the sun goes behind a cloud, I'm done."

"I want a good defensive position for the night," Falconer said. Almost to himself, he added, "I want to work west. To the coast."

Conway had expected something of the sort. Everything Falconer had said during the arguments over leaving hinted at an intention to explore and actively seek contact. He asked, "Why the coast?"

"It was the closest large population center. It's a milder climate, and we've got no winter gear. Primarily, though, because I think that's where we'll find the most advanced culture. Shipping, either riverine or maritime, is a keystone for growth and development."

Tate said, "If they're using bows and arrows, they're not what I'd call advanced."

Falconer reached inside the open collar of his blouse. The arrowhead dangled from a cord around his neck. He held it out. "That's not a one-time effort," he went on. "It means mass production and standardization."

Conway said, "Okay, so we decide to head for Puget Sound. Where's the pass through all that?" He gestured uphill, indicating the wall of the Cascade Range to the west. Snow still capped many of the peaks.

"That's one reason why I was wishing for binoculars. Our best hope is that we'll find friendly locals who'll guide us."

Tate said, "What's second best?"

"We spend our summer exploring."

Conway frowned. "The coast didn't come up when we debated leaving the cave. Everyone assumed we'd find a friendly tribe, or at least a good location for a camp."

"That's first priority. I'm not asking everyone to go with me. I think we all should, but whether anyone else does or not, I am."

"You'd break up the group?"

"Certainly."

They matched stares before Tate put a hand on the arm of each. "That can all wait. We've got to prove we can even function in this environment first."

They agreed. Conway knew his own response was halfhearted. He could only wonder about Falconer's.

The sun was centered in the sky when they reached the creek, and Leclerc christened it Noon Creek. With that, Falconer insisted everyone set his or her watch accordingly. Despite having been out of the crèches for almost a week, it was the first any of them had considered time as something to be measured in increments smaller than mealtimes or guard shifts. The first real laughter of the trip came as they realized the disparity of the timepieces and joked with each other about who'd been cheated out of the most sleep.

Late that afternoon their line of march was forced away from the creek-bank by a steep bluff. They crested that high ground and found themselves overlooking the exact campsite they sought, where their smaller stream fed into a river. The flood plain on their side was scoured flat, a lush meadow. There were numerous large droppings from cattle or buffalo; possibly both, Leclerc guessed. He remarked on the size of them, and the absence of any sighting of the animals.

Across the river the ground was rougher. Flood currents had formed long, narrow hillocks topped by tufts of alder and willow that made Conway think of unruly haircuts. The dry channels between them were weedy expanses of tumbled, round river rock.

The chafing of packs and incipient foot blisters were temporarily forgotten. They hugged and congratulated each other, then hurried to the junction.

Falconer soon had them dug in militarily, with two-man foxholes in perimeter and a central command post. The digging took place under great complaint. Conway conceded the necessity for it and grudgingly admired Falconer's ability to sway his reluctant crew.

As the lowering sun neared the mountaintops, Karoli detached himself from his near-constant attendance on Bernhardt and strolled downstream to some alders where he noisily hacked free a branch. Using the metal lid from an empty ration jam can and his pocketknife, he fashioned a workable barbed head. A strip of cloth from his shirttail bound it to the branch. In a few minutes he'd fashioned a fish spear. The offhand ingenuity pleased Conway out of all proportion. It was a minor accomplishment in the grand scheme of things, but it was exactly the way they'd have to survive.

Conway also saw Falconer's irritation, understanding the soldier considered it a breach of discipline for someone to leave without notifying him. He considered going to Karoli to intercede and explain the need for security, but decided against it. That sort of thing was Falconer's responsibility. Anyhow, he was tired, and they'd seen no sign of anyone, or even any large animals, except grazers.

Falconer continued to glance Karoli's way from time to time, and when the larger man moved farther downstream, Falconer trotted to Karoli's foxhole. Whistling, he held up Karoli's vest, helmet, and weapon, gesturing for him to return.

Karoli looked back, grinned, and kept going. Falconer ran after him, carrying the equipment. Coming up behind the other man, he turned him with a hand on his shoulder, thrusting the military gear at him. Startled, Karoli took it. In the next instant he threw it to the ground. Conway half rose, as did Tate, ready to break up a fight.

Standing on the riverbank, the two men argued, faces almost in contact. Abruptly, Falconer stepped back, spun on his heel, picked up the equipment, and stormed back toward camp. Karoli nonchalantly proceeded in the opposite direction, disappearing beyond a rock outcrop. Everyone was suddenly very busy as Falconer reentered the perimeter and dropped into his foxhole.

Tate turned her attention to the alcohol stove, saying. "Too bad. Things went pretty good there for a while. Karoli ought to know the Colonel's really looking out for him."

Conway said, "Maybe Karoli thinks he can look out for himself."

Tate looked over her shoulder at him. Her smile was condescending, and Conway bridled, ready to strike back. However, all she said was, "Maybe so. I just hate to see our first day ending like that. When it started I was looking at how pretty everything is and thinking how well we're doing, too."

He looked past her, out where the sunset spilled color across the sparse clouds. A reflected golden glow warmed the spring green, hinting of the rich summer to come. In the river a large fish rolled, the splat of the tail a signal for a flock of swallows to swirl over the camp. She was right, of course. It was beautiful. He watched the swallows, thinking how thick the animal population was. It spoke well for livability. He wondered if Karoli was having any luck. Another steelhead dinner was a far more appetizing prospect than another load of freeze-dried glop, no matter how nutritious.

Bernhardt called to Falconer, attracting everyone's attention, pointing. Karoli was returning, empty-handed, moving at a heavy trot, looking over his shoulder every few steps. From the brush behind him rose a yapping, yodeling howl. "Coyote," Leclerc said. Answering cries came from somewhere between the group and the now-running man. He would have to pass the second one to get away from the first. The only alternative was to head for the river.

He put on a lumbering burst of speed.

The first arrow hit his left leg, the one away from the river. He took it very well, staggering only slightly, the protruding shaft no encumbrance.

Bernhardt screamed. No one else reacted; all were frozen by the unfolding spectacle.

The next arrow missed Karoli completely, but the third hit him fair in the side, just below his ribs. He lurched badly at that, slowing to a shuffling jog. Two more arrows, one from behind and yet another from the side, stopped him in his tracks. He still refused to fall, turning, turning, tugging at the shafts. His chin was almost on his chest, and he was close enough for them to hear his panting efforts.

When the two men broke out of the brush and sprinted toward him, the sight galvanized the group. Leclerc fired first. Without appearing to aim, he dropped both men with two shots so close together that the rolling, battering noise was almost a single explosion.

They were small people, and the impact of the high-velocity flechettes threw them whirling and tumbling to the ground.

More howls came from the brush, and Falconer pointed. "Boops! Two rounds each!" The designated gunners fired. After the crackling blasts, they were rewarded with screams and moans from the bushes.

Bernhardt ran for Karoli before anyone was aware of it. Conway followed, watching for more arrows. Bernhardt had eyes only for her friend. She cradled his head, but Conway snatched her upright, grabbing Karoli's collar. They hurried back, dragging him, ignoring Falconer and Leclerc, who passed them, heading away from the perimeter.

Conway and Bernhardt were trying to make Karoli comfortable when the other two returned, dragging one of the dead warriors. Bernhardt looked at him and gagged. "Why?"

Falconer said, "We have to know as much about these people as we can. I'm going to check his weapons and everything else." He turned a grim, unblinking look on Conway. "Any chance for Karoli?"

Conway shook his head.

An arrow whistled down among them, quivering in the dirt. For a second they gaped at it. The eager whisper of the second sent them scrambling for their holes. In the failing light Conway scanned the circle. The withdrawal he'd seen in the expressions before had toughened to determination.

Then he looked at Karoli and the other dead man. They lay on their stomachs, heads turned toward each other. Lifeless, startled eyes looked into identical eyes.

He hoped no one else saw them as he did.

Across the river on the knoll overlooking the scene, Clas angrily waved back the two women holding the horses before snapping at Gan, who lay beside him. "Of course I heard the thunder! You think I'm deaf?"

Gan heard the fear sharpening the anger. It made him feel better, because the way the two Devil warriors had seemed to come apart had almost made him shout his terror. The women were still buzzing agitatedly.

Gan said, "They killed the Devils. Like lightning."

"It's lightning. I saw the flash. We've all seen lightning kill."

"Much the same." Gan avoided complete agreement or argument, then asked, "What about the soft noise, and the big noise later, far away?"

"We can't know everything. These things take time."

Gan held back a bittersweet smile at the sound of the voice his father had always used when he didn't know the answer. He said, "I never saw clothes like that. Do you know their tribe?"

"No. I can't understand what they are. Clumsy as hamstrung cows. I'm sure there're women among them. Strange clothes—and weapons that kill at a distance as surely as a knife in the throat." He pursed his lips and nodded. "They die well. He was like a bear."

"What should we do?" Gan asked. He knew what he wanted to hear, wished he could express the force of the thing that had been growing in his mind since Col first mentioned the prophecy. From that moment he'd had a feeling of a future hurtling toward him. Now he knew these strangers were part of it. The certainty of what he had to do drummed in his head, while at the same time, he thought with wonder how a few days ago he'd have deferred instantly to Clas in any similar situation. Now he had to convince, to lead.

"They'd make strong allies," he said.

"We don't need allies. If the Devils attack, we'll wait till it's over, then get away. They'll probably leave. Two dead, and at least two more wounded by weapons that work like magic, ought to convince even them to go home."

Clas slid noiselessly back off the ridgeline.

Gan was drawn back to the encircled group.

They were important.

His scalp prickled at the *fact* of it.

He joined Clas as he grained the horses, and when his friend turned an expression of puzzled expectation on him, he blurted, "Everything that's happened to us—Faldar Yan, the Rose Priestess coming to us, the duel in Earth Heart, the strangers here; could there be a reason for all of it?"

"A reason?"

"Something makes weather; we don't understand what. Are we like clouds, pushed by new winds, bringing changes we don't understand? Could there be a *reason* for what's happened?"

Clas' eyes narrowed. He continued to pour grain into the nosebags, but much more slowly. A breeze eased through the branches with mocking chuckles. Gan felt his shoulders tighten in defensive reflex. Clas' answer was restrained. "I know what's behind your words. My life is fighting. The reasons why a man lives and his enemy dies are very clear, so a man learns to respect only what he can see. Church comforts. Readers and Seers and other babblers bore me. Except for your mother. She knew things she couldn't know." He looked away. "And you're her son as much as Col's."

Devils yapped coyote calls near the strangers. Clas' speculative look disappeared. "It's time to eat," he said.

Gan called his dogs. He picked up some food from a saddlebag and moved away from the others.

Clas was cutting an apple into thirds, sharing it with the women. They made muted exclamations of pleasure.

He wanted to join them. They all liked him; he knew that. Still, ever since the thing with Faldar and Bay, they acted as if he was different, somehow. He remembered the way Sylah looked at Raggar before he killed his man, and how differently she looked at him afterward. Silly. He was the same dog, wasn't he?

And Clas. He was more like his father every minute, hard to please, always looking for reasons to find fault.

When he turned for one last look before leaving, Neela was watching him. She turned away. Her hair caught the touch of day's failing light.

Gan rose swiftly, moving downhill to his watch position. He reminded himself that his only reason for living was to lead the Dog People.

Friends weren't important. Not really.

CHAPTER 27

Raggar was nervous. Several times he'd heaved his bulk upright, looming dark against the night. Gan knew part of his irritability stemmed from uncertainty. He still wasn't comfortable with Cho, and as far as Shara was concerned, he'd made it very clear he tolerated no youthful fools. The gangly pup already nursed a nipped thigh and had learned to keep Gan's horse between himself and Raggar while they were on the move. Once again Raggar padded off into the night. Cho groaned softly as she rose to follow. Gan made Shara settle back. He'd lost count of the times the adult pair moved off together in silent investigation, and the immature animal needed more rest than that.

They were all tired. Still, they'd been lucky. There was no pursuit; the storm apparently cloaked their move north. He shifted his position, and a twinge in the shoulder reminded him that the wound was still there, but no great problem. Even Neela had been helpful in that regard. That was a pleasant surprise. For the most part she said no more to him than was absolutely necessary.

He understood. Better than he was able to admit to anyone. In her place, he'd be much harsher with the man who killed his father.

One of the advantages of standing watch was the dogs. He wished Neela had a similar benefit. The dogs didn't understand the details of his problems, but they understood his moods better than any human.

Neela had sacrificed everything but life itself. Her losses were more bitter, more devastating, than anyone's. Yet she never complained. Her retreat from contact was the only sign of the turmoil he knew must rage in her. She'd even put aside her outright hostility toward Sylah. He felt sure there was a rebuilding going on between them, and the relationship might even prove stronger for it. He hoped so.

The only other time she approached her brightness of old was when Clas had time to relax and joke with her. She hung on his words, made soft, feminine sounds of amusement or amazement at everything he did.

As often as he told himself that was typical woman-stuff and it shouldn't bother him, it still did. He worried about her when she didn't communicate, and hated it when she did. Especially with Clas.

Which was stupid.

The dogs returned almost at a trot, Raggar's low growl presaging their appearance. Gan felt their excitement. Raggar stood beside his master, looking down where the river and creek were hidden in darkness. He growled again.

Gan rose to all fours and sniffed the air, trying to scent what had Raggar so troubled. He detected nothing.

A Devil warrior hooted a reasonable imitation of an owl. Another answered. Gan cupped his hands behind his ears, thought he detected movement. It could have been the breeze, or a creature disturbed by the false owl cry. Gan was torn: If the Devils were preparing to attack, the strangers might all be killed; if he left his post to assist, his own people would be left sleeping, unguarded.

He woke Clas, explaining quickly he meant to take the dogs and scout the strangers' perimeter to see if they survived.

Clas' eyes were black holes in the pale oval of his face, the normally demanding tattoo nothing but a darker smudge. His voice had a soft, concerned quality Gan had never heard before as, instantly wide awake, he said, "Tell me only one thing. Do you think these people are so important to you, or do you *know*?"

Gan hesitated, then said, "I know."

"Then we go. If a man knows something he cannot know, he must act. Leave the pup with the women."

Gan woke them and explained what was happening. Their calm acceptance made him proud of them. He wished he had time to tell them so.

Flanked by the dogs, they moved in a silence that filled Gan with the giddy feeling that with each noiseless step he grew beyond himself, became spiritlike. Shadows rose to shroud him. It was all he could do to suppress the growl of pure pleasure at the back of his throat.

They entered the river a good distance above the strangers' camp, coming out across the smaller creek from them. Leaving the dogs on guard, they crawled through the shallows, inching onto land with murdats drawn.

There was no need for Gan to speak aloud to inform Clas when he discovered the abandoned fighting hole. Generations of unending conflict had forced the Dog People to create combat communications. On the march in quiet circumstances, they had arm and hand signals. In battle, or at great distances, they had a combination of shrill whistles, signal pennants, and war drums that was almost as detailed as speech. When absolute silence was required, they used hand language. It was a code based on touch, using hand grips, clasping of fingers in a particular manner, or a series of short or long pressures. The grammar was rudimentary and the vocabulary limited, but it enabled warriors to plan, organize, and strike with the terrifying soundlessness of owls dropping from the night.

He told Clas, "Stranger place here. Stranger gone."

There was a splash on their left, coming from the far riverbank directly across from their location. On their own side the angry chitter of a raccoon alerted them further. A fish slapped the surface downstream.

Clas signaled "enemy" on Gan's arm. Together they crept to the edge of the hole. It was still heavy with the scent of its occupants.

The raccoon chittered again, directly ahead. Gan flexed his sword arm, savored the pull of muscle on bone. He signaled, "Enemy. I," to Clas, and moved forward. He imagined himself transformed into a man-animal from the campfire legends.

If the Devil on the riverbank heard anything, it was the faint hiss of the murdat. Gan took his bone and eased him into the water.

When the slapping fish sound was repeated, Gan prepared to move across the river, but Clas materialized beside him, insisting they go back. They crossed the stream, gathered the dogs, and then proceeded up the main river, keeping to the bank. They had to allow for the current on their return swim, and gauged their trek so that, having made it across, they came out about a hundred yards upstream from the abandoned perimeter. Gan figured the current would have carried the fleeing strangers about thirty yards downstream from their starting point. Thus, when it became light, it should be less than two hundred yards to where they were hiding.

He put the dogs downwind so their wet coats wouldn't screen out other smells. While they waited for activity, he admired the skill of the strangers' move. They might be better fighters than he thought.

Time passed until daylight enabled him to distinguish individual leaves on shrubs. The dawn brooded. Mist breathed up from the surface of the water, tumbling in slow waves across the flood plain. When the sun touched the horizon, the blank whiteness turned silvery as it poked and prodded inquisitively across the rocky ground.

A hoarse call came from one of the elongated mounds that rose a few feet above the scoured surface. The dogs moved to a half crouch, eyes jerking from the direction of the sound to Gan, waiting for a command. He gestured them back down. To Clas he touched, "Understand talk?"

Clas gripped his fingers in a negative sign. When there was an answering shout from another clump of brush, they both winced at the tactical mistake. The Devils now knew their prey was separated and confused.

A figure appeared near the riverbank. In the dim light and the knee-high mist, it appeared more beastlike than human. It headed inland in a series of clumsy lurches. Sharp thunder crashed. The figure wobbled but remained upright. At the next crack the head jerked, then lolled sideways to rest on its shoulder.

It was a trick, a rough decoy to draw the strangers' lightning. The man moving the dummy, submerged in the mist, lowered it with a loud, choking gurgle. Voices hidden in the fog erupted in derisive laughter.

Drumlike thumps, like the ones of the night before, came from the strangers' two widely separated locations. Moments later the earth erupted with smoke and sound at several points. Plants whipped and danced as if caught in a storm.

Something that buzzed like an angry wasp struck a rock in front of Gan and spun to a stop on the gravel directly under his nose. It was metal, with bright, jagged edges. He picked it up and dropped it instantly, exclaiming surprise before popping scorched fingers in his mouth.

Increasing light exposed a cautiously advancing warrior. Within moments Gan counted four more. When he turned to Clas and held up that many fingers, Clas was frowning. He pointed east and held up a full hand three times, adding hand-signing saying that many horses and riders advanced toward the river.

Craning, Gan saw them and understood what was planned. The hunting party had left a man behind to hold their horses; Gan spotted him on the far bank, close to where he'd struck down the warrior. The remainder intended to hold the strangers in place until the larger element could attack.

Suddenly, with no warning whatsoever, a stranger was upright and walking. Gan almost spoke to Clas in his surprise. His friend hissed in startled disbelief.

The stride and shoulder-length hair suggested a woman. The voice confirmed it when she called out. She addressed the vacant space before her, and even though he understood no words, he heard the cajoling, pleading tone of a mother calling a toddler.

His throat tightened. She must have gone mad.

She moved forward again, unaware that one of her companions, a smaller figure, was also visible now, crouched at the edge of the bushes where they'd both been hiding. Frightened shouts came from another mound about fifty yards farther away from where Gan hid and watched.

Carefully, she raised her hand. A white cloth fluttered appeal.

A warrior not ten feet from her rose slowly, keeping her body between himself and her companions. They quieted when he revealed himself. He conspicuously put his bow on the ground, but made no move to drop the sword he wore on his hip. It was the short weapon they called a ma, used for fighting afoot. They were as good with it as they were with the deadly sodal. He stood perfectly still while she came to him, waving her flag. Her teeth flashed in a smile. She raised her free hand and shook a scolding finger.

The second figure, another female, rushed to join her, setting off renewed cries from her friends.

The warrior reached for the larger woman with his left hand. His right eased toward the ma. She put her hand on his where it gripped her sleeve and pulled to release herself. The warrior held on, taking a backward step. The smaller woman leaped to grab his arm.

The thunder cracked again. Rocks danced up from beside the warrior's right foot, and something howled away with a noise that Gan reacted to instinctively by dropping his chin to the ground. He continued to watch, however, and saw the warrior whirl the ma through two glittering slashes. He dove to cover in a shallow depression even as the small woman dropped. The taller one sagged, then rolled backward.

Hollow noises rolled from the bushes. Blossoms of white smoke like huge tufts of cotton sprang up all around where the warrior lay hidden. He leaped to his feet, screaming, beating at a body that suddenly, unbelievably, spouted flame and smoke. Gan bit his fist an instant before the lightning weapon spoke again. The Devil tumbled through the air, lying where he fell. The broken body continued to smoke.

There was no time to dwell on it. The mounted Devils were on hand.

Leaving a man to handle the horses, they moved to close on the stranger's mound farthest from Gan. They meant to eliminate one group at a time. Unless he stopped them.

Distant movement, something out of place, drew his eye. Something moved on a ridge that sloped down from the paralleling hills to the bank of the river. He ignored the cries and sporadic battle sounds to concentrate.

He saw it again, rapid, straight-line movement through the trees, a column of riders moving to the sound of the battle.

The Devils were unaware of them and in no hurry to close with the destructive power of the weapons turned against them. They loosed occasional arrows, backed by obscene promises of how their enemies would die. Gan and Clas both remarked at the discipline of the strangers. They unleashed their power only as often as needed to keep the Devils at bay.

When they came closer, the new arrivals were easily identified. Only Olan cavalry carried such heavy lances or wore conical helmets.

Gan slipped away before Clas could do more than bang his fist on the ground.

He circled wide, running hard. The dogs followed easily, long legs swinging in their deceptively swift, untiring wolf pace. After a while he turned and began a cautious stalk toward the ongoing action. The thrashing of the newly arrived horses led him directly to where they were secured to scrub trees by their reins. The slam of the lightning weapons terrified them, and they pawed the ground and tugged at their restraints. A single guard tried to control them.

Gan ordered the dogs to wait.

He advanced in short rushes until he could launch himself across the last yards in two straining leaps. Warned by some sense of danger, the man turned, eyes widening. A shout of alarm died on the point of the murdat, and then Gan was bounding to free the straining horses. He cut loose ten, letting them flee. He led the remaining five away. Raggar moved automatically to a guard position between Gan and the fight. The other dogs joined him.

Cries in the distance told him how narrowly he'd beaten the arrival of the Olan cavalry.

He tied the horses safely before flinging himself on the ground beside Clas. He was gasping for breath.

Clas punched his shoulder. "Look," he said, "the Devils are in battle frenzy. They're taking on the Olans, too. Some of the strangers are caught in the middle and the others are being held in place by only a few—uh!" He stopped with a grunt as one of the strangers sallied from the nearest mound and charged in their direction, away from their other group. As soon as Gan recovered from his surprise, he recognized it as a counterattack, designed to clear an avenue of retreat. It was a brave, risky move, something a fighter would do rather than wait to be picked off. Even Clas was forced to mutter approval.

Warriors rose to shoot arrows. They also appeared to fly before falling to the ground as the lightning blinked from the weapon and the now-familiar thunder roared.

When the tempo of the noise increased so dramatically, warriors from the larger attack party ran toward the activity.

The stranger retreated back into the cover, reappearing leading a second person who was doubled over clutching his stomach. A flurry of arrows from the arriving warriors narrowly missed them.

They ran, every step distancing them from their surrounded friends. The Devils exulted as they gained on them.

More lightning sent the pursuit hurtling for cover. The Devils continued the chase with more caution.

Clas started to rise. Gan restrained him, but he pulled away, saying, "They're coming right at us. We have to hurry or get caught up in it."

"We're going to help them escape."

"*Strangers?*"

"There's no time to argue, Clas. Believe in me. Help me."

Clas afforded himself a brief groan. His new expression reminded Gan of the odd exchanges that used to pass between him and his father. "How?" he asked resignedly.

"We let the strangers pass and ambush the Devils."

"There are six of them."

"By the time they know we're here, there'll be fewer."

"So you say." He tested his bow.

Obscured by brush, the strangers crashed headlong past on their left. Hurrying to intercept the warriors, Gan and Clas simultaneously spotted the clearing the Devils would have to cross. There was no need for words. They took cover and readied their bows.

The Devils poured into the clearing almost perfectly abreast. The first Dog arrows struck while the next ones whirred toward their targets. Of the pair of warriors who survived, one literally hopped in indecision. Clas ended his quandary with another arrow; Gan's flew harmlessly wide as the sixth man, more decisive, was already in retreat, crying alarm.

Gan and Clas ran to recover the horses. Raggar hurried to assure himself Gan was all right before he and Cho took guard positions to the rear.

The fight continued to rage behind them as Gan and Clas easily traced the heedless flight of the strangers. A steep slope marked the limit of the flood plain. The undergrowth was heavier at the edge, much thinner uphill. Gan elected to stop just above the thicker belt.

Looking back, they saw the Olan cavalry quartering the far end of the plain, more interested in driving off the remaining Devils than in running them down. Clas growled disappointment at their lack of aggressiveness. It left survivors to pursue the strangers and the stolen horses.

A sapling bearing a white flag poked up from the defended mound. A stranger came out, carrying it in one hand and a slightly different-looking weapon slung over his shoulder. Tucked under the same arm was another object that looked like a black board.

The Olan cavalry troopers moved closer. The flag bearer turned his back on them, trotting to the place where the couple Gan and Clas saved had been hiding. Next he examined the bodies of the fallen women, retrieving their weapons. Then he amazed Gan by running to the Olan leader to tug at his horse, trying to get him to help find the missing pair.

The cavalrymen closed behind him, swords drawn, but the commander ordered them off. The man afoot let go of the horse, gesticulating violently. The Olan indicated the strangers would give up their weapons and come with him.

The man pointed across the river. A Devil there was still holding the original hunting party's horses. He screamed insults at them. Putting the board-thing on the ground, the stranger raised the weapon to his shoulder, looking along its length. Its roar was the loudest of all, and it made the Olan horses caper like goats. The Devil warrior bucked and crumpled. His horses stormed away.

When the Olans got their mounts back under control, the commander compromised. By sign, he made the man understand his people could keep their weapons, but they were to come with him. The stranger picked up the flat thing and shouted. Five more strangers filed out of the brush and immediately fell into an active discussion that could only have been argument. A cavalryman blew a signal on a brass horn that ended it. He was lowering the instrument before the last notes reached Gan and Clas.

Horses and riders closed around the strangers. The lackadaisical hunt for the surviving Devils broke off, and those troopers galloped to join the main body. The strangers strained to look outside their escort, and two of them actually raised their hands above their heads, waving.

Gan and Clas continued their pursuit of the two they'd saved. From a hole between a boulder and the base of a towering fir, one of the weapons pointed at them. Clas backed his horse until he was shielded by a tree. "They found a good place to die. Now what?"

Gan looked uncertain. "They understand the white signal. Do you have anything white?"

"No."

Taking a deep breath, Gan advanced with his three horses in tow. Riding slowly through trees so sparse he might as well have been in the open, he held the led horses' reins out to the right, making it clear he was offering them. Cautiously unsheathing his murdat, he held it between thumb and forefinger, pointed at the ground.

He was twenty yards away when he offered the reins, saying, "For you."

The stranger rose slowly, lowering the front end of the weapon. Gan nearly dropped his murdat. Not only was she obviously a woman, she was *black*.

He was still blinking disbelief when the man came out. He was unarmed, Gan noted, and pale as frost. His voice was soft, full of hurt.

He stepped forward, open hands raised to shoulder height, wearing a pleading expression that practically invited aggression. He took the reins, mumbling something Gan was sure was gratitude. When he pointed back the way he'd come, the woman agreed emphatically, her words mere babble, but the meaning clear.

Clas spoke from down the hill. "I hear Devils shouting down there."

Gan touched his ear and pointed toward the sound, and then at the strangers. Slowly, he drew a finger across his throat. He was pleased to see how quickly they grasped his meaning.

The woman spoke sharply, and the man mounted when she did. Her eyes rounded as Clas and the dogs appeared. His response was no less than hers. He stared, dumbstruck. The dogs sniffed suspiciously, keeping their distance.

Neela and Sylah hurried toward them as they reached the camp. After assuring themselves that neither man was hurt, they sprayed questions at them about the strangers, hardly waiting for answers before asking more. With a boldness Gan found downright embarrassing, they inspected these fascinating, exotic travelers. The newcomers remained close to each other, shying from contact when Sylah tested the texture of their clothing and reached to touch the odd, tubelike weapon. Both Sylah and Neela tried to rub color from Tate's skin, which she accepted with what Gan could only think of as fierce amusement.

Sylah turned from her. "The legends speak of black giants as well as white and yellow ones. I've seen dark-skinned people, but never anyone black."

All agreed it was a marvel.

To Gan, Neela said, "I'm glad you saved them. The story will live forever."

He kept his composure until Sylah favored him with a quiet smile that made his face burn and his stomach move peculiarly. He felt more like a bumbling fool than a warrior.

Clas saved him, reminding everyone that pursuit would be coming fast.

As they organized the column, Clas said the woman should be disarmed. Gan disagreed, and as he was doing so, he noticed that she immediately perceived the subject of the argument. Her reaction impressed him. Without being obvious, she edged between the Dog group and her companion. She never touched her weapon, but she was prepared. Then, when she sensed they weren't talking about her any longer, she relaxed a bit.

Another possible trouble point threatened as Neela saw how the black woman intrigued Clas. However, when he drifted back to take the rear guard, she immediately feigned disinterest in him. When they were ready to move, Gan dropped back to learn the woman's name. He shot a glance at Neela. This time she was much more disapproving. She jerked Sunflyer around and flatly refused to look his way. It irritated him that she'd be jealous of Clas but save her censure for him. It was the sort of unfairness his father had practiced. At least Col had a reason for it; Neela was just thoughtless.

He learned the woman called herself Tate and the man was Jones.

The incident slipped from his mind as he led the column north, and he enjoyed a vague sense of accomplishment. There was more to the Tate person than the awful destructiveness of her weapon, he was sure. She was different from anyone he'd ever heard of, and it wasn't a matter of her color or language or equipment. She gave the impression that she was consciously *learning* all the time.

She would help him. As he'd told Clas, he knew it.

The man mystified him. He was as different as the woman, but it wasn't a difference that gave him any sense of comfort.

And what of the six on their way to Ola?

As the waiting mountains grew closer, mile by mile, uncertainty sliced away at his earlier satisfaction.

Eventually the Dog People would have to confront Ola's dreams of expansion. Would the other six help that kingdom?

He turned to look at the ones he'd saved. What solid, logical reason did he have to expect their help?

His gaze fell on Sylah, then on Neela. Sylah had her own goals; so did Neela. They might help him, but their major effort would be in their own behalf.

And what of Clas? Would his anger over the loss of Col slowly sour in his guts, infect him, turn him against the one responsible?

Gan gritted his teeth. He promised Col he would conquer.

The peaks ahead watched him come. His vision swam, and he saw them as white-headed, ancient men with eyes of ice and teeth of stone. He blinked away the image, and told himself it was the west wind, and nothing else, that made him shiver.

BOOK II

Warrior's Gamble

CHAPTER 28

Awareness that they'd been riding deeper into Devil country for a week pressed against Gan's back like a cold hand. He imagined their best Man-hunters leading the way after them while the rest of the warriors loped along behind. They were probably hoping he'd have them urge the horses to greater effort. That would only tire the animals, and they had to retain as much strength as possible. If the Devils closed on his party, enough energy for a sprint might be a deciding factor.

He looked to the Priestess, swaying with fatigue in her saddle. Even she might share the danger now. The Devils were more superstitious than religious.

He shook his head. Thoughts of her and thoughts of Neela were clouding his mind. They snared and tangled all others.

At the head of the small column Clas rode with deceptive calm, choosing their route. Gan couldn't help thinking of the man's great fall from his proud position to a member of this tiny group split by multiple motivations—some known, some hidden—as well as differing origins.

It made Gan think of leadership as never before. He'd only had a romanti-cized notion, really. One did right things. Others followed that example. Even when he knew Faldar Yan was challenging his father, he'd never genuinely understood exactly what was taking place. He cursed his childish-ness. Belatedly, he understood that many people would tolerate evil if they smelled personal advantage.

Clas waited for Gan to ride up alongside. He had stopped at the war crest, the point on a slope that afforded an unobstructed view to the valley floor. The geographical crest was usually ignored or avoided; it provided a scenic outlook but silhouetted a figure for any eyes that cared to see. Clas gestured to the strangers, positioning them where he could watch them while he conferred with Gan. Tate pointed while talking to Jones, almost as if she were explaining the use of the ground to him. It was an unlikely thought, but the strangers were unlikely in all their aspects.

Clas indicated the distance. "If we break east through that scattering of wildcows, they'll destroy our tracks. As soon as we get into the main part of the herd, we'll go north again, then cut back west."

Gan said, "You feel the Devils behind us, too."

Clas drew a hand across his face. It pulled the skin taut, stretching the tattoo out of shape. The altered features accentuated an air of weariness that Gan knew came more from the mind than the body. Clas nodded and said, "I've been thinking of that, and how the Olans attacked them. Why'd they do it? It wasn't their fight."

"Think like Bay," Gan said. "Even if you believed your sister ran away with your enemies, wouldn't you tell the people you want to be your allies that she was kidnapped? The tribe hunted to the west for us. They must have ridden all the way to that place at the pass summit where everybody trades in the fall. You told me about the big fort there, and all the Olan troops. I'll bet that's where Bay or Likat told the Olans that she'd been taken. The Olans don't want the Devils to get her; she'd be the perfect hostage until Bay could ransom her. Ola wants Bay free to work for Ola, so their cavalry's ordered to find her. When they run into the fight between the strangers and the Devils, they have to interfere, on the chance Neela's there. When it's all over, they have no way of knowing we were in the area. They take the other strangers and leave."

Clas added, "And we have Devils on our tails. If we don't get away from them, none of this heavy thinking means anything." He heeled his horse toward the wildcows at a sharp pace.

As the column moved, Gan mused over how the strangers did their best to move quickly, although it was clear neither of them knew the first thing about riding a horse. They were a mass of contradictions, and Gan wished he had the time—and the language—to speak to them. They were sufficiently relaxed now to exchange a few words, and their speech was unlike anything he'd ever heard. It lacked the clicking nervousness of the Peddlers, and bore no resemblance whatever to the flat drawl of the Olans. There was no trace of the rasping sibilance of the Mountain People, either. He wondered if they might be of the fabled Nions, but doubted that. Every story agreed that Nions were the color of good bronze and their eyes slanted.

He urged his horse forward to get a better look at Tate. Her eyes were different, but not much. She was aware of his scrutiny, he could tell. She refused to turn and acknowledge it, but there was a stiffening in her bearing. He dropped back to his position, disappointed by lack of any Nion slant to her eyes but impressed by her character.

Jones, bouncing along, threatened to tumble out of his saddle. Tate moved to support him. He still looked sickly. Gan was further impressed by the way she cared for him, but puzzled. There was no possible explanation for his being unarmed. More, it was disgraceful for him to accept so much attention when he wasn't wounded. For a moment he wondered if the stranger might be diseased. The concern passed quickly. The strangers were different, but no one associated with the ill. Whatever outlandish place they came from, they certainly had Healers to deal with that problem.

He tried to imagine sending a warrior on a mission with such a weakling, and almost laughed aloud when he realized he'd granted the woman the status of warrior; he sobered at the recollection of her behind her rock with her weapon pointed at him. It would be a mistake to think of her as anything less, he decided. There were some like that in the tribe, women who managed to be feminine, yet strong. Neela was a good example. Women like her had occasionally risen to Horse or Dog Chief, although they were never allowed in Earth Heart or men's secret councils. There were several families, though, where the unacknowledged control was a woman.

Neela was a fighter, that was certain. She'd probably never acquire the cunning a woman needed to be a successful leader. Even a man had to have some cunning. A woman who would lead couldn't hope to survive without a double portion.

He nodded to himself in time with his horse's stiff-legged progress down the last few yards of steep slope to the valley floor. Looking around, he caught Tate adjusting her weapon on her shoulder. Without the thunder and lightning crashing around it, it was coldly sinister. Its smooth surfaces and joinery were awesome workmanship, but it lacked the heart-feel of a good sword or knife.

Clas led through the wildcows, the animals snorting and tossing their sweeping horns nervously as they trotted out of the path of the riders. Their heavy smell thickened the air. It would help cover their passage. Gan hoped one of the bulls wouldn't decide to assert his territoriality. The dash for safety would be hard on the horses, for one thing, and it was unlikely the strangers could hang on, for another.

He wondered if he'd made a mistake in seeing them as important.

They left a swath through the animals that pointed out their course as clearly as an arrow on the ground. When they'd traveled approximately a mile, Gan stopped while the rest continued on. When they were a long arrow shot away, he rose to stand in the saddle. Using his whistle and arm signals, he directed Raggar and Cho to positions where they could drive wildcows back across their trail. On order, the dogs charged, enjoying this work. Shara literally danced with excitement, rising on his hind legs to see more clearly. He held fast beside Gan's horse, though.

When enough wildcows had run across their path to obscure the trail, Gan whistled the dogs back. Clas was already angling north. Looking back, Gan was pleased to see the herd still milling, the agitation of one group affecting another, so the whole valley was alive with activity. Not even a wolf would be able to track through such a mess. He hurried to rejoin the rest.

They continued generally north, not stopping again until late afternoon. Gan took the dogs to inspect their back trail as a precaution. When he returned to report no sign of pursuit, it was long past sundown. Only Raggar's nose saved him from stumbling about while trying to locate the dark campsite. Clas' bed of coals in its sunken cookpit was invisible until one stood directly over it.

Everyone else was already asleep. Clas offered up the last of a steaming soup of seasoned dried beef. Gan savored the fiery pepper-and-salt. In one of the bags beside Clas he found the dogs' dried goat meat.

He imagined continuing such a life, free and unbeholden.

It wasn't the way.

Like the stars above, he had his course.

Wearily, he got to his feet and padded off with the dogs to stand watch.

CHAPTER 29

Tate woke with a start, squinting directly into the rising sun. Unmoving, she watched the distant figure of the warrior called Gan rise and face that direction, then touch his forehead and heart. She assumed it was a religious gesture, and was certain of it when he muttered what could only be a prayer. He turned to walk back to camp, the dogs materializing to follow. She rolled over just as Jones was waking. She told him what she'd seen, asking, "Could it be vestiges of Catholicism? The Vatican's certainly east of here. The practice could've changed to something like that. It's as we were saying last night, whatever they speak, it's got the sound of English—the rhythm and style—even if the words are different."

"It's English," he said. "I guarantee it. It's nothing like we ever heard, or should have lived to hear, but it's what happened to our language when the people who spoke it were fragmented and left to re-create the world."

"This part of it, anyhow," she amended, and Jones agreed.

"Of course," he continued, "I'm sure the English spoken in Pennsylvania now is only rudimentarily similar to the English spoken here. They've had centuries to create accent and pattern, if not actual dialect."

"At least we should pick that up fairly easy," Tate said. "When I think how much we have to learn, it scares me."

"Watch!" Jones alerted her. "The tattooed one's getting up."

Clas performed his morning ritual quickly, unaware of their interest.

"See?" Tate said. "That's what the first one did. It's some sort of morning prayer."

Jones said, "In that case, we should watch the woman in the black robes carefully. I have the distinct feeling she's a religious of some kind."

"Maybe. Forget the two troopers," Tate said. "If they've got religion, it's the kind that says you go to heaven for killing bad guys. I'm aching to know how Gan got that wounded shoulder. And what about Clas, him and his square tattoo? I'll tell you, we had some hard-looking cases in the Corps, but these people make them look like Sunday school teachers. No offense, Pastor."

"None taken, Donnacee. In fact, I've been thinking about what we've seen so far. 'Brooding' might be a better word." He flashed a wan smile. "I'm worried sick about our friends, although they seem to have fallen in with a somewhat more advanced culture. They're certainly not in the company of fugitives, as we clearly are. But the thing that troubles me is that I see no sign of anything but hostility. In fact, every aspect of this world seems hostile."

Wryly, Tate said, "And that goes for their dogs, too. They look at you like they're daring you to make a move. The only thing that keeps me from running from them is the way they mind. I swear Gan can make them do anything. The horses, too—the ones they ride, not the ones they stole from the people who attacked us—they're like an extension of the rider. But those dogs. I never heard of anything like those monsters."

Jones said, "They look like the pictures of the old Irish wolfhounds." At Tate's blank expression, he went on, "There used to be several breeds of giant dogs. People owned cats, too. My parents had a book about it. The Anti-Pet Ordinances eliminated all dogs over fifteen pounds, and all cats. It was when we were just children."

Tate said, "Someone must have had enough heart to keep this breed alive."

The remark brought Jones' head up. "They were useless animals. They ate food needed for people."

"I read about the debates, Pastor. I wondered then if more people was the answer to an overpopulated world. I still do."

"Human lives were at stake; they had to be protected. Would you have imposed controls on births? Who would choose who had children? You? Tell me your criteria."

Angered, Tate lashed back. "I didn't say I had the answers, Pastor. But take a look around; this is what your nicey-nice got us. Are you really that proud of it?"

"Overpopulation was not the only cause—"

Tate grabbed his shoulder. "Our hosts are watching. It's not clever to let them see us arguing, okay?"

"You're right. Sorry. My fault."

"Equally mine. It's the stress."

As if understanding their situation and anxious to forestall trouble, the black-robed woman smiled at Tate, indicating she should accompany herself and the blond girl.

Jones said, "You'd better go along, Donnacee. She's doing her best to be friendly."

Dubiously, Tate rose, and he added, "Some things never change. Ladies still have to have company to go to the powder room." She shook her head in a gesture of tried patience and hurried to catch the others. They seemed a bit uncertain as she joined them, but they were all smiling by the time they made their way around the shoulder of the closest knoll.

When she came back, Jones had rolled up the sleeping bags, but remained in place. She veered off to Clas' small fire. He'd spitted five birds she guessed to be a kind of partridge, and they were sizzling over the practically smokeless heat as Jones approached. She repressed the urge to call him closer; he settled just far enough away to exclude himself, and it was obvious their hosts resented it. Glancing up, Clas afforded him a flat stare before turning a brief smile her way. He pointed at her, then one of the birds, and rubbed his stomach. Tate grinned broadly before squatting across the fire from him.

He touched his own chest, then pointed at Gan, who was feeding the horses grain, and named him. Next, he pointed back the way they'd come. He drew a finger across his face from the right temple across the forehead to the left eye and down to the cheekbone. Even before he closed his eyes and sagged, she knew he was telling her they'd lost a member of their group. She nodded, and he indicated Gan again, then gestured back the way they'd come.

Okay, she thought; back there. The past? Oh—his father. Then Clas confirmed her guess. The word he used wasn't exactly *son,* but it was so close she decided to try an experiment. She pointed at the horizon. "Sun," she said, getting as close to his sound for *son* as she could. Then she pointed at Gan and repeated the word.

Clas stiffened, staring hard into her eyes. She knew she dare not break that contact. Suddenly a torrent of words sprang from him. They carried the bite of angry accusation. At the edge of her vision she saw Gan step away from the horses. He moved slowly, with his hand on the hilt of the vicious-looking sword that seemed as much a part of him as his arm.

Tate forced a smile, tried to appear ignorantly innocent. She cursed herself for leaving the wipe lying beside the sleeping bag. She pointed at Gan and Jones. "Son," she said, then pointed at Clas, repeating it. Then she indicated herself, shaking her head. "No son," she said, and pointed at Sylah and Neela. "No son."

Clas relaxed slowly. He looked to Gan, said something, and shrugged. When he faced her again he wasn't smiling, but the tension was draining from his features.

Trying to reinforce what she hoped looked like unconcern, Tate poured water from her canteen to her aluminum cookpot and sat it on the fire. It had taken a long time to get around to sharing each other's fire, and now that the ice had been broken—albeit not without a bad moment—she was determined to make an impression. She'd seen the way their noses twitched when they got a smell of the combat rations. In a few minutes she had hot water, and she added three packets of freeze-dried coffee crystals, stirred the mix, and offered it to Clas. She got a suspicious look in return, so she took a sip herself. "Not the best I ever had," she said, keeping her tone light and smiling pleasantly the while, "but hardly worth a look like that, you tattooed rhinoceros. I'm not trying to poison you."

He took it when it was offered a second time. His eyes lit up and he grinned like a child at the taste. He handed it back with great dignity, managing a covert glance at Gan. Tate took the hint, calling him and extending the pot. He was less impressed. Clas steadfastly and regretfully refused any more.

When Jones finally eased close enough for conversation, she reviewed what had happened for him. "They're completely unpredictable," she finished, while they accepted their roasted partridge from Clas. "Brutally direct about their feelings on one hand, and refined as dukes on the other."

Jones said, "We're going to have to walk carefully."

"Maybe more so than either of us guessed. I found out this morning the woman named Sylah's a nun, or something. That rose on her left shoulder is her rank. I didn't get the full drift, but unless she's a lieutenant colonel, I've got centuries of seniority on her, so we won't worry about it. The girl's name is Neela, and I think she's under the nun's personal care, maybe on the way to a convent, or whatever they have now."

Stopping his tearing at the small bird, Jones said wistfully, "I wonder where the nearest Protestant congregation is? I'm glad we're not the last humans on earth, but I don't know how I'll respond if I find out I'm the last Methodist."

Tate laughed easily, then fumbled in her pack for a moment, bringing out a salt packet. When she let their hosts taste it and offered it to them before using it herself, the entire party murmured approval. They rationed themselves very carefully, so there were still a few crystals left when it completed the circle back to her. A similar packet of pepper created delighted consternation. They couldn't get enough of it, sniffing until they sneezed explosively, pouring it into the palms of their hands and licking it off while tears of pleasure glittered in their eyes. When Jones displayed two more packets, they clapped their hands in unabashed delight. Clas even accepted another taste of coffee—in celebration, as Tate put it.

With breakfast out of the way, they mounted up once more. Jones moaned in pain as he struggled aboard, and when the horse tried to bite him, he almost fell off in his efforts to avoid the clicking teeth. Once they were under way, Tate said, "From now on, we study the language as much as they'll put up with us."

Jones winced. "Don't you think we'll find our way back to the others?"

"We can hope. And work. We start by learning to talk."

Gan brought up the rear of the column, and he seemed more than simply pleased to have Tate's company. In fact, she thought, he acted as if he'd been waiting for her. The largest of the three hounds was less forthcoming; he paced threateningly close by for several minutes before Gan noticed him and sent him off to the flank. The dog obeyed immediately, but went with many a look over his shoulder. As they plodded along, she spotted him from time to time, always just as the dog flitted out of sight. The female—her name was Cho, she discovered—and the young male named Shara ignored her.

The first hours went quickly. Tate was overwhelmed by the richness of the land. They wandered past immense herds of longhorned cattle, beasts that made her think of history books and cowboys. There were antelope, as well, delicate animals that watched the party until they judged the range was too close, when they'd snort and slip off with effortless bounds, flashing white powder-puff tails.

The cattle were another story. Once, a territorial bull made a bellowing, bluff charge at them. Tate swiveled the wipe quickly, chambering a boop round. When Gan saw her expression and readiness, he nodded soberly, lowering his head and mimicking the head-tossing rush. Then, in a gesture she was beginning to think was far too common among these people, he drew his finger across his throat.

Even as the significance of that signal made her contemplate her situation, she got another example of the ethic of this world. A subgroup of cattle, grazing far to their right, suddenly broke into a bawling stampede. Tate rose in her stirrups to see a tiger overhaul a yearling calf. They went down together in a swirl of dust, and a pair of half-grown cubs boiled out of the brush that had shielded the female. They clawed and bit at the agonized calf like kittens with a mouse, learning their strength and perfecting their technique.

Turning away, Tate was dumbfounded to see the rest of the herd grazing again, although still occasionally prancing about nervously. The bereft mother cow stood off alone, bellowing in helpless loss.

Of the entire group of savages, only the woman named Sylah spared more than a glance in the direction of the kill, and Tate was sure her interest was only to assure herself the tigers were keeping their distance.

The incident was an insight into more than the harshness of the land. It revealed the core of her new companions.

They understood survival.

They understood predation.

If she and Jones were to survive, learning by itself wouldn't save them; they must understand.

By noon she'd acquired a vocabulary of several nouns and verbs. She tried them on Sylah, who enjoyed her efforts so much she laughed till she wept. Neela was polite and distant.

The midday meal apparently had no name, nor did breakfast or dinner. When Tate and Jones indicated three meals, the savage party agreed unanimously that this was their custom, but for each event they used the same word. Jones explained. "I guess they don't differentiate that much—food's food. Always has been, always will be. Seems to me I remember a Chinese greeting that went, 'Have you had rice?' They didn't have a hello, and as far as they were concerned, when you said rice, that meant eating. Period."

Tate said, "Speaking of words and meanings reminds me—I believe those longhorns are called 'wild cow.' I'm going to do an experiment." Hands to her head, forefingers extended, she tried to pronounce the word as she heard it from them, with an almost aspirated *w*, the *i* hard, and the *cow* similar to "goo." Their companions laughed, but they applauded and nodded.

"Beautiful." She hugged herself in accomplishment. "It's coming together. We can work out a pronouncing guide between us, and then we'll be riding high."

Jones moaned, rubbing his rear. "If it's all the same to you, I'd rather not ride any which-way. The cowboy's life is not for me."

Clas watched and listened with a heavy frown. Turning to Gan, he glowered and spoke rapidly. Gan said something that sounded placating, but Clas ignored him.

Jones smiled ruefully. "They really don't like me much, you know. They can't figure me out. I'll be glad when I can explain that I'm a religious person. They'll understand that."

"I'd be careful," Tate said. "They can be understanding, all right, but I don't like the look of these people when they're being tense. You didn't see them when I made the connection between *son* and *sun*. Take it slow, please. Will you do that for me?"

He laughed aloud. "I won't do anything rash, Donnacee. Goodness, my specialty is keeping others from being rash. It's my life."

She accepted the mild rebuke with an understanding smile, but when Gan put an end to the whole thing by saying something that sent his companions moving to break camp, she was pleased to have an excuse to turn away from the anxiety shining out of Jones' tired eyes.

CHAPTER 30

As it ever did, the mountain winter mightily resisted the change of seasons. The late storm shrieked in the night. Its winds clawed at the towering firs. When the fiercer gusts howled through the pass, even the squat fort seemed to lean.

Altanar told himself once more that the vibrations were his imagination, only to have the heaviest blow of the storm ram the building with such strength the roof beam groaned complaint.

He clutched both handles of the copper tankard and drained it almost dry. With his head tilted back, his eyes made contact with those of a trooper manning the balcony that circled the room. The man blinked and spun away quickly. Altanar lowered the tankard, letting his gaze linger, mentally daring the man to peek at him again. When he realized the soldier was too cowed to risk another glance, the disappointment fueled his growing irritability. He turned his attention elsewhere, surveyed his surroundings for the hundredth—thousandth?—time.

The fort marked his border with the Dog People. It was two stories tall, with a first floor of fitted rocks crowned by a second level of yard-thick logs cut from the neighboring forest. The top overhung the stone base, and both levels were pierced with tall, narrow weapon ports along their length. The overhang of the second story was similarly slit, so attackers could be engaged from above as well as frontally. Iron-bossed doors of thick, rough timber led outside. They were proof against any man or weapon, save a battering ram. The power of the wind, however, set them to mumbling in their frames.

The design of the place was simple and defensible, and on a night like this even the spacious major room was cozy, what with a huge fireplace blazing away a few yards from the long plank table and benches that were its primary furnishings. Candles gleamed from holders on the walls. The rich mix of burning wax, the fire, and the faint remaining aroma of dinner's excellent roast would be a perfect atmosphere, Altanar decided, if the accursed wind would give them a moment to enjoy it.

The rest of the building was through the smaller door to Altanar's right. Beyond it, stairs led to living spaces on the second level. Storage and stables occupied the first. To his left, outside the heavier iron-bound door, lay the highland meadow that surrounded the building. Somewhere on the lee side of the fort were the tents the Dog warriors, the captured strangers, and the Olan cavalry shared. Horses wouldn't eavesdrop, so they were all stabled indoors under the fort's sleeping rooms.

For a moment he considered sending one of the remaining interior guards to fetch the interesting newcomers with their even more intriguing weapons, but he abandoned the notion quickly. The fewer eyes and ears involved in this meeting, the better.

Altanar wished the strangers were the only reason he'd come to this forsaken outpost. Bay Yan. He repeated the name to himself as he wiped beer suds from his lip. The informant had described him: "A large man, strong as a buffalo bull, and as dangerous. His dead hand is always on his mind. Maybe that's why there's more cruelty and cunning in him than any of us ever suspected. Be careful."

Of course, the information had to be weighed. What was an informant, if not a liar or a traitor?

Usually both.

His witticism pleased him, reestablished his perspective. His evaluation counted. Others could afford to be wrong. Kings must be right. That was why he dealt with informants and people who had the brains of buffalo bulls.

Bay Yan, an ally. It depressed him.

An unsophisticated savage, a man who equated drawing a weapon with drawing a conclusion.

At that moment the double doors to the outside flew open, driven full wide by the force of the wind. They crashed shudderingly against the stone wall, admitting a blast of air that bent the candle flames horizontal and sent sparks from the fireplace roaring up the chimney.

Only raw shock kept Altanar frozen to his seat and prevented him from embarrassing himself.

Bay Yan stood in the doorway, cloaked in the hide of a prairie bear. The snarling head formed a hood for snow-flecked features.

The moment of fright passed, and Altanar rose gracefully to greet his guest. For the moment, he kept his eyes on the bear head, trying to imagine what the Nion traders would pay for that, alone. He sighed; the coat was worth a fortune. The skill of the Dog People with leather and pelts was legendary, a craft that approached art.

Bay slammed the doors shut, dropping the crossbar to secure them. He walked to join Altanar with a rolling horseman's gait, sweeping off the cloak with a quick gesture. The inner lining was quilted wool; Altanar knew there would be down under that. For all its attractiveness, it required strength to wear something so heavy.

Even without the hide, the man suggested wildness. Altanar found his close-cropped hair amusing, and the gaudily embroidered wool shirt and the equally garish trousers tucked into knee-high boots were bright enough to endanger the eyes. Nevertheless, he felt no inclination to laugh, even when Bay carelessly flung the outerwear on the table and sat down without taking off his boots and replacing them with indoor slippers, as any civilized person would.

It was the sort of thing he had to expect. He resigned himself to an unending string of similar offenses. Surreptitiously, he sniffed at Bay as he settled himself on the opposite side of the table with his back to the fire. He could never understand their to-do about cleanliness; right now he smelled so strongly of herbs it was easy to imagine him sprouting leaves.

He comforted himself with a glance at his own elegant, efficient clothing. The quilted underwear didn't show, of course, but he wished it did, the better to show the savage what good construction was. He stroked the outer garment of intricately patterned knitwear executed in understated gray, black and white traditional designs. He wondered what Bay would think of the cream-smooth fur of his own sea otter coat.

Another gust twisted more groans from the timbers. Altanar gulped the remainder of his tankard and called to the captain of the post, who'd come out to stand by the fireplace. "Have the kitchen scut bring beer."

"Not for me," Bay said.

Altanar shrugged. "Tell her to bring me both, then."

There was no need to repeat the order. The woman, mate to one of the soldiers who manned the post, scurried to the table. The Captain accompanied her, hovering nervously as she served.

Yet again the wind struck the building, the most prolonged thrust yet. The Captain raised his eyes to the ceiling. Altanar started, as well, but when he noticed the Captain's action, he smirked up at him.

"What's this, Captain? Afraid of a little wind?"

The man stiffened. "No, sir. I was concerned for the King's safety. And for his guest."

"Of course." The sarcasm was unmistakable. From the corner of his eye he watched Bay, and was pleased to catch a faint glimmer of approval. That was the purpose of the whole scene, actually. He wanted to impress his guest, but more than that, he wanted to understand him better, learn what he liked, disliked. Feared. Without understanding, one couldn't hope to gauge when cooperation would end and betrayal begin.

And it would begin. The trick would be to get as much use as possible out of him beforehand, and dispose of him before he had a chance to do harm.

Altanar decided to give him a display of true authority. He told the Captain, "Empty this place so we can talk."

The officer stiffened. Altanar looked up, frowning. "Well?"

"Empty, sir? Outside? Now?"

"War Chief Bay Yan and I want to talk; I'm not having simpleminded soldiers listen in so they can bawl their guts out to every whore in the kingdom. Get out!"

The woman put a fist to her mouth and backed away. A ring of white expanded around the Captain's thinned lips. He swallowed before speaking. "It's over fifty yards to the tent. The snow—you can't see—"

Altanar rose slowly to his full height. "One more word, Captain. Just a hesitation, and I'll have you executed to make your rank available to someone who doesn't argue. Must I?"

"No, sir."

"You're happy to obey me?"

"Yes, sir."

"Louder, Captain. I want to hear enthusiasm."

"Yes, sir!"

Altanar dismissed him with a quick head movement and sat down. He took a long draught from his tankard before remembering his guest. "It's always like that," he said. "Give them some authority, even if it's command of a dunghill like this, and they forget who their masters are."

He ignored Bay's sage agreement and glowered in silence as the Captain rounded up the interior guard and herded them into the night.

Bay smiled at the Captain's departing salute. "My men will feel a little less abused when your officer arrives to share the tent with them." He laughed ponderously. "Even I was a little concerned tonight, and we understand snow better than you westsiders. And what about your prisoners? They didn't impress me as being very strong people."

"They won't be allowed to die. Or leave. Not until I know more about them. My cavalry captain insists their leader killed a Mountain warrior at least five bow shots away, and he did it with thunder and lightning. Either the whole troop was drunk or there's magic taking place. In either case, we're going to find out. And use it."

"Against the Devils."

Altanar heard the flat challenge in the statement. He reminded himself to keep his temper. Nevertheless, the man had to be kept in his place. He said, "Col Moondark's escape has created some unexpected problems."

"Col Moondark is dead. He is disgraced. His son and his friend still hold my sister and your missionary hostage, but what problems can such men cause?"

Altanar almost choked on his beer. He covered his confusion with an elaborate show of sipping more.

Why had his informant failed to tell him of Col Moondark's death? It was unforgivable. Unless . . . of course. The man was more clever than he thought. It wouldn't do for the King of Ola to be unsurprised by everything the new War Chief had to say. It was a good move.

Clever Likat, who scouted ahead for his new War Chief.

He said, "My congratulations. I knew only that he'd fled with Clas na Bale and his son, and kidnapped the women."

Muscles bunched in Bay Yan's jaws. *"Only?* You're well-informed."

"Don't be concerned. Troops exchange tales, and I'm informed about what my troops hear. I do not spy on my allies." Altanar stifled a grin, thinking how Bay Yan would scourge his warriors the following day and how the poor savages would wonder in vain whose gossip brought down such anger on them. It would be amusing to see the arrogant scum hop, even if it was just one of their own cracking the whip.

Bay wrapped his damaged hand protectively in the good one and leaned forward. "The half-breed and Clas na Bale will be dead in days. I promise you."

"I don't understand that such men would even try to run away. I hear they're the sort who die facing forward." He held up a hand as Bay Yan attempted to interrupt, then went on. "The day after their escape, when your warriors arrived here with the news of what happened, my captain had the good sense to send a rider to me and a search patrol for the escapees."

Altanar felt obliged to explain how his cavalry troop had heard the sounds of the fight between the strangers and the Mountain hunting party. He covered it quickly, anxious to get back to his main concern.

"Is it possible Gan Moondark will attempt to deal with the Mountain People?"

Bay said, "Not even Gan would try to talk to Devils. Anyhow, he knows nothing of us or our plan. Nor does my sister."

"I hope so. In the meantime I must maintain the appearance of neutrality.

I'm already working to smooth over the incident leading to the capture of those strangers." Bay frowned, and Altanar rushed on, getting his position stated as rapidly as possible. "Nor can I ask you to move, with the Mountains ready to strike at your flank. Or worse, at the people you leave in camp, almost undefended. I can't move against Harbundai without your strength beside me. Until we assure ourselves Moondark hasn't betrayed our plan to the Mountain People, we can't move."

"We had an agreement!" Bay levered himself off the bench, leaned threateningly across the table.

Altanar smiled easily. "I'm not breaking it. I am delaying it. And not because of something Ola did, my friend. Remember that."

"Gan knows nothing! He can't."

"The Rose Priestess was in the main camp of the Mountain People before she joined you. She's shrewd. She may guess our true plan. For now, the Mountains believe I'm working with them to destroy you. Think about them. Between us, you're by far the better hunter; how will our quarry react if it suspects a trap?"

"Charge like a wounded tiger." Bay stared at the table and eased to a sitting position. He massaged his scarred wrist. "We'll be ready for them, but I can't afford to take losses. Not now, not yet. Would the Priestess tell Gan her suspicions? Her vows . . ." He gestured uncertainly.

"Priestess or not, she's a woman, all guile and weakness. However, I have a solution." He drew the words out, purposely lazy, enjoying playing with Bay's straining impatience. "They seem to believe they can hide in the country of the Mountain People while they wait for the opportunity to exchange your sister and the Priestess for safety. Now, I pay certain Peddlers to keep me informed of what they see and hear during their travels. With spring coming, those who wintered away from the sea will be traveling to Ola with furs and other trade goods from the interior. I can send Messengers to intercept them and tell them of your search."

"Messengers." Bay Yan spat the word. "Any time we see them, we expect trouble. They smell out death."

The quick irritability confused Altanar. "But you do see them frequently? I mean, if you need to contact me, there won't be an unacceptable delay? I want the Peddlers to report directly to you."

"To me?"

"Yes. No one must know I have any interest in them, you, or the Dog People. If we don't keep the Mountain People lulled, they may fall on you without warning. If that happened, I'd try to assist you, of course."

"Of course."

Altanar thought he detected a hint of disbelief in the tone, and scrutinized the face across from him, but continuing anger shielded any other expression. He dismissed the possibility as far too subtle for the man as Bay continued, "How long can you delay the campaign against Harbundai?"

"No later than Summer Day. Once the sun starts moving south, our time will have passed for this year. Why do you ask about delay?"

Bay's chin rose. His tone turned defensive. "Never think we avoid fighting. Dog warriors can go to war any time. Our people always have supplies hidden. We don't live our days tied to a plow or a fish net, like you who live on the rain side of the mountains. But honor demands I kill Gan Moondark, and the country of the Mountain People is large, with many places to hide. He could avoid us for a long while."

"Don't worry. We're leaders, working for the future. If we're forestalled by a year, we'll simply improve our plans. Do your best, my friend, and never doubt that I'm with you at all times."

Bay was impressed. He rose heavily. "You are the ally the Dog People have needed. You'll never regret your confidence in us." He left for his quarters.

Altanar watched him go, lifting the tankard to his lips, keeping it there until the door to the sleeping area closed. A most enlightening chat, he mused. Lessons about Likat, as well as the new War Chief. One would think he'd fear the redoubtable warrior Clas na Bale, but he clearly worried most about the boy. Revealing.

Now to learn the why of it.

He glanced at the door Bay had passed through, taking another hearty drink. He muttered, "Uncultured brute," into the tankard's depths, staring at the fire's embers. "If I could depend on the accursed Mountains for one instant, you'd be meat for the crows." He chided himself that talking aloud when alone was the sort of act that triggered many other tongues. He scoffed at the concern; the sound of his own voice was calming, reassuring. And the only other person in the building was Bay, probably snoring his empty head off already. He downed some more beer. "I wonder what would happen if I convinced the Mountains they should raid Harbundai all this summer? Bay Yan's hotbloods would lose much faith in him, for one thing. Maybe enough to get rid of him. Likat's much more manageable." He brooded over that prospect, then rose abruptly, pitching the remaining beer onto the coals. The fire hissed and spat, giving off clouds of steam that smelled of scorched grain and yeast. "No matter what, the escapers have to be killed, and quickly. The more I think about it, the more I dislike the look in Bay's eye when he speaks of the boy. Something about—what's his name? Gan has a hold on him." Again he fell silent, getting up to go around the table and poke at the fire.

Very quietly, he resumed his monologue, the words hardly loud enough for
him to hear. "If you have prayers, Gan, pray the Mountain People find you
first. They'll kill you. You'd prefer that to having my protectors pry your
secrets out of you."

CHAPTER 31

"We'll have to camp nearby for a while," Clas said. His gesture at the
creek was an unnecessary underlining of the reason for stopping. The roaring
torrent was grayish-green with the discoloration of meltwater and runoff. Its
banks were cluttered with brush, and where the course of the creek bent
sharply, entire trees were wedged into rock traps that held them fast. The
party was a good fifty yards from the stream and a hundred feet above it.
The sound was awesome. Gan dismounted and was immediatley aware of an
insistent tremor in the earth. Where the water was shallow, he saw erratic,
almost hidden, movement below the surface and it took him several seconds
of puzzled observation before realizing the stream bed itself, ranging from
pebbles to boulders, was a moving mass, grinding downhill. Spring rain and
thawing snowpack had created an irresistible force.

Gan remounted. "The passes are probably under watch, anyhow," he said.
"We need rest."

Sylah said, "Is this what the Mountain People call Two Bear Creek?"

Clas nodded, surprised. "I think so. You know of it?"

She explained. "A Messenger told me of passes he uses to avoid the
Mountain People. I think at least one of them would be unguarded."

"Could you find one?"

"There are three, north of us. I think I could find all of them."

He smiled approval, then led the way back over the ridge to the slope away
from the creek. As they dropped below the crest, the noise subsided dramatically. The vibration was much reduced, as well. Gan continued to walk,
leading his horse, and he was pleased when the trembling finally disappeared.
He didn't like the way it plucked at him; it made him think of whispered
conversations.

They busied themselves with the routine of setting up camp. The strangers were part of the activity by then, even using a few words intelligibly.
Tate watched everyone else as she carried out her chores, moving quickly to

help as soon as she understood what was needed. Somehow, she and Sylah communicated well, laughing together in easy friendship. Even Neela showed moments of warmth toward her.

Gan moved away to cut a sapling for a lean-to rooftree, grinning to himself. He'd asked Clas directly if he was interested in the black woman, and Clas had nearly laughed himself out of the saddle. When he calmed down, he confessed a great curiosity; she seemed to have a sense of tactics, he said, and he'd noticed she rode trailwise, watchful as a warrior, although she sat her horse with the grace of a bundle of sticks.

Gan trimmed the last branches from the trunk, carrying it to the shelter site. The pole was lashed to two trees, and from the juncture of each end a side pole was angled to the ground. The wedge-shaped shelter went up quickly, roofed with blankets that were then thatched with boughs. The latter were selected from trees and shrubs at a distance from the campsite in order to avoid noticeable stripping of nearby trees. They made two such structures, complete with interior firepits.

With the shelters completed, the women went to collect more boughs and needles for bedding. Gan took Jones to look for firewood. They crossed the ridge and dropped down to the riverbank. Driftwood required no chopping and was free of sap, if one picked properly. By the time they returned, spitted wildcow steaks dripped fat in the flames of the evening cooking fire. A breeze dispersed the smoke well, but when Gan walked downwind, the smell of the camp and its cooking was thick for a hundred yards. He moved on a bit farther for his watch position and turned slowly, marking those things that would give him bearings in the darkness.

When he arrived back at the lean-to, Sylah was in earnest conversation with Clas, scratching in the dirt with a stick, describing the routes to the passes. Gan listened to the river, telling himself it would be at least two days before they'd chance crossing. Unless, of course, they were discovered. If that happened, the river might prove the least dangerous enemy.

Clas called him over closer to listen to what the Priestess was saying. They squatted on each side of her, frowning down at her sketches until Clas had to smile, thinking of children being taught. Tate drifted closer, keeping a discreet distance but making no effort to hide her interest.

Clas' unexpected chuckle broke into his thoughts. Gan looked up to see Neela had joined them and he'd missed an exchange between those two. Again, resentment burned in him. Was Clas so blind he couldn't see Sylah already hanging on his every word? Ever since their first ride out of the Dog camp, the time Clas found the sign of Devil scouts, she'd watched him. Covertly. Quick, soft glances when she thought no one else was looking. Why wouldn't Clas pay more attention to her? She was beautiful. Different.

Why must he go out of his way to charm Neela, as well?

As quickly as those thoughts crowded his mind, so did the feeling of self-degradation. He told himself he was misjudging Clas. He was misjudging all of them. The hurt lingered, nevertheless.

Neela's fleeting smile for him only aggravated the situation. He seethed with complex, contradictory feelings: fear of disloyalty warred with a vague sense of betrayal; anger over her attention to Clas clashed with his need for approval and affection from both of them.

Now, of all times, he had to be clear about everything.

He welcomed the return of Sylah's lecturing voice. She continued right through the evening meal, which was brought to them by Neela and Jones. She repetitiously described routes and landmarks until the food was eaten and the dogs were crunching the steak bones. Gan made her ask questions, and they took turns answering until each could sketch the necessary map. When she reached into her saddlebag and flourished a north-needle, they explained politely they had no use for it. Actually, they were offended. The session broke up soon after.

As he made his way to his post, Gan followed the ridge paralleling the stream. He decided he could afford to sleep for the first hour. The dogs would remain alert.

His conscience warned him he was being derelict, and for a while he almost convinced himself that was the reason he couldn't sleep. He shifted his position, getting away from a rock pressing between his shoulders. The stars were bright flecks that appeared and disappeared randomly as a gusting breeze moved the fir branches. A small owl, the one called the darksinger, quavered up and down through its call. He remembered how his people said it cried so sadly because it read the true heart of sleeping humans, and despaired. It was children's talk, of course. Nevertheless, he sat up.

Raggar's head rose in quick interest as his master spoke. "The man's my friend, more important to me than my own blood." Raggar responded to the tone by leaning away warily, but when Gan stood up and threw a stick into the trees, the dog unobtrusively got to his feet and found a more comfortable distance for his watch position.

CHAPTER 32

The rains came again in the morning. The wind was no factor, working only hard enough to slowly muscle the clouds along, west to east. It was what Gan's people called a buffalo sky, a mass of dark, rounded forms that jostled shoulder to shoulder.

His morning ritual accomplished, he whistled in the dogs, watching the scene above him while he waited for them. He wondered if rain fell on the camp of the Dog People, and who manned his Nightwatch post, and if the man was careful.

For a moment he was very homesick.

The return of the dogs from their last sweep of the area brought him back to the necessities of the moment. Shara trailed Raggar, holding place off the larger dog's right hip, while Cho trotted easily by his shoulder on the other side. It was apparent the pup was still no more than a burden in Raggar's view, and Gan would have sworn Raggar looked exasperated as he padded up the hill. Shara wagged his tail, but made no move to pass Raggar, which was good. It meant the young one was learning. Raggar set the example in all things, including how to get one's ears rubbed without appearing to be eager about it. Gan greeted and petted them in proper sequence.

Raggar affected great unconcern. Gan smiled at the pure fraud of it. He knew if he touched either of the others first, the gray hound's eyes would follow him with dignified reproach until he was satisfied Gan had made the necessary amends.

On the way back to camp he reflected that Shara was learning well. There had been almost no time to work on the pup's training, but he seemed to understand what was wanted, and Raggar was certainly quick enough to let him know when he failed to comply. Still, there was pride in the pup. Gan was sure no other dog would ever be allowed to discipline Shara as Raggar did. Sometimes he wondered if they'd ever seriously fight for dominance. As for Cho, she did her work without fuss. Her quiet strength was a blessing, a reassurance on those occasions when the two males were being stiff-legged with each other. After a quick meal of leftover steak and some soup, Gan went with Clas and Tate to inspect the river. There was no change.

With another day to spend, Gan decided to put the time to use. Signing Tate to follow, he led the way back to the lean-to where he rummaged in his baggage until he located the bundle of twenty sticks. As soon as she saw them she pointed at the bow, then pulled an imaginary arrow. Gan nodded and felt around until he located the small glue pot and the leather packet of hawk feathers. There was a separate, smaller bundle in with them.

Tate took one of the shafts and examined it, then sighted its length, following that with a second, then a third, all the while looking more puzzled. Turning back to Gan, she held a shaft at both ends with her fingertips, rotating it rapidly. She looked a silent question.

Gan pointed out the saw marks at the ends of the shaft, then indicated additional lengths, now missing, where pins had held the rough wood. He mimed the action of a man working at a foot-powered lathe. Tate smiled, nodding understanding.

Next, Gan tied a rock to a piece of cord, then hung it from the end of one of the blanks while he held it with his fingertips at the other end. In a few minutes he had a half-dozen that bent equally under the weight of the rock. Again, Tate looked puzzled, so he patiently demonstrated how a released arrow bends under the impetus from the string. Accuracy required shafts that shared the same bending characteristics.

Taking the hawk feathers out of the leather packet, he selected the one he intended to use, splitting it along the length of its quill with an obsidian chip. From half of each long feather he cut three arrow guides of exactly the same size. It took several arm-waving attempts to make her understand that using pieces of the same feather assured the identical curvature necessary for equal spin rate.

Fixing the guides to the shaft was a painstaking process. Gan smeared the quills with glue from the pot, smiling at her reaction to the stinking mess. He attached the feathers, then swung the arrow over the heat of the fire to set the glue quickly. He chanted the appropriate blood prayer, pleased to see her grow very serious and straighten perceptibly. For a moment he thought he saw a twinge of fear, but decided she was only being respectful.

As soon as the glue was set, he went to his gear again and returned with six new steel heads.

She seemed very excited by them, which made no sense to him. Their own weapons were obviously of steel, and made by a very accomplished smith; why would she be so intrigued by something as plain as arrowheads?

After painting the unfeathered end of a shaft with glue, he forced the hollow cylinder at the butt of an arrowhead over it. While that was setting, he showed her the lightly oiled sawdust at the bottom of his otter hide quiver. The arrows rested head down in the sawdust, which kept the heads from rubbing and dulling each other. The oil prevented rust.

Laying out the arrows to dry fully, he said good night, making a joke of his odd hours. Tate knew the conventional phrase for "good night" quite well, but there was just enough confusion, considering the time of day, to create a comical pause. She made a face at him, and he laughed, feeling a bit closer to her for the exchange.

Jones was waiting when she came out. He fell in beside her, and they strolled aimlessly. She made conversation by telling him what she'd just seen. It was clear, however, that his thoughts were elsewhere. She waited for him to bring it up at his own pace.

He looked around nervously, making sure they were well clear of any listeners, before saying, "This is the first time I've felt free to talk. They frown and growl if you talk while we're riding, and by the time we stop, I'm exhausted. This nervous stomach . . ." He made a helpless gesture. "This isn't the sort of life I was intended for, I'm afraid. Not exactly urban academic. Have you figured out what they're running from?"

"Not a clue." She shook her head. "I'm just glad they saved us from that other bunch. I get the feeling they're not usually this hospitable." At Jones' stare, she went on. "I can't pin it down. Sylah's helpful with language, and she's got so much interest in naming parts of the body, I have to think she's some sort of doctor, or something. The girl's all right, but she can be a snotty little twit when she remembers to work at it. She's got a crush on Clas."

"You're sure? How can you know that?"

She gave him a sideways smile. "It goes like this. I see him look at me, okay? Then I see her looking at him looking at me, and I *know* she's jealous from the tips of her nifty leather headband right down to her fancy beaded booties."

"I saw him watching you, too."

"Curiosity. He can't see either of us as women. Sylah's got him wired. Which means Gan's moon-eyes for Neela may work out yet."

"Oh, God." He lowered his head to his hands, shaking it slowly.

Tate said, "Nothing we can do but keep low. What've you noticed while I was checking out everyone's love life?"

"Contradictions! You tell me their arrow shafts are turned on a lathe, but the points are hand-forged. Nevertheless, they're made of excellent steel. The cast head Falconer found by the river was bronze. The cavalry we saw wore helmets and armor. I'm beginning to think we're seeing the mutated cultures we wondered about in the cave. The people we're with have made a total adaptation to nomadism. The cavalry has to represent a more complex, civilized culture."

"I thought the same thing. About their cultural development, I mean.

Everyone I've seen looks physically normal. By our standards. But they sure don't know what to think of a black person."

"Survivor bands would have bred out any minority racial characteristics."

"They eliminated them somehow, that's for sure." When he turned, she was waiting with a thin smile. She went on, "Do you see anything in these people that's not solid white genes? Do you?"

"The minorities were absorbed, that's all."

"Sure. All I know is, you can joke about being the last Methodist on earth, but I may be the only black on this continent."

He smiled, attempting to be placating, and was spreading his hands to answer when she pushed her face within inches of his, eyes blazing. "Don't you dismiss me! Don't you ever condescend to me! I don't take that from anyone!"

He inched back, very slowly. "I was going to point out we're both minorities here. Your color may even give you an advantage. Your military skills certainly do."

The glare broke as suddenly and unpredictably as the collapse of a wall. The glass-hard eyes were overrun with tears. Even through sobs, her admission rang with angry strength. "Damn it, Pastor, I'm *scared*!"

"So am I, Donnacee. It's only norm—"

"Shut up! I don't want your damned niceness, can you understand that? Just listen to me." She pulled an olive-green handkerchief from her trousers pocket and dabbed at her face. In a few seconds she was back in control. She said, "I thought I knew all about being afraid, thought I'd beaten it. I lied about the cry program. Cheated. They said it was dangerous, but I asked around, you know? And they said it didn't hurt." She paused, wrapping the handkerchief around her hand in an unending coil. "I figured I was committing suicide. We all knew we were going to die in the war, didn't we? And going to sleep beat hell out of being fried or puking your guts out from some bug no one ever heard of. So everybody said I was a hero, and I let them say it. Why not? Now I'm here, and they really are dead, and there's nothing I can do. Except I don't want to die. Not anymore. Not again."

He gently led her downhill until they were on a huge boulder overlooking the raging creek. Only when they'd been there for several minutes did he start talking. "I believe *you* believe what you said back then. Still, deep down, I think you meant to survive. Remember, I came out of a crèche, too. All of us feel some guilt."

Something in his tone brought her head around, speculating. He half smiled. "We're going to have a positive influence here. Contribute to a second chance. I'm sure of it."

"You sound like Colonel Falconer. Or Madge Mazzoli."

"I suppose I do. But think about it. We know exactly what'll happen if the world goes the way it did before."

They were halfway back to camp when Clas hailed them. He gestured for her to get her weapon, but at the quick consternation he created, he only smiled and mimed eating.

"Wow." Tate's tension drained away in the single word. "He wants to go hunting. For a second I thought that other crowd had caught up to us."

Jones said, "So did I," hurrying to keep up. She took two magazines for the wipe. As she checked the action of the piece and her equipment, she spoke with an attempt at casualness that just missed its mark, "I hope you're right about us, Pastor. We have to step lightly, though. Don't do something that'll get me left here alone, you hear?"

"No fear. And we'll be with our friends soon. Things'll look better then."

Her departing smile was quick, the need for physical release hurrying her.

As soon as they were mounted, Clas set a fast pace for the valley floor. Within minutes Tate regretted being included. Riding at a walk had given her some time to get used to horseback, but she was still tender, and the jarring downhill trot was excruciating. At the valley floor, when he indicated they were to dismount, she had to stifle groans.

Clas pointed out an unsuspecting herd of about twenty wildcows no more than fifty yards away. She raised the wipe. He caught it. Shaking the weapon, then touching his ear, he indicated the hills around them and pantomimed others listening.

Tate's mouth was suddenly dry.

On all fours, she crawled along with him as quietly as possible, doing well enough to draw only a few sour glances. They were within twenty yards, she estimated, when Clas inched up to a shooting position. The nervous cattle sensed a predator. The bull, his coat a striking pattern of white splotches on red, circled the cows, nose raised to test the wind. Every few steps he paused to paw the ground. One old cow, her back scarred and one ear reduced to tatters, snorted angrily and searched the brush.

Clas' arrow struck a yearling perfectly, just behind a shoulder, angling forward. The animal bawled and leaped, but even as it started running, the second arrow struck.

Tate was ready to give chase, but Clas stopped her, gesturing animatedly at the bull. It lagged behind the fleeing herd, looking back. As if on cue, it spotted them. With astonishing agility for something so large, it whirled and charged. The closest protection was an old apple tree. They sprinted for it, scrambling up into the branches like monkeys. Sitting there, making faces at the raging bull, Tate changed her mind about the monkey imagery. Monkeys would have better sense.

When it was satisfied they weren't coming down, the bull trotted off, tossing his head.

Tate was surprised to realize how the excitement of the hunt absorbed her. She'd been hunting once before, and it had left her cold. Now she scrambled through the brush, sweating, dirty, eager to find the quarry before Clas, who clearly enjoyed watching her excitement. When they did locate the animal, she suffered a severe setback when it became clear they had to butcher it to transport it. Swallowing hard, she let him show her the best way to create manageable portions.

That done, he demonstrated how to lash the load to a horse so it was properly secured and in balance. Tate was sure she'd seen almost exactly the same thing before, and suddenly the picture was clear in her mind.

In an old textbook, one dealing with mountain warfare, there had been a picture of a man loading a packhorse. The lashing holding the equipment was called a diamond hitch. This was identical. For a moment the juxtaposition of something from her world into this world threatened to overwhelm her.

From the corner of an eye trying to mist over, she saw Clas' gesture. She went to retrieve the bow and its quiver of arrows from where it rested. On the way past her own horse, she stuck the wipe into the murdat scabbard they'd adjusted to fit it. She turned when she heard Clas' horse whinny, and was just in time to see it gallop off. At the same time, her own horse bolted, nearly knocking her down. Struggling to retain her balance, her only thought was of the lost wipe. Literally sick with loss, she twisted around to call Clas.

Between them a bear rose on its hind legs, so massive she froze in stunned terror.

It was concentrating on Clas, who was struggling to hold onto the packhorse. His back was to the bear, and he was totally unaware of its presence. The horse, already giving Clas trouble because of the smell of the cow's blood, had a clear view of the threat. It screamed, bucking wildly, sending meat flying in all directions. The lunge that finally broke it free pulled Clas off his feet, spun him around and dropped him in a sitting position facing the bear.

Daggerlike claws on its waving forelegs glinted. The runaway hoofbeats faded. Then the bear growled.

Motionless except for his eyes, Clas sought Tate. Seeing her empty-handed, his face sagged to disappointed resignation. He moved to draw his shortknife, the hand creeping toward it with infinite slowness.

The three of them formed an irregular triangle. To reach the bow and arrows in a direct line, Tate would actually shorten the distance between herself and the bear. Relying on its interest in Clas, she essayed a tentative step.

The movement gained the bear's attention. When it turned her way, she saw the broken stub of an arrow protruding from its jaw. The entire area was a suppurating wound. The way the tongue lolled out of its mouth, she was sure it was unable to swallow. Maddened by pain and thirst, it wanted revenge on anything and everything.

Swiftly, threatening, it moved to intercept her. When she stopped again, it immediately swung its head back to Clas. It was as if the animal knew which opponent would be most effective. It was in no hurry. It meant to deal with them in order.

CHAPTER 33

The bear charged.

Clas scrambled to meet it, extending his knife. Unable to bite properly, the animal succeeded only in butting him. It was more than enough to send the man sprawling.

Tate raced for the weapon. With blinding speed, the bear swatted at her almost carelessly. The blow caught her back as she ran, lifting her off her feet, driving her forward. The armored jacket prevented the claws from tearing her flesh; still, the blow shocked every part of her body. There was hardly any pain, but everything seemed to stop for an instant, and then the world was drifting past in syrup-slow detail. She dove face first into the ground, and rose spitting dirt and litter, reaching for the bow and arrows.

The bear had Clas down. Even though its jaw wouldn't close, the exposed teeth raked him wickedly. The man hacked and slashed with the knife. The bear's roaring seemed to indicate far more rage than hurt.

Tate had never shot an arrow in her life.

She ran toward the melee until she was close enough to touch the animal. She released the arrow at the juncture of spine and skull. The bear screamed and rounded on her; once again it batted her away. As she wobbled to her feet, cowering, expecting the blow that would kill her, her vision cleared to reveal the animal tumbling about wildly, clawing at the shaft. It rose upright again, extending loglike forelegs and advancing. Clas lay unmoving.

Tate still couldn't focus properly. The bear's image refused to form into a solid whole. She fumbled another arrow into place and shot.

The animal leaped forward, taking her to the ground in a crushing embrace. Hot, fetid breath flooded her nose, her lungs. She tried to scream, but a smothering shoulder muffled her cries. She thrashed wildly until she was simply too spent to move.

Only then was she aware the bear was still.

She opened her eyes. Then the pain came, a crashing wave, and she groaned. Slowly, she managed to work her way free. It took a while longer for her to get on her feet. A drink of water worked wonders. She made her way to Clas. Water helped him, as well, and in a few minutes they were leaning on each other. She belatedly checked herself for wounds, and save for a nasty scratch on her forehead, she was only bruised. Clas was a different matter. One cheek was badly torn, an ear dangled loose, his scalp was ripped in several places, and at least a dozen deep claw marks crisscrossed his torso. She was amazed that the man continued to function.

What came next made her question her reason. He washed his hands from his waterskin, then poured water on the chest wounds, washing away the debris. Once they were clean, he dropped his chin onto his chest and mumbled under his breath. The words were indistinguishable to Tate, as she expected, but there was a singsong rhythm to them that she was sure was a chant. It was an eerie picture, the man sagging as if dying, half singing, half talking, and all the while, blood running down his face and neck from the scalp wounds.

That was when she realized the chest wounds weren't bleeding any longer. The wounds were already clotted.

He repeated the performance with the scalp wounds. Finally, he used his headband to put his ear back in place. By then it was no longer bleeding, either.

With all that accomplished, he set about reclaiming his weapons. Tate could only watch, awestruck.

He examined where her arrows had gone, pointing out to her where the second had glanced off one of the lower teeth and punched upward through the roof of the mouth into the brain. She shivered, realizing how fortunate she'd been; no other shot could have killed the animal so suddenly.

Clas made a fist, grinning approval, then touched his chest over the heart before smearing his hand in the bear's blood. Tate swallowed audibly as he smeared some on both their lips. When he licked his off and made it clear she must do the same, she told herself to think of something else. Her stomach rebelled forcefully, but she managed to avoid being sick.

Next, Clas whistled. Swollen lips necessitated several tries, but within seconds his horse appeared. He whistled again, and to Tate's surprise, the animal wheeled and disappeared. Unable to ask questions, she slumped to

a sitting position to wait for developments. It was only a few minutes before
the horse returned. This time it herded the other two. She could hardly
believe it. She'd had opportunity to admire the training of the Dog horses,
but this was beyond anything she'd seen. Together they moved out to take
control of the animals. She wanted to cry with relief at the sight of the wipe
safely in the scabbard. Then, moving with a pained determination that made
the bear's attack just another unpleasant interruption, Clas started rounding
up the scattered meat and tying it to the packhorse.

He was peculiarly silent on the ride to camp. Tate understood his frequent
sweeping scan of the valley as they rose above it—after all, the arrow in the
bear's jaw had come from a human source, and the group was fugitive. What
was more disturbing was his frequent sidelong glances at her, as though he
was making up his mind about something.

Their arrival at the camp created consternation. In seconds the women
had them bundled into the lean-to and were ministering to them. Clas
ignored their washing and scraping. He not only didn't seem to mind, he
talked animatedly, with gestures. For her own part, Tate resented having to
breathe, because even that hurt.

Sylah worked together with Neela, and Tate found herself in a halting
bilingual discussion of her own treatment as well as Clas'. She was quite
surprised to see that the girl had free access to the woman's medical kit.
Further, she responded quickly to Sylah's instructions, so she was trained.
Tate knew next to nothing of shamanism or any other primitive medicine,
but she'd heard it was supposed to be very secretive and mysterious. Sylah
simply attacked the problem. The only time she appeared to trouble with
prayer was at the outset, when she scrubbed her hands fiercely with boiled
water. She used more of it to bathe their wounds. As each was cleaned, she
smeared it with salve.

Finally, with a flourish, she produced a slim, lacquered box. Tate and Jones
exchanged knowing looks then, certain the magic was about to begin. Instead, their eyes popped wide when Sylah opened it and they saw the array
of tiny needles and the silk thread on its ceramic spool. In response to Tate's
unabashed curiosity, Sylah handed her one of the needles to inspect, while
she nonchalantly threaded another and dipped the arrangement in the
boiling water.

Tate held the needle out to Jones. "Can you believe this? And I'll guarantee you the thread's pure silk."

Jones said, "I have to believe it. Who made it? How?"

Sylah started sewing Clas' wounds. When she coolly pulled together a tuck
of flesh and stitched it, Tate winced. Gan saw her reaction and said something to Clas, who looked away from watching Sylah to laugh at her. There

was a good-natured sound to it, with no hint of scorn. Gan, joining in, mimed cutting his own skin while looking disinterested, then pointed at Clas.

Jones said, "I believe that. The man's got more scars than a cheap golf ball."

Sylah sternly shushed them all, bandaging the repaired injuries with a boiled cloth. Her last chore was to salvage Clas' ear, which she managed with stitches so tiny they almost disappeared against the skin.

As soon as she finished, Clas launched a graphically detailed account of the morning's events. Tate took the opportunity to question Neela about his remarkable recuperative powers. The language problem made it very difficult, but in the end, Tate pieced together the story.

Neela explained about the Siah who rescued the tribe and forged them into a nomadic raider group that started the generations-long trek north. Among other things, he taught that the mind is the master of the body. Much of their tribal medicine and all of the men's hunting and fighting skills centered on that concept. Clas was the very best at it, Neela assured her, and Tate was quite willing to believe it. The memory of the wounds seeming to dry up as she watched was still fresh.

When Tate pressed for information about any particular women's use of those teachings, Neela was reluctant. She spoke as if carefully fencing off areas as safe and unsafe, telling Tate that everything she was about to hear was "woman's mind," deliberately hidden from men. She claimed that many of her tribe's women could avoid conception by what she called cold thought. As nearly as Tate could determine, the principle was to mentally change the womb into a cold, lifeless place, a thing to reject life and creation. (Tate got the impression of a lake, or pond, where the water looked no different than any other, but was unsafe to drink.) All women suffered little in normal childbirth, and some few women not at all.

Neela hinted there were other secrets, things she'd had no time to learn. Tate tried to discover more, but beyond a reference to "women's food," the younger woman would say no more. She made an awkward excuse to leave, and the conversation was over.

Tate made her way to Jones' side, summarizing what she'd seen Clas do. For some reason, she felt obliged to withhold what Neela said of the Siah and women's secrets. She asked him if he saw a connection between controlling bleeding and the pain threshold.

He stroked his chin. "He can obviously control pain well. I don't see how he could do much about his clotting rate. I mean, with sophisticated training and proper equipment, an advanced culture might—just might—approach that capability. These savages? They can't even control their tempers." He laughed dryly. "I'd bet against any such thing."

"It wouldn't surprise me," she said, then paused. "Yes, it would. Everything about these people surprises me."

He murmured a sympathetic response she didn't bother to listen to. She snapped at him without turning. "I'm okay. Look, don't worry about me, all right?" Immediately, she apologized. "Sorry. Tension. A little pain, too. Sorry."

Jones smiled understanding. A slight tug at her sleeve startled Tate. She turned to find Sylah there. The woman acted subdued, a shade apprehensive. She indicated the lean-to with a tilt of her head, then cut her eyes at the Dog men.

Clas was still talking to Gan, gesturing frequently in Tate's direction. Gan appeared to be very favorably impressed. Neela was intent on his every word, as well, but there was a hint of disapproval in her manner. Nothing hostile, Tate was relieved to see, but definitely cool.

By now Clas was pantomiming and speaking at a furious rate. He got to his feet, urging Gan along. The other two women ducked inside the lean-to so swiftly Tate was left standing alone. Clas grabbed her arm as he passed, pulling her with them. They only walked a few yards before they stopped. Facing east across the valley, he struck a pose. His manner of speech changed, as well; he seemed to be speaking to an audience. As a finale, he closed his eyes and folded his arms on his chest, imitating a death pose. When he opened them, he reached for Tate's hand, and before she could do anything about it, drew a scarlet line across her forearm with his short-knife. Startled, angry, she protested loudly, pulling away as he cut himself the same way.

Easy for you, she thought: you don't even feel it.

Chanting in a low, solemn voice, Clas smeared blood from both cuts on the three middle fingers of his right hand. Sylah and Neela made soft, keening noises. From the corner of her eye Tate saw Sylah reach out to pull Jones close to them. Gan and Clas continued to look east in a rigid attitude Tate could only think of as military attention.

Then, with the stained fingers, Clas touched her forehead, then above each breast, and a point just below the center of her rib cage, leaving three distinct spots at each point. He repeated the sign on his own body and stepped back. Facing east himself, he changed his chant to an almost conversational tone, first raising his arms as if in welcome, then folding them on his chest and closing his eyes in the death pose again. He stayed that way for perhaps ten seconds, then relaxed, as did Gan.

Gan came to put a hand on her shoulder, speaking in a slow, dignified tone. She heard her name, and that of Clas na Bale.

Clas spoke again, smiling, despite fat beads of sweat growing at his temples. Suddenly it was pouring from him, as if he stood in an oven instead of a cool forest. He walked slowly to his sleeping place and stretched out. Tate was certain he was asleep as soon as he closed his eyes. However the man's mind denied his pain, she mused, the body still managed to display its need for healing sleep.

It struck her as an overwhelmingly good idea. She barely made it to her own space.

Gan was careful to hide the frown trying to force its way onto his face as he watched them both lie down. It should have been him fighting the prairie bear, not Clas. Now the stranger was adopted; what should have been his own privilege had been usurped by a man he considered his best friend. Clas had even invoked the One Who Is Two, not caring that there were women within hearing. It was almost frightening in its implications. Would Clas feel more beholden to Tate than himself?

He felt cheated. And resentful. Clas should never have put Tate at risk, nor should he have taken a woman hunting. Tradition warned of bad luck, and he almost caused the loss of one of the lightning weapons.

Hours later he was still brooding, sitting near the women's lean-to. Tate's weapon lay beside her. It couldn't do any harm to touch it, he thought. He looked around carefully. Neela was coating the wildcow meat with ash to discourage flies, prior to hanging it in a tree out of reach of animals. Sylah was off looking for herbs. Clas snored away in the other shelter.

He sidled closer until he was squatting beside the weapon. Studying its smooth lines, he felt the power of it pulling him. Almost by itself, his hand stole to it, caressed the solidity of the black part that went to the shoulder. His fingers moved along its surface, thrilled at the cold menace of the steel. When they use it, he remembered, one hand holds the front, and the other is here, in the middle.

He lifted it, marveling at how light it was. His hand closed over the middle, encompassed the semicircular bar that protected the black tongue where it protruded from the bottom. Was it important, like the releasing arm on a rabbit trap? Do they open a door with that, to let the death out?

Something stopped him. Looking up, he met Tate's eyes, the whites luminous around the dark, staring pupils. She, too, was holding her breath. He wanted to set her at ease, make her understand he was merely curious. He pointed the weapon at her, shaking it. Her eyebrows jerked up. Her lips pulled back, baring her teeth. In a flash she pushed the front of the thing away.

It was very insulting. He tensed to jerk it back from her as she gently moved to lift it from his grasp. Then he was suddenly and painfully aware that the weapon had possibilities he'd failed to consider.

Was there a special prayer that held the thundering death caged? Could it strike at its handler if angered?

He put it down slowly, but when he tried to release it, a finger was caught inside the bar around the tongue. He wiggled it to get free.

She made a sound like a mouse, and then she was gripping his hand. Without a word she reached to push at an irregularity on the steel surface he hadn't noticed before. It moved, clicked. When it did, she let go of his hand and leaned back, breathing as if she'd been running.

He started to leave, but she waved him back, kept him there until she stopped trembling. She picked up the weapon and called to the others. Clas woke quickly, reacting to her quiet urgency. Sylah and Neela hurried up with Jones.

When they were gathered, she did something that made the long, narrow iron box on the bottom of the weapon fall out of its cavity. The box was packed with tiny, jewel-bright darts that made Gan think of wasps huddled in their hive. Tate flipped out one for each of them. Jones smiled and refused, walking away.

Neela asked if they could be made into necklaces.

Tate made them understand that the small things were what caused the noise and the death. Neela dropped hers. When Gan rebuked her for being disrespectful of another's weapon, she surrendered it to Tate gratefully. Tate put it back in its iron box, collecting the others and returning them, as well.

Replacing the box in its cavity, Tate demonstrated the other things next, the ones that looked like fat, comical versions of the darts. She imitated the hollow noise of their departure and the crunching, destructive boom of their landing.

Gan turned to Clas. "I have to know more about these things. How powerful they are!"

Clas rubbed his jaw, looking judicious. "Man-killers, that's all. They change nothing. You must find ways to change people, not kill them."

He bit back response. It was just like before. Now it was Clas instead of his father. Always a correction, an argument. He nodded and turned away.

Had he looked back, he would have seen the aborted gesture from Clas, the half-raised hand that beckoned. Uncompleted, the movement turned to a frustrated cutting motion.

The patrol came on the morning of the tenth day, eight Mountain warriors leading their mounts. They drifted up the valley as fleeting figures, visible sporadically through screening forest, then up the bed of the stream that passed the camp.

Sylah hugged the ground at the very crest of the ridge, wishing she could disappear into it. Downhill from her Gan, Clas, and Tate were settled behind cover. Only Clas watched the warriors advance, reducing the possibility of detection to its barest minimum. Sylah watched him, prepared to relay information to Neela and Jones, who were holding the horses downhill behind her. The dogs were off to her right.

Tate moved slightly, catching her eye. The memory of the brilliant lightning dart in her hand excited her.

Magic.

Church eliminated magicians who presumed to be anything more than entertainers. What would Church make of this wonder?

The leader of the Mountain patrol spoke. They were abreast of her, on the far side of the stream—which had settled to a nearly normal flow two days earlier—and he was carelessly loud. The words were indistinguishable, but the sound carried well. Sylah was certain he was bored, perhaps even discouraged. They had the look, hiking along in no particular order, weapons dangling from saddles. True to Mountain practice, they were both gaudy and dirty, their beadwork fraying and their leather outer clothes stained. She shuddered at the memory of the woven shirts and trousers they wore under the leather.

Only one man actually watched the ground for sign. He did it carefully, however.

Two of the warriors started a rock-throwing contest, laughing and jeering back and forth.

She looked to Clas, and her breath caught as she saw his hand clench on his bow. It was an extremely difficult shot, downhill at an angle. Worse, it was unnecessary. They were far better off remaining undiscovered. He had to know that. Nevertheless, her oblique angle brought out the hunter's glitter in his eye.

She leaned forward, willing him to hold. Her movement was enough to divert his attention. He eased the bow as he turned, and when he saw her, he smiled. It was a pale covering for the violence behind it. It drew her and repelled her.

She looked away, back at the warriors.

They continued upstream.

When they were out of sight, Clas moved downstream on their own side to ensure no one paralleled the first group. Gan and the dogs trailed the patrol.

Tate held her place. Sylah moved to sit beside her. Tate immediately made her speak, threw herself into trying to understand. Sylah was amused to realize Tate was directing the stress of the situation in a different direction.

Church taught formally what Tate was doing instinctively; the term was deflection. She remembered the first time she'd come screaming out of a nightmare to find the Iris Abbess, who was a mere dormitory supervisor then, shaking her awake. That night and on several others, the Abbess carried her away to soothe her. In the peace of her room she explained that whatever force affects the mind, the mind can turn to advantage. They spoke of the nightmare, and together they composed an ending that satisfied instead of frightened.

In time, after unending patient coaching from the Abbess, she *believed* that a dream rising up to terrify her sleep-mind was only a challenge to her imagination.

"The mind wants to be well, child," the Abbess had said. "It can do miracles." She'd laughed at Sylah's expression. "Yes—I've spoken of miracles, and that's blasphemy. Now you know a secret about me."

When Donnacee Tate channeled the energy of her fears to concentration on Sylah's words, a spark leaped between them. In hushed tones, as if discovering wonders, they spoke of the plain things around them—the sights, the smells, the textures.

The sun was almost directly overhead when the sound of Gan's return interrupted them. He was frowning. "They're crossing over the ridge, continuing north and east to pick up the next valley. They'll be coming back tomorrow."

Sylah started explaining to Tate what had been said. The woman was nodding understanding before she finished, and Sylah realized she'd caught the gist of the conversation already. She hugged her impulsively, and even Neela, hurrying up, was moved to smile when she realized what was happening.

Clas came in at a trot shortly after. When Gan told what he'd heard, they agreed it was time to move. If the scout party retraced its steps, they'd be reasonably safe. If they came down the campsite side, however, they had to discover it.

The lean-tos were dismantled and all equipment packed on the horses in minutes. Clas disposed of the lean-to poles far downhill in the brush. Gan swept the site with pine-bough branches, rearranging twigs and ground litter. In less than an hour Sylah would have sworn they had just arrived, rather than lived there ten days.

The warriors were less impressed. Gan sniffed at the ground, almost making her laugh, until he straightened, grumbling. "We'll need a good rain to get rid of the smoke and people smell," he said. "Any Manhunter would know who we are and how many."

Sylah thought of the Mountain warrior called Fox. He bragged he could track fish downstream. If he examined the valley . . .

There was no time to worry. Gan led them away. Clas brought up the rear, doing what he could to cover their tracks.

Once they were across the ice-cold creek, Gan stopped, ignoring all of them to look back. When he turned to lead them on, they fell back of one accord, leaving him to his thoughts.

The route alongside the stream was idyllic, an easy grade through trees so massive they shaded out most undergrowth. The party moved well, with the quiet trail sounds of oiled leather, the even breathing of the horses, the scuff of hooves on soft ground. The air, thick with moisture from the water shattering against its rocky channel, was spiced with cedar and fir, laced with the fern-soft taste of high-country spring.

At one point Sylah slowed to ride beside Tate and Neela. As if taking strength from the arrival of her friend, the girl spoke, keeping her voice conspiratorially soft. She used basic words, including Tate in her remarks. "I fear. Gan different. Not right. You understand?"

Tate's gaze drifted up to him. "Understand," she said. "Today new. Yesterday gone; today not same. Never. Gan never same again."

Sylah nodded. She wondered if Tate realized how much that was true of all of them.

Chapter 34

Altanar waited for the crowd in the King's Hall to grow absolutely still, letting the suspense build. He posed, knowing what a splendid scene he'd created for the moment. Behind him, hanging from ceiling to floor, strings of iridescent abalone shell disks swung between him and the throne altar, which was also flanked by twin bloodred screens. Behind the latter, two men with fans kept a breeze flowing across the decorations. The trembling, rotating disks spiked the air with a rainbow of constantly shifting colors.

He wore the ceremonial garb of Guardian of the Inland Sea, a feathered robe of black and white, simulating the killer whale. His black headband featured a spray of filmy white egret feathers. Rings of gold, silver, polished stone, and glass glittered on every finger.

To his right front a timber platform jutted from the stone wall. Musicians perched there like birds, waiting for his signal. There were ten of them, all men, as required for state music. Two faced individual semicircular arrays of drums. Three sat before racks that held suspended gongs, while another stood by an instrument that featured wooden bars of varying size with hollow boxes under each to magnify the sound. There were two copper horns; their players stood on each end of the group. The tapered instruments were at least ten feet long, mounted on rests, angled toward the front entrance. For the occasion, all candles except those nearest the throne altar were extinguished, leaving the firepits to provide illumination. The sweating, nervous faces of the musicians gleamed almost as brightly as the polished metal instruments.

At Altanar's signal, they shattered the silence. The percussion instruments supplied both rhythm and melody, with the horns affording a sonorous base for the music to weave through. The packed humanity trembled under vibrations that seemed to move the flesh on its bones.

It stopped as abruptly as it started.

Altanar signaled again. Troops from his personal guard marched in through the main door. They came in two columns, each a single file, with a four-foot gap between the columns. A drum beat a slow march cadence. The crowd pressed back, creating a passage between the main fires.

The men looked directly ahead, glowing in ceremonial polished breast plates and helmets. They carried swords vertically before them at arm's length. Classic in line, the weapons were austerely plain. Their simplicity failed to lend them elegance, managing only an image of brutal efficiency.

There was a break in the twin columns after the first twenty men. Falconer, Conway, Leclerc, Anspach, Carter, and Bernhardt entered as a group. They were followed by more guards. The second element of soldiers carried the wipes and Falconer's sniper rifle, but the strangers still had their pistols in hip holsters.

People pushed forward for a better look. The pressure of the scrutiny struck the group like a physical wave, collapsing them against each other. Falconer's head came up and his back straightened. He spoke sharply to the others. By the time the troops were peeling away to each side, leaving the six centered at the kneeling board, the prisoners were considerably calmer, respectful in manner without any indication of being cowed.

As the last guards reached the walls, Altanar stood. Music burst from the orchestra again. The six knelt.

When the music stopped, Altanar spread his arms. In the deep, straining voice of ceremony, he said, "Leaders of Ola! You think you have been summoned to a celebration feast in order to see prisoners from a land so distant we know nothing of them. The King alone knows what will be done and what will not be done. You have been summoned to a feast, but not to see prisoners. Altanar has no need of prisoners. His needs are those of his people."

He clapped his hands, and one of the guards carrying a wipe broke ranks, trotting to the kneeling rail where he dropped to his knees, bowed his head, and offered the weapon with both hands. Altanar stepped forward and accepted it. The man retreated to his position.

Altanar raised the weapon over his head. "Why would a king bring his most important men to stare at six people? Three are women, not even Healers, not even Church. Would Altanar embarrass you with such a mean reason for a feast?"

This time the pause was broken, first by a cry of "No!" and then by a shouted, "Live, Altanar!" Another voice joined in, "Why are we here, King? Lead us: We follow!" The shouts blended into outright cheering, and Altanar basked in the growing volume. At the first faint slacking of the sound he immediately gestured for silence.

He signaled Falconer to stand. When he rose, Altanar waved him forward, and the entire room gasped as Falconer stepped over the kneeling board. It was a liberty reserved only for specific, defined occasions. The gathering reacted with stunned silence.

Falconer accepted the weapon with a respectful bow, taking a position to Altanar's right front. He broke the weapon open, inspected it, and snapped the piece together. The metallic clatter echoed in the watchful silence.

Altanar said, "You will see the power these new friends have put in the hands of your king, who will use it to bring you wealth and authority beyond your dreams. Behold your future!"

Falconer waited as a drum sounded the signal for another detail from Altanar's personal guard to march in. The first men carried planks, fully two inches thick and three feet long. The second group staggered under the weight of a huge ceramic urn on a litter that resembled a stump-legged table with handles; water sloshed out the top of the urn. A third group carried still more planks. In minutes they had them all lashed together, creating a wall in front and back of the water container. Their work completed, the troops cleared the crowd away, leaving the odd construction standing alone.

Smoothly, Falconer raised the wipe and fired three rounds in as many seconds. Splinters of wood, geysering water, spinning bits of ceramic all flew away from the impact. The plank that was Falconer's aiming point snapped its lashings and danced crazily before falling to the ground. The rest tumbled over wearily. Noise roared from wall to wall and back again.

The throne hall erupted. Men trampled each other in a rush for the door. Screams replaced the earlier cheers. Guards, the normal hall troops as well as Altanar's personal detachment, shouted and flailed about with the flat sides of their swords to restore order. Altanar, laughing hugely, signaled the orchestra again, and the familiar, reassuring rhythms began to affect the panicked crowd. The sight of the troops forcing a passage for slaves burdened with baskets and litters of food was the final calming step.

Healers slipped in behind the slaves, hurrying to the sides of the injured, tending to the few who still lay on the floor. More slaves loaded the worst cases on stretchers and hurried them out.

Altanar, holding his hands out toward the hall, shouted for attention. When he could be heard again, he said, "These men are wards of the King. They will live with us and be afforded the highest respect. You will consider the women as important as Healers, sacred as any raised in Church. Altanar withdraws to celebrate his triumph and make thanks. Celebrate! We conquer!"

Still smiling for the crowd, he spoke quietly to Falconer. "My guard will bring you to me. Wait with the others."

Falconer bowed, then moved to rejoin his companions. Leclerc was smiling. "That woke them up, Colonel. You should've seen Altanar. Even when he knew what was coming, he nearly jumped out of his fancy costume."

"I wish we could have put on a different demonstration," Falconer said. "Simple firepower isn't a good example. We've got to run out of ammunition someday, and using rounds for a sideshow is a terrible waste. We can't afford it."

"You didn't have much choice," Conway said. "He's in charge, as you said."

"We've got to get better at getting what we want."

Anspach said, "I agree, but I think we have to keep reminding ourselves we're in an extremely sensitive position and not push too hard. We especially need better language skills."

"I'd say that was where we've excelled. Especially you."

"For all the good it'll do her." Carter's features were as bitter as her words. *"You're* saviors. *We're* women."

Falconer said, "He said you're important."

"You didn't hear him say equal, did you? And you haven't been exposed to the 'ladies' of this so-called civilization. They sell women here, Colonel."

"I know that. Don't attack me, Carter. And don't attack them, either. We could go from privilege to prison in seconds. Would that make you feel better?"

Before she could answer, a man from Altanar's personal guard was at Falconer's side. His steel breast plate was engraved with the stylized bear of an officer. He grinned broadly at them, tapping the design. "The King ordered. Captain, his guard. For find you." He spoke very slowly, not ready to trust the growing fluency of his former prisoners.

Falconer said, "I'm glad, Eytal. You're a good soldier."

They followed him through a side door, where a torch-bearing slave waited to light their way. Outside, they proceeded along a gravel path under a roofed walkway. Altanar's palace was fifty yards away, its upper levels looming above a surrounding torchlit stone wall. The dim illumination gave the mass a brooding, suspicious air, and the few windows that gleamed with internal light seemed to glower at the darkness. Guards at the massive timber-and-iron gate passed them through the smaller pedestrian doorway. They were actually penetrating the wall at that point, with another gate at the end of what was essentially a tunnel. Above them was a false ceiling of more stone, pierced with slits. An attacking force that broke through the outer gate still had its twin ahead of them—and archers directly overhead. The entrance was a death trap.

When they were through the second gate, everyone unconsciously straightened. Their pace slowed.

The palace's design was similar to that of the mountain fort, although on a much larger scale. The lower wall of stone was fully twenty feet high, too smooth to offer any foothold. Like the fort, it was designed for defense, with arrow ports in the overhang as well as in the facing wall. More guards ushered them through the actual doorway, a six-foot-wide affair of cedar planks a full ten inches thick. It was deeply carved with a representation of salmon.

Conway indicated the workmanship as they passed. "Has anyone else been surprised to see how closely this art resembles the ancient Indian art from this part of the country?"

The answers were more revealing than conversational. Anspach merely remarked that she knew nothing of Indian art. Bernhardt barely glanced that way, mumbling obscurely about violence everywhere. Leclerc wondered if it could have started with an attempt by the original survivors to establish a common past. Carter sneered that simpleminded imitation was the best anyone could expect from barbarians.

Another slave waited inside. He wore the robe of the King's household, a yellow woolen tube that reached from high collar to the ankle, with long sleeves. He pointed at their feet, shaking his head. Grumbling among themselves, they bent to remove the offending boots. Each of them already sported the customary belt-slung shoebag of the Olan upper classes. The boots went in, and the rolled up, delicate doe-hide slippers came out. Properly shod, they were guided along a hallway past several rooms.

Altanar himself opened the door at the knock. Rid of the cumbersome costume, he greeted them in a richly embroidered tunic and trousers. He gestured the group inside, then proceeded to a table where he unrolled a map. Torches in wrought-iron holders stood at each corner of the table, providing plenty of light. In addition, a fireplace crackled just beyond it. To help the flames repel the chill of the stone walls, the two long walls of the room were hung with heavy tapestries depicting hunting scenes.

Altanar waved a hand over the chart, beaming pride. "The world," he said. "Years of work, hundreds of reports." He punched with one finger. "Kos." There was smugness in the word. "They think we know nothing of their land, but we know all."

Falconer bent forward eagerly, and then he paled. "If this is accurate, the Bay area's been completely altered. Look, here—the whole southwestern coastline looks different."

Anspach touched his arm. "Burl, don't think about it. Remember—" She failed to finish the sentence.

When he looked at the pain in her eyes, he nodded briefly. "You're right. Probably no one we knew was alive to be affected. Maybe no one at all was alive." He massaged his temples. "My mind keeps leaping from time to time. I'm sorry."

"Speak so I understand." Altanar's lips were ringed by a white line of control. His lower jaw jutted.

Falconer bowed, apologized. "King Altanar surprises. We think only we know the south lands."

"You know? You from north, east. How know Kos?"

"Our king send people like us here." Falconer indicated a southward course down the eastern side of the Rockies. "No go to Kos. Other people speak Kos."

Suspicion clouded Altanar's renewed smile, but eagerness overwhelmed his reservations. He bent over the map, gesturing the group close. "Here, Harbundai. Generations we war for Inland Sea. *My* sea. This summer, kill all. You help." He pantomimed raising a rifle to his shoulder. "Boom! Harbundai." He laughed, then turned to the map again.

For the next hour he lectured them on the explorations and spying expeditions that went into creating it. In some cases, he was able to point to a blank space or an area only sketchily covered and give the name of the spy who'd died attempting to garner more information. He also had an exhaustive knowledge of the politics and the strategic and tactical significance of the geography of the vast area. Conway caught Falconer's eye, and they exchanged looks indicating renewed respect for the man.

A knock on the door interrupted him, and he shouted for the party to come in. A female household slave entered, head down, looking at nothing beyond her next step. Altanar's eyes narrowed and he pursed his lips. The combination hollowed his cheeks, accentuated the sharp features. "You dare? You knew I was busy with guests."

"The gift woman, King. You left word."

"Oh. Yes, I did." He turned back to the map for a moment, irritable and indecisive. Then he smiled at the men. He explained, with gestures. "A custom. Spring. Tribes give gift. Woman for king. Live here until with child, then go home. King's blood mix with all tribes."

Carter's voice crackled with restrained temper. "The women choose to do this?"

Altanar answered the question, but ignored her, speaking to the men. "Holy. Too important for woman mind. My Master of House selects."

Carter said, "Where we come from, men who get women for other men are called—"

Falconer grabbed her arm and barked her name. She turned on him, her fury momentarily stilled by shock at his roughness. Slowly, control returned to her features as he lectured sternly. "You forget yourself. Women have their place here. *We all do.*" Then he apologized to Altanar. "We never discuss such things, King. My friend is tired, almost speak secrets of our people. Please forgive."

Altanar's languid wave fooled no one. He indicated the slave. "I leave that to guide. Stay as long as you like."

"Thank you. Before go, King—your men find our friends?"

"Killed by Mountain People? No. You must be very glad my men saved you."

"We are, King. We thank you."

At the door, he offered them a sly smile. "Gift woman is Lapsa tribe. Very religious. Tomorrow, I be very tired."

He smirked his way out of the room and Bernhardt opened her mouth. She caught herself, glaring at the slave before turning to stare at the fire, muttering under her breath.

Falconer returned his attention to the map, becoming very thoughtful. Finally, Carter could contain herself no longer. "Thinking up ways to help your friend, Colonel? Some interesting perks, right? Maybe if you do a good job you can help with—"

He whirled on her. "Shut your mouth." The others stiffened at his vehemence. Carter's eyes flew wide open. When he spoke again, it grated as if the words were dragged through the stone of the surrounding walls. "I despise this man. Nevertheless, he holds our lives. Our only hope is to be useful. That is exactly what I intend to do."

Leclerc was suddenly tugging at everyone's arms, glancing at the servant, who remained fixed in place. He worked the group into a tight, confidential circle and said, "Look, Colonel, we all have to know where everyone stands all the time."

Falconer nodded. "You're right. I'm sorry, Janet; I shouldn't have turned on you. Look, we can't stop Altanar. We can't even slow him down. We *can* look for weak links. We've all remarked already on the stress between him and the local Church, and did you listen to that cheering during the ceremony in that hall? Those were shills getting the crowd going, I'd bet my life on it. He's feared more than respected. Still, his army's good, and it's apparently loyal. I don't know where we'll find advantage, but until we do, we work for him. At least, it has to look that way."

Conway was dubious. "We're mixing in situations we don't even know about. What if he loses this war he wants us to help with?"

Falconer's smile was as raw as a fresh scar. "We've already been mourned, Matt, and the people who did it have been dead for hundreds of years. What's left for us?"

In his quarters, submitting to the ritual undressing and inspection by the Healers of the Lapsa tribe, Altanar stared unseeingly at the portrait of his father on the wall. It was unbearably degrading, but the Laws gave them the right to ensure the King was correct in all particulars.

He didn't mind this time, he decided. In fact, it emphasized his irritation, and made his decision easier.

These things were never accidental. He was sure of that. Every time he had to take an unpleasant action, something happened to irritate him. What could that be, except a message from a greater power? The One in All might not speak to him directly, but surely messages were there to be interpreted. He was fortunate to be able to see them so clearly.

The one called Falconer was too observant, too quick, and far, far too much in control. The others didn't always agree with him, but they listened to him. He had the ability to understand what was needed, and what the group capability was.

He was a leader.

He would have to be eliminated.

The Healers brought in the gift woman in the traditional sheer collar-to-knee robe that proclaimed modesty, but only heightened sensuality. She was a delight, a beauty. More than the Master of the House had said. And shy. It was always so much more pleasurable when they trembled and pleaded reluctance. If she were as exciting as she promised to be, he decided he'd give her to the Master of the House for his own enjoyment, once they were sure she was pregnant. He was always grateful, and there was no sense in wasting her.

He made a mental note to take it up with the Guard Commander in the morning. Along with the Falconer matter.

CHAPTER 35

Gesturing at the wall, Altanar next held a warning finger to his lips. The Iris Abbess, barely visible in the gloom, moved gingerly in his wake. The dank stone of the passageway seemed to emit a presence, something just beyond vision, waiting to clutch at her. Dampness tormented her aching joints, and the irregular floor conspired to trip her. Stumbling along, she was constantly obliged to keep a reluctant hand in contact with the clammy rock. Nevertheless, she kept her gaze fixed on Altanar's back; it was better than seeing the scuttling creatures her fingers occasionally disturbed.

In the wavering light of Altanar's shielded candle, she saw his brittle expression, the one she knew from bitter experience that meant he was one phrase, perhaps one word, from fury.

Banishing that concern, she stretched to fix her eye to the peephole when he indicated it to her. Her face burned with embarrassment. That, in turn, brought a rueful smile that barely moved one corner of her mouth. Here she was, ashamed to be spying on the strangers, and she'd spent her life spying on the man who ordered her to do it.

They were arguing. She wished she could better understand their outlandish tongue. Trying to learn it through occasional conversations with the women and covert lessons from the slave girl seated by the door was little better than useless.

Suddenly the stranger named Anspach was looking directly into her treacherous eye as if she would read everything in her soul.

The Abbess shrank back with a muffled gasp.

Altanar smiled, then whispered. "Unnerving, isn't it? If someone glances at the elk in the tapestry, it's as though they were looking directly at you. Be easy, Abbess; they see nothing. Now, pay attention. Eytal is coming."

"The Captain of your Guard? The one who rescued them?"

"I rescued them, Abbess. Captain Eytal discovered them and made them prisoners. I declared them my personal wards."

"Why am I being made aware of any of this, King?"

"Listen. And look. Explanations later."

The slave opened the door at Eytal's knock. The group waved him over to join them. He said, "The King said I stay with you. Guide. Help with language. You understand?"

They reacted with signs of pleasure, and the Abbess turned at Altanar's touch on her shoulder. He pointed at his eyes and ears, then beckoned her to follow.

They left through the same door they'd used to enter the passage, and this time the Abbess saw the tunnel led in the opposite direction as well, disappearing in darkness. She shivered at the implication. How many times had her conversations been watched, listened to, in this building? Were there any rooms that weren't open to observation?

She wished she knew nothing of what she'd been shown. Experience had taught her that ignorance—or the appearance of ignorance—was the surest survival technique in Ola. Knowledge was power, but accumulating it was synonymous with climbing a tree; the higher one went, the farther one saw, but each upward gain made a single misstep all the more deadly.

Awareness of the passage in the walls was the sort of rotten branch that could bring her to a fall.

Torches brightened the room they entered. Smoke curled up to the ceiling and disappeared through ventilation vents. She envied its escape.

Altanar settled onto a large, soft leather cushion that molded itself around his weight with a gusty sigh. He waved the Abbess to a similar seat. Mindful of the abuse inflicted on her joints and muscles by the dank passageway, she chose a hardbacked chair instead.

Her careful posture amused him. "How prim you look, Abbess. As always. Which is why you're here. Propriety. The moral influence on my ambitions. Which is why we're going to be closer allies than ever before."

She raised one skeptical eyebrow, and Altanar laughed. "This time we have exactly the same goals, if not the same reasons for them. Captain Eytal is bait in a trap. If these strangers are going to trust any of us, it's going to be the man who accepted their surrender. Eytal took their word, let them keep their weapons."

"I understand nothing of trapping and baits."

He chuckled. "You've been snaring souls longer than I've been alive. You're the cleverest person in the kingdom, next to me. I mean to keep it that way. I must know *everything.*"

"What use am I? Surely, with Eytal providing you information, plus—"

"I've kept them all together here in the castle long enough. I want them separated. The women will stay with you at your abbey. Cultivate them. What they confide to you will be matched against what I learn from the men."

"My king! I'm as loyal as any, but you ask me to prostitute my vows. I cannot."

"Of course you can."

She'd been prepared to fight and surrender, conceding what she must, trading off for privileges and allowances. The very mildness of his reaction thoroughly frightened her. He went on in a similar tone. "These people trouble me. You should be more worried than I. Item: Their language is incomprehensible, yet there's a ring of familiarity that tickles my ear. The next time they speak, don't try to understand, but *listen*. Item: The power of their weapons is wonderful, yet they're surprisingly shy about exercising it. Questions: How much of this power do they actually have? Does it only last a certain time, like oil in a lamp? Can they create more after they use what they have? More questions: Why do I doubt they came from this distant kingdom to the northeast that none of us has ever heard of? Why am I sure they know more—and less—than they reveal?"

"They seem to want to be cooperative. They understand they must serve you."

"Everyone knows what's good for them, Abbess. Including you. But you surprise me. You've talked to the strangers; haven't you been curious about the two who disappeared?"

"I thought little about it."

"Unlike you. And a mistake. They said one was black. I never heard of black people, except in the legends of the giants. They also said one was a man they called Pastor Jones. I haven't heard him called Pastor for quite a while, and I'd swear they stopped just after one of your Healers spoke of Church and its insufferable assumption of supreme authority in all matters of religion. Does that suggest anything to you?"

She shifted in her chair. Her strength wasn't what it should be, and in the face of younger, harsher pressure, she knew she was crumbling. What had she missed? What difference did it make what they called the man, then or now? She was suddenly less troubled by pain than an overwhelming weariness. She wished she could go home. She said, "I don't know what a Pastor is, King. Should I?"

"Someone should!" His sudden lurch to his feet set her back against her chair. He leaned into her face. A wine-purple vein squirmed under his right eye. He said, "It has to be religious, old woman! We have our conflicts, you and I, but between us we control this kingdom. These people have brought in a new religious figure, and it's a *man*. Think of that, Abbess—a man with the killing power of these strangers and who speaks for the One in All. Church has been women's strength. If Jones lives, the seed of your destruction may have arrived. That is why you'll be the closest friend these women have." When he was silent, she wanted to believe he was finished, but a corner of her mind warned her to hold her tongue, to wait. It was well she did.

"If it's in your mind to object, let me point out your own judgment is open to some question just now. You chose Rose Priestess Sylah as missionary to the warrior tribes. What if your runaway Rose Priestess has aligned herself with this new religious figure? These strangers we have here may be our only defense against the man Jones. I want them bound to me, if at all possible. If I can't have that, then I'll have the answers to their powers. We must be patient. Observant. Do you for one heartbeat believe they've shown us *all* they can do? No, Abbess, they have even stronger powers they're holding back, to unleash on us if we frighten them. I'm sure of it."

He struck a fist into a palm with such sudden vehemence she flinched and almost cried out. Unaware, he continued. "If I have to, I'll risk it. They're human. My protectors will bring them under control. Once I own those weapons . . ." He let the thought trail away, then spun to point at the Abbess. "You will immediately demand that Church cast out Rose Priestess Sylah. I want her here."

She rose, drew herself erect, denying reawakened pain and the beat of a heart so agitated it was practically a flutter. She said, "The weight of responsibility makes you question the complete loyalty of one such as me. I understand that what the King needs, Church needs. Every word and suspicion will be reported to you. The matter of the Rose Priestess will be attended to. May I withdraw?"

He waved her out.

In the long corridor the hall lamps made her shadow a lying silhouette that transformed her halting progress into a carefree dance. It wavered and flowed, pain free, first leading, then falling to nothingness, only to pop up gaily and follow. It taunted her mercilessly.

Angrily, she denied the possibility that Sylah could betray her or Church. Nevertheless, she was very glad Sylah couldn't identify any contact in Harbundai, but only because any torturer would force her to reveal one, in time.

There was no similar protection for herself, though. She'd treated many who'd endured questioning by Altanar's protectors. Sometimes she imagined she heard their moans in the sea winds of winter, sometimes caught herself with her head cocked, momentarily immobilized by the suggestion of their screams in the shrieks of gulls. Walking a storm-lashed beach had been a treasured pastime before she became a Healer.

And Altanar had forced Church to deliver up a sister once before. It had been long ago, and she'd always suspected he faked the charge to show his strength.

Many times she'd compared that long-dead sister with Sylah. The woman broke, of course; confessed to anything and everything. On the execution stage, though, she spat on the swordsman and declared herself innocent. She died cleansed.

It was the way that sister carried herself at her last moments—the Abbess thought—she and Sylah had the same carriage, the conscious pride and life defiance in even the smallest tilt of the head.

She stopped abruptly, frightened, no longer interested in bravery, but remembering instead the woman's groans as the protectors lifted her onto the execution stage.

If Altanar got his hands on Sylah, his vengeance would rain on everyone connected with her.

The Abbess looked down at her bent hands, tried to make a fist and grimaced, stopping before the gnarled fingers had moved a quarter of an inch. There was so much pain already. Could she stand any more? For how long? And—most shattering question of all—to what purpose?

The door leading outside was across the entryway. It seemed a thousand miles too far. Leaning against a convenient statue, she used the chant to clear her mind.

She turned to the present.

So Eytal was an informer. Very well. She wished she could tell Altanar to his blustering, arrogant face that the mousy servant woman had her own value. "Barren trash," he'd called her two years ago when she failed to conceive his get. How little he truly knew, much less understood. Someday he might learn that the girl cheerfully chanced execution to procure and eat the herbs that guaranteed she'd never bear any child of his. The women of her tribe secretly whispered her name with awe and pride, embracing her courage as their own.

The guard opened the door for her, and she stepped out into the night. Her feet were sure on the path. Church's great goal was still attainable. The plan to achieve it was threatened, but only at its shallowest level. All would go forward again when the time was right.

The Old Book of First Church said: No mystery is so great that it cannot be solved by Church, as Church is the mother of all mysteries. Her stewardship will be challenged, her servants oppressed, her holy places crushed to dust. Yet will she rise, and one among her many will illuminate the truth again, again, again, so long as humankind exists.

Time was not the issue. Nor pain. Nor even life.

She pictured Sylah's face for one brief moment, saw again that commitment, the blue-fire eyes that burned into a future she wanted and feared, as women have always wanted and feared a birthing.

Chapter 36

Sylah's knowledge sent them north across the huge spurs and fingers that formed the east-west buttresses of the Enemy Mountains. Moving against the grain of the land measured every mile of advance against grueling hours. Rainfall, broken by infrequent skies of dazzling clarity, was both blessing and curse. The Mountain People knew they were on their territory. More, they had determined their general line of march. The rain and wind were the greatest allies in covering their tracks. It also made them miserable, particularly Jones. Never well, he was now seriously ill. Only Tate's strength kept him with them.

No one spoke of it, but it was in the hidden glances and averted faces of all; the majority wouldn't be sacrificed for him.

On the third day a lone scout actually passed within twenty yards of where Clas crouched, arrow notched to bowstring, waiting. The breeze that rippled the Mountain warrior's badger fur cape brought his scent to the dogs with a strength that threatened to overcome their training. Raggar trembled violently, lips curled in a silent snarl. Shara half rose from his down position, and Gan had to put a hand on the dog's head to steady him. Cho simply waited, eager eyes darting from Raggar to Gan to the warrior.

It seemed as if the narrow escape was a signal for other troubles. They spent most of the day afoot, tugging and shoving the scrabbling horses up to a knife-sharp crest where they faced an equally sharp descent on treacherous scab rock. Once they were on lower ground, exhausted, they were forced into a canyon so narrow, they crossed the same stream seven times in a span of three hours before finding a route that provided access to a broad ridge above.

High ground was an additional burden to the strangers. Although Tate and Jones had been provided with what extra clothing the original party could spare, they still suffered from the cold. It was another puzzle for Gan. Wherever they came from, there were weavers of miraculous skill, but apparently no one knew much about wool or leather. Even their strange footwear was mostly cloth of some kind, unimaginably tough, but clumsy and absolutely undecorated. For people who looked and acted with remarkable individuality, they dressed with disappointing sameness. And ugliness.

Nagging doubts about their importance pecked at his mind.

When they reached the ridge that was the last major obstacle on that leg of the journey, he drew in a breath that stretched his lungs to the point of pain. The ridge routes might be unpleasant for the strangers, but he welcomed them. He acknowledged they were dangerous; even though forested, they were easily observed by searchers. Still, he much preferred them to the confining valleys.

One of the problems with such grueling travel was that it eliminated conversation and provided too much time for inward thinking.

Neela said he had no friends. His father said he must be a leader. They defined nothing, merely created other questions. The truth was that he had no idea who or what he was, much less how he was to become anything.

He believed he would survive. And his mother had said survival meant glory.

He looked back over his shoulder at the group. This was the way of greatness?

He would find out. If they ever got out of these mountains.

They broke out onto a route far easier than anything they'd seen all day, and covered more ground. Toward evening they made a final descent. His horse relaxed under him, whickering softly as he was at last able to stretch his legs properly on the near-level high valley floor. Gan patted his neck sympathetically.

The sun brushed the slopes to the east with the hues of sunset. Had they been willing to travel the more moderate terrain beyond those foothills as they headed north, they would have been able to enter the valley through the almost hidden eastern gap. The more difficult route enhanced the chances of remaining undiscovered.

The rising ground at the western limit of the valley would be a good place to rest prior to the assault on the pass. He glanced at the sky again, sniffing the air, resolving to double check with Clas, hoping they were out of danger from any late storms. If not . . . He shrugged away what he had no control over. They would rest, prepare, and cross according to plan. If they were flushed by the Devils before they were ready, they'd fight as much as they had to and run for their lives.

Sometimes the world was a very simple place.

He examined the area as he turned west. There were trees everywhere, hard-budded, expanding in tempo with spring's warmth. Soon a new whiteness of blossoms would cover their branches, a lightness that would make them appear to float, in contrast to the weighty snow that so recently burdened them.

His attention was drawn to Raggar's growing nervousness. He was sure he knew the cause. The younger trees, many of them apple and cherry, were well browsed, the lower shoots and small branches neatly pruned. Many of the wounds oozed amber sap. Browsing deer caused that. Where deer were plentiful, wolves were sure to be handy.

He slowed to allow Clas to catch up. They continued on, ahead of the others, the pace a walk now. "You noticed the signs?"

"Yes. Many deer. The dogs smell wolf?"

"I think so. I—" He stopped with a sharp intake of breath. "Here they are."

It was a large pack, fourteen magnificent animals directly ahead, standing in a crescent formation with its forward points stretched beyond the flanks of the human group. The dominant male was at the center, forward of the line. He sat, unmoving.

Raggar's stiff-legged stalk to the front of Gan's horse was the only movement. It brought the wolf to all fours. The two animals looked at each other, then away. Gan estimated the wolf outweighed Raggar by a good thirty to forty pounds.

Softly, Clas said, "I don't recognize any of them. Do you?"

"No. I'll have to be careful."

"Careful?" Clas was shocked. "We back away. They leave us alone, we leave them alone."

"We're on pack territory. I'll make them know we're friendly."

"This is Devil country! They don't know us. If they come for you, I may not be able to stop them."

"It'll be all right. They respond in the proper ways. They're brothers."

"Brothers to a fool, then. Be careful!" Clas signaled the rest of the group back. He took Gan's reins as he dismounted. Next, Gan ordered Cho and Shara to guard the others. Shara's mane bristled defiance.

Slowly, never looking at the wolves, Clas retreated. The two dogs moved with him. Standing alone beside Raggar, Gan was left with no weapon but his sheathed murdat.

The pack leader stretched, tongue lolling across teeth that made Gan think of new spear points in the smith's tent. The pack's mounting tension surfaced in a flurry of yawning and panting. They looked as if they all enjoyed some private joke. Obeying Gan's hand signal, Raggar held his ground and watched his master advance toward the center of the crescent. The pack closed on him, heads down. It could have been a stalk.

Gan avoided eye contact. When the leader stared at him, he turned his head a full forty-five degrees, studying the mountains over the heads of the wolves ranged almost alongside him now. Carefully, as slowly as a flower turning to the sun, he moved to face the leader. Politely, the big male turned his head, pretending intense interest in a grasshopper.

Sylah could stand it no longer. She whispered to Clas, "What's he doing? Why doesn't he at least draw his murdat?"

Without turning, Clas spoke naturally. "Calm. There's no point in whispering. At this distance they can hear the blood in your veins. You've seen him do this before. Everything's going well—look."

Nothing could have made Sylah turn her eyes elsewhere. Gan was absolutely still, no more than a yard from the wolf's shining black nose. Her skin crawled as the animal leaned forward, almost touching Gan's legs, and when it took a tentative step forward, she made a sound in her chest that brought a warning glare from Clas. Without thinking, she clutched at his sleeve.

The wolf, tail high, circled Gan with precise, measured steps. All the while, his eyes burned up at the man. Gan glanced at him occasionally, no more than an indication of awareness. When the animal was satisfied, it moved toward Raggar.

Gan inhaled very slowly. This was the part he feared. Raggar was more than proud, he was arrogant, and for all the difference in their weights, he believed the dog would kill the wolf in a fight. That wouldn't solve the problem, however.

He needed the wolves.

Contrary to etiquette, Raggar's tail remained as high as the dominant male's. Worse, he refused to expose his neck in proper submission, choosing instead to circle and sniff as an equal.

The angry wolf's hackles rose and a rumble sounded in his chest. Raggar, unimpressed, braced himself and growled back.

Gan took a step forward, drawing the murdat as he did. He let it dangle at his side, bright in the last light of the sun. "We want no fight, brother. The dog is with me and I am with the dog. Our way isn't the same, but we are still brothers. We leave you in peace. We will hunt. We will eat. Raggar. Come. To me, Raggar."

The dog trembled, lip curled in a snarl that somehow expressed his willingness to fight and his desire to obey. He moved as if it hurt, but he stepped back. The pack leader watched him go. He made no move to pursue. Raggar stopped when he was abreast of Gan.

Due to the earlier circling about, the move had created an awkward situation, however. Gan and Raggar now stood with their backs to the bulk of the pack. It grew restless, and the young males began to edge toward juvenile hysteria. The wolf, realizing his back was to the human group, looked at Gan with an almost human puzzlement, as though asking for a dignified way out of the situation.

Gan said, "Softly, softly. We all move together." He hand signaled Raggar, and moved slowly to his left.

Several wolves growled and shifted.

The pack leader sidled to his left. Little by little the three regained their original positions. Gan sheathed the murdat. He said, "I'll be back, brother. We'll hunt."

The wolf made a noise in his throat, not a growl, not a bark. Then they dispersed. One moment they were in plain view, and the next they were a jumble of grays and blacks and browns against the undergrowth. An occasional moving leaf or swaying twig was fading testimony to their presence.

Gan put his hand to the dog's head. For a moment he couldn't be sure if it was his hand or the dog trembling, then laughed when he realized it was both of them. Raggar looked askance, unaware of any humor in the situation.

Clas was of a similar mind. "You should laugh. All madmen laugh."

Sylah realized for the first time her hand was on Clas' arm. She jerked it away.

Gan was mounted by then, and he fell in beside Clas as they resumed their march west.

For a long while after the incident, Sylah kept looking over her shoulder, but no matter how hard she tried, she saw no further trace of the wolf pack. She was unable to rid herself of the feeling they were still there, watching. It came to her that her entire life had become an awareness of things unseen and unwanted. The thought helped her regain perspective; wolves were the least of her troubles.

Eventually weariness overcame worry. The evening was soft, unexpectedly warm. Bundled in her robes, Sylah almost dozed as the slow, steady plod of her horse lulled her. She half dreamed, mixing reality and fantasy. She pictured the Dog camp as a sort of haven, despite its rigors and her misfortune there—as opposed to the luxury of quarters in Ola. From that, it was no step at all to thoughts of Clas.

Such a complex man; when the Devil patrol came looking for them, he'd *wanted* to shoot. No. She corrected herself. To kill. And yet she couldn't stop feeling there was something like desperation in the look he turned on her. It unsettled her to realize how clearly her mind held such images of him and how strongly they affected her. Her face warmed as she thought about it, and she was remembering muscles bulging, as he seemed to swell with restrained strength.

The warmth that had touched her face spread through her body, and she was remembering more, wondering more, imagining things she had only heard described in whispers in the dormitory nights.

She snapped upright in the saddle. Clas was there, reaching toward her in concern. "Are you all right?"

"I'm fine." She twisted away awkwardly.

His eyebrows rose in surprise at her swift rejection, and he urged his horse forward to rejoin Gan.

The wolf pack chose that moment to erupt in a chorus of howling. It brought Neela to her side. Sylah greeted her with a smile of reassurance that was totally false.

The move for companionship was a good sign, though. Hardship was welding them into a whole. She began to believe they were going to get to Harbundai.

The wolves howled again, and wavering echoes resounded through the canyons leading out of the valley. Her heart ached at the freedom it expressed.

"And me," she whispered to herself. "Please. Someday. And me."

CHAPTER 37

While they waited for spring to soften the pass for them, they camped on a relatively level shelf high above the wolves' valley. It was a good site, with a nearby stream and well concealed. Almost every night for three weeks the pack sang, letting them know there were no intruders. It was a time of rest for all but Clas, who'd immediately left to scout ahead for the first week. It seemed to Gan he'd been eager to leave. He asked no questions. Clas knew what he was doing.

He returned bearded and smelly. Snow restricted his movement, and he penetrated no great distance up the pass. Discouragingly, the Devils were thick, traversing easily on skis and snowshoes. On returning, Clas bathed and shaved in the nearby creek and slept a full twenty-four hours. He was still rather withdrawn. Gan put that down to living alone and silent for so many days. This particular morning when Gan came in from nightwatch, the sun was hidden by a white mass of cloud that shrouded the camp in its damp embrace. Mist wasn't unusual—it was another reason why Clas' scouting had taken so long—but this was different. It pressed against the earth heavily, loading the branches of the firs with accumulated water that dripped as steadily as slow rain. Gan sniffed at it and watched it creep through the trees and around the lean-tos, and a suspicious frown creased his forehead. He told Clas, "I'm going down the mountain and get meat. And hide, for snowshoes."

Clas looked dubious. "It's been mild. The pass is clearing well."

"I'm taking no chances."

Clas jerked his thumb at the lean-to. "Bad weather'll kill that one. I won't carry him. That's final."

Gan looked in at Jones, who was shivering under every piece of blanket or hide they could spare. He said, "He doesn't fight to live."

Clas said, "And I won't fight for him."

Gan watched Clas stalk away, then instructed the dogs to wait. He rode downhill a full two hours before he was low enough to let the other hunters know of his presence. He threw back his head and howled.

The answer drifted to him through the mist. Faint, complex music made the gray air tremble. When it faded, silence palled the valley, an acknowledgment by the hunted that the hunters were prowling.

Gan picked a stand overlooking the convergence of three trails.

Looped over his belt at the back, he carried a cloth cape, woven in a zigzag pattern of black stripes on brown. When he sat down to wait for game, he draped the material over his body from chin to ground. The pattern, its symmetry broken by wrinkles and folds, made him almost invisible against the forest background. A piece of oiled brown cloth covered his bowstring to protect it from moisture.

A howl floated up the valley's right side. It was answered with a cry from the left that was almost a bark. The pack would move toward him slowly, quartering back and forth. Some prey would double back through gaps and some would slip past the stand. There would be those that came to Gan's arrows.

A drop of water caught on his eyelashes, distorting his vision for a fraction of a second, and when it cleared, he was staring at a young doe. She stilted along the trail from his right, a difficult shot. Her head was up and her ears flicked continually. Without seeing him or smelling him, she still sensed something wrong. She continued to advance, and Gan decided to let her pass. The pack would provide better quarry. Or none.

Less than an hour passed before a buck picked his way down the trail on Gan's left. He shot it easily, and it fell with hardly a struggle. Gan was rising, reaching for his shortknife to bleed it, when a movement to his right froze him. A huge boar trotted down that trail, hurrying along with the deceptively dainty trot of his kind. He was unaware of the man watching him, and only slightly disturbed by the wolves in the distance behind him. His tusks would discourage all but the hungriest of packs. Then it saw Gan. For an instant it wasn't sure what it was looking at, but then it made up its mind. Its squeal of alarm filled the valley, and Gan realized the stand was compromised beyond recall. He also needed the deer for his own purposes, and the bond between himself and the wolves demanded they share in his kill. Two arrows assured the pack a pork dinner.

He hurried down to the deer, slashing the throat to drain the blood. Working quickly, he first removed the genitals, then cut the colon free, tying it off. Both acts were necessary to prevent fouling the meat, as was excising the musk glands on the hind hocks, to keep the strong, acrid musk from rendering the meat inedible. After scrupulously cleaning the knife blade, he sliced through the hide of the abdomen from rear to the front until he struck the brisket. He moved quickly, from much practice, but with care; a fraction of an inch too deep with the point of the blade, and he'd slice the wall of the intestine. That, too, could ruin the meat. It was harder work cutting through the brisket, but soon he was able to turn the animal on its side and pull out the internal organs.

He decapitated it, then cut through each hind leg about two inches below the second joint. Running a leather strip through the cuts, he heaved the other end of the line over a branch and hoisted the deer clear of the ground.

He first ringed the hide on each hind leg, then split the skin on the inside of the hams from leg to leg in one long cut. In a series of smaller cuts, constantly tugging and pulling the hide, he stripped it from the hind legs, then peeled it all the way down to the shoulder blade. Repeating the same long slash on the inside of the forelegs as on the hams, he finished the job by pulling the skin over the neck.

Despite the chill mist, he was sweating, and the job of quartering the animal to carry it back to camp was still ahead of him. He continued swiftly, careful to keep as much hair and litter off the meat as possible.

He pondered the amount of waste from this kill, and it depressed him. He hated to waste anything, especially something that had died by his hand. Myriad products could be made from what was going unused; the antlers alone would provide buttons, toggles, utensil handles, awls, flint-knappers—the list went on and on. There was no choice, however. They needed the meat and the hide, had neither time nor opportunity to use the rest.

As a final move before leaving, he hacked off several thick branches from a dead apple tree nearby. He used the leather strap to tie it to the outside of the hide-wrapped meat, and was carrying the bundle to his horse when he sensed the pack's arrival. He reached the animal before he actually heard them behind him. When he turned, their eyes gleamed with the still-surging excitement of their own kill. Full-bellied, they nevertheless watched with devoted interest as he lashed the carcass behind the saddle.

They knew food as a function of their skill and nature's fickle smile. They knew hunger as routine and starvation as a frequent specter. Enough was always very temporary, and the man before them had meat. They stirred restlessly.

The horse snorted and tugged at its reins. Even as Gan silently berated himself for bringing one of the Devil nags instead of his own mount, the pack leader casually rose and stretched, yawning. Two others followed his example.

The horse was now so nervous that securing the load became a struggle. When Gan finished, he was surrounded.

The leader advanced stiff-legged, tail high. He growled softly when he stopped, only a yard away, sniffing ostentatiously at the man, the horse, and the still-dripping bundle.

It took all Gan's strength to control the horse with his left hand, while the right crept to the handle of his murdat. Finally, either from sheer resignation or at Gan's urging, the horse stopped jerking and rearing, settling down to uninterrupted trembling. A solid rim of white circled its eyes. Lather made it look as if it had run all day.

Gan spoke soothingly to the leader, avoiding his eyes, fixing his own gaze on the ground in front of him. "Brother, we hunted together today. The pack is fed. We share in peace."

A snarling, snapping scuffle broke out between a pair of males, an eruption of uncontainable aggressiveness. The activity pulled at Gan, but he kept his eyes fixed on the same spot. An animal yipped, and the incident was over.

The issue had come to wills. Gan knew the dominant male needed to show his followers he was a controlling factor; if he didn't dominate, he created terms.

Gan untied the reins and wrapped them around his fist. The other hand drew an inch of blade free of the scabbard. He said, "I've left what I don't need. I'll fight for what I have."

The animal's upper lip trembled at the sound of the voice.

Gan led the horse away, careful to avoid making the leader move. It was a moment when any affront to his dignity meant instant attack. The others moved aside, panting, uncertain.

He forced himself to clear the place slowly. The feeling of the pack behind him played across his back like feathers. He was ten yards away. Then twenty. At fifty, he stopped and turned.

Only the leader remained, watching. Gan waved. The wolf continued to stare. Continuing up the mountain, Gan took a long drink from his water-skin.

Dealing with the brothers was always a sensitive event. This was a new behavior, however. Something had disturbed them.

He'd traveled only another few steps when he saw motion far down the valley. He thought it must be a prairie bear, so powerful it roamed without thought of concealment. Only when the brush thinned was he able to see it was a man on horseback, leading a string of three burros.

A Peddler. Everyone else existed within some sort of social framework, but Peddlers wandered with nothing to insulate them from the cruelties of the world except their own fingers-of-the-hand family.

This one actually traveled completely alone. Gan repressed a shudder. No bond to any group was beyond reason. Even now, renegade, he saw himself as Dog tribe.

He eased into an alder patch to watch the man come. The sun burned a hole in the overcast, spilling light into the valley. Blossoms painted the ground, rioting in undisciplined swirls of yellow and white and pale blue. The numerous fruit trees were pink-flushed snowdrifts. Through it all, the bearded Peddler rode bundled in a heavy coat of raccoon furs, with hat to match. He whistled short passages, then sang to himself. His horse flicked its ears politely when the man occasionally stopped the music to talk to it. Gan didn't even realize he had a smile on his own face when the man suddenly reined up, barely ten yards away. He nearly fell out of his saddle at the sight of the warrior watching him. Speech gushed through the beard in a torrent.

"You look friendly. Are you? I don't have anything worth dying for. Take anything you want, and good luck to you. May it do you more good than it's done me. I've traveled miles and miles and miles, and not made enough profit to—" He stopped instantly at Gan's raised hand.

Gan said, "Who are you? From where, and where headed?"

The man's jaw worked in advance of his words, and the effect was like watching the whiskers ripple in a high wind. "Why, anyone can see I'm a Peddler, son of a Peddler, grandson—" Again Gan's hand rose, and he stopped, resuming with, "Yes. Well, that's what we are. Always were. I wintered with the Buffalo Eaters. On my way back to Harbundai."

"It's early for the pass. And you didn't give me your name."

"Nor you me, young Dog." He chuckled, and the nervousness partially left the shining green eyes, replaced by a shrewdness that seemed far more natural. "Took me a minute. I'm Bilsten. I know you, Gan Moondark." He rose in the stirrups, looking about. "The rest hiding nearby?"

"What rest?"

This time his look was confident. "There was you, the fighting instructor, Clas na Bale; Neela Yan, the daughter of Faldar Yan, that you killed; your father, Col, the real War Chief; last one's a Rose Priestess from Ola, named Sylah. Oh, yes—you've got three dogs with you. Now, where are the others?"

"My father died, Peddler."

There was genuine sympathy in the Peddler's reaction, and Gan regretted the harshness of his statement. Still, he reminded himself, the man was what he was. He said, "How do you know so much?"

"What I know keeps me alive."

"What you know of me could change that. You're clever enough to realize it. There's already a bargain in your weasel mind."

He nodded vigorously. "Good! I like it. No haggling. Truth. Bay Yan's promised a hundred horses for each of your heads. Except his sister's, of course. Two hundred for the sister, alive and unharmed. No market for the Priestess. Too much trouble from Church, don't you see? Lot of horses, a hundred. Dog horses, too."

"You want my head?"

The man was indignant. "Suspicious. Young fellow like you. Shame. Here's my idea. Suppose someone—you, for instance—killed a Mountain warrior, maybe even a pair of them. If they were left where the weather and the animals could get at them for a few days, a man—a Peddler, maybe— could go to Bay Yan with the head—or even two, like I said. Young Bay, he wouldn't want to look too close, now would he? And if he did, he couldn't tell nothing, could he, especially if there was something like that bow of yours, or that murdat, to sort of *prove* who the head belonged to? Why, a man would be a hundred horses—maybe even two hundred—to the good. And all for a dead Mountain warrior."

"Or two," Gan supplied wryly, and Bilsten's grin flashed again. Gan went on. "I'll think on it. What other news?"

"I sell news, young Moondark."

"And I give arrows away."

"See what you mean. Good argument. Well, the Buffalo Eaters are at it with the Muddy River tribe. A chief named Plenty Iron—he's High Chief of the Farm League—is pushing the Muddy's west, into Buffalo Eater territory. Plenty Iron's an Upriver man. You know any of these names?"

"I've heard of the Buffalo Eaters; that's all."

Chin in hand, Bilsten frowned. "Hm. Not much to tell you, then. Oh— the Mountains looking for you told me some lies you might enjoy. Claim they had a battle with people who fight with thunder and lightning. Claim they killed two, and would have got the rest, but some Ola cavalry showed up and rescued six and the other two ran off. Showed me some strange clothes and boots and stuff, but no weapons. Almost had me convinced they believe their own story."

"You haven't told me where you're going."

Bilsten slid to the ground, leaning back against his patient, immobile horse. "You must be getting anxious to try the pass. How'd you like me to get you through? Safe and quick."

"What would you charge to guide?"

"I won't guide you." At Gan's frown, he held up a warding hand. "Don't get skunky. Patience. If I arrive on the western side with you, everyone knows I guided you. The Mountains would hear, soon enough, and my next trip, they cut my throat. Slow. But if I leave an easy trail along a path they don't usually watch, who's to blame me if you follow it?"

"What do I owe you if we succeed?"

"Bay Yan thinks you're each worth a hundred horses dead, so that's two hundred, and we both know he'd go up to three for the girl. But I'm a generous man, to my eternal cost and sorrow, don't you see. Instead of the five hundred I'd get from Bay Yan, let's say you promise me five fifty and I'll leave a trail you can follow in the dark." He waved his hands as if erasing the words from the air as Gan, face aflame, opened his mouth to speak. Bilsten was contrite. "Ah, no—that's greedy, you being trapped here, and all. Make it an even five hundred; call me a soft-hearted fool for the rest."

"Five hundred *Dog* horses? For a trail you mean to follow whether we do or not? Four, Peddler, and not another word, or you guide us across on the point of my murdat."

Bilsten drew himself erect. "Harsh. You might give a thought to my risk, taking the word of man who's likely to die before he can pay his legitimate debts." He made a Three-sign quickly, and Gan noted it had the offhand grace of reflex. He went on, "Four fifty it is. And when?"

"Come to our camp. Eat. No more argument. I can't promise when, but I promise four hundred and fifty."

Bilsten swung aboard his horse. "Thank you. While we ride, tell me all about your travels."

The dogs watched their arrival with mild interest. "I'm Bilsten," he called to an openly hostile Clas. "Clas na Bale, I imagine."

"Clas na Bale no matter what you imagine." The answer was more growl than speech. To Gan he said, "Where'd you find this? Why bring it here?"

Bilsten was quickest. "And thanks for your kind welcome. May I ask to meet—" The smooth chatter died in midair. Tate helped Jones out of the men's lean-to just as Sylah and Neela appeared in front of the other. He made a valiant effort to recover, doffing his hat. "I know you, Rose Priestess Sylah, and you, Neela Yan. I'm Bilsten, a Peddler, as was my father, and—" He glanced at Gan and quickly finished, "—and so on." He shifted his attention to the strangers, the green eyes practically crackling with curiosity.

Tate said, "We know you, Bilsten. I'm Donnacee Tate. This is John Jones."

Bilsten straightened in his saddle, flourished the cap in a grandiose gesture. He turned slowly to Gan, "So the young man bargained the poor Peddler into marking trail for six, and not just the three Dog people and the Priestess. Bilsten won't forget."

"What bargain?" Clas demanded.

Gan recounted their meeting and conversation.

As if working to dispel anyone's qualms, Bilsten slid off his horse, his ingenuous smile beaming at everyone. To the strangers he said, "You're the ones got away from the Mountain People. Is that your real skin, Donnacee? I've been a lot of places, seen a lot of things—even heard stories of black people that lived in the times of the giants. Taking your kind heart for a fact, I'm saying you're not a giant."

She said, "Call me Tate."

"Where are you from?"

"East. Very far."

"How'd you get here?"

Clas opened his mouth to interfere, but a quick hand gesture from Gan quieted him. The casual evasions of the strangers had been irritating, and Bilsten, with the brashness of his kind, would root for details, and never mind good manners. Jones, looking more uncomfortable than ever, edged back into the lean-to. Tate remained unruffled. She said, "Walked."

"Past the Muddy Rivers? The Buffalo Eaters? Are you Upriver People?" She never blinked. "From farther east. We were careful to avoid others."

"Careful? You must be ghosts." Bilsten turned to Gan. "How'd you meet them?"

"When they saw us, they knew Dog People were the ones they wanted to be with."

"Why you? There are other—" Gan's change of expression snapped Bilsten's mouth shut. He recovered quickly. "Of course. Superior tribe."

Clas said, "You've a very nimble way with words."

Bilsten was unabashed. "Sometimes words are even quicker than steel."

"Don't bet on that very often," Clas said, and disappeared into the lean-to.

Sylah stepped forward. "We're making our way to Harbundai. Did Gan tell you?"

"That, and little else, Priestess. You're from Ola, aren't you? The Iris Abbey?"

She ignored the question. "Cloud Rest Pass—we're going the right way?"

He nodded. "How'd you know of it?"

She considered a moment, then explained about her patient. When she finished, he stroked his beard, thinking, then turned to Gan. "Curse my soft heart, I do have to say what I believe is best for people." He indicated Jones. "That one won't make it. It's early for a pass this high. You have to be strong."

Tate was close enough to overhear. "He'll make it."

Bilsten shrugged. "You're not to mention me. Not to anyone, for any reason. It's worth my life, don't you know?"

Gan nodded. "You have my word."

Bilsten bobbed his head at the others. "Of course. And theirs?"

"I'm responsible."

The sharp eyes narrowed to challenge. "That confident of your authority?"

From the corner of his eye Gan saw the worried frown net Sylah's brow. He said, "They trust me. I trust them. It's the way."

Clapping his hands, Bilsten got to his feet. "The very answer! Now, with your permission . . . ?" Without waiting, yet managing to suggest the greatest civility, he half bowed and made his way toward the strangers.

Gan chuckled, watching him. "The man pries for answers like a magpie trying to crack an egg."

Sylah was thoughtful. "He's cunning."

"So long as he gets us across the mountains."

She looked deep into his eyes. "You're learning to use people. It's a dangerous knowledge. Use it *for* your people." She turned away, leaving him to stare after her.

He was unaware of Neela's approach until she spoke, practically at his elbow. She revealed her eavesdropping with no apparent concern. "Yes, Gan, how will you serve your people? Fight them? Bring them more misery? At least I have some hostage value. I can hope to be used to buy some peace for them."

He sat frozen in shock for a long breath, and when he reacted, he flung himself over to his horse, hacking through the lashing, sending the bundle of meat, hides, and wood tumbling to the ground. Then he mounted his own horse and trotted back down the trail. Heedless, wanting only distance from Neela and the hurt of her words, his anger mounted with each step, so that when he reached the valley floor, it exploded within him. He flogged the horse into a breakneck gallop, thundering through the trees, hacking at the blossom-studded branches with his murdat, leaving a flurrying, weeping trail of petals.

The mad ride lasted until the staggering exhaustion of his horse brought him to his senses. Vaulting to the ground, he led the animal to a stream, pulling it back before it could drink too much and harm itself. While the abused animal heaved for air, he held its neck and apologized. He hoped the foolishness of his ride hadn't undone the benefits of a good rest and good grazing. Letting the animal drink deeply again, he led it back toward the upper end of the valley.

About halfway there the wolves fell in behind. For a while he expected trouble again, but instead the leader held the pack at a respectful distance under iron control. They were tense, but not aggressive.

On the small bluff overlooking the game trails, he turned to see them gathered in a group below. Lethargy swept through him as they sprawled in the sun. Suddenly, he wanted to rest, too. Fumbling, he tied the reins to his wrist before slumping to a sitting position against a fir.

He felt the dream coming even as sleep collected him.

Clas was beside him. They faced a council of fierce men. Their faces refused to focus, came to him as scars and hard-formed character. Clas was there, the only one he could name. Still, the Gan who sat with them knew them all.

They waited for word from him.

Beyond them he sensed a vast expanse, although he couldn't actually see it. He knew it was dark, a blackness that gleamed like obsidian. He was drawn to it. The Gan he saw knew exactly what it was.

A man stood alone, facing the dream Gan. Menace thickened the air.

There was a weapon, a slim, steel-handled axe. The threatening man raised it to throw at him. Gan saw the smallest change of every muscle in the bare arm.

A sound came from beside him, from Clas. His sword, not a murdat, hissed through the air, struck the axe thrower directly under his ribs. His weapon fell, rang wildly on stone.

Time stopped. The heart of the Gan in the dream raged with hatred for Clas, the man who saved his life.

He woke with a start. An echoing, denying voice confirmed that his own shout had wakened him. The sun was low.

He rose gingerly, half expecting pain to be connected with a dream so harrowing.

What could it mean? he wondered, and decided the imagery was only a sign, not a sight.

As that thought registered, it was as quickly forgotten in his realization that the wolves had encircled him. As if by command, they padded back to form behind the leader. They were calm now.

He started away as the sun's light paled. Its departure drew color from the earth. Darkness already claimed the depths of the flanking canyons.

He trudged upward, still leading his horse. Wolf-song followed, filling him with loss and loneliness.

High above him Neela heard the chorus and shivered. Sylah, across the small fire warming the lean-to, looked up anxiously. She said, "Don't worry. Those are his friends. You've seen that."

She nodded. "I know, but I can't help it. They always sound sad to me. I hate that sound." She pounded a fist against her thigh. "I hurt him. I didn't want to, but I did. Why am I such a fool?" Then, with hardly a pause, she added, "He should have known, should have understood."

Sylah moved to take her in her arms. "That's always the trouble. We don't understand ourselves, and expect them to; they don't understand themselves, and expect us to. Maybe it's enough if we just care."

CHAPTER 38

Sylah watched Tate's routine evening polishing of the lightning weapon. She wiped it with its special oily cloth, as usual, then opened it in the middle—it made a noise, as if breaking a stick—to peer studiously into both hollow tubes. It seemed an odd thing to do, since it was immediately obvious the tubes were empty. What was even more curious, she invariably looked through them from both ends, as if something might sneak in there while she turned the thing around.

Sylah bent to arrange her bedding—secretly envying Tate the amazing thing she called a sleeping bag—and when she straightened up, she was surprised to see Neela already entering their lean-to. Neela said, "Jones is stronger, I think. He took more broth tonight."

Tate said, "You've been good for him." She paused, forming the words carefully. "He responds to you." She busied herself with the small weapon she carried on her hip, taking it apart to rub the pieces with the oiled rag. Sylah didn't realize how intently she was staring until Tate returned it.

At that, Sylah lifted her chin and decided simply to acknowledge her curiosity. She said, "You have the weapons of a warrior. Jones has none. This is very confusing. Can you explain?"

Tate said, "In my time—" and caught herself. She faked a small cough. They appeared to be waiting normally, and she resumed. "I mean, in my country, when I was growing up, there was much fighting. Sometimes women had to fight beside the men. We were taught."

Neela said, "We're taught, too, but we don't have murdats, as I do now. Did you fight? Like a warrior, I mean?"

She debated trying to explain that her experience was limited to administrative matters. There had been plenty of combat training, of course, and she'd studied military history intensely. That wasn't what the women meant, though; they were wondering if she was an asset. They were thinking of another fight with the tribe they alternately called Mountain People and Devils. She lied easily. "Yes, I'm a warrior."

Sylah asked, "You volunteered? You were not ordered? Would they let you make children?"

Again, how would they comprehend an overpopulated world? She said, "Yes, I would have been allowed."

Neela laughed. "Of course, she'd be allowed." She turned back to Tate and explained. "In Ola, when they say a woman's 'allowed' to make children, it means she's been given to a man. Women who don't make children are shamed. Dog women choose a mate, and even among us, children are a woman's pride. Sometimes—" She stopped abruptly, turning suddenly fearful eyes on Sylah.

Sylah smiled softly, making a calming gesture. She rose as she did, signaling Tate to help her lower the leather cover across the front of the lean-to. When it was lashed shut, she spoke in a whisper. "We should know more about each other, we three. Come close. The men must not hear."

With their heads almost touching, faces barely discernible in the ruddy glow of the coals in the firepit, she quizzed Tate extensively on her rights and obligations in her "tribe." In the darkness the matter-of-fact answers, the almost automatic assumption that everyone was as free and privileged as herself, forged a hardening tone of resentment in Sylah's questions. Even Neela, proud of a culture Sylah considered practically unfettered, was moved to frequent mutters of surprise.

Tate was too perceptive to miss the effect of her answers or the root of the questions. After answering for a while, she interrupted. "Your questions make me think women aren't very free in Ola."

The silence that followed was thick with the necessity for judgments. Sylah's first words came hard, because they shamed her. "You're right. In my country, we are bought and sold."

"Jesus," Tate said.

Neela half screamed, jerking away from her, falling sideways in her effort to escape. Sylah thought her heart would leap into her mouth. Shock kept her immobile long enough for Neela to untangle herself from her bedding and start backing out of the lean-to. Sylah lunged, catching an ankle. A sharp twist brought her down, and Sylah clamped an arm around her shoulders, covered Neela's mouth with a hand. She snapped orders at Tate. "Get outside! Clas will come. Tell him you heard a noise—an animal. *Hurry!*"

Tate was just in time to meet Clas, the murdat a sinister shadow in his hand. She told her story, and he muttered something about nervous women and returned to his own quarters.

When Tate rejoined them, Neela was silent, her eyes huge in the increased light thrown by some shavings added to the firepit. As soon as Tate sat down, Sylah jammed her face within an inch of hers. "You used the name, the forbidden name. What if *they* heard? They would have to inform on us!"

"I just said—"

"No!" Sylah grabbed her shoulders, shook her. "Church forbids. The name must not be spoken by us, or by them where we can hear!"

Tate swallowed noisily before speaking. "We use that name often. He's our friend."

"Of course. He's everyone's friend. But men killed Him, and for women to speak the name is to remind them. Since the Purge, it's forbidden. You said you have Church in your tribe; how could you not know?"

Tate hesitated, then said, "We're not taught that."

Neela gasped. When she spoke to Sylah, her eyes continued to dart back to Tate. She said, "Maybe they didn't get the Purge. Maybe they still have Teachers!"

Sylah was gruff. "Enough. If we're to talk religion, leave it to me. It's far too dangerous for you."

"They can't hear us."

"There is another here. Always. *He* was a man."

Neela drew herself up in a tight ball. Sylah went on. "You angered Clas when you spoke of 'sun' and 'son' because Church makes us know the face of the sun is the face of the One Who Is Two, the son of the One in All. No woman must speak of Him. In my country, if a woman says His name, as you did, the King's truth protectors come for her and she disappears."

The tale caught in her throat, and Tate reached for her hand. She said, "It's all right, Sylah. Don't—" She stumbled, trying for the right words. "Don't hurt. Or fear. I understand."

It was as though the words had the same firmness as the physical contact. Sylah was convinced she could depend on this unpredictable new friend.

As Sylah explained her mission to the Dog People, she felt her earlier resentment and distrust drain from her, even though, in her heart, she knew Tate was lying to her about many things. She wondered why she lied, and what about, but felt no fear for herself or her confidences. It grew on her that Tate lied to protect them all, as well as herself.

But why?

When Sylah stopped, she waited a long time while Tate silently digested what she'd heard. At last Tate said, "Tell me what to tell Jones and what I must not tell him. Then tell me how to help you. Tell me about our goal and about Church."

The following morning Sylah noted the blue hollows around Neela's eyes and the way she picked at her food. She settled back to wait for the girl to come to her. With ill-disguised aimlessness, Neela did just that. Once there, she looked at the ground and seemed to hover, as if unsure whether to speak or to flee.

Sylah supplied a nudge. "You didn't sleep well."

Her reserve broke. She sagged. "I didn't sleep at all. What you said to Tate made me think. About leaving my people, breaking away from my family. It seemed so *right*. Now I'm not sure. People are supposed to avenge a death, not run away with the killer. The tribe doesn't know about Likat. Or Kolee. They don't know I want to stop a war. And I don't think I can anymore. I'm not that important." She lifted her eyes to Sylah's, and tears trembled in them. "Will Bay even care what happens to me? Are we going to die, and no one even know?"

Sylah sighed. "I don't know. We all seem to be tangled together, and I don't know how it's going to unravel." Looking past Neela, she saw Gan approaching from his watch downhill. She said, "I don't know how it happened, but we seem to be drawn along by that one." Neela turned to look, and the tears came then, rolling free. Sylah turned her around. "Don't let them see that. We're as strong as they are. And never doubt yourself. You did a brave thing; the right thing, as you said. You'll see. I promise. Now let's go get that venison smoked."

She was relieved to see the small smile of acceptance. And sorry she'd been so quick to promise something that gave her so many qualms of her own.

They'd treated the meat already, soaking it with a salt brine that also featured fiery dried peppers. They carried the sliced meat to the stream, where it was rinsed, then brought it back to the smoker. A network of fir boughs formed a frame, with a twine network for suspending the meat over the smoke. Neela built a small fire in a pit, and once it burned to coals, the apple wood was cut into chips with a hatchet, soaked, and dumped on the coals. Moving quickly now, they lifted the frame over the hole, and as Sylah distributed the meat on the twine netting, Neela thatched the structure with fir boughs. As soon as Sylah was finished, Neela completed the thatching on that side of the smoker, and then they draped one of the leather front entrance covers from a lean-to over the whole thing. Before they settled down beside it, Neela hurried to the stream, returning with a waterskin. The apple-wood chips would never be allowed to catch fire, and the temperature would be monitored constantly over the next four hours or so, in order to dry the meat without dehydrating it while it absorbed the flavor of the smoke.

A short distance away, obscured by a massive tree, Tate and Jones had been watching. It was Jones who finally spoke. "I was afraid they'd see us and think we were eavesdropping. Not that we'd have to hear anything to know Neela's depressed."

Tate rolled her eyes in mock disgust. "Who isn't?"

He chuckled softly. She looked at him askance. He continued to smile. "I hadn't even thought about my depression this morning. Is that progress or regression?"

"Progress." She was firm. "The more we mope, the shorter the odds on tomorrow."

"Right. You know, the thing I'm most worried about now is fitting in with whatever develops when we get where we're going."

She laughed, a hard slash of sound. "What a bunch of jerks they were— the clowns who picked us to go in the fridge. They really believed they'd bring us back to a place that was a sort of miniature of the country when we went in. Nothing was going to be changed but the numbers."

Too casually he said, "You never said what you were expected to do."

She looked at him until he was forced to turn away. It was several seconds longer before she heaved a sigh and leaned back against the tree. "Not everyone trusted Colonel Falconer or the people who asked him to volunteer for the crèche, okay? I did. He's no traitor. Couldn't be. But some people were afraid he'd use the troops to either take over or set up his own man. They set up two counterforces, one in the Blue Ridge crèche, another in Iowa. Part of my job was to watch Falconer, go back east with him, report."

"You didn't like the idea."

"Hated it. It's spying."

"You must be a pretty good soldier."

"I'm no Field Marshal. I studied and worked."

"Why'd anyone mistrust him so?"

"One-track mind. People say watching him run an operation's like watching a wolf deal with a lamb chop. He can be ruthless."

"Who would have guessed?"

The sarcasm earned him a lopsided grin. He changed the subject. "What're your thoughts on this Peddler, Bilsten?"

"He looks like Mr. Hommerbocker."

"Hommerbocker?"

She laughed aloud. "My sixth-grade teacher. Nicest man I ever knew. This bird's a cold-blooded sucker; forget the jolly stuff."

"I was glad we'd had time to rehearse a story. I was very glad he asked nothing about religion. I have to tell you, this has been very difficult for me—I mean, really—facing east, crossing themselves, and in three different ways, if you please; and they pray at, for, and about everything. It's sacrilege."

She considered telling him some of the things she'd learned. He was a good man, trustworthy.

Then she wondered. Not that he'd run to tell the other men what he knew of the women's conversation, but some day, sometime, he might say something that could be traced back to Sylah, through herself.

It stunned her to realize she was beginning to think like *them*, Sylah and Neela. Women against the men.

Why not? The question twisted like a knife in her mind. Was it so much different than being black in a white society? Or the female officer in a unit full of infantrymen? So she was a minority, and on the wrong end of the stick. So what else was new?

She looked at Jones from the corner of her eye. He waited for her to rejoin their conversation. Patient. Forgiving.

She'd protect him as best she could. But he'd have to learn to do a better job of taking care of himself. They both would. If they ever got out of these freezing mountains.

Taking him by the arm, she walked him away from the camp, trying to make him understand that Church was a very real, very important thing in this new world. He tried to comment once, and she told him to shut up, purposely rude, not wanting to argue because she had too many pieces of information to sort out. He had to know enough to survive. She didn't dare tell him any secrets. Sylah had been clear on that.

And Church was the one refuge she felt she could depend on. He had mankind. If he didn't throw it away.

As she finished bringing him up to date on what she'd learned of customs and boundaries, they each heard the wind mutter in the trees. There was a wet, tough smell in the air. Their voices mingled in the hope it wasn't a storm.

They covered less than half the distance back to the camp before the gusts grew unruly. Groans and complaints of heavy timber joined the excited tenor of branches and needles.

Tate said, "We may be wasting our time worrying about the future. Right now's got me concerned."

Jones nodded, ducking into the men's lean-to. The front cover was downwind, so still in the raised position. Gan was there, sitting on his bedding, leaning back against a slumbering Raggar. Shara and Cho stretched out beside him. Raggar peered at the new arrivals sleepily, favored them with a solitary thump of his tail, and closed his eyes with what Tate was certain was a self-satisfied smirk. She settled to the ground, sheltered from the wind, and watched Gan work off his cold-weather boots.

The ingenuity of the footwear fascinated her. The calf-high outer boot had a supple, fringed top, stitched to a shoe of hard leather. Then there was an inner boot; it was made of much finer, softer leather. The outer boot was large enough to accommodate insulation. Before putting on the outer boot, the inside of the sole was padded with dried grass, and once it was on the foot, more of the same was stuffed between the inner and outer components.

She pictured herself in them, and was struck by a vagrant thought of herself wearing out her technologically perfect, manufactured-material equipment, hoarding tattered swatches of ripstop nylon, simulated leather, moisture-barrier cloth. She'd be dressed in a hodgepodge of natural and lab-created material, as piebald as one of the Dog horses. She wasn't sure if that was funny or not.

Once he was finished with his boots, Gan gestured her closer, tugging a bundle from behind Raggar. He opened it and handed her a half-finished snowshoe. She accepted it gingerly, not just because it was made with the hide of the recently killed deer, but because she remembered the one time she'd worn them. It was at cold-weather training camp, and she'd ached for days in places she'd never been aware of before.

They were the style called bear-paws. Nearly round, they lacked the tail of the trapper type. She remembered them as the easiest to use, if such a thing could be said of either kind.

When she looked again, he had some branches and more strips of hide on the ground between his outstretched legs. He spoke slowly, so she could follow his instructions, but his hands seemed to flit through the motions of bending the supple branches and lashing them into the near-round shape he desired. She struggled to mimic him. Next, he showed her how to lash the cross-struts in place. He was patient and encouraging, pointing out how he knotted the sinew bindings and discussing the advantages of properly tanned leather compared to the rawhide they were forced to use for the webbing.

Her hands continued to follow the required patterns, but her mind was still reaching, searching, too troubled by what had happened the night before to be lulled by handcraft alone. It wasn't until she noticed that Jones was sound asleep that she realized how little actual conversation was passing between herself and this enigmatic young man. She was thinking of him as a friend, and it surprised her.

Could a woman be a man's friend in this world? It wasn't a pleasant line of thought. She'd had few men friends in her own world. There were men in their eager plenty, but few friends. And the best of them was married to the best of her women friends. Bittersweet? No. Just bitter.

Then, inexplicably, she was in another time, sitting in her father's lap, smelling the familiarity that was him and no one else. He had his every-evening-after-dinner glass of whiskey in hand while he was teaching her to read, hearing him brag to her mother about how quickly she learned.

She hadn't thought about him for years. She'd thought he knew everything. One of those people who read everything, he had a catchall mind that erupted facts. A steady man, a bureaucrat. Faceless to the world, he was the tree that sheltered her and her brothers until they were ready to face the future and find a place for their own roots.

The future.

There was a taste of bile at the back of her throat.

It startled her when Gan's voice penetrated her reminiscence. He was asking what "her people" knew of his part of the world. She couched her answer in generalities. She asked as much as she told, learning that he knew of a people with bronze skins and different language who lived beyond the Great Sea. She told him that her people said the land he lived on extended to another Great Sea, but she had no name for it. When she knew of the Mother River that ran through the Dog People's land, and into the sea, he was pleased. She chanced asking him about the dams on what she knew as the Columbia; was there an old building that stopped the river?

He laughed at the joke. Everyone built fishing weirs across small streams, but the Mother River? There was some giant work there; the river tribes mined it for metal. But not even the giants could have interfered with the Mother River. When he told her his mother had been of one of those tribes, she saw the cloud pass over his face.

She brought the conversation around to the Dogs. It was a surprise to learn they did some minor farming along with their animal husbandry, but until Col's time, they were primarily hunters and gatherers. And raiders. They understood speed and striking power. She caught his sharpened interest in her questions, and when she asked about fundamental matters—miles per day, what rations a man carried, tactical formations—his hands slowed at their work and he looked directly into her eyes when he answered.

She was able to field his questions about her "tribe" with honest numbers; the average combat trooper's load in the infantry units of her time was within ten pounds of the weight lugged around by the Roman foot soldier. Gan was disappointed to learn she was infantry-oriented, but politely acknowledged that the might of her weapons made up for some of that misfortune.

The snowshoes were finished, a pair for everyone. She was amazed at what they'd accomplished. He examined them critically, with much dubious head shaking. The limited amount of salt available for treating the deerhide particularly troubled him.

As they stacked the snowshoes, she studied him covertly. She genuinely liked him. Tattooed Clas, too, for that matter. They were crude, powerful, honest. Force was their way.

No.

She corrected her shallowness. They were men of goals and ambitions. Casting them as stupid weapon-wielders was wrong. They were complex, but they'd learned to coordinate their energies, to single-mindedly drive through obstacles.

They were survivors.

Donnacee Tate was a survivor, too. A winner. She hadn't cheated the war and the crèche to wind up a loser. Not now. Not after all this.

Straightening with the last of the snowshoes, her gaze met his. He reached for them with both hands, but for some reason she made no immediate move to release them, nor he to take them. She smiled. Something moved in his eyes, a swirl that disappeared before she could be sure of it, but it left her thinking of the delight of a child discovering an eagerly anticipated gift.

CHAPTER 39

Sylah woke softly, rising to consciousness into a muffled silence that lulled her into a lethargic relaxation. For a moment she had trouble remembering exactly where she was.

When she opened her eyes, Neela still breathed regularly in sleep, golden hair a filmy net across the side of her face where it peeked out from the mounded blanket and hides covering her. Beyond, the contrasting darkness of Tate's features were still, her breathing so shallow it hardly moved her covering. Sylah remembered hearing her slip into the lean-to after her watch.

She thought back to times when waking had been a pleasure, when bright sunrise opened a door to the prospect of some enjoyment. The memory was so dim it seemed to be from another life. And it was, she thought, with grim humor.

This life demanded watches. Gan at nightwatch with his dogs, the women and Jones sharing two-person camp watches until the last one, when Clas took over alone.

Neela sighed heavily, and Sylah rolled up on an elbow, looking down at her. Sleep tried to reassert the unburdened innocence of childhood, but new patterns marked her, the signs of adulthood's armor.

Wrapping herself in her quilted down coat, Sylah swept aside the hide cover over the mouth of the lean-to and stepped outside. The fog brought a routine grimace that shifted quickly to wary speculation. Yesterday's wind had a peculiar smell. This was different yet, thicker, laden with a smell of rocks and ice.

An indistinct shape loomed a short distance away, coming toward her, resolving into a smiling Bilsten. He bowed low in flamboyant imitation of Olan court manners, eyes full of challenging amusement. "Good morning, Priestess. Seeing your lovely self first thing in the morning gives the day a proper start. Adds strength, don't you know?"

She smiled back at him. "I see how you survive in your travels. What do you say to the old women who've lost their youthful beauty?"

"Youthful? Ah, Priestess, isn't the beauty no eyes can see the most important? Doesn't it say in the Apocalypse Testament—let me see; yes—'Man must learn place. When man sees domain as the only beauty, all that is foul will claim him, and the righteous are commanded to shun him'?"

Frowning a fierceness she didn't really feel, she said, "We're taught the Evil One quotes scripture. I thank you for reminding."

He winked, turning away, and then she noticed his heavy clothing for the first time. "Why so warmly dressed this morning?" she asked.

He pointed past her, and she turned to see his animals already packed and ready for the trail. Concern tightened her voice. "So soon?"

"That wind yesterday . . ." He pulled on his beard, all humor gone. "I fear a snow. Snow, and then a warm spell. That means avalanche conditions, and I want to be ahead of that. And if the Devils *do* find you here, I don't want to be part of what happens."

"Isn't it more dangerous to travel alone?"

Shrugging, he said, "Alone's easier. If there's trouble, I only have one person to worry about." She saw his beard moving. It took a second for her to realize he was chewing on his lower lip. When he spoke, he was abrupt. "You watch that young Moondark man, Priestess. He's got more ambition than even he knows. Be careful." Quickly, he was all smiles again. "Have to go. Wish I could talk longer."

"Perhaps in Harbundai."

Brittleness edged in his laughter. " 'Perhaps.' Every day's a throw of the dice."

Moving quickly, he said good-bye to the arriving Gan and to Clas when he stepped out of the lean-to. He passed close to Sylah with a final "Good luck," and then the mist swallowed him. For a few seconds the sounds of hooves and the squeak of leather load harness drifted back to them on the warm ammonia smell of his animals. In the void that followed, the fog seemed to grow heavier.

She entered the lean-to for her toilet articles. The rustling of the hide brought Neela to a wide-eyed sitting position. A shortknife peered from under the bedding where her right hand remained hidden. Tate mumbled sleepily, squinted at them from one eye, and rolled over. Neela asked "What's wrong?" in a voice still clotted by sleep.

"Nothing," Sylah said. "I was just getting up. Everything's quiet."

"Too quiet." Neela slipped from under the covers, sheathing the knife as she did, and moved to kneel beside Sylah and look outside. "More fog."

Sylah said, "Bilsten's gone. I think Gan and Clas are trying to decide when we should follow."

"The sooner the better." Neela frowned in the direction of the mountains. "I don't trust him. He said bad things about Jones."

"We all have to keep up. He's a burden."

"He's gentle. I never talked to anyone like him. He told me that where he came from his work was to help people who were confused and afraid. I asked him if that was all he did, and he said yes. What sort of place can that be, where a man does nothing but help other people?"

"Church does it."

"For the sake of Church." She made a face, contrite. "And women. He says he worked for anyone in trouble."

"He's not strong. If he puts us in danger, you know what he must do."

"Yes." The answer was almost inaudible. It was custom the Dog People embraced with dark pride. In any retreat, those who would encumber the survivors either died by their own hand or staged a suicidal attack to cover the withdrawal of their companions. The family of such a man made a new pala drum and gave it his name, that his voice would live as long as the clan lived. Sylah tried to explain that the custom existed precisely to prevent good-hearted people from dying to help someone beyond help. It allowed the injured to die with honor, and the healthy survived to avenge him.

Leaving Neela to finish dressing, Sylah decided to walk past Gan and Clas. They squatted before the morning cookfire. She called to them, and they greeted her with faint smiles. Gan forced heartiness. "At least the weather's holding mild. Maybe the pass won't be as difficult as we thought."

Clas shook his head. "You know better. I only hope your precious new friend won't slow us down. I wish we'd never seen him."

Gan stared into the fire, and then, so quickly he startled everyone, he reached across it to put a hand on Clas' shoulder. "More than any other, ever, I need you by my side."

Clas stared at the hand on his shoulder as if he feared its touch. He shifted his gaze to Gan's eyes. He said, "When I promised your father, I promised you."

Sylah backed away, not wanting to stop watching the scene before her, equally unwilling to intrude. They'd spoken instinctively, impulsively. She heard the commitment in Clas' voice, the plea in Gan's. More than the unexpectedness of the exchange, she was awed by a passion in them she'd never suspected. She admitted to herself she was shaken by it. Until then, she had seen Clas' alliance with Gan in the sense of a bargain; an agreement of integrity and import, but still a matter of words. What she'd heard, those few words flung out so plainly, made her know this went beyond logic, beyond what they might will.

Turning, she made her way through the fog to the nearby stream. Preoccupied, mentally scrutinizing the relationships within the group, she suddenly became aware of her heedlessness. She'd been paralleling the streambank for some time and had no notion of where she was. Somehow she'd managed to intercept the stream too far downhill, past the normal washing-up place. The fog distorted everything, turned the familiar awry. Still, she wasn't terribly concerned. Finding her way back to the campsite was a simple matter of following the same stream uphill. She'd wash here and get her breath—she really *had* walked some distance, she realized, with a twinge of uneasiness—before returning.

The water was so cold it burned her hands. The first splash on her face drew an involuntary gasp, and she laughed at herself. With a small cloth she scrubbed her hands and face, then put her cloak and boots aside to better reach arms, legs, and feet. Another cloth served as towel. By the time she was finished with it, briskness had given way to a persistent clamminess that crept into her bones. She rushed to get completely dressed again.

She pulled on her boots and was just getting to her feet when she thought she saw something upstream. The disturbed air above the tumbling stream created a shifting, sliding sort of tunnel through the fog. She bent to peer into it, mildly embarrassed that her friends were searching for her.

A gust opened the gray curtain dramatically, revealing the death-painted Devil warriors huddled on the bank. They wore white cloaks that robbed them of form, made them all the more frightening. All looked uphill, toward the campsite, save one who walked toward them, parallel to the stream. He pointed an accusing finger at the ground. At her last clear view of them before the fog closed again, they were on both banks, moving downhill.

She could shout at them, warning them they pursued a holy person, inviolate, a Rose Priestess, a War Healer.

They wore the death paint. They knew who they sought. They knew what they meant to do.

She tried to scream and failed, then nearly choked at the realization that a single sound from her would bring them on her in a rush. She'd be dead before anyone in the camp could move, much less rescue her.

She ran.

At every glance behind, another swirl of mist took on the shape of a lunging Devil. Her heart pounded as if it would rip apart. She stopped, listening. A squirrel barked angry warning. She ran again.

Suddenly she was at a cleft in the earth, a drop of at least fifteen feet to where her stream intersected another. Scrambling down one side, she clawed her way up the opposite face, then raced headlong uphill, away from her original watercourse.

Her mistake registered within a few dozen yards, when she found herself crawling across jumbled, broken rock. Pieces were slabs the size of huts, ranging down to unstable little bits as small as her fist. There was no choice but forward, and she struggled, scrambling, leaping recklessly from boulder to boulder in her need to distance herself from the danger behind her. The finality of her error was a scarred rock wall, the source of all the rubble she'd crossed. It soared out of sight, disappeared to left and right into the fog. Remorseless, it blocked her utterly.

Unreasoning anger flooded her. She pounded on the wall with her fist, quickly abandoning that futility to step back and search for a place to climb.

Something metallic clattered below her.

She found a handhold, then a protrusion that formed a step. She crawled upward, tearing nails, pressing herself against the rock until she felt the grain of it must be etched into her flesh.

Inches. Feet.

And there was the ledge. By craning her head back she could see it, waiting for her.

Hoarse voices filtered through the fog. She heard their confidence.

Agonizingly, she hauled herself from purchase to purchase until one hand triumphantly gripped the ledge. Panting with exhaustion, she dragged herself onto it, rolling into the tiny hollow behind it.

She lay there, too frightened to move, until the rough cry jerked her head around. There, rushing at her from the grayness was a dark, menacing shape.

She almost cracked into hysterical laughter as the startled raven saw her and fluttered wildly, turning away. For an instant its bright, malicious eye held hers, and the fog parted to let her watch it fly to its brethren in a nearby tree.

Death birds. They croaked and chuckled among themselves.

The warriors spoke directly under her. The ledge that had been so distant when she wanted to reach it was now perilously close to the ground, no more than fifteen feet up the cliff. She risked a look. The four of them were directly below, arguing. As one gestured at the wall, she shrank back. In a few moments she heard voices fading in the distance, and dared hope, only to crash back to reality when the rasp of heavy breathing indicated a pursuer was started up the wall.

She pushed herself into the cranny and drew her shortknife. She tried to think clearly, picturing him raising up to look over the edge. He'll need both hands to hold on, she told herself; I can lunge at him before he can defend himself.

The warrior understood his predicament as clearly as she did, and when he got a grip on the edge, he flung himself up and in in one move. That swiftness and the shock of the horribly painted face thrust almost in contact with her own momentarily froze her. Belatedly, she struck. He caught her forearm with his empty hand. Still, the space was so cramped, his weight on his other elbow prevented him striking with the ma pinned under him. They struggled, and his superior strength drove the tip of the blade irresistibly toward her stomach, inch by inch.

Abruptly he stopped. His eyes bulged, as if he recognized her. Slowly, almost absently, he relaxed his grip on her wrist. The ma sagged, scraped rock, and was still.

He slumped against her. The feathered shaft of the arrow in his back snapped off when he rolled onto his side.

She cried then, unable to stop until after Clas had climbed to the ledge and assured himself—and her—that she was unharmed. After he'd pulled the body of the warrior free, it took his firm hand on her shoulder to coax her to the edge and steady her descent. Once on the ground, her legs refused to hold her up, and she embraced his supporting strength. Then she remembered the others.

"Three," she said, choking on the word. "Three more. That way." She pointed.

He nodded. "I know. I followed."

She drew back. "You *followed*?"

"I was foraging. I saw the Devils. I knew they were tracking something. When I saw your footprints and knew it was you they were after, they were too spread out for me to risk shooting at one of them. I had to wait."

"You should have attacked! You let them follow me, frighten me! I thought—"

He crushed her to him. "You were very brave. You saved all our lives by not screaming."

"I couldn't. They chased me like an animal." She shivered, and he patted her shoulder.

"We have to hurry," he said. "This is going to make things even more difficult. At least it'll keep the Devils from following us."

She looked up, puzzled by the last, and realized it was snowing. She'd been too excited to notice the wind had come up alarmingly. Fog whipped past in tattered banners.

Clas carefully snapped off the arrow that had killed the Devil, then stripped the cloak from him. He handled it gingerly, wrinkling his nose at its gaminess. He shook off the quilted white jacket under that before collecting the short, white skis propped against the cliff. There was also a long coil of plaited leather line, and he took that, as well. His last act, after breaking the warrior's weapons and throwing the blades as far as he could, was to take his trophy.

Sylah turned away, and when Clas was beside her again, he said, "You missed the tattoos on his forearm. A bee and an eye."

She frowned. "I know the meaning. He's a southerner, and a Manhunter. They never range this far north."

He nodded, silent. Then they moved away as quickly as possible, the snow making the going more difficult every step. It obscured the rocks they had to traverse, then doubled that hazard by making them slippery.

Before they reached the shelter of the trees, Clas was shouting in her ear that they needed shelter, and quickly. When they came to an especially large boulder, he led her into the shelter of its overhang, and they joyously discovered the entry to a roomlike cave. At first she stiffened at the prospect. Although it was far larger, it was all too reminiscent of the cleft where the warrior had trapped her. At his urging, she crawled in and settled against a wall, unsure if her shivering was primarily from the cold or nerves.

As soon as she was settled, he left, rejecting her plea that he stay. He returned in a few minutes, covered with snow, carrying firewood. Striking sparks with flint and steel into some of the tow he carried in his pouch, he quickly had a fire burning just inside the entry.

The flames had a magical effect, made her feel isolated and secure. The storm could only bluster. In fact, it was their friend, hiding their trail. Muscles loosened, setting off small aches that faded quickly. She leaned against the firm resistance of Clas' shoulder, luxuriating in the shared warmth of the contact. The events of the morning clamored in her mind, but where there had been terror was now a delicious excitement, a feeling of danger beaten. Relaxing even further brought a soft drowsiness, a delightful hazy peacefulness.

The first touch of his hand on her cheek was even more pleasant, and as it drifted gently down her neck and her shoulder, she knew his intent. Nevertheless, the touch of it on her breast startled her. She reached to push it away, but he resisted. The moment was swift, the clash a travesty. The dreamlike lassitude reclaimed her. She felt more than the little fire's warmth now, and a power in her called for more yet. With her eyes closed, she interpreted his movements, knowing he was taking off his fur coat, putting it on the ground beside her. Then he was turning her shoulders, laying her back on it, lying beside her. He was on one elbow; when he fumbled at the laces of her blouse with both hands, she almost smiled to herself at how wonderfully she perceived everything, every touch, every thought, every heretofore imagined mystery unfolding under the spell of this moment.

Then, in one blazing instant of pain and pleasure, she wanted to understand no more, cared nothing for any thought. There was only Clas.

She had no idea how long they'd been in their shelter when she first realized the sounds of the storm had ended. The fire was dull coals. Her face warmed; she didn't care how long it had been. She wished it could all happen again. She looked down at him, sleeping as soundly as the rock all around them, the scars of too many battles tracking across his body. She was shocked at how near-deadly some were, and wondered why she had to fall in love with a man whose path kept him so near the edge of life. And why had he the power to raise her passions so, why would he choose her, of all women?

She tried to move him aside as gently as possible so she could dress. Her first touch brought him awake, and he grabbed for his own clothes, awkward in his haste. She took his face in both her hands, brought it around to her own and kissed him lightly on the lips. He flinched.

She said, "It was going to happen, Clas. We've both known it."

He shook his head stubbornly. "I didn't." He half turned again, then dropped his head and tried to smother a smile. "I hoped it would. Not like this." He took her hand, kissed the palm. "I feel like a thief."

"I know your thoughts. You're not a man to hide things, and we don't dare speak of this."

"They'd understand."

"Possibly. It's a risk we can't take."

Urgently, he asked, "When will we— I mean . . . ?" When she pretended alarm, he went fiery red.

She laughed and took back her hand to continue dressing. "Not soon enough, my love. When we can."

Grinning, he embraced her. He only held her for a moment, though, before hurrying to look outside. "It's slacking off," he said. Then, chuckling, "Good timing."

She said, "Can we get back to camp now?"

"Yes. If the storm doesn't regain its strength, we'll be all right."

"And if it does?"

He continued to look away from her. He said, "Those Devils'll bring their friends, and quickly. We have to warn the others. We're in a race now, from here to Harbundai. If we don't get back to camp, we lose before we start."

She joined him, peering out at the blowing snow. "Promise me you won't let anyone know."

"Can I tell you I love you?"

"As often as you will. As I love you." She reached up to touch his lips. "Our secret, though. If they guess, we deny."

He nodded and scrambled outside, leaning into the wind. When she followed, he reached with one hand to scoop her against his back. "Hold onto me," he said. "Don't let go." He started walking. She bent forward, sheltering behind him.

Nothing will ever make me let you go, she thought, and felt strength from the words.

CHAPTER 40

Gan poked at the fire irritably. Smoke whirled up from the disturbance, writhing through the thin gaps between the hide front curtain and the frame of the lean-to. A few feet away Neela sat on the ground and worried at the fringe on her boots. Gan said, "You shouldn't have let him go after her alone."

"He didn't go after her!" Her face flamed. "Not at first, anyway. She took her things to wash up. He went foraging."

He lifted the curtain to peer out. The women's lean-to remained closed. Letting the hide drop, he said, "It's gotten stronger again. It looked to be dying off, but it was only resting." He hoped Neela would continue to believe Clas and Sylah were tucked in some sheltered spot. He had no intention of pointing out that if they had found shelter, and then been lured out by the false lull, they could be in greater danger than ever. As for the possibility that they'd run into a Devil patrol, he was trying very hard not to think of that himself.

"You usually stay awake awhile after coming in from nightwatch. He shouldn't have had to go after her by himself."

Neela managed to sound accusatory and defensive at the same time, and he lashed out thoughtlessly. "So it's my fault? That's all you care about— who's to blame."

She recoiled.

He waved his arms. "All right, I'm sorry."

Immediately she was placating. "I shouldn't have said that. I didn't mean it. I'm worried."

"I can't sit and wait any longer. You stay with Tate and Jones. Tell them what to do."

She clutched at him as he rose. "You'll never find them in this storm. You'll get lost yourself."

He lifted her hand from his arm, held it a moment before letting go. "I'll be careful. Take care of the strangers, keep them alert. You'll be in command."

The words hung between them, shocking. It wasn't what he'd meant to say, certainly nothing she'd ever expected to hear. He bit down hard to avoid correcting himself, and she lifted her chin to say, "No fear."

She left as he busied himself dressing for the search. Extra protection was a must. He began by stripping off his normal leather shirt and trousers, putting on the quilted cotton winter underwear over his regular wear. The trousers were first, with suspenders. The jacket overlapped them, and laced up the front, providing a snug but not tight fit. Buttons at the sides kept the two items aligned, helping prevent bunching. Clothes that were too tight didn't provide room for warm air, and clothes that bunched up invariably led to cold spots on the wearer. A cold spot could go from an irritation to a threat in short order. It bled the body of strength as surely as a wound.

The leather outerwear was next. It stopped the wind, as well as providing insulation. Slipping into the sheepskin coat and adjusting the earflaps on the raccoon fur hat, he slung his murdat across his back. There was no point in carrying a bow in this visibility.

Outside, the dogs were three tightly coiled bundles, each lying in the lee of its own tree. They knew, however; three pairs of eyes waited for him as he lifted the flap. They rose as one, shaking, sending snow flying back into the storm. The oval indentations they left in the snow began to fill immediately.

The dogs took positions they'd never assumed before, with Raggar immediately beside him on his left, perhaps a yard ahead, while Cho and Shara were in the rear and to the flanks. They were close enough for good visual contact, yet they were obviously creating a spread formation. He thought about setting them in their normal wedge, with Raggar to the front and the other two abreast, but decided to let them have their way. They wouldn't change a routine for no reason.

The snow drove into their faces relentlessly, sometimes throwing up an almost impenetrable wall, other times slacking to a spiteful softness that tantalized him with the hope that it signaled the storm's end. It never did. He'd gone a hundred yards below the washing site when he saw the broken branch. Only because the sharp ends pointed away from the wind did he notice the lighter color of newly exposed wood. He squatted by it, brushing the snow aside to see if there was any other sign.

Raggar's low growl, almost at his ear, brought him to his feet, murdat in hand.

The lead wolf stood just at the limit of his vision, watching. Dim shapes beyond him could have been the rest of the pack or tricks of the shifting light.

After a moment Gan sheathed his weapon and moved forward. The wolf's sides heaved from heavy breathing, and it was apparent he was very tired. His tongue lolled as he watched Gan advance until only a few feet separated them, then he turned and started down the mountain, looking over his shoulder.

Raggar looked at Gan as if approving. Together they followed, the other dogs still in their rear-guard positions. The shadows that might have been the pack materialized and disappeared randomly. Then, as suddenly as he'd appeared, the lead wolf was gone. Ahead, where he'd been, Clas and Sylah stumbled uphill.

Clas said, "What're you doing out here?"

"Looking for you, of course. What happened?"

"Four Devils." He jerked his head back downhill. "They chased Sylah, I followed them. Killed one—Bee Clan, Manhunter, painted for a fight. Sylah's wearing his snow cloak. These are his skis and coat. The storm caught us on the way back. You shouldn't have come looking; what if you'd missed us?"

Gan looked around. "Where are the wolves?"

Sylah melted closer to Clas. "Wolves?"

"They led me right to you."

Clas grunted. "Good for them. Never saw them. Give me a hand with Sylah, will you?"

Gan sent Shara and Cho ahead, so the others were waiting for them when they arrived. The women swooped down on Sylah, but before they could get her inside, Gan turned to see the wolves again.

Eyes walling, the horses danced anxiously at the ends of their tethers. Neela ran to them, her sure hands and voice bringing a semblance of calm.

A thick ammonia-and-wet-fur smell rose from the wolves' bodies on clouds of steam. They were obviously exhausted. Several lay flat. From the rear a young female practically slunk forward. She was very afraid, and as soon as she dropped the arrow she carried in her mouth, she scuttled back into the pack.

That was when Gan realized they were fewer in number, as well. The leader looked over his shoulder at the remainder, turning his great muzzle from side to side, as if marking the losses. When he faced Gan again he snarled.

Beside him, Raggar stiffened. Gan put a hand on his head.

A large male broke away from the pack, swinging uphill past the campsite. The remainder streamed after him, dark smoke eddying into the obscuring snow. The leader scratched earth, sending sticks and dirt flying before following.

Clas picked up the arrow. "Devils," he said.

Tate came to stand beside him. She looked pinched and cold. "They brought you the arrow to tell you that?"

Gan said, "It must be so. They never did it before. They led me to Clas and Sylah, too."

Everyone was talking at once then, demanding to know what happened. Something about the way Sylah glanced at Clas and deferred the tale to him sparked an unpleasant twinge in Gan's mind. He immediately looked to Neela, and was sure he saw the tail end of an identical reaction. They all crowded into the men's lean-to while Clas related their story.

As soon as he finished, Neela said, "They'll be back as soon as the storm lets up."

Gan disagreed. "Two, at the most. One has to report."

Tate said, "Has anyone else thought about Bilsten?"

Gan smiled crookedly. "Yes. He leaves and the Devils arrive soon after."

"He left a trail, all right." Clas' laugh held no humor. "Straight to us."

Gan said, "We have to cross the mountains. If Bilsten informed on us or not, we go for Cloud Rest Pass. It's a race. Pack. We leave now, so the snow can cover our tracks."

"Or us," Clas added, already stuffing gear in his saddlebag.

*   *   *

They made good time, despite the weather, the first day. The following afternoon they were plodding along at a steady pace. The best news was the lack of pursuit. So far.

The weather had warmed; Gan was sure of it. Not enough to make a difference, but the snowflakes seemed fatter. They fell more vertically, as well, not skating past on the wind. The air still had a steel-cold smell, though. Odd.

Beneath him, his horse moved steadily, almost silently, pushing through snow that reached almost to his hocks. He thought of the hard country ahead; steeper grades were certain. If the snow deepened, the animals might be unable to cope. Unconsciously he patted the animal's neck. It was hard to remember a time when they weren't companions. They knew each other. It snorted and tossed its head, and he laughed to himself, wondering if it wasn't meant to reassure him.

Gan's mind turned to what Bilsten and Sylah said about Cloud Rest. More a low spot in the mountains than a narrow gap, its width would force the Devils to cover much ground to intercept the party. Bilsten had promised to mark a "safe" path, one that paralleled the main route and was unlikely to be observed.

Their dilemma was the need for haste and the need to scout the way as carefully as possible. Pursuit was probably under way already. The Devils would consider the storm a minor event. On skis and snowshoes, they'd come like the wind.

He looked back at the rest of the group. Neela rode a short distance in front of Clas, who was rear guard. She was unrecognizable in her heavy bearskin coat and the woolen hood mask. Listless, she rode as if disjointed, staring at the ground. Sunflyer reacted to her attitude, as usual. He was unsettled, walking almost on tiptoe, popping his head up and down as if pecking. She toyed with his mane absently, her eyes seeing past the beauty of the thick snowflakes against the rich fur of her beaver mittens.

Gan gestured for Clas to take the point and waited for her to come abreast. She jumped when his words broke her concentration. He said, "Don't worry so much."

"About who? Oh—*them*, the Devils. I'm not afraid of them."

He laughed softly. "You're braver than I am, then. They scare me."

She pushed back her hood and removed the mask. Her smile was a tiny movement. She said, "I had other things on my mind." Ahead, Clas dismounted, indicating the horses needed a rest. When everyone had snowshoes lashed on, he led the way forward once again. Still preoccupied, Neela lagged. Gan stayed with her, saying nothing until the silence between them grew oppressive. He tried to draw her out. "Something's troubling you. Can you talk to me about it?"

She'd been walking with her head down, staring at the ground, and at his question her eyes flicked toward the head of the small column. When she glanced to see if he'd caught her, there was apprehension and embarrassment in her expression.

Gan was sure he understood. He said, "Oh, Sylah. I know we almost lost her, but she's fine now. Learned her lesson, too; be sure of that. Even if there was a chance she didn't, Clas'll never let her forget. I don't think he knew himself how much he cared for her, until she was missing. Sometimes people never see what's closest to them."

She stopped as if she'd hit a wall. Even when Sunflyer reached the limit of the reins and jerked to a surprised stop, she merely swayed without taking her eyes from Gan's face. Her whole manner suggested he'd spoken in some unknown tongue. Then she started to laugh, a harsh rattle that tore at him like a saw. Confused, he reached for her, but she pulled back, stumbling clumsily, backing into her horse. One of her hands went to her mouth, stifling the awful laughter. The other cracked on the side of his face with a report like a breaking branch.

Instantly, before he could even react, she lurched forward and flung her arms around him.

She was crying. He was so confused his mind felt empty, robbed of all thought.

He lifted his arms to embrace her, making sounds he hoped were comforting. The group continued on, leaving them alone. Gradually he felt the sobs lessen, felt her regaining physical control. He risked asking what he could do to help.

"Just hold me, Gan. Hold me tight."

It was exactly what he wanted to do. He put a hand behind her head, pressed it to his shoulder. The warm scent of her hair was as if spring had come to their snowy trail.

She moved against him, and the wound her brother Bay had given his shoulder twinged slightly.

The brief pain set off a string of thoughts.

For the first time in his life he held a woman in his arms. Her father had died by his hand. Her brother had tried to kill him and would again.

So be it. She was the sole woman he wanted in his arms, like this, always, and families and tribe would have to make their peace with that any way they could.

Now he understood that she'd been thinking of Clas and Sylah and the time they were alone, and how they looked at each other since then. She'd been thinking of them, but also of him and herself. He remembered the first night they'd both known Sylah, how he'd been so impressed by her arrival, such dark beauty, and a Priestess. He'd spoken so foolishly to Neela then, asking her embarrassingly revealing questions about the older woman.

And then he remembered how he'd gone into Neela's tent when Sylah asked. He also remembered that, on the night they escaped, Neela said she'd come to Sylah only after she heard Clas' name.

Clas and Sylah had found each other. And Neela was crying.

But she was in *his* arms.

He realized he'd let his grip slacken. He tightened it. She'd come to him, and that was sufficient. It was everything.

A corner of his heart, a place so small it could barely make itself felt, wondered if she could ever cry for him the way she cried for Clas na Bale.

CHAPTER 41

Gan insisted they push on until it was almost too late to build a shelter. As it was, they had to rush. The new snow was heavy, and fortunately packed well, so the snowhouse went up quickly. Gan and Clas handled the actual construction while the others formed the blocks. After stamping out a flat surface, the two warriors used murdat and shortknife to put the finishing touches on the blocks, laying them row on row in ever-diminishing circles. Soon they had a domed dwelling with a tunnellike crawlway entry, snug against wind or cold.

They were surprised to learn that Tate and Jones used the old word, igloo, to describe it.

Neela insisted they all eat, explaining solemnly to Tate that hot food was necessary to replace heat stolen by winter's cold. Using a powdered mixture from a large leather sack, she prepared a stew. Tate apologized once more for her—and Jones'—inability to contribute. Neela brushed aside the comment, saying everyone had enjoyed their food very much, while it lasted, and complimented her on the way she'd unhesitatingly helped with the foraging. She reminded Tate that it was she who helped Clas bring in the yearling wildcow that had fed them so well for so long.

Tate was glad to let the matter rest there, and went on to point out that this was the first prepared food she'd seen them use—everything else had been fresh forage.

Neela said they always carried rations, and when the opportunity provided, prepared more, such as the smoked venison. Prepared food was hoarded against such a time as this.

When Tate asked what was in the powdered mix, Neela said it was a family recipe that her mother made up every summer, sun-drying all the ingredients herself. The meat was chicken and rabbit. There were tomatoes, potatoes, onions, garlic, and some other vegetables.

As it simmered, Tate raved about the delicious smell, and she saw how intensely the three Dogs and Sylah watched as she sampled it. The attention made her a bit nervous. It took a moment for a searing blast from the first sip to let her know that much of her "replaced" heat was to come from some absolutely violent pepper seasoning. She sputtered, choked, and knew from the laughter she was the butt of the day's joke.

She made the most of it, scolding and carrying on, glad to see everyone, including Sylah, break free of the weight of concern that bent their shoulders ever since the Devil scouts had discovered them. Then she really pleased them, revealing that she loved spicy food, laying into the broth with gusto.

They slept well that night, well fed, protected from the weather, and thoroughly drained by their long path higher into the mountains. The leftover stew made a nourishing breakfast, although Sylah noted unhappily that Jones complained to Tate about it. He got some down, but he seemed to object more to the quality than the taste. That irritated Sylah, and she quickly reminded herself to think about something else. Minor disturbances became dire offenses in such situations.

She turned her attention to Clas, smiling wryly at her realization that she did that far too often, and was pleased to see the way he helped Tate. She wasn't very adept at living in the snow, and he was anxious to assist. That was as it should be. They'd exchanged blood because she saved his life. Thinking about that brought her to Gan. He tried very hard to hide his resentment over the closeness between Clas and Tate. The others saw nothing, she was sure. There were signs, though, if one looked carefully; now, for instance, as Clas joined her to scrub out the eating bowls with fir needles and snow, Gan measured grain into the horses' feed bags less than carefully, continually glancing away to watch them. She almost felt sorry for him. He respected Tate and he loved Clas. He was pleased to see they were friends. But he wanted their loyalty. He had a destiny. Theirs was part of his. She wondered how long he could exist with that thought and continue to be a normal person.

They were under way quickly.

The breeze was soft and warm, as if apologetic. Gan knew it for a liar.

Its sly whisper loosened snow on bent fir branches, cascading it to earth. Some of the burdens were heavy enough to injure. Even a small one could make one's clothes wet, opening the door for the "soft death" that almost painlessly stole life before one realized what was happening.

As they plodded along beside the horses, beset by the unremitting muffled drumming of the falling snow, they were forced to admire the beauty of it even as they worried about it. Columns of sun sheared through the trees to catch the particles, turning them into white-fire plumes that brought small gasps of delight from the women. Their furs, bristling with ice crystals, seemed to vibrate with energy. The almost horizontal light limned each tree behind them with a glow that made it appear to retreat into its own darkness. To the sides, similar rays were blades of pure brilliance.

It was a dangerous beauty. On the crests above them, invisible through the trees, unimaginable tons of snow poised in delicate balance. The gentle breeze, the beautiful sun, touched the mass with seductive softness. They brought the melting that would unbalance the cornices, create deadly shifting.

The trail itself wasn't as bad as Gan expected. He began to think they'd actually get all the horses through, after all. They were as high on the south shoulder of the pass as they'd have to go. If Bilsten hadn't lied. Still, Gan felt it best to let the horses continue unridden, conserving their strength.

The trail they left gave the impression that lumbering, belly-dragging beasts were attempting to scale the mountains. Manhunters would read it and tell the physical condition—and probably a great deal about the mental state—of each person and animal.

Gan considered the possibility of ambush. Longingly he watched excellent positions on each flank approach and then recede. If he broke to the side to reach one, the trackers would know immediately. Dropping back was an option, but only if the situation became desperate. A one- or two-man ambush, no matter how effective, would be quickly cut off and eliminated by the skiing Devils, leaving the group that much weaker. If the entire group participated in the ambush, it became no more than a surprise attack. That would either lead to destruction or headlong retreat and pursuit. Their only reasonable chance was to keep distance between themselves and their pursuers until they escaped to some sort of shelter.

Late that afternoon they crossed a stream, a crashing roar of silver froth and crystal-shining water so cold that when they bent to scoop up drinks, its touch made finger joints crack. To taste it was like having a tiny knife drawn along the line of contact between teeth and gums. They had traveled only a short distance beyond when Clas, riding point, threw up a hand to halt them, then pointed. In sight was the last shoulder they'd have to navigate before starting downhill to Harbundai.

Bilsten had marked trail well to that point. While the horses shuffled and pawed the ground, hopelessly prospecting for something green to eat, they scanned as far as they could see, and there was no further sign of a trail. Clas' hand clenched and unclenched angrily around the handle of his murdat. Gan was grim.

Raggar walked to a tree to the west of them, sniffed it, then looked up at the trunk, cocking his head to the side. Gan watched him idly, then with more interest as the dog backed away, still looking up, then returned to his original position and raised his leg. He seemed confused, and strained at his work so hard Gan wondered if he were going to fall over. And then he understood.

"You see what Bilsten's done, Clas? That coyote's son marked a trail. He marked it the way a dog would, and stood on his horse to do it, so even the heaviest snow wouldn't cover it up. Lucky Raggar didn't injure himself, trying to reach up there."

They moved on confidently then, following the dogs, making as good progress as could be hoped. There was only a little daylight left when Gan indicated a rest break. He used hand language with Clas to say he intended to scout the route ahead and below. Clas seemed surprised by Gan's sudden interest in a silent rest, but asked no questions. In fact, he appeared nervous, more concerned, somehow, than Gan could ever remember him.

Gan proceeded west until he was satisfied there was no patrol nearby, then dropped downhill to a point where he could view the main trail. During his scout he heard an occasional bird call—magpies, pheasants, an eagle—and once he thought he heard a deer bark alarm far away. There was no large animal sign, however, save one tree a tiger had clawed, but the scars were old. It was the *absence* of things that bothered him, as if the wilderness was holding back, waiting.

Compared to the challenge of Bilsten's secret path, the regular route was a road. Gan signaled the dogs and advanced from tree to tree at a crouch, bow slung across his back now, murdat in hand.

He would have missed the man if the jay hadn't complained. When it first rose, squawking, above the trees, he was inclined to dismiss it. They were undependable, as likely to scold another bird as a man.

A single warrior, on foot, appeared on the bank of the creek on the other side of the main trail. He scooped a hide bucket full of water and was back out of sight in seconds, but the action told Gan what he had to know. If the man was getting water in a bucket at this time of day, he was assuredly carrying it to a campsite hidden in the trees. The route was guarded well.

He hurried to rejoin the others.

Gathering everyone close, he told what he'd seen, and they were on the move again in minutes. They soon discovered the reason for the Devils' camp location. With expressions ranging from despondent to disbelieving, they huddled together at the edge of a burn heretofore hidden in a deep bow in the mountains. Featureless, a snow desert, it stretched at least a half mile in front of them. The Devils, from their position in the valley, had only to look up occasionally to see anything moving on its face.

Gan admired Bilsten's courage for crossing such a place with a laden pack train, but he'd put them in a terrible position. Falling snow hid him during his crossing and covered his tracks afterward. For the group, there was nothing.

It was Clas who gave words to the obvious. "We fight our way through the blocking site or cross at night."

Gan backed everyone into the protective forest. Once again they put up a snow shelter. Tate hurried Jones inside just as a fit of coughing seized him. When she came out, defiance blazed through her exhaustion. Her expression silently dared anyone to criticize. Gan broke the uncomfortable silence. He rubbed his wounded shoulder as he spoke. "We'll go tonight."

Neela made a small sound, and he turned to her. "Even with surprise, we'll lose someone if we have to fight. There must be warriors behind us, and they have to be catching up."

Two people at a time shared the watch on the back trail. The rest packed the small shelter, sharing a cold meal of smoked venison. The dogs accepted their meager ration with disappointment, but it was the reproach in the eyes of the horses that troubled Gan. He shared the job of graining them with Neela, measuring out the last kernels almost one by one. She asked quietly, "Do you think these poor things can make it across there?"

"I don't know." She had her hand curled tightly in Sunflyer's mane. He went on. "We're not going to leave them on this side. I can't promise. You understand."

She nodded and turned away, leaning against the animal. Gan added, "I'll do my best, Neela." He reached out, couldn't bring himself to touch her. The hand lowered to his side. "I want you to know I'm sorry about . . . everything that happened. I wasn't very smart. I've learned a lot." He wished he could find the courage to tell her he was aware that he sounded like a fool, that his own words ridiculed him.

Turning slowly, she looked at him with a controlled, unreadable expression. She said, "You're a true friend. And I will always be a friend to you, as long as we live."

That wasn't what he wanted to hear, especially the soft reservation in the latter words. In that instant he decided that she must be part of the prophecy, part of the future he was expected to create. Otherwise, he wanted nothing to do with it. *He* would include her, and the dream must.

Without further comment, she turned away from him, began removing the empty feed bags. She dropped them on the ground, and he bit back a protest at her wastefulness, realizing, as she had, that with no more grain, the leather sacks were only excess weight.

A beaten-silver half-moon rose in a cloudless sky. When Gan and Clas moved away from the others to sit by themselves, Tate's frayed nerves sent her rushing to Neela for answers. "What're they up to? Why are they talking?"

Neela shushed her, then answered in a whisper. "We call it nara. When a warrior has time to pray before a fight, he asks for courage, and thanks the One in All for giving him brave men to test him. He asks that his mind be strong enough to control his body and all his thoughts."

So, Tate thought, we've got meditation. And biofeedback. That links up with the ability to slow the blood flow, and ignoring pain. It *doesn't* necessarily explain that unreal clotting time; that ought to be a purely physical adaptation. If this is what they've become in five centuries, what'll their descendants be like in another century? Another five?

What'll I be like in another year?

Will I be alive tomorrow?

Neela's hand on her shoulder brought her to her feet in a flustered rush, checking her weapon, staring into the night. She moved away quickly to rouse Jones, getting him on his feet, bundling him up against the cold. "As soon as you feel yourself warming up," she said, "undo some buttons. Ventilate. Don't overheat, understand?"

He mumbled, and she made him repeat his answer until she was sure he understood.

The Dogs and Sylah were all making Three-signs as she turned, and then they were gesturing her forward.

The brightness was frightening at first. Distant peaks loomed in cold clarity, while even the dark valley seemed ready to open all its secrets. Ice crystals twinkled, mimicking stars.

They were less than a third of the way before Gan was sure all of Church's fearsome claims for the Land Under were overstated. No punishment could match forcing the straining horses over this treacherous snow mass. Even the snowshoes slipped. Their progress was a series of falls and rises, each more draining than the last. Clothes grew sodden, giving off steam that mingled with the clouding breath of humans, dogs, and horses. Jones was already wrapped in a hide; the women saw to him, two dragging, one walking beside to keep him faceup. Gan hoped he'd remain silent in his semiconsciousness.

The first tinge of dawn fell across their backs as they staggered and fell into the protective cover of the forest. Two of the stolen Devil horses marred the white bald, slaughtered to end broken-legged misery. Gan urgently gestured everyone past him, dropping behind a stump that gave him a view of the back trail as well as the Devil camp in the valley. Shara and Cho curled up against him wearily. Raggar took position under the snow-laden canopy of a young fir. Gan dozed in spite of his efforts not to, until the deep, mournful drone of a Mountain war horn jerked him to a fuddled, unsure wakefulness. The sound echoed weirdly. He turned to see the others stirring where they'd collapsed. Still secured to trees as Clas had left them, the horses were scrambling to their feet.

Coming to stand beside him, Clas gestured lazily across the burn. "Must be a good number, to bring a horn."

"They salute," Neela said. She stood erect, proud and sure. "Clas na Bale is our finest fighter. Gan and I are the children of War Chiefs."

Below them the camp leaped to life. Through the screening forest, they glimpsed men and horses scurrying like disturbed ants.

Tate joined Gan and Clas. They heard shouts. The pursuit had reached the other side of the scar. She said, "I think I can stop them."

Gan shook his head. "There's no time for a stand. The ones from the valley will come up to cut us off from the route west if we wait."

"They'll ride us down if we don't stop them," Clas said. "Look, they're leading extra horses. And they've all got skis."

Tate pointed and said, "Maybe I can make that snow fall."

Gan was skeptical. "Our crossing didn't do it."

Tate said, "I want to try. All of you should be away from here."

Gan tensed. She was a friend. But the prophecy was in control. He believed she had a bearing on his future. Was she to create escape? At the cost of her own life?

The beliefs and dreams were true or they weren't. "Do what you can," he said, and left.

Tate pumped a boop round into the chamber and aimed at the base of the snow mass. The sound of firing didn't faze the Devil warriors, and when the round thumped harmlessly far away, they screamed taunts and threats. At a wavering blast from the war horn, they streamed out onto the open space, some leading horses that towed teams of skiers, while the rest cut swiftly across the snow under their own power. There were at least thirty. Two labored under the weight of the huge brass war horn. It was at least ten feet long. When they stopped to sound again, the bell rested on one man's shoulder while the other blew into the mouthpiece.

Pieces of snow broke off, high on the mountain. Someone yelled at the horn men, and they came on again, but without noise.

Tate fired again, with no more result. The warriors picked up their pace.

She fired again, and prepared to shoot at the advancing column.

The mountain breathed.

It sounded as if the earth gasped, a shocked, liquid noise. And after that, the rumble.

Tate ran. She prayed she wouldn't stumble in her rush away from the terror thundering down the burn. Trees around her whipped and cracked as hurricane winds struck their tops. Smothering, choking billows blinded her.

An arm of snow shot free of the body of the avalanche to playfully swat her off her feet. She rolled upright and kept running.

When she overtook her companions, they had to grab her. Sylah held her, calming her babble, a distraught Clas circling in the background. Actually, it was Jones who brought her out of it. He stirred on his hide sled, querulously asking if there was any hot soup, since they weren't moving anymore. Tate's burst of laughter earned her a solid shake from Sylah, and then she stepped free of her help. She continued to lean against a horse, her control still tentative. When she said, "You can forget about those warriors now," ragged laughter cracked in her voice for a moment.

Neela stayed with her as they resumed their hurried march away.

Gan became a man possessed. He ranged their small column, exhorting, demanding, tongue-lashing. The dogs slunk off to become shadows that ghosted through the trees at what they considered a safe distance. Jones was lashed to Neela's horse, sprawled across a blanket where she'd thrown off the saddle in partial compensation for his weight. At the limit of their strength, they stumbled on. Two horses, one of them Sunflyer, bled from the nose, leaving a ruby-spotted testimony of exhaustion.

When Gan gasped out the evidence of a trickle of water running with them, their first indication they were actually moving downhill, the only sound that greeted the announcement was a strained, wavering screech from behind that indicated the Devils from the low-ground camp were on their trail.

The chase lasted for hours. Another horse went down, thrashing weakly. Clas dispatched it almost absently, then looked at Gan. When he spoke, his voice rasped.

"Far enough," he said. "I won't be cut down running, too weak to fight."

Gan swayed, caught himself. "True." He made a sound that could be laughter. "We'll give them something to sing about, right? Those boulders there, at the bend of the river. Good defense."

The women moved Jones into the center of the rock jumble. Neela came out, led the horses a few yards downstream, then flapped a blanket at them. The captured Devil horses ambled away. The Dog war horses trotted off on command from Clas. Copper shied, then refused to leave until Neela stoned her. Sunflyer was even more reluctant. He kept trying to make his way back to her, dodging her thrown rocks. He whinnied piteously, too weary to rear. Finally, dispirited, he backed off, shaking his head in near-human confusion. Tears coursed down Neela's cheeks as she made her way back inside the rock formation, and when Tate and Sylah tried to comfort her, she pushed them away.

Gan watched her, saying nothing, and suddenly she turned, as if she felt the pressure of eyes. Her tears were gone. No steel ever looked harder, he thought, and he had a premonition that he might never truly understand her strength. He tried to tell her he understood why she chased the animals away. She rejected the sympathy.

"I didn't want to kill them. They've worked too hard."

"The Devils'll get them."

She held up her murdat. "At least one Devil won't."

"More than one. And maybe we'll get your horse back."

Her smile humored him.

The dogs trotted out of the forest, joining him. He roughed their heads, and they wagged their tails before settling down, looking east. They were bred for this moment. They understood.

A warrior ran out of the trees to stand on the riverbank upstream. He wore death-mask paint. His barmal armor was painted white, with black ribs and a bleeding red heart painted on it. He carried a ma and a small round shield.

Jones force himself up beside Tate. He said, "Can't we at least try to talk? He's out of range, isn't he? Don't shoot, Donnacee."

"He'll get closer."

"How can you tell?"

"I can smell it. He's showing everybody he's not afraid. He'll come to me."

Other warriors flitted through the trees. The exposed one danced closer, shouting, beating a rhythm on his shield with the ma.

Tate wiped him.

The man sprawled in the river. There was a frozen silence immediately after the report, but as the first echo rolled back from the mountains, literally hundreds of crows erupted in screaming excitement from a nearby rookery. Simultaneously, a great shout went up from the warrior's companions.

Tate turned a fierce slit of a grin on Jones. She said, "Party time."

"Don't try that on me," he snapped with surprising vigor. "You were telling me how frightened you were just a few days ago."

In the silence following the last echoes of the shot, her laugh seemed quite loud. With a quick flourish she picked a yellow flower from its patch of green among the rocks and tucked it in a buttonhole. She said, "Being scared only makes sense if you don't know how the deal ends, right?"

Several seconds passed before Jones looked at her and said, "What a waste. You're a special lady."

"Thank you, sir." She waggled her fingers at the enemy, not taking her hand from the piece. "Outlive a war, die in a fight. Does make you think about fate, don't it?"

"It shouldn't be this way. Never should have, not for anyone."

"Right. Now get over there out of the way."

The Devils learned. They set slingers and archers in covered positions to keep a steady rain of missiles falling on the group. Sliding from person to person, Gan predicted they were waiting for nightfall, when they hoped to cancel the effectiveness of the lightning weapons. Tate swallowed her thoughts, unwilling to admit how effective that would be.

She was also awed by the slings. Three feet long, they dispatched river-rounded stone missiles with accuracy and astonishing velocity. Those that missed hummed overhead, while those striking the boulders cracked like gunfire. Some shattered, throwing splinters that could make a nasty cut, as she discovered.

Unexpectedly, it was only late afternoon when the warriors burst out of their hiding places, screaming and brandishing weapons. It caught the group entirely by surprise. Tate blew gaps in the first wave with the boop, switching to the wipe as the shrieking Devils poured in on them. Then it was bayonet work, with everyone in the same whirling, screaming mass. A warrior grabbed the muzzle of her weapon, twisting it, nearly breaking her trigger finger. She struggled to pull it back, and another warrior charged up to finish her. Cho, a roaring fury, leaped to clench the raised sword arm in her teeth. Tate regained her weapon, dodged a blow, lunged forward with her eyes closed. When she opened them, there were two Devils at her feet, and Cho was gone. Another warrior was charging her.

Gan felt something hit him behind the knees. He seemed to drift downward, and the sodal coming at his stomach moved as slowly. In contrast, Clas' murdat was a flicker of steely light that traced an arc across the front of the Devil holding the sodal. The painted warrior stared, stupefied, at the spouting blood where his forearm used to be. Gan hit the ground, rolled upright, cut down another man. One staggered toward him with Cho on his back, and Gan slashed him as he went past. Raggar bowled into yet another, and Gan's sword completed that attack, as well.

Even more suddenly than it started, it was over, with Devils leaping away over the rocks, splashing through the stream in retreat. The last casualty was a particular fool who vaulted a boulder into their midst and impaled himself on Neela's murdat. She calmly rolled the man over the rock out of sight, cleaned her blade, and doubled up with spasms of dry heaving.

Shrill, brassy music from down the valley set off an intensified flurry of slingstones and arrows. Sylah shouted to the others. "Those are Harbundai trumpets!"

The Devils screamed back and forth, arguing about whether they should attack. Tate fired a boop round in the direction of one particularly belligerent voice who called himself Hawk Cedar Eight. He cried out once, then failed to answer several calls before another voice reported him dead. The arguments favoring attack grew less insistent.

The Harbundai troops were still out of sight when the Devil war cries and frustrated threats faded away upstream.

Clas found the strength to whistle. From downstream their horses whinnied response.

Gan turned to Clas, then Tate. There was a film over his red-rimmed eyes and a distracted cast to his smile, as though he saw something that was particular to him alone. He said, "So, my friends. Now I know it will all happen."

Tate giggled at Clas' quick Three-sign. Poor, superstitious man, she thought. And Gan was obviously so exhausted he was hallucinating. What more could possibly happen? she asked herself, and spoke aloud without realizing it. She said, "At ease, people. The Marines have landed and the situation is well in hand."

Even the dogs stared at her. She giggled again. Then she passed out.

CHAPTER 42

The group bowed to the Iris Abbess, and she acknowledged them with a stiff, controlled nod. Her ornately carved highbacked chair was positioned to sit in the beam of sunlight coming through the window behind her. Turned slightly, it kept her face in shadow while allowing the light full play across the rich blue-and-green robe with its interwoven gold thread. The heavy gold bracelet with its amethysts glowed on her wrist. As soon as the group was properly introduced and the young Chosen who escorted them had left, closing the door behind her, she said, "The King has kept you well isolated these weeks you've been with us. It sharpens curiosity. I must ask: The name Falconer? Is the bird your clan protector?"

"No, Abbess. We don't have clan protectors in our country."

The answer was sluggish, and Conway could have sworn he looked weaker than he had only an hour ago, when they were summoned to the meeting. Falconer went on, "We have symbols—eagles, bears, and the like—but they're not religious symbols. But I have a question for you, please. We're told Church is in contact with people in all the kingdoms here. Have you heard if our friends escaped the Mountain People?"

She told him she'd heard nothing, but her attention was taken by the attitudes of the others. The smallest of the women, Carter, was most intriguing. She stared and fidgeted like a hungry mink. It wasn't surprising when she was the next to speak, but what she said was shocking. "We ask your help, Abbess. The King keeps us prisoner. We're not allowed out of the castle grounds. We have no work."

The Abbess composed her answer carefully, thinking of what was to come later. "You wouldn't be here if King Altanar hadn't decided to use you." She paused so they could fully appreciate the implications of that remark, then continued. "My frankness troubles you, I see, but you've all observed that the King and I are adversaries in some things, allies in others."

Falconer said, "You embarrass. I underestimated you."

She waved languidly, the easy grace of her arm in contrast to the arthritic hands. "Careful you don't overestimate me. Of course, I can only deal with the women. I asked you men to come to see I respect your status, and in order that you might approve how we want to use the knowledge and skills of your women."

Carter fumed. "We need no approval."

The Abbess looked away to steady herself. The slave girl had spoken of this charade, of course, but she'd expected even strangers to be considerate enough to avoid insulting the intelligence of an abbess. "Need no approval" indeed. She looked directly into Falconer's eyes. "Altanar will never give direct permission for the women to do anything. That way, if their abilities gain too much influence, he can blame me and direct me to stop their activities. By having me—that is, Church—stop them, all women will see that Church can only exercise as much authority as the King allows. You understand the basis of our problem?"

Sue Anspach made her first contribution to the conversation. "Church is woman's power, but man sets the limit on that power." Delighted, the Abbess beamed. She said, "Exactly. Your mother taught you this?"

Anspach shook her head. "I've been watching, thinking. And listening to you."

Even more pleased, the Abbess looked to Falconer. "Would you permit the women to remain with me for private discussion?" Before he could respond, she was speaking to them again. "By helping me, you attract the King's attention. That is not a path for carelessness. There are those who will attempt to use you. Trust no one."

"We're all agreed on that," Conway said.

The tone of the answer brought her head up. He met her gaze with appealing boldness. She looked back to the women, saying, "I'll try to warn you away from danger, of course. Still, I'm an instrument of Church, the servant of our Sister Mother. Never forget that I have obligations that reach far beyond you. Or me."

Falconer tried to gesture and winced. He said, "We understand. We have obligations of our own."

Anspach said, "Thank you for your honesty."

Absently, she nodded at Anspach, then bending forward, asked, "What troubles you, Falconer? You're weak, feverish; just now you felt pain. Where?"

"My arm. An insect bite. A flea, probably. It seems to have gotten infected. It stayed the same for a while, but it seems to be getting worse." He rolled up his sleeve to display the area.

"Unseens," she said.

Conway asked, "Can you help him?"

Taking the arm she felt the flesh around the sore, smelled it. "Go back to your room. Go to bed. I'll send a War Healer. Do you mind if the women stay with me?"

He agreed, and with Conway and Leclerc flanking him for support, they left without further conversation.

With a small bell the Abbess summoned the Chosen waiting outside and gave instructions for Falconer's care. That done, she gestured the three women closer and indicated they should be seated. Then she said, "We must put aside Falconer's problems for now. Forgive me. There are important matters at hand for us. If you're willing to do as I tell you, we can be of help to each other."

Without hesitation Kate Bernhardt said, "That depends on what you tell us to do and what sort of help you want. Before we discuss that, however, we have a minor question. What do you call your language?"

The Abbess stared. Of all the things she could have asked, that was certainly the strangest. "Call it? Why, speech, of course. It's the way everyone talks. Almost everyone. I know your version is unintelligible to us, but I understand it's still speech. At least it's not like that odd click-clack of the Nions. Then there are the Hents, who live months away, to the south. They don't have proper speech, either; sounds more like singing, to me. Travel north and east as far as you want, though, and everyone has speech. What a strange question. Who *names* the way we talk? Do you?"

They exchanged glances. "No, but many of your customs are different here. We wondered. It's not important." She grew quite stern. "You'll tell us now what you want of us?"

"Of course. First, I want to know more about your country. For generations Sister Mother has sent missionaries ever farther from her Holy City, yet you know nothing of Church. That is strange."

She watched them exchange glances as they silently decided which of them would answer, and was surprised when the least aggressive, Anspach, took the lead. "We've only heard stories of your Church. The slave assigned to us is a young woman named Tee. She warns us constantly not to speak to anyone until we speak to you, especially of religion and rights. In our country, we aren't allowed to discuss our religion at all. That's a matter for the leaders."

What a clumsy lie, the Abbess thought; how intriguing. Are they really so bad at it, or do they believe their power will protect them? Surely they weren't so foolish. She sighed. They'll have to learn. But after I have some answers. She asked, "You have a Sister Mother in your Church?"

Anspach said, "We've several religions among our people. Almost all religious leaders are men."

Carter bent forward. "Three of the main religious groups don't allow women to perform the most sacred rituals."

This time the Abbess saw truth in their faces. A sudden disquiet brushed her with chill fingers. How long ago was it? A year. That was when the rumors surfaced about a new, secretive religion. A thing of night and the moon, it demanded blood, knew only followers and enemies. The rumors had said it started far to the east, beyond the Ocean River. Men were its priests.

These strangers came from far to the east. Sylah might be with one of them, the one Altanar said was a religious figure.

She said, "Here, women are Church and Church is women."

They exchanged the looks that said this was an area of disagreement among them. Again Anspach spoke. "In our country, women do more than Healers and more than Church. We . . ." She paused, and the Abbess clenched her fists in anticipation of real insight. The pain of her afflicted knuckles nearly made her cry out and spoil everything. Anspach finished lamely, "Very often we're considered the equal of men."

Biting back anger, the Abbess waited to answer. The early lie had been clumsy. This was simply brazen. She marveled that they'd survived a long journey. It must be more than the weapons.

A quick thrill of fear ran up her spine. Were they Seers, all of them? No, that was impossible. If they were, they wouldn't have been surprised by the Mountain People, and they'd know what happened to their companions. Perhaps they were just unbelievably lucky.

In that case, she'd draw them out just a bit more; it would make the forthcoming jerk on the leash all the more effective. "What is it you would like to do here in Ola?" she asked, and was even more amused than before at their exchange of transparent, conspiring glances. She leaned back in her chair, anticipating the entertaining lie. When she thought of what was in store for them, she actually felt a twinge of embarrassment.

Then, with a confidence that soared beyond arrogance, her face bland as a babe's, Anspach said, "We thought it would be best if you assigned us to work with the children, especially the ones you call Chosens. In our country, we were all teachers."

The Abbess' breath caught in her throat. The room was too small, closing on her. She stood and took a few steps. A deep breath steadied her.

When she was able, she faced them. "Haven't you even spoken to any other tribes on your journey?"

The three heads shook no in unison.

She made her way back to her chair. "What did you make people know, please?"

"A little bit of everything; all ages up to twelve. Arithmetic, reading, writing, Eng—" She cut the word off, correcting herself. "—language."

"And you?"

Carter said, "We had other jobs, but we couldn't do them here. Your culture's different."

Her smile failed to take the sting out of the rude remark. Just because they were allowed to have Teachers was no excuse for open contempt. These were not *Teachers,* not in the sense of those wonderful, mythical figures who brought skills and knowledge to the lives of all they touched. The learning these three passed along to the children of whatever land they came from was important, but it was far short of what the Teachers promised.

Disappointment was bitter on her tongue. Still, knowing that one thing about these women made them warmer, more sympathetic. Children were clearly very important in their culture. For a moment, she wondered how their dreadful weaponry was involved in that environment, and wished she had time to pursue the question. Perhaps later; there was no time. Hastily, she fumbled out a charcoal stick and a scrap of parchment.

They were extraordinarily well schooled. In truth, they surprised her with their understanding of letters and numbers. Writing posed no problems at all for them, and when she tested them on numbers, they actually laughed and chattered their way up to long division as if it were the simplest of games. In no time, their hands were grimed to the wrists with charcoal, and the sorry little scrap of parchment was so soiled everything was running together. She wished she had time to press them harder. Their careless, near-patronizing manner suggested they knew even more than they admitted.

There were more pressing issues. They had to learn about their present environment. And quickly. Feeling stronger, she said, "Come," and led them out of the abbey. When they tried to keep the conversation alive, she responded with vagueness and evasion. For them to understand, it was necessary for them to see.

They'd been walking for several minutes when Carter asked where they were going. The Abbess wanted to say, I don't like you; I'm awed by you, but you're in my country now. You need me. Instead, she answered with a tinge of vindictiveness. "Just a little farther and we'll be there. It's called the Beach of Songs."

She hoped it stayed quiet for a few more minutes.

There was a crowd on the weedy ground at the edge of the forest. Clear sky beyond them marked where the Inland Sea began. The Abbess moved through the people with the certainty of privilege. Some objected to the initial pressure from behind, but at the sight of her, men as well as women stepped aside. Every face had a welcoming smile for the strangers. Whispered comments bubbled in their wake.

Parting the front row of people, they were on the edge of the man-high bluff that marked where the sand beach began its slope to the waters of the Inland Sea. She was barely quick enough to drive an elbow into Anspach's side and arrest the cry she saw forming when the woman looked down on the singers. Fortunately, Bernhardt and Carter were too stunned to do more than sag against each other.

Fifty feet away a man and a woman hung naked, vertically spread-eagled, on two of the many square frames ranging the beach. The couple faced each other, only inches apart, held in place by wrist-and-ankle lashings.

Congratulating herself on her timing, the Abbess noted the approach of the two men on unblemished white horses. They were dressed all in white— jackets, trousers, and hoods. The horses were hooded and rigged in white also, and in the bright sun the most arresting thing about them were the black holes of the eyes and the glistening black coils of the whips dangling from the whitened saddles.

Quietly, the Abbess explained. "Those are King Altanar's truth protectors. They question prisoners and inflict whatever punishment is required. If you ever have occasion to hear one speak, you'll notice the peculiarly toneless manner of it. They are death, authorized to kill any who resist or refuse to obey."

The men dismounted, trailing the whips on the sand. The ends were splayed into three smaller tails. The woman twisted and strained to see them. The man was still, eyes squeezed shut.

Carter said, "They're wearing *white.*"

"Of course," the Abbess said. Her smile was a grimace. "The color of purity shows the blood better."

Wincing, Carter turned her head, and the Abbess pinched the soft underside of her arm. She blinked at the sudden pain and tried to pull away, but the Abbess held fast, forcing her farther forward, away from the crowd, signaling the others closer with a look. When sure they couldn't be overheard, she said, "All public punishments take place on the Beach of Songs. The protectors are very ingenious. And you spoke of being a teacher." She indicated the scene in front of them. "That woman broke the law. She learned reading, writing, and some numbers to help her husband in his business. His crime? He didn't report her."

Carter swallowed hugely. Tears trembled in her eyes. Facing the Abbess, she strained for defiance. "They can't make her forget, though, can they? I mean, no matter how hard they whip her, she'll still remember what she learned." An afterthought almost choked her. "They're not going to . . . ?" The question fell away.

"Kill her?" the Abbess finished. "This was her first time. If she's caught again, they'll blind her."

"No." The sound was soft. The Abbess caught herself admiring the taut, hard little woman. There was compassion in her, and toughness. Maybe I'm being spiteful, she thought, and gestured for them to follow her away from there.

Few paid any attention to their departure; all eyes were on the guards testing and inspecting the whips. The four women cleared the last rank of spectators, and Anspach couldn't resist turning for one last look. She was just in time to see a guard take a full-armed practice slash at one of the frame's uprights.

She jerked as if she'd taken the blow herself.

When they were alone on the path through the forest, the Abbess said, "It is like this in every place known to Church. You have much to learn if you want to survive. Later, I will tell you the full legend of the ones called Teachers. First, however, learn this; we find many things the giants left behind that carry letters. Personally, I believe some of the slaves were even allowed to read and write, because those who dig in the godkills occasionally find a sort of parchment with letters on it. The letters are far too small for giant eyes. But where Church's blessings are accepted, anything—*anything* —with writing or numbers must be brought to Church immediately. Anyone caught hoarding such material is apostate and dies. Church is responsible for destroying the stuff. It's done in a ceremony called the Return."

Carter said, "What are you returning it to? How's it destroyed?"

"We burn it, then dispose of the ashes in running water. And I have no idea what 'return' means. It's the name of the ceremony. Must it mean something?"

Bernhardt looked confused. "How can there be such a ceremony and legends of teachers? They contradict each other."

"Contradict is the exact word. That's why the Teachers are only a legend." The Abbess twitched her head to indicate the scene behind them. "If they do this to a woman who teaches herself, what do you think they'd do to a woman who taught another?"

The woman's shriek blended with the man's hoarse cry moments later. Carter's tears burst free.

Stiffly, the Abbess turned her head. Whippings were distasteful, of course, and no one liked to hear other people suffer, but tears? They must have come from an unbelievably soft society.

She was asking herself how such easily affected people could have traveled so far without being discovered when she corrected herself. They weren't merely easily affected, they were stupid. If it weren't for their outlandish clothing and those monstrous weapons, she'd never believe they were what they claimed to be.

Nor would Altanar. So what did he plan for them?

She watched the three of them hurrying along, arms wrapped around each other like pea vines. It occurred to her it was probably because the screams were constant now. She'd closed it out of her mind. The strangers seemed unable to do so.

Taking them under her wing had its risks, she thought. Then she brightened. If they were able to speak so freely of teachers in their country, perhaps they knew something of the Door.

The Door.

The swift arrival of the burning sensation behind her eyes caught her off guard. A twisted smile forced itself on her, as she thought how she'd scorned Carter's tears only moments earlier.

It was several moments before she was able to think calmly of either the Door or Sylah. Yet again she acknowledged her love for the strange waif who'd come to her so hungry for love, so afraid of love. And there *was* love between them. The Abbess had brought her up to be more than just another

Healer, and the things done to her were things that were to make her great in the eyes of all. She was born to risk, raised in cunning. It couldn't have been otherwise.

Even if she hadn't loved Sylah, she thought angrily, how much more exciting she was than these contradictory, *valuable* strangers!

If only her mission to the Dog People hadn't been such a desperate failure. Now she was a liability to any who might consider giving her shelter.

Poor child. Poor Sylah, who always believed her determination to solve the mystery of the Door was her own idea.

CHAPTER 43

Falconer sweated on his bed. The Healer sat on it beside him, a small pot of soup steaming over a firepot on the cabinet next to her. In her lap she held a copper basin of water mixed with alcohol. From time to time she soaked a cloth in it, wrung it out, and wiped his face or torso where it showed above the sheet. Neither the alcohol or the essence of sage used as a deodorant could mask the scent of his suppurating injury.

The War Healer offered him a spoonful of soup, and he rejected it with an angry mutter. Stoically, she slid a carrying rod through the handles of the firepot and carried it out of the room with the food just as Conway and Leclerc appeared at the door.

Rolling his eyes, Falconer was able to see how the poison from the injury was inching up the veins of his arm to his heart. The tiny bite mark was now a pair of crossed slits, where the Healer had opened the wound to relieve pressure and allow access to the affected flesh. The Healer didn't know that everything in the group's medicaid kits failed to faze the infection.

Falconer looked at his friends at the foot of his bed. He put together a smile for them. "Can you imagine this? After everything else, gangrene, of all things?"

"It's not the same." Leclerc's lower lip protruded. "I've seen that, and this is different. Our kit should have fixed you. They did something, Colonel. Somebody did something to the germs, made them different. They cheated."

"Whoever it was is long dead, Louis. Remember that. Whatever you do, remember who we say we are." He cut his eyes meaningfully at the door the Healer had gone through.

Conway said, "Would you like us to move you out into the sun? That seemed to help yesterday."

"Helped me. Didn't help the arm." He turned his head on the pillow. "I was yelling again when you woke me up out there in the sunshine. I remember some of it. Exactly what was I saying?"

Conway, red-faced, acted as if he was inspecting the arm. "Nothing at all. Just noise."

"That's a lie," Falconer said, and Conway flinched at the heat that flared in his eyes, as if the fever had suddenly concentrated there. The Colonel went on. "I was telling the troops to get in the trucks. We were going to the airport, on the way to the cry project. How much could you understand?"

"Nothing."

It was no good. The more he tried to lie, the more he realized Falconer saw through him, and when he lifted himself on his elbow and demanded the truth from Leclerc, the smaller man broke down completely. "There wasn't anyone there but us. You were just issuing orders. You weren't even loud. Not really. Honest." He backed out, apologizing to Conway with face and gestures.

Falling back, Falconer gulped air greedily. Sweat ran off of him. Conway said, "Burl, that's enough. You're hurting yourself."

He grimaced. "I'm worried about hurting the rest of you." In the following silence, his grating breath was unnaturally loud. He said, "Security's got to be priority number one from now on. Something funny's going on. They've got their hospitals, what they call healing houses. Why's Altanar insist I stay here? I know I rave. What if I yell in their language about the cry project? Or nukes? Or where we come from?" He fell back on the bed and was asleep immediately, his breath rasping in his throat.

Conway wished there were some way to reassure the man. The truth was, he had them all terrified. They'd drawn up a schedule, guaranteeing that he was never alone. The delirium came with startling suddenness, the day after the talk with the Abbess. Conway often wondered if she didn't realize how desperate Falconer's condition was. She would have hid it well, he was sure, just as she hid what she meant to show the women on that day. Carter still couldn't talk about it.

And now the man supposed to be the strongest of them all, the acknowledged leader, was dying.

Staring at the mean, gray stone walls, Conway thought back to his panic at Falconer's first outburst. Tee, the slave girl, overheard. She didn't understand, but she read his expression and intuitively knew secrets were being revealed. She warned him of stories about them, tales that said they were magic, from a place where no one visited and returned. When Conway asked her if people would feel threatened if they were too different, she assured him that was correct. He knew how the people of this world reacted to feeling threatened.

Falconer received good treatment. Altanar insisted they have anything they asked for, and he made good, including having the room cleaned.

Tee made herself indispensable. When no Healer was present, she took over whatever chores she could perform. Falconer asked after her if she was absent for any length of time. Conway appreciated her, too. She was quite pretty, and enjoyed explaining local customs and helping with language. She was, he thought, overly suspicious of Altanar, and her attitude on that subject didn't help Falconer. He suspected it was she who got Falconer worried about being overheard in his room. It was possible; the trouble was, there could be a dozen reasons why Altanar might want him kept there. He might not want the people to see how vulnerable his new friends were, for one thing.

Conway grimaced, remembering starting to inspect the walls for spy holes to placate Falconer. The guard captain, Eytal, almost caught him. That would have been the end of it, he thought, and surprised himself with the casual knowledge that he'd have killed the man instantly if he'd felt threatened.

Threatened.

He was becoming more like them. Like the ones who created this world, sentenced him to live out his life in it. What had someone said once, way back in history? "We had to destroy the village in order to save it." Was that what man was eternally fated to do? Was that what he must become?

The Healer returned. Conway mumbled something to cover his departure, nearly running for the outdoors, where there was sunshine and clean air.

Behind the tapestry Eytal bent awkwardly to watch. One hand brushed nervously at the stone, as if he'd enlarge the view, make the scene and voices clearer. He'd learned to interpret a good deal of what they said in their own gargling language, but the matter of eavesdropping was brutally difficult. He argued with himself over whether he should hurry to the King with what he'd learned so far. He thought of the smell of the soup, and his stomach growled.

He left.

The guards in the antechamber of the King's work quarters submitted him to routine search before passing along his request for an audience. It was approved through a small, grated inspection port, and they swung the iron-strapped door open without expression. Immediately inside was a barrier wall that stretched almost to the adjacent structural walls. It was wooden, covered with copper plates. Torches on both sides gave the polished metal a soft glow, but the black scowling eyes painted on the surface warned all who entered.

Eytal walked around the barrier. The chamber itself was a dark airless cube. The trappings of luxury only emphasized its isolation.

A massive oak table dominated the center of the room. Altanar's chair was at the head of it, a raised thronelike piece of rich walnut, with carved jade salmon armrests and an ivory eagle topping the tall, leather-cushioned back-rest. The floor was completely covered with a carpet of bearskins, and a polished silver candelabra of exotic geometry provided light with dozens of candles.

Altanar stood beside the chair, drumming impatiently on the table. When Eytal finished, he asked, "Is that all?" in a voice that promised more than it asked. Eytal shrank noticeably.

"You said to tell you of anything important, King. The man Falconer is afraid of what he might say. They talked about where they came from, of a 'project.' " When Altanar continued to glare silently, he finished weakly, "It's hard to understand them."

Altanar advanced slowly, mocking the shaking soldier in a sneering fal-setto. " 'Anything important, King.' 'Afraid of what he might say.' Oh, yes—'a project.' " He stopped directly in front of Eytal. "You mindless garbage. You've left them alone to come here and tell me you've learned nothing. Is he awake now? What is he saying?"

Eytal stammered, his entire body involved in his search for an answer. His eyes sought the exit longingly.

Altanar slapped him. "Try to understand. I'm *glad* he's dying. It saves me the trouble of having him killed. I'm glad he's delirious. He'll say things that tell me how to question the others. Go back. It's important that I know everything he says. When he sleeps tonight, report to the protectors. Tell them I want you flogged well enough to remind you of your duty, but that you must be able to work tomorrow. Do you understand?"

Eytal nodded, mute, and Altanar kneed him. "Answer!"

Doubled over, Eytal gagged with pain, and Altanar slapped him again and again, demanding he speak, until Eytal was finally able to croak an acceptable response. Breathing hard, beaded with sweat, Altanar screamed at him to get out. Eytal stumbled into the hall, enduring the smirking guards as a final indignity before reaching the sanctuary of an empty passageway. He leaned against the wall, pressing the side of his face to the cool stone. Slowly, painfully, he came erect. His right ear wouldn't stop roaring, and when he put a hand to it, the fingers came away smeared with blood. He studied it very thoughtfully.

*   *   *

Conway was back again when Falconer woke. He acknowledged his visitor, then stared at the ceiling for a long time before turning his head to look at him again.

"I'm not going to make it." The weak, panting voice was surprised. When Conway tried to protest, he waved him to silence. "This is hard enough, without turning it into a comedy of manners." For a moment the command presence was back. It faded quickly. "I keep thinking how we nearly wiped out the Indians in America when we brought them smallpox. Just my luck—this time the invader's the victim."

"Don't talk like that. I know how bad it looks, but you have to beat it. We need you."

He shook his head. "No. I need you."

The dark suspicion flitting across Conway's face amused Falconer, but when he tried to laugh, it broke down into a coughing fit. A drink of water helped, and he went on. "I wouldn't ask you to kill me, my friend. I've got a really hard job for you."

Conway said, "I don't like any of this. Wait until you're better; then we'll talk."

"We'll talk in hell, then. No, I'm saying my piece while I can. I'm laying off my responsibility on you."

"You're still thinking about that idiot who said someone had to put the country back together, aren't you? You're crazier than he is. Was. There is no country, hasn't been for centuries. Everything's different."

"Ideas don't die, and we were an idea. A dream." He reached across his body, clutched Conway with a dry, hot hand. "Everything needs a place to grow, Matt. You're the only one. The rest—good people—the best. Not leaders." The hand fell free, limp.

Conway looked down at the wasted frame, shocked to realize the face was little more than flesh stretched over a skull. Closed now, the eyes were sunk in sockets nearly as dark as the lines of infection discoloring the swollen arm.

Suddenly Falconer was struggling to sit up. He stared wildly, trying to gesture with the injured arm as well as the other. "Set up the machine gun there! Base of fire, those trees! Antiarmor, here!" As quickly as he'd risen, he fell back, breath wheezing in and out. His chest vibrated with rapid heartbeats.

Conway bathed him with the alcohol-and-water mix. The toll of the brief physical effort showed in the flaccid, sagging muscles. He spoke without trying to turn his head. "I can't help it, Matt. It's all so real, and as soon as it passes, I know it was another damned hallucination. That's the sort of thing that could get you tortured. Altanar wants to go along with the story that we're from another place. Let someone start talking about us being more than that, supernatural or something, and he'll be forced to ask us questions. His way. And we'll answer."

Calmly, rationally, Conway argued. Falconer lay with his eyes closed, unmoving. Conway wasn't even sure he was awake until the man gave a shuddering sigh and said, "Unless we find a way to get people moving in the right direction, everything's going to repeat itself. We've got to try. I want to hear you say that's true before I die."

Conway bolted to his feet. "That's a miserable, unforgivable thing to do."

Falconer tried to smile. "That's what I wanted to hear. I win."

"I won't do it, damn you. I'm going to live any way I can as long as I can. I won't be tricked or shamed into your stupid crusade, get that straight. You die, and you lose."

He opened his eyes. "You'll do it. Not the same way I would, but you'll do it. We're no more alike than black and white, my friend, but we want the same things. Now let me rest."

For several seconds Conway stood over him, clenched fists working furiously. He was in a positively foul mood as he spun on his heel and stalked to the door. Before he could open it, a sound from Falconer stopped him. When he turned, the other man said, "I'm giving you a chance to make an exit, just like they used to do it in the movies, remember?" He stopped abruptly, making a noise in his chest Conway couldn't identify. He continued, "I just wanted to say I wish . . . ah, nothing. Wishing just wastes time. See you." He let his head fall back.

Conway closed the door softly.

When Conway was gone, Eytal kept his eye glued to the spy hole. The roaring in his right ear all but deafened him. Rubbing it helped the pain a little. It was so deep inside his head he couldn't really do much about it. The ache in his groin was almost gone, though.

It was one thing to be abused; it was something else to be shamed. When he closed his eyes, the faces of the guards swam in his vision. When he opened them, he remembered the night in the mountain fort, and how Altanar had forced them to walk to the tent in the storm. He wondered if the woman kept any of the fingers the frostbite got. He doubted it. If he hadn't gone back after her—

The door was opening slowly, stealthily. It was the slave girl assigned to the strangers, peering in. Cat-quick, she slipped inside, checking the hall behind her before closing the door. She hurried to the bedside, and Eytal was surprised to realize Falconer obviously expected her.

Straining, pushing on the wall, he wanted to yell at them to speak up. If he failed to hear them, Altanar would be worse than ever.

The woman bent over him, and for a moment Eytal thought she was going to kiss him, but then he realized she was fumbling at her leg. When she straightened, she had a knife in her hand. He was drawing breath to shout at her to stop when she handed the knife to Falconer. This time she did kiss him, on the forehead. As quickly as she'd come, she was gone.

Eytal cursed himself even as he admired her cunning. Only now could he appreciate the real reason for her eagerness to be taken off the list of people allowed or required to visit him. When Falconer was discovered dead, Altanar would have everyone on duty tortured, seeking the one who brought him the knife. No one could confess to what he didn't know, and Eytal was certain there would be several people to testify that little Tee was far away the whole day.

Falconer tested the edge of the blade.

Something stung Eytal's eye, and when he realized it was sweat, he also realized he was soaking wet, despite the cold clamminess of the passageway.

Falconer planned his own death. To protect his friends from what he might say when the poison in his blood brought the madness. That was brave.

A great calmness slid over Eytal.

If he shouted and revealed the hiding place, Altanar would quite possibly have him killed. If he ran to the room to stop the suicide and was too late, Altanar would very probably have him killed. If he did nothing to stop the suicide, Altanar would certainly have him killed.

In any event, Altanar would have him tortured until the slave girl's name was revealed. She would provide prolonged entertainment for the protectors.

Eytal straightened. For several minutes he stared into the darkness. When he looked into the room again, Falconer had done what he meant to do. Stepping away from the hole, he repeated the ritual reserved for a clansman who died well. "Go easily. Take our respect on your journey. Please leave your courage for us who still fight."

He wasn't sure why he felt compelled to say the words for Falconer, the strangest of strangers, but he felt much better for doing so. He retreated down the passageway.

CHAPTER 44

Conway and Leclerc gazed out over the landscape from their viewpoint, and the taller man said, "That's got to be Mount Rainier, but I can't get used to looking at it with a round top and a notch in its side."

Leclerc nodded. "And how deep the river bed is. Almost a canyon. The trees are smaller here, too. I figure she blew a couple of hundred years ago, and this whole valley floor's mud and lava from the blast. See how level it is? Hardly a bump, all the way from the mountain to the Sound. I wonder if anyone lived here when it went."

Conway said, "I doubt it. Isn't that ironic? Homes, factories, fields—no one knows what was there. The people who built it saw it destroyed, but not obliterated. The people who live on top of the ruins don't even know there was a civilization here." He paused for a moment, scanning all around. He said, "Snowfather Mountain. Interesting. Rivers, lakes, the earth—all female. The mountains are male. Maybe they're saying the things that bring life are feminine and things that bring death are male."

"Could be, a long time ago. Women still bring life, but that's about all. While we're on the subject, I'm worried about Carter. She won't be able to take this place for long."

"She'll take it as long as she wants to live. That old abbess'll keep them busy. They'll be helpful, too."

The last phrase had a hard ring to it that brought a quick lift to Leclerc's eyebrows. Cautiously, he said, "I think you ought to explain exactly what you have in mind."

"We'll only survive here as long as Altanar needs us. Once he understands our weapons, he'll take them from us."

Leclerc continued to look at the mountain, studiedly casual. "Colonel Falconer laid it on you, didn't he?"

Conway felt his neck grow warm. "That's not what I'm saying. Don't assign motives to me until you hear me out."

"I'm listening."

Conway wished he'd thought out what he was going to say. There was so much he wanted to express; the plain patriotism that swelled in his throat when he thought of the country that was his, gone, and the new one waiting to be born; the group, its future so bleak in the face of Ola's barbarism; his inability to think of a safe escape. He stumbled through it, feeling ever more inadequate.

When Conway stopped talking, Leclerc cut his eyes at him. "Like I said, he laid it on you." He gestured away protest before it could start. "Admit it; there's no alternative. You already said he'll dump us as soon as he's got no more use for us. Can we make ourselves indispensable?"

"We have to."

Leclerc nodded, as sober as if discussing chess moves. "And that means we help him in his wars, and that brings us to the President's order to reunify the country." His composure finally broke, and the smile that twisted his features was agonized. "I can't even remember his name. We're the only people who ever heard of him, ever heard of the whole damned *country,* and I can't remember the President's name."

"It was a good country. It ought to live again."

"Are you nuts? You think this savage moron is going to rebuild Independence Hall, or something? Look, I volunteered for the cry project 'cause it was a way out. I was a nobody in a nothing job, and the war was going to snuff me like everyone else. So I figured if I made it through the project, I'd have a chance at real adventure. Some figure! This is a helluva lot scarier than I wanted. Okay, okay—it beats catching a bombload of AIDS Six-A or watching your radex badge change colors while you soak up gammas. If it's excitement you want, I'm with you. Scheme to take over Ola, and I'm in, up to the hilt. But reunite a continent?" He swung an arm, including Snowfather Mountain, the valley, the eastern horizon in the gesture. "We don't even know what it looks like anymore."

Conway started walking. "Let's go back to the castle. They get touchy if we're away too long."

It was a two-hour hike back. They enjoyed the exercise even more than the fresh air and scenery, despite being under constant observation. Their accompanying guards made no effort to be discreet, although they kept a distance that permitted private conversation.

Nor was there any restriction on where they went or their contacts. The Olans weren't an unfriendly people, they'd discovered, and they treated the strangers with patience and humor. Nevertheless, they kept a wary eye on the guards; they freely admitted that they'd be questioned about their conversations. Among themselves, Conway and the group expressed amazement at how greatly the people feared Altanar, yet how eager they were to know more about the world beyond their immediate vicinity. Travel was strongly discouraged and strictly controlled.

Today, strolling beside a stone-surfaced road, Conway remarked on the Olan's engineering skills. Stone and timber were the favored building materials, but they had yet to perfect the arch; windows and doors featured lintels, some of them marvelously large. Leclerc spoke of their preference for strength over grace or balance. The road itself made his point. It was arrow-straight and clearly had an excellent foundation, or it would have long ago collapsed under the pounding of the huge timber wagons that rumbled up and down its length. Nevertheless, the stones were irregular in height and angle, creating a bumpy, difficult surface. Scornfully, he said, "Why would anyone be like that? I mean, when they need square, they can do it, but they build this herky-jerky highway and deal with it by just tying more horses to the front of the wagon and putting more slaves on the push pole in the rear."

He had to raise his voice as he finished. One of the wagons pulled abreast, the driver swearing lustily at his plodding forty-ox team. His assistant sat at the rear of the load, regally atop the six-foot-thick butt of the single log. His job was to crack a whip over the sweating backs of the thirty slaves chained to the push pole. Conway wondered what the weight of the entire mass might be. The wheels alone were staggering. They were more than six feet in diameter, with wooden shoes a good six inches wide. Scorch marks on the wood showed the iron tires were hammered on red hot, and they rotated so slowly one could see the massive countersunk rivets that secured them in place. Spokes as thick as a man's leg radiated from a hub that looked like a barrel. The truck bed was itself made of timbers a good four inches thick, reinforced with iron strapping.

In unspoken agreement, Conway and Leclerc waited until the squealing, groaning wagon was well ahead before resuming their walk. He looked off to the city as it passed.

Rising on a flat plain in front of them, it overflowed the level area and spilled down a fairly steep slope toward the glittering blue of the Inland Sea. Its gray-black stone walls were a half-mile long and fifteen feet high. Outside them was pasture, a full two hundred yards of flat, grazed ground, offering no cover to an attacker. Inside the walls everything was straight. Nothing had been allowed to disturb the lines of the grid, except for official buildings that needed to stretch more than one block. Those had been designed as steps on the grade, so the roof of one building created a pedestrian terrace for the one immediately above it. Streets that ended at the wall of a building began again on the opposite side.

A circular racetrack and athletic field combination was inside a two-by-four-block rectangular area. More impressive than that was the even larger, equally geometric reservoir.

The jewel of the kingdom was Altanar's castle within its own wall that abutted the western city wall. The castle's interior grounds were parklike, with a gate accessing the Inland Sea, so that there were actually five gates in the city wall. The four public gates, much larger, were named Sunrise, Sunset, North Star, and Summergold, the last one named for the way its polished brass plates reflected the sun. The river, with its docks and warehouses, was to 'that southern side.

Far beyond that rose the Glass Cliffs, ever-present, unavoidable, two hundred yards of mirrorlike fused ground. Whatever had been there, man had unleashed his thermonuclear hell on it. When first seeing it, the group had debated heatedly over the probable name of the community or the likely function of the target that warranted such a massive strike. Bernhardt was the one who steadfastly insisted it was a stray missile.

It was clearly a radpad, as such things were called. They all commented on the fact that no one really knew what it meant. The radiation danger was long over, but so was the knowledge of what radiation was. Waxing philosophic, Conway remarked that education is a tender garden, whereas ignorance is weeds. History—the old history—was full of examples proving that, when civilizations fell, learning was the first thing to disappear.

They were all shocked when Leclerc pointed out how callous they sounded. His voice trembled and his gestures were agitated, almost spasmodic. "We turned whole hillsides into glass," he said. "Don't you see? We corrupted the very *earth*. Who cares what was there? Look what's left; it's obscene!"

They had seen it then, the shining horror of it, the sparse, starved trees that littered, rather than decorated, the cliff's crest. They avoided looking at it after that. And never spoke of it.

With the wagon far enough away to allow conversation, Conway and Leclerc started walking again. They'd traveled about a mile when Conway pointed at mounded earth off to the side of the road. "Know what that is?" he asked.

Leclerc didn't.

Conway said, "Do you remember the family we saw in the marketplace about a week ago? We said they looked like they were from a different tribe, and people weren't very friendly toward them? Well, I asked Tee about them. They're called Peddlers." He described their strange nontribal existence, adding, "They've got a rotten reputation. One of the things she called them is 'godkill pickers.' " He stopped and jerked a thumb at the mounded earth. "That's a godkill. A place where a village or town or city used to be. It ended up being overgrown, buried, burned—whatever. The Peddlers hunt for them. When they find them, they start looting them. They always get run off by the locals, but they manage some pickings first. Godkill."

"I thought we were giants."

"Me, too. I didn't get to ask her about that. What's even more interesting about the godkills is that some of them were also called radpads. The Peddlers were the ones who learned when they were safe. Probably by watching for animals to move back into the area and survive for a few years. Hard folks. Tee also called them 'dead-thieves.' It's no wonder they're not liked."

At Leclerc's suggestion, they wandered over to see what happened at a godkill. Their first impression was of an open pit mine, with men laboring away on tiered cuts. On the lip of the hole were several piles of material, and they walked over to inspect them.

Their observers hung back, satisfied to keep them in sight.

The largest mound was construction material; bricks and cement block were stacked, to be used in their present form. Reinforced concrete was hammered apart, the rebar painstakingly claimed as steel, which was then carried to a central dump for metals. Copper pipe in good condition was separated, under guard. Both men already knew it was valued as jewelry, as was the other material stored with it, ceramics and glass.

Men working on the mining tiers delivered their salvage to a central location, where it was hoisted up to ground level by a crane. As Conway and Leclerc watched, the loader below shouted up for his partner to take away a load of the more precious goods.

Leclerc said, "Will you look at that thing? A vee arm sticking out in the air from a guy pole. One pulley. And can you believe it, not even a windlass? The guy just muscles the rope, and—"

Before he could finish, the man pulling lost his hold. With remarkable speed he grabbed a coil of the line piled beside him and threw a braking loop around a post obviously provided for that purpose. Despite his quickness, the falling sling struck the loader below before jerking to a stop. The stricken man dropped in a quivering heap. Glass and crockery crashed and tinkled.

Until then Conway and Leclerc had assumed the supervisors standing around were simply that. Neither had noticed the clubs at their waists. Three of the supervisors came running now, however, weapons in hand. The crane operator darted first one way then another, desperation shining in his face. As they closed on him, he fell to his knees, screaming for them not to hit him. They ignored him.

Leclerc reached for his pistol. Conway batted his hand away, saying, "Don't be a fool!" before running toward the prone figure and those beating him. At the sight of one of Altanar's strangers approaching, the supervisors stood back. They grinned, obviously pleased by their efforts.

Leclerc hurried up. Between them, he and Conway talked the three supervisors into describing the operation. As they walked, the bloodied worker crawled away, struggling to his feet soon after. But he headed back down into the pit.

That was when they discovered the workers were all slaves.

"There must be a hundred of them," Conway said, and one of the supervisors nodded happily. "Exactly ninety-three," he said. "Most from Harbundai, some from the Mother River tribes. We're the largest pit godkill in the kingdom. Lots of giant stuff down there."

Leclerc said, "We saw drinking cups in the pile. They didn't look giant-size to me."

The man looked surprised. "Of course not. Nobody knows where they actually *lived*. This is a godkill, one of the places where their slaves lived. When they tried to escape from the giants, their gods killed them all. Don't you folks have godkills where you come from?"

"Certainly." Conway drew himself erect, offended. "*Our* giants never left anything behind in godkills, though. Our giants would never enter a slave place."

"Oh." The man looked crestfallen, then recovered enough to say, "Well, there's just small giant stuff here. Some steel. The slaves must have stole it."

"That's probably it," Leclerc said. His tone failed to match the words.

Conway made their good-byes. Back on the road, they were silent for some time.

"Why didn't she tell you it was a slave place?" Leclerc finally demanded.

"I don't know. I'll ask her."

Leclerc sneered. "I'll just bet you will." He was ready when Conway spun around to glare at him. "You'll have plenty of opportunity to ask, won't you? Tee's her name, isn't it? That's where you go when you wander off by yourself. Some lady. If she wasn't like the rest of these savages, she'd have known how upsetting something like that could be."

A pulse jerked in Conway's neck. He said, "She's a slave herself, Louis. She doesn't like it, but she knows it's part of this world. Does that make her 'like the rest of these savages'?"

The rest of the walk through the city and into the castle grounds was practically a sprint, both men fuming. They parted at the door to Leclerc's quarters, where he turned on his heel to enter his room as Conway continued down the hall.

Six days later Conway woke to a resounding knock on his door. Prepared for anything, he picked up his wipe before calling, "Who is it?"

"Me." Leclerc was cheerful. Excitement rang in the single word.

Muttering sleepily, Conway flung open the door. Leclerc hurried in, grabbing Conway's arm. "You're not dressed," he observed, and bubbled on, undisturbed by Conway's exasperation. "I've got something to show you. Simplest thing in the world. Can't imagine why I didn't think of it sooner."

All of Conway's questions earned the same knowing grin. Soon he was smiling, too. The other man's enthusiasm was irresistible. He washed and shaved quickly, then allowed himself to be led off the castle grounds, across the meadow outside the walls, and into the city. Ducking through a low doorway cut into a board fence, Leclerc practically pulled Conway after him. When the taller man straightened, they were in the yard of a large workshop. Leclerc was pointing triumphantly at a tall, gawky contraption.

Conway's good humor evaporated. "What's this all about?" he demanded.

Confused, Leclerc continued to point. "That," he said.

"It's a crane," Conway said, and was surprised at the way Leclerc's brightness returned.

"No, no." He dragged his friend closer, pointing. "Look—a double-pulley arrangement. Think of the mechanical advantage. But here's what's really important." He trotted to a windlass. "This adds even more leverage," he said, giving it a twist. There was a clacking noise from the device mounted above it, and he beamed when Conway looked at it. "That's the thing I was talking about. A simple ratchet. See how it pivots on its pin? And the way the hook grabs these gears on the windlass shaft? That means this thing can only turn one way, Matt, unless you manually disengage the ratchet to lower the sling. Now those poor devils in that pit can lift more, lift it easier, and never worry about dropping it."

Smiling once more, Conway moved closer to inspect the machine. "Great," he said. "The sort of thing we ought to be doing for these people."

Leclerc said, "We're already working on an improvement, a lifting arm that pivots, so people don't have to reach out to pull a load sideways. I thought of it when I noticed the stone walls. Most of the rocks get smaller as the walls get higher, 'cause it's so much work getting heavier stuff up there. I can figure out how to make portable or collapsible cranes; I know I can. We can raise walls—stronger walls—anywhere we want. And aqueducts. There's no limit—"

"Yes, there is," Conway said, leading Leclerc away from the workers gathering around them. "We have to be careful we don't help too much. Remember, this Altanar's a murderous tyrant. If we build up his walls—"

Leclerc interrupted, winking. "If we build them up, we know where the weaknesses are. Anyhow, walls are defense. Defense is for football, not war. Anything I show these folks will spread like a grass fire, Matt. It's always been that way. Some secrets can be held, but anything another man can see, he can duplicate. Or improve on. It's not like I'm giving something *only* to Altanar."

"It helps him."

"We have to be useful; you've said that yourself. Anyhow, you can't stop knowledge."

"You can if you're the only one who has it."

"If I'd made this crane two weeks ago, that slave'd be alive."

"That's not the point."

"I think it is. I think we have to do what we can, judiciously, to improve things. Even if some of the improvements aid bad people and good people at the same time."

"And I say there must be a better time and place."

"I'm here. Now. No less concerned about this butcher Altanar than you. But I'm concerned about other things, as well."

Turning away, Conway studied the improved device, trying to find his way through the thicket of moral questions. When it occurred to him that the entire argument originated in the development of a thing as simple as an automatic brake, a wave of depression surged through him.

"Do what you think best, Louis," he said, making peace. "Think about the ramifications, though. Will you promise me that?"

"Sure." Leclerc slapped him on the back as he turned to leave, and when Conway passed through the doorway on the way out, the smaller man was already engrossed with his workers, drawing pictures in the dirt with his finger.

Back at the castle Conway idled the day away through the evening meal. Shortly after that he made his way to a tiny enclosed garden. Encircling stone walls held pockets of earth planted with ferns and flowers. The wall opposite the main entry was an artificial waterfall. Glassy sheets of water shattered on a rock ledge before draining into a sun-warmed pool.

There was a second, hardly noticeable entry to the garden behind a clump of rhododendrons. It was serviced by a path that was obscured by a solid hedge of lilacs. It led to a gardener's shack some distance away. He made himself comfortable on a bench in the corner opposite the waterfall and waited.

He was there long enough, and was still enough, that three birds failed to recognize him as alive and landed to bathe in the splash of the water. They were as large as crows, but a beautiful pale green, a species unknown to him, and which he was sure was no part of the Pacific Northwest of his time. Their exoticism stirred up a dim memory. A summer day, a place that smelled like this, of plants and water. There were animal sounds. A zoo. A child laughed.

He rose swiftly, clumsily, sending the birds squalling up and over the wall.

They were still carrying on when Tee slipped through the secondary entry. She advanced with the tense poise of a deer, dark skin, black hair, long robe shadowy against the shrubbery. She displaced branches and leaves so soundlessly she might have been coming through mist. She hurried to him.

He described the meeting with Leclerc, linking it to the earlier event at the godkill. Throughout, he avoided looking directly into her eyes, trying to avoid the simple, devastating effect of her presence. When he told of the one slave's death and the other's beating, however, he made the mistake of watching her face, and winced at the dead acceptance that hardened her features.

He thought he'd only been so affected by a woman once before in his life, and was embarrassed to find himself having to work to remember how he'd felt then. He struggled to tell himself that he wasn't being disloyal, that the other attraction was better, somehow.

Unaware of his trial, she said, "I'm sorry you had to see. It's not only Altanar who mistreats us, but almost every noble in the kingdom. If you still want to help us, I've spoken to some friends. They're willing to meet you, if you'll follow instructions."

The suddenness of the announcement banished all other thoughts. He laughed softly. "I can imagine how your friends protect themselves. What sort of instructions?"

"You must come alone, with me. You must be unarmed."

"Impossible." The word leaped out, angry. He clamped his mouth shut behind it.

"It's the only way they'll meet you. That or nothing."

She turned away, too late to hide the sudden wash of distaste that surged across her stoic determination.

The reaction pleased him. She didn't like the ultimatum any more than he did. With that conclusion firmly in place, he took a hard look at his situation.

If she chose to lead him into a trap, the only way he could fight his way out of it would be with gunfire. Even if he escaped, Altanar would know his captive had been prowling about in the night. The delicate tissue of deceit and mutual fear that bound them together would be irrevocably torn. Altanar would throw aside all pretense and simply torture their secrets out of them.

A quick shudder raised the hair on the back of his neck. Altanar would do exactly that, sooner or later, if they didn't become as much his creatures as were the white-clad protectors. Unless he found a way to break them all free. Trusting Tee was no more than a bet on long odds as opposed to a bet against a sure thing.

The irony of it was, he did trust her. The admission still surprised him. He was afraid of what the night might bring, but he was happy to be sharing it with her. He believed in her.

He managed to smile, knowing he looked sheepish. He said, "Maybe it's not so impossible after all. These people—are they all from your tribe?"

"No." She saw the satisfaction in his nod, and asked sharply, "Why? You don't like the For?"

"Easy, easy. I was only thinking I'd like to know people from different tribes, that's all."

"You'll meet some."

She was still irritated, and Conway patted her hand. She jerked it back, but he spoke as if he hadn't noticed. "I want to be the friend of all the tribes."

"Too many." She made a face, shook her head so the sleek hair swayed. "We all want something different."

"You all want to be free of Ola, and kings like Altanar."

"Yes! Oh, yes. That we all agree on."

More to himself than her, he said, "Point one," then, briskly, "How do I know when to meet you here?"

"You know the guard-change signal?"

"The bells? How can you not know it—they ring all over the city."

"Yes. One hour after the first guard change, come here. I'll be waiting."

He nodded, hoping the water clock in their quarters was close to whatever one she used. They parted without good-byes. As he left the small garden, he paused to knot a loose bootlace.

Despite taking that time to inspect for watchers, he missed the form lurking behind the massive cedar in the distance. If he had seen, he would have been particularly disturbed to realize it was the one position in the castle enclosure that afforded a view not only of the main entry to the little garden, but along the otherwise hidden path from the gardener's shack, as well.

Chapter 45

Conway felt his way down the dark passageway leading to the outside door. He had to avoid the guards posted to watch the approaches to the King's living quarters and the random two-man patrols that walked through the entire castle and its surrounding grounds.

The sound of one of those patrols froze him against the wall momentarily. The practice of wearing only slippers indoors made them extremely quiet. Carrying his own boots in the customary bag made him feel burdened and clumsy. He wished he had Tee's skills. She was a For, a forest tribe, she said, and the way she moved proved it. He wished now he'd never listened to her. Not that she was terribly forthcoming. She said little about herself, but when she did, the underlying rock of her character broke the surface appearance of cowed humility. She was a slave inside Altanar's castle, and she had connections with the resistance. That took incredible courage.

Resistance. The word had its own memories. Resistance was a code word, the one they used to destroy his reasons for living. Innocents, who knew nothing of "the sacred cause."

Resistance meant murdering—for good reason, of course—such as, in the name of compassion.

He arrived at the garden and was settling to wait for her when she rose from her hiding place behind a bush a yard away. It occurred to him he'd never seen her first in one of their late night meetings. As he let her take his hand and lead him away, he noted the coiled line over her shoulder.

She stopped at the base of one of the permanent ladders leading to the battle walk on the inside of the castle wall. They hurried up.

The walkway was six feet below the wall's full height, scored with firing notches for archers about six feet apart. The platform itself was wide enough for two men to walk abreast. There was no protection on the inner side, the rationale being that, should an attacker scale the wall and get onto the walkway, he was vulnerable to arrows and slingstones from inside the castle grounds.

Tee moved quickly to place a grappling bar across one of the notches, and Conway tried not to think how flimsy that purchase looked as he scrambled to the ground outside. She followed, dropping the last few feet to land beside him as soundlessly as a bat. A flip of her wrist brought the bar and line down to them. She picked it up and, taking his hand again, raced off across the open meadow. Without hesitation, she burst through the open door of a shepherd's shanty at its far edge.

Conway ducked to avoid the low doorjamb. It brushed the back of his head, and he was telling himself how lucky he was to have noticed it at all when the building collapsed on him. By the time he realized the walls had sprouted hands to tie him up and tongues to curse his struggles, he was bound, gagged, and wrapped in what felt like a blanket that assured he couldn't see, and could barely hear or breathe.

Sick with anger over his stupidity and the girl's treachery, he fought to remain calm, to think. At least he'd come unarmed; no weapons were lost. They'd certainly have done him no good, he thought ruefully.

What did they expect to accomplish by kidnapping him?

He was bodily hoisted at shoulders and feet, carried, then dumped on hard boards that rattled. Squealing wheels and the clop of hooves identified a horse-drawn cart. The driver hurried, completely unconcerned that the trip was jouncing the wits out of the passenger.

For the next ten minutes he was either being bounced or listening with his captors when they stopped. At such times, he felt their tension as clearly as he felt his own helplessness. Far off to his right he heard loud laughter and party sounds. In the midst of listening, he was lifted out of the cart. The noise stopped abruptly. He had the impression a door had closed it off behind him. Two people carried him like a log down a long flight of stairs.

They propped him in a sitting position. An indefinable sense warned of an approaching mass. There was a sound like the retreat of a broken wave. After that, silence.

He flinched as someone seized him. He tried to pull away. Powerful hands roughly tore free the heavy sack. It took his eyes a second to adjust, and then he saw a black-robed figure retreating to join a knot of others, all dressed in identical dark floor-dragging cloaks. They exuded hostility. He estimated fifteen of them.

Each had the cloak's hood drawn over his head and folds of cloth pulled across the lower half of his face. One couple stood revealed; Tee beside a huge man. The uncovered face sported a full beard as black as his cloak.

At the sound of a small bell, the group turned from Conway, their attention going to a raised dais at his left front. It was flanked by small candles that drew the eye but provided scant light. Conway had the feeling he was underground. Massive ceiling beams crisscrossed above him. The weak glow from the front of the room emphasized yawning blackness elsewhere.

A shrouded figure drifted silently up the steps to the dais. He spoke in a voice too soft for Conway to distinguish; the audience hung on his speech.

Raising his arms, the figure led the group in a slow, solemn melody. There was a hypnotic power in the music. Conway fought the pulling insistence that he let go, join the group in its solidarity. Suddenly, shockingly, there was a series of metallic clashes, as from a struck cymbal. The silence that followed was broken only by the shuffle of feet, as the group turned and advanced on him. Forbiddingly silent, it formed a looming semicircle that enclosed him.

The bearded man stepped out of the mass. With one hand he tilted Conway's head back against the wall. He held a long, thin dagger in the other. Expressionless, he slid the point from Conway's jaw up under the cloth gag. It went slack, and Conway spit it out. The man then cut the ropes binding his hands and feet. Finally, his gaze still frozen to Conway's eyes, he rested the blade on the bone at the base of Conway's throat, the tip sharp against the stretched skin. He lowered his face to within inches of Conway's. "Why are you here?" he demanded in a bass rumble.

Conway swallowed, and the knife pricked the moving flesh. He said, "I was going to ask you that."

The whiskered man blinked and said, "You're Altanar's dog, come sniffing after us, and you think you can joke?"

"I belong to no man." He looked past his questioner. It was a nightmare scene. The mass of shapeless forms waited, threatening. Even Tee had found a robe. He was relieved that she, like the bearded man, continued to leave her features exposed.

He looked back to the man. "How do I know you're not Altanar's people, trying to trick me into saying something against the King?"

A murmur ran through the crowd. He couldn't tell if it was a compliment to caution or anger at accusation. Tee answered. "You've seen my life. Would I let myself live for any reason except revenge?"

Conway said, "I'm as much a prisoner as a guest in the castle. Tee's told you that."

"She has. We've seen no proof that you're not working for Altanar."

"If my friends and I are forced to it, we will." The crowd leaned forward, and he instinctively tried to back away. The dagger point never lost its contact with his flesh. Trying to sound unperturbed, he went on. "My responsibility is to my people. Altanar will use us, as he uses everyone, but freedom is our goal."

The man made a sound deep in his chest. "And you'd inform on us to earn it, wouldn't you?"

Deliberately, Conway reached to push the dagger away. Then he said, "I came here as a friend." As slowly as he'd moved the blade, he rose. The knife moved with him, no longer in contact, but patiently present. Once erect, he asked the man holding it, "What's your name?"

"Wal," the man said. "You'll never tell anyone, though. You can't get away."

"That was my guess," Conway agreed. Then he gave the crowd a leisurely wave. He added, "If you wanted me dead, I'd be on the ground by the castle wall. Why are you doing this?"

Furious, Tee answered. "I told you he wouldn't be frightened. I hope you're satisfied. You embarrass."

Wal sheathed his dagger and glared around the room, looking for someone to share the blame. Almost mumbling, he said, "We have to be sure of him."

"I'm sure, and I'm the one who lives inside the walls. You'll be on your ship and gone before we get back. Deal with him properly or we leave." Scorn danced across Tee's mobile features. Conway was startled by her performance. In all their meetings, her expression had been unrevealing, her words slow and deliberate. Now both were volatile, lightning quick.

"Enough!" Wal turned to Conway again. "I'm Tee's cousin. If she's wrong about you, our tribe will get its hands on you, you understand?" He glowered, but Conway saw he was posturing now; form was being observed. He responded in kind, including the others in his assurances that Tee's life was as important to him as to them. She looked as if she didn't know if she should be flattered or amused.

Conway continued, "I have to ask—do you have plans to overthrow him in the near future?"

"Overthrow? You make another joke. We can't even disturb his sleep. We're weak, his spies are everywhere. But we're building. Yes; one day we'll destroy him." There was more wish than conviction in the last.

"Tell me about the kingdom. When I go out of the castle and speak to people, they seem afraid, but they don't seem ready for rebellion."

Before answering, Wal spoke to a man behind him, who then circulated through the gathering. As he left, they broke up into small groups. Wal said, "You're talking to Olans." For the next hour he lectured Conway on how Ola was originally a loose organization of eight tribes. Several generations earlier an Olan chief had united them under his rule. Two tribes, the Lapsa and the For, both living on what Conway realized used to be called the Olympic peninsula, still retained some autonomy. The others had essentially been absorbed. Wal was a For. He called his homeland the Whale Coast.

He went on. "The Nions across the Great Ocean—you've heard of them?—Altanar won't let us trade with them. We do, of course. We're smugglers, the best. But some Nions know we can't complain, and they rob us or kill us. Sometimes they even raid our whale-killers. Altanar does nothing to control them, but sometimes he sends troops to destroy our villages, looking for what he calls contraband."

Conway interrupted. "Aren't the For a forest people?"

Tee spoke up. "They are, and the Lapsa call themselves the children of the ocean. The tribes have always intermarried. We have two cultures, but we're like one people."

Wal picked up where he'd left off. The problem was Altanar. His father had been a tyrant, and Altanar was worse. "His nobles take our land. Tax collectors crush us. Young Olan men—and there are almost as many Olans as the rest of us put together—rush to join the army for the pay and privileges. Men from other tribes join to escape poverty."

"Is the army loyal?"

The question earned a brief smile. "Discipline's very harsh. The army's Altanar's most worrisome weakness. He has to use it to enforce his rule, but soldiers have families, clans, tribes. Let's say they're not disloyal. Yet."

The big man stopped then, suddenly hesitant. He looked to Tee, who stared back in flat challenge. He sighed, facing Conway again. He went on. "Tee said you could be a great help. We need you." He studied his knuckles. "I thought we should test you."

Conway said, "It's what I'd have done. Forget it. There's talk in the castle of war between Ola and Harbundai. What do you know of that?"

Wal winced. "Altanar wants it." He scratched a rough map on the wood floor with his dagger. "Look, here's the Whale Coast, here's the Inland Sea, here's Ola and Harbundai. Harbundai controls these islands here in the north—the Sea Stars—but she doesn't interfere with traffic between the Inland Sea and the Great Ocean, except to charge a small toll. The Nions think if they get rid of Harbundai, they get rid of the toll. They don't realize what it'll be like to deal with Altanar in order to trade anywhere in the Inland Sea. Altanar will grab for the coast to the north, too, sooner or later."

Tee interrupted. "Tell him about the pirates."

He shot her a frown that would have sent most men scrambling for cover. She met it placidly. He said, "A few honest smugglers and whalers shelter among the islands. Sometimes they attack a fat Nion trader or an Olan freighter. Nothing important." He jabbed at the map again. "If Ola conquers Harbundai, they control the whole Inland Sea. The insignificant sailors Tee calls pirates will be hunted down by Olans and Nions. The Lapsa and the For will be squeezed to death."

"How long before the war starts?"

Wal stroked his beard thoughtfully. "Hard question. It's said an inland warrior tribe called the Dog People was supposed to help Altanar, but something went wrong. Another story says the Mountain People were supposed to help, but they backed down. No one knows. All I can tell you is that Altanar's got his troops trained and ready, with supplies in city warehouses. He can launch an attack in hours."

"Does Harbundai know all this?"

Tee burst out again. "Their king is a fool! He thinks he can bargain with Altanar. He knows there's enough trade and land here for everyone; he won't believe Altanar wants it all."

"That doesn't answer my question."

Wal gestured Tee to silence. She tossed her head, fuming. Wal said, "Harbundai knows Altanar wants to attack. I don't think the army's very loyal to their king, though. They feel he's weak."

"You think Altanar can beat them."

"If Harbundai's king can control his barons and finds the courage to fight, Altanar may win, but only at great cost. That's why he wants the Dogs or the Mountains to help him. And we won't know if they're joining him until they actually strike."

"It's a more complex problem than I realized. I'll think about it."

Conway was surprised to see Wal bristle. "There's nothing for you to think about. Don't interfere, and never let us catch you or your friends in a lie. You're not one of us, and we're not ready to trust you. Not now, perhaps not ever."

Conway saw Tee was torn, afraid to advance, too nervous to be still. Her hands fluttered aimlessly, reaching and retreating. He said, "I understand your feelings. I'm willing to earn your trust. But *you* understand something: Never speak to me that way again." He spun to face Tee. "I'll walk back. Blindfold and lead me, if you want, but no carrying and no cart."

Wal apparently passed some sort of signal, as two men stepped away from the crowd to put a cloth over his eyes. After that came a hooded cloak. They were careful leading him up the stairs. Tee fell in beside him, warned him to step back. He felt a current of night air and assumed it was from an opened door. Then another voice was telling him the hood was coming off. The voice said he was to walk with his head down while two men supported him. The blindfold would be removed when it was safe. After a long walk of turns and twists, it was Tee who removed it. The escort was nowhere in sight by then.

The trip through the now-quiet streets was uneventful. It was the first time he'd seen them at night. The one they were on, and most of those they crossed, were the narrow sort used for residences and small businesses. Brick or stone walls crowded the cobbled way, leaving only a strip of star-studded sky for illumination. An infrequent window light provided a welcome help in walking the irregular surface. Wider boulevards featured tanneries, brickmakers, woodshops, and other manufacturing facilities, as well as administrative buildings. Sparks danced into the air from the chimney of a potter's kiln. An occasional dog's bark marked their passage, but no one challenged them. There were few other pedestrians. Occasionally they saw the lights of taverns in the distance, but Tee chose a route that avoided such places.

They crossed the field outside the castle wall in a crouching sprint. Tee flung the grappling bar over the top with surprising ease and accuracy. After a quick tug to test its hold, she went first, silent and swift, a darker part of the night. Conway scraped and clumped along after her. Freeing the bar, they hurried down the ladder. Conway was coiling the rope when he heard her sharp gasp.

He whirled to find himself staring at a wipe in Leclerc's hands. The short man spoke in a calm whisper. "I think you want to tell me what's going on."

Conway said, "The gun's not necessary, Louis."

He put out a hand, and Leclerc knocked it away with the barrel, swinging it back to almost touch his navel. "Don't try that again. I'm too nervous for it."

Conway turned toward the castle. As he moved away he looked over his shoulder to see Leclerc shove Tee along until she was beside him. He followed them, the wipe poised. They rushed across the grounds, then made their way cautiously through the halls to Conway's room. Like Falconer's, it was a small rectangle with a bed, two chairs, a cabinet for clothes, and a table. Falconer's equipment was still draped on a deer-antler rack on the wall. In spite of the situation, the sight of it made him feel guilty for not at least packing the things away. After Conway lit the wall candles, Leclerc indicated Tee should sit in the larger chair, with Conway on the floor in front of her. He took the desk chair for himself. When they were all settled, he said, "Let's hear it, Matt. Make me believe."

Conway said, "I didn't mean for the situation to develop this way."

Leclerc shook his head. "That's a bad start. I knew you were meeting Tee. At the beginning I assumed it was man-woman stuff. Today when she left you she was inspecting that wall like her life depended on it. I watched you go over. You risked all our lives. Why?"

"She took me to meet the resistance."

The wipe lowered fractionally. "That's pretty much what I thought. What I hoped. Why not tell me? We're supposed to be in this together."

"It just happened. I wanted to tell you—meant to tell you—but I kept putting it off. I wasn't working behind your back."

"Yes you were. That's exactly what you were doing to all of us." He rose. "It's best the women don't know. If we're caught, ignorance may save them. I'll keep my mouth shut and leave things to you. For now. Don't make us have to protect ourselves from you, Matt." He pointed at Tee. "It's disturbing to see you trust her more than us, that you think you need her more than us. You used up a lot of good faith tonight."

Leclerc left, and for a full minute neither of them moved. Then she went behind him, standing over him, and put her hands on his shoulders. He jerked at the touch, the already tense muscles drawing even tighter. She kneaded them with soothing pressure. His head lolled back, and she moved her forearms closer together, cradling it. Soon she edged forward on the chair, accepting the weight of his head against her body, reaching down to massage his arms and chest.

At first the half pain, half pleasure of her probing fingers eased him, freed mind and body of stress. When she moved forward, however, he felt a stirring in the pit of his stomach, and even as he told himself he must move, it was too late. She bent over him, her breasts brushing his head, the smell of her flooding his nostrils, and the growing heat in his vitals spread, then seemed to fall in on itself, concentrating again in his groin.

Her touch there was almost more than he could stand. His lips felt hot and dry, and when he licked them, he tasted salt. She flicked open the buttons of his trousers. A shudder of release ran through him at sudden freedom, and then she held him between hands that delighted, promised, built ever greater fire at each touch.

He turned, clasping her to him, lifting at the smock, heedless and rough in his hurry. She managed to force his head back and fixed her eyes on his. "Undress," she said, pushing him back. By the time he finished, the smock and her shoes were on the floor and she was naked on the bed, watching him with unreadable, hooded eyes. She extended her arms, and he went to her.

There was no time in his urgency for further preliminaries, and their coupling was a violent, demanding conquest from her first back-arching thrust that met his need to the mingling groans and muffled cries of climax. Not until long after they were spent did he feel able to move, and only then did he raise from her stillness under him and see the way she looked at him.

It seared him, forced him to the edge of the bed. She lay still, watching him. He felt awkward, and he pulled on his trousers and dropped into the larger chair. When she asked softly, "Are you well now?" he heard undertones that inexplicably shamed him. He muttered a yes and thanks that sounded coarse and crudely inadequate. At the sound of movement he looked to see her dressing. He marveled at her, her smooth grace, her unsuspected beauty. Nude, arms extended overhead with the robe, she was the most erotic thing he'd ever imagined. And yet now she was as distant as the stars.

He had held her. He hadn't possessed her. He wasn't sure if the same was true of himself.

She surprised him by sitting in the chair to face him, instead of leaving. He felt clumsy, unable to move.

She said, "You're a good man, Matt Conway. I think now you fear you may have hurt me in some way. You must understand I'm to be used. You know my history. I didn't bear Altanar's king-child, and that makes me a thing. A tool, perhaps." Self-mockery steamed in the words.

"You're more than that." It was such an inane, inadequate response.

"I'm his property." She reached to straighten his hair, pushing, studying, as if concentration on something else might lift her out of her thoughts. She went on, though. "It made me feel good to help you, make you forget for a little while."

"You did. I wish . . ." He gestured the rest away.

She took a deep breath, gathering herself. "We have much in common. My people don't trust you. Your people don't trust me. I thought this way I could make you see I'm being honest with you."

He stared at the floor, unanswering. She paused by the candles. "You can't share, can you? I sorrow. Good night." She blew out the candles as she left.

He slumped on the bed, too much in turmoil to bother taking the trousers off again. A flung-out arm fell on the clothes trunk, across a carelessly dropped rabbitskin jacket. The texture sent him whirling through time, and the earlier zoo came to him again. He saw a children's area, with animals to be cuddled and petted. He heard excited laughter, shrill joy, and a mother's loving, cautioning murmur.

Sleep came as retreat.

CHAPTER 46

"**I** won't allow him to be moved again," Sylah said. She hovered over Jones' litter. A cloth draped over the side of his head protected the wound caused by the slingstone. She was pale with exhaustion, her face tightened to rigid planes of obstinacy. Gan thought he'd never seen her so unattractive, or realized how protective she could be. And all for the useless Jones.

The setting for the scene was in direct contradiction to the temper and hazard of the situation. All around them rhododendrons were coming into bloom in brilliant reds and whites of all shades. Some plants were the size of small trees. At a distance, obscured by intervening growth, they were ghostlike smears of color adrift in the forest. Meanwhile, the noise and litter from the ill-trained Harbundai soldiers offended sight and hearing.

Gan tried to explain once more. "It's been three days. The Devils are following, growing bolder. This Harbundai baron's threatening to leave us."

Neela rose from her seat by the fire, where the morning grain porridge was just beginning to bubble. She came to stand beside Sylah. "I stay with her."

Sylah sent a quick look of gratitude at her, then said, "It's my duty, Gan. You know that. And what will the King of Harbundai do if this Baron Jalail deserts the daughter of a War Chief?"

"Probably nothing. Not when he's anticipating a war with Ola."

"Let him go, then," Neela declared, sneering. "If there are Devils following us, why aren't your dogs excited? These so-called soldiers are just anxious to get away."

As if responding to a cue, the Harbundai night guard crashed through the brush and into camp. Gan had been aware of their approach for some time. He stared coldly at them. Two of the five carried their armor draped on spears over their shoulders. Clas joined the group around Jones, muttering, "Now they're in camp, maybe they'll shut up. I heard them talking to each other all night out there."

"Fools." Gan made a quiet curse of it, but the Baron's sharp glance caught his expression. The short man drew himself as tall as possible. In spite of the gray at his temples, his rounded, undefined features called to mind chubby smiles rather than scowls of authority. Even with fire in his eyes, he appeared more like a petulant child than an angry, middle-aged noble. Still, he held uncontestable power, and the group watched apprehensively as he approached. He planted himself in front of them, feet widespread. "I've watched your disapproval for three days, young man—yours and Clas na Bale's. You owe us your lives. You show appreciation strangely."

Embarrassed, Gan was defensive. "I've spoken no criticism, Baron Jalail."

"Not in words." The Baron pulled on his armored jacket. It was leather, with rows of small metal plates attached by rivets. The plates overlapped, in the manner of fish scales, and as he shrugged it to a comfortable fit, they rubbed together with metallic sibilance. "That's not what I want to talk about. I told you when we met, the King sent me with these fifty men as all he could spare because he expects Ola to attack any time. If the Mountain warriors following us decide to come at us, there are no reinforcements."

Gan said, "The Rose Priestess says Jones musn't be moved."

The Baron stiffened. "My tactical decisions don't acknowledge the whims of women. We move in an hour."

"You move," Gan said. "Please explain to your king that Neela, sister of

Bay Yan, couldn't accompany you because it would risk the life of someone
she holds very dear. As for the War Healer, if the Devils kill her after you
took her under your protection, Church will decide if you fulfilled your
proper obligation. We are honor bound to stay with them, so we will.
Naturally."

Jalail's round cheeks wobbled and turned a startling red-purple. Visibly
controlling himself, he said, "Your women are more problem for my king
than you realize. The Queen Mother and Church have tormented him for
years, urging unnecessary 'reforms' for the females of this kingdom. We're
already enlightened, unlike that pig, Altanar. But they're never satisfied.
Now the Queen Mother is ill. Her influence wanes. As for your Rose Priestess, she deserted an assigned mission. Church will deal harshly with her.
We'll argue no more about them." Spinning on his heel, he walked away a
few paces, back stiff, hand on his sword. The action put Gan in a quandary.
If the Baron was sending hand signals to his men, a surprise attack might
come momentarily. If that wasn't the case, he could easily create a nasty
situation by appearing too anxious to fight. He saw that Clas read the
situation the same way. He was outwardly unconcerned, but his posture was
subtly altered. He was ready.

Gan's low whistle brought the dogs to a standing alert.

Baron Jalail returned to them slowly, his features controlled. In fact, Gan
had the distinct impression of amusement when he spoke in the clipped, flat
accents of his people. "Since you understand so little of negotiations, I will
tell you that there's merit in your argument. Surprising for a Dog."

He turned away, shouting orders to his men. Smarting from his remark,
Gan opened his mouth to retort, but Neela's tight grip on his shoulder pulled
him around. She smiled faintly as she shook her head. "Let him have his last
word. And tell the dogs to relax."

Gan signaled them, grumbling under his breath, stopping at the sight of
Sylah tending to her patient. Prior to the argument with Baron Jalail, he'd
seen her uncompromising, fixed features as unattractive, even ugly. Now he
saw that inner strength filled her face with a different beauty.

Tate returned from her morning wash-up, going directly to Jones, who lay
on a blanket, his only sign of life a rapid, threadlike pulse in his throat. Sylah
removed the bandage from his wound. The entire top of his head on the left
side was grotesquely swollen, giving the close-cropped hair the appearance
of bristles. There was a cut in the middle of the swelling, insignificant
compared to the visible damage surrounding it.

Sylah called Neela to her without looking up, then spoke as the girl knelt
on Jones' other side. She said, "He's gotten worse. See how that yellow liquid

comes? He feels hot, and he vomited several times last night. I'll have to try something drastic."

Tate was hostile. "Do something," she snapped. "War Healer." There was sarcasm in the tone.

Neela defended Sylah. "He won't even stay awake to eat. He hardly speaks, and if he does, he doesn't make sense."

Sylah said, "You noticed he's having trouble breathing? I'm sure there's bone pressing on his brain."

"And you have to make it go away?"

"Exactly." A fleeting smile praised Neela's understanding.

Tate asked, "How? Is that what you mean by 'something drastic'?"

Sylah spoke with soothing softness. "I have to expose the bone, get rid of what's creating the pressure. It's very dangerous."

Tate asked, "What if you leave it alone?"

Sylah shook her head, absently brushing some perspiration from Jones' temple.

Harshly, Tate said, "Tell us how we can help," just as Gan joined them.

"Boil some cotton cloth. Wash your hands. Everything that comes near him must be perfectly clean. While I work, everyone must recite the Protection Against Unseens prayer. Don't stop except to ask for instructions or answer questions. Neela, get my bag, please." Her body tried to obey the wearied mind's commands with normal briskness. Instead, the action was abrupt, jerky. She thrust her hands in the bag and, prior to turning her back on everyone, was already moving her lips in silent prayer.

Then she was handing Gan a piece of material and a sealed bottle. "I'll want clean cloth to put over the wound. Tear that in half. Boil it in the oil in this bottle. When I tell you, take the cloth out to cool, then squeeze it as dry as you can. I don't want to have to wait for it. You understand?"

He hurried to obey. She gave more cloth to Neela and Tate, saying, "When I open the wound, there's going to be much blood, much yellow liquid. You clean it while I search for the trouble. Don't faint or get sick; we don't have time for it. Gan, go get Clas; tell him to keep boiling water ready for washing the cloth they use."

Next, she took a large chunk of obsidian from her bag. With a piece of limestone, she gave it a sharp blow. A gleaming black flake the size and shape of an alder leaf split off. Another small pot from the seemingly inexhaustible bag supplied soap, and she scrubbed the area around the wound before shaving Jones' head with the obsidian.

For several seconds she poised over the man on the blanket, her head thrown back, eyes closed, the glittering black blade offered up in extended, trembling hands. When she stopped, she was composed. "You're all ready? Water, oil boiling?"

There was a murmur of assent. She nodded. "Start the Protection prayer." Listening closely, she coached the three Dog People until the hum of the words was a rising, falling cadence.

Sylah cut swiftly, the touch of the blade leaving a tiny line next to the wound. She started another cut as the first pulsed open. Even Clas blanched at the corruption that spewed out. The two women were shaken, Tate's eyes rolling whitely and Neela struggling to maintain the prayer. Still, they worked efficiently together.

With quick assurance Sylah created a flap of scalp and lifted it back. The large, roughly circular section of bone the slingstone had broken was driven inward, an obscene dimple. Sylah probed into the boiling water to pull out a small metal hook. She used it to engage the pieces of bone, lifting them free of the fibrous outer cover of the brain. The hot blade of a slim knife cauterized blood vessels. She also used it, when it was cooler, to work free two large clots. At one point she turned pleading eyes on Clas, who immediately wiped away the sweat running down her face and held up a cup of cool water for her. After that she had only to turn and he was there, waiting.

When she stopped to inspect her progress, Gan was stiff. Only when he looked to the position of the sun did he realize how long she'd been working. Reaching yet again into her bag, she produced a pear-shaped metal bottle about three inches long. There was a wooden stopper in the neck, so tight she asked Gan to pull it. When he did, and handed it back to her, she shook dust from it to settle on the wound.

Tate was completely under control now; involved in the operation, actually. She asked, "What's that?" indicating the powder. Sylah was sewing the wound shut, her hands slightly unsteady.

Talking to Tate seemed to relax her, and the tremors eased appreciably. She said, "It's made from a mold. We grow it on cabbage leaves, scrape it off and dry it." She looked up, meeting Tate's interest. There was sympathy in her look. She said, "Usually it keeps out the unseens well and helps people heal very quickly. Sometimes it doesn't. Other times . . ." She let it fade away. The final stitches were quick and sure. Once more she dusted the wound, then gave the bottle to Gan to replug and replace.

Protesting weakly, Sylah allowed Clas to lead her away while Neela and Tate completed the bandaging. When she was in the shelter, Gan noticed how many of the Harbundai troops had gathered a short distance off, watching intently. He was puzzled by their attitude, but Neela's sharp call for the oiled cloth quickly sent them from his mind.

She folded it to fit the shaved area on Jones' head. With that in place, she wrapped him in more dry cloth. It took her only a few minutes, and when they had everything cleaned up and restored to Sylah's bag, Gan wondered again why the pale, near-dead man should mean anything to his life. He couldn't think of anything more unlikely.

The following day Baron Jalail examined the patient and complimented Sylah. Still drained, she responded with a wan smile, continuing to bathe her patient with cool water from the neighboring stream. A gruff command from the Baron stopped her.

"I must speak to you," he said, then to Gan added, "Come with us. This affects you, as well." Tate took over the bathing chore. The Baron led them to the sand and stone beach beside the stream. He was careful to position himself with his own back to the water, giving him a clear view of anyone who might attempt to overhear. The soft features were bland, noncommittal. Nervous hands that seemed unable to rest gave away his agitation.

"Priestess, I have bad news. I just learned that your abbess sent a delegation to Sister Mother asking that you be expelled from Church. I sent a rider to tell my king I'm offering you residence in my barony until the matter is decided, on the condition you conduct no Church business."

Gan almost reached to steady Sylah, who swayed as if slapped. Barely audible, not entirely believing, she asked, "My abbess? What reason?"

He shifted uncomfortably, seemed to gather himself for a difficult task. He said, "They say you put your interests before Church. I don't believe it. I watched your attention to the wounded man. There's no War Healer in my lands. I need one."

"Me?"

Baron Jalail misinterpreted her surprise as reluctance. He said, "I'll protect you." When she continued to stare at him, he said, "You'll have your own healing house." Then, exasperated, "It's as much as I can offer!"

Sylah waved her hands, overwhelmed, struggling for words. Blurting, "Thank you, Baron," she managed a weak, "I accept," before hurrying off toward Jones.

He turned to Gan. "She's crying. Last thing I expected."

"Two shocks so quickly, Baron; it's no wonder. And she's a Chosen. Church has been her life."

"Oh, she was in no danger here in Harbundai. We're much more understanding than Olans. Some noble was sure to make a place for her. She's attractive enough. Unless she's barren, of course. Even then she might have found some tradesman who'd use her, maybe even marry her."

Gan breathed a silent thanks Clas wasn't present, then said, "You should know that she and Clas are very close."

"Well, then, there you are. There never was a problem, was there? At least, not that kind."

"You have another kind in mind?"

"Walk with me." Baron Jalail ambled along the water's edge. "I'm afraid of this war with Ola," he said. "That's treason, of course, but you'll keep it to yourself. You're a leader, young man. When there's a question, your group looks to you."

Gan kept silent. The Baron nodded approval and went on. "Harbundai is a country waiting to be conquered. You've seen my men; they'll fight for their own homes, but that's about all. I'm not a warrior, and neither are my three sons. Except the youngest, but he wants only to fight. He has no *goals.*"

He fell silent then, walking faster, driving his heels into the rocky beach as if the jarring strides would shake the turmoil from his mind. A startlingly blue kingfisher flashed past, headed upstream. Its rattling, derisive cry earned an offended glare from the Baron before he said, "You and your friends must declare yourselves my servants. If Neela Yan doesn't stay with me, the King will choose someone. She'll be more comfortable in some of our castles, but nowhere as welcome. Or as safe, because by electing to serve me, you stay with her."

"What if the King won't allow your plan?"

Baron Jalail smiled. Gan was startled at the quick cunning that slid across the normally innocent features. "There are barons who'd support me. He can't afford any internal squabbles now."

"You want us to make warriors of your men. You see your son defending Harbundai, not just your lands."

Pulling an ear, the Baron said, "You've a clever head. Take care your tongue doesn't separate you from it. If the King or one of his informers heard you say that, we'd both decorate his hanging tree."

"Hanging tree?"

"You know—where they hang criminals. By the neck?" He demonstrated with his hands, made strangling noises. "It's how we get rid of them. How do you do it?"

Gan explained about the Journey. Baron Jalail shook his head. "You'll never get our people to do that. Just make them fighters, that's all I ask," he said, heading back toward the camp. "The black woman and her lightning weapon will be our backbone, my son will be our heart, my men our muscle. As we grow strong, others will join us. My son will lead them all. In strength, Harbundai can prosper without fear."

When Gan asked why none of the barons had done any of this on their own, Jalail explained that life and power in Harbundai was a question of balance. No baron would tolerate ambition in another, and would ally himself with any other baron to confront it. The King, on the other hand, constantly juggled all of them to assure enough support for his crown. Presently, everyone would be preoccupied with the Olan threat. By the time the tension subsided, he, Jalail, would be strong enough to attract supporters.

Later, Gan repeated the conversation to the others, finishing with, "I agreed to it. It's the only way we can be sure to stay together. And it's the base we need."

Tate said, "He's asking us to discipline and train men who aren't used to it. We're all strangers. He sees you as the leader, and you have to admit you're young for the job. And what about me, a woman and black? Are you sure this is a good move?"

He leaned forward. "Some will call me 'boy.' Only the bravest will say it where I can hear, and none—I promise you—none will say it a second time. I am a leader. I was born for it. I say that as an invitation. Believe in me. Believe in *us.*"

The words came unbidden. He watched the doubt wither in her expression, to be replaced by something like surprise, and then growing conviction. Something like joy shone from Clas.

Sylah's Priestess-trained gaze was hooded, secret. He was sure she was afraid though, because he was equally sure she, too, felt the invisible forces controlling all of them.

When he looked to Neela, the inner vision collapsed to sadness. Whatever came, he couldn't enjoy it without her. And she would always want to be somewhere else.

CHAPTER 47

For three more days Sylah insisted Jones couldn't be moved. Several times during that delay she found herself trembling on the edge of hysteria. No matter how hard she worked, the same grating voice searched through her mind, chanting, *Cast out! Cast out!*

It was a living execution.

She had *belonged* to Church. All her life she had been Church's object, and hated it. That was gone. She'd longed to be free. Instead, she was abandoned.

Night was a time of torment. As she fought to sleep, her brain pulsed with chaotic thoughts. She saw her mission to prevent the Dog People's attack on Harbundai as a hollow, terrible success.

More than that, she'd unleashed a force. If she'd never gone to the Dog camp, Gan would never have come to Harbundai. Now, when he spoke of commanding Baron Jalail's men, the look of a conqueror was in his eyes. Power was coming to him, building. She couldn't look at him without thinking of the first tumbling, insignificant rock that starts the landslide.

That was the sort of imagery that came when exhaustion finally turned to sleep—visions of the damage she'd done, and of battles and fires to come.

Clas was the strong chain that bound her to hope. But how could she burden him with a cast-out woman?

They were preparing to leave when Neela approached her. She spoke as if each word cost her hard effort. The clashing din of the soldiers breaking camp formed a discordant background. Neela said, "If I ask you one question, will you promise to answer honestly?"

"If I can."

"Did you ever think that perhaps I loved him, too?"

For a second that felt like an eternity, Sylah refused to believe what she'd heard. How could she have been so blind, so utterly uncomprehending? She let her own concerns, her own plots and schemes, destroy the last of Neela's dreams.

She saw her expression had answered for her, and Neela spoke before she could. "I'm glad you didn't," she said, and Sylah tensed. How could that be? If someone stole Clas' love from her— She rejected the thought, the hatred that seethed behind it.

Neela said, "I loved him the way girls love heroes. He was my friend, always nearby, so I could be close to him and admire without being obvious." She laughed, and the quiet end of it was discordant. "I must have done well, if my closest friend failed to see."

Sylah said, "You're not angry? You forgive?"

"Forgive? There's no need. The only person to harm me is myself. When I saw how Clas loves you, and how you love him, I wanted to hate you. I couldn't. Then, when I thought our journey might end, I felt a great sadness. I feared for the happiness you'd found with Clas. I feared the honors that should be Gan's would never find him. I—" She paused. "—I thought of many things." It was a clumsy evasion, and she blushed.

Sylah took her arm, led her away from the noise and toward the soothing murmur of the small river. At the water's edge Neela picked up a handful of pebbles and, one by one, tossed them out to create their concentric circles, watching them sweep downstream. "I don't know what to say to you, Neela.

My thoughts run everywhere, like spilled milk. I'm sorry we caused you pain, yet I'm glad it opened your eyes to other things. Have you spoken of this to . . . anyone else?"

Neela's earlier color returned. She shook her head. "I can't. If I told him now, he'd think everything I did was because of him. I wanted him for myself, or had ambitions for us."

"Do you love him?"

Slowly, almost imperceptibly, she nodded.

"Then trust him. Tell him how you feel, how you felt."

Quickly, like a startled animal, Neela stepped back. "About Clas? His friend? No." She drew the word out, a sound of anguish. "What if I came between them? You heard Gan say it yourself—he needs Clas beside him. If he ever thought I cared for Clas, it might affect his judgment of him just when he needs him most."

"Why must he be different from you? If you can love and trust him, why can't he do the same?"

Neela clutched her arm, begging with her eyes. "You must never tell him. He doesn't know how I feel; he's always thinking of other things. When I saw you together with Clas, when I knew about you, Gan comforted me, but he thought I was only reacting to your escape. He never guessed how I thought I felt about Clas, and he'd never guess how I feel about him. Up at the pass he said I'm his friend. Perhaps someday he'll see me as more than that. But he must never suspect about Clas. What I've told you is our secret, Sylah. Please. Promise me."

Sylah said the words, even though she believed the promise was a trap that would never lose its danger for any of them.

They walked back to the campsite arm in arm. The more Sylah thought about it, the more she wished Neela would simply be honest with Gan. She was being stubborn, as much as concerned; it showed in the set of her chin and the way her stride sent the golden braids slashing across her back. She wanted to tell her: I know what love can become when too long denied. The repressive atmosphere of the abbey created many complex situations for the women who lived there and were attracted to men who lived more normal lives. Some budding romances smoldered for years, suddenly bursting forth as consuming flames. The terrible part of such a flash fire was that no one could predict when it would come, or even what form it would take. Love didn't have to become hatred to be dangerous. Suspicion, or jealousy, or envy could all serve.

The loading progressed rapidly, the Baron's troops anxious to get home. The Devils left them alone, but no one doubted they were watching.

The weather grew worse. Clouds drifted in from the west, their thickness muffling the pleasant sound of the river, hiding it from view. Moisture slicked the branches of the trees. Droplets condensed and pattered down in simulation of rain. Sylah hadn't remembered the forest as so foreboding, and it seemed far colder than the time of year required.

She was supervising the litter bearers when the Baron approached. He invited her to ride along with him, and called to the others to join them. He was voluble, once moving. "I'm told this was a busy trade route long ago," he said. "Now we depend on Peddlers like Bilsten to use it so it's not lost." He laughed at their surprise. "Yes, I know him, but he didn't come to me about you. He went to the King because that's the only place he'd get a reward. The King sent me after you because this is my land. A point the Mountain People dispute. However, as I was saying, the Peddlers are our only trade link to the east. It's not a good situation."

"You have good trade with others?" Gan asked.

"Even with Ola, unless we're warring. Access to the east grows more important, though. Our population's growing. Our climate doesn't favor grain, corn, or meat animals the way yours does."

Gan asked what they traded with Ola, and the Baron launched into a monologue about everything from the exchange of products to a commentary on the near-constant skirmishing between Ola and Harbundai to determine who controlled the Inland Sea and the Whale Coast beyond it.

Sylah watched Gan. He said no more, having steered the conversation in the direction he desired. His expression was the clue. She was delighted with herself for catching him. The more the conversation interested him, the less expression he showed. When the discussion turned to the thrust and counterthrust of the opposing land and sea forces, he looked straight ahead, bland as milk, but undistracted by anything.

She was also watching him when Neela's horse stumbled, making her cry out in surprise. Gan's concentration broke on the instant. How could she be so unaware of the truth that glowed through that worried, anxious look?

She winced inwardly. How many times had Neela looked at her with hurt? Or jealousy? She'd never seen that, and she was trained to catch the most subtle physical nuances.

Another thought came to her, even more disturbing. She'd already asked herself how she could ask Clas to live with a cast-out Priestess, but now she must consider if Gan's caring for Neela could make him vulnerable. Until now, he was Gan, alone with a fate that somehow involved them all. What would happen to the rest of them if he was distracted at some important moment by concern for her?

That thought generated yet another, more chilling question: Could *she* herself endanger Clas? Sylah wouldn't believe it. She glanced behind, where Jones rode on his litter, the four men who carried him striding along steadily. He was an example of her power to sustain and preserve life. How could she be a danger to the man she cared for most?

Gan left Neela's side, moving abreast of the Baron once again. He turned for one final glance at Neela before attending to the conversation between them. As his head swung back to the front, his eyes caught Sylah's, held the contact. It was a piece of time too small to measure. She wished it had been too small for her to see the confused longing in him. Sadness washed over her, left her yearning for the comfort of Clas' touch.

CHAPTER 48

Raggar was supposed to be working far in advance of the column, and his appearance, particularly since he was so close, was an unpleasant surprise. He swung his head first toward Gan, then back in the direction of the march. It was an odd display of uncertainty. Gan watched him for a moment before signaling him back to work, and the dog wheeled and obeyed immediately. It was only a few minutes later when Cho and Shara, operating together on the flank away from the river, similarly popped into view on a ridge. He whistled them away.

The incidents aggravated his tension. He didn't like the forest. Trees crowded the narrow trail, scorning the puny figures winding past their ancient strength. Even their fissured bark spoke of unimaginable time. Blackened patches and scars were proud testimony that some resisted the fury of forest fire. Above the marching column, interlocked branches blocked so much light they created a thickly scented dusk at ground level. The very sky contributed to the oppressiveness, masking the sun with gray persistence.

And the forest talked. Sly, gossiping breezes whispered tantalizingly just outside comprehension, so that he never quite understood what they were saying, but couldn't avoid hearing. There was little animal life. The occasional scold of a squirrel or call of a bird split the air with unnatural volume. He tried to concentrate on the troops plodding along in front of him, envying their boredom even as he deplored their unpreparedness.

Raggar's next appearance was more dramatic. He came around a distant bend in the trail, running to rejoin his master. He sounded no alarm. It was unheard-of behavior, and it was compounded by the return of Shara and

Cho, the younger dog leading the female, both at top speed. Alarmed, Gan rode to join the Baron at the head of the column. He listened impatiently to Gan's urgent recommendation for an advance party and flankers. Gan had nothing to base his fears on save the inexplicable behavior of the dogs. "I've never known Raggar to act this way. He's nervous and confused," he confessed.

"And you?"

The Baron's condescension shocked Gan, who snapped, "Confused, only. Let me lead your advance."

"No. My troops carry out my orders." The Baron rose in his saddle and called a grizzled soldier from where the men were already sprawled on the ground beside the trail. The man ambled over, casually brushing leaves and dirt from his backside as he did. He shot an appraising look at Gan, then turned his back to slouch against Gan's mount and look up at the Baron. The horse trembled at the unwelcome liberty.

The man nodded up the trail. "Dogs got you spooked, Baron?" he asked. Gan was so surprised by the man's observation, he forgot to be offended by his disrespectful attitude.

Baron Jalail's round face puckered in a prunelike frown. "Gan thinks there may be danger ahead."

"This close to home? The dogs probably smelled our chickens and come looking to him for orders."

The Baron turned away. "Take five men ahead as advance. Send another four to the right flank. We won't worry about the river side."

"I ain't worried about anything but wasting my time."

Gan's touch on his horse's neck sent it lunging forward, and the soldier was suddenly without support. He dropped flat on his back. By the time he started to rise, red and fuming, Gan had turned the mount completely around, and the unshaven, twisted face found itself only inches from a ground-pawing, tooth-gnashing war-horse. Speaking calmly, forcing the man to scramble backward too fast to regain an erect stance, Gan said, "Watch a real warrior. Learn. If I don't get you with my murdat, one blow from the horse's hoof should cripple you. Unless you'd rather hurry along and carry out the Baron's orders." He reined in the aroused horse. It continued to prance and snort.

The man straightened cautiously. Stepping back, he finally raised his eyes, and surprised Gan once again. Something suspiciously like amusement pulled at the soldier's scowl as he turned away, and then he was trotting to the troops. His commands came back to Gan as a series of growls, and when one of the younger men moved too slowly, the older one dealt him a blow on the helmet with the flat of his sword that rang like a blacksmith's maul.

Several minutes after the security units had set out, a still-seething Baron said, "Of all the men I command, you have humiliated the most reliable. You're well on your way to being useless to me."

Gan shook his head. "My usefulness depends on obedience in battle."

The Baron grunted and waved the column forward. Gan continued to ride beside him.

The decision to embarrass the man might have been a mistake, Gan conceded to himself. Still, there was a limit to what could be accepted. And there was that peculiar look in the man's eye.

He debated sending the dogs out again as Raggar automatically loped ahead to scout. He called the dog back. Whatever lay ahead, it was strange; let the Baron's people sort out their own problems, he thought, giving way to the anger picking at him. His dogs were too important to risk around armed, undisciplined fools. He bent down to ruffle Raggar's ears, and the hound glanced at him before pretending to be unaware.

The Baron watched. He said, "You treat those animals better than you treat men."

The censure required an answer. Gan listened to the careless clatter and chatter of the column as he formed the words. He thought of Nightwatchers, stealthy as owls, of men who planned raids with the silent hand language, who saw battle as joy. A wave of loneliness threatened to overwhelm him, and then, as suddenly, it was replaced by determination. He said, "Affection has nothing to do with goals. You and your son can have their love, if it matters to you. I want only their battle skills."

Baron Jalail laughed harshly. "What reason do I have to believe you won't try to subvert my men to your own goals, then?"

"My word, Baron." Gan had to force the words past lips stiff with outrage, and he repeated to himself that he was entering a world where there were more motives than stars in the sky.

"I want to believe you," the Baron said. His thoughtful tone drew some of the poison from the atmosphere. "Understand, my country's had no connection with your people for almost a hundred years. We hear you're warlike and proud. And honest. If you're to help me, the first thing to learn is that lying is an art in Harbundai—or wherever men call themselves civilized." Gan's eyes flashed, and Baron Jalail chuckled. "Oh, I know that offends you. To you, civilization is courage, sound customs, and honor; to us it means buildings, bridges, and sewers."

Gan said, "We live as free men must."

"Don't you think everyone says the same thing? We're all convinced *our* way is right."

It was Gan's turn to be thoughtful. "I never thought about it. We say a man can only live as the One in All shows him."

Shouting ahead jerked them both upright. In seconds one of the advance guard was sprinting around a bend, headed toward them in a flurry of arms and equipment as he tried to get into his armor on the run. The sound of alarm rang clear in his incoherent shouts. The Baron spurred forward. Gan was beside him.

Racing past the man, Jalail and Gan halted abruptly after rounding a bend that brought them to the point where the trail started descent into a wide, flat valley. Approximately a mile away smoke spired lazily from at least twenty burning buildings. The individual plumes rose to combine in an elongated black smudge that pointed accusingly southeast.

"Slaving raid." Baron Jalail lashed his horse back into motion. Once more keeping pace, Gan turned to see Clas and Tate galloping behind them.

When they caught up to the advance guard, there were only two left, one of them the man who'd been so insolent. The remainder had left for their homes.

They came across the first survivors moments later. A woman clutching her side and holding a child by the hand stumbled toward them. The Baron stopped, swung down to steady her, offered her a drink from his waterskin. When she recognized him, she tried to bow, stopping suddenly. Blood seeped between the fingers of the hand at her side. The child, a boy of about ten, looked at it, then at the Baron. His eyes were clear, unteared, but there was terrible accusation in them.

The Baron cleared his throat. "How long ago? How many?"

"Perhaps an hour. How many? Twenty? Forty?"

He said, "The King sent troops here, to guard. Where were they?"

She looked at him blankly. "There was no one, Baron. Old men, boys. Some cripples, like my husband, the leatherworker. They tried to fight the raiders."

Gan said, "You escaped. Your husband. . . ?"

She shook her head. Gan said sympathetic, automatic words. His eyes were on the child, who still supported his mother. Gan eased her to a sitting position. Kneeling, he was eye to eye with the boy. He told him, "A War Healer comes, a woman all in black, wearing a red rose. She'll help your mother."

He started to rise and the boy blurted, "The one who did it, he had a scar, like this." He traced a mark on his arm. The mother reached for him, said, "Hush, son," and the boy resisted, determined to have one last question. "Will you catch him?"

"I don't know," Gan said. "If I do, you'll have his sword."

The boy nodded solemn approval.

They rode off as Clas and Tate joined them. Gan repeated the woman's story for them. By the time he finished, they were at the limits of the village. The entire complex was no more than fifty yards long, shoulder-to-shoulder buildings facing the trading trail. It was totally ablaze. Riding around it, they found the least-injured survivors tending to the others. There was little noise. Exhausted youngsters slept or stared in shock. A woman wailed, a heart-rending rise and fall. One old man fought his way almost to a sitting position to shake a feeble fist at Baron Jalail as he passed. The Baron affected not to see him.

From the edge of the village Gan saw the Baron's castle. It was quite distant, but there was no mistaking the blunt, square shape. Pennons flying from the corners made it even more obvious. A rider burst out of its protection, pounding toward them. They hurried to meet him. As soon as he was close enough for the Baron to recognize him, he paled. "That's Ops. Something is very wrong if he comes himself."

He spurred his horse to greater speed. Gan and the others hurried to catch him, and as Gan looked over his shoulder, Tate called to him. "Did he say Ops?"

When Gan said that was what he understood, she deliberately changed her expression from amazement to mere curiosity. "Strange name," she said.

Then the newcomer was skidding his mount to a stop in front of the Baron. He raised his right fist to his jaw to speak, the back side of the hand out. He was an older man, and his face was drawn with worry and weariness. The Baron returned the odd greeting as Ops said, "Your son is in pursuit, Baron. I tried to stop him."

"How many with him?" The Baron said as he headed for the castle at a trot.

Riding alongside, Ops said, "It was the castle watch, Baron. All twelve," and when the Baron whirled on him, he blanched and repeated, "I tried to stop him."

"What happened?"

Ops pointed north. "They took four women and three boys. As soon as your son heard, he rode that way. When the raiders struck here, they saw the smoke and came back."

Gan interrupted. "How far north?"

The man looked at him, then at the Baron, who nodded at him to answer. He said, "Eight or nine miles."

"So he'd ridden sixteen to eighteen miles by the time he got back here. He changed horses at the castle?"

Baron Jalail said, "We're not cavalry, we're infantry. We don't have enough horses to change every time one gets tired."

Gan turned to Ops again. "The men with the Baron—they're warriors?"

Highly agitated, the Baron spoke for him. "Children. The oldest is fourteen, the youngest only eleven. The sons of my sons. 'Castle watch' is just a term, a thing to make boys aware of future responsibilities as men."

Baron Jalail read Gan's failure to comment. "Twelve children. On tired horses. We have to overtake them."

"When the horses drop. The slavers were mounted, weren't they?"

"Of course," Ops answered. A touch of scorn colored his voice. "A wagon, too." At Gan's quickened interest, he explained, "To move the prisoners."

To the Baron, Gan said, "We have a chance," and to Ops, "Show me which way they went." As the other man pointed, Gan was using the silent whistle, calling the dogs.

A few minutes later they were south of the village, the stink of its burning a constant companion. Ops pointed out the path leading south. Gan studied the tracks, noting one lame horse and one with a peculiarly notched shoe. One wagon wheel left a distinct mark, as well. He directed Raggar to smell the sign, then gestured him on. The animal padded away, concentrating on the scent trail. Shara and Cho flanked him.

Gan explained that they'd track until they sighted their quarry. Raggar would then return to Gan, while the others kept contact. He called to Clas and Tate to accompany him. When the Baron called Ops, Gan suggested the older man might be more help to the villagers.

Agreeing, the Baron fell in with Gan. They moved out at a controlled trot, but the strain became too much for the Baron. "We've got to go faster. My son's up there with my grandsons. We have to hurry!"

"We can't." Gan continued the steady pace. Baron Jalail had to slow in order to hear him. "Our animals are tired. We have to stop soon, water and feed them. Look at the tracks of your son's riders. Their horses are exhausted."

"You can't know that!"

Quick irritation stirred a sharp retort in Gan's mind, but he swallowed it and continued easily. "The hoofs drag. Look, on this bush; saliva. Over here, sweat. This is where one stumbled. No wonder—it's carrying a heavier load than the others. A bad rider, as well."

"Anancha," the Baron almost whispered. "A large-boned boy, a bit overweight, perhaps. He'll be a huge man." The hope in the last was prayerlike. He looked to Gan. "If the horses fail, they'll have to stop, won't they? We'll find them waiting for us."

"I hope so."

Baron Jalail broke into a gallop. He urged them to keep up.

Gan said, "No."

The Baron made a sound of disgust and frustration, whipping his horse into a run.

Clas joined Gan. "Doesn't he know anything?"

"Not about horses," Gan said. He slipped out of the saddle, examined the tracks more closely. When he straightened, Tate was looking at him with silent question. Gan said, "Look here. The slavers have spare mounts. In ten miles the boys' horses will begin to drop. If they stop when the first one goes, they can at least make a stand. The Baron may even overtake them before the slavers double back on them." He slapped the neck of his horse and led him to a stream.

Tate came to stand beside him. "Do you have a man you call Ops in your tribe?"

Gan said, "No, we don't. You've heard it before?"

"Yes." She hesitated, then added, "Not exactly. There was a time—we had a man called the Operations Chief. He made war plans."

Gan nodded. Whatever she was saying wasn't entirely the truth, but it wasn't anything she felt compelled to actually hide, either. Puzzling. He said no more, setting out afoot, leading his horse.

While they'd waited for Jones to get well enough to travel, Gan had made new feedbags for the horses. He put a measure of grain in his now, letting the animal eat as it walked. The others did the same.

As they continued on, he thought about the raid. Something about it had the smell of a trap. He argued with himself; he'd never experienced a slave raid. Constant preparedness had spared his people all but the most fleeting attacks. And all people knew that the Dog tribe exacted heavy revenge for injury. Nevertheless, the notion that the scene was wrong refused to leave his mind. It seemed a great number of raiders for so few slaves. They'd gone far deeper into the barony than was prudent or necessary, and the destruction they'd wrought was out of all proportion to the mission.

There was more to it. He wondered what it might be.

The sun was low when they came across the dead horse. Reading the tracks, Gan shook his head in disbelief. "One of them took the rider; they're doubled up."

Clas said, "They're determined to die together."

Moments later Raggar appeared, trotting toward them, panting. Gan patted his head. He listened to the dog's breathing, felt his heartbeat. "Not far away," he told Clas. "He's calm. Maybe the raiders decided to just keep going and escape."

Clas nodded, noncommittal.

It took only another hour for them to reach the next two horses. They lay within fifty yards of each other. Crows and ravens complained bitterly at being disturbed. The boldest, caught on the ground, flapped up into the trees, blacker shadows against the darkening forest. The second horse was the Baron's and it had died of an arrow in its throat.

A few yards off the trail they found him. Another man was sprawled beside him, an outflung arm on the Baron's bloody chest, as if comforting him. Clas grunted. "Slavers left a rear watch, just waiting for some other fool to come riding along."

"He's not dead," Gan said, not bothering to hide his surprise.

A sip of water revived the Baron. He rolled his eyes from Gan to the dead Olan and back. "Ambush." It was a croak. "Ribs broke. Leg, too, I think. Played dead. He thought he'd rob my body." He half rose, fell back again. "Leave me. Save the boys."

Gan studied him thoughtfully for a long moment before gesturing to Clas for help. Between them they got him into the saddle on Tate's horse, lashing him in place, ignoring his pleas that they leave him and press ahead.

When Gan faced Tate, she lifted her chin and spoke before he could. "Don't send me back with him. You may need me. You know I can fight. Sending me back weakens you by more than just one person." She hefted the wipe meaningfully.

He took her arm and led her a few paces away. When he spoke, his voice was softly insistent. "He needs help. I have to send you or Clas. Think what this man is to us. If these children are dead, who knows what struggles will erupt in the barony? What happens to us if *he* dies? Keep him alive. Protect him. He's our shield."

Her agreement was so grudging he had to smile at her spirit. She left her horse as a spare for them, and he watched her with true admiration as she left. She was as innocent as a babe in some respects—he winced as she underscored the thought by tripping noisily—and uncannily wise in others.

For that matter, he was surprised by his own foresight. A month earlier he'd never have thought about the prospects of a power struggle among the Baron's sons, much less the effect it could have on him and his friends. Now its importance was a matter of course.

He sent Raggar on ahead, fell in behind Clas. The afternoon sun broke through the low clouds, creating oblique columns of light that turned the forest luminous without improving vision.

As if responding to that strange, unrevealing glow, he felt his thoughts drift away from the immediacy of the moment. A sense of duality pulled him, left him with the feeling that he was fully alert to the present, yet free to let his mind wander. He imagined himself standing to the side, watching two warriors. The younger of the two was hot-blooded, a tiger that lived for the hunt as much as it lived by the hunt. The other warrior was a stalker, too, but cold and logical. Without knowing why, Gan was certain the second was the truly dangerous one.

The brawling sound of a fast-flowing stream intruded on his thoughts, brought him back to the necessities of the present. They let the horses drink freely and munch some more grain.

Shortly after that, Raggar came in again. He leaned into Gan's legs, growling. It was a warning of danger ahead. Both men hurried off the trail, continuing their advance by paralleling it at a distance.

There was little undergrowth because of the gloom under the fir canopy. Swordlike ferns managed to grow, and infrequent spindly survivors of other species sometimes reared up from the dark litter. Slugs flourished. Their silvery slime trails were an incongruously beautiful netting across everything.

The horses moved gingerly, unused to the uncertain softness of the decaying duff.

Shara and Cho slipped up on them quietly, weaving through the ferns as though born to it. Shara whined and made a tentative rush forward, stopping abruptly at Raggar's growl. Gan hand-signaled both of them to lead the way.

The dogs took them to where the children had found their enemies. A man was moving from place to place, busily bending to retrieve things from the ground. Deliberately, Gan fitted an arrow to his bow. He shouted an instant before releasing it. The man was straightening just then, and it struck him as he turned, startled by the noise. The dogs were on him before he could fall.

Clas looked quizzical. Gan said, "I wanted him to know it was coming."

Calling the dogs off, Gan walked over to inspect him. Rings and bracelets and a gold necklace littered the ground around him. He also had a peculiar scar on his arm. Gan took his sword as they picked up the jewelry. Then they looked over the site of the massacre. The bodies were flung about like toys thrown down in a pique, the miniature armor lewdly bright and gay. Gan couldn't help thinking how cruel the sun was, to settle on this, of all places, picking out color and vitality in the midst of such grim loss.

The boys had come down the trail from the right. There were eight horses dead of arrows here; Gan assumed the others were on the part of the trail they'd bypassed, just as dead, either from arrows or exhaustion.

The ambush was hook-shaped, the shorter length across the trail, the longer arm at a right angle, so its men were ranged along the length of the route. When the first victim reached the men barring the way, a flight of arrows struck the column from the front. Immediately, the long axis of the ambush swept forward, driving into the flank of the startled children. In the silence Gan's imagination echoed with the screams.

So young, so unready.

Clas said, "They fought hard. The Baron said there was his son and twelve others. I count one missing."

It was Cho who found him. Gan watched her move with deliberate intent toward a downed tree some distance from the ambush. He was already on his way to her when she turned and whined. As he pulled the unconscious youth out of the cramped hole under the trunk, he wondered at the instinct that drew Cho to such helplessness. Her tail flailed wildly and she licked the boy's face as Gan dragged him clear. The broken shaft of an arrow jutted from his back. The metal plates of his small armored jacket were crimped inward, pointing at the blood oozing from the hidden wound. They got the jacket off. Gan decided to leave the treatment to Sylah.

While Gan was lashing the boy in his saddle, he couldn't keep his eyes from the small bodies. They could have been pretending to be casualties in the endless running, shouting, battles of boyhood. Today they'd seen the truth, in all its viciousness. The glory, the excitement they'd sought and been taught to expect, was swept away in a few shattering moments of pain and terror before they were old enough to understand the meaning of any of the words.

"Poor fools," he muttered under his breath. Then, seeing Clas in the distance signaling all clear, he sighed and added, "Like the rest of us."

CHAPTER 49

Baron Jalail's castle was somber against the dawn as Tate broke clear of the trees. She fought the urge to hurry, telling herself the worst was over now. Even so, as she turned to check on the wobbling form of the Baron, she purposely avoided looking back into the forest. The hushed sounds and the wet smells still seemed to cling to her. It made her flesh crawl. Hurrying farther into the field, she inhaled deeply, filling her lungs with the rich scent of farmed earth. This was land that was willing to share the sun instead of greedily absorbing it. She thought of kissing it, and laughed. It was shrill, tainted with hysteria. After a night of jittery wakefulness listening to the Baron's rasping breath, she was at the limit of her stamina.

Striking out purposefully, she steadied him and checked his pulse with the same hand. It was weak but steady.

A man stumbled out of the nearest farmhouse when she was only a few yards distant. He was on his way to the outhouse, tucking in his shirt, scratching sleepily. At the sound of her voice he jumped. When he saw her, he froze, mouth agape, eyes wider than seemed possible. She repeated her message.

"Send someone for help! Baron Jalail's hurt!"

The man's arms windmilled wildly. Tate screamed, "Move it!"

Leaping straight up, the man came down running and shouting. "It's the black one! She's got the Baron! She needs help!" He disappeared inside the house, his voice taking on an ethereal, echoing quality, and then he flew out the front door, headed for the castle, calling out his news at every step.

In minutes Tate had more company and assistance than she needed.

Neela and Ops led the group that rode out from the castle to meet her. Neela insisted Tate ride her horse the last few hundred yards. She walked alongside, explaining that Sylah was working on patients. "She sleeps sitting in a corner," she said, "and every other word is to ask if Clas is back." She paused, then went on, "Gan and he were all right when you left them?"

Tate nodded, afraid she'd mumble if she tried to speak. When Neela asked if she'd slept at all, she felt the nervous laughter crowd her throat again. Sleep? she wanted to say, I was too frightened to blink. She closed her eyes to shut out any more such foolishness.

When she opened them, she looked up at the timbers and planks of a ceiling and could barely remember being helped to the room. She clutched the blanket to her neck and sat up. The cubicle was very small, but neat, with a bed, table, and chair. Sunlight streamed in the single window. Her clothes were next to it, draped on hooks extending from the stone wall. She hurried to get dressed, uncertain of the time. The windowsill was hot, so she assumed it was afternoon.

Pulling open the door, she looked across the narrow hall into a placid face that smiled a greeting. "I've been waiting," the woman said.

"For what?"

"For you, Traveler. I'm yours."

The answer was so assured it left Tate feeling a bit stupid. She responded with unwonted sharpness. "My name's Donnacee Tate; don't call me traveler. And what do you mean, you're mine?"

The woman looked flustered. "I'm a prisoner. They said I was to look after you." She was rising as she spoke, and now she put her hand to her jaw in the same gesture Ops had used the day before. So had the farmer; Tate remembered it clearly now. The woman followed that move with a low bow, saying, "My name is Myrs Talasho, your servant. And we always call friendly strangers Traveler. I was told you're friendly. I offend?"

Tate gestured her into the room, pointing out the chair. Myrs stood by it uncomfortably until Tate insisted she sit.

The woman was well into middle age, and she folded and unfolded tired, blue-veined hands in her lap when she settled. Her dress was a scoop-necked single-piece robe that hung to ankle length. It was black and white in broad diagonal stripes, of a heavy wool that made Tate want to sweat just looking at it. Her hair was gray and her eyes were coffee-dark.

Tate said, "Are my friends back from the forest yet? How's Jones? Is the Baron all right? Where are Neela Yan and the Rose Priestess?"

Myrs assured her that everyone was well, but the two Dog savages were still out.

When Tate asked for something to eat, Myrs suggested they visit the castle's kitchen. She said that was where she usually worked. When Tate asked how long she'd been there, Myrs replied vaguely that it must be almost a year. She also mentioned that her assignment—all assignments—came from a member of the Baron's staff called One. Tate stopped dead.

Myrs turned quizzically. Tate asked, "The man who sends people to different jobs is named One?"

"It's not his real name. He's called that after the Baron gives him the job, just like the man who looks after the Baron's supplies and things becomes Four."

Tate's head spun. It was military terminology, from her own time. She told herself to be casual. Myrs confided, after glancing about to be certain she wasn't overheard, that the man who controlled the Baron's spies was called Two. He traveled a great deal, using what she called commers as messengers back to the castle; sometimes commers worked on their own assignments away from Jalail. It was a quick leap for Tate from *commer* to *communications*. With that, the fist salute was obvious; they were acting out holding a radio handset.

She was still preoccupied by her new knowledge when they entered the sprawling kitchen. It was another major distraction. The staff, all women, were clothed uniformly in wool blouses and skirts featuring the same stripes as Myrs' robe. When Tate commented about it, Myrs said all staff wore the Baron's colors.

They were eager to feed Tate. There was a blue-marbled cheese with a bite that was an effective eye-opener, along with sourdough bread to accompany it. Another plate held sliced apples, and there was hot tea steaming in a thick ceramic mug. Tate thought she detected a hint of cinnamon in the tea, a possibility that suggested a far more developed trade system than she'd imagined. She wolfed it all, while the women bombarded her with questions about her trip, the fight with the Mountain People, and her own origins. At Myrs' request, she let the senior cook try to rub some color from her skin.

She wondered how long she could stand that particular examination, then reminded herself she had very little choice.

She asked Myrs to take her to Sylah and Neela, knowing that was where she'd also find Jones and the Baron.

On the way, Myrs told her Sylah insisted the Baron was to be kept in the healing house until she released him. He'd complained, but he was still there.

Tate studied her surroundings. The defensive stone wall of the castle was farther from the main building than she'd realized. There were several buildings backed against it, and the way they ringed the dominating bulk of the castle made her think of a rural town square. She heard the clatter of a metalsmith in the distance. From a shop with a wooden representation of a boot hung over the door she inhaled the smell of leather and heard a hammer's rapid tap-tap-tap.

Everyone stared at her, bluntly curious, although friendly. The women were dressed in blouses that hung below waist level, worn over full skirts draped to mid-calf. A belt outside the blouse gave the costume shape, and they exercised full imagination in their color, pattern, and material combinations. Purses, equally varied, dangled from the belts. The men wore plain full shirts and trousers in darker colors. The latter were bloused above bead-and-bangle-decorated boots, some positively gaudy.

They were passing a large, plain building that shouldered up against the castle wall when Myrs said, "That's where I live now."

An underlying sadness in the words made Tate look closely. It was an ugly place of rough, weathered wood. The sloping roof was as high as the battle walk, and its blank walls lacked windows. It reminded Tate of Myrs' comment that she was a "prisoner." She'd also said she "belonged" to her. She'd accepted the terms with the mental reservation that they must have a unique meaning here. The stark building made her wonder.

Ignoring Myrs' distracted tugs at her sleeve, she walked to the door centered on the end of the building. The other door was straight ahead of her. The only light in the entire, barnlike structure came from the shielded ventilation breaks under the overhanging eaves and dozens of small candles that flickered in the gloom. They reminded her of distant campfires in a valley.

As her eyes adjusted, Tate realized each candle sat on a tiny table, and from behind each one, a pale, frightened face looked at her. It was the silence that made her aware of the smell, the peculiar dead air of a large room full of immobilized people. Memories flew through her mind, images of classrooms where eye movement was considered a breach of discipline. She'd hated them.

She hated this place.

A hushed whisper ran through the room, the sound of trapped birds. With her vision adapting to the gloom, she saw the faces were those of women, all dressed the same as Myrs. She turned to her. "Prisoners?"

Myrs nodded.

Her spine tingled. "What did they do?"

She let herself be dragged outside and away by the frightened Myrs. When the older woman finally slowed, Tate planted her feet and refused to move. "Now, I want to know: What are their crimes? What was yours?"

"You shouldn't have gone in! The lockup is off-limits to everyone but prisoners."

The familiarity of the jargon, even in the exotic accents of this world, jarred her. Roughly, she grabbed Myrs by the shoulder. "Tell me," she demanded.

Myrs looked down where her hands twisted folds of her robe. "I was a good wife," she said. "I was careful with the children, I don't care what he said."

"What who said?"

The question surprised her. "My husband."

When Tate said no more, Myrs continued, looking off into the distance. "Ten little babies. None left. I loved them all. So many troubles. The sicknesses. The slavers." Her lips thinned until Tate could only think of a scar. "At least my pretty didn't live for the filthy slavers to carry away. It was better for her to die. But why should she have to? Or her brothers and sisters?"

Tate's stomach wanted to rebel at the singsong recital, but Myrs wasn't finished. "He had me arrested for refusing to have more. I was fifty-two when we lost the last one."

"What? How could you go to the lockup for refusing to have children at that age?"

Myrs clutched her arm, looking around in renewed fright. "We're not allowed to speak of that time. I mean, our time, what happens to women. It's classified."

Again, the familiar jargon, twisted by this looking-glass environment. Taking Myrs' elbow, Tate made her walk, continuing to question her.

Myrs' husband proved he could still be a father by getting another—much younger—woman pregnant. In Harbundai that meant Myrs was at fault. She went to the lockup, sharing her disgrace with the barren, as well as the adulterous and those who simply stole. Tate noted murderers weren't even mentioned, and chose not to pursue the matter.

When Myrs spoke of the imprisoned widows, however, it set off another outburst. *"Widows?"*

Again, Tate's ignorance shocked Myrs. "Certainly. An honest woman needs a protector, doesn't she? Usually someone takes just the children, and if it wasn't for the lockup, a widow might be forced to steal or sell her body, or something awful. It's for her own good, isn't it?"

"Why can't she work, support herself?"

"And keep a man or a bearing woman from a paying job? That's what the lockup's for; we sew and weave and work leather, and the Baron sells it." She glanced over her shoulder. "If you work in the castle, sometimes you get meat."

Tate leaned back against the healing house, letting the sun's warmth in its stone loosen muscles that had drawn taut. She thought of nights in the lean-to listening to Sylah speak of the harshness of life in Ola. She said Harbundai was *better*. Carter, Anspach, Bernhardt. They had the three men with them, but would that be enough? Without them, the women would be helpless. She shivered. "Helpless" took on a new density in this world. She'd never thought how much it sounded like "hopeless."

Before she could go inside to find the others, a hubbub arose from the direction of the main gate. A bell tolled from a tower. Sylah and Neela hurried out of the healing house, looking up at her with pleased surprise. "They must be coming," Neela said, hurrying her along. "Gan. With Clas, and the boys."

Their path took Gan and Clas through a village similar to the one that had been raided. People streamed out of the houses and fields to watch them pass, some offering water, others food. Almost all asked about the fate of the wounded boy's companions, and the answer left a wake of tears and angry muttering behind the three plodding horses. A voice shouted for men to ride with him for the bodies.

This was the first good look Gan had at the people of Harbundai. He'd noticed the variance of skin coloration in the Baron's troops and wondered if everyone in Harbundai ranged from very dark to very light. The villagers confirmed it; they were nothing like as similar in color as his tribe.

The general attitude of these people puzzled him. Everyone appeared reasonably well-fed and healthy, and the children were active and energetic, but there was a listlessness about the adults. At first he attributed it to the effect of the recent events, but it was the houses that convinced him it was a thing of long standing. The buildings weren't dirty or tumbledown so much as unkempt, as if the owners afforded them the barest maintenance necessary. There was almost no decoration. Flowers were conspicuous by their rarity, although even the smallest hut had a vegetable patch. The eager green of the young plants contrasted embarrassingly with the drab surroundings. The paint of some business signs was flaked; others were aged almost to illegibility.

Gan looked over his shoulder past Clas. The black-green of the forest rose up against the sky. Farther away it scored the horizon to the front and flanks, as well. He had the feeling it waited, eager to reclaim what it considered its own. The village seemed to sense it, too, and it crouched like a small animal in a den, afraid to stray outside, even more afraid of what might force its way inside.

When they were close to the castle, servants in their striped dress hurried out through the massive twin doors of the main gate to take the small figure wrapped in Gan's cloak from his horse. Their weeping and lamenting grew in volume when he had to tell them the boy was the sole survivor.

They both waved at the three women, and Gan asked one of the servants about the Baron's condition. The man made the peculiar gesture Ops used, the closed fist with the fingers turned to the jaw. This man, however, shook the fist, then shook his head. It was all done in silence. By then Tate and Neela were beside him, and the black woman said, "He's greeting you. When he shakes his head and hand that way, I think he means he can't talk to you. Or doesn't want to."

Neela said, "I overheard a servant say the survivor's not the Baron's son."

Gan said, "We didn't know. I wish it had been."

"There's worse news." Neela seemed to pause to steady herself, and before she could continue, Clas was out of the saddle, hurrying to Sylah. She was already examining the boy, and she looked up at Clas' worried expression with a quick, weary smile.

When Sylah moved off with him, Clas accompanied her, leaving it to Gan to hear Neela's news. Speaking to Tate, as well, she said, "Ola attacked while the Baron was gone. The King threw everyone into the battle."

Tate knew something important had been left unsaid. A terrible premonition struck her. "Did something happen to another of the Baron's sons?"

"Both were killed. The King's using it as an excuse to send in 'help' for the Baron; an ambitious nephew. No one will say it aloud, but everyone knows it's a naked move to replace him."

Tate called to Sylah, "How is Jones? And the Baron?"

"The Baron's body is fine. I worry about his heart, after so much loss." She made a face. "Jones, too. He heals. But something—there's a *look* about him. And the Baron blames him for the delay in getting back here. I'm worried about it."

It was a subdued trio that brought each other up to date in quiet tones as they made their way to the healing house.

When servants came for the horses, Gan turned over the salvaged jewelry. He also gave one of them the sword, with instructions to find the leather-worker's son and give it to him. "From the Baron," he added.

He tried not to show how much the size and construction of the healing house impressed him. The number of patients was much greater than he expected, too. The slavers clearly intended to sow terror among those they left behind. He picked his way carefully between the rows of trestle beds. He'd already noticed how much cooler it was inside the thick stone walls, but it was the snowdrift ranks of white sheets that made him chilly.

The Baron occupied a corner of his own. Gan spotted him easily, the round figure sitting up in a high-backed chair. When they drew closer, he saw the fan-shaped section over the Baron's head was carved with a hunting scene of a spearman killing a tiger. It was inlaid with polished stones. The handholds on the arms of the chair were spheres of jade.

The Baron's flushed cheeks were vivid against pale features. He said, "You heard of my king's generous offer of 'help'? If I even object, he'll call it a disloyal act. There are other barons who'd march against me for favor. Or loot. Or just to see another man fall."

Gan said, "You know if the King's man comes, he'll never leave."

"Of course I know that. Because I was fool enough to wait while your War Healer wasted my time and my son's life on your madman, don't think I'm a fool always."

Gan spread his hands in a gesture of apology, and then said, "You've spoken of these other barons and the lands they control. Is that a map?" He pointed at a rolled paper in the basket beside the Baron's chair. The older man handed it to him with ill grace, frowning suspiciously as Gan rolled it out on the floor.

From the corner of his eye Gan saw Tate edge closer. He was first amused by her eager curiosity, then puzzled by what looked like a swift wash of intense pain. It was gone quickly, but he knew he'd seen something deeply revealing. Once more there was a sense of secrets she'd like to share. Why did she keep herself—the important part of herself—walled off that way?

He concentrated on the map. It was exhilarating! The Inland Sea! So huge this drawing showed only a part of it, but seeing even a picture of that much water excited him.

The land mass shown was only a fraction of the vast distances his own people roamed. Memories rushed to mind, long evenings with his father, arguing over the significance of land forms, alliances, campaigns, defenses. His ears drummed with the taunting demands for reasons, the scornful bite of embarrassing rebuttal. How often he'd stormed away from those sessions, hating his father's twisting, probing questions. How much had he learned? How much more had his temper cost him?

Tate crowded close to him as he studied the map, and between them, they poked and prodded at the helpless image as a weasel tumbles an egg. And, like that, in the end they broke through the shell of confusion around it. Each one pointed out a consideration, and the other noted how it tied in with something else. Baron Jalail's holding bordered the mountains to the east, Ola to the south, and another barony, called Malten, to the west. Malten extended the Ola-Harbundai border to the Inland Sea. The other six barons of Harbundai ruled to the north, from where the King's New City held sway. Baron Jalail, when asked, answered that the normal Olan avenue of attack was close to the coast so Olan ships could resupply the troops, as well as plunder the fishermen and merchants who tried to escape by sea. "Then Malten's flank is very important," Tate said, musingly. "Your king's feelings about removing you isn't just a political whim, but calculated determination to realign the kingdom's defenses. He wants a strong force here, east of the standard Olan route of advance. If Ola moves north, Jalail can drive west into the exposed flank. He could even cross into Ola and strike at the column's rear base."

Unnoticed to that point, Ops' cough drew the attention he sought. He said, "All that's true, but I'm not certain the King can afford to attack us. His position isn't very strong right now. If he wants the Baron out, he has to win fast and decisively. He has to avoid anything like a civil war."

Tate asked, "Why now? Is something special happening?"

"The season," Ops said, surprised at her ignorance. "He can draw some men from the fields. The loggers won't want to be pulled from their work, and the trappers must market their catch. As for the fishermen—when they see this fine weather . . . " He threw up his hands.

"It's the same here in Jalail?" Tate was intent now.

"Of course."

"Is there anything like a registration list? I mean, does anyone know how many men are in the barony? By age? And what their occupations are?"

Baron Jalail said, "My nobles have a good account of the people in their holdings. They're not always honest, but Ops has a good idea of what's going on all the time. Don't you, Ops?"

The flattery nearly staggered him. He managed a blushing, diffident smile.

The Baron turned away from Ops, the warmth of his expression dwindling away to a burnt-out sadness. He said, "My sons . . . There's no one to succeed me. The people will welcome the King's interest, and a strong leader."

Gan looked to Tate. He saw her read his silent question. It was meant to be a test, and he was sure she understood that, as well. Her response delighted him. She grinned and winked. The wipe was slung over her shoulder, and she shrugged it free. It dropped into her hands with a most satisfactory clatter.

Facing the Baron, Gan indicated her with a nod, saying, "The King will have heard of us. It'll give him something to think about." To Tate, he said, "Your thoughts?"

Tate said, "I need information. Ops, which nobles can we depend on? Any we should watch? Is there any friction? Do the nobles owe the Baron a quota of men for war? How many can you fall in without calling on the nobles? I want to know how many and what quality of men the King will send with his nephew; get me all the information you can about the troop commander and the nephew, too. And I'll need to see what sort of stores we have. What and how much of it do we feed the troops around here. No one goes hungry in this outfit. We'll be needing supply wagons. Pack horses. But foremost, I need to know how many men of fighting age there are in the barony. That'll be my planning base."

"Slowly, slowly!" Gan laughed, holding up a hand.

She looked surprised momentarily, then joined in his laughter. "Excuse us, please, Baron," she said, "and you, too, Gan, if you will. I think Ops and I are about to have a very long conversation." She took the stunned Ops by the elbow and practically lifted him to his toes to escort him out.

The Baron was scathing. "You, Clas, her, and whatever you can scrape together expect to defeat the two or three hundred men who'll escort the King's nephew?"

Pacing, Gan asked, "Does everyone here fight as you do, on foot, with spears? A few archers ahead and on the flanks?"

"Of course. We always—"

"We'll change that." He grinned at the Baron, almost mischievous in the quick resurgence of exuberance and certainty. "Your king surprised you. We'll surprise him. Clas na Bale is the best trainer of fighting men that ever lived."

Caught for the moment in Gan's enthusiasm, Baron Jalail laughed, the round body jerking with the pain of the movement. He groaned when he stopped. "At least the King doesn't cause me pain." Sobering, he shook his head. "I wish I were young enough to be hopeful, as you can be, but there's neither reason nor time for opposition."

"He'll wait at least a month." Gan ignored the Baron's confused surprise, explaining, "Postpone the funeral services; use any excuse. Send Messengers to the other barons, with gifts of appreciation for their support in the past and invitations to the ceremony, and decree a thirty-day mourning period to follow it. The King won't dare move until all that's over. Oh, and send a declaration to your people that you'll collect no taxes for a year, as a memorial to your sons. It'll give them all the more incentive to support you. We can save your barony. You must get us time."

The Baron's face had hardened while Gan spoke. He met his stare with equal coldness, even though he sympathized. It must have been like being torn apart to hear the funeral of his son discussed as a tactical tool, especially by a stranger. Gan told himself sternly that it made no difference; the Baron was doomed unless he fought with every weapon he had.

And he and his friends were endangered.

Baron Jalail's full features were tightened in an austere dignity Gan had never imagined. His lips barely moved. "So. I use the death of my son to shield my weakness. Should I weep and claw myself bloody, like a woman? Show the injuries to my brother barons to buy their pity? Better yet, I can have a poet write the details of my youngest son's first and final battle."

Gan's resolve bent under the honest contempt. The Baron said, "As much as I admire you, Gan Moondark, there's menace about you. I see myself putting out my hand to you as a thirsty man reaches for a cup of water. Yet you are many things—many cups—and in at least one of them I know there is poison. Many men will think they have used you and be none the wiser until too late."

He drew a deep, full breath, letting it out in a long sibilance. "It will be as you suggest. If I must fall, I'll go with a war cry."

CHAPTER 50

Sylah braced herself against the hospital bed. She stretched and rolled her shoulders. She pictured her aching muscles cracking like old leather straps.

A servant passed carrying a mop and a bucket full of what was essentially a strong mint tea. Some said the solution killed unseens. She wasn't sure of that, but she welcomed the stinging aroma that masked the heavier smells of the crowded hospital. She supposed she should be thankful it was warm; at least the weather allowed for open windows and ventilation.

The woman on the bed opened her eyes. Sylah was surprised to see how bright and alert they were, because all the while she'd been treating her injuries, the woman had given no sign she was conscious, yet her disdainful gaze was not that of someone just waking. She said, "I'll thank you for your help, Priestess, but it won't change anything."

"Change?" It was an unexpected comment.

The woman fumbled at the silver chain that disappeared inside her blouse. She flourished the polished silver disk at the end of it. "We're not afraid of you," she said.

The circular piece was thin, the chain links small and crude. There was no great value represented, but it was a more expensive piece of jewelry than Sylah expected to see on a farm woman. The sight of it stirred her memory. She seemed to remember seeing it when treating the woman's injury. Had there been necklaces like it? She thought so, but couldn't remember. There were so many victims, and she was so tired. Why did the woman speak of fear? Intrigued, Sylah reached for the object. The woman jerked away with a vehemence that pulled at her broken ribs, made her wince openly. "It's not for Church to touch!" she snapped.

"I'm sorry." Sylah's apology was automatic, but sincere, which made the woman's harsh laugh more offensive than it might have been.

"You're sorry we're strong enough to defy you. You think you can treat a few small injuries and we'll flock back to you."

Sylah had enough. "I don't know what you're talking about. I want nothing from you."

"Except my mind, my body, and the tax money the Baron squeezes out of us to keep himself and people like you fat and comfortable." The woman raised up on an elbow. "Well, nothing's what you'll get from me, and if the Baron had sense, it's what you'd get from him. He's still one of yours, though, so you'll go on living well."

The hair rose on Sylah's neck. "I think you'd best say no more. This is dangerous ground."

"Not for me." She smiled challenge. "I'm a Moondancer."

Sylah could only say, "I don't know what that is."

Disbelief washed away the smile. "Don't know. . . ?"

"There's no such thing in Ola, nor among the Mountain or Dog People. If you call it a religion, then you know it's forbidden. Your soul is at risk."

The woman made a spitting sound. "Threats of your Land Under don't frighten us. Misery's here, now, while we live. But there's pleasure, too, and wealth. Moondance gives us strength and leaders. Soon we'll take all we want."

There had been whispers in the halls of the abbey, furtive words telling breathless stories of sects and cults that openly defied Church. She'd only half believed them. They sent the other Chosens into fits of praying. She'd occasionally wondered what it would be like to face sin of such enormity. Now it was here, and the superficial reserve she'd assumed when she was safe inside the womb of the Iris Abbey dissolved. She wanted to run, to find help. Not until she bumped the bed behind her did she realize she was backing away.

Worse, it was Jones' bed. Even the malice of the strange woman dimmed at the prospect of another blistering diatribe from him. He slept as if he'd never wake, yet when he did, he still complained he'd had no rest. From a man who'd been diffident and self-effacing, he'd become cruelly abusive. He made a deep, growling sound, but continued to sleep.

She'd had time to muster some composure. She forced her legs to move her forward, reminding herself she knew exactly where Clas was. He'd had to leave for Gan's side when he saw the discussion with the Baron growing tense. It would be the simplest of matters merely to raise her eyes and look to him. Just to see how close he was, that he could help her if she needed him—that would be all the reassurance she needed.

She rejected the idea. This was her fight, to win or lose in her own strength. And she knew nothing of this woman who was so determined to be her enemy. She said, "Tell me of this Moondance."

"So you can run to your Sister Mother, if she even exists, and tell her what you've learned?"

Sylah deliberately asked her question with the mildness of one leading a child to reason. "Would you care if I did? You say you have nothing to fear from Church, but doesn't your response sound fearful to you?"

Coloring, the woman said, "We claim the night. You sing about the wonderful sun and life, but you never speak of the Virgin, and the son she's supposed to have given the world. And why? Because men rule and won't let you tell the story of a woman who could have a child without one of them. Everyone knows you think it's your secret, but the men tolerate it because it keeps you quiet, like cows in your stalls. Men can talk about the One Who Is Two, the Son in the Sun, but what would happen to you if you did?"

Visibly pleased by Sylah's white-lipped shock, the woman went on. "Our idol is the moon. He gives us all the light we need in our chosen time. We reject your light. We are darkness."

Sylah had to strain to answer. "Every man's hand will be against you. Church will root you out like weeds in the fields."

"There are as many men as women among us. More come all the time. Haven't you wondered why there's no Church person in the castle? Because we told her to take her false tongue and her ointments and get out while she had her life. And you'll do the same."

"I don't think so." Resentment brought strength. She was tired of running.

The woman closed her eyes, smirking. For a while Sylah waited, then became aware of the weariness reclaiming her. If she was to be effective, she'd need her wits. Patients would need care. There would be other Moondancers; she'd have to watch her every word, analyze everything she heard or saw. Vigilance.

She was nearly asleep on her feet.

Someone had said she had quarters—who was it? Oh, yes, Neela. But when? The hours were a blur, a mosaic of hurt bodies and heavy decisions. If only she knew more, understood more.

For now, she needed sleep. The rough stones of the floor seemed to tilt under her feet, to reach up and snag the soft leather soles, making her stumble frequently. A firm hand grabbed her forearm in the middle of a particularly awkward lurch, bringing her up short. When she turned to thank her benefactor, she was happy to see Clas.

He said, "You're going to bed now, aren't you?" At her nod, a smile eased some of his troubled look. He went on, "I've been worried about you. I'd have ordered you to stop, but I knew you'd ignore me."

"We could have had our first argument."

He grinned. "We'll have other chances."

A hoarse shout interrupted their progress. She turned reluctantly. Jones was struggling to a sitting position, tossing covers to the side. Before Sylah could head back, Tate was hurrying to him. Neela came from a different direction, and, seeing Sylah, waved her off. In silent accord, Clas tugged her arm.

She paused at the door, not knowing which way to turn, and he asked, "You don't even know where your room is, do you?" She confessed she didn't, and he turned her to the right, practically holding her upright in his grip.

He'd been to the castle while she talked to the Moondancer. He chattered about it as they went, the thickness of the walls, the size of the rooms, the length of the halls. She was amused, thinking how small and rough this place was, compared to Altanar's castle. Soon, however, the scene with the woman drew her mind back to that unpleasantness.

The Moondance cult would be a problem for Gan, as well as herself. He meant to make himself master of the Baron's fighting men; she knew it as clearly as if he carried a sign. More than that, she knew that wouldn't be the end of it. The only question in her mind was the magnitude of his ambition. Bilsten said he didn't know himself, and she was inclined to agree.

Gan couldn't see the eagle glare of his own eyes. In his own mind he remained no more than the vengeful son of a wronged War Chief.

She tripped on the entryway doorsill and clutched at Clas, reaching across her body with her free hand.

"I have you," he said, and brushed her hair with his lips, adding, "They have showers here. They're almost as nice as the ones in our camp."

Again she had to hide a smile. The Baron's soldiers disappointed him, so it surprised him to find anything likable about them or their country. In his mind, a man who fought well was sure to have good qualities, even if one had to search for them; a man who didn't fight well would be expected to have bad habits that shouted for attention. Still, he'd been fair-minded enough to appreciate what the Baron's people were able to build, and admired them for that work. She faced him to answer, pausing, thinking to herself how much she treasured each discovery about him, how she simply enjoyed thinking about him. He began to look worried at her silence.

She said, "Yes, I'd like a shower. Where can I get soap, and towels?"

"They're already there. With a fresh robe I borrowed from a lady near your size." He grinned with pleased self-consciousness. "In case you wanted."

She squeezed his hand and let him lead her to the entrance, where he settled himself against the opposite wall as she closed the door.

The individual shower stalls were stone partitions jutting out from the main structure. They were just as tall as she, although the roof itself was a good three feet higher. A cloth screen provided privacy at the entry. A handle controlled the single pipe overhead, and she turned it gingerly, hoping the water wasn't too cold. She was surprised when it was almost uncomfortably hot, bringing with it the scent of hot bricks and sun. It was cistern water from the roof, its thick aroma reminding her of freshening rains falling on the sharp, broiling buildings of Ola.

Feeling her body relax under gentle pressure, she remembered how the Abbess disliked the heat, and wondered how she'd fare through the summer, with its stresses piled one on another.

Her thoughts flowed from the Abbess to her own problems, and for a while she tried to think about the call to have her cast out of Church. Her inability to concentrate on the matter startled her. It startled her even further to discover that the reason was a lack of concern. She simply didn't care.

She stopped to consider that, posed with the soap in her hand pressed against her neck while unseeing eyes studied the blank wall. It was quite a while before she absently resumed bathing.

Perhaps Church wouldn't be so severe. Her primary requirement had been to keep the Dog People out of Altanar's war against Harbundai, and that was done.

She decided her lessening concern over that possibility came from the growing feeling that she was on a truer path than ever before.

Somehow, Gan's progress was linked to hers. He was the storm, pulling them all in his wake, pulling her closer to the Door. She didn't know why she was so sure, but she was.

Toweling briskly, she retreated to less dire matters.

Neela was bearing up well, despite Gan's deplorable masculine blindness and lack of understanding. It was incredible that he could overlook the myriad signals the poor girl displayed. Similarly, she sighed over Neela's too feminine refusal to simply make her feelings known and let the truth sort things out.

She smiled wryly. That certainly hadn't been her own technique. Well, she'd have to remember that, and try to act accordingly.

As she dressed in the clean robes, she turned her attention to the other woman in their group. Tate was an even more intriguing question, a person who watched, listened, and kept her own counsel. Sylah tried to recall another woman who spoke as knowledgeably of warfare, and couldn't. In fact, Tate had a physical grace and confidence that suggested personal combat skills. She was deeper than that, however, and as troubled in her way as Neela. It showed as an unexpressed, smoldering anger that gave her eyes a smoky, inward-looking distance when she thought she was unobserved.

She put on the robe, bundled up her clothes and went into the hallway.

Clas jerked upright, pretending the wait had been so long he'd fallen asleep, and she made a face at him, linking her arm through his. He took her up a flight of stairs, then down another long hall. He said, "We're here, finally. You can rest." He ushered her into a cubicle, not much more than a study cell in the Iris Abbey. He made a sweeping gesture. "It's all yours," he said. "You don't have to share with anyone. Even the closet's empty."

She was ready to snap at his clumsy humor when she realized he was completely serious. She turned to put her arms around him, face up for his kiss, and was taken aback by the lack of fire in it. She broke the contact, hands against his chest, lower lip pushed out in an irritable sulk. He shook his head in a slow negative. "I don't dare," he said. The words scraped like gravel. "If I hold you in my arms for more than one heartbeat, I don't know if I can let you go. Please, sleep. You need rest, and I need you."

That was better, she thought, and this time she kissed him, a lover's kiss, swifter than she wanted, but full of promise. On his way out he fumbled clumsily with the door handle.

It was a thick door, oaken, with iron reinforcing bands, and when it hit the jamb, it made a solid thud that should have been comforting. Such a door would bar any entry but the most determined assault, assure privacy against any prying spy. Such a door should have represented sanctuary.

With its close, however, Sylah felt as if the open window behind her had slammed shut, too, and that both air and light had been magically sucked from the room. Instead of protection, the door's wooden slabs and iron bars were suddenly prison ware, and she was trapped.

Pinned to the back side of the door were the roses, bloodred.

It was the signal, the one the Abbess promised.

This was no sign of protection, however. This was terror. The roses hung limp, blasted, as if their delicate freshness had been burned out of them. A single strand of black thread held the green stems together. They were all very carefully snapped at that point, so they dangled slackly away from the wood, pointing at her like three raw fingertips. Tied to the loose end of the thread was a rattlesnake's rattle.

CHAPTER 51

Gan looked out over the assembled men and hoped his true feelings didn't show. After a week lost arguing with the Baron about the necessity to gather them, and another week spent rounding them up, he found they were a sad excuse for a crowd, much less the nucleus of a fighting force. Clumped in five groups of a hundred men each, they were selected members of the barony's seventeen- to twenty-year-olds. Gan's information from the man called Two revealed that men from a district had historically fought as a unit, and his first inclination had been to keep that system. Then Tate pointed out, very discreetly, that their latest behavior pattern was to desert together. It seemed reasonable to attempt to stop that, so he was pleased to accept her suggestion that men from each district be randomly distributed throughout each hundred.

They stood awkwardly on the ground below him, outside the castle walls. He wished they didn't remind him so much of bunched wildcows. They had the same air of sheer muscularity, but, like the wildcows, it was a twitchy, uncertain strength that could as easily become panic as valor. He tried to dispel his depression by telling himself they were simply unsure of themselves and their companions.

Clas groaned audibly beside him, and Gan shot an elbow to his ribs. "Don't let the Baron hear you," he whispered. "He could send them back to their farms and forests."

"Unbearable loss," Clas muttered, bearing down heavily on the sarcasm. "Oafs and fools I'm expected to make into warriors, most of them barely able to seat a horse. They'll never see a day when they're not outnumbered by Ola's professionals, and we're supposed to not only fight those iron turtles, but beat them."

"We must." The brittle vehemence in Gan's voice earned him a sharp look from Clas, who seemed to consider a remark, but then shrugged in resignation.

Baron Jalail mounted the small platform built atop the castle wall for the occasion. The murmur of the men and their officers subsided to a waiting silence.

The Baron's speaking platform was unlike anything Gan had ever seen, and if the audience hadn't shown such genuine respect for the situation, he would have laughed at it. Instead of an ordinary stage to raise him above the protective parapet, it had an additional square thing, of narrow boards, that looked like a window attached to its front. He centered himself in the square to address the gathering. When he spread his arms, he almost touched the sides.

Down on the ground inside the wall, a man called the House Director sprang into action. He was responsible for organizing the staff's activities and special events. For this occasion he wore a sleeveless jacket of red-and-white checks over his black-and-white uniform. He was further adorned with a necklace of iridescent dentalium shell circles.

As soon as the Baron had positioned himself, the House Director gestured frantically, and a crew threw themselves at the main gate. Huge hinges groaned and squealed, and the Baron's military band marched outside. Trums blared and flutes shrilled. Small drums struck up a staccato rattle. Compared to the drab, shambling men watching them, the musicians, immaculate in the Baron's stripes, glowed in the bright sun. They flourished their instruments, making them flash and glitter. Long-feathered plumes, in the same black and white, waggled atop leather helmets as they chopped along in a rapid half-step. Billows of dust eddied lazily behind them. The band turned smoothly to face the men.

Fifteen feet below the Baron, the officers shouted commands. The untrained men surged forward to form a tight semicircle at the base of the wall.

The House Director, after launching the band, had sprinted up the inner stairs to stand beside the framed platform and the Baron, who remained immobile, arms still outstretched. At another gesture from the House Director, the band fell silent. He paused dramatically, then, in deep, rolling tones, shouted, "Listen, all! Baron Jalail speaks!"

After such an introductory ceremony, the speech was short and uninspired, little more than explanations. The forces of Ola had fallen back from the border, but three of their best divisions remained poised close enough to attack without warning. The barony needed a force that would stand ready to intercept any attack. The men collected there were part of a new policy; from now on, all able men of seventeen would be required to serve two years. The barony would maintain a permanent armed force of five hundred men. Although the barony was officially in mourning, and would be for another two weeks, their training would begin immediatcly.

The Baron stepped back on the platform. Gan and Clas both gaped in surprise as the House Director yanked a hitherto unnoticed cord, and a black screen rolled down from the top member of the frame. Behind that cover the Baron sent the two Dog warriors a perfunctory nod and then made his exit. The men at the base of the wall were called away by their officers.

Clas was the first to speak. "Why couldn't he just walk away, like anyone else? These people love to make a fuss," he complained. "All this foolishness, just to tell this herd they're going to be taught to defend themselves."

Gan said, "I want to see the officers who brought these men here. Have them bring fifty of the most likely leaders to the armory. Our first requirement is some organization." Gan heard the cold precision of his own voice and was repelled by it. Clas reacted, too. His features jerked in aggrieved surprise, then closed down to expressionless obedience. He left without a word.

Gan turned his back. Since his father's death, he'd felt the growing struggle within himself of two completely different people. His orders to Clas bordered on insult—*orders,* to a man who'd taught him, helped raise him— but the new personality demanded obedience. He snapped at Clas, and the Gan he thought of as himself hated it. The other man was pleased only when his orders were carried out instantly.

The spirit-voice that was his mother said it: *Life has made me two hearts in one body, I leave you with a son who is the same.*

Was this what she meant, this steel-souled man who ignored the love of friends in the name of authority? Was that what he was born to be? Was it love or hatred that moved her?

Far to the southeast the fractured crest of Snowfather Mountain gleamed snowy white. Even farther to the northeast was his brother, The Destroyer. The Dog People knew him mostly by reputation, rarely ranging far into his surrounding mountains. The soaring splendor of both peaks spoke to him of the world on their far side, the world he knew as a child. This land was nothing like his prairie with its vast silence that freed the spirit to soar. Here was a place of boundaries and enclosures, of people devoted to schemes, their lives and history a tangle of shifting alliances.

His memories might be of a past that could never be again.

Whatever filled men's minds with the need for ever more power, it was part of the Dog People now. It was a need that had led to his father's killing. It made his best friend and himself exiles. It made him hurt that friend.

And Neela.

She seemed to have used the experience to her own advantage, and grown. He missed her complete spontaneity, true, although her laughter was coming back. She could remind him of spring when she laughed, bring brightness to dispel the meanest gray. For long days—and longer nights—he wondered if she'd ever admit to joy again. Just recently, though, she seemed to be regaining herself.

That was another two-faced situation. The Neela he wanted to see was the lighthearted Neela, the girl-woman who sang at life and knew her heart and mind. Yet that was the Neela who loved Clas na Bale.

It was a wrenching thought that sent a red flash searing across his mind. It blotted out reason for a moment.

He was jealous. It chagrined him to admit it, because he acknowledged jealousy's destructive force, yet he also knew that identifying the problem offered the only hope of avoiding the more dangerous possibilities.

The very logic of his reaction depressed him further. He wanted to be furious, to rage and strike out. But at whom? And why? Clas had done nothing to harm Neela. He seemed hardly aware of her.

For that matter, when she looked at Clas, her face was neutral, a mask that expressed interest when necessary, friendliness at all times, and even the proper amusement, if required. It was because her eyes were watchful that he knew her manner was sham. Why else would she guard her reactions, be so careful to show exactly what was expected?

He knew.

Deep inside, she still reached for Clas.

The new Neela favored him with her company. Her smiles were warm, her attention exciting. More and more he found himself recalling the memory of her golden head pressed to his chest, her slim, firm arms around him, the way her body molded to his. He longed to hold her so again, and was ashamed to admit that he didn't care if she came to him out of joy or misery, but only that she came.

Just knowing she believed he could do things gave him confidence, knowing she cared multiplied his determination. He'd taken to stopping by her quarters after his sessions with the Baron. They were tiring, worrisome meetings, rife with the Baron's indecision. In spite of everything, he openly yearned for compromise and accommodation with his king, alternating that with periods of bleak depression over the loss of his sons and the forces ranged against the barony.

Neela was relief. She listened to him, pointed out flaws in his approach, weaknesses in the Baron's arguments. More than that, she sympathized. Never once did she mention the uncertainty of their lives, or speak of the terrible loneliness that crowded into their every unguarded moment. She bore her pain and shared his without a murmur.

Those hours with her were his strength.

A shrill whistle cut across his thoughts. Clas was just removing his fingers from his mouth when Gan looked down at him. The signal was to let Gan know the men he'd asked for were waiting for him. His first reaction was irritation. He wanted to establish a solid dignity on this first meeting with the men, and being whistled to attendance could start things off badly. The thing to do was use the incident, he decided; it was important the men learn battle communications, and the Dog technique of whistling was far more effective than voice. He'd point out how easily Clas reached him. That would eliminate any thoughts that he was a man to be considered lightly.

He called the dogs to him and walked to his first command.

Gan was preparing for dinner when a servant came to his quarters, telling him the Baron requested his company. As soon as the woman was gone, Gan sat down, pensive. The Baron normally ate alone with his wife, a pleasant, quiet woman who'd withdrawn even further into herself with the loss of her sons. Sylah reported that she spoke frequently of retiring to the abbey in New City, but the Baron refused to let her go. Gan understood why. His wife was one of the few people he could relax with.

Change was probing the entire kingdom, challenging all the old ways, seeking fertile ground. Neela had heard tales of a new religion spreading through the villages. Clas' conversations with the men who'd fought the Olan regulars indicated a growing sense of helplessness in the face of their professionalism. The skirmish that killed Baron Jalail's sons had been a minor confrontation, in terms of kingdoms, but the defeat had disheartened Harbundai out of all proportion to the casualties involved.

Gan felt that raid was merely a preliminary. Giving credence to that, there were recent reports of Devil war bands seen in Ola. Not all was bad news, however; there were rumors of growing unrest in some quarters of that country.

The most pressing problem of all, however, was the King's continued insistence that the Baron accept his agent in the castle to act as "advisor."

The dinner was a perfect example of the Baron's refusal to deal with his problems. Instead of a war council with food, it was a quiet, elegant affair. Where Gan would have had scouts and spies gathered at the table, available to contribute what they knew of the situation, the Baron had musicians strumming stringed instruments off in a corner. There was even a singer, a little girl who trilled like a bird about love and spring and true hearts.

The Baron restricted his table talk to the food, although even that was more to the Baron's taste than Gan's. The farmers and fishermen of Harbundai were good at their work, and the Baron's cooks were the finest. The table was set, then whisked clean, with a succession of dishes. The salad was mixed greens, with nasturtiums for color, as well as their peppery flavor. Then came a fish chowder, followed by another soup, chilled cherry. The main course was a pork roast. Gan found it much milder, less satisfying, than the wild pig eaten in the Dog camp. And the vegetables were cooked past their best. Gan's people believed the less one did to vegetables, the better. The Harbundai approach was to boil them to near mush before covering them with a rich sauce.

During the last course, beer and cheese, the Baron finally stopped his clumsy, self-conscious conversation. He dismissed the servants and musicians, saying, "You impressed the new men."

Gan nodded, waiting. The Baron played with his fork, then finally continued, "They compare you and me. I don't do well." He tried to smile, but it broke under the weight of the conflict behind it.

"They're young."

The Baron laughed shortly. "You're barely more than a boy yourself. They sense what I do—leadership. They have no reason to fear it."

"Nor do you." He stood up. "I'm your weapon. I'll serve you until we both agree I may leave with honor. I've told you I will return to my people one day. It will be a day of my choosing—or yours. If you decide to fight your king, I'll be beside you. If not . . ." He shrugged. "I'll wander farther."

Baron Jalail impatiently waved him back into his seat. His features tightened to shrewdness. "Doesn't a threat like the King worry you?"

"Any threat worries me. And every threat's an opportunity." He leaned forward in his eagerness. "I've been talking with Clas. And Tate. She has an unbelievable knowledge of how other people fight; their tactics, weapons, organization. With these five hundred, we'll keep the King's man out of here, and I promise you that within two years, *all* the other barons will come to you for allegiance."

"I believe you could do it." The Baron downed his beer in one last, large swallow, patting his lips with his napkin. "We'll never know, however. They're gathering around the King now, coyotes watching for the tiger's kill."

Gan slammed the table. "You said it yourself, once. He's too concerned about Ola to move against you right away. And we're preparing a trained force."

"You won't have time to train. I won't let you jeopardize my people for nothing, Gan. I won't risk a civil war I'm convinced I'll lose. No risks for glory. If you wish to help preserve my barony, I welcome you, but only on my terms. Is that clear?"

"I need some concessions," Gan said, and the Baron held up a peremptory hand.

"No more men," he said. "Your demands—"

Gan cut him off. "The women," he said, and the Baron's mouth stayed open in surprise. Gan went on, "Some of the men are newly married. I want your permission to house their wives near our camp."

"Near the camp? Housing? Who's to build it? And what are they to live on?"

"The unit will build the houses. Neela and Tate have agreed to organize the wives who join their husbands. Some will be support people—cooks, uniform repair, shoe repair, some weapons work—and the barony will pay them. Others will be taught to make products for sale. All money goes in a common pool to be divided among all families. Ask yourself what these men will do for you if they know you'll protect their families."

The Baron shook his head stubbornly. "Families are already taken care of. Children are claimed, women have the lockup."

"What if you died? Is that what you'd want for your wife?"

"You go too far! I'm a noble! The Baron!"

Gan took a step toward the door. "Please think about it, not as a baron, but as a man. With your permission, I'll leave, and we can talk again."

"There's nothing to talk about. You have your men. If you train them well enough, you may convince the King to leave me in command here. It's enough for me to dodge this blow; there's no reason to cut off his hand."

Gan's last view of the Baron was the round, furious face glaring at him as he swung the door shut. He walked to his quarters, absently fending off the delighted welcome of the dogs, ordering them to follow. He needed to get away and think. The guards at the gate passed him through with their peculiar salute. One called a warning to be careful.

Gan knew he referred to wild animals. An occasional tiger prowled out of the mountains to make an easy kill of some farmer's stock, and bears sometimes came looking for the beehives they smelled from the forest. It was unusual for anything like that to happen so close to the castle, but not unheard of. Gan checked his murdat, relishing the solid glide of it in the scabbard. At the same time he noted how frisky the dogs were. He wondered if they, like himself, felt they were growing too accustomed to the easy confinement of the castle.

Under a full moon he hiked along, letting the dogs run free. They gamboled in the silvered night like pups, sometimes invisible, their presence given away by the hoarse breathing and heavy pounding of their running. That sound hurtling toward him in the dark never failed to make his heart beat a bit faster.

He resigned himself to trying to puzzle his way out of the present maze. After miles of trudging, deep in thought, he was no closer to an answer. There seemed to be no sure way to forestall the King. Baron Jalail wouldn't fight, and without his orders, Gan couldn't.

Or so it appeared. "I must be ready," he said to himself, wanting the reassurance of hearing his own words. Raggar stopped abruptly beside him, making Shara veer off awkwardly to avoid a collision. He reached down to scratch the larger dog's head. "I wasn't talking to you, old friend, but I will. You listen better than anyone, don't you? The thing is, I don't know what's coming. Tate has some good ideas about how to fight in this country, and how to use men to do it, but I can't stop the Baron if he decides to surrender, or if he becomes nothing more than a straw figure for the King's man. I have to have followers."

There was more he meant to say, more he wanted to say, but the words caught in his throat. Snowfather Mountain shone in the moonlight, a torch that called, a wall that blocked.

How was it he'd put it to the Baron? "I'll wander farther." Such a short statement. Perhaps he'd already wandered too far.

CHAPTER 52

Tate sat alone in her room, dressed in a loose smock. She held some material in her lap, and she was sewing and talking to herself at a furious rate. Animated expressions chased each other across her face. She emphasized her remarks with physical action, jabbing the needle through the material, yanking the thread, tugging the stitches just so.

"I'd give my eyeteeth to know who set up this society. That baron, up on his stage. And the House Director; never gave the title a second thought until I saw him working yesterday. Fool me. A television production, that's what it was, with himself in the middle of the screen. And a *blackout* when it was over. TV as ancient social anthropology. I'm dying, just—flat—*dying.*"

She held up the skirt, turning it for scrutiny in the light from the solitary window. It was similar to the dress of the local women, with some personal flourishes. She took off the smock, stepping into the skirt, then pulled the blouse over her head. When she added the combat belt with its automatic pistol, she made a face at it. "Now, there's a fashion statement that's a loser."

Twisting and posturing, she struggled to get an impression of the whole by piecing together reflections in a small hand mirror. Any observer would have reassured her. The blouse was a dark blue, with a random lighter blue thread in the weave. Collar and three-quarter sleeves were trimmed with an embroidered geometric design in the same lighter color, as was the skirt. The latter was the gray-silver of weathered wood. Gone were the heavy government-issue boots. In their place were new ones, calf-high, of soft, supple leather, laced on the sides. Her dramatic features and the short, darkly glittering hair made her an exotic figure.

She pulled off the blouse to improve a hem. Her thoughts drifted.

Shreds of the past; they're like psychological sniper rounds, she thought. Every event like the Baron's TV show, or even something as minor as a familiar phrase, makes me go crazy wondering about the people who originated this hybrid culture. What was it like to realize you'd made it through the shooting war and then get hit with one rotten plague after another, never knowing if you'd found a place with a livable radioactivity count? Adults'd be too concerned with staying alive to worry about getting their facts straight when they passed on stories of "the old days" to the kids; myths and legends would take over. And the big ticket for everyone would be the supreme importance of *your* group.

"When was it ever different?" she asked aloud, and heard her own cynicism.

Faces swam into her mental vision—Falconer, Anspach, Conway, all of them. What were they doing? Were they even alive?

Falconer and Conway. There was a team. They'd make a lot of sparks between them. They'd create change, too. Progress.

Maybe she could do something.

What? She remembered Madge Mazzoli. If she'd suspected then how wrong Madge was, she'd never have agreed to leave that peaceful valley. These people knew more about engineering than she did. And weaving. Farming. Whatever. She lifted her chin, spoke to the wall's stones. "I can navigate by the stars. I can tell time by the sun. I know unseens are really germs."

She picked up the mirror. The face that stared back was frustrated. Maybe a bit humiliated. "I know more about warfare than anyone in this kingdom. Wonderful. This whole world needs another soldier the way I need a wart on the end of my nose."

She flung down the mirror, leaping to rescue it when it bounced on the bed, terrified at the prospect of breaking it.

War was where these people did their best work. The best steel went into weapons, the best building went into forts or castles. Even the most valued dogs and horses were the ones trained to fight.

It didn't have to be that way. They called Sylah a War Healer, but she was a healer, first and foremost. She saved Jones from certain death.

She smiled to herself. She'd been sure Sylah was killing him.

Suddenly she was wondering if Sylah had done the best thing, after all, and the unworthiness of the notion stung like a scorpion.

It was only reasonable he should be cross.

She might as well be honest. The man wasn't cross, he was deliberately perverse, argumentative, and abusive. There: she'd admitted how she felt, and it was a relief.

But how hard it all must be for him! A man who *knew* peaceful reason and compromise were the way to solve people's problems. He believed all his life his soft, white Jesus was the answer to hate and violence, and then they made him watch the world kill itself. And after all that, he wakes up in this slaughterhouse. He's the greatest victim of us all.

That wasn't true, either. Mazzoli and Yoshimura paid higher prices. And Harris and Karoli. At least Jones was alive. He could make an effort to be glad about it, think of a way to live a useful life.

She walked to the window, looking out. The small house where Jones lived now was barely visible, hidden in a clump of trees at the edge of the closest village outside the enclosed grounds. She leaned on the windowsill and sighed. She had no choice but to go see the man.

Around him, one gave no signs of self-interest. He was mean-spirited even when you worked to make him believe your every thought was of him. If he suspected you were thinking of anything else, he was positively vicious.

All of which was unimportant. The inescapable issue was that he was her only connection with the reality of herself.

This was not her world. She came from an existence no one here could comprehend. Without Jones, without the reinforcement of his presence, she was afraid she'd go mad.

Unexpected tears of resentment welled suddenly. She wiped them away with swift, hard strokes. Dry-eyed again, teeth clenched, she looked out the window. An eagle stroked its way across the middle distance, bright against the mountains in the background. There, she told herself, that's reality, and in this place there is beauty, there is life, and the past is nothing more than yesterday.

She turned to face the door, and took a deep breath before starting out.

Jones insisted on maximum privacy, and the Baron was pleased to have him out of sight. As a reminder of his son's misfortune, Jones was unwelcome under the best of circumstances. His newfound irascibility literally made him a danger to himself and others. Tate was relieved when he was allowed to move out, although everyone understood it was more of a banishment than release. Sylah had arranged for a two-room house and a full-time nurse-housekeeper.

The walk to and from the village was the best part of any visit with him, Tate reflected ruefully. The people accepted her now, albeit with rather more curiosity than she preferred. On this occasion it amused her to see how several of the women stared pointedly at her clothes; she could almost hear the scandalized gasps from some and the speculative evaluations of others.

The attentions of the livestock were as blunt, if not quite so personal. She frequently stopped on her walk to pick a particularly attractive bunch of greenery and offer it to them. It had taken her a while to adjust to the llamas—they were still zoo animals, in her view of things—but she couldn't resist them. She was half convinced they'd all talked it over after she fed the first one, because from that time on, they crowded to the split-rail fence and fastened their soft, heart-melting eyes on her whenever she passed. She scolded them for making her walk through the boot-scuffing weeds, and they nodded impatiently, eager for their handouts.

Jones greeted her from a cot outside his house. He lay in the shade, drinking from a tall ceramic cylinder. "Come to sympathize with the invalid? Come to compare, so you can go away and revel in your own good health?"

Tate spoke quickly, heard the nervous chatter in her voice and hoped he didn't. "John, you know it's not good for you to talk that way. Anyhow, you're stronger every day."

His face cracked in a sly grin, and he touched a finger to his temple. "Our secrets," he said. "Mustn't let everyone know."

In spite of herself, her eyes went to Jones' pointing finger, and before she fully realized what was happening, the turbanlike bandage was whipped off and she was staring at the pink depression in his skull. Shaved clean, it seemed to pulse, the red lines of the stitched scar looking far too delicate and inadequate.

Jones traced it slowly, caressing it, his eyes burning at her. "Ugly. Grotesque. That's what you're thinking. Considering the primitiveness of these savages, it's also a miracle, right? But you wouldn't say that, would you? No, you wouldn't. You already think they're ordinary people. They're not. They're lost souls. Cursed."

Tate knelt beside him, put a restraining hand on his chest as he started to rise. He allowed himself to be held in place. Veins stood out in his neck, and the flesh over the injury seemed to grow translucent. She turned, averted her eyes, afraid she'd see through it to a throbbing, fever-hot brain.

A spot of white froth sparkled on his lip. "Take your hand off me; you know how I hate touching." He twisted to glare in all directions, falling back flat. Breathing heavily, he went on, "Don't worry, I know better than to discuss religion when one of these pagans can hear." Then, whispering, "They don't know I'm the one. They mustn't suspect until it's time. I'll save them. Their ways are weak and ignorant, and I'm to bring them strength and wisdom. You and the others—if they're alive—you'll do what you can to challenge their ignorance. You're limited, of course, because you came from such a technical society. Fortunately for these people, however, I know the truth. The problem is that I can't afford the luxury of persuasion. Kingdoms are being forged, and from them will come empires. I know you'll all babble about democracy. I can't be concerned with your political games. Surely you see such things are, for me, mere childishness. I am directed— No, that's not what I meant, not what I said. Don't you put words in my mouth! Don't you dare look at me in that superior way!"

Tate tried to soothe him, and he pushed her hand aside. "Oh, I know all about you," he snarled. "You're more interested in your comfortable daily existence than your immortal soul."

"You shouldn't put words in my mouth, either. I want you to get well. I'm trying to help."

"Well, don't expect me to fawn over you for it, even though I'm directed—required—to use any resource I can. I'll get along without you if I have to, don't worry."

Her chin came up instinctively, and she carefully reined in her temper and spoke with the voice of conciliation. "Just be careful. Sure, use your skills; you're a persuader, a leader. If you want to do me a personal favor, make these people understand that women have souls, too. I'm not sure they know it."

He was instantly sly again. "I know some who do. And more come to awareness every day. They come to learn the new way of seeing. They understand—" He stopped as if cut off, forcing himself up on his elbows to glare about him, jerking his head from side to side. When he lay back down, he sneered at her. "Never mind. Maybe some other time, when you've earned the right." There was a new quality in his voice, a totally unexpected menace that stroked the back of her neck with a clammy hand. "I'm tired now. Remember, though, you always have a home at my palace, if your warrior friends turn on you. *When* they turn on you."

She rose, saying a quick good-bye, walking with measured dignity and a fierce resentment that wouldn't let her turn to even wave in departure.

The last jibe hurt more than Jones could know. For all the trust and confidence shown her by Gan and Clas, all other men clearly regarded her as a freak. Clas accepted her fundamentally as a warrior; as far as he was concerned, there was only one woman on earth, and that was Sylah. End of story. Gan was another matter. Sometimes he looked at her or spoke to her from a different place. That was the only way she could phrase it. When he was like that—and she couldn't even describe any physical change in his appearance—the word that came to her was "mystic." Not like Jones' new babble about saving and curses, but a sense of headlong, *unpreventable* action. She felt Gan was riding it, and she had no more choice than he did.

The women were a delight, though. Neela was as friendly as their differing cultures could allow. Sylah was even more, a person of true intellect, in addition to being a friend. She was someone to watch, Gan's psychic opposite. Where he seemed to have a sense of hanging on to a whirlwind that was taking him where he wanted to go, Sylah wanted control of herself and her destiny. Sooner or later, Tate told herself, those two are going to run head-on into each other. I hope they're going very slowly when it happens.

In spite of friendship, however, and despite their shared hatred for the role society assigned them, no woman of this world could imagine, Tate thought, her particular mental anguish. The few times she'd been rash enough to expose her views on marriage and shared responsibilities within couples, they'd listened with the polite tension of people learning unpleasantries about the family. At first it amused her. When they neatly closed her out of the rest of their conversation, the depression set in. Now, by unspoken mutual consent, they avoided that subject.

It wasn't the same rejection as racism. The hurt was exactly the same, though.

She stopped to feed her favorite among the llamas. He had a brown face with one white-circled eye. It gave him the supercilious air of a monocled aristocrat. She scratched his chin, and he stared off into space contentedly. She said, "You know, Your Lordship, sometimes I think the only difference between us is that you just don't care. I'd have to be a fool to envy someone just for that, wouldn't I?"

Back on the roadway, she turned to look at him. He was still braced against the fence, and when their eyes met, he shook his head back and forth, as clear a disagreement as she'd ever seen. It should have been funny, but she couldn't bring herself to laugh about it.

CHAPTER 53

The rataplan of drums and blare of trums from the castle so nearly overshadowed the muffled groan beside her that Sylah felt she must have sensed Clas' discomfort as clearly as she heard him express it. They were at a considerable distance from the arranged biers.

In a gesture of solidarity, the Baron had arranged for all the youngsters who died with his son during the slavers' raid to be cremated together. His son held pride of place, to the north of the others, his coffin raised several feet higher on its single pole. To the east, sitting in prepared stands, the King waited with his entourage. A body of troops was bivouaced beyond them.

She reached to cover Clas' hand where it rested on the pommel of his saddle. "They're not going to bother Gan," she said. "The King's given all the barons strict orders to observe the courtesies."

"Courtesies," Clas scoffed. "Baron Jalail trapped him. If any of the other barons make trouble, they'll be offending the families of every one of those children. A ceremony for all of them at once was a clever move."

"Is that what Gan thinks?"

"Certainly. He said it himself. But I still don't like having him so close to so many people who don't like him. Especially when I'm not allowed to be there."

She started to speak, thought better of it. They both knew his assignment. Clas was watching, with the new unit hidden in the forest, waiting for a signal. If there was treachery, their first combat would begin immediately.

She noted the sweat on his brow. The weather wasn't that warm. He worried about Gan and the barely trained men who'd have to race to his rescue if it came to that. They'd grown enthusiastic under Clas and Gan's leadership, but they were unskilled. She'd overheard Clas' analysis of one of their horseback exercises one afternoon, and she was still amazed by the inventiveness of his language. She'd thought of him as taciturn, but it

appeared that, when angered, he became quite eloquent. Her face warmed
at the recollection of some of the phrases. Perhaps "forceful" was a more
appropriate description. No matter, she decided, sniffing; he'd made them
understand.

Gan appeared as the procession continued to wind out of the castle. A dog
stalked on each side, with Raggar in front. His horse pranced regally, aware
they were the focus of every eye. Tate followed in a flowing robe of scarlet
and yellow.

She smiled; the black woman's bearing always made her remember a
younger Iris Abbess. That, in turn, reminded her of the reason she wasn't
participating in the ceremony. The smile disappeared. She was just as glad
to be free of it, she told herself, denying the small voice that insisted she
hated being left out of such an event. The Baron had made it clear the King
would tolerate no appearance of disobeying Church. The Queen Mother had
finally lost her lifelong struggle to influence her son. What oppressive barons
had been unable to do, time had done for them. Her reason, which had led
the fight to blend Church and women's rise from servitude toward equality,
was fading. With it went the organization. Church was further in disarray.
Women were fearfully silent, waiting for a new leader.

As for Sylah's own relationships in this new situation, the King made it
clear that while her case was being decided he wanted nothing to do with
her. If Church decided to disown her, decisions would be necessary. Until
then, she was to keep out of his sight.

The column flowed closer, a river of color in the soft sun of evening. Baron
Jalail led. When he reached the gathered spectators, they parted to let him
by. He moved through them slowly, nodding acknowledgment to what Sylah
assumed were sympathetic comments. The King rose to return his greeting.
The nephew he'd selected to share the responsibility for ruling the Baron's
lands stood beside him. Sylah thought she saw Baron Jalail stiffen at the other
man's smile, but she told herself it was pure imagination. They were too far
to see any such thing. Nevertheless, it was clear that the other barons were
keeping a careful distance between themselves and their host.

Experience had taught her to recognize that behavior pattern as readily
as Clas read weather signs. The other nobles would be polite, inoffensive.
After all, Baron Jalail might find a way out of his present danger, and why
create an enemy unnecessarily? On the other hand, if it became worthwhile
to stab him in the back, that was done more easily if one gave him no specific
reason to expect it.

"Look at them," Clas said disgustedly. "Those other barons. They hang
behind that king exactly like coyotes behind a bear."

The remark embarrassed her. He saw what she did; she'd assumed he couldn't. Her face warmed, and she was glad he continued to speak as the rest of the castle's personnel filed into the stands. "I don't think much of these burning customs, either," he went on. "It may hold a lot of meaning for them, but it looks too fancy for me. Even the coffins look funny."

She said nothing, but the truth was, she agreed with him. Arranged in a vee configuration, each coffin was a smaller vee. All pointed north. The central section was a rectangular box, and that held the body. There was an odd triangle centered on the top at the back, however, and there were two larger triangles attached to the length of the box, one on each side. The effect was like wings and a tail; the coffins didn't look exactly like an arrowhead or a bird, but gave the same impression of speed.

The practice of treating the bodies with preservative oils and herbs and then wrapping them in cotton bands was different, too, as was delaying the burning for thirty days. She breathed a silent thanks that it was a custom normally reserved for nobles. She knew of no culture that did anything similar, so great was the fear of disease and contamination. A final concession by the Baron was to include two youngsters in the group who were below the status normally required for this ceremony. The people approved heartily.

She studied the King while the last of the column settled into the stands. Even at a distance, the light-dance of his jewels was dazzling. He wore polished metal torso armor, set with dentalium, obsidian, and amethyst. The exposed material of his shirt and his trousers was red; the Baron's wife had been flattered to learn he'd wear that color, as it was the mourning hue of the Baron's clan. In addition to the bejeweled armor, his hands were adorned with several rings. Bracelets ringed his arms up to his elbows. Golden pendants dangled from each ear. The other barons, including Jalail, would normally have been considered gaudy. In the presence of the King they looked positively drab.

A low, insistent humming noise intruded on Sylah's observations, and she looked around for the source. Clas was doing the same thing, and they exchanged puzzled glances in silence. Simultaneously they identified it as coming from the crowd. It was a shade louder then, and it continued to grow. There was an insistent, demanding quality. It irritated her quickly, and then she was a bit frightened. She edged closer to Clas, and, as if expecting her, he put out an arm and pulled her to him, still watching the cremation site.

"It's voices," he said, "just voices. It must be part of the ceremony."

"It is." She remembered she'd been told of it, and was relieved to be able to put a name to the strangely moving behavior. "That's the departure song. When it's just right, they light the fires."

He looked at her. "What's Church think of this?"

"All people have their own ceremonies. Church has no objections."

He shrugged, turning back to the scene. The humming was a roar now, everyone in the crowd standing with head back, making the loudest, steadiest sound possible. Bass rumbles mixed with the highest sopranos in a leaping river of sound. There was urgency in it now, a straining for release. A hysterical scream cut through it, a razoring screech that lifted the hair on Sylah's neck. The muscles in Clas' arm tightened, pulling her against him so hard it threatened to crush the breath out of her.

The Baron stepped out of the stands, accepted a torch from the House Director, and threw it across the open space between himself and the piles of timber at the base of the coffin poles. Both Sylah and Clas knew the wood was oil-soaked, so they were prepared for a quick flame, but neither expected the sullen crush of air that leaped at them, nor were they fully prepared for the breath of heat. The Baron, much closer than they, visibly staggered and backed away hurriedly, hands protecting his face. Those in the stands ducked or turned away, and the crowd, which had been pressing forward, retreated from flames that leaped to engulf the coffins on their poles.

Now Sylah saw that the poles were so slender the heat actually made them move. Swaying, rocking, they seemed to be leaning toward a journey. Soon they began to topple, and each fall brought a wail from the crowd. As the last one tumbled down in a storm of sparks, those observers not seated in the stands began to move away. There was no visible signal Sylah could identify, but as one they turned their backs on the pyre and walked off. Another song rose from them, however, one far different from the earlier single-note chant. This was soft, sad, and its gentle decline as the crowd dispersed across the fields brought tears to Sylah's eyes.

The families and official observers trailed out of the stands. There would be a formal dinner that night for the Baron's guests, while the people would enjoy a feast provided by him and the families of the other deceased. As they rode toward the back gate of the castle on a route that would keep them out of the King's way, Sylah said, "I'm glad we're forbidden to attend the rest of the ceremonies. The gathering at the funeral would have been bad enough, with their questions, but the dinner, with all the talk . . ." She finished with a shiver of distaste.

Clas smiled sympathetically. "I feel that way most of the time." At her look, he went on, "The only thing I've learned since we got here is that these people's situation is even more complex than the mess in our camp. I never know what to say to anyone."

"Be yourself. If you're honest—"

He cut her off. "I make everyone angry. Gan says I'm too blunt."

Sylah opened her mouth to deny it, then closed it quickly as she thought about her own honesty. "I wouldn't say you're *too* blunt." That kept her within the realm of truth, anyhow. She added, "He'd best be careful, or he'll become like the rest of them, unable to tell the difference between tact and lying."

"Not him." Clas didn't have to pause for thought. "He knows their rules now. He may let another person think what he wants to think, but he won't lie."

And what makes an open mouth that lies different from a closed one that hides the truth? she wanted to ask, knowing she never would. Even when defending Gan, Clas unwittingly defined a man growing into changes. She watched him, seeing the stern set of his jaw, the determination to concede no weakness in his friend.

The strength of that conviction turned her mind inward to other questions: Was she jealous of the friendship between them? She wanted Clas to be hers, entirely and irrevocably hers. It was senseless to admit less.

Without warning, he leaned over to grip her hand in his, reining in both horses. Hers shied a few steps at the suddenness of it, but he controlled it easily, never taking his eyes off her own. For several heartbeats he stared at her, as if his will would peel away her mental privacy until her innermost thoughts were totally bared. She hated that stare, literally feared it, and yet she was powerless to break free of it. When she tried to protest, the words scraped to a stop in her throat.

He said, "I want you to be my wife. I love you." At last he released her from that stare, letting his eyes slide away to gaze at their linked hands. He went on, "What happened in the mountains, when you were trapped, and now, the way I creep to your room at night, from shadow to shadow—I'm not proud of it. I want you beside me. I don't want to have to hide the most important truth in my life."

They were in an orchard, riding between the thick-scented lanes of gnarled trunks and arching branches. Fat, round clouds studded a perfect sky. Clover carpeted the ground, and the drone of feeding bees pressed in on her in mumbling counterpoint to the sudden pounding of her heart. His first words rolled across her mind, the rest of his comment recorded, appreciated, dismissed. Only that he asked to marry her was important.

She absorbed the moment, let her senses pull everything to her, wanting to lose nothing of this time, wanting to be able to recall it all, savor it as long as she lived.

Warmth filled her, brought joy on top of joy. She wanted to laugh and to cry. And she knew there must be nothing held back, no misunderstandings allowed to flourish under what appeared to be an unmarred surface. She said, "I love you, Clas. More than I thought I could love anyone. But marriage

. . . Our lives are different from other people's. We're escapers. More, Church may order that I be given to King Altanar."

Clas laughed, swung his free arm in a wide gesture to the east. "The road toward sun's rise has no end. If we're to be escapers forever, so be it."

"You don't know Altanar. He'll send men after me."

"It'll take months for Church's decision to reach the King of Harbundai. Many things can happen by then. There may be fighting. Altanar's not immortal."

Nor are you! The thought seared. It recalled the unexpected, unwanted image of the solitary Gan sending his faithful Scar to the next world. Once more she remembered the flames of the just-ended ceremony, saw the coffins and the swirling sparks as they fell. The red flames came together in a shape, and she realized she was now imagining the fearsome bloodred roses fixed to her door.

She reached to kiss him, putting her hands on his shoulders, savoring his solidity, the reality of his presence. Tomorrows had a way of disappearing, or coming in a guise no one expected. She said, "I'll marry you. With pride and gladness."

CHAPTER 54

The weather held good all that summer. Only in the border areas, prowled by Olan slave-takers, sporadic Olan army probes, and even more infrequent Devil raids, did the kingdom have difficulties. The relatively peaceful summer worked very strongly in Baron Jalail's favor. With such a great opportunity for a prosperous season, the King was unable to generate any enthusiasm among his other barons for the manpower he needed to occupy Jalail's holdings. The people worked at their lives, and the King impatiently marked time.

An unusual number of travelers and traders found their way into Jalail's holdings that summer. Many were men with nervous eyes, full of questions, interested in the new fighting force being built up by the Baron's Dog warriors. One was foolish enough to offer money to a recruit, asking nothing more in return than regular reports on the state of training, a description of equipment, and the names of any disgruntled members. No one ever heard if the stranger reached his next destination, but it was known that when he left the barony, he had a limp he hadn't brought with him and had left part of an ear behind.

Harvest time was a feast. The young men of Gan's command were missed in the effort, but the crops were gotten in with no loss, and food would be plentiful for winter. Livestock grew fat and bred healthy young. Shad and salmon glutted rivers and streams. Wild and cultivated fruits all bore heavily, especially the blackberry canes and huckleberry bushes, which nearly collapsed under the weight of fruit in their season, filling the air with perfumed sweetness.

As the first breath of fall sighed new colors onto the leaves of vine maple and alder, every village was blanketed in the white pall and mouth-watering smells of the smoky fires used to treat meats and the more subtle scent of drying vegetables.

On one such day Gan trotted at the head of a snakelike column of troops. He estimated how long before the men would clear the small village they were passing through, then turned to the man next to him. "I'm dropping off here," he said. "Halt the column when you reach that large rock beside the stream ahead. Put out security, have everyone eat. We'll move again in an hour."

"I hear." The man raised his hand, touched his ear. It was the signal Gan had directed they all use to acknowledge that an order was heard and understood. Tate had suggested it, as she suggested adding mirrors to their array of communications techniques. Most of her ideas improved effectiveness. He watched the men, their tired, expressionless faces streaming sweat, and thought to himself how desperately they needed that effectiveness. They would have to offset numbers with superior skills and equipment.

He waited for the officers bringing up the rear to come abreast of him, then gestured for them to fall out beside him. One was Tate, unique in the mottled clothing she'd brought from her own land. It amused Gan to see how she cherished it. She washed it personally, as careful as if the incredibly tough material was the most delicate lace. Any tear, no matter how tiny, was repaired immediately. Still, everything was showing wear, and any new sign of it brought lament. He'd decided long ago there was probably some tribal significance to it, so he never teased her, nor would he allow anyone else to do so. She was entitled to her foibles.

She still resented not having a command, and insisted on being included in all the training. He refused to consider putting her in a position of risk, but he freely admitted he wanted her present. It was a tricky matter.

Not so for the troops. From the earliest days, when she'd gone on a training run and stayed in with the best of them, she was accepted. When they saw how fiercely her Dog warrior friends watched over her, however, potential interest of a more personal nature quickly matured to a distant, but warm, respect.

The other officer was the grizzled man who'd leaned on Gan's horse so impudently the day they'd ridden toward the castle and learned of the slavers' raid. He looked tired now, but he was clean-shaven, his hair cropped, his equipment in perfect order.

The column moved away, the thudding feet like a heartbeat pounding dust out of the earth. The two men leaned against the wall of a convenient house, and Tate grinned at them through her weariness. "Well, how're we doing, so far?" she asked, obviously aware things were going well.

"Very steady. Five miles every hour."

Tate laughed soundlessly. "If anyone'd ever told me—"

She stopped, and for an instant he thought: There, she did it again. For that instant there was a yearning. I can never be sure what creates the mood, and it never lasts more than a few seconds, but there's so much pain. Why can't I just reach out to her, assure her she's with friends?

Then, as always, Tate caught herself up and continued as if nothing had happened. "If they'd told me I'd see a day when I ran twenty miles between breakfast and lunch, and expected to run another fifteen before dinner, I'd have said they were blind drunk."

"Wish I was." It was the second man, and bright eyes belied the glum scowl. "Thirty-five miles! Don't see why you don't feed us oats, and have done with it. Maybe then we'd at least get a rubdown, like real horses."

"Hmmm, oats. I wonder . . ." Gan said, mock-serious, and the man spat on the ground.

Tate said, "Emso, you give him another idea like that, and the rest of us'll elect you to permanent nightwatch."

Emso managed a wobbly smile. He said, "You've been good for the young ones, Gan. These are proud, strong men. Best soldiers I ever saw, and I've had to run away from Ola's finest. Clas' made fighters out of them. Used to be I could outsword every man in the barony. Now I believe at least half of these youngsters would do me."

"They're getting better. I wouldn't bet against you, though. You're too crafty."

"Me?"

"You. I still remember the way you baited me the day the slavers came."

Emso's lined face cracked in a richer smile. "Was you dumped me on my backside. That *I* remember."

"You wanted to see if I'd do it. You wanted the men to see."

"Figured it out, did you? Thought you had. Thought the men ought to know you'd show some muscle if you had to. Didn't have to put the horse on me, though. Not what I expected."

"The unexpected's always worth more than muscle. You know that."

Tate straightened, stretching and groaning. She stopped abruptly, head tilted back. "Someone who knows what they're doing is smoking salmon. Garlic. Honey. And—and . . . yes, pepper." Moving as if pulled by the nose, she went around the corner of the house. Behind it an older man and woman were taking wood chips from a leather water bucket and dropping them in a hole. Gouts of steam and smoke boiled out of it, and the man quickly covered it with a metal lid. Mounded earth marked a tunnel running from the firebox to the smoker itself, a squat earthen square a few yards away. Smoke began to ease out of its upper vents as they watched. That was what Tate smelled, the carryover that brought the smell of the fish and its cure along with the wood.

The couple looked up, startled, and the man quickly executed the unique salute of the barony. Gan returned it, then nodded slowly to the woman. "We were on the road," he explained, then indicated Tate. "My friend had to see what you're doing. None of us ever smelled anything better."

The woman beamed. "Thank you. People seem to like it."

"Comes from choosing the right fish. Took me years to learn how," the man said. He caught the hardening of his wife's jawline from the corner of his eyes, and added hastily, "Wife has a secret blend for the cure. Makes all the difference. Nothing like it." He smiled at her and got a chill return.

She faced Gan again, holding a hand up to the smoking vent as she did, explaining, "We smoke slow and cool. Meat keeps longer that way."

When Gan spoke of open smoking and sun drying the woman clucked sympathetically. She refused to let him be deprived further, despite his protestations that he'd tried salmon many times in Harbundai. The husband was equally insistent, declaring that, until he tried theirs, he hadn't tried the best. And it was good. Tate named a dozen herbs, trying to discover the elusive flavors she achieved, and the woman laughed herself weak at Tate's confusion.

Preparing to leave, Gan moved toward the well, where he meant to draw water to wash his hands. He saw the man move to assist him, and the woman checked him. They argued about something, heads together, glancing anxiously at their guest. The man braced himself as Gan returned. "My wife . . . we have a request."

At Gan's nod, he went on. "Our son is one of the young men the Baron called to service. His wife lives with him in their camp." He hesitated, then turned a confiding grin on Tate. "He was home for a day a while back. We heard about you. He says all the training they do is to your plan. True?"

"I work with Clas and Emso. In my country we had to train inexperienced men. The knowledge has been helpful here."

The man grunted. "If they're all as improved as my son, you do magic. I wouldn't have known him. Got a pride in him I never saw before, and he's half again as strong. He's not just a farm boy with a sword, either. I could tell—he's a warrior now, a man other men recognize." He turned his attention back to Gan. "The other thing he told us was how hard you worked to get all the men a camp where their wives can be with them, and how the wives are learning to do things that make them some money. We're indebted. My request is that I be allowed to ask one of your men to carry some of our smoked salmon back to our son. We'd like to send some to the man named Clas, too. And we'd be honored if your party would take some. It's not much, but it's a way for folks like us to let you know how proud we are that our son's one of your Wolves, and to say thank you for what you've done for them, Murdat."

"What?" Taken completely by surprise, Gan blurted the question. The man's eyes widened and he jerked, as if instinct told him to run and the mind refused to obey. Gan said, "What did you call me? What Wolves?"

Emso spoke up, covering the man's tongue-tied stammer. "The five hundred have heard tales of you and the wolves. They say they can't be Dog warriors, so they're your wolves. And they call you Murdat because a leader should have a title."

Gan's glare speared Tate. He ignored the now-quaking couple. "You knew of this, too? Clas knew? Who else?"

Tate said, "Everyone but you, I think. None of us was sure how you'd react."

"I'm Gan Moondark. That's title enough."

Tate and Emso shook their heads in solemn disagreement. She said, "That's not the way the men want it, Gan. Your father wasn't just Col, he was War Chief."

Emso added, "Sign of respect. Reject it, you reject them."

"Wolves." Gan's emotional turmoil erupted as scorn. "They've never been in a fight. What can they know?"

"They'll fight." It was the householder, surprising everyone, himself more than anyone. As all eyes went to him, he swallowed loudly, then pressed ahead. "They've grown up seeing the Baron and his sons grow weak. Instead of fighting off the other barons, Baron Jalail makes alliances, the same as our king. When the Olan slavers come, our nobles are useless. They overtake no one, and if they do, they're driven off. My son says things will be different now. We've had years of practice in learning how to hide from the slavers. Worse, we've always known that someday Ola would come at us in full strength. To take our land. Probably our lives, too. Now, my son says, we believe we can stop them. Because of you." He stopped and swallowed again, making up his mind about something. He added, "Murdat." It was defiant.

When Gan looked at him, Tate was grinning. She tried to swallow it and failed miserably. Gan considered more argument, but thought of Emso's advice and checked himself. No one knew better than he did about the nature of respect. When the young men of his own tribe rejected his father, they blamed it on Col's determination to find peaceful solutions. That was merely the excuse. In truth, they were afraid they'd lost the respect of their traditional enemies and might be attacked when they were least prepared.

Dimly he heard Tate saying, "We'll take the fish for your son and Clas. They'll enjoy it as much as we did, I'm sure."

The woman spoke to Gan directly, demanded his attention. "We were angry when you took him," she said. "Now we wish you—and him—success. But I still wish he was home."

Gan thanked them for their hospitality, and the man for his information. Then, bending forward, he kissed the top of the woman's head. "I wish your son was home too, Mother." He turned away quickly, calling the dogs, leaving Tate and Emso to make the good-byes.

That night they all ate in Clas and Sylah's new house. It was small, only slightly larger than the nearby houses of the married Wolves. A major distinguishing difference was the windows. Every home had at least one window of glass, mined from a godkill. They were usually a patchwork of pieces, sometimes of varied colors and thickness, held together by pitch or resin. The poorer huts used oiled paper or cloth. Clas and Sylah had glass in all but one of their six windows, and one was an entire single piece as big as a man's chest. It was shaped rather like a chopped-off pyramid, but everyone admired it, commenting on how there were no dizzying wrinkles in it.

Gan realized he was bad company and recognized the levity of the others as forced because of it. Neela, in particular, seemed anxious to jolly him out of his mood, and he couldn't help thinking she was a bit more attentive to him when they visited Clas and Sylah in their new home. He told himself it was a reaction to the obvious affection flowing between the other couple, that it stimulated her. A part of him wondered how much of it was brought about by jealousy.

As if sensing the unfortunate turn of his mind, Tate moved the conversation to a subject that never failed to brighten him. Aiming her remark at Clas, baiting him, she said, "With all the unit and individual training you've given your men, you know the thing that's made them better fighters is the program we set up for the women. The troops know we're supporting them."

Nodding wisely, Clas said, "The women are better off. No one appreciates it more than we do. With their own houses, they'll pay more attention to their cooking, and that'll make them healthier, and they'll have bigger, better babies, and—uh!" He grunted and jerked away as Sylah jammed her thumb in his ribs.

Tate turned her attention to Gan. "Remember we told you we'd be teaching them to make products they could sell in New City? Neela sent off the first load of baskets this morning. Sylah's teaching all the women basic medical things. We're calling it first aid treatment."

Gan said, "I think the Baron will change the law about the lockup for widows, too. Once we prove the unit can earn a lot of its own keep and that we'll take care of our people ourselves, he'll see we can add to his community, instead of draining it."

Neela said, "We do have a problem, though. The Baron's nobles don't like us. They say we keep to ourselves too much. They resent losing young men to your unit, and they're very upset about the land the Baron's giving each married man."

Gan slammed a hand on the table. "The land and house belong to the unit; if a man goes home, it'll be given to another married couple. And what if we keep to ourselves? None of them's made a move to befriend any of us."

"They've been good to me." Nervousness tightened Tate's normally relaxed tones. "A few are good friends."

"Friends of yours or Jones'?" Gan's question froze everyone's expression.

Tate was slow to respond, and her manner was deliberate when she did. "Both of us, I hope. They listen to us, they try to understand his message."

To Sylah, Gan said, "Jones is involved in some new religion. Will Church tolerate it?"

Tate opened her mouth to respond, bleak with anger, but Sylah gestured her to silence. "Let me answer, Donnacee," she said. "It's a point we've been avoiding. You don't know our ways, and because you're my friend, I've avoided the subject. We may as well have it said plainly. Church will attack anyone who challenges her leadership."

"Jones is talking reform, equality. Aren't those Church's goals?"

"Certainly, but—"

"Then help him."

Sylah wrung her hands. "I can't. You mustn't. Change and learning must come from Church, from those appointed by Church."

"Is that why you have this thing you call the Return, where you burn everything people have dug up that has writing or numbers on it? I see you use the stones and bricks from the buried buildings. Church doesn't object to that, and I saw a piece of stone the other day that had a word on it."

"It's not the same. Those are things the giants left, and no one will ever understand them. Church only wants to direct the power of learning into the proper hands. By rights, she should control all learning; only she is ethically qualified to oversee all people, because she has no ambitions, no desire to rule."

Seeing the sincerity of her friend, Tate bit back her retort. She wanted to tell Sylah that her speech was pure propaganda. More, it was a blunt statement of the determination to command, and the instrument was education. She also wanted to remind Sylah that Jones was her countryman.

Strangely, the word *friend* came to mind, but it slid away, suddenly elusive.

Gan stopped listening, stricken by a disappointment that approached despair. He'd never felt close to Jones. Tate was different. She was companion, ally, and—he still had difficulty acknowledging it—advisor. If he forced her to choose between Jones and himself, she might abandon the other man, but Gan would never know how comfortable she was with the decision.

The thought brought a wince. There was a time when it wouldn't have occurred to him to wonder about another's loyalty. How far away was that world, where friends and enemies were identified, and a man knew which was which?

The word that changed it all, of course, was "man." With the pure certainty of youth, the boy knew the distinction was solid and unmistakable. The man was confused; he'd learned that a separation existed, but it was a hazy, treacherous line that could create a picture as deceptive and dangerous as a mirage.

Resentment replaced his earlier disappointment. He'd never asked for any of this. His dreams had always had him defending his people, not attacking them. Or anyone else. In fact, he was sure he'd rather have remained a Nightwatch all his life, responsible for no more than his sector, alone with his dogs and his own skills. This talk of power, these responsibilities for training hundreds of men, bringing them to the peak of their individual and combined strengths, knowing he must throw them into battle and not all of them would survive—it was all more than he ever dreamed could happen.

Questions generated more questions, and then someone hammered on the door, bringing him back to the present and the still-boiling discussion. He noticed that everyone had become involved, and wished he'd paid more attention. Clas, closest to the door, opened it. One of the black-and-white-clad servants stood there, impatient. "The Baron wishes to see Gan Moondark immediately," he said.

Gan rose swiftly, reading the trouble in the man's face. "What's wrong?" he asked.

The man glanced significantly at the others, then back to Gan. He made the signal for not hearing. Clas said, "I'm coming with you. If he wants to talk to you alone, I'll wait close by."

As they left, Gan was relieved to hear Sylah say to Tate, "I think we're going to be needed," and Tate's murmured agreement. The hostility between them was at least put aside.

The Baron was extremely agitated. "I wish you'd come alone," he said petulantly, "but I suppose it makes no difference, really. You'd have gone directly to them, after all. It's not important. Still, I sent for you, not everyone." There was more along the same line, and Gan waited patiently for it to stop, hoping Clas wouldn't let his temper force words out of him. When the Baron got to his point, it was shocking news. "It's worse than I expected. The Olan troops—you remember the three divisions we were told were left near the border?—are moving this way. That's two thousand infantry and five hundred cavalry, twenty-five hundred men."

"What route? Are they coming through the barony to the west, or sliding along that border until they reach us? How do we know they're aiming at your lands?"

"The King's spies learned it. What difference does it make what route they're taking? There's no time to call up any more of my men. The other barons say they can't spare anyone, except Baron Galmontis from the northwest holding. He's promised to be here in ten days with a thousand troops. And of course the King himself is coming—with the appointed assistant to 'help' me defend the barony and administer it after the battle."

"If there's to be a battle."

The Baron glanced at him shrewdly. "The same thought occurred to me."

The whole thing smelled to Gan as if it had been lying in the sun too long, and he said so. It had taken weeks for the King's spies to even discover where the Olan divisions were encamped, and now, suddenly, as soon as they moved, he knew where, when, and even why. More, he was prepared to react, but only with troops from a barony so far away it couldn't create a confederacy with Jalail to confront him.

Baron Jalail jerked upright out of his chair, paced nervously. "I'll just have to accept the King's assistant and hope I can get rid of him somehow."

Clas made a half-strangled exclamation, and Gan spoke quickly to override it. "We could meet the other baron's troops at the border, deny them entry to your lands."

"Deny?" The Baron stopped almost in mid-stride, bent over, head twisted awkwardly to stare at Gan in shocked disbelief. "They're with the King! If I even interfere with them, all the barons will have their excuse to accuse me of treason. They'll have the barony divided among them in a week! No, no, no." He shook his head. "We've avoided the King's plan for my land this long, but now there's no more evasion. We'll accept the assistant, and just outwait him."

"Baron, even if the King intends to let you live, can you really believe his pet won't kill you eventually?"

The round figure sagged as the blunt words struck like fists. He dragged himself to his chair, slumped in it. His gaze went to his family banner, limp on the pole jutting from the stone wall. Moisture gleamed at the tight line of his eyelids when he closed them in a grimace. He wiped at them carelessly. Eventually he said, "I must trust my king. I won't strike at him." Shockingly, he laughed, a sharp, almost shrill sound. "Listen to me. 'Strike at him,' indeed. With what? Five hundred against a thousand and more? Five hundred half-trained boys? And what if there *are* Olan troops planning to attack the kingdom? I'd be a traitor, stripped of all lands and honors." He drew himself erect, a sudden dignity banishing the self-pitying tears, the beaten appearance. "If this barony changes hands, no one will ever be able to say it was for treason. Let the King and his coyote live with the knowledge they stole it from the last Jalail. The shame of it will follow them. Disband your troops. Send them home. Make whatever preparations you wish for yourselves. Now go."

Gan nodded, and almost brought himself to use the Baron's salute, but even in this circumstance, he was unable to do so.

In the hall Clas turned to him. "His courage is broken. He's a dead man. Where do we go?"

CHAPTER 55

Gan still hadn't answered Clas—indeed, hadn't made a sound—as they strode down the hall toward Gan's quarters. Unconsciously they walked in step, and the heartbeat cadence of heels on stone was the only sound to be heard. The rhythm pounded in Gan's brain as he silently repeated Clas' question: Where do we go? Where do we go?

Suddenly, a voice drifted to them from a dark side hall. Despite its insistent urgency, Gan had to listen closely to be certain it actually called his name. He knew that passageway led to a storage room, a place with one door and four windowless walls of solid stone. With one hand he pulled Clas' arm, stationing him behind and to the left, simultaneously using hand language to tell him to watch their rear. He moved forward cautiously, straining to see. The light from the torches in the main hall lapped past the passage, giving him no view beyond the black mouth.

"Come out of there," he said, and with his free hand half drew his murdat.

In answer he got a soft chuckle. "I don't think so," the voice said. Gan knew he should be able to place it. The irritation spurred his tension, and he drew the blade free. The voice laughed some more. "No need for that, young Moondark. Not just yet, don't you know."

The familiar phrase brought Gan up short. "Bilsten?" He squinted into the darkness. A subtle shifting of the black space resolved itself into the familiar figure. "What are you doing here? How'd you get in?"

"Not so loud, young friend, or I may not get back out." A white hand touched Gan's sword arm. "A man like me isn't allowed to go just anywhere, but I have to live, so I learn to go where I must. I got you away from the Devils, didn't I?"

"We fought our way out. And they knew we were coming." Clas spoke past Gan, edging closer as he did.

Gan waved him to silence and asked Bilsten, "What do you want?"

The Peddler seemed to fade as he slipped back into the darkness. "I bring you something you may find valuable."

"I can't pay."

Again, soft chuckling. "When I ask, you will. I'll not forget you owe me, and you're too proud to cheat on your debts. I came because I heard you and your friends were brought here by Baron Jalail and you're training a band of fighters for him."

"You heard right."

"The King of Harbundai isn't pleased. I hear he wants this barony in his family, that the Jalail line is dead and must be replaced."

"So?"

Bilsten made a sighing sound of approval. "Better, young friend; neither confirm nor deny. I do believe you're learning. However—onward. Baron Jalail's told you the Olan troops to the west are moving east, which will put them on his border with Ola—"

Gan's outthrust hand took Bilsten just below the throat, wadding up his blouse. He pulled him forward, finding himself stopping short of dragging the man into the light. It would have been easily done, as the Peddler made no more resistance than an empty sack. Slowly the bearded man reached up and disengaged Gan's fingers, then slid back into the darkness. Calmly he continued, "I was guessing. Why else would he call you tonight, unless it was to share important information, and didn't I have to ride my poor mule almost to death to get here by this time myself? And isn't it convenient for the King, what with him looking for a reason to bring his nephew here? Doesn't it make you wonder?"

"It does. And so do you. What're you leading up to?"

"I have some knowledge of precious items," Bilsten said, and Clas made a harsh noise in his throat. After an offended pause, Bilsten went on. "A week ago an Olan general called me to his tent. It happens his troops made the attack that killed Jalail's oldest sons. They were camped on high ground above the mouth of a river called Bear Paw. You know it? It's named that because it forms a flat, five-streamed delta—a marsh—where it empties into the Inland Sea."

Gan nodded and Bilsten went on. "He showed me a dagger. No scabbard—had it wrapped in a cloth. Asked me if it was valuable. I recognized the workmanship and the material immediately, of course. In fact, I recognized the piece. It's Kwa goods, from up north, and the other time I saw it, it *had* a scabbard. With jewels worth more than the stuff in the blade handle. It belonged to the royal nephew who's to replace Baron Jalail."

Grinning, Gan said, "You've just committed several acts of treason. I could have you flayed and thrown to the crows."

Bilsten edged out into the light. The wavering glow of the torches gave his skin a cast like old gold. He dropped his voice even lower. "I'm worth more than entertainment for a bloodthirsty mob."

"Perhaps. Now, tell me what I have to know about this Olan movement."

A white tube appeared from inside Bilsten's robes. "The route and destination are on this map. They should arrive there in three more days. They move slowly, with no security." He thrust the paper into Gan's hand, then sighed. "That's the way it is. I give away the key to the future of an entire barony, yet my own requests are the most humble of wants."

Gan felt his back muscles draw tight. "Ahh, now we come to it. What's the price?"

"A message. For the Rose Priestess. You will tell her this: 'Never forget; the rose path leads to the unexpected door.' "

"That's all?"

Teeth gleamed and disappeared. "It's quite enough. You'll tell her? It's a small enough favor, isn't it?"

Bilsten was already blending into the darkness. "Please, go. I've dallied too long here, don't you know."

For a moment Gan balanced the map, burning with curiosity. Then he turned on his heel.

"We ought to go after him," Clas said, following reluctantly, adding, "I don't trust him."

"Neither do I." Gan didn't break stride. "He's using us. As long as we both benefit, it's fair."

In Gan's rooms, where the women waited, Tate swooped down on the unrolled map like a fox discovering a mouse. Sylah and Neela looked on with high interest, but without her sense of purpose.

Tate said, "This is quality work. Look, he's shown routes leading to good intercept points where we can drop on the column. He's even marked the best observation points."

Dryly Gan said, "You can be sure there are other, unmarked, trails. Bilsten will have his secrets."

With Clas, they discussed the terrain, and through it all, Gan felt he was failing to see something. The proposed Olan camp appeared a reasonable site, with access to trails leading into Harbundai as well as good roads roughly paralleling both sides of the river.

Tate pointed out an interesting feature. "Look. There's only one trail leading east from the campsite into the Enemy Mountains. If the Olan commander's attacked by Devils, he's got no chance of effective pursuit."

Clas sneered. "He's not worried about them. They're probably allies by now."

Gan jerked upright. Suddenly, the map presented him with a totally different picture. It was as if he had been staring into a thicket, and one chance movement revealed the living creature there. He bent forward again, piecing together the rest of the beast.

Tate said, "What is it, Gan? What do you see?"

He asked, "Why were so many Devils camped at Cloud Rest Pass?"

She looked blank, and he said, "Not to capture us. There were far too many for that, and they were settled in too well. That camp's a place for warriors to shelter, to prepare for an attack to the west."

Tate inhaled slowly. "You're saying Ola's not cooperating with the King's man, but seducing him, instead. It makes sense. The troops 'visiting' Baron Jalail can't stay here more than a month or six weeks, and then they have to get home to take care of crops or business or whatever. If they leave a bodyguard for the King's man, it can't be more than a couple of hundred men, right? So the Devil warriors at Cloud Rest and the Olans strike at Jalail when the main force has gone home. In two weeks, probably less, they control the whole barony. The barony to the west is outflanked. Ola and its Devil allies would be in perfect position to drive a surprise column north along the foothills of the Enemy Mountains while another force strikes along the traditional coast route. Harbundai goes up on both horns of the bull."

Gan grinned broadly. "You see it, too. Good."

Clas pointed out there were no bridges over the Bear Paw so far east, and no fords until well upstream of the Olan's intended bivouac. "They mean to ferry the divisions across the river."

"We can catch them as they land," Gan said. "They'll be disorganized and vulnerable."

Tate and Clas exchanged glances. Unsure, troubled, Clas looked away. He frowned, clearly wondering what to say next. Tate was bolder. "The river's not a wall," she said. "Even if it was, we can't defend as well as we can attack. We can't think of it as a tripwire to make them stumble, but as an anvil we can smash them against."

"Smash them?" Gan was dubious.

"Absolutely. They have the men to force a landing whenever they want. We can hurt them, but we can't stop them. So let them come. See how the ground rises on our side of the crossing site? We give ground, bring them to us on our terms. When we've beaten them, they've nowhere to retreat."

" 'When we've beaten them.' " Gan winked broadly at Clas. "How do we argue with such confidence?" Nevertheless, he smiled at her. "I agree; they can make the crossing. Even your lightning weapon wouldn't guarantee we can stop them. For that matter, I don't want you using it unless the wind of the battle turns against us. I want it to come as a surprise. Now, knowing that, what magic do you have for us?"

"No magic, Murdat. Study. The work of my life. So a woman can compete in this male world." Her hands darted across the map, a contradictory flow of grace and sinister suggestion as she described her vision of the battle to come. "We rely on trickery. We give ground to create the battlefield we must have. In our terms, we call it a double envelopment, where we strike the enemy from both sides."

Gan nodded, sober now, the smiles and pleasantries forgotten. He said, "My father spoke of it as the noose. It takes great leadership. I don't know if I have the strength to make such a plan work. If I fail . . ."

"You will not. We will not." Clas almost growled the interruption. "You are our leader. When we see the ground, you will perfect your plan. We will fight by your side. It is the way."

So softly as to be almost unheard, Sylah spoke for the first time. "Must this way always be *the* way?"

Clas said, "We were given no choice."

Gan said, "So now we find out how good we are." He rose, rolling up the map as he did. "Wake the men. We leave in two hours. Silently."

Neela broke the shocked silence. "Gan! They're the Baron's men. You can't."

"We'll be gone when he wakes. If we win, he won't punish us. If we lose, he won't have to." He shrugged.

Coldly, Tate asked, "And me?" His answer didn't come quickly enough to suit her, and she gestured angrily. "I've worked as hard as anyone. Harder. I deserve some consideration."

He said, "You don't want consideration. You want battle."

"Don't pick at words with me. I want to lead the men I've helped train. It's only fair. I've spent my life working for the opportunity. They cheated me out of it once. It can't happen again."

"They? Who?"

"My people. I studied hard. I was trained by the finest. Then my opportunity to prove myself was taken away. Still, I did my duty. Since we met, I've served you loyally. Don't treat me as they did."

"You're worth any number of fighters to me. When we first came here, it was you who questioned the Baron, determined how many men we could draft and train. What of Clas? And Emso? Your learning from your culture helped them create a superb training system. Who helps them if you die? Why should I risk your skills?"

"Because I'm one of your Wolves, too, and I ask it. Or am I a prisoner?"

His face flamed, and for a moment his expression was pure rage. It took several seconds of tense silence for balance to return, and the thoughts that ran through his mind as he waited were heavy. She spoke the truth; she deserved whatever she asked. The men probably understood that. Nevertheless, taking orders from a woman in combat—in their first combat—was asking a very great deal. Further, there was more to her demand than the need to prove herself. That was one of the factors spurring her, assuredly, but he wasn't willing to bet that even she could describe all the forces driving her so fiercely. He wished he could supply whatever it was she needed to fill the emptiness that sometimes threatened to swallow her. It wasn't killing. Of that he was certain. Yet she would go where the killing was.

So be it. Sadness tainted his growing battle-fever. He had to force heartiness into his words. He said, "You'll command a wing. I expect you to avoid personal combat until I need you to use the lightning weapon. Understood?"

She nodded, unsmiling, accepting her due. He admired her all the more.

Clas merely told her they had to hurry and get ready. They left at a trot. Neela watched them go before turning back to Gan. She said, "I'll go to the women, keep them quiet. Sylah, will you come with me?"

"Of course." Sylah's eyes remained fixed on the door where Gan had left. She rose, following only when Neela gestured. When she reached Neela, she stopped. No words passed, yet Gan knew a message had been exchanged. Neela's color heightened almost imperceptibly. Sylah continued on alone.

Neela faced him, stiff, her face a kaleidoscope of changes that moved too quickly for him to interpret. He knew she wanted him to speak, but he couldn't imagine what to say and was literally speechless at the prospect of using the wrong words. He managed to mumble, "If we don't come back—" and she was clinging to him before he realized what was happening. Her body trembled against his. Her breath was rapid, almost like small, sharp sobs. He held her tightly, unspeaking. Little by little she calmed, and when she stepped back, he had to smile at the proud set of her jaw.

She spoke with controlled assurance. "You'll come back. We have things to discuss, you and I. There are plans, goals. Mine aren't so grand as yours, but they're just as important to me. And should be to you."

He heard it as a crushingly disappointing statement, words of nothing more than ambition. He realized with a terrible, sick sensation exactly how much he'd hoped she'd say something about him, about them. He wanted her to care about *him.*

An image struck him, seemed to twist time at its roots.

Neela sat with her arms around a golden-blond boy in her lap. His face was a miniature of hers. They both fixed him with a straightforward, steady gaze full of uncomprehending hurt.

The image disappeared.

He gulped air. He yearned to tell her of his own hurt, his thoughts, his feelings, as he had wanted to since the moment he'd first held her in his arms.

When she realized she'd lost Clas.

Fool, he shouted inwardly; she could never love you as she did him.

He lowered his hands to his sides and stepped back. He said, "I understand about your plans. I promise you, when we return to our people, your family's name will be as honored as it ever was. As you say, we'll do it together."

She paled. He was sure she was thinking of the enormity of the challenge ahead of them. Stretching, she kissed his cheek, and he was about to turn when she suddenly kissed him again, full on the lips. It was clumsily done, and the unexpectedness of it staggered him. With her hand to her mouth, blushing furiously, she watched him regain his balance. The tears she'd fought so successfully finally escaped, slipping in shining paths down her cheeks. Then she ran.

When he reached the billeting area, it was a hive of mumbled curses, clattering, and growled orders. There was no light, not even a shred of moonlight, but he could tell things were going well. Picking a place so far from the castle had been wiser than they'd realized. He also told himself it was well they were having no major problems. The frustrations of the meeting with Neela gnawed at him disconcertingly.

A few questions led Gan to where Clas already had the horses saddled, waiting for him. The dogs greeted him with excited, joyous leaps. Tate and Emso found them all together and reported the lead company was within minutes of being ready to move. Clas would bring up the rear with the cavalry and the light supply wagons.

Gan was checking progress in the other companies, moving toward Clas' end of the column, when a lantern winked on and off in one of the married men's houses. Idly, he wondered if that was where Neela might be, or Sylah, and suddenly he remembered Bilsten's message.

He heeled his horse ahead, picking his way through the milling, muttering troopers. Finding Clas, he reminded him of the exchange with the Peddler, and they both tried to recall the exact words. Finally, sure he had it, Clas turned over control of the cavalry unit and trotted off to find Sylah. Gan retraced his steps to the head of the column.

Sylah was sure the man riding toward her was Clas long before he was close enough to recognize properly. As he drew near she called softly, and he slid out of the saddle to take her in his arms. He kissed her, then said, "That's the best reason I had to come looking for you, but there's another, as well. That old weasel, Bilsten, had some sort of message for you. In all the excitement, we forgot about it. Sorry. Anyhow, it's from your abbey, I guess—he wouldn't say exactly."

She willed herself to speak calmly. "Clas, *tell* me."

Offended, he said, " 'Never forget that the rose path leads to the unexpected door.' "

She gasped. His face loomed as he bent closer. "Does that mean something?" he asked, and she lied instinctively. "No. I mean, yes, of course it *means* something, but it's not important. My abbess is just telling me that life is unpredictable and I should never lose hope."

"Well, then why didn't she say that? Seems silly, to me. I have to go." He kissed her again, and for that moment she forgot the withered roses nailed to her door, forgot her goals, could think only of him riding into the night, perhaps never to return to her. She clutched at his jacket as he pulled away. He unlocked her fingers with the gentle strength that always surprised her. His teeth gleamed in an off-center smile. He said, "Don't worry about me. Take care of yourself."

"There's something—" She stopped. "Never mind. You'll do what you must. And I'll be proud of you."

He squeezed her hand one last time, and then he was mounted, riding away. Dwindling hoofbeats mocked the continuing pounding of her heart.

Gan heard the hoofbeats, as well, hoping no one else was abroad at such a late hour to report seeing the secretive departure. Just in case, he picked up the pace to a trot. It would tire the men, but distance was the most important factor just now; they could sleep tomorrow.

CHAPTER 56

Rolling peacefully through its broad valley, the Bear Paw River was a dark sheen against the gray, dawn-lit forest on its banks. A huge heron soared above it, gracefully weaving its own pattern back and forth across the flow. The decrepit road on the north side of the river was empty, except for a small Olan guard detachment. The men were lax, either cooking breakfast or rolling up bedding.

Farther downstream, on the south bank across from Gan's viewpoint, the Olan division's camp was an ant heap of activity. The man standing beside Gan said, "Just beyond that fir with the lightning-blasted top is where they cut the timbers for the rafts, Murdat."

Gan winced. Even then, when the approaching battle should be the uppermost—the *only*—thought in his mind, the title set off a complex series of disquieting emotions. He'd finally decided it was because it made him look at himself in a different light. To everyone else, it identified him. To Gan Moondark, it was an alien, unknown person. He had just begun to discover himself; he had no idea who the Murdat was.

The man went on. "They didn't build many, because they don't feel they have to move many horses at once. You can see the boats they've requisitioned over there, pulled up on the bank."

Gan said, "When will they start crossing?"

"Today." The scout was certain, and Gan looked at him quizzically and got a smile in response. "They're packing the cooking equipment. That means they won't be making any more meals on that side of the river."

"They could go without, or eat cold, as we have for the past two days, just to be sure no one sees smoke."

The man shifted his feet, looking at the ground. Gan slapped him on the back. "But I think you're right. You did well. Tell your commander I compliment him."

Touching his ear, the man said, "I hear," and trotted smartly away. Gan was pleased to see him break into a self-satisfied smile when he thought he wasn't being observed.

Leaving his viewpoint, Gan considered how important that sort of spirit would be in combat. Outnumbered, his men faced a confident force, one accustomed to winning.

He was still trying to quell growing uncertainty as he reached the place where Clas and Tate waited with the dogs. Forcing firmness, he said, "Today," and they both nodded. Then he asked, "All the commanders are sure of their assignments? One mistake," he held up a finger, "just one, and we sleep in the next world tonight."

Tate said, "It's a good plan. It'll work."

Clas was primed to fight. Unnaturally bright, widened eyes betrayed his temper even before his gruff answer. "Take care of my feelings. I made them fighters. Whatever orders you give, we'll do our job. We'll destroy our enemy."

Gan reached to grip his friend's taut sword arm. "Your fighting is the one thing I depend on without question, my friend." He drew away a few yards, turning to where the sun was streaking fire along the tops of the Enemy Mountains. He went through his nara meditation with great difficulty, having to fight clear of persistent images of fighting. His mind cleared at last, however, and he was able to see inside himself openly, without disturbance. With that, he was ready to respond, unburdened by preconceptions or hesitation. He was one thing, made of many, as a season is a total of all its days. When he felt his soul rise in him and reach to embrace the day, he made his Three-sign. That done, he returned to where the others waited and said, "Everyone to positions. Clas, attack with your unit when you judge it's time. If you're discovered before that, retreat. We'll try again somewhere else. We agree?"

"Yes." Clas used his own vocal response and walked away without saluting. Gan grinned at his back. Clas would never be anything other than what he was.

Turning to Tate, he said, "I'll signal you with the war drums. I want you to use your lightning weapons only in self-defense, and I want you to remain behind the men. I'd rather the Olans not know about you."

"I hear." Tate winked as she tugged her ear, then made a face in the direction of the retreating Clas, sharing the moment's humor at Clas' studied insistence on his own ways. Gan laughed, and for the first time in weeks felt free. It was as if a chain binding him to a world he neither liked nor understood was suddenly broken. Had it not been for the absolute necessity they not alert the enemy, he'd have screamed his war cry in anticipation.

Returning to his position on the hill, he watched Clas' column slip toward the river, holding to the lowest ground and best cover. Then, crawling on their bellies, they made their way into the field inland of the north-bank ferry landing. The land sloped upward gradually from the river's edge for a good half mile and paralleled it for about the same distance.

The irony of the situation tugged at his concentration. If the Olan slavers hadn't made the area unlivable, the field would have been without cover now, either harvested and cleared of crops or grazed by livestock. Their raids drove off the farmer, and that meant nature could reclaim the land. Today it was rank with autumn-blasted weeds and brush almost shoulder high. And because Clas could hide, the Wolves had a chance.

He grinned to himself. Wolves. They'd learn.

The first Olan troops moved to the ready boats and the ferry on the south bank.

The soft breeze disguised the movement of Clas' force, although to Gan's eye the subtle irregularities in the movement of the brush that told him the men were getting in position were all too obvious. He pictured them spreading out at extended intervals, unrolling the three-foot-long slings, adjusting the leather slingstone sacks at their sides. He imagined he could hear the scrape of metal on metal as some tested the fit of murdats in scabbards.

His forehead was drenched with sweat. When he reached to wipe it, his hands were equally wet. As if sympathizing, Raggar nudged him, whining softly. "Be ready, old friend," Gan said, ruffling his coat. Shara came up, demanding equal attention, and the older male surprised Gan by making no objection.

He had no time to dwell on it. Tate was on the move, leading her unit into the forest at the northern limit of the field. Clas' pitifully small force of slingers seemed much too far south.

Gan asked himself what more they could have done to pick a battlefield, what more they could have done to prepare the troops, what equipment they might have developed to help them.

A sinister smile twisted his features as he thought of Tate's innovations. Her people must be incredible warriors, he thought; she knew tactics and equipment like no one he'd ever heard about. Sometimes he couldn't believe anyone so young, especially a woman, could have learned so much about combat.

The new shield was a perfect example. Made of wicker and hide, they were backed with thin metal. They'd turn any arrow or sword. The upper edge was a razor-sharp band of steel. In close fighting, it would slash as well as a sword. A stubby blade projected from the center of the shield's face. On the inner side, in its own sheath, was an eight-inch battle knife with a lead ball on the end of the handle that made the butt a weapon that could crush a skull. She'd even improved on the slingers, having the metalsmiths prepare wooden balls studded with long, protruding spikes. They reminded Gan of spiders. However they were thrown, they landed with at least two points up. If they hit a man, so much the better, but their purpose—and he hated to think of their horrible effectiveness—was to simply lie on the ground and break up cavalry charges.

His eye drifted to the rear, where Emso commanded the Wolves' cavalry. There wasn't enough open space here for the Dog style of wide-ranging, wheeling cavalry work, so Emso could handle it perfectly well. Clas' steadiness would be more important at the point of first contact.

Emso's rigid bearing was unmistakable, even though his face was obscured by one of the new war masks like those traditional to the Dog warriors. The men had been allowed to decorate the basic design to suit themselves. They presented some interesting visages.

The second wave of boats was preparing to leave the south bank. Men heaved dozens of them across the cobbled shore. They made Gan think of ungainly animals lurching toward the water, but once launched, they were suddenly graceful again. Troops crawled over the sides, grabbing oars, pulling toward the north bank. Even at this distance the hubbub of thousands of men and hundreds of horses created a unique sound. For all its confused rumble and lack of urgency, there was a presence of violence in it.

He jerked himself to his feet, dry-mouthed, wondering again at how unusually hot the morning seemed, despite the high overcast that blocked most of the sunlight.

As the Olan infantry landed, they moved inland a short distance and formed in companies before sitting down to wait for other units to join them. The edge of the field in front of Clas' hidden troops filled with men who spread like a leather-brown stain, as if the river itself was moving up its banks. The noise grew louder with their numbers, and the boats continued to scuttle back and forth across the river.

The first indication most of the Olan troops had of any danger was the screams of the wounded in the front ranks. Clas' slingers responded to the three-note whistled signal by rising in perfect unison, the long leather thongs of their weapons humming angrily, and then the first missiles were whizzing among the packed troops. It was impossible to miss at that distance, and the heavy rocks did fearful damage. Dozens of men dropped, some continuing to move or cry out, many forever stilled.

Carnage created panic. Overrunning the officers who tried to set them into defensive formation, the mass of survivors of the initial onslaught streamed back toward the river. Clas' men moved forward, the first ranks drawing swords for close work while the remainder continued to sling stones with deadly effect on the Olans farther away. Gan sucked in his breath as one of his men tried a sweeping sidearm stroke. His opponent caught it easily with his square shield. In that instant the young Wolf slashed upward with the lethal edge of his own shield, exactly as he'd been taught. The Olan tumbled backward with a cut throat.

The Olans at the river's edge couldn't retreat farther. Cooler heads were forming shield walls, settling the rattled troops. Forewarned units tumbled out of the boats in armor, ready to fight. Bending under the continuing lash of the slingstones, the Olan regiments seemed to be coiling.

Gan signaled Emso.

Slingstones began arcing back toward the Wolves, as well as arrows. Something else glinted ominously, flying from the Olan ranks. Gan recognized them as chings, the razor-edged throwing disks. A full six inches across, they could behead a man if they hit just right. Any blow guaranteed a nasty wound.

A Wolf fell. Another. The field was carpeted with Olan casualties—he estimated at least three hundred—but they could afford twice that many. The Wolves could spare none.

"Get back," he muttered, not hearing Raggar's sympathetic growl. "Fall back now, Clas." He was pleading, his hands clenched in helpless fists.

The earlier fiery elation turned to a cold bitterness on his tongue. He spat continuously despite a raging thirst, trying to get rid of that taste. His men were dying, his Wolves, who expected him to lead them to victories and glory. He imagined he could identify individual cries of the wounded, and heard himself screaming wordless, mindless rage.

And then he was calm, his nara gripping firmly. What had been bitter was no longer, but the cold remained.

He mounted his horse, spurring it to where his units waited for him. Storming up to them, he saw their eyes, orbs of raw fear behind the fake ferocity of their masks. To those close enough to hear, he said, "Your comrades have done their work well. The Olan's are regaining their balance now. We'll strike in a few minutes, along with Tate's force. Then Emso will come in."

The ones who heard shook their murdats. It was an eerie, almost soundless enthusiasm; they knew surprise was their most precious weapon, and only silence could protect it. A muted buzz ran through the unit as the information filtered from one man to the next.

By the time Gan eased to a hidden observation post at the edge of the forest, the elements of Clas' strike force were literally running from the enemy. The Olans were barely under control, eager to overtake the upstarts that had hurt and embarrassed them. Horns and whistles sounded commands to close formations or slow the advance. They went unheeded.

Gan's lighter-armed and quicker men stayed far enough ahead to avoid close work, all the while maintaining a galling hail of slingstones and arrows. Soon, however, they were nearing the looming forest border of the field. The Olans redoubled their efforts to overtake.

At Clas' signal the men slowed, formed in defensive ranks. A cheer went up from the Olans when they saw their quarry would stand.

Gan thought of a prairie dog he'd watched try to escape a bear. Caught away from its burrow, it ran until the bear overtook it. Then it turned, raising on its hind legs, chittering defiance and terror. It nipped the bear's nose, and the prairie calm shattered at the bear's unbelieving roar of pain.

It swatted the small animal once.

The final image was clearest of all in his mind as the bulk of the Olan armored infantry clattered forward to claim their vengeance.

Olan cavalry, riding hard, swept up from behind the infantry and passed them, eager to be the first to strike. A few Wolves raced away to the rear. The Olan infantry cheered again at the sight, failing to notice that the runners stopped short of the forest. They were also too excited to worry about the sudden gaps in the cavalry ranks when the slingers littered the field with the spiked balls. Horses tumbled. Many of the riders failed to rise again.

At Gan's quick hand signal, an archer in hiding released a whistling arrow, then a smoke arrow. They were such small specks in the panorama of the battle that Gan was afraid they'd be lost. He was vastly relieved to see movement as Emso's cavalry headed for the river in response.

Gan directed his detachment forward at a rapid trot. The noises of battle and the drone of Olan war horns drew them forward in crouching anticipation, and the accumulated sound of their passage through the forest was a vast, anxious whisper. Not until they were clear of the trees and actually in the field did the mass of Olans even suspect their presence. At the sight of them, the cheering checked. The war horns and whistles signaled urgently.

Then Tate's wing appeared on the other side of the field.

They, too, appeared in grim silence, advancing rapidly.

To the front of the Olan forces Clas' men drew abreast of the men who'd run away earlier. Suddenly the mass of Wolves were lining up between them, where they held fast. At a whistle signal, they knelt to the ground in the face of the cavalry nearly on them. As if by magic, they formed a wall, raising the huge spears that had remained hidden at their feet until that moment. The longest, held by the men in the rear rank, were fully twenty feet long. The first and second ranks held correspondingly shorter ones, so that when the spear butts were braced against the earth, the points were a uniform barrier of waiting steel. Unable to stop, and with many too brave to try, the first horsemen crashed into it. Those behind them piled into them. Instantly, the Wolves were into the tangle of struggling men and horses, murdats flashing.

The Olan infantry's triumphant cries took on a different, confused tone as the Wolf units closed on both their eastern and western flanks. Worse, the surviving cavalry bolted in retreat, spurring through the milling troops as they tried desperately to rally their formations.

That was when Emso's men, howling, charged their rear. Simultaneously, Gan and Tate struck. Arrows and slingstones hummed overhead. Clas advanced as well, many of his men now mounted on Olan horses, their spears turned to devastating lances.

Surrounded, crushed against themselves, the superior numbers of the Olans were worse than useless. Those on the fringes fought well, but they were beset by men who'd seen their people and land tormented too often.

It was more than a defeat, it was massacre. The Wolves attacked at first with the ferocity of men who knew they must win or die, then with the abandon of men discovering that they need not be forever beaten.

Gan signaled with more smoke arrows, directing Emso to open the way to the river, and the first Olans warily eased away toward what they believed to be escape. The crush of men in the trap felt the easing pressure at their rear. Automatically they moved in that direction. A war horn blared to maintain order. A war drum's command created a rallying center. Gan shouted at his dogs, hurtling into the melee with them, determined to silence it. With Raggar roaring at his side, Shara and Cho guarding his rear, he saw the first man to stand against him clearly; after that, they were a blur—a sword to block, an exposed place to strike. He was instinct and training, more a force than a man. His Wolves saw, howled approval, redoubled their efforts.

Gan cut his way to a knot of men. One of them held the war horn high, trumpeting instructions. The drum was next to him on a stand. Oblivious to everything else, the drummer sent out his message. Another man, wearing armor far more ornate than any Gan had seen before, thrust himself forward to protect those two. He was an excellent fighter, and he battled with the fury of a proud man who knows his cause is lost. A command to the dogs protected Gan's rear and flanks, leaving him free to engage the officer. It was well they did. Twice Gan's armor saved him; a blow at his throat nearly cut his war mask in half. Both he and his opponent had to dodge a secondary struggle as Raggar and Cho eliminated a spearman in a tumbling, screaming muddle. Then Gan saw his opening. His man knew it as soon as Gan did, and he was shouting a denial before the murdat cut him down. With the same momentum, Gan whirled and slashed the drum. The man carrying the war horn threw it to the ground and fell on top of it, covering his head with his hands. Gan edged back out of the melee as a howling cheer burst from the Wolves. The collapse of the Olans was a visible thing, a shudder through the units like ripples in water.

Panic was the Wolves' ally, and she clawed the Olans mercilessly.

The numbers streaming through the opening Emso created for them grew. In minutes they were a flood.

The Wolves pressed after them, hanging on the flanks, destroying the brave few who tried to cover the retreat that quickly became a mindless rout.

And carnage.

When Gan directed the Wolves to break off, no more than two hundred Olan survivors huddled on the riverbank.

Leaving a silent, menacing guard over the shattered remnant of the Olans, the Wolves moved back across the battlefield, picking up their own dead and wounded; Tate brought up the rear. She was alone when she discovered the body of the fallen Olan commander with his helmet beside him. Its gold and silver trim was scratched and dented. She dismounted and picked it up. For a few moments she turned it idly, thinking how much it resembled similar objects she'd seen in museums and history books. Looking away from it, she gazed across the battlefield's destruction. Without the fear and excitement of combat, it was mindlessness. It was the world she'd fled.

She wondered about the others, and a weight of loneliness threatened to crush her. How were the other women? Was Falconer schooling the Olans as she was the Wolves? If he was, would they find themselves fighting each other?

She thought of Jones, her sole contact with the truth of her existence. And he was going mad. Suddenly, irresistibly, she had to try to let her friends know where she was and what she was doing. Drawing her bayonet, she considered scratching a message on the helmet, then stopped. Writing would be too revealing simply by its existence. She had to think of a way to speak only to her people. Two Wolves passed her, chattering excitedly. Although she heard little of what they said, it was enough to solve her problem. With the tip of her bayonet she scratched an ugly, but anatomically explicit cow. To the right of that, she drew two quill pens.

Gan had decreed no looting or mutilations, although all weapons and armor were to be collected. Unwounded prisoners were to be allowed to join the forces of Harbundai or be assigned to work gangs; there would be no abuse. Wounded were to be returned to Ola. As for the dead, men were already gathering wood for the ceremonial pyres.

She turned her attention to the rest of the gear belonging to the man at her feet, and she noticed he was lying with one arm covering a knife on his belt. Squirming inwardly, she detached it and its scabbard. According to Gan, Bilsten mentioned a knife that strongly suggested a bribe paid to the Olan commander. She stuffed it inside her armor jacket, then continued on. Her thoughts returned to the helmet, and she wondered if her decision about it might be something she'd regret. What she was doing could be seen as communicating with the enemy.

She sought out Emso and awkwardly thrust the helmet at him. "I want this to go back to Ola with the wounded prisoners." He said nothing. Her explanation burst out. "Make sure it gets to their king. It'll tell him we killed his commander here." By now Emso was turning the thing over and over in his hands. At the sight of the scratching, he was suddenly concerned. Anger glinted in his eyes when he looked his question at Tate. She spread her hands in helpless pleading. "It's a message, Emso. My friends there'll understand. No one else will, I swear. I want them to know I'm alive, that's all. If they are," she finished, dropping her gaze to the ground.

Emso asked, "Why would your friends see this?"

She brightened again. "The King would keep them close, wouldn't he? And even if he didn't, people will talk about the symbols. Everyone'll be curious about them. My friends will hear, for certain."

"Not that certain."

"All right, then—not that certain. But it's a chance. Please, Emso; for a friend?"

"Gan's friend to both of us. Said he didn't want the Olans knowing you were about."

"The Olans won't. Only my friends. What can it hurt?"

"Don't know." He frowned at the helmet, blaming it, then he was staring into her eyes. "I'll think about it. You're never to mention it again, understood? You don't tell anyone else, you never ask me what I decided. None of this ever happened."

Unspeaking, she nodded. Emso's stiffness as he turned away shamed her, and she half raised a hand at his retreating back before letting it fall to her side. When she did, the knife in its scabbard shifted under her armor, reminding her that she harbored still another secret.

She told herself the knife was a legitimate souvenir, the spoils of war. The whole thing about the helmet was just a gamble, at best. Emso might pitch it in the river; she'd never know. There wasn't even any guarantee anyone would catch the significance of the message. The whole thing was in the hands of fate.

Nevertheless, she felt dirty.

On her way to rejoin Gan, she caught a glimpse of movement on the far shore. It was unclear, a suggestion of something that didn't belong. She was surprised at how nervous it made her, that the furtiveness of it sent sharp, tingling sensations running across her joints. She tried to appear as if she wasn't watching, and was rewarded by seeing a figure on horseback slip across an open space. Suddenly she was seeing more of them, at least twenty.

Their manner puzzled her. The Olans at their launch site, a few hundred yards downstream, made no attempt to hide. This mounted group was different. They filtered through the forest like wild creatures who expected to be unobserved. And then she knew who they were. Devil warriors.

She raced to tell Gan, describing their location without pointing, and was humbled by how easily he picked them out. Clas was even better at it, counting their numbers as if they were on parade. Neither said much, although Clas suggested they might as well remount the cavalry and run them down. Gan dismissed the suggestion, and then Tate remarked that they must have heard the battle and ridden to investigate.

Gan shook his head. He seemed pleased about something. "They were here," he said. "I thought they would be." He nodded, confirming something in his own mind.

Tate wondered what it might be. Of one thing she was certain—he'd already planned his next move.

CHAPTER 57

The victory celebration began with the appearance of the first returning Wolves as they marched clear of the forest on the final leg of their return. People lined the road from that point to the walls of the castle. Emso and his cavalry led the column. The cheers of the crowd were a substitute for the rest they hadn't had since the battle ended; heads rose, backs straightened. They grinned at friends, relatives, and everyone else. When the infantry appeared, the cheers continued, rising to a crescendo when Gan, who rode at their head, drew his murdat and waved it, then pointed it at the men. The troops drew their own weapons to wave them then, and when one began to pound a cadence on his shield, the idea spread quickly. Soon the entire body moved to the clash of steel on steel, and their chanted "Murdat! Murdat!" threatened to drown out the spectators until they, too, took up the cry.

Gan absorbed it all. There would never be another moment such as this, he realized. More battles, certainly; never another first victory. His vision seized on details and fixed them in his mind. He discovered he could close his eyes for a moment and recall individual characters vividly. A girl, long hair flying, skirt billowing, flew from the mass and shoved past two ranks of soldiers to reach the man she wanted. She kissed him with quick passion before scampering back where she belonged, and by the time she disappeared into the crowd, she was blushing with a color that would daunt any rose. A small boy raced out to touch Gan's boot, blinking up at him with a combination of trepidation and adulation that made Gan laugh out loud.

An older, worried face scanned the oncoming ranks. The woman, gray-haired, had her hand on the shoulder of a man as troubled and aged as herself, and she strained to remain on tiptoe. Gan was sure it was her husband, and he turned to see if any of the troops responded. One did, a squad leader. For a second the soldier's eyes met hers, then her husband's. Sadly, solemnly, he shook his head. After that he looked directly forward, refusing to look their way again even when he passed so close they could have touched. The constant roar of celebration drowned out the anguish Gan saw pour from the open mouth in the old woman's agonized features. The husband wrapped his arms around her to keep her erect. Tears streamed unhindered down his cheeks.

This is what we do, Gan thought. Every victory is marred by its terrible, soul-cracking defeats. We try to forget them, because if we don't fight, we become slaves. And yet the old woman and her husband are slaves now, imprisoned by loss.

He thought of his father, dead at the hand of his own people because he'd been wise enough to construct peace with honor.

Someone in the crowd called his name, and he glanced that way, waving automatically, and realized his thoughts had brought a frown with them. He forced a smile, and told himself he should leave off thinking about things that confused the main issue.

The sight of the old couple had shaken his enjoyment, however. His mind would no longer be placated by the sweetness of acclaim. It drifted on to different troubles.

The Devils had expected to combine with Ola in a surprise strike and an easy conquest. The Wolves had shown them that both were impossible. Unfortunately, the Dog People would feel the backlash of that disappointment. Every sign they'd seen on the escape to Harbundai indicated that King Altanar had planned to have the Devils ambush the Dog warriors as they crossed one of the passes toward Harbundai. A Devil victory there would have swept the Dogs from the board, allowing Ola to expand into their territory as soon as Harbundai was brought under control. The Devils were prepared for a war and loot. It would be up to Altanar to fight beside them

or lose them as allies. The only likely victims for their combined enmity were
the Devils' traditional enemies, the tribe they hated most of all.

Winter would be harsher than usual for the Dogs.

He thought of them. His people. He remembered the pain of the old
woman. Had she lost a son? A grandson? How many Dog women would
suffer identically that winter?

He remembered the feeling of utter waste that came over him at the sight
of the Baron's castle guard of youngsters, cut down by the slavers. Interrogat-
ing prisoners after the battle confirmed certain suspicions. The attack that
killed the Baron's two older sons was launched because the Olans knew the
Harbundai units were unprepared and undermanned. More than that, three
days before the attack, a squad of their cavalry was sent to the ferry crossing
where the battle with the Wolves was fought. Their missions: provide security for a returning slave party, and scout the area for a large-unit crossing.

The Olans also knew their general had actively worked to convince Altanar that a combined attack by Olan troops and Mountain warriors on Jalail
would lead to the fall of Harbundai. The general had insisted he lead it
himself. The prisoners were sure he'd suggested the Bear Paw ferry attack
after the skirmish with Harbundai in the eastern barony.

Later, when Tate handed him the jeweled shortsword, Gan had the
answer to the general's behavior. At the first look, he knew it was the weapon
of Bilsten's tale, the treasure that had been used to bribe him. The blade
for the first attempt, the scabbard to finish the job.

Gan carried it under his jacket now.

The appearance of the Baron and the official greeting party interrupted
his thoughts, and the sight of Neela chased everything else from his mind.
She wore riding trousers and a blouse of a black-red color that made him
think of sun-warmed blackberries. Against the fall chill, she'd draped herself
in a cloak of bright yellow. Others wore equally bright colors, but to Gan
she stood out, unique. He didn't know how long she'd been waving at him
before he stirred himself to return it, but by then most of the troops were
waving at someone, and his was one arm among the hundreds.

The party was a brave sight, alive with color and action. The Baron's
personal insignia, a spread-winged raven against a white background, billowed in the brisk wind. The truth was, Gan didn't approve of the Harbundai
banners. They were cloth, forming a square with sides about the length of
a man's arm. Braces at top and bottom held them rigid at the top of their
carrying staff; this made them difficult to handle in the wind, as the staggering bearers illustrated. Carried facing the enemy, they were easily recognized
from front or back, but impossible to read from the flanks. They did little
more than identify the force to the enemy, and served as a dependable guide

only to troops far in the rear. Wryly Gan thought that too often in the past that had been the eagerly sought position of the Baron's men. The Wolves carried much smaller, unbraced banners. They were long and narrow, more easily rolled and hidden until needed for action. Once unfurled, they didn't get in the way.

In response to the Baron's approach, Gan signaled that his wolf's head standard be presented. He affected not to hear the louder cheer that greeted the snarling mask as it lofted upward at the head of the full five-hundred-man division. The Baron heard, and across the fifty yards still separating them, Gan saw him stiffen in his saddle.

Reining up, the Baron halted his group, allowing the mounted band to ride around them and take up position to the side. The war drums took up the cadence of the Wolves, adding their rumble to the crashing of swords on shields, and the brass trums brayed their welcome. It was the first time Gan had seen the barony display all its pomp, and he was impressed. The horses gleamed in polished gear, the musical instruments flashed in the thin fall sunshine, and the ornate costumes of the Baron's nobles seemed to glow. Even the troops looked better, he thought, as he glanced around. Several were surreptitiously trying to wipe smudges from jackets or flicking mud off boots or shields.

He made a mental note to prepare for ceremonial entries in the future.

Emso wheeled the cavalry away from the band, then turned it, so that Gan rode up to the Baron between the two units. He halted and gave the closed-fist salute. In the background he saw Neela smiling and waving. Sylah was beside her, much more composed, but her eyes were only on Clas.

The troops stopped their racket, and the war drums paused. An expectant silence followed, and then the war drums throbbed mightily, giving way to a flourishing salute by the trums. The Baron nodded, and Gan advanced alone as the music stopped. His horse capered excitedly, full of the moment. The dogs, in contrast, shambled along as if bored.

Gan expected no warm greetings from the Baron, and received none. Austere, the Baron complimented him and the Wolves on behalf of himself and the entire barony. The only time his eyes showed anything but suppressed anger was when he mentioned that a Messenger had arrived from the King the previous day. He brought a warning that Olan forces might move into the vicinity of the ferry crossing on the Bear Paw River. The King had also assured him the Olan force was minimal, but that he was sending reinforcements under the command of his nephew "to assure stability in the barony." The Baron went on, "It pleased me to send the Messenger back with the information that three Olan divisions had attempted to invade Harbundai and been destroyed, and that I felt quite able to defend my land.

Two tells me the 'reinforcements' have already turned around."

"Your men fought well," Gan said. "We lost only nineteen dead, twenty-three wounded. All but seven of the wounded will fight again. It was a fortunate day."

"Miraculous," the Baron corrected. "I want to hear the details. Come to my quarters when you've rested. We'll talk. Two nights from now will be the official celebration. My people have hungered for a victory for a long time."

At Gan's salute he wheeled his horse and made his way through the opening the entourage cleared for him. Gan gestured for Neela to go to the billeting area, ignoring the knowing smiles and smirks of the watchers.

The Wolves had expected none of the ceremony that greeted them, and now, marching at ease, they talked animatedly about it, about the upcoming festivities, and about their part in the battle. Gan was amused to hear how much greater it seemed as they rehearsed the stories they'd tell. By the time they reached the housing area, he would have sworn they'd defeated at least twice as many divisions, and in half the time.

He saw to the hospitalization of the wounded and the final orders to the troops. As much as he disliked doing it, he directed that security not be allowed to fall off. The established patterns of nightwatch would be maintained. The major difference between nightwatch in the barony and the routine of the Dog People was the lack of dogs. To compensate for loneliness, the Wolves stood nightwatch in threes, one man awake at all times. The troops grumbled, but they'd done the impossible; now they would accept the disagreeable.

Gan was delighted at the tone of their complaining. His father had always said no man is as indomitable as one who's proving he can accept abuse and triumph over it. He wished Col could listen to this lot; he'd expect them to want to conquer the world.

Neela swept into the small hut he used as command headquarters, and imitated the Wolves' salute. He grinned up at her, returning it with mock solemnity. She said, "Is this what I have to do to get your attention? Should I bang a sword on a shield to make you remember I'm waiting for you? There's nothing more for you to do here. Come back to the castle. Now."

He rose with a leap. "As you command. But only if we walk. I want to be alone with you as long as possible."

She smiled and hurried outside without answering, and when he followed, puzzled, he found her tying Sunflyer's reins to his tent-pennon staff. "I'll send someone after him," she said, looping her arm through his.

On the way to the castle she asked about the battle's conduct. She listened without interrupting, saving her questions for when he paused, or was about to move to another phase of the action. Finally, when she was satisfied that she knew what had been done, she asked about his personal participation. He explained that his function was to assure that all had gone according to plan before he could even consider participating. He spoke of the charge to quiet the Olan war horn, neglecting to mention that he cut down the commander, essentially sealing the fate of the battle, in the process.

He told her of the shortsword, explaining how Tate had found it and brought it to him, adding his belief that it was the same weapon used to bribe the Olan commander, as Bilsten had described. As he finished they were about to enter the castle, but instead of heading directly for the gateway, he led her to the side. Facing the wall, protected from view in all directions, he pulled the scabbard from under his jacket and showed it to her, gratified to see that it was as compelling as he remembered. Without being aware of it, he bent his shoulders forward, as if he'd draw himself around the weapon in a protective circle of his own flesh.

He partially drew the blade from the ornate scabbard, so she could admire the steel, and it was only when he turned to see her reaction that he became aware of her misgivings. There was no discernible change in her face or voice, but he sensed a confusion and resistance in her, as if she'd seen something repellent and couldn't bring herself to turn away from it.

It made no sense; there was nothing to see but the rich beauty of the weapon, yet he couldn't get rid of the feeling that something had disturbed her deeply.

As he replaced it she added to his puzzlement by smiling up at him and taking his arm once more, leading him off to the castle gate while she spoke softly of her pleasure in seeing him ride up. "You looked wonderful," she said. "I was as happy for you as I was happy to see you come back safe, I think. That doesn't sound quite right, but what I mean is that I know how much it means to you to grow strong enough to avenge your father."

They were inside the walls by then, besieged by shouts of welcome and greeting. Hugging his arm, she applied a gentle pressure, and he went along more than gladly until they were inside and away from the well-wishers. Someone was showering as they passed the shower room, and suddenly he was exhausted, as if the stresses he'd been denying since he rode out of here to go to battle had caught up to him all at once. The sound and smell of the rushing water tore through the wall of denial he'd built around his fatigue over the past several days, and he stumbled.

Neela's strength steadied him, and she tilted her head to ask, "How much sleep have you had?"

"I don't know," he said, thinking the lie wasn't important. It wouldn't please her to know he'd slept only three hours of any twenty-four since he'd left, and only once had he felt confident enough to sleep for two hours consecutively. At her frown, he added, "There was a lot to oversee. I'll rest now, before dinner."

"You certainly will," she said, her tone scolding. She practically shoved him into his quarters, waiting until he came out in a robe. "You shower," she ordered, "and I'll be back before you're finished."

He was too weary to ask where she was going. Still, when he was on his way back to his room, she came hurrying down the passageway, carrying a small bag. "What's that?" he asked, suspicious; she had a motherly look that made him nervous.

Her answer didn't help. "This will make you feel much better," she said, and followed him into his room. When he found out he wasn't going to have to swallow some foul-tasting medicine, he was relieved, and allowed her to turn him around and make him lie on his bed. He made a show of protest though actually much intrigued and vastly pleased by the attention. She pulled the robe off his shoulders, baring his arms and upper torso, then climbed on the bed, kneeling between his legs to massage his back and neck. The bag held scented oils, and he luxuriated in the pressure of her fingers, amazingly strong, as they reached deep into his muscles and kneaded pain and discomfort away, leaving a drained, spent feeling behind that was almost hypnotic. The room filled with the aromatic tang of the cedar-scented oil.

She talked as she worked, almost as if she were alone, but in the one corner of his mind that remained alert, he realized she was making suggestions without being intrusive. She spoke of the implications of the Baron's dual victory over Ola and his own king. It would be a while before any of the other barons would want to disturb him; they'd be afraid of him now. There would be many councils and secret discussions to redraw the lines of power. While king and barons were arguing might be a good time to strike at the Devils in their new war camp. They were the most likely danger at present.

She paused for a moment, and even as he struggled against the languor overtaking him, he hoped she'd continue. A new scent drifted through the room, and it took him a moment to identify it as the softer smell of balsam. Somehow, she'd heated the oil, and where he'd felt she was gripping his muscles before, now the sense of her eased through skin, flesh, and blood, taking away not only pain, but concern.

Her voice lost consistency, became a distant hum. The aromatic richness pillowed his mind.

A sword flashed toward him. Shara leaped.

The presleep spasm nearly lifted him clear of the bed, and then he was gone. Neela rose carefully, plugging the bottles as she moved around to look at him while he slept. Taking a cloth from the sack, she wiped her hands, kneeling to bring her face close to his, inspecting the way his eyebrows seemed to swoop across his forehead and the way the new stubble of his whiskers caught the light, each one reflecting it in its turn as she moved slowly back and forth in front of his closed eyes. His lips were full, barely parted to reveal the strong, white teeth. Coming closer yet, she was aware of his breath. It had a thick, moist smell that made her think of animal strength and conjured unformed images of heaviness and muscularity, images even more suggestive than those that came to her while her fingers had probed and mapped the ridges of muscle under his surprisingly supple skin.

She closed the remaining distance between them, kissed him with the softest of touches, then quickly rose and hurried from the room.

Chapter 58

Gan sat with Neela at the Baron's table, finishing the dessert that marked the end of the meal. It was made of blueberries, baked inside a featherlight crust that flaked at a touch. The summery smell of the hot fruit blended with the honey-sweetened raspberry tea that accompanied it. The lively fragrance clashed with the almost palpable tension that had made the evening a stiff, difficult time. The Baron's wife had begged to be excused, pleading a headache. Conversation had limped, and on several occasions Neela's hand had sought his, curling in his grasp like some small, troubled thing seeking shelter.

Throwing himself heavily against the back of his chair, Baron Jalail raised his hands, then splayed them flat on the table. Gan was chagrined to realize he'd never noticed them before. Now he saw how large they were. Signs of great strength struggled to assert a presence almost obscured by fat. The roughened web between thumb and forefinger could only have come from hard sword work. It was losing tone, just as the callus was softening on the palm. Heavy knuckles were thick and stiff, and there was a wealed scar on the left hand. Altogether, they suggested loss, the erosion of once-solid determination by decades of compromise and uncertain maneuver.

Gan resolved to commit the lesson to memory.

The Baron said to Neela, "I asked you to come with Gan tonight because you're part of what I must face. I'm sure you heard I had a Messenger in here today. The King has canceled his visit—'matters of state interfere,' he said. That's a lie. It's been barely ten days since our men destroyed the Olan divisions, but everyone's heard about it. No one's willing to chance a fight with the Wolves. And that's the problem."

Puzzled, Gan waited for the explanation. Jalail said, "The Wolves feel nothing for me." He indicated Neela with a nod. "She and that black woman and the Priestess have their women selling the things they make in their own stores. I happen to know they've a plan to buy a boat so they can send merchandise directly to the Inland Sea. Your men and their women are the envy of the entire barony. And beyond. Yet no one celebrates *my* name." His breath wheezed when he paused.

Gan tried to keep the hurt from his voice. "We're your people. Your men know who approved the women's plan. And as the women earn money, they build your strength. The battle at the Bear Paw was fought to benefit you."

"To benefit me? It was fought without my permission! Am I to merely watch what happens in my own barony? Am I to have no feelings except gratitude? And what of the madman, Jones? He moves to confront Church—how does that benefit me?"

"You don't like Church. You said so." Neela's soft-spoken determination pulled his head around to her. He glowered. "I don't want a brawl with them. I'm already harboring a renegade Priestess."

"Church may not cast her out. Then you'll be in their good graces."

"You omit the alternative, child." He redirected his attention to Gan. "Don't misunderstand. I trust you completely. Right now. Sooner than you think, however, the King will suggest that you might be more comfortable if you didn't have to answer to me. He'll lure you with dreams of independence, then trap you in a spider's web of alliances. You mean to destroy the man who stole your father's position. To do it, you need men. A base." He paused, searching Gan's face with sad, understanding eyes. His brief smile opened his face like a wound. "Poor Gan. You want so much, and you're just learning how cruel you must be to take it. In the meantime, you'll serve me. But the King *will* offer his golden hand."

Gan inhaled noisily. "No man who wants to live will try to bribe me."

The Baron laughed. "He's puzzling over what to offer you already. Never forget; I don't fear your ambition, I fear his."

"I could never betray a man who's been so good to me."

"Minds such as yours put together such words with ease. Minds such as mine believe them with difficulty." The sadness reclaimed the Baron's eyes. "Never mind. I always say these things badly."

Neela asked, "Has the King complained about the women's self-support work?"

"Not yet. He's aware, of course, and disapproves. If his mother . . ." He shrugged. "Two tells me she's very excited by your little effort." The round face wrinkled in a bitter frown that unmistakably expressed his feelings for the Queen Mother's attitude. Gan was ready to let the whole matter pass when the Baron added, "The King's not ready to prohibit the work yet."

Gan bristled. "Prohibit? The Wolves will have something to say about that. So will I."

"Those women are breaking customs we've always followed. Not even Church suggests such radical changes."

Unimpressed, Gan said, "Customs that don't have any purpose deserve to be broken."

Very softly the Baron said, "I'm sure that's exactly what Faldar Yan told himself while he plotted your father's downfall." When Gan started out of his chair, he waved him back almost carelessly. "Never attack the truth, and never forget that ambition always finds reasons to justify its actions. It would sadden me to lose the friendship of a young man who makes me think my sons would have grown to be like him. And now I think we end our conversation."

Gan agreed gladly. These weren't new thoughts for him, but coming in another's voice made them harder to accept. It was as if the Baron had wormed into his thoughts, saw too much of him.

When he caught Neela's glance at him as they walked the hall toward their quarters, he realized she was studying him, as well, and his heart sank at the prospect that she might see into him as easily as the Baron. Just as quickly, he realized that was impossible. If she could, she'd know how he felt about her, and he'd seen nothing he could believe was a sign of that.

She liked him. She trusted him. In time she might even recover from her involvement with Clas. Life would be complete if she'd ever care for him similarly.

He must be patient. He could win warmth and affection, if he couldn't win love.

She smiled up at him when he took her hand in his. He made a small joke about the Baron's nervousness, and she laughed easily. There was concern in her comment, however; she sympathized with the man, she said, because the loss of his children was so devastating. And retaining his lands would be a terrible struggle. She squeezed Gan's hand, telling him she hoped neither of them would ever get caught up in that sort of scheming.

The realization that they already were caught up in the Baron's plans, as well as their own, struck them both simultaneously, and there was no more conversation until they exchanged subdued good nights at her door.

In his own room Gan sent his servant off for the night. With the man gone and the heavy plank door securely barred, Gan went to the rough desk under the room's solitary window and drew out an object wrapped in cloth. When he let what was inside tumble free, it burst into the light like living, multicolored flame. The bejeweled scabbard and ivory handle of the knife from the battlefield gleamed up at him. It was cool on his damp palm when he picked it up.

It was indeed a handsome bribe.

Gems and metals made the scabbard and handle precious. The value of the blade, despite its ornamentation, lay in its cold menace, however. A full foot long, it was thick-spined, razor sharp. The steel was unlike anything he'd ever seen, the cutting edge marked by a sinuous line that made him think of the round-topped standing waves of a river. It ran the length of the blade, and the portion above the line was a subtly different color. The change spoke to him of secrets, of hidden knowledge, just as the river's murky waves kept its depths unknown.

Polished, honed, the knife played with light as a child plays with fire.

Gan held it toward the candles, moving it through abbreviated slashes and thrusts. The movements were short and swift, the muscles in forearm and hand bunched hard. Still, his expression was distant, and his eyes had a smoky, sensual look. The soft reflection from the blade danced on the dark stone walls until he resheathed it. He deliberately let a finger slide on the edge, opening a tiny slit that released a single drop of blood.

When the knife was safely tucked away, he continued to stare at the wooden face of the drawer.

Again, as he had every night since Tate gave him the weapon, he told himself he should give it to the Baron. At the very least he should tell him Bilsten verified it was the one the King's nephew had used to bribe the Olan general.

He knew he wouldn't. Every night it was easier to admit he never would.

He wanted it. He wished there were two, so he could give one to Clas. He knew no other man who would understand how important it was to have such a weapon, how necessary it was to give proper honor to so terrible a beauty.

Baron Jalail would carry it to show people. The Olan fool who'd let it buy his integrity never even thought to use it, relying instead on a plain Olan sword that had the quality of a brick.

It must stay in hands that appreciated it.

Yet as he lay down to sleep, a small, sneering voice scraped at his consciousness. It, too, was a regular nightly companion, coming at the moment just before he fell asleep, when he was too disoriented to argue.

"Keep the knife," it whispered, raising gooseflesh on his arms. "You killed the man who fouled it by taking it as a bribe, didn't you? If you keep it, perhaps you'll confront the man who disgraced it by offering it as a bribe. It's correct for you to hold the knife, smarter still for you to hold its secret. Wise Gan, learning to protect his own back."

He went to sleep with sly laughter dying in his ears and his teeth clenched so hard his jaws hurt.

In a similar room Sylah sat in a bulky, straight-backed chair, her back to the door leading to the hall. There was a small table on her right, with burning candles, and she appeared to be leashed to the wall in front of her by a strange contraption of strings and square cards that tied to her belt. At least that was Clas' first impression when he entered. He stopped, staring, and she turned to look over her shoulder at him, then smiled.

"I'm weaving," she said, and his frown only darkened.

He said, "How? There's no loom. Are you all right?"

"Come." She gestured him forward, laughing, until he was kneeling beside her. She showed him how the warp threads, leading from a hook on the wall, ran through a hole in one of the cards. There were four holes in each card, and a total of twenty cards. The holes were all numbered, one through four, and she showed him how all were aligned so the numbers matched. Each strand of yarn—she called them all the "warp"—ran from the wall, through a hole in one card, then to the belt around her waist, where it was tied off. She turned the cards away from her all at once, as though they were all on a central axle. That created what she called a shed by lifting some warp strands while others remained in place. She pulled a separate strand—this one called the "woof"—through the gap. After turning the cards again, she pounded the resulting weave.

The pattern was a series of blue arrowheads on a red background. He grinned at her, proud of the effort. "It's too tricky for my hands, but you do it perfectly. Look, you even made it go backward—half the design points one way, half the other."

She kissed his cheek. "It has to be that way. Card-weaving makes the thread twist around itself, so every so often I have to turn the cards in the opposite direction. That reverses the pattern. See how simple it is?"

"For you. It makes my head ache to think about it. I'm happy just to look at the finished product. And you." He rose, went to another chair a few feet away, taking an apple from the basket on the cabinet where he stowed his armor and weapons. The fruit broke with a loud crack when he bit into it, and she turned at the sound.

He said, "I've been trying to figure out why you fell in love with me."

She felt her face burning, and she almost lost the tension in the card-weaving band by standing up, catching herself just in time. Her voice caught, coming out as a shocked squeak. "Clas! Of all the vain, self-centered, arrogant—" She stopped in mid-outburst, checked as much by her own search for words as his wide-eyed surprise.

Swallowing a heroic mouthful of apple, he rushed to explain. "Not like that! I mean, I've been thinking about Gan. I think he's unhappy, or not as happy as I am, and I know why I am, and I think that's why he's not."

Carefully she said, "Do I know what you said?"

"Us." He gestured with the apple, took another, smaller bite. "We have each other. Gan and Neela seem to get close, but there's something missing. And both of them are acting—I don't know—different."

She started detaching herself from the weaving, using the time to prepare her response. "You're right. I think she had some plans for you, once."

The black tattoo nearly disappeared in the flush of color to his cheeks. "She had her pick of every man in the tribe. She'd never look at me."

"Oh? And I would?"

She wouldn't have believed he could actually grow even darker red. He tried to speak, failed, tried again. "Don't be like that, Sylah. You know what I meant." He threw up his hands. "How'd this happen? All I wanted was to ask you how we could find a woman for him. Now I don't even know what I mean."

"I do." She went to him, sat on his lap. "I think I always know what you mean, my Clas, even if I don't always understand the words you use." She drew his shortknife and took the apple, cutting slices for each of them as she went on. "How has Gan been different?"

"He's growing. Not just size, although sometimes I think that's happening, too. You can see by the way he grabs ideas, by the way he gets inside the men and understands their problems. You know what he did today? We lost two married men at the Bear Paw. Both widows have two kids. He visited our weavers' workhouse today. The woman in charge suggested the widows bring their children there every morning, and they could take care of all the weavers' children during the day. Gan agreed on the spot. The new widows don't have to go to the lockup and their children don't have to go live with someone else. Believe me, the Wolves are happy about it."

"If he's doing so well, why are you worried?"

He described outbursts of temper, periods of withdrawal, and, most disturbing, incidents of what sounded like deep depression.

She decided it was the weight of responsibility growing on him, and was startled again to think how little time had passed since the young warrior had so boldly risen to confront her on that cold, frightening prairie. Gan had indeed grown, and was still growing, but his burdens were multiplying in size and number.

She kissed Clas' forehead and returned to her weaving, seeking relaxation in the orderly repetitions.

A smile pulled at her mouth as she thought of Gan's visit to the weavers. He'd never know how hard Tate worked to plant the idea of the visit in his mind, or how hard they'd all rehearsed the little scene where the woman would suggest the widows act as keepers for the children.

Clas gave her no time to dwell on their small triumph. Hands on her shoulders, he bent to her ear and spoke of his need for a good night's sleep. She laughed aloud at the utter failure of what he thought was subtlety, leaning against his presence. For a few moments she put him off with teasing insistence that sleep would indeed be better for him than what he obviously had in mind. With unassailable logic she threw his words back at him, telling him that it was he who mentioned sleep, and if he felt that way about it, then sleep was what he should have. It delighted her that he enjoyed the sparring as much as she, that he sought and found pleasure in anticipation. As she freed herself once again from the backstrap and its woven band, she wondered at the contradictions in him, the clumsy strength that somehow translated to adroitness when they made love. Who was the inarticulate brawler whose normal means of expression was shouted orders, and what happened to that man when she was with the one who inexplicably found exactly the right, tender, flaming words that set her own blood burning through her veins?

Then she was free of restraint and in his arms, under his hands, and her robe was falling to the floor and there were no more questions.

The following morning they made their way together to the kitchen. She saw he was still uncomfortable with the eating arrangements, and once again suggested they could use the fireplace in their house.

He said, "The Baron insists. I suspect some of the nobles have convinced him I should make a daily appearance. Someday I'll find out. For now, it keeps the peace."

She dropped the subject. Until leaving Ola, she'd never known anything but communal meals, so it wasn't a problem for her. In fact, she rather enjoyed going into the kitchen with its mouth-watering smells and appetizing sights. She especially liked the enormous copper pots, all bright and shining, bubbling with stews or soups. The food itself was intriguing, the heavy strings of aromatic onions and garlic, the bright orange of carrots opposed by the brisk green of broccoli or chard or the softer tint of lettuce. And the mornings always featured bread; there was no finer aroma, she decided, surreptitiously pinching a piece from an unwatched loaf.

The difference between the kitchen at the abbey and this one was that one chose the food in the Baron's castle. Eggs were prepared to order, there was a selection of fruit—fresh in season, preserved if out—and usually there were what the people of Harbundai called jacks. She knew them as cakes, which was the correct name, of course. Where Clas' people came up with the term wheats she couldn't imagine. In any case, they were all the same, and the sight of their flat round forms browning on a griddle convinced her she'd have them, and no argument.

A servant brought the meal on thick ceramic plates, along with heavy mugs of hot cider. For an instant Sylah remembered sharing the exotic osh with the Iris Abbess.

It was a bad memory for that place, turning the stone walls to imprisonment. Even the fire crackling in the large fireplace failed to cheer her, and the colors of the bright banners draping the chimney lost their vigor.

Clas noticed the change immediately. "What's wrong? Is it the food?"

"No. It's just a memory." For once she was glad of the class system that placed them at one of the court tables. Those used by the commoners and servants were too crowded for confidences.

"You were thinking about Ola."

Sometimes he was almost eerily perceptive. She nodded. He said, "Some of the things you've said about your life there—the way Church treated you, and the way they're treating you now . . ." He paused and shrugged. "It surprises me that you'd have any memories nice enough to make you look so sad."

"There were some good moments. None to compare with what I have now. And I'm not worried about what Church decides about me."

The confidence in her voice pleased her at first, and then she was quite startled to realize it was almost true. She applied herself to her meal quickly, withdrawing from Clas, anxious to examine this changing attitude.

It came from Bilsten's message, she was sure. Only the Abbess knew of her interest in the Door, and that meant she was the one who had entrusted the message to him.

For a moment she thought of Priestess Lanta of the Violet Abbey, who saw other's minds, saw pieces of the future. If Bilsten had similar powers . . . It was too frightening to contemplate. She forced her thoughts elsewhere.

The message was obviously stated as a riddle in order to prevent Bilsten from understanding its meaning. The trouble was, she wasn't certain of it, either.

When she'd finished eating, Clas said, "Do you want me to walk to the women's area with you?" She accepted the invitation, and was especially pleased when he understood she needed some quiet time within herself. As they approached the workplace, two women were already at work, loading pottery into a horse-drawn cart. The man who owned it looked at Clas, then at the women, then back to Clas before making a helpless gesture, as if silently asking for an explanation to cover a world going by too fast for him.

Sharing a grin with Sylah, Clas grew serious before saying, "I don't know exactly what's troubling you, and I promised myself I'd never ask you about the past. Don't think I fear it or don't care about it. I want you to come to me to talk about it when you decide it's time. You understand?"

"Yes. Thank you."

He squeezed her hands in his and left.

She was still watching him out of sight when the woman in charge of the weaving shop approached. On arriving, she leaned forward to speak confidentially. "There's a person to see you. Someone who claims to know you."

"Knows me? Here?"

"Come." The woman took her arm. "She has little time."

Sylah bit back questions, hurried along, aided by the woman's grip and long, country stride. Ducking through the low door of the pottery workshop, she glanced around. Everything looked perfectly normal, women at each wheel, more at tables applying designs to turned but unfired articles. Suddenly she was whirled around and almost thrown down on the seat of one of the wheels. A woman sat beside her, an apprentice, cleaning the equipment. The woman who'd brought Sylah in was leaving before she could ask questions.

The apprentice pulled her hood back, and Sylah barely repressed a shout of surprise as she stared into the eyes of Priestess Lanta. All she could think of to say was, "I was thinking of you just this morning!"

A smile tried to form on Lanta's face, but her nervousness overrode it. "I had to reach you. The Iris Abbess asked me."

Sylah interrupted. "You're here to explain the message?"

Lanta blinked. "I have only my own message. The Abbess managed to delay King Altanar's request to the Sister Mother that you be cast out. Now, because it's such a long trip, and so dangerous, no one will be sent until spring."

"What else? Nothing for me from her?" It took all Sylah's will to resist the urge to shake the answer from her.

"Of course." Lanta looked away, her eyes suddenly dull and vague. She went on, "She asked what I saw. I told her, 'Sylah will know shame and glory, loss and triumph. She will rise above destruction to creation.' " Her voice altered as she spoke, so that she finished in a thin whisper. Her head fell forward, the movement bringing the hood over her hair, so that in the gloom of the workshop, she looked like an unkempt bundle lost on the floor.

Sylah put her hands on Lanta's shoulders, straightened her up, brushed tears from her eyes. "Hush," she said. "You can only repeat what's revealed. The Iris Abbess asked you to See for her?"

"Yes. She's worried for you." She frowned. "I felt terrible when I had to tell her what the voice said, but she seemed almost pleased. When I asked her what she thought you must lose, she said she couldn't imagine. I don't want you to have to lose anything. I hate saying you will."

"She understands things we cannot. So, what brings you to this country?"

"My abbess sent me as missionary. When the Iris Abbess heard, she asked me if I could get here, and I said I'd try."

"You came so far out of the way? You'll be late arriving at New City. Your abbess—"

"You will do good things." She made a helpless, confused gesture. "What I see is frightening; it speaks of trial. Yet I *feel* good things will come from your work. Your abbess felt it long ago. She told me. A little risk to help you is nothing. My duty."

The shop manager was approaching at a run. Sylah read the urgency in her, and lifted Lanta to her feet. "Someone must be coming."

The woman, close enough to hear, nodded. "Out the back way," she snapped. "We'll take care of you."

She practically carried Lanta to two more women at the door, and they were all quickly out of sight. Sylah grabbed the manager. "Who's looking for her?"

"Her escort. They lost her three days ago. We'll see they get directions that'll help them find her this afternoon."

"What do you mean, 'we'? I don't understand. She's risked her life to come to me, and—"

The woman stopped her with a raised commanding hand. "Many people risked their lives to help her, many more still are. You say you don't understand; do you always understand everything you know? I think not."

"Who are you to speak of what I understand?"

Imperturbably, the woman said, "Nobody, true enough. But I think you should mind what you don't know, because there's a great deal of it, indeed."

When the woman turned her back and stalked away, Sylah was tempted to pursue her, but suddenly the uselessness of that, and of so many other things—of trying to decipher the riddle of the roses on her door, of the possible action of Church, of finding the meaning of Lanta's Seeing, of the mundane uselessness of trying to force this rawboned woman to confide in her—all crashed down on her, and she slumped back onto the potter's seat, cradling her head in her hands.

Lose.

Lose Clas? The Abbess? Her dream of the Door?

What could it be? Which could she sacrifice to avoid losing another?

CHAPTER 59

Small boys shouting woke Gan, and for a moment he was tense with the awareness that he'd slept far into daylight. He jerked upright with a hard knot of dread in his stomach, then realized where he was. He relaxed, chuckling to himself; he couldn't remember ever sleeping so in his life. Another first. Swinging his feet out of bed and onto the floor, he walked to the window to investigate the noise.

A group of boys had kites in the air, their colors sun-jeweled against the clean blue of the morning. They were small, unlike any he knew. Almost perfectly symmetrical diamonds, they swooped and dodged in a display of control he'd never seen before. The kites of his boyhood had soared. These were almost like birds at the end of a string, except that the boys directed them in their maneuvers. As he watched, one sent his blue diamond careering across the sky after a scarlet version that dove frantically in its attempt to escape. The tiny sound of their collision brought a cheer from the boys. A moment later the red one, staggering valiantly back aloft, launched a counterattack. The rip in its material whistled shrill defiance.

Pulling back from the window, he busied himself with getting ready for the day. Or what's left of it, he told himself, still amused by this difference in his schedule.

An hour later he was leaving the kitchen, and Neela appeared. They both struggled with a slight embarrassment, trying to gauge the other's thoughts. He glanced around quickly, determining they were alone, and took her in his arms, kissing her with a soundness that startled her rigid for a moment, and then she was returning it. When they parted, they continued to embrace, but scanned the hallway to see who might be watching. Seeing no one, they looked back at each other, then realized what they'd been doing and broke into laughter.

Gan spoke first. "Thank you for helping me yesterday."

She lowered her eyes. "I enjoyed it. You were so tired."

"I'm rested now. Ride with me. Did you get Sunflyer back?"

"Yes. He's in the stables. Where do you want to go?"

The words caught in his throat. "I don't care. So long as we're alone. I have to talk to you."

Stepping out of his arms, she took his hand in hers. "I've been wanting to talk to you, too," she said, and at her quick turn away, he read what he hoped was the same shyness, the same uncertainty he felt. The thought filled him with guilt. How could he be glad to see her feel as clumsy as he did? That wasn't what he wanted. He only hoped she was nervous because she was experiencing the same feelings he was. But that would mean she was as miserable as he was.

Why did it have to be so confusing? None of it made any sense at all. A few days ago he led hundreds of men into mortal combat, and the moments of uncertainty were frightening, but this was different. That was action. This was immobility. She never left his mind, and he couldn't seem to *do* anything about it. It was ludicrous. How could someone he'd known all his life, liked all his life, turn him into a gawking, mumbling bear cub? Especially someone so small. And so soft, and pretty.

All he wanted to do was tell her he loved her.

He tried to stop thinking. His knees were threatening to melt.

The stable hands saddled their horses while he made desperate small talk about the kites that were still slicing across the sky above them. He pointed out a woman selling cakes from a tray at her waist. He babbled enthusiastically about the unusual number of bees still around at this time of the year. She talked along with him, but he couldn't shake the feeling that beneath her quiet responses was a flood of laughter waiting to drown him. As they rode off he growled orders at the dogs in a tone that offended Raggar into a tail-down sulk. His mood improved rapidly as they rode out onto the lanes bisecting the fields. The freshening wind brought the cool taste of rain and the rustling sighs of an earth preparing for a winter's rest. Smoke boiled out of chimneys, adding the smell of burning alder and cedar. Just as they reached the bank of a small stream, a flight of geese approached. They heard them before they saw them, faint gabbling drifting down from their passage. Several flocks flew over, their vee formations wavering and rearranging so the entire sky seemed to be covered with unending writing.

He remarked on it to Neela. "The way the lines change—it always makes me think of the way Olans write things on paper. My father showed me a message done that way when I was a boy. Ever since, I watch the geese and swans and imagine they have their own language, and people aren't allowed to understand."

"Animals don't need language," she said as she was dismounting, and he followed suit, looking askance at her last comment. She smiled. "They don't have to talk. Your dogs know when you're happy or angry. Sunflyer can see me a hundred yards away and know how I feel."

"That's not the same as talking."

She shrugged, turning to look him in the eye. "Why is talking such a wonderful thing? We leave what's important unsaid; when we find a way to say it, we do it so badly no one knows what we mean."

Three simple words. So important. She was right. He wanted to say them so badly he was afraid he'd burst, but he couldn't. Finally, in the face of his silence, Neela continued in a small, injured voice. "Sometimes I think I've spent my whole life not saying what I wanted to say, and saying things everyone else wanted me to say, instead."

They walked out on a log that formed a natural bridge across the stream, sitting down to dangle their feet inches above the surface. The stream bed turned sharply a few yards away, the force of the water glancing off a large boulder and driving into a pocket it had created for itself in the bank. A continuous eddy growled and swirled there, and during the water's calmer moments, the sleekness of a large trout could be seen, hanging stationary, waiting for what came his way.

Neela was so close to Gan their bodies were in contact from shoulder to hip. She turned to speak, and the subtle variations in her pressure against him so clouded his mind he almost missed the words. "You said you wanted to talk to me."

He was falling into the blue depths of her eyes. He said, "I don't know how to start. I can't even think the right words to myself."

Solemnly, she nodded. "I have the same trouble sometimes. If I just say it, even if I say it wrong, I always feel better."

He half turned, taking her face in his hands. She seemed to shiver, or move, almost frightening him into letting her go, but nothing more happened, and he plunged ahead. "I'll say it, then. The only way I know how. I love you."

Her eyes misted and he thought his heart would freeze, but she smiled. More confusion. Perhaps it would be better if his heart did freeze. She said, "I'm glad. You can't imagine how glad. I love you, too. I've thought about it and thought about it, and I believe I always have and just didn't realize it. Sometimes I think about what would have happened if I'd stayed with our people, done what Bay wanted me to do." She leaned forward to put her head against his chest and her arms around him. There was a sound like crying in her voice as she continued. "I want to be with you, Gan. Whatever happens to us, I want to be beside you."

"I promise you that," he said. "So long as I live."

She lifted her head, smiling, and he kissed her.

Gan watched the preparations for the official celebration of the Bear Paw victory with a feeling of detachment. It was all under the conflicting orders of the men called One and Four, with accompanying disagreement and contradiction from Ops and the House Director. Each claimed to have the authority for every morsel of food or assigned position or instruction to workers and servants—until something went awry; then they yelled and blamed each other. In spite of their wrangling, however, it was all taking shape. Because of the bountiful harvest, there was no reason to skimp, and squealing wagonloads of fruit, vegetables, meat, and game started unloading at the site just outside the main gate of the castle early in the morning. Tents popped up like multicolored mushrooms. Picket lines were established for tying up the horses of those who came mounted, and soon they were filling up. Small boys ranged the lines, earning a few coins by keeping the animals fed and watered. Hour by hour the crowd grew. Musicians on flute, trum, drum, and a half-dozen different kinds of stringed instruments competed for audiences and cash on every hand, while jugglers and coin-toss gamblers offered their brand of entertainment. There were even three acrobats, two brothers and their sister, who battered a drum and a split, weird-sounding cymbal to gather a crowd. They leaped over and under and past each other in an unbelievable fashion. Gan marveled at the girl, in particular, who seemed to have neither bones nor fear. She twisted her body into positions that made him ache just to watch, actually bending over backward so far she brought her face forward between her ankles, then straightened up, all without help. Then, with an angelic smile, she submitted to having her brothers toss her about like a slingstone.

Shaking his head in wonderment, he turned away to continue his walk. He'd watched the panoply build throughout the morning from the top of the wall. Now, having wandered about for an hour, he started back inside the castle wall.

The activity made him uncomfortable. He was responsible for the whole celebration, but he wasn't part of it.

And he was mightily distracted in his own right.

All this and a marriage, he thought, and once more wondered if he could get through it without his nervousness betraying him. If his men knew how afraid he was— He shivered.

The massive brass bolts that joined the timbers had been polished to golden glitter, and he lost himself in contemplation of one of them. He braced himself with one hand against the rough timber and stared and wondered if any woman had ever been so lovely, if any man had ever been so much in love, had been loved by such a wonderful woman.

There had been a time when love was a comedy. He'd watched others buckle under it, staggering around as if their minds were so full there was nothing left to control the muscles. Almost every week saw a fight, men injuring each other over the exclusive right to pursue a girl who might just as easily tell them to leave her alone. It used to baffle him. It seemed so senseless, at the time; there were girls everywhere one looked. Some were prettier, or stronger, or smarter. The truth was, he'd regarded them as in the way. Worse than that, when he got older and attended the puberty ceremony in Earth Heart, he saw the glazed, almost clubbed look on the faces of some of the adults when the talk got around to sex, and he suspected that anything that rattled otherwise intelligent men so totally must be downright dangerous.

He thought back on those times, then remembered the sickness in his heart when he believed Neela wanted only Clas.

The question was, which is the most dangerous, love or sex?

Was he wracked by pain at the thought of her loving Clas, or by the thought of her in his arms? When he thought of losing her, or never having her, which part of him dominated his mind?

But he wouldn't lose her, never had to fear not having her. She'd never be in Clas' arms. She'd be in his.

That thought broke the wall holding back the burning, spine-tingling fantasies he'd denied so long. Once he'd looked at her as something so beautiful she should be admired. If she were to be touched, it must be with reverence. He still thought of her in those terms. Something else had forced its way past his reserve, however, past his control. He looked at her and saw the full rise of breasts, the play of firm muscle under skin as smooth and soft as down. The long, plaited hair down her back drew his eye to the sway of buttocks, the easy stride of long, graceful legs. Sometimes he watched her and his soul sang at the gentle loveliness of her. In an instant that could change, and the world was forgotten in his private image of the two of them entwined in a sweating, sliding, mindless ecstasy. The things he'd never dared think now plagued him. They seized his mind at the most inopportune times, set his body throbbing with desire. He feared them now, too, worried that the rage of the sexual appetite in him could make him hurt her.

For a moment he almost felt sorry for Clas and Sylah. They might be getting married at the same time, but they couldn't know the same passion, the same tenderness, as he and Neela. It simply wasn't possible.

Neela came up unnoticed to take his arm. He turned, his eyes still dazzled from the polished brass, and saw her face in a glowing nimbus, indistinct, but radiant.

She said, "Well, aren't you going to speak to me?" and he realized he'd been staring.

The silly grin stretching his face out of shape was suddenly very tiring. He tried to force a serious expression and felt it struggle and fail. He said, "I was going to ask you: Would anyone miss us if we ran away from all this foolishness?"

"How I wish we could!" She glanced past him at the growing tent city. She was dressed for riding, in beaded doeskin blouse and trousers. The cape draped over her left shoulder featured the Baron's raven, but on a light green-and-blue-striped background. For a moment he visualized her on her horse, the cape and the blond hair, freed of its braids, streaming behind her like sun breaking through clouds. She added, "This must be what the Olan trading grounds look like in the spring," before returning to his question. "It would be a terrible unkindness to the Baron. He's gone to a lot of trouble."

"Most of it to celebrate the victory. The double wedding was an afterthought."

"Certainly it was. The barony's his. Our lives are ours. He didn't have to do anything for us."

He put his arm around her waist and they walked into the castle grounds. He said, "You're right. He's been good to us. I'm saying we shouldn't forget that we earned it."

"You earned it." He looked at her, half expecting some sort of teasing, but she met his eyes with complete seriousness. "You're the leader, Gan. I don't care what your mother's prophecy said, and I don't care what your father said. You're what you are, and you need nothing more than that."

"I need you."

She squeezed his hand. "I hope so."

Tate's voice stopped them, and they both craned over their shoulders to see her coming almost at a run. She didn't look happy, and as soon as she was close enough to speak in a normal voice, she made it clear she wasn't. "Neela, how're you going to be ready for tonight if we don't get started? We've got sewing to do yet, and the women are waiting."

"I got tired of sitting and waiting. It's only been a few minutes. Anyhow, I wanted to talk to Gan."

"Where I come from, it's bad luck for the bride to see the groom the day of the wedding."

Gan said, "Then how do they get married?"

"Until the ceremony, I meant. Don't be smart. You may be Murdat to the troops and some sort of hero to the Baron, and this poor child may have fallen in love with you, but you're just another *man* to me, running around with your tongue hanging out like a wet sleeve. Let the girl be. We've got work to do."

Bowing, Gan straightened and backed away, winking at Neela. When he said, "Take good care of her for me," to Tate, she sniffed and hurried Neela off.

The celebration was well under way long before the official start of ceremonies, so that when the Baron made his appearance inside the official frame erected on the stage for that purpose, he was greeted by the full-throated cheer of thousands of people who were eager to be entertained.

He signaled the appearance of the Wolves. A trum blared, and the noise of the crowd subsided to an expectant rumble as they were forced back to create an opening. Men hurried forward with piles of straw and wood, laying a series of small bonfires that stretched into the darkness. In the distance a trum answered, the rising three-note call to advance. The second repeat involved all ten of the division's instruments, and then came the crash of the new war drums. Two distant fires flared to life simultaneously. They were almost all the way to the billeting area, so the figures moving between and past them were small and indistinct. Quickly, however, another pair of fires was alight, and it was apparent that, as the front rank of ten men approached the prepared wood piles, they were being lit as markers to illuminate the advance.

When the first rank was about two hundred yards away, the men began to beat their swords against their shields in a delayed cadence, slower than their trotting pace. The drums boomed accompaniment.

Breaking onto the cleared area in front of the stage, the regiments formed into their individual hundred-man units. They sheathed their murdats as they did, so that the clashing sound that built to a crescendo at the edge of the presentation field faded away, regiment by regiment, until only the drums maintained a beat. The cavalry came last, taking position across the rear, the drums between them and the foot troops. The entire action was conducted by the sergeants, and as soon as the senior man was satisfied that the ranks were straight, he announced to Gan, who stood beside the Baron, that the Wolves were present. When he saluted, the drums rolled furiously and the crowd cheered with one throat.

Mounting his horse, Gan moved to take his position in front of the unit. The other officers, including Clas, Tate, and Emso, formed a separate line behind him. They, in turn, saluted the Baron, who gestured Clas forward.

He rode to within a few feet, then vaulted out of the saddle. Standing in front of his horse, he raised his murdat in tribute. Again the crowd screamed approval, but Gan was only interested in the Baron's reaction. It was a spontaneous gesture, and the older man accepted it with a surprised, pleased smile. He called to Gan and Clas to join him and their brides-to-be on the stage. In a short speech, he thanked the Wolves, who beat their shields in answer.

When he was introduced, Gan had no idea exactly what he was going to say, and the steadily increasing silence of the crowd drew strength and thought out of him, until, behind him, he heard Neela's admonishing cough. He cleared his throat and began.

"You are the Wolves. There will be others, there will be hundreds, even thousands, more. There will never be any others who were the first. You have won the second most important battle in the history of the Wolves, the first one. We must work to guarantee that we win the most important of all, the last one. We, your officers, are honored to lead you. If our skills match yours, if our courage equals yours, no force can defeat us. I salute you."

When some order was restored, he continued. "Tonight Clas na Bale marries Rose Priestess Sylah. Neela Yan becomes my bride. If any man of you thinks I'm going to waste this time talking to you, you don't belong with the Wolves, because we recruit no fools. Now—a cheer for Baron Jalail!"

Again the night air was split by voices, this time aided by drums, trums, and anything else people could seize on to make noise. Gan stepped back into place beside Neela, who looked up at him, smiling, embarrassed to be the center of so much attention, proud to be exactly where she was. He kissed her quickly. The Baron waved at the crowd with increased good nature, unaware of what was going on behind his back and interpreting the crowd's merriment as somehow connected with him.

After giving the order for the Wolves to break ranks, Baron Jalail himself conducted the marriage ceremony. It had been explained to all of them, and when they saw how solemnly the Baron treated the matter, they accepted the alien words. Sylah pointed out that they differed little from those of Ola or the Dog People. Her comment finally swayed Neela, who told the Baron bluntly that she had no intention of sacrificing her Dog woman's independence for the servitude of Harbundai. The Baron's wintry smile at her declaration collapsed to shock when he saw Gan's fierce pride in her.

Now, on the stage, in front of thousands of people, the two couples held hands and crowded together for mutual support as the Baron repeated the prescribed phrases. It was the last part of the ritual that Gan focused on. The words were, "You are become one, but your strength is multiplied, not added, because in all things you will be more than two. Swear to each other that your love would prevent this marriage if you were ill. Swear to each other that your love will require you to confess if you become ill. Swear to each other that you are husband and wife in heart as well as mind, in truth as well as law." He waited for their murmured oaths, then faced the hushed crowd. He raised his arms and shouted as loud as he could. "I say it for all to hear and acknowledge: Gan and Neela are married; Clas and Sylah are married!"

This time the applause was longer, fading only when the foursome agreed to join the crowd and accept congratulations. Strains of music forced their way above the hubbub, only to be swallowed by it. At the edge of the presentation field a juggler threw blazing torches high in the air, creating a circle of blazing circles. Fragments of the crowd drifted off into the tent area where the food and drink waited. Others crowded around the juggler. Some musicians formed an impromptu band, and more people moved to them and started dancing.

Gan edged toward the darker shadows at the side of the stage, where his horse was tethered. Together, he and Neela shortened their responses to well-wishers. They made slow progress in their escape, but they never stopped moving, edging away. From the corner of his eye Gan saw Clas and Sylah trying to break free, as well. When there was a momentary lull, he grabbed Neela's arm, whispering, "Now. Hurry to the horses." They sprinted the last few yards, almost in the stirrups before the laughter and shouts started. They galloped off to a chorus of bawdy suggestions, laughing like children freed from chores. Gan looked over his shoulder once to assure himself there were no followers, and was relieved to see none. He'd had all the communal involvement in his wedding night that he was willing to accommodate. His glance stole to Neela, riding beside him. Her white clothing shimmered in the pale light of stars and a new moon. She was indistinct, but the mere sense of her presence made him shiver with anticipation.

They passed through the gate into the castle grounds at a quick trot, and Gan leaped from the saddle to hit the ground almost in a run. He pulled Sunflyer to a rather rude stop, handing the reins off to a waiting stableboy without even seeing the youngster's ill-hidden smirk. Helping Neela down, he tried to act calm and hurry her at the same time, and she leaned back, setting her own pace. He had the good sense not to press the issue, and they reached their new quarters against the west wall of the castle all in good time. Shadowy, giggling figures scampered off as they approached.

A solitary rose-scented candle burned in the bedroom, its light easing through the open door into the main room, where it barely augmented the muted glow of the alder coals in the fireplace. There were herb leaves strewn on the new wood floor, so that every step released the fragrance of thyme and marjoram, lavendar and tarragon, to mingle with the fat smell of the fresh-cut cedar and fir of the house's construction. Two cups of dandelion-root tea steamed on the hearth in front of the fireplace. Whoever had arranged all that had also left a pile of furs conveniently in place there, as well.

Neither of them seemed to be willing to break the silence. Gan closed the door behind them, joining Neela at the table. They sat on the furs next to each other, his arm around her shoulder, and watched the black shadows crawl through the embers. They sipped at the tea, then put the mugs down in unspoken agreement. A moment later he turned her face to him and kissed her gently, wanting to reassure as much as communicate his growing need. She returned it with similar tenderness, yet he felt the tremor that ran through her. He was prepared for her look of concern as she pulled back from him. "I'm afraid," she said, and turned quickly to stare into the coals once more. She picked some of the leaves from the floor and threw them into the fireplace. They crackled and curled, disappearing in tiny red dots that gave off coils of aromatic smoke.

"So am I, a little," he said, "but only because I don't want to make any mistakes."

"That's what I'm afraid of."

"I thought you were afraid I'd— Well, they say men are rough sometimes."

"You'd never hurt me." She took his hand between hers. "I want to be everything you want me to be, and I don't know if I am. Or can. Or anything. See, I can't even say it right." She half turned, pressing her face against his shoulder.

He said, "It's not something we need to talk about," and the husky voice sounded like nothing he'd ever heard before. His free hand seemed to take on a life of its own. It rose to the collar of her blouse, and he looked down past the soft gold of her hair and the pale outline of her features to see his fumbling, frustrating efforts to undo the buttons. It occurred to him that he could save a great deal of time with one honest pull on the material, but at that moment the button gave way and spared him that error. The others followed quickly, and he lifted the cloth aside to expose one breast, then the other, the flesh washed roseate in the firelight, the aureoled nipples like dark, inviting buds. He moved to hold one of them, unready to believe its soft firmness was truly captured in his hand. Her sigh, almost a moan, told him it was so, and his need grew to irresistible strength. He shifted away from her, lowering her to the furs, stripping off his clothes. As he did, she raised herself to remove the blouse, an enigmatic half smile playing across her lips. The soft light accentuated the full, almost languorous expression, added to the aura of eager vulnerability about her. She removed her own boots by the time he'd done the same, and he slipped the skirt away, kneeling above her just long enough to imprison the naked beauty of her in his memory forever, and then he lowered to her.

It was a clumsy moment, unsure, both of them afraid, but too driven to speak or pause. Gan was sure she would insist he wait, and even more sure he couldn't possibly. Then, suddenly, she was guiding him, helping him, and he entered her. She gave a small cry of pain, and he hesitated. She only clutched him tighter, however, her hands splayed across his back, her demands challenging his as she arched to meet them.

When it was over, he lay spent, while things that were not true memories, but as vivid as present time, crashed and stumbled through his mind. There were remembered words, the lingering impression of sensations that defied reality in their intensity, and a faint, mocking remembrance of cries and words spoken.

He had never been delirious. He had seen it. He thought that if delirium could ever be pleasure, this must be what it would be like.

Neela stirred under him, her hands in his hair. "I love you," she said, and he raised his head to look into her eyes and say the same thing. She was shy, nervous.

He said, "I never imagined. I can't say anything."

"Good. I was surprised, too. Everything the older women told me was true, but they didn't say enough." She giggled and pulled him back down to her breast. He buried his face in the golden tangle of her hair, and was pleasantly surprised to find himself suddenly and totally untired. When she laughed again, it was a throaty sound, spiced by more mischief than nervousness. She nipped his neck with her teeth.

He wasted a moment wondering if they'd ever find their way to the bed that night.

BOOK III

Who Dares
Define Victory?

CHAPTER 60

$\mathbf{A}$ waning moon and the dying fires of the merrymakers combined to throw a muddled glow across the nearly abandoned site of the celebration. Most of the troops had long since either gone back to their quarters or succumbed to the seemingly limitless amount of beer available for the occasion. People slept on the stage where the wedding had taken place. A few horses remained tethered to the picket lines. Voices, laughter, and music still etched the night, filtered through the cloth of faintly glowing tents.

Tate stepped outside, leaving one such diehard party. She walked a while, distancing herself from the noise, then stopped and stared up at the moon.

People lived up there once. Humans, who worked, played, and even conceived children on that dead-silver place. She knew one of them. Had known. Used to know. What difference did it make? It was all so far in the past, it had outlived legend.

In all these months, she'd never thought about the colony once. The moon was simply the moon. It wasn't a place of scientific accomplishment or a source of national pride. No one poked and prodded its airless secrets, no one up there scanned the earth for the telltale pimple that was an intercontinental missile lancing into the sky.

Or did they?

She shook her head. The colony was never self-sufficient, and the most heroic efforts to produce enough food to sustain life would only have postponed the inevitable. Anyhow, a couple of reports had sifted past the censors saying a missile had eliminated everything.

Eliminated. Another flash from the "good old days," just like the intrusive memory of a friend who lived on the moon. People here died; they weren't wasted, blown away, disappeared, bugged, or nuked. Violence took them with appalling frequency, as it almost took Jones, but at least violence here had the integrity of honest combat. No one poisoned the air. No one made the earth an emitter of invisible rays that riddled the bones and peeled away the flesh that covered them.

And she missed her time. Alone in the darkness, she pressed her fists to her temples and swayed with the unbearable pain of unending loneliness.

Her world. As terrible as it was, it called to her. It had destroyed everyone and everything she ever knew, but this strange place, for all its unsullied air, its crystalline water, its unnumbered birds and animals, would never be home.

At one time she'd blamed that on being separated from the others, and on Jones' grating new personality. She'd come to acknowledge that it wasn't so. She was an exile. Not an entirely unhappy one, but one who knew she was never—could never be—like those around her.

The weddings nearly finished her. Her friends. So happy. And her? Alone. A freak. Oh, Emso was good company, and a couple of the other officers in the Wolves made it clear they found her interesting. She admitted to herself that she actually wanted for nothing, and in the same thought envied Sylah and Neela so bitterly, the emotion was practically a cold flash of hatred. Immediately, she was ashamed of herself. They weren't to blame for her inability to find a man who attracted her.

What was to blame? The thought had taken on a more worrisome cast lately. She smiled ruefully; maybe it was the onset of winter that was getting to her, and she just didn't want to face all those cold nights in a single bed. But it was more than that, she knew. The trouble was, she didn't know what. She'd been out with white men, so that wasn't the whole problem, although the complete lack of black men preyed on her mind. Again, she was forced to be honest with herself and admit it was that lack, rather than the lack of other black women, that troubled her the most. So at least some of her reactions seemed to be standard, she thought, and tried to make a joke of it, tried to lighten her own mood. It didn't work, and she set out for her quarters, determined to think of other things.

Perversely, her brain shifted her center of attention from herself to her fellow crèche survivors. She knew they were alive. Or, more accurately, that more than one still lived. One of the Olan prisoners at the Bear Paw insisted they'd have won the battle if the strangers with the lightning weapons had been present. Gan had insisted she remain out of sight, not wanting to let them know of her existence, thus keeping her weapons a secret, but he'd let her listen in on the interrogations. The prisoner was tough, with an unflinching eye, and he'd promised them Ola would avenge his dead comrades—with thunder and lightning, as well as blades. She wondered if the etched helmet had been returned to the capital. She doubted it. In a way, she hoped it was at the bottom of the river. The sense of having wronged Gan troubled her more all the time.

A breeze came up as she approached the small village where Jones lived. It stole the warmth from her, and she shivered, hunching her shoulders and jamming her hands in the pockets of the short jacket she'd made for the night's occasion. In a moment of whimsy she'd told the women she was working with at the time that it was a common style in her country; they called it an ikejacket. She'd seen another one at the ceremony, and the wives of two Wolves had already asked to borrow hers so they could duplicate it.

Donnacee Tate, stylist to the savages, she thought, but when she tried to smile at herself, the wind gusted and burned her eyes. She was wiping away the moisture, telling herself it wasn't tears, and if it was, it was the wind's fault, when she saw movement and stopped immediately. Something warned her. She obeyed it without hesitation. Quickly she dropped to a squat, so anyone approaching would be silhouetted against the stars or the wan remnant of moonlight. For a long moment she froze, listening to the steady whisper of wind and grass. She searched then, turning her head, using the corners of her eyes, where the best night vision registered. The thing she'd seen failed to repeat itself, but she'd had time to think about it, and she was sure it was the movement of a shielded light. It was furtive, something someone didn't want seen. After a full two minutes she rose and resumed her way, with her murdat in her hand. She kept to the center of the narrow roadway, forcing someone to cross open ground to reach her.

The first hut at the edge of the village was barely distinguishable when she saw the bulky figure edging away from its protective blackness and toward the road. Anger washed away her fear as she saw how confident he was that she wouldn't see him. He apparently didn't expect her to be able to resist very effectively, either. Wrong, mister, she thought, and raised the murdat so it crossed her body diagonally, ready to slash or deflect. The figure disappeared behind some brush, but she knew where he was. She continued on.

He stepped out, blocking her way, a blocky, featureless form. Taking two long strides, she brought the blade forward, it's point pressing into the softness just below his ribs.

Two hands went directly skyward. A voice said, "Not a friendly greeting for an old friend, Donnacee. Especially one who's waited for you so long his bones are ice and his eyes weep for a bit of rest." Even in a hoarse whisper, he managed to inject his customary mix of injury, accusation, and the suggestion of sly mockery.

"Bilsten," she said, matching her voice level to his. "What're you doing here, you fool? I could've killed you."

"I was betting you'd hesitate. And you did, don't you see."

She lowered the blade a fraction of an inch. "Gan told me how you popped up in the castle. Were you betting he'd hesitate?"

"Different. I called to let him know I was there. Startle that one and you'll find he's given you the worst surprise of your own short life. But I didn't want to come to you in the castle."

"Why come to me at all?"

"Sit and listen." He moved off to the weeds at the edge of the road and knelt on one knee. He was as smooth and silent as a cat, and she began to suspect he'd wanted to be seen heading for the confrontation on the road. She resented that more than her earlier assumption that he didn't respect her skills. When she was settled, he went on. "Tell your friends that the King has allied with three barons in a plan to lure the Wolves into a trap. The bait will be Malten, the barony to the west of Jalail."

"Baron Malten's his best defense against Ola! What's he—"

"Shh!" He cut her off with a hand on her shoulder. "Not so loud. He fears Gan more than Ola. I'm thinking he's right about that. And I'd thank you for forgetting I said it. Now, then, Gan also has to know that the Devils cut up the Dog camp."

Tate listened with growing dismay. The first element rode in fast, not caring that Nightwatch spotted them and gave the alarm. As soon as they had drawn most of the defenders to them, another element struck from a different direction, and then a third from another side. He finished with a grim casualty count. "Over thirty warriors dead, mostly Gan's own North Clan. Eighteen women. Two men, twelve boys, and eight women of bearing age missing. Separate raiding parties hit the kennels and the corrals. They surprised the Dog Chief and killed more than forty dogs. The Horse Chief heard them coming, so they didn't get any of the trained animals."

She shook her head. "You tell him."

He chuckled. "I'll be gone by daylight, and I think I'll not bother him this night, don't you know. But I've some good news for him. Tell him the defeat on the Bear Paw touched off some resistance over on the Whale Coast. Tell him Ola won't be looking to help the Devils this winter." He paused, and she caught herself leaning forward expectantly. When he resumed, it was with a different tone. "Now we'll speak of religious things. King Altanar is saying Sylah is involved with a new religion here. It's frightened both him and the King of Harbundai; they're talking about an alliance to crush it. Church has no one here, so doesn't know what to believe. Perhaps you know?"

Tate shook her head. "She works at the healing house. There's no time for her to preach, or anything like that. They're probably upset because we've helped the women here."

"Does she spend much time with you?"

There was something in the question that warned her, exactly as the half-seen light had earlier. She said, "More than anyone else except Clas and Neela. Why?"

"As much time as you spend with Jones?"

She raised the murdat to touch his stomach. "I think you'd better tell me what you're saying."

He sighed. "Other Peddlers hear Jones is involved in the new religion. *Very* involved."

"That's crazy. He's a— Never mind. Listen, leave him alone. He's still sick. Anyhow, what do you know? You brought everyone your cheery news, so why don't you get out of here while you're able?"

He rose, and she moved with him, keeping the murdat pointed at his midriff. Carefully, he raised a hand in salute, then edged past her and walked away, toward the Enemy Mountains. She was turning to leave when she heard a heavy, dull sound. Holding her breath, she strained to hear more. Twice that night she'd felt warned, and now it was an alarm in her brain that threatened to push her into panic flight. She moved forward reluctantly. After a few tentative steps she convinced herself her imagination was running wild. Five yards, she thought; I'll go five more yards.

She stumbled and fell, almost crying out, managing a sideways cut at nothing with the murdat before she hit the ground. She rolled, came up in a defensive crouch.

Nothing. Silence. Even the breeze was gone.

What had she tripped over? She shuffled back, hand outstretched. Touched something furry. Wet. She recoiled, scrubbing the hand on the rough dirt of the roadway. The thing groaned, and she brought the murdat up in case it attacked.

"Someone's brought me an accident." Bilsten's choked whisper seemed to rise from the earth. "From the feel of it, my head's entirely broken. From behind. Wouldn't have been yourself, would it?"

"No! I came looking for you!"

He moved again, retched. After a moment he said. "Well, I'm found. Unless you're here to finish me, I could stand to be away from this place, don't you know."

She moved to get her hands under his arms, tried to get him to his feet. "You've got to help," she said, and realized he was dead weight.

Hating him, she started dragging him, waiting for his attacker or attackers to come back for both of them. After what seemed hours, she was far enough into the village and among enough people to risk calling for help. She sat

down beside him, yelling her head off, fighting back tears of anger and
confusion and fear and the return of the aching sense of *alienness* that had
started the whole damned, damned, damned thing.

The Abbess had arranged a special trip for the strangers. They were all up
early, and she watched them riding away from the palace together thinking
how they treated the outings with the unfettered delight of happy children.
As with so many things, it made her wonder what their country must be like,
because the humor was freely exchanged between both men and women, and
each sex was equally attentive to the other. In fact, she was quite sure the
men deferred to the women sometimes. It had taken her quite a while to
assure herself that this was the case, but now she was certain. And more
confused than ever.

She'd learned next to nothing about their individual backgrounds, and
that rankled. If she was acquainted with someone, she expected to know
everything about them. These people resolutely rejected any attempt to pry
into their past. It was all very unsatisfactory, especially since they seemed so
knowledgeable. The small man, Leclerc, had already shown the stoneworkers
how to set up more efficient and safer hoists. Conway had, of all things,
convinced Altanar to institute a program of road repair, financed by tolls.
Produce and material were moving much more efficiently throughout the
kingdom. And Altanar was convinced they knew more than they were willing
to share.

She hoped they continued to keep him content.

More than that, she hoped she'd learn everything she could from them
before he decided to have them killed.

She liked them. They could be as clever and amusing as the little man-
squirrels that sailors sometimes brought to port from the lands to the faraway
south. Today they were all on horseback. She was sorry she had to have her
own litter. She'd liked riding once, but her bones wouldn't allow it any
longer. Conway had been riding beside her, chatting pleasantly, but then
he'd seen something he wanted to examine more closely and he'd galloped
off. She liked him most. He was the greatest challenge, especially since the
death of the one called Falconer. For all his affability, there was a sense of
tension about him since then, as if his thoughts had a purpose beyond his
words. He made no pretense of his wish to know everything about the
kingdom and its people. Altanar wasn't entirely happy with his poking about,
but he was so open and friendly about it, he'd given no one any reason to
criticize. And the people liked him. Altanar was shrewd enough to use that.
He pretended Conway was his favorite, as well, letting him roam where he
would.

Predictably, Altanar discouraged travel by the women, saying they should respect the customs of Ola. In fact, the women, for all their willingness and hard work with the Chosens, had retreated into a closed circle of their own ever since their exposure to the Beach of Songs. They'd suffered the loss of Falconer badly, but recovered well. It was the scene at the beach and the protectors that they spoke of in the hushed tones of horror. She'd felt badly when she realized how strongly it affected them, blaming herself for introducing them to the truth protectors so forcefully, but before long she decided that it was something they were going to have to accept, and how they discovered the facts was immaterial. Still, it was unpleasant to see a woman as strong as the one called Kate Bernhardt reduced to exclusively associating with children—and her two friends. As for those two, the reversal of positions was shocking. The little spark, Janet Carter, seemed to go into some sort of emotional decay after the show at the beach, and the Sue Anspach one grew as the small, dark one faded, until now she was more a guardian for Carter than her friend. She invariably asked for Carter's advice or opinion in everything. More often than not, Carter claimed to be too busy to decide, or to have too much on her mind to be bothered. The fact was, she left decisions to Anspach.

The most disturbing thing was Carter's sudden and intense determination to never be separated from her weapons. It was as if she believed the protectors might come for her any minute. Altanar was very nervous about her behavior, and his blundering attempts to convince them they needed no other protection except his goodwill had only convinced the other two that her way was best. They weren't as fanatical about keeping the weapons in hand, but they were never more than a few steps away from them. They watched each other, too, constantly ready to react.

Sooner or later Altanar would decide he had to have more control over them. Over the weapons, actually. She didn't like thinking about the implications of that distinction.

She sighed, shifting about to find a more comfortable position in the litter. Before she could settle, a hot stench rolled over her, making her eyes water. Her throat seemed to close on itself, and she coughed. Conway and his friends saw her discomfort immediately and shouted at the litter bearers to hurry. In a few seconds the smoke was gone and then they were telling the bearers to stop.

"What are you doing?" she shouted up at Conway where he sat his capering horse.

He grinned impudently. "It's a world of surprises," he said, and despite the tears still blurring her vision, she caught Leclerc's quick start and tiny frown of disapproval. There was more to Conway's statement than his friend approved of; for a moment her irritation was pushed aside as she wondered what else was involved. Conway's voice pulled her back to the business at hand. He was pointing at a peculiar brick thing. It looked like an immense brick muffin. Heat waves danced all around it and smoke boiled from vents in the top. That was the source of her coughing and tearing spell.

She didn't know what it was, but she hated it.

Conway said, "A gift for Altanar." She looked at him sharply. Had she heard a touch of disapproval? He went on. "One of the requirements for good steel is a hot fire. Louis and I built this to help. We call it a coke oven. We put in coal and heat it to drive off all the impurities. It's like making charcoal."

"It stinks," she said.

"That can't be helped," Leclerc said. "And a little smoke's a small price to pay for cheaper and better plowshares and hinges and stoves and—"

Interrupting more harshly than she meant, she said, "Knives. Arrowheads. Spear points. More of men's toys."

Conway winced. "We know he won't use it all for peaceful purposes, Abbess. Our hope is that the smiths can make more tools, faster."

He wasn't that happy with it, after all, she realized. There was an appreciation there that Leclerc seemed to ignore. Or was more able to hide.

One never *knew* about these people.

She looked to the women. There was no doubt about them. Their faces were illustrations of dislike. Poor little Carter visibly despised the whole thing. Good for you, she thought, and wished she could tell her how much she agreed.

Trying to salvage some goodwill, she asked Leclerc, "How'd you get that round roof on there? That's brick, too, isn't it? What holds it up? Why doesn't it fall?"

He almost swelled with pride. "That's a true dome. I measured off what we'd need, and had workers build a dirt pile the right size. Then the brickworkers cemented all the bricks in place, right on top of the pile. Once the mortar set, we dug out the dirt. It's not the best way to make it, but I remember some pictures—" His runaway enthusiasm choked to a stop, and he sent another apologetic glance at his friends. When he resumed, he was considerably more controlled. "That is, I remember some examples from our homeland. I'm working to improve this technique. It's a great design. Strong. See that pattern there, where we bricked up the loading door? That's what we call an arch, that curve at the top. The whole building is a load-bearing device. There's no posts or props inside, and a dozen men could dance up on top there. Wouldn't bother it a bit."

She sent him a look that dared him to trifle with her intelligence. He said, "It's the truth, Abbess; no kidding."

"No what?"

This time all the others glared. Leclerc started to sweat. "An expression. We use it. My family—my clan, that is. It means, if I'm lying, may my goats never have young. We say it all the time."

Another naked lie. Yet he was obviously telling the truth about the stuff he called "coke" and his foolish little brick toadstool. His friends were watching to see if she accepted his explanation.

"I never heard that phrase," she said. "Tell me, how does this oven work?"

She almost smiled at the way his relief burst forth as unrestrained pleasure. He lectured her about their good fortune in finding a supply of what he called "bituminous" coal, explaining that most of the local material was too impure to make coke. She wanted to tell him that coal is coal, and that was the end of it, but he was already far ahead of her. They put a layer of coal inside the oven, he said, heating it to drive off what he called gas and tar. She assumed he meant something like steam, because he said those things went to the top of the oven—she understood that, easily enough, having seen the accumulation of soot in fireplaces—where the intense heat set them aflame and the bricks reflected that heat back onto the coal below. It took three days to complete the process, he finished.

"Has King Altanar seen it?" she asked.

"He knows about it, of course. We wanted you to see it first," Conway said. "It's important to us that you understand our goal is to help the people, not the King."

She nodded, and when he suggested they continue on, she agreed readily. It was that nasty sulfur smell that put her off, she decided; it made her think of the Land Under. Perhaps that was why her original impression of the building had been so negative. Rightly so, too. Weapons would certainly come of it.

Thinking about weapons—and the strangers—always led to the same point. Altanar would decide to eliminate them eventually.

Conway spared her any further brooding by riding off to chat with some shipbuilders at work, then hurrying back to take a place beside her to explain that he wasn't familiar with seagoing vessels because there was no ocean coast in his homeland. He called Leclerc to his side, and between them they worked at recalling construction details where they came from. They set her mind spinning with their talk of sails and cats before she put it all together and understood that their "cat" was some sort of boat, and when they said "outrigger," they were talking about the thing properly called a balance bar.

Then she asked herself why they'd be familiar with a seagoing style of boat when they weren't familiar with seagoing.

They were not at all what they seemed. Everyone noticed. Were they really so blind they didn't realize that?

She was still wondering about that when they reached the dock and the boat she'd arranged for the trip. There were several pods of killer whales cruising the Inland Sea now, and she wanted them to see the greeting ceremony. Not that she approved of it. Not at all.

Killer whales were sacred to Altanar's family line, his personal protectors. Twice each year, in the spring and in late fall, any pods in the Inland Sea were approached, and offerings of fish and flowers were thrown to them. The whole symbolism of it galled her. Fish and flowers, indeed. Food for the powerful—meaning the males, or rulers—and useless flowers for the weak—meaning the females, or subservient. Church approved because one of Altanar's ancestors had been smart enough to make the claim that he only acknowledged the whales because the One in All supplied them. It was a bald lie, but it patched up a rip in the tapestry of shared power.

Conway had asked to see, so here they were. The women were more relaxed and carefree than she'd seen them in a long time. They helped her aboard, and within minutes the sail was up and they were under way. The crisp, clear water chuckled as the hull knifed through it, and the rigging sang its secret song. Huge jellyfish, unhurried, uncaring, pulsed to the beat of their own needs as they swept past. Scores of black-and-white sea birds skittered away at the boat's approach, leaving widening patches on the water where feet and wingtips whipped up silver spray. Far to the south a half-dozen sails of the greeter's boats leaned almost into the water as the boats tacked in their search for the whales.

Suddenly she was aware of another ship bearing down on them. It flew no pennant, and only a man at the rudder and another in the bow were visible, but the steadiness of its approach made her nervous. She couldn't swim. The only sails besides the greeters' were even farther away. She called to Conway. "Can't we change direction? That other boat seems to be coming right at us."

Calmly he said, "It is, Abbess. There's a man on her I'd like you to meet."

"What?" It was a gasp.

By then the other boat was just behind them. Its sails blocked the wind, slowing them almost to a stop, and then, as it swept past, so close its balance bar almost struck their hull, a man with a beard as black as a bat's eye raced out onto that part of the ship and nimbly hopped aboard their boat. Conway greeted him warmly, each man gripping the other at the elbow in the salutation of the For people.

She struggled to maintain her dignified reserve as they approached. The excited babbling of the other three women was no help.

Conway said, "This gentleman would rather you not know his name, Abbess, but he's a friend. He hates Altanar as much as you do."

Her heart bounded like a rabbit, tried to knock the breath out of her. She recoiled. Conway was on one knee in front of her in an instant, whisking a small bottle of ammonia under her nose. She winced and pulled away, striking ineffectively at his hand. "Don't treat me, you puppy! What do you think you're doing? Don't you understand you've killed this man? And yourself?"

The black-bearded one said, "I think not, Abbess," and he was actually amused. He went on, "It was rude to surprise you, but we decided this was the only way for me to meet you safely."

"Hah! What do you know about safety?" She threw a significant glance at the helmsman and his two crewmen.

"It might be best if you knew my name. I'm Wal. Those are my men."

"As I suspected." She blasted him with a smile of triumph. "Great proud lump. See how easily I make you tell me what I want to know? And you speak to me of safety."

Wal looked helpless anger at Conway, who laughed aloud. The sound startled her, and in spite of the present drama, she couldn't remember ever hearing him do that before. Conway said, "Abbess, you know Altanar means to get rid of us as soon as he's satisfied he knows all there is to know about our weapons. I learned there's resistance against him. I've spoken to Wal, and we agree on many things, particularly Altanar. We also agree that Church—and women—should have more freedom. He can organize fighting men from the Whale Coast tribes to help us. He can throw his independent shipmasters into the effort. We don't ask you for anything, but we know you have many sources of information and powerful friends. If you can't help us, please don't fight against us."

"Don't you think you ought to consider an army to fight Altanar's? Or will you wave that lightning weapon at them and make them run away?"

Instead of answering, Conway produced a small box with a charcoal stick inside and drew a nonsensical picture on the planks of the deck. The first was a cow, with a huge udder to assure identification. The second was two vertical feathers; their quill ends were sharpened, and a drop had been drawn at the tip of each. The three women crowded forward to examine it, while Leclerc and Conway grinned in conspiracy. Wal looked dubious. Conway said, "That's a message from a woman named Donnacee Tate. It was scratched with a knife into the helmet of the division commander who died at the Bear Paw River battle we've all heard about."

She scoffed. "Message? It's children's pictures. What's that mean?" She jabbed a crooked finger at the feathers.

Conway looked severe. "The message is a secret, of course. But it's from her. Only we understand."

She looked down at the pictures and watched him without appearing to. He certainly looked serious. And there were people who wrote in pictures or strange symbols. She looked at the fierce frown on the one called Wal and shivered; *there* was seriousness. She had little choice but to go along with them. She peered up at Conway again, and strange, barely remembered vibrations danced along her ribs, up and down her spine. She actually wanted to join them! She hadn't felt like this since . . . She bit her lip. Since Sylah said she'd be willing to try to stop the alliance between Altanar and the Dog People.

Conway was going on. "The Harbundai troops were commanded by a Dog warrior. Tate must be helping him. He'll fight Altanar, when the time's right. We have to be ready to help from here, and we have to weaken Altanar any way we can before that battle."

She straightened and sniffed. "I promise nothing. If you live, I expect you to live up to your word, however. About women and Church."

"For nothing?" Wal's growl seemed to come from the ship's timbers.

She glared at him. "I said I promise nothing. I didn't say I'd do nothing. I'll do what I can, and you must live up to your word."

Unimpressed, he said, "I didn't speak. I gave no word."

"Then do so, or leave with an assurance of nothing. Will you agree to what Conway said, or not?"

He chewed on his whiskers, then, eyes flashing, he said, "I do." Then, as suddenly as a break in a storm, he was laughing. "I'm glad you're on our side, old woman. You're worth a division of the best, you are."

She composed her sweetest smile. "Any woman knows that. And you're still a great lump. Leave my ship."

Shaking his head, roaring with laughter, he walked to the stern. His boat was a good half-mile away, but without hesitation he slipped over the side, waving once before letting go. In seconds they could barely pick him out. The other ship changed course to cruise his way.

Anspach said, "Can he make it? The water's so cold. Why didn't he jump back the way he came?"

"Too dangerous," Conway said. "If the two boats came so close together twice, too many eyes might notice. Once will look like plain carelessness. And Wal swims better than most fish, I think. He's survived three wrecks."

"You know a great deal about him," the Abbess said. It wouldn't do for him to know how much she admired what he'd accomplished. Best to keep him humble. "You choose very unlikely friends."

Bernhardt said, "How'd you do it? And how can you tell that message is from Tate?"

Before answering, Conway said, "Abbess, will you excuse us? This really is secret."

Bitterly, she waved them off. On top of everything, the wretch spoke so softly she couldn't eavesdrop. He was really a bit too clever.

Conway, ignoring her irritation, made his explanation as brief as possible. "Both Tate and I are history buffs, especially about the American Revolution. There's a particular place where we won a battle against the British; a small group of Americans, mostly militia, encircled an experienced group of British regulars and defeated them. The place was called Cowpens. Tate sent a message that was foolish sketches to anyone in this world, but something that has meaning to me. The clincher is that Harbundai used the same battle plan at the Bear Paw. You can be sure she had a lot to do with it."

By then the others were grinning, except for Carter. Her sneer lacked the fire it used to have, but it was a brave attempt. She said, "See what we've brought to the new world. The same tired stories of victory. More war. Wonderful." She stalked back to the stern.

Anspach straightened, smiling sad apology. "She'll be all right. I'll talk to her." She retreated, as well.

Bernhardt caught Conway's arm as he turned to rejoin the Abbess. "Thanks," she said, "I'd about given up. We know this Altanar's got a number for all of us. I thought we were going to just wait for it to come up. You've given us something to do. Win or lose, thanks."

Leclerc said, "I told you, Matt. You watch, Carter'll come around. She's always been more dovey-minded than the rest of us, but she's no fool. She understands, deep down."

"I'm not worried, Louis. I'm sure she does. Now, what do you say we go watch some whales?"

The Abbess turned sharply at the laughter. It made her joints twinge. Conway was beside her in a flash. "You need something warm for those hands," he said, hurrying off. He was back in a few seconds with a steaming hot cloth. "I had the crew heat some of these," he said. He wrapped it around her hand, and immediately the luscious heat steamed out some of the pain. She closed her eyes and offered up the other hand, lying back in her chair. She felt the boat change direction under her as they rocked south. For a moment she squinted up into the pearl-glow of a cloud, luminous against the blue of the sky. The perfect shaft of the spruce mast sketched a wavering pattern across both. She closed her eyes again, absorbed by a feeling of release, as though she could will her awkward, painful body to rise and float, like the cloud, and leave aches and worries behind.

She almost giggled. For the first time in her life she'd actually committed herself to a dangerous act to be committed by a man, and now he was swaddling her like an infant and she was loving it like some moonstruck maid.

It was either the silliest beginning of a rebellion that had ever occurred, or the best. She rather hoped it was the latter.

CHAPTER 61

Winter hauled itself across the contending kingdoms of Harbundai and Ola with a ferocity that revived all the legends of the Beginning and its summerless years. Snow fell with unremembered frequency, clogging roads, obliterating the passes across the Enemy Mountains. It was as if the sky itself was trying to impress on the opposing rulers the futility of their puny wars. Men of importance take little notice of such things, however, and although neither kingdom could mount any sort of sustained activity, both continued to hone their forces.

Life was different among the common people. For the first time, the complete lack of Healers was driven home violently, as the unusual cold struck down the unfit, the unwary, and the careless. Sylah worked harder than she ever had, because the weather brought injury as well as illness. And there were other hardships. Fishermen became very cautious, and their catches dropped. Vegetables that normally wintered over in the benign marine climate either rotted or were frost-blasted and inedible. Many old fruit trees lost limbs or toppled. Surpluses from the bounteous harvest melted faster than the drifts. The seemingly endless parade of gray days and storms even insinuated itself into everyday speech. Mothers pointed at each new snowfall and used it to discipline their children: "Behave yourself, or the evil giants will make the wintertime stay, like the story says! You wouldn't want that, would you?"

The answer was obviously no, but the children noticed that the snow came whatever they did, so they continued to act exactly as they always had.

The great similarity in behavior patterns between men of importance and little boys wasn't lost on Sylah as she watched her husband and Gan school the Wolves.

Prior to the first snow, she'd been surprised by how eagerly they seized the opportunity to strike at the Mountain People's encampment in the foothills of the Enemy Mountains.

Not long after that raid, Two's spies brought in reports of continuing Devil attacks on the Dog People. The two-edged benefit of the camp's destruction was apparent then. The warriors killed by the Wolves would raid no one, which included the Baron's subjects. In fact, the braver loggers had been only days behind the Wolves, harvesting the best cedar and getting out before the first of winter's snows.

The Baron led Gan through some tangled diplomacy throughout the season. Whenever the weather permitted, there were visits to the adjacent baronies in the north and west. Sometimes the visit was official. More often Gan rode without the older man, taking only Clas and Emso, and occasionally Tate, to observe. They traveled in light chain-mail armor, under rugged commoner clothes, and they scouted carefully, going afoot through the densest forest, leading the horses, ghosting the ridgelines in silence, unseen, noting everything. Gan learned the approaches into all three baronies touching Jalail. He committed fords to memory, saw where major routes were channeled between obstacles. They were caught by several storms, but only at risk once, when the horses were unable to move through the drifts. They barely lasted, and they carried much more grain after that.

Gan learned. He practically destroyed the suffering Baron's social life by keeping him up almost all night every night while he asked for explanations of everything they'd seen or done during the day. Baron Jalail privately complained that traveling with Gan had all the charm of having one's brains pulled out through one's ears, but he always provided answers to questions and pursued any ideas his young aide originated. His pride in Gan became a source of considerable concern to his contemporaries. There were infrequent, but disturbing, whispers that some nobles in his own barony were envious of the newcomer's influence.

When Gan was at the castle, he interrogated Two almost daily, driving that poor man and his commers as they'd never had to work before. By the time of the shorter days, when the passes were completely blocked, Gan already had a detailed knowledge of every noble in Jalail, every baron in Harbundai, the King, the Queen Mother, and most of the nobles in the other baronies. He could rattle off figures concerning trade with every group known to Four, and startled both the Baron and Four by projecting how profitable their sales of coal to Ola would be if there was uninterrupted trade across that border. When he suggested using that profit to buy jade from the northern tribes for resale to the Nions, the Baron simply goggled at him. Gan realized he was thinking far ahead of anything the Baron had ever considered. He said no more; everyone knew he hadn't stopped thinking.

He was less forthcoming about his thoughts on his scouting trips, until one night when the harsh winter was in its last throes.

They stopped early, high enough on a timbered slope to look out past a sprawling river delta onto the Inland Sea. While the others chatted among themselves, Gan walked away to stand alone, gazing at the scene. Windows gleamed from the small settlements and separate farmhouses, the glass ones more dazzling than gems, while those of oiled paper were as rich and yellow as butter. Smoke lazed straight up. Where the land met the sea, a pattern of irregular flashes moved up the coast, then turned and swept south again. A flock of shore birds, wheeling through maneuvers more precise than any military effort, made wild display of their skill. Invisible when they presented their dark upper surface, they jeweled the dusk when they turned, all at once, to reveal the whiteness of their bellies.

The green-black Sea Star islands beyond them were like stones set in moving silver. They blurred, merging with the water as the sun slid low enough to bloody the clouds and the white teeth of the Whale Coast's mountains.

Tate watched him the whole time. There was a feeling in the air around him, an energy that failed to alter the stolid, unchanging features. For some reason, she knew he was wrestling with a great problem, yet for all the emotion he showed, he could have been made of stone. Then she remembered Sylah remarking once that sometimes his eyes gleamed unnaturally bright. It was what she called his conqueror's gleam.

Tate concentrated on his eyes after that. She was the least surprised by his words when he rejoined them.

"I mean to rule here," he said.

The day's earlier conversation had largely been of inconsequential things and routine remarks about the terrain. The ordinary comfortable silence of the evening only added to the shock of the statement.

They were all huddled around the firepit of the abandoned trapper's shack that was to be their shelter for the night, cooking chunks of seasoned beef on spits. The snap and sizzle of hot grease was the only sound that greeted his announcement. No one so much as looked up.

He continued to stare into the fire, turning the meat stick over and over. After a long pause, he went on. "My father brought us peace, but too many young men were afraid of being attacked by one of the enemies that always seem to be on all sides of us. What if Harbundai, Ola, and the Dog People had a single ruler? Even the Devils would see the pointlessness of making war on such a group." He looked up, his eagerness begging for agreement. "Imagine Ola's armored infantry providing an anchor for the quickness of our Wolves—and all of them screened by the finest horsemen in the world, our own Dogs. Who'd dare attack us?"

The pause was thick with uncertainty. Clas looked away. Emso cleared his throat, then said, "I'll tell you who. The first War Chief who decided he wanted to control our fur trade, or wanted our lumber, or who thought we ought to train horses for his cavalry instead of our own, or who wanted our fish, or—"

Gan cut him off. "Enough! I grant you I can't stop other people's greed, but who could *defeat* us?"

"Ourselves." It was Clas, and the word appeared to hurt him. Still, he pressed on. "Look what we're doing right now. When Baron Jalail was weak, the King wanted to replace him. We've made him strong, we four. And what are we doing? We're scheming to put together alliances that'll make us stronger yet, so we can replace the King. Listen to yourself! You're becoming one of them!" He rose, too agitated to remain seated. "We should fight one more battle for Jalail to make sure he's able to hold his lands. We owe him that much. And then we go home. Our people need us, Gan. Think of them."

Gan stood up to face him, neither man aware that the pressure of their passions pushed Tate and Emso into a stealthy retreat. Outside, the dogs whined anxiously, pawing at the door.

For several long, eerie moments they stood transfixed, hands lingering just in touch with murdat handles, leaning toward each other as if held back by invisible bonds. Then Clas moved. It was as if something surrendered inside him. He seemed to grow smaller. Bunched muscles fell slack and lost definition. The warrior's grimace slipped from his features, leaving an almost baffled, embarrassed cast. "I won't fight you."

Gan's answer was almost a snarl. "Not because of my father! I'm my own man, not his! I'm not my mother's prophecy!"

"I swore an oath. It doesn't matter to me how I die to honor it. Do what your fate demands."

Gan half turned, his hands dropped and his shoulders slumped. He looked up at the rough ceiling. Tate was sure she'd seen a sudden tear. He drew a long, shuddering breath, then said, "I asked you to be next to me always. Now I've done this. I'm ashamed."

"Never that," Clas said.

A thin, uncertain smile added some life to Gan's face as he looked at Clas again. "No man deserves such a friend. Forgive me, please."

Clas shrugged. "It's forgotten."

Then, acting as if nothing had happened, they sat back down at the fire. Tate and Emso exchanged glances and edged back to their original positions. The door stopped shuddering under the weight of the hounds.

It was Tate's turn to take the first watch. She was pleased to get out of the shanty, although the freshening wind combined with the dropping temperature to make her pull her sleeping bag around her. She sat down, jammed up against the base of a tree, choosing a spot that afforded her a clear view of three sides of the building. Raggar and Shara were on the fourth side. She kept Cho with her, pulling her up close. "Us girls have to stick together, dog," she said. "You help me, I'll help you." She was surprised when the animal swung its head up to plant a wet lick on her cheek, and she gave her an impulsive hug. "Some fierce beast. A dumb old lovebug. I guess I'm supposed to protect you, is that it?" Cho responded by turning around several times, finally settling with her head on Tate's lap. Cold or not, Tate felt obliged to scratch her ears, and she almost laughed aloud at the way the dog accepted it, and yet she watched the surrounding forest with her full attention.

Tate let her mind wander, and it found its way to Jones immediately. He'd grown more and more distant all winter. There was no doubt he'd found friends in the barony, and she'd finally admitted that they were coreligionists. People came to Sylah frequently with information—and even more frequently with wild tales—about the growth of the group. Sylah always kept Tate informed. No one spoke the fact, but everyone understood that whatever trouble Jones made, some of it had to rub off on his "countryman." Sylah's anxiety to provide Tate with every opportunity to protect herself touched her deeply, as did Neela's unfailing friendship.

She'd found her own friends, she reflected.

Jones only complicated things. How could she warn him of the ill feeling building toward his associates if he rejected her?

And some of the things said about the Moondancers were disturbing. One man had come to Sylah with his back flayed by a brutal whipping. He'd come too late, however, and he was dying of infection. He clung to Sylah like a child, pleading for her assurance that he wasn't going to eternal torment.

Jones had been there when he was whipped, he said, and then rejected all questions. To the last, he refused to name anyone else or say any more about the group.

That had been Tate's first intimation of their power. The second came from Bilsten. Sylah wasn't at all shy with her opinion of all Peddlers, but she treated him with the same gentleness and attention she gave everyone. The night he was attacked, he suffered what Sylah called a cussing, which gave

Tate considerable difficulty until she recognized the treatment as proper for a concussion.

It was when Bilsten was able to travel that his respect for Jones' friends revealed itself. He planned his departure in complete secrecy, only telling her minutes before he walked out of the building. "I've been waiting for this full moon," he said, his hand drifting up to rub the site of his well-healed injury. "They'll be leaping and yelling like goats somewhere, and that'll give the poor Peddler a chance to slip away. I've a feeling they don't approve of the likes of me."

His manner frightened her. She compared this reaction to his behavior when he offered to scout a trail for them through the country of the Mountain People, and this was a different man. He'd clearly feared the Devils, but he'd shown confidence in his ability to deal with them. There was no such faith evident now.

She'd gone with him to saddle his horse and harness the burros. He melted into the night, leaving her with the lonesome sound of his little caravan shuffling down the road. For a moment she thought she saw him turn, and she quickly half raised a hand to wave back, but it was only a trick of the light.

Once he was gone, there was no longer any reason for her to deny her growing conviction that the covert light she'd seen the night he was struck had been in Jones' house.

CHAPTER 62

The first flowers of spring rose through the melting snows of winter. They were crocuses, and Tate was no less surprised by their number than Gan and Clas. "We have these," Tate said, "but they come later, and never so many." In some places they carpeted the ground, but it was on the hillsides that they especially excited her. They seemed to be trying to climb to the sun, luxuriant swirls of yellow-orange and purple, the color so vibrant the slopes seemed to tremble at the force of their vitality. Once, looking at them, she felt a sudden pang of loss. For several minutes afterward she couldn't imagine where such a contrary reaction could come from. Then she was remembering a trip through a museum in Washington, where she'd been drugged by the beauty of dozens of exuberant impressionist works that sought to capture similar scenes.

The colors of spring were also reflected in the energy of the people. Lingering nostalgia kept her at a distance, and she scolded herself for not being able to join in. Finally she was jollied into a proper state of mind by Neela. Her argument was that Tate might as well enjoy herself; it would be good conditioning for the really big celebration, which would take place in a few weeks, on the official first day of spring. In an unusually friendly move, Baron Jalail had asked Sylah to preside over the sun-welcoming ceremony. When Tate looked confused, there were some embarrassing questions about celebrations in her country, but she'd grown very adept at dodging such issues. Sylah salvaged that moment, explaining that Church was responsible for fixing the dates of all holidays, and that included changes of season. Spring was the most important of all. It symbolized the beginning for people after the giants left the world.

For now, however, the warming days were a signal for activity. Some farmers barely waited for the snow to melt before they were in the fields with their plows, getting the earliest possible start for their peas. Tate watched, curious, as ramshackle pole towers ten to twelve feet high began to appear in the fields. She soon learned they were there because the crows were as canny about man as nature. They flocked to perch in trees, on rooftops, on fences, even on the castle walls, in their raucous, cawing thousands. It was the duty of farm children to perch in shelters atop the towers and yank at a network of lines strung across the fields and their seeds and, later—it was explained to Tate—the succulent sprouts. All manner of chasers dangled from the lines, from disturbingly realistic snakes of woven grass that writhed in the breeze to brightly colored, whirling propellors. And still occasional birds penetrated the defenses, tumbling from the sky, rapidly pecking at an exposed pea, then squalling triumphantly in escape. The children had help in the battle, however, in the figure of small dogs. They roamed the fields, alert to the pesky birds, and raced to do battle with every one they saw attempting to land. Tate never saw a dog catch a bird, but she did see several fall madly in love with a particular female, and until the owner removed her, the crows wreaked havoc.

The Baron spent the better part of a morning rendering judgments over the incident. Still, as bitterly as the farmers wrangled over whose dog trampled whose pea bed, and whether it was the female's fault for luring or a male's because he started the fight, everyone managed to enjoy the proceedings.

That evening there was no humor in the Baron's manner when he set in motion the operation that would put him irrevocably on the road to revolt.

One of Two's commers came for Tate as she worked with the wives of the unit in the new childcare building. He would say only that the Baron needed her at the castle. On the way she saw Neela and Sylah hurrying along ahead of her. By the time she arrived, they were already seated in his conference room. They weren't at the long table, but against the wall, across from Gan, Clas, and Emso. Also seated at the table, with their backs to the two women, were Two, Ops, and Four. She wondered why the other women were needed yet were excluded from the actual body of the meeting. It struck her as an ominous arrangement, but she let the idea go in order to examine the stranger in their midst.

He sat next to Baron Jalail at the head of the table. He was clearly a man of great wealth. His clothes were heavy wool, and a sea otter coat was draped across the back of his chair. Thick gold bracelets peeked out from under ornate decorative shirt cuffs, and a large enamel brooch dangled from a gold chain around his neck.

The Baron gestured her to a seat beside Emso, and introduced the newcomer. "I'm pleased to introduce all of you to Noble Malten," he said. "He's Baron Malten's brother, from the barony to the west. You'll be interested in what he has to say."

Within a matter of a few sentences Tate was more than interested—she was amazed. The man was a four-square traitor. As he spoke she could almost see him ooze malice. He dabbed at his face with a linen cloth continually, using each dab to change his eye contact from one person to the next. The eyes were dark, as intense as knife points.

He claimed the Malten barony was his by rights. His brother, in some unspecified manner, had cheated him of it. Now his brother meant to betray Baron Jalail. He unfolded a story that verified Bilsten's report; the victory at the Bear Paw frightened the King. He meant to lure the Wolves into a march west and ambush them. His hope was to convince them to surrender their officers. If they agreed, they'd be hired on by the King as his personal troops. Should that effort fail, they were to be slaughtered to a man.

At that point Baron Jalail said, "My man Two has already informed me of this plan. His men have been busy. To be honest, Noble Malten, they've told me of your dissatisfaction."

"Then they've not served you well," he said, and the Baron's eyes widened. He went on, "A man who's dissatisfied doesn't give you his brother's head on a stick. A man who's enraged does that."

"I see your point." The Baron looked uncomfortable. "However, I assure you, I don't want anyone's head. What I want is peace in my barony. The question we're all waiting to hear answered, however, is what do you want?"

Noble Malten's upper lip curled delicately. It was too tiny a movement to be properly identified as a sneer, but the piercing gaze chilled any mistaken notion that it was a smile. He said, "Your Wolves are our greatest weapon against the Olans. I want to see them protected, I want to see the King's treachery fail, and I want my brother overthrown before he loses my land to the King, or worse, to the Olans."

"You expect my Wolves to do that?"

"I merely suggest, Baron. I suggest you strike him and be in good defensive positions before the King arrives with his three helpers."

Mildly, Gan asked why they shouldn't simply send a Messenger to the King and tell him they'd uncovered the plot. Why should they fight anyone, especially countrymen?

"Because if you don't try for the bait, they'll bring the combined forces of all four barons here after you." He faced Jalail. "I think you can imagine what that many men looting and burning will do to your people. Even if the Wolves magically drive them off, the damage will take a decade to repair."

Gan's color heightened at the insult aimed at his men, but he said nothing. The Baron rose. "We'll confer. Your quarters are immediately next to this room, so you may rest knowing no one will know you are here. I'll give you my answer in the morning."

As soon as he was out of the room, the Baron gathered everyone else to his end of the table. His hands were joined on the table, each finger raised in a small bridge that twitched and trembled with enthusiasm. He said, "My first reaction is to leap at this opportunity. I wanted to avoid conflict with the King. He plans to attack me. There's no treason in self-defense. I still suspect Baron Malten knew Olans planned to attack us last fall. I've been the victim of my own enthusiasms before, however. That's why I have you men to advise me. I'll abide by your collective judgment."

He asked each man in turn, starting with his staff. It was apparent that all would have let Gan speak for them. As it was, the Baron forced everyone to speak individually. He asked questions, as well, assuring that everyone gave solid reasons for any advice. He saved Gan for last.

"Well, Gan," he said, "you've heard the arguments. We all have reservations. What do you think?"

Surprise and disappointment washed away the Baron's look of pleased anticipation as Gan shook his head, staring down at the tabletop. When he looked up, he said, "We have plenty of time to arrange a defense. We don't know if a new baron on our flank will be any more reliable than the old one. If we move, you can be sure the King will wonder where we got our advance information, and you can be equally sure this Malten is prepared to deny he was ever here. If the King chooses to attack, we'll be ready. If he sees we're prepared, and elects to leave us alone, everyone's better off."

The Baron was silent for a long time, massaging his throat as he thought. Without preamble, he turned to the wives. "Sylah. Neela. You hear the thoughts of the people. What do you know of their attitudes?"

They exchanged startled looks, and then Neela nodded, and Sylah spoke. She was almost shy, at first, but a quiet determination added force to her words, and her tentativeness disappeared little by little. "As women, we fear any battle, because we fear for the men in it. We also fear for all our sisters." She gave a quick gesture at the Baron's frown, hurrying on. "Life is better for us here in Harbundai. We have no advice for you, but assure us that you'll protect us from Ola, assure us that you'll help us secure our rights as people, and our sisters in every barony in the kingdom will help you any way they can."

The Baron gave her an acid smile. "Help us? How? By refusing to sleep with anyone who attacks us?"

Tate half rose, but Gan's quick grab held her in check. She was startled to see he'd reached for her without even looking; his attention was riveted on Neela, and he was struggling to keep back a grin.

Neela came out of her chair in one swift, flowing motion. Her blue eyes were as bright and forbidding as ice. She said, "The Wolves know their wives and children are protected by the Baron's word, should anything happen to them in the Baron's service. The women are grateful for the opportunity to work and profit from their efforts, and all they ever asked of the Baron was land to build houses and plant gardens. They're the envy of every woman in the kingdom, not because they have houses or land or husbands, but because they have *dignity*. Their men know that, and appreciate them—and you—all the more." She blushed and then added, "And the other thing you suggested has its merit, too."

Everyone else laughed as she sat down, and eventually the Baron joined in. He made a face, acknowledging he'd been bested, and waited for the moment to subside. Next he told Gan to prepare to march. The opportunities outweighed the dangers, he said, and ended the meeting.

Gan and Neela returned to their quarters. He piled some wood on the fire and started a blaze before settling in his chair. Neela busied herself breaking off chunks of bread and putting them on a wooden platter, then added some chopped onions to the covered iron pot in the fireplace. It was suspended from the right angle of an iron arm, the vertical end of which was fitted into a tube attached to a large metal plate bolted to the floor. She had to swing it out to add to it, and it grated and squeaked when it was moved. That brought all three dogs to full attention where they lay on the floor by the bed. They knew the sound meant cooking, which usually led to scraps. This time nothing more came of it. They resumed dozing.

Neela settled on the floor next to Gan, resting her arm on his thigh and her head on the arm. "Did I say too much?" she asked, looking into the fire.

He stroked her hair. "What you said was exactly right."

"You're so quiet. I thought you might be angry. People here aren't used to hearing a woman argue."

He chuckled. "I respect your judgment."

He hoped she'd let the conversation go at that point, and she seemed satisfied with his answer, so he was allowed to return to his thoughts. It took him a moment to regain his concentration, with the mouth-watering smell of venison stew already beginning to fill the room.

Food was one of the myriad things he'd have to arrange for the march. They'd be able to supply themselves with some food from the land, but much would have to go with them in wagons. Squeezing food from the locals was out of the question, except in an emergency, and they'd have to be repaid somehow. The men's equipment would have to be inspected thoroughly, too, and shortages made up. Now that clothing was standardized, it was much simpler to assure that everyone had what he was supposed to have. Anything extra was permitted, but its maintenance was the individual's responsibility. Personality tended to be expressed in decoration. He was proud of the handsome display they made on the march, although the staggering variety of hats tended to give the columns a raffish look.

He was also proud of their clothing. It had been chosen with great care after many consultations and experiments. Footcloths were an excellent example. The Dog People wore foot coverings that looked like cloth tubes, with a reinforced heel and toe. There were no weavers in Jalail who could duplicate them. They used a square cloth, folding it over the foot and around the ankle. It was Neela who pointed out how much more easily they washed, dried, and stowed for carrying. He'd grown a few blisters learning how to wrap them properly, but now, like every other Wolf, carried six such cloths. They also carried two strips of tough cotton material five feet long and three inches wide. Wrapped around the legs, they kept trousers from flopping about, and if a man was wounded, they made good bandages. If needed, a number of them could be tied together and used to hoist or lower articles. Every man also carried an additional shirt and trousers made either of leather or the oddly mottled dark brown cloth the Baron's people called kam. They seemed peculiarly attached to the stuff, although Gan found it ugly. It did, however, blend excellently with the forest. The men were most proud of their boots. They were high-topped, thick-soled, crafted by their own women in their own shops under the supervision of a man regarded as the best shoemaker in the barony. The women took pains to guarantee they were made of the best leather available. What little surplus they'd generated was avidly sought by locals and Peddlers alike. A man who lost a pair of boots carried the shields of four of his fellows everywhere the unit went until he paid for new ones.

As a last item each man carried a sewing kit to keep his gear in order.

Gan smiled to himself, remembering how Four carried on when he learned how much soap would be required for the unit. When he heard more than half of it was for the households—at Sylah's request—he almost choked. But he provided it. And the people in the villages were already commenting on the lower winter-sickness rate of the Wolves and their families.

He shook his head to clear his mind, forcing himself to face the real problem bothering him.

The Baron's decision was exactly what he wanted. He'd answered honestly when he advised against it. The victory at the Bear Paw didn't change the basic fact that his Wolves were a small unit. They were in the position of a small man in a fistfight with a big man. The small man must land a blizzard of punches and constantly avoid getting hit, because he can only wear down his opponent. Let the small man make one mistake, however, and the big man needs land only one blow. So it would be with the Wolves. They could win a dozen battles and still either Ola or the united barons of Harbundai would have the sheer manpower to overwhelm them, if they made that one, fatal error.

In his heart, though, he wanted the confrontation. Noble Malten was a traitor. His arrogant dishonesty was his weakness, as fear of the Wolves' growing strength was the King's. Playing their game was a risk. The stakes were irresistible.

At his knee, Neela was braiding her hair, letting it fall free, and he coiled a soft bundle of it around his fist, savoring the blood-surge that swept his body. There were times when he thought of his happiness, and caught himself staring off into the distance, as foolish as any spring colt.

And yet.

They were living on the edge of a knife. Without their contributions, Jalail would have left this world before winter, yet they lived at his sufferance. Guests or partners, they were dependent. Freedom was relative, he'd come to realize. Jalail put fewer demands on him, physically, than Nightwatch. Tribal demands had been natural to him, part of his life because he was part of the tribe. Here, where he was accepted and admired as he'd never been among his own people, he was constantly aware of being different. None of them spoke of it. He saw it, though. He saw the quick hurt in Clas' eyes when the other officers spoke of festivals or simple family interrelationships and he was ignored. They didn't do it out of unkindness, but through the ingrained habit of excluding anyone not "us" by birth. Sylah took it with less difficulty. He supposed her life as a Chosen had trained her to be an outsider.

Neela suffered the most and said the least. The other women treated her much as the men treated Clas. They seemed honestly to welcome her company. The wives of the Wolves knew how much she and Sylah and Tate had done for them, and they treated all of them like queens. Sylah had her healing house, and Tate her responsibility for training the unit. Neela worked long, hard hours with the weavers, potters, clothesmakers, and child-care women, but, like Clas, she wasn't one of them. They brought her the first flowers of spring where they worked, they made special shawls and blankets and pottery for her, but they never came within twenty yards of her front door, nor did they ask her to their homes. Several times lately he'd seen her when the afternoon sun streamed into their front door, sitting just inside the opening, her fair skin and bright hair alight in the glow. The first time, he'd held his breath, unmoving, not wanting to make her move while her beauty filled his eyes. Then he'd looked closely and seen the sadness, the tender yearning that pulled her hands from her lap out onto her thighs, as though she'd reach across the hundreds of feet separating her from the knot of laughing, talking women. Their gestures flashed white in the sun, lifting, darting, and each time one of their hands brushed another's arm or settled onto a shoulder, his wife winced in loneliness.

Later, with Neela asleep at his side, he stared into the unanswering darkness as on so many other nights, and asked himself yet again why his feet had been chosen to walk this path.

He asked himself if he knew the truth anymore. Once he'd been sure. Always. Now, he could never tell.

The darkness reached for him, touched his skin, his muscles, his very bones. It knew. It understood who he was and where he was going. It wouldn't tell. The light spring rain chuckled against the window. The night wind whispered, "Time. Patience. Time."

CHAPTER 63

Spring came to Ola with the same beauty it brought to Harbundai. Under the expected and eagerly awaited promise of renewal, however, there was tension. The kingdom knew Altanar meant to avenge the loss of his divisions, and he meant to bring Harbundai under control once and for all.

In the city itself, forges making weapons and armor smudged the sky with their smoke from dawn until darkness. After that, the fires provided entertainment for the children who'd gather to watch the showers of sparks whirl up from the chimneys. Parents who interrupted their fun in order to put them to bed were less amused. They led the children away, glancing back over their shoulders with the sort of grim resignation that comes with understanding the ways of power. As Conway made his way down a crowded street, he stopped to watch one of the smiths for a few minutes. The smith looked at his visitor and smiled pleasantly, but said nothing. Conway made no effort at conversation, either. Anyone he spoke to received a visit from the protectors. Nothing had ever come of it, but he'd learned not to put people at risk for the sake of a few words. Unwillingly, his eyes were drawn to the two men lounging nearby. At least they didn't wear the white clothes of their organization.

Altanar had given all five of his so-called guests the freedom of the city, but it was a carefully supervised freedom. To leave the abbey, the women had to ask permission—which had never been withheld, Conway had to admit—and then wait for an escort. The men could leave any time, but not until the requisite pair of followers was provided. The number of guards never varied, which led to the rule that anywhere the "guests" went, they were forbidden to separate. On the occasions when they'd discussed losing those constant companions, the talk was full of emotional gusto, but in the end they understood that any apparent resistance would only draw attention to themselves. Further, they knew that Altanar had a legion of informers who worked to stem the growing dissatisfaction of the populace. Even the Olans, his own tribe, were restive under the weight of increased manpower levies and taxes.

Conway and the others accepted their status, pretending unconcern about their restricted freedom. They felt the increasing stress, however; particularly Conway. His nocturnal forays were still unknown to the women. It troubled him more and more to deceive them. Things had gone on too long. He couldn't face confessing his duplicity. More than that, he was afraid he'd risk his link to the growing forces of resistance. Ironically, their greatest hope was their greatest danger. Once again—he was doing it a lot—he told himself he was handling everything fairly well.

Of all of them, Carter had proven to be the greatest surprise, he thought, turning his back on the forge and continuing his walk. He'd first noticed a change in her manner in the fall, at the big harvest feast. Altanar paid them another of his visits, and Carter, who'd vigorously avoided contact with the man up to that point, not only listened closely to everything he said throughout his whole visit, but when he singled her out, she answered his questions quietly and forthrightly. Later, she'd been more like her old self as she explained that the only way to deal with him was to soften him up, find his vulnerabilities. Conway warned her that Altanar had no more vulnerabilities than Dracula, and fewer friends.

The more he thought about it, the more he believed that evening had been some sort of psychological watershed for her. Her personality, formerly aggressive and occasionally even abrasive, had continued to soften. She was as bright and incisive as ever, but almost reluctant to state a position. When she did, however, it was invariably backed by sound logic and perception. In fact, he remembered, it was she who suggested they take as conciliatory a position as possible on all issues, making compliance their camouflage. She'd also proved to be almost as adept as Leclerc in introducing fragments from her world into this one. She was a master of the intricacies of cat's cradle, a game completely unknown among the Olans. Young and old, they responded to it with great glee. More than that, she knew several different names for each pattern, and could weave a story incorporating the intricate figures as smoothly as her flying fingers changed her web from one appearance to another. The children begged for her tales.

The Chosens were her favorites. She learned their names, their likes, their personalities, and spent at least part of every day with them. Several of the crustier Priestesses complained to the Iris Abbess that she was too influential. The Abbess told them to learn from her. It was a wise decision, but not a popular one. The few adult Church friends she'd acquired drifted away. Still, she had her children, and, as Conway had noted on at least one occasion, her stories for them had some interesting morals buried in them. Caged birds sang their way to freedom, noble animals saved households, ladies were saved from dragons by heroes, and mice organized themselves into a team of cat-belling daredevils. He smiled, thinking of it. He was determined to let her go on with her secret as though he'd never noticed what she was doing, but it was perfectly clear to another adult that she was guiding them to create their own standards and dispute the ones they saw around them.

Carter's greatest conquest was a recent event, however, one that amazed everyone. Far too often for it to be coincidence, Altanar began happening by the Chosen classes when she was telling her stories. From the very first, he was as rapt as her six- and seven-year-old charges. The next thing anyone knew, he was taking part. When she finished, he "explained" what she'd said, casting himself in the heroic roles, pointing out how the tale reflected his position, his accomplishments, his goals. Carter wisely never contradicted him, and was too shrewd ever to explain to the children that another interpretation was possible. In the meantime she jollied Altanar as no one else dared. Conway had only seen her act twice, and both times his lungs had ached from repressing laughter, the same heart-in-mouth humor he associated with memories of a high-wire clown.

Kate Bernhardt and Sue Anspach were more direct in their integration into the culture, and although their efforts weren't as dramatic as Carter's, they were effective. For a while Anspach visibly suffered when Carter, who was her closest friend, drew away from her and found her niche among the young Chosens. Bernhardt saw the problem and responded, providing attention and a friendly presence. Anspach still made occasional attempts to reestablish closeness with Carter, but something of Carter's need for Anspach's form of caring seemed to have disappeared.

So it was that Bernhardt and Anspach threw their efforts into working with the Healers. Remembering Falconer, they insisted they not work with the ill. The Iris Abbess accepted their reluctance as perfectly reasonable, and assigned them to the War Healers, where they dealt exclusively with injuries. It turned out to be an unexpectedly beneficial move. Traveling to treat victims, they observed everything, comparing with each other to fix the details in their minds. Dealing with victims in the healing house, they probed for information. By the time the snows were gone for good and the daffodils were speckling the fields with their yellow cheer, they had learned the best escape routes to the north and south, and had created a shared memory bank of data on every noble family in the kingdom.

Leclerc, like Carter, had undergone a change. Once his improved hoist system became known, he was approached by one of Altanar's generals, who wanted to talk about the engineering problems of siege machines. Leclerc had gotten carried away, and his discussion of a moving tower, with sketches and mathematical calculations to predict stresses, had frightened the poor general speechless. Any arithmetic more complex than long division was considered to be related to the time of the giants, and therefore evil. Leclerc's cabalistic x's and y's that equaled s's and t's had the grizzled old warrior backing away with both hands wiggling Two-signs to ward off witchcraft until Leclerc was able to convince him that it was nothing to be afraid of, just words from his old language, and so forth. The general left muttering to himself, and Leclerc spent the next forty-eight hours sitting bolt upright in a straight-backed chair, wipe aimed at the door, determined to blast a few protectors when they came for him.

When that threat didn't materialize, he asked Conway to help him get assigned to the palace farm operation. Altanar's fear of poison had led him to have a farm created where almost everything he ate was grown. It was also a large horse-breeding facility. Leclerc was granted his request. He threw himself into his chores with his characteristic energy, and within a week was supervising the construction of a huge chicken house. He confided to Conway that he'd improve the local stock through careful genetic controls and show the people how to create a better fertilizer from the droppings.

Conway visited the place once. The people working there clearly liked Leclerc and his continual bustling about, although they were bemused by his preoccupation with manure. He showed Conway his methane production tank with the pride of a man discussing fine jewelry.

The shock came when he led Conway into what he called his "office." An out of the way cranny, Conway wasn't at all surprised to learn it had been a stall before Leclerc claimed it for his own. Now it had a new window, freshly cut in the wooden wall, and long worktable that stretched the length of one of the long walls. The opposite wall was fitted with shelves. The slot remaining in the center was just enough for a man to move and turn about. The table was littered with jars of all sizes and shapes, a large mortar with pestle, and a crude scale. Leclerc had posed at the far wall, directly under his window, grinning like a child with a secret. Conway finally had to ask him what he was supposed to see.

Leclerc was crestfallen. "You didn't notice? Can't you smell it?"

Gently, Conway said, "I haven't smelled anything else since I got here. I have to tell you, Louis, it doesn't intrigue me."

Laughing, Leclerc said, "Not the manure. This!" He hoisted a sack off the shelf. "They use it all the time. For the soil. They doctor the horses with it. They smoke apples with it before they dry them."

Mystified, Conway looked in the bag. "Sulfur?" he asked. He heard his voice questioning Leclerc's sanity.

The smaller man was even more amused. "You just don't see it, do you?" With his hands on Conway's shoulders, he forced him back into the huge barn. "Look at the walls, the lower part, where it's made of stone. Don't you see that stuff?"

Conway guessed. "You mean the white junk? Like salt?"

"Salt." Scorn dripped from the word. "Didn't they teach you anything but vehicular density and traffic lights? That 'white junk' is saltpeter, Matt. Saltpeter is potassium nitrate. Remember me showing you the charcoal ovens? Remember the sulfur? Now this—potassium nitrate? Doesn't that suggest *anything* to you?"

"Oh, Lord," Conway said, breathing hard. "Black powder. You're working on black powder?"

Leclerc practically trotted back to his office, leaving Conway no choice but to follow. He showed him jars of the white powder, then pots with a black, grainy substance. "The white scum on the manure settling ponds is the same potassium nitrate. I've got a pretty good supply now, but I can't get the mix to work right," he said, banging one of the jars on the table and sending

Conway into an instinctive cringe. "This is good charcoal. Willow. I seem to remember that's what they said was best. And this sulfur's straight out of Snowfather Mountain, pure as the morning dew." As he talked he was dumping dabs of each in a different pot, stirring it around with a stick. He poked at it viciously, making the pot roll drunkenly.

Conway grabbed his arm. "Be careful," he croaked.

"What? Oh, don't worry. This is only good for starting fires. It burns okay, but no oomph, you know?"

"If they catch you, it's going to be a problem."

"If we don't find a way to keep our 'lightning weapons' in operation, we won't have any more problems ever. We need a hole card. This stuff will help. When I get the formula right." When he dumped the newest batch into his tiny firepit, it sizzled and spat blue flame that smoked horribly. He shook his head sadly.

Still, his argument couldn't be denied. Conway had agreed to help in any way he could. He only hoped they had time to do something—anything—to forestall Altanar's latest move.

The need for safety forced reminiscence from Conway's mind as he continued his apparently aimless stroll along the narrow street. He reminded himself he must continue to appear nonchalant.

He wiped a quick flush of sweat from the palms of his hands on his trousers and wished Tee could be with him to keep an eye on things. She trusted no one in the castle, and, of course, was never allowed outside the wall. Conway's contact with the underground was a do-it-yourself activity. He'd gone over the wall a few other nights with her, but that risk was made even worse by winter. The cold might keep the guards huddled in sheltered cubbies when they were supposed to be patrolling, but a sudden snowfall could turn their footprints into glaring evidence even the sloppiest security would notice.

They'd managed to work out a system of signals with the underground. If Conway had information to pass to Wal, he stopped in a particular tavern and ordered beer. He said no more than that, and spoke to no one else, but when he left there, his meandering walk eventually led him to the market, where a contact would be made.

Conway's walk led to the city's major market, according to the plan. The next step was for him to bargain with someone for fruit. The contact always wore a green scarf and a silver earring. It was never the same person, and was as likely to be a man as a woman.

Today it was a man, and he was selling dried apricots, apples, cherries, and peaches from wood-slat baskets. Conway spotted him as soon as he stepped into the eye-shocking, ear-pounding tent. The market's furor always dazed him momentarily, the sensory impact of its activity a physical blow. Nevertheless, as if his eye was drawn by some force, he saw his man instantly. His gaze simply cut through everything else, and the immediacy, the ease, of the identification jolted him like the touch of a knife point. He paused, taking time to collect himself, then began to move casually up and down the aisles.

As always, the market took him out of himself. He enjoyed wandering through it more than anything else he'd found in Ola, because the people were alive, enjoying themselves, bursting with energy. Not only was it like nothing he'd ever seen before, every visit taught him something new about the world he lived in now. Today a man was selling a spotted fur that Conway was sure was a snow leopard's coat. When he asked the man where he got it, he looked at Conway as if he'd lost his mind. "Up in the mountains, to the north. That's where they live."

Conway smiled and nodded before walking away, hiding his surprise. If there were leopards in what used to be the Cascade range and was now the Enemy Mountains, it had to be the handiwork of the Williamsites and their cell banks. If the war had started with the all-out nuclear exchange everyone had expected, they'd never have had time to complete their work. Apparently, by choosing the most isolated sites possible for their centers, they'd been able to release breeding numbers of all manner of creatures. He was already used to seeing as many as six different kinds of pheasant hung in stalls, their blazing iridescence as fine as any enamel. All but one, the ringneck, were exotic creatures he only vaguely remembered from zoos, on TV, or in pictures at species preservation banks. Tiger and bearskins were impressive and in good number, but not as commonplace as seal, beaver, mink, and caracul lamb. Wool was abundant, llama and alpaca as well as sheep and goat. Butcher stalls offered at least a half-dozen different kinds of meat, from rabbit to hog. Most of the handicraft products were crude by his standards, but they were done with care and appeared to be sturdy. Woodworkers hammered and sawed while waiting for customers, potters shaped their bowls and plates, and there were even jewelers, soldering and polishing and twisting metal.

When he stopped in front of the fruit peddler, he kept his eyes firmly to the front. It was the Peddler's responsibility to know if it was safe to talk. If he wasn't satisfied that he'd identified the watchers, he'd simply bargain with Conway and send him on his way. Today, however, he was eager to confront him, so eager he almost forgot to control his expression. Conway's first irritable glance calmed him, and the man stepped back into his role as merchant. After a moment he held up a handful of dried peaches, as though displaying them. Instead of a sales talk, however, he said, "Wal wants to know if Altanar has taken your weapons from you."

Conway grunted in surprise, then shook his head. "No. Way too much."

The man went on. "The protectors are collecting men for the army and adding members to their own strength. One of Altanar's favorites has said the attack on Harbundai will come earlier than anyone expected, and if you and your friends don't lead the way with the lightning weapons, someone else will. Wal's very worried about you."

"About the weapons, you mean."

The man grinned, holding up another handful of peach slices. Conway thought they looked like old ears. He said, "He thinks they'll be useless without you."

Helping himself to a slice, Conway bit off a chunk. It was as tough as the bark of the tree it came from, but delicious. He said, "What's he expect us to do?"

"Be ready to leave. There won't be much warning. And you better leave here, too." The man's gaze flicked past Conway's shoulder. In a louder voice he said, "I'll make a gift of the one you've eaten, but that's my last price. Three cash is cheap."

Conway counted out the money, and the man wrapped his purchase in a square of paper, tying it off with twine. "See you again, I hope," he said. He flashed an innocent smile, offset by a twinkling eye as bold as a jay's, then Conway left.

The walk out of the market was one of the most difficult things Conway had ever done. His thoughts were chaotic, leaping from subject to subject, and he thought of the red, burning sparks twisting away from the chimneys of the smiths. He was as helpless as they were. There was a great chance that he'd end up consumed by darkness, as well, exactly like them. He tried to think of his friends and how they'd respond to the need to escape. It was going to be like leaving the cave again, he thought; too dangerous to stay, and yet leaving threw them into the unknown.

He was embarrassed to discover that he couldn't concentrate on them. Always, Tee superimposed herself.

All winter long he'd denied what was happening to him, even on the nights when he waited for her to come to him and she'd failed. Sometimes he didn't sleep at all on those nights, and if he did, he invariably woke with a wrenching start, heart pounding, shivering with a fear that made his bones ache. The worst part was over in seconds, but the fear stayed with him, a poison that made it impossible to eat or think clearly until he saw her and knew she was all right.

Even then he'd told himself that he was afraid for her because he was afraid for anyone who lived at the whim of Altanar.

On the nights she stayed with him, he knew a pleasure and a satisfaction so total he found it easy to deny that Matt Conway had ever been anyone else, lived anywhere else. In the bright light of day he told himself he was lonely, and that she was, too.

The nights they lowered themselves over the castle wall and made their way into the city, he feared for her far more than himself, yet took inordinate pride in her swiftness, her strength, and her indomitable courage. Their danger-forged closeness on those nights was a bittersweet emotional orgy.

The massive doors of Sunrise Gate loomed in front of him, and now he told himself that he couldn't bear to leave this place without her. His face grew warm, then hot, but he smiled to himself, because he realized that was the first time he'd told himself something about Tee that was honest. It felt very good.

CHAPTER 64

For two days Conway debated whether he should alert his friends to the impending escape. There was little they could do to prepare, he reasoned, and if they showed any signs of unusual activity, the protectors could become suspicious. More suspicious, he corrected himself wryly. They already suspected everyone and everything. With good cause. Many of the people hated Altanar, but it was the sort of hatred one directed at a river that drowned a child, or a fire that swept a house and its accumulated memories. There was an other-world sense of power about the King. The protectors brought Altanar's cruelty down to a personal basis. When Altanar ordered pain, they inflicted it. Wherever they went, eyes watched for their misstep.

On the morning of the third day one of them came for Conway, saying only that the King wanted him. He was dressed in the white trousers, shirt, and cape of official business, and Conway felt the muscles in the small of his back draw tight. The protector fell in behind him, giving one-word directions as they proceeded. The King's orders came from their mouths without life or color. They had authority to kill anyone who refused to obey.

Entering the King's work chambers, Conway hardly bothered to glance at the scowling mask painted on the inner wall. He walked around it briskly, smiling an ease that was a lie. Altanar greeted him amicably, bubbling with small talk that only heightened Conway's conviction that something was brewing. The point came quickly. "I've had to change my plans for the war with Harbundai," he said. "I'd planned to use you and your friends to decide the action at the critical time and place. I intend the first battle to be the final one. My goal is annihilation of Harbundai's army. In the end, it saves the lives of my men. You agree?"

The inference that they weren't to be used was a relief, especially since Conway knew Tate to be somewhere in the country to the north. Still, he heard a threat under the words. He agreed cautiously.

Altanar laughed appreciatively. "I sense a reluctance. Good. Our wars aren't your concern. To spare you involvement, I'm asking you to train some of my men to use your weapons." He formed an expression of false regret, then went on. "I've always agreed that the weapons are yours, and you use them on my behalf. But we have a new problem."

"What is 'our' problem, King?" Conway emphasized the word, bringing a sudden glint of irritation to Altanar's eyes. It faded, replaced by one of his more unpleasant smiles. "I've located your friends," he said. "The two called Jones and Tate are living on the lands of a fat little coward who names himself Baron Jalail. You should have told me the woman is black; such a curiosity should be shared. Anyhow, they arrived with the disgraced son and best friend of an ousted Dog War Chief. The Dogs are responsible for the treacherous surprise attack that embarrassed three of my divisions. I can't ask you to fight Harbundai, knowing that your friends will be involved on the other side."

"And you want us to train others to fight our friends, instead?"

"Of course not!" Altanar was injured. "At my own expense, I'm sending a Messenger to tell this so-called Baron that you're in my service. I'll give him an opportunity to find a way out of the battle, and let him know I'll be very well disposed toward him, if he does. Secondly, if he presumes to have some sort of honor, and insists on resisting the inevitable, I'll warn him that I'll show no mercy to the defeated. Lastly, you'll tell your friends that you're not engaging in this war, as it's not your affair, and you ask them to do the same."

"But you'll have trained men to take our place."

Altanar's smile was avid now; he was enjoying a larger prospect than toying with his listener. "One surprise in a battle is worth more than two divisions. The surprise of your weapons should be worth at least five." He sobered quickly. "The most important thing, however, is that we spare your friends."

Conway already knew what he had to do. Argument would only fan the flames of Altanar's paranoia. So would too quick an agreement. He said, "We can train no more than two men, King, and we must retain possession of the weapons until the battle itself."

They haggled, finally agreeing on three trainees. Instruction would start in three days and last for seven. Conway gave ground on the possession issue, conceding that the men be allowed to carry them when they left Ola. Altanar grudgingly agreed that Conway could accompany them.

After the meeting, hurrying back to his quarters, Conway's mind raced through the implications. Tate and Jones were the lever to pry the group from the weapons. He knew they wouldn't dare fire into the confusion of battle, knowing their friends were somewhere in the mass. And Conway knew no Messenger with a warning for Tate and Jones would ever leave Harbundai. Once those three men proved they could handle the weapons, the lives of the strangers would be counted in minutes.

Sabotaging the weapons so they killed the Olan handlers was out of the question.

Wal was their best hope. The prospect of trying to escape had looked grittily dangerous just a few short days ago. The question now was, could Wal arrange anything soon enough?

Altanar walked over to throw some more wood on the fire, pulling up a chair to sit by it. He pulled his cloak tighter; the hard fist of winter still clenched the stone of the castle, resisting spring's warmth. Even had it been pleasant in the room, he thought, the fire was necessary. Fire purified, and staring into its infinite shifting cleared his mind of distractions. There was truth in fire.

He smiled at that thought. The protectors certainly found fire helpful in their quest for truth. For a moment he wondered if other people's private thoughts were as witty as his. It was rather doubtful. He couldn't remember anyone who'd amused him for any length of time.

Conway's reaction to fighting his friends had been precisely as anticipated. That was good. And he didn't simply agree to hand over the weapons, which meant he was truly concerned and bargaining as best he could. There was no evasion in his argument.

Or was there?

There couldn't be, he decided. The man was no fool. He had no choice, and was struggling for terms.

Sometimes he wondered if Falconer might not have been easier to deal with. Conway hid his feelings well.

Falconer. It was infuriating that he'd managed to get his hands on that knife. They never should have been allowed in the kitchen. The chief cook paid for that, but the damage was already done. He wished the cook had lived longer. Much longer. He deserved it. And the new woman didn't understand meat preparation half as well.

He moved in the chair again, berating himself for letting his mind wander. Conway wasn't especially concerned about training men to use the weapons in seven days. That was good, too. The lightning weapons would be vital in two weeks. Three, at the most.

The fire danced and wavered across the logs. He reached for the poker, unmindful of the craft that went into the smooth hand-fitting handle or the stylized snake of the iron body. Poking about, he asked himself why he was still bothered by the conversation with Conway.

Seven days of training. There was something about the way he looked, the way his eyes moved. He wasn't pleased with that number. Not upset, but unpleased. Why would that be? Of course he claimed he needed ten days, but people always said they needed more of everything than they really did. Altanar sighed. They were all so foolish; it was a wonder he was able to accomplish anything.

Seven days. What difference did it make to him if he had seven days, or ten, or twenty? Aloud, he said, "I saw something. What was it? What was there about the training time that was so important? He argued for more time, but weakly; why did he never tell me it would be my responsibility if the trainees didn't learn the job properly? Any reasonable man would have tried to hide behind that logic. Something's wrong."

He drew the heavy poker from the coals. The snake's forked tongue and head glowed a dull rose color. A wisp of smoke rose from a place where a tiny piece of wood adhered to it. He knocked it off, then lowered the end of the poker to the fur at the edge of the stone hearth. Individual hairs blackened and writhed away from the heat, sending up billows of acrid smoke. He twisted the handle, crushing the carbonized fur aside, exposing the naked hide. Small blisters erupted on it, and the leather charred. It sizzled and crackled. He continued twisting the handle, jabbing with the snake's tongue until the noise stopped. As he replaced the poker in its rack, he bent forward into the still-rising smoke. It filled his nose.

"Truth," he said. The sound was soft, sensual. "Fire bares truth."

An hour later Altanar was standing outside the room where the woman called Carter was telling the children a story. It had to do with a rabbit and a blackberry thicket. He peered in, amused by her seriousness, the intensity of her manner. The story was so much like her—like all ordinary people, actually. They invented their little tales to give themselves a sense of achievement. The rabbit would trick the fox, and live another day. Ordinary people admired the rabbit, wanted to be just like him. A man of intelligence fought to be a clever fox.

When she was finished she attempted to follow the children out of the room and into their play yard. From his position against the wall he stepped in front of her, blocking her way. He startled her, and she clapped a hand to her mouth, almost smothering the small cry. Her eyes were wide, fright-ened. It pleased him that they stayed that way even when she recognized him.

He said, "I didn't mean to surprise you. Come, sit with me for a moment. I have news that will please you." He took her wrist and attempted to turn her, but she resisted.

"My children," she said. "I can't leave them alone."

He continued to force her around. "I arranged to have Priestess watch them. You're free until I have to leave."

She let herself be led back to her chair, only once glancing at the door. When she sat, she drew in her elbows and feet, shrinking into the smallest space possible.

Altanar chose a chair and swept into it, flaring the embroidered cape in a brave show. Its bright green embroidered lining contrasted perfectly with the glory of the reds and yellows of the sunburst on the outer surface. His blouse and trousers were also embroidered, featuring an intricate interwoven chain pattern of white against the blue-green material.

He asked her about the children, steeling himself to bear her prattle as long as he could, then changed the subject to herself and her friends. She assured him that all was well, sounding almost as if she believed it. In turn, he explained how it was only the custom of the land that kept them practi-cally imprisoned. "If it wouldn't offend my entire nation," he said, taking her hand, "I'd never make you ask for an escort. I have complete authority, of course, but, as a king, my people's customs must influence my every thought." He looked down at his doeskin slippers. "I was talking to Conway just a little while ago. I think he'd like to leave us. As much as I'd hate to see that, I couldn't stop you, of course. You're my guests; you leave when you choose. But I'm frankly puzzled by his lack of gratitude for the protec-tion I've offered you."

She started to protest, and he touched a finger to her jaw, forestalling her. He went on, "I know you'll defend him, and in truth, I've never suggested I want anything from him, except some training for some of my people, so we can defend ourselves against Harbundai. He agreed to that, but I rather expected him to offer me one of the weapons. Not now, but certainly he could spare one when you all decide to leave us? You already have more of them than there are of you."

She said, "I wish we could give you all of them. I wish we didn't need them, and I wish you didn't, either. I hate all this killing. The pain—" Her eyes sparkled with sudden tears.

He released her hand and strode to the window. A pair of protectors nearby assured there were no listeners, so he said, "I wish you knew how much I hate to be the one who inflicts these things on my people. They force me to it. My lifelong ambition is to provide them happiness and security, but to do that I have to have the power to create a society. So many resist me. And do they want to help people? Never. They want everything for themselves, just as Harbundai blocks us from our proper rights in the Inland Sea."

Rising from the chair, she moved to stand behind him at a respectful distance. "I thought your war with Harbundai—I mean, I heard you say it was a conquest."

"It is. Or will be." He turned, smiling down at her. "As far as their king is concerned. But the people will welcome a ruler who understands their needs. I can't sound too conciliatory to my people—they have to fight the war, don't they?—but I know I can tell you the truth. It makes me feel better to be able to say it. I hate war and killing. I hope we can end it quickly, and build something good."

"Oh, I do, too."

"I especially hope so now." He gave her a slow, wise wink. "Did I tell you I had good news?"

"There's more? What you told me about yourself—" She stopped, coloring slightly, embarrassed by what she'd revealed of her thoughts. Her lips remained slightly parted as she stared at him, and he saw her as a fish, convincing herself that bait wasn't really bait. He stepped closer and held out his hands. She raised hers for him to take.

He said, "I haven't said anything because I didn't want to raise your hopes, but I've been searching very hard for your two missing friends. I found them."

"Donnacee? Jones? They're here?"

"No, no. But I know where they are. They're prisoners of a Baron Jalail, one of Harbundai's ugly little nobles." He watched her delight weaken and die as he told of the danger they'd be in during the next battle. Then, letting go of her hands, he gestured her to silence. He practically ran to the door, peering up and down the hall, repeating the process at the window. Returning to her, he sat in one of the chairs, pulling her down to the one next to him. Leaning so close his lips brushed the hair tumbled over her ear, he said, "Only my most trusted spies know I'm negotiating with three of Harbundai's barons, arranging for them to desert with all their men. They hate their king, you know. And they're deathly afraid of the lightning weapons. I have to make it *look* like I'm declaring war, but I hope I can force Harbundai to surrender without bloodshed. It sickens me to be so underhanded, but kingship's a game of patience as well as great skill."

"You can do it." Impulsively, she put her hand on his arm, too excited to notice the way he almost imperceptibly pulled away at the contact. She said, "I'm so glad you told me these things. When I saw your truth protectors at the Beach of Songs, and what they did—" She blinked and shivered before continuing. "It makes all the difference, knowing you can't help any of it. And trying to negotiate a peace! That's wonderful news. That's exactly what has to be done. I knew— No, I didn't know anything. I'll be as honest with you as you've been with me. At first I thought you were cruel. I hoped and hoped there was goodness in you, and after a while I thought I saw the real you behind the cruelty, the King who suffers because he must do these things. Now I know. You want what's best for everyone, and you must be firm to get it."

He rose, stroking her hair once, thinking it was remarkably wiry. It conjured some interesting images.

Later, you naughty boy, he thought.

He said, "I trust you. Please, don't say a word to anyone. Especially Conway. He's very proud of his leadership, and I don't want to offend him."

Her eyes flashed. "I know all about him. I won't tell anyone anything."

He was humming as he left.

CHAPTER 65

They were walking on the grounds inside the castle wall. From their first days in Ola, Falconer had insisted they arrange frequent meetings, the more the better. People came to expect to see them in a group, and what was commonplace was eventually accepted as nonthreatening. It was the safest way possible for them to exchange information. Conway continued the pattern. Falconer had also told him personally that if any outsider ever attempted to interfere with their meetings, he should interpret it as a very bad sign. Altanar was unable to hide his dislike for the practice, but he was equally unable to forbid it. Not and maintain the pretense of treating the group as guests. It was a weird game, one that everyone knew could only end badly. Altanar was determined to have the use of the weapons, and he still hoped to twist his "guests" around to serving him. Failing that, he'd torture what he could out of them. They knew it. He knew they knew it. And, until now, they'd all continued the charade, each side looking for a way to win. First Falconer, and now Conway, had treated a running escape as the worst possible case next to being imprisoned.

Well, he told himself, preparing to break the news, we're one step away from the worst. It's time to try for next-to-last. He tried to sound confident.

"We're getting out of here," he said. The three women looked at him as if he'd spoken a different language, and Leclerc's audible gulping sound was the only thing that interrupted the sibilance of the spring breeze through the spruces lining the path.

Leclerc recovered first, however, and asked one question. "When?"

"Tonight. Altanar left an hour ago to ride north and inspect the divisions getting ready to move against Harbundai. Part of his personal guard's with him, so security's under strength. The ones that are left won't be as alert as usual. We'll never have a better chance."

Anspach asked, "How will we get away? They'll be after us as soon as they miss us." The question wasn't unexpected, but the flat, calm way she asked it was a mild surprise. He looked at her before answering, embarrassed that he was belatedly recognizing significant changes in the old Sue Anspach. It wasn't just the shorter hair, combed back, that gave her that leaner look, nor was it the sunlight accentuating healthier, ruddier skin. She was as soft-spoken as ever, the sense of caring still there—she seemed to have a capacity for worrying about others, and it still shone through. The new woman had an overlay of surety, as well. This one knew she had strengths to counterbalance weaknesses. He'd liked the other one. This was an improvement.

"We've got help." Conway heard himself being smug, and couldn't help it. "Louis knew I'd met the local underground. I never mentioned it to anyone else because I didn't want you responsible for anything if I got caught."

There were a series of exclamations, not all entirely pleased, as he expected, but the real outburst came from Carter. She was very angry. "You've been meeting with the King's enemies all this time? Risking all our lives, without even the courtesy of telling us about it? Now you say these rebels we're just hearing about are going to whisk us away. King Altanar is sure to find us, and when he does, we'll all be blamed for trying to escape, for dealing with outlaws, for lying to him. Why should we even try to run away? Who would we run to?"

There was enough truth in her accusations and enough logic in her questions to hurt. Conway was conciliatory, although he did defend his position, telling her that the people helping them were far less savage than Altanar, and nothing like the Mountain People. He emphasized that he and Leclerc had been teaching Altanar's men how to use the wipes. They could only stall for so long, he reminded them, adding that Altanar had selected some of his best for them to instruct. He ended by saying, "We're at the end of the line. They know enough now to take over."

"Good," Carter said. "I'm glad. We shouldn't be fighting anyone anyhow. This whole stupid war's just so he can get control of the Inland Sea. You all know how I despise even the idea of war, but the sea really is his. Let him have the guns. He told you he only asked for his men to have them because he doesn't want us to chance shooting at Tate and Jones. We haven't needed weapons here. We don't need them now. I'll be glad if we never see them again."

Suddenly she recognized the disbelief and burgeoning antagonism around her, and she drew back as if afraid. The silence was awkward, painful, and when she laughed, the trill was as sharp as breaking glass. Her gesture of dismissal was a tight arc across her body. "I know what you're thinking. I'm not defending him. That's ridiculous. I'm only saying how terribly dangerous it really would be to run away from here. We should calm down and ask ourselves very rationally if we've ever considered that Altanar's as trapped as we are. We've seen cruelty, but have we ever even thought that maybe he *has* to do the things he does? Or that he doesn't actually do them himself? He's been genuinely considerate of us. After all, he's involved in a war, and to him we're potentially dangerous aliens."

Leclerc said, "He's treated us like calves being fattened for slaughter. What's it take to convince you? Do you want to be spread-eagled on one of those racks at the Beach of Songs?"

She paled and her mouth flew open. For a second she looked comical, an effect that stopped at the fury in her eyes. She controlled herself very well, however. She said, "I say we vote on it."

"Of course." Conway concurred immediately. "But we have to stay together. Majority rules, and if we go, we all go. Agreed?"

All nodded. He put the question to them, and only Carter wanted to stay. She accepted the judgment with no comment and with apparent grace. Conway launched into a short discussion about the need for appearing perfectly normal, but he watched her. He thought he'd seen a glimmer of something surly. He remembered back to the arguments about leaving the cave; she'd resisted that, too. The thing that outweighed everything else, however, was how the Beach of Songs affected her. He decided he was borrowing trouble. She just needed time to adjust to the idea.

Bernhardt was asking how he intended to coordinate their departure, and he told her there was no strict schedule. "The people helping us have to wait for an opportunity. All I know is that we've got to be out of here by moonrise. That reminds me—don't forget to blacken faces and hands. Check each other for white or shiny gear. Pack so nothing rattles. Be ready any time after dark."

Anspach said, "These friends of yours—is what Janet said true? Haven't we even seen any of them? And where are they taking us?"

He said, "The answers are yes, no, and I don't know. And now you're wondering if we have a chance. Chance, yes. Choice? Not really."

She smiled and gave a small shrug. Carter ducked her head and pretended to study her boots when he looked her way.

When they parted, they all worked hard at being unaffected, and Leclerc managed to appear practically nonchalant. Conway wondered how they felt about his own good-byes. He was a bit more optimistic than they were, he was sure. He smiled, thinking of how proudly Tee diagrammed a four-person cell and told him how only one person in a cell knew how to contact one other cell. She was so sure no one before had ever designed anything so clever.

The memory set off one of the draining fits of depression that were beginning to worry him more and more.

Despite all the opportunities and advantages simply lying at mankind's feet in this world, the people weren't a shade different from the ones who'd burned and blasted and diseased the race almost to extinction. With millions of square miles of land to provide them with an almost unimaginably rich existence, they were still warring and killing, greedy for every tiny advantage over their fellow man.

And he was part of it. He'd already killed at the battle by the river. He knew, given the chance, he'd kill Altanar. The world would be better off for it.

Was Matt Conway any better a man for having blown up a murderous savage? Would Matt Conway be any better a man for doing it again?

Irresolution ate at his soul. The feeling that nothing was worth anything clutched for his mind, wanted to erode his will to fight for survival.

The race *had* survived.

That raw fact restored his balance, got his feet back under him. He consciously straightened. The old saw about "Where there's life, there's hope" was true. Man would always have the capacity for evil, and good men must always be willing to face the evil ones and overcome them. If armed resistance was the only way he could contribute to Altanar's downfall, or the destruction of anyone like him, then that was what he'd do.

Brassy descending notes from a war horn on the castle wall announced midday and broke his reverie. He stopped his aimless wandering and headed for the kitchen. He had no appetite whatever, but reason said it might be a long time before his next meal. Sitting alone at one of the long trestle tables, he put away an exceptionally hearty load with workmanlike steadiness. It was excellent steak, with rough-cut slabs of fresh bread and butter. There were assorted jams, as well, and cheese. There were apples, some still dry, others plumped from soaking. Finishing, he rose, draining the last of his dandelion-root coffee. He thought wryly that he might be eating his way into a real handicap; if he ate that much again at the evening meal, he'd be so full he couldn't run.

"It's good to see you smiling," Tee said in her soft, high voice, and the suddenness of it, coming from right at his shoulder, startled him so badly he almost dropped the drinking mug.

"What are you doing here?" He scanned the room as he spoke, his underlying nervousness breaking through his relaxation of the previous moment.

She said, "There's nothing to worry about. I work here. It's natural for me to speak to you, but you should frown. Anyone watching will assume you're criticizing me."

"What a place." He glared at her. "Is everything going well?"

She lowered her gaze to the floor, looking contrite. "Everything is ready." All he could see of her face was her cheek, and when its color heightened, he frowned in earnest, wondering what caused the change. Then she said, "I wish you weren't leaving," and he understood. He almost reached for her.

"I want you to come with us," he said.

She jerked, turning a wide eye on him for a second before stepping back, cowering as if she expected him to strike her. Her voice was choked. "Don't say that. Please, go." She turned to get away and he grabbed her, struggling to appear angry.

"I had to say it. It's true. I have to talk to you. I can't leave without you."

With an agility that took him completely unaware, she slipped out of his grasp.

Did she simply want the scene to end before it became dangerous? Was she telling him that she wanted to leave with him but couldn't?

She rushed off before he could articulate any of his questions, and he was in a foul mood by the time he reached his quarters. He stormed in and threw himself on the bed, hating Ola, hating the fate that put him there, hating the resistance for using him. Yes, he thought, that's exactly what they're doing. How do I know they're not as vicious and cruel as Altanar?

It was something that had never occurred to him, and it jerked him upright like a puppet on its strings. As he started to pace the room, the simile seemed more and more appropriate. They'd strung him along well. The sophistication of it was admirable. The courageous little woman—make that pretty, too—with her hard-luck story. And then all the mumbo-jumbo to introduce Wal, so he'd feel he'd passed some sort of test when they said they were willing to deal with him. Then the big seduction scene, made all the easier by her up-front admission that she was only doing what she was supposed to do. He'd bought every word of it.

And would again.

His need for her cared for nothing else.

He didn't even want to think about loving her.

Sweating, he forced himself to other questions. What of his friends? If this escape was no more than exchanging one imprisonment for another, how could he face them? What had he led them into?

He was being a fool. Angrily, he slammed a fist down on the small table, sending his mug and the sheathed hunting knife dancing off the edge and onto the floor. The mug shattered on the stone. He was glad to see it. Picking up the pieces would give him time to steady himself.

She was there when he straightened up. Like a man at a play, he saw himself pile the shards on the table. He opened his mouth to speak and she put her finger to his lips, silencing unspoken words. She stepped closer, raising the other hand to smooth his eyebrows. Still moving as if caught in a dream, he reached to embrace her. Contact with her body shocked him out of his strange state. It ignited something in her at the same time.

They struggled together to get the robe over her head until, desperate with desire, he simply gathered it up from the bottom and pulled it off. For a moment he stared, held by the gleaming loveliness of her, of rising breasts and flat hard stomach. The dark patch of her sex was still damp from her bath, and for the first time he was aware of the scent of roses and the more subtle, driving aroma that was her. Clumsily, they stripped off his clothes. Their lovemaking was the feast of starvelings, a thing of need and violence and the melancholy joy that comes from pleasure that counts its seconds.

She left as silently as she'd come. He was never allowed to speak. When he was alone, he thanked her for her love and wisdom.

There could be no words.

When he woke, it was late afternoon. He got busy organizing his equipment. After a quick meal, waiting for the darkness, he cleaned his two wipes, the sniper rifle, and his pistol, oiling them, breaking them open to peer down the diamond-bright barrels. He loaded the magazines, testing the spring tension, thumbing the rounds out. They spun to the tabletop, where they landed with eager glinting. He reloaded and checked the weapons again, comforted by the authoritative clicks and clacks of machined parts. Hours passed. He honed the knife. Of all the make-ready exercises, it was the one that passed the time best. He'd purposely saved it for last. Circular strokes, one hand carefully holding the angle, the other steadying the small ceramic sharpener. Round and round. Hypnotic rhythm replaced thought. The room echoed the thin song of edging steel. Its wordless melody set cold feet dancing on his skin.

He held the blade to the light, conscious of the irony of being soothed by an act which had as its sole objective lethal violence.

He held up a corner of the fur on his bed, slicing at it. The knife cut through it effortlessly, and he sheathed it.

There was nothing left to do but wait. Alone. Again.

CHAPTER 66

When the knock came, it was almost an anticlimax. Conway went to the door slowly. He couldn't be sure it was his guide, so to assure he didn't alarm anyone simply checking up on him, he left the wipes on the table. As he reached for the latch, he also considered that the plan might have been compromised. Before opening the door, he eased his pistol out of the holster and held it out of sight behind his back.

One of the guards stood there. Conway's eyes went immediately to the bloodstained sword the man held at his side. He swung the pistol up. The man's face contorted. His voice was a muted squeal. "Wal sent me! I come from Wal! To show you the way!"

Conway lowered the weapon. The guard pointed down the hall with his. "I had to kill the man who was with me tonight. We must hurry."

Rushing to scoop up his pack and the weapons, he surprised himself with the controlled speed of his movements. He wondered if anyone could look at him and understand how hollow he felt.

The guard swept down the hall, Conway following. For once, he was happy about the leather slippers and their soundlessness, although he could have done without his boots banging on his thigh at every step. Soon they came to a small door leading out. The guard opened it boldly, stepping into the night as if investigating. When he saw nothing, he gestured Conway forward. Discarding the slippers to don their boots, they ran, doubled over, from cover to cover until they reached the abbey. The women slept in a small house of their own, a concession to their unique status—and one that made them easier to keep under observation. There were no guards on that night; the force had been stripped to provide escort for Altanar. As the women hurried out to join them, their faces were indistinguishable in their blacking, but Carter stood out by virtue of her smaller size and he was sure Kate

Bernhardt would be carrying the extra wipe. Conway hurriedly blackened his hands and face with charcoal.

As they slipped away into the night, Conway pictured Altanar fixing the blame for the lack of security.

Within a few yards he realized they were headed south. That meant they were on their way to the southernmost city gate, the one called Summergold, with its brass panels. Beyond that was the farm where Leclerc lived.

They made it across the castle wall and all the way across the intervening city without incident, and were within a few short yards of the city wall when a dog yelped from an alley. The guard whirled and shoved the first person behind him into the same alley. He had all the women in there before they could make any sort of protest, but Conway, bringing up the rear, was ready for him. He braced to resist, and a voice from the direction of the wall shouted, "Who's there? Come here, you!"

When the guard pushed again, Conway was already headed down the alley, forcing the women along ahead of him. He had no idea where he was going, except away from the alert voice. Suddenly, ahead, he saw movement, black against black, and had the impression an object had moved to block their route. He slowed, confused, and the guard squeezed past them to duck inside the open door Conway had seen and couldn't identify. They hesitated to follow, but when the voice behind them shouted again, they tumbled inside. The door closed quietly behind them. In the pitch-darkness a woman said, "Hold onto each other." There was a moment of fumbling, and then she said, "Say nothing. Follow."

Tripping, scraping against rough lumber walls, they allowed themselves to be led along. A flight of stairs leading downward set off a flurry of dismayed gasps and murmurs. A door closed behind them when they reached a dirt floor, and a small candle threw just enough light for them to make out faces. The guard was still with them, as was a bent old woman. Roughened skin and gray hair spoke eloquently of many long, hard years. She was glaring at all of them, the guard in particular.

"How could you be so careless? Are you so eager to sing on the beach? The protectors must have discovered they were missing as soon as they were over the wall."

"I wasn't careless!" the man replied, defending himself. "We weren't seen. Ask them."

"They didn't have to see you." The woman bent to move a large chest, and the guide hastened to help her. She continued to berate him between grunts of exertion. "Fire. At the women's quarters. Minutes after you left." She straightened. "That's far enough." A square hole lay exposed at her feet. The top of a ladder was barely visible, leading into a blackness so dense it appeared solid. The woman ignored it to speak to the women. "Which of you left something burning?"

The three exchanged glances, shaking their heads. Carter said, "Was it a bad fire? Was anyone hurt?"

The woman said no, and Conway was sure he saw some of the tension drain from Carter. Then she was saying, "They don't know we're trying to escape. They only know we're missing."

The old woman said, "It was put out quickly. Your belongings were gone. They're not smart, but they're not completely stupid."

"But they don't *know* where we went. They don't know why, either." Carter put a hand on Anspach's arm. The charcoal smeared on the faces around her and the dim light combined to create eerie, mysterious expressions, yet the eyes of all were clearly filling with growing horror and realization. Conway and Bernhardt imperceptibly pulled back from her, while Anspach stood frozen, as if immobilized by the light touch on her arm.

Carter went on. "Don't you see? If we hurry back, maybe we can make them believe we just ran away from the fire. Even if they don't believe us, all we have to do is explain that we didn't actually go anywhere. When they see we came back voluntarily—"

The crack of Bernhardt's palm on her cheek split the dank air like a curse. The wipe on Carter's shoulder was dislodged by the effort behind the blow, and she caught it as it fell to the crook of her elbow. She staggered sideways and bounced off the wall, standing slump-shouldered, trying to focus her eyes. Almost conversationally, Bernhardt said, "You stupid bitch. You bought into it, didn't you?" To the others she said, "It's such a pathetic old story. The prisoner who comes to identify with the captor. We should have seen it."

Conway put his hands to his temples. "How could I have been so blind? She practically told me."

Anspach said, "Don't blame yourself. Kate's right; we all should have seen it. It's too late to worry about it. What do we do?"

Conway looked to the old woman. "Is this the way out?"

"Not directly. The tunnel below here takes you—"

Carter flung herself on him. "Don't listen to her! If you go down there, you're finished! We'll be caught. They'll torture us. We have to go along with Altanar. We haven't done anything wrong."

Roughly, he jerked free of her. He wanted to shove her away, but he knew if he raised his hands, he might very well strike, and the emotions building in him made him fear himself. Tee was back there, and she'd organized this entire operation. She was at some risk before, but Carter's warped logic had redoubled her danger. Altanar might have been willing to believe they'd suborned a single guard, but when he learned that suspicious figures had appeared near Summergold gate, only to melt into the darkness and avoid his protectors, he'd smell a conspiracy.

There would be retribution for all, innocent or not, until names began to surface. Tee's might be one of them.

He had felt hatred before. He had never been close enough to look into the eyes of those he hated. Now that he could, he saw only fright and a desperate grasping for life.

The fact that he felt sorry for her only made him feel guilty.

The old woman grabbed her by the shoulders, and Conway was surprised to see the strength of her grip immobilize the younger Carter. The woman said, "You'd best leave this one to me and my friends upstairs."

Carter's eyes threatened to leave her head. Her entire face became a silent, shocked appeal, and she swiveled from Anspach to Bernhardt and back again. They, in turn, looked at Conway. Anspach said, "We can't do that," and Bernhardt nodded agreement. To the old woman Conway said, "She's one of us. We can't do that."

"Just leave me," Carter said. "I'll go back by myself. They'll understand about the fire, and the trying to run away, and everything. And I won't say a word about which way we went, or this place. You can trust me."

The guard said, "The protectors would steam you open like an oyster. You've betrayed us, and the organization." Cat quick, he struck her with his fist. The sound wasn't nearly as dramatic as Bernhardt's open-handed slap. Carter seemed to lift, then slumped to the floor. The guard faced Conway. "If you want to save your traitor, carry her. Don't lag, though. I'll leave you if you do." He was into the hole and started down the ladder before anyone could even speak.

Bernhardt rushed to follow, and as she disappeared, she gestured at Anspach to help Conway. When he got to the bottom, he was gratified to find the guard waiting for them, his temper apparently better under control. He held a candle high enough for them to see each other, as well as the brooding mouth of another tunnel, branching off from their own. "That dog you heard was a signal that our chosen wall-crossing was too closely guarded. Some friends will keep the protectors and the troops busy in this area. That'll draw people away from other places. Hope that our second choice is one of them, or we're finished."

The tunnel was narrow and low. Conway soon discovered that the only way they could carry Carter was for a person in front to hold her ankles while the one in the rear carried her under the arms. Even the women, shorter than

Conway by several inches, were forced to scuttle along bent over like crones. Worse, the guard set a brisk pace. In short order their backs were complaining mightily.

Despite everything, Conway found time to marvel at the construction. The only light came from the guard's candle, up ahead, so he knew he was missing a great deal. Some of what he glimpsed made him glad he couldn't see everything. Cobwebs, gilded by the candlelight, seemed drawn to his face and neck. Trickles of water stained the walls, and once he tripped over a pile of dirt that had scabbed off next to such a place. Several times he was sure he heard shrill rat noises in the distance. He stared with amazement as they trotted past intersecting tunnels, and on three different occasions they burst out of their confined run to find themselves in large, forbidding rooms. One was large enough to return their labored breathing as echoes, and he was sure he saw stacks of swords and armor. It had to be an armory.

Soon after that the guard stopped at a ladder that was held to the earthen wall by pins of some sort. It stretched overhead out of sight in the gloom. After setting Carter down, Conway gave it a tentative shove. It wobbled frighteningly. The guard grinned a challenge. "Wait here," he told them. "I'll see if anyone's outside waiting for us." Handing Anspach the candle, he started up, awkward with his sword still in hand. When the rasp of his boots on the rungs faded into silence, the tunnel seemed colder and clammier than ever.

After what seemed ages, the quivering ladder announced his return. "No one there," he said, and scrambled off. They could hear him rummaging about, and when he returned, he wore a long coil of knotted rope draped across his body, with a grappling bar tied to one end. He explained that when they got to the wall, they must climb it by clamping the knot between their feet and standing up. Then they should grasp the highest knot their hands would reach and pull up until they could stand on the next knot.

Anspach was shaking. The dim light couldn't disguise how pale she'd become. She said, "I don't know if I can do that. I don't think I can. I've never been strong." Her gaze found Carter, and she seemed to find hope in the smaller woman's helplessness. "What about her? She won't be in any condition to climb a rope. Why not leave us here until it's safe for us to be smuggled out in a wagon, or something? I'll take care of her. We'll be safe."

"We all go," Conway answered for the guard.

Bernhardt reached inside her jacket and drew out a coil of quarter-inch nylon line. "I thought this might come in handy. I'll go up ahead of you," she said. "Loop this around your upper body. I'll pull. You're going to be all right."

Anspach said nothing, her lack of conviction clear in her expression.

The wavering ladder brought them to the surface inside a hollow stack of firewood standing outside a potter's shed. They got out of it by simply taking apart one wall of the split wood. Leaving the group to repair any signs of disturbance, the guard hurried to the base of the wall. The distant shouts of the search for them added even more urgency to their situation.

Conway followed him up the rope, Carter and the two wipes draped over his shoulders. She moaned softly once, but aside from that, she was an inert weight. He dropped her on the battle walk and hurried back down. He was sweating when he reached the ground and watched Bernhardt work her way to the top. The nylon line hissed down beside them, landing with an unsettled thump. They quickly wrapped it around Anspach and got her started.

She managed two of the knots before giving up, quivering with fear-induced exhaustion. Conway could hear Bernhardt straining at the line. He forced his head up between Anspach's legs, getting her on his shoulders. Between the three of them, they muscled her steadily to the top.

Going down was a repetition of the climb. When the guard gave the rope a flip to disengage it, however, the bar rattled and refused to disengage. No amount of tugging or flinging about would get it to release. Finally, the guard scrambled back up, practically dropping down in his haste. "Line looped around a loose spike in the battle walk," he said, pulling it free and coiling it as they ran.

Conway and Bernhardt strained to keep up, still carrying Carter, who groaned occasionally at the jouncing. After a few minutes of that, they were into an apple orchard. Another man waited for them there, holding the reins of five horses. He handed them over to the guard, then left at a run. In seconds they had Carter lashed to a mount and the rest of them were in the saddle, moving through the trees. Once they were clear of the orchard and on the road south, the guard dropped back to join the others. He said, "I don't think they'll have ridden out to the farm to look for your friend yet. If they have, though, he'll have to fight alone. Whoever was sent to let him know we're coming will run if there's trouble. Those are his orders."

"What good is he, then?" Bernhardt's normally commonsense voice was brittle with anger.

The guard said, "If a resistance member is identified, dead or alive, the entire family pays. Imagine your father and mother on a frame. Then ask yourself how many chances we'll take to save the lives of people who've done nothing for us." He heeled his horse forward, leaving them behind. When Bernhardt made as if to resume the conversation, Conway held her back. Muttering, she subsided.

They were still very far from the farm when the rank stench of Leclerc's fertilizer experiments struck them. It was bad enough to offset the morale-raising effect of a newly risen quarter-moon that brought some light. Suddenly there was a sharp whisper from a patch of brush on their right, and Leclerc appeared on horseback. Another mounted man appeared from the thicket to stop beside him, jerking in his saddle so nervously his horse was affected, and it, too, jittered about. The guard rode close to the stranger, and the hard edges of his angry questions clipped the night silence. After listening to Leclerc's companion for a few moments, the guard said something softly, and the man wheeled and dashed away without a word.

Leclerc said, "That fellow saved my bacon. He got edgy, hanging around waiting for you. We just got here a little bit ago, about two minutes ahead of a big war party. They went thundering down the road toward the farm. Won't be long before they realize I'm not there."

The guard made a quick mental computation, then said, "We'll have to go this way. Follow me."

When Leclerc hurried to the thicket and came out leading a packhorse, the guard was furious. Leclerc listened quietly, then said, "There's stuff here I have to take with me. That's final."

At first it seemed there had to be a potentially destructive argument. Carter picked that moment to regain consciousness, however. She retched violently and then pleaded to be allowed to sit in her saddle properly. While the two women helped her, she was told they were out of the city. She pivoted about anxiously, peering into the night before lapsing into an unresponsive silence.

They followed their guide across some fields and then along a narrow, shadowed trail through forest, breaking clear of it on a bluff overlooking the Inland Sea. Conway had purposely positioned himself behind Carter for the ride, in case her foolish belief in Altanar should lead her to try to break away. Watching her vague form move through the darkness maddened him. He'd risked the lives of the entire party to save her. Tee, who'd made it all possible, was trapped. Waves of self-contempt flooded his mind, made him ashamed of the weakness that enabled him to abandon the woman he— He what? Loved? Did he?

He couldn't even find the courage to admit his emotions.

Signaling a halt, the guard forced him back to reality. Below them two balance bars rested on the moon-silvered water, creating a scene of such quiet peace it mocked the night's tension.

It was a cruel illusion, as well, because the first sounds of pursuit erupted behind them.

Rushing now, they went south until they reached a more gradual slope, then started a sliding, treacherous descent. They were almost to the beach when the Olan riders stormed out of the forest and raced after them.

The boats from the balance bars seemed to crawl across the water toward them, although they could hear the yells of the oarsmen and knew the crews were giving their best. Then, from above them, arrows whirred in sinister song, plunging into the water with the sibilance of doused firebrands. Worse was the meaty thud when they struck the wet sand; it was too reminiscent of the sound they made when they hit flesh. It was Carter who dismounted first, saying, "Get off the horses. Get them between us and the archers."

It worked until Anspach's horse screamed in pain and broke free, an arrow in its side. Instantly, the other horses were in a panic, tearing at the reins, lunging. Bernhardt was knocked spinning. Carter had to let go or be dragged away. The guard and Conway managed to hold onto their animals by sheer strength.

That was when Conway recognized the folly of their position. No more than fifty yards away a pile of driftwood provided excellent cover. Too far from the water's edge to be an acceptable defense—they could never make it to the boats, once it was time to retreat—it was well within range of the rapidly approaching Olan mounted archers.

Leclerc was frantically unloading his packhorse, dropping gear all over the beach. Conway managed to get beside him. "You're not going to be able to take all that. What is it, anyhow?"

The answer was harshly abrupt. "Why don't you take a couple of shots at those yahoos and quiet them down? Let me worry about this."

Three wipe rounds brought no cries of pain, but the number of arrows dropped dramatically. The cavalry, however, was spilling onto the beach in the distance. Bernhardt and Anspach launched a boop round apiece in that direction. The horsemen split into small groups, riding hard for the driftwood barrier.

Suddenly Leclerc was charging in the same direction, waddling across the softer inland sand under a load. Conway shouted at him to come back, knowing it was wasted breath. The smaller man scrambled up onto the piled logs, apparently looking for something, and Conway thought he saw the flare of a match. Then Leclerc was dashing back toward them, and Conway turned to see the boats lurching up onto the sand. Leclerc reached them as they sprinted through the water to clamber aboard. The oarsmen were headed back out to sea while they were still throwing in packs, weapons, and tumbling clumsily over the gunwales to join them.

The archers from the bluff, as well as the beach, unleashed a rain of missiles. An oarsman screamed and slumped. Another yelled and stood erect, setting the boat to rocking as he yanked an arrow out of his thigh and threw it into the sea. Another yelled for them to get their backs into their work, just as Conway looked over the side and was dismayed to see they were making almost no progress. He'd thought they were slow coming in, but now he saw that was mere suspense. The truth was that the tide was against them, holding them within range of the arrows.

He aimed at the men brazenly standing on the bluff. Leclerc put a hand on his arm. He said, "Save your ammunition. I left the lads a surprise."

"That junk? They won't stop shooting at us just to loot—"

A sound like distant thunder startled him to silence, and then there was a sense of pressure, as though a giant hand had forced him down in the boat. Logic and experience told him it was an explosion, but it was unlike anything he'd ever known. The general effects were right, but there was no harsh crack, and the flash was more of a blossoming, fiery glow. Whatever it was, it sent massive logs tumbling. Men and horses screamed and sprawled. Those who were able retreated with all possible speed. The galling arrows stopped completely.

Everyone in the boats sat immobile, slack-jawed, staring at the cottony white smoke eddying up from the beach.

"I *thought* I'd finally gotten it right," Leclerc said.

When an arrow fell astern, the man in charge of the boats regained enough composure to shout at the crews to start rowing again. They moved with renewed vigor.

Leclerc said, "Let that be a lesson to you. Never trust a man who tells you he *likes* to be surrounded by chickenshit. Got to be something devious about the rascal." He was chuckling at his joke as he finished, but Conway heard something sorrowful in the laughter. When Leclerc's gaze swept back to the dissipating smoke and the survivors struggling to help their comrades, he sighed raggedly. "Another escape. Another contribution to man's progress, huh, Matt?"

Conway wished he had an answer.

CHAPTER 67

Every few years the border dwellers living at the point of contact between Harbundai and Ola trickled north in a sort of human tidal flow. Rather than stimulation from moon or the season, theirs was a move spurred by presentiments of war.

This year found Harbundai stumbling through the earlier weeks of spring in a veritable fog of such rumors, although there were fewer actual border incidents than usual. Nevertheless, just as the animals have their inexplicable ways of predicting weather, the borderers knew. For one thing, there was wary communication between them and their erstwhile enemies. Some of them provided services to the free-ranging slavers who headquartered in Ola. In order to live, they closed their eyes to the suffering of their countrymen farther north. Some even told themselves they were helpful because they bargained to buy back anyone they recognized. The fact that they couldn't afford to buy back *everyone* they recognized was discussed less openly. Still, the borderers survived. Over the decades they became cunning, inbred, and clannish to a fanatic degree.

This year they were in full retreat, and, as usual, they were as welcome among their new neighbors as a pack of wild dogs. The circumstances of their lives generated an almost inborn sense of guilt in each of them that took very unkindly to taunts about flexible ethics and cowardice.

Whenever they were displaced north, their countrymen affirmed their own moral superiority by mercilessly gouging them on the price of everything. The borderers responded by stealing anything within reach. They stole to eat, and once they were no longer hungry, they stole for gain. For lack of any other excuse, they stole to keep in practice.

Sylah's healing house welcomed a steady stream of broken bones, bruises, and aching heads from both communities.

Gan attacked the problem, roaming the entire southern flank of the barony, arbitrating disputes and settling grievances. Trust in him grew. Soon, riders came to him, each asking him to help a particular group. The word developed among all, borderers and their unwilling hosts, that this new Dog warrior-leader was as fair as he was iron-willed. They spoke with pride of his concern, and with awe at the way he came among them with no escort save his regular companion, Clas, as though the two of them, with their hot-eyed war-horses and the three dogs, need fear no numbers. All except the greedier merchants further applauded his efforts beyond roving justice. He set up camps where the newcomers could associate in governable groups. He had them choose their own leaders. He arranged markets where they could purchase food at honest prices. The Wolves helped them with their dwellings, and he suggested, in the strongest terms, that the wives of the unit show some hospitality to the border women. Wolf recruiters worked among the men. More and more, Gan was emphasizing a volunteer corps, and although there were few young borderers available, those who took the oath were tough, grateful for the consideration afforded their people, and eager to prove their worth.

Baron Jalail was pleased. "We've never had such numbers move north," he said one morning, strolling through the bustling Wolf camp with Gan.

"We've never had such a peaceable time of it, either. You've done a fine job."

Gan thanked him, wondering if this was the opportune moment he'd been waiting for. He decided to chance it. "Most of the problems seem settled. I've waited to ask you something. I'd like your permission to move into Malten now. We can be on the road in two days."

Baron Jalail frowned. "You're not supposed to march for another week. Noble Malten may not be prepared."

"Exactly. Two tells me his best informants in the Malten barony have gone silent. One of his commers was sure he was being watched before he left to come home. I don't trust the Noble."

"You don't think he truly wants to rule in his brother's place?" Baron Jalail's sarcasm was soft.

Gan refused to be baited. "Oh, I trust him on that count. It's everything else I think he's lying about. If he's our ally, we won't hurt him by joining him a bit early. If I wait for the King's coalition to arrive, I could find myself facing all of them at once."

"Why would he bother with such an elaborate ambush? Why wouldn't he simply go to the King and offer the same arrangement?"

"I don't know. There are too many possibilities." The air of logical discussion fell from him like a cloak, and he was the young, impassioned warrior. His hands and features grew animated. The measured stride became a lithe glide. He went on, "I want to disturb his plans, force him to make a mistake, then pounce."

"So much for the coldly rational Murdat," the Baron observed dryly, but he wore a pleased grin when Gan turned to look at him. Then he asked, "You have your own commers supplying you information?"

Gan flushed. "I don't hunt on Two's land, Baron. If I ever have reason to distrust his work, I'll say it openly."

"Of course. Sometimes you move so fast one wonders."

It was yet another stinging reference to the night march that led to the battle of the Bear Paw. Gan was resigned to paying for that decision for the rest of his life. Still, it rankled to be reminded he'd been less than honest.

Suddenly, the image of the bribe weapon was in his mind, turning, glittering at him with all its jewels and gold. He shook his head to get rid of it, and the Baron stared at him in open concern.

"Something troubles you?"

"Nothing important. Have I your permission, then? If you send a Messenger to inform him we're on the move, he won't be able to say you tried to deceive him."

The Baron considered, then exhaled heavily. "If you think you must, then yes, you have my permission."

After thanking him, Gan continued to walk with him just long enough to be polite, then whistled up the dogs. They stopped their gamboling and raced to him. He loved to watch them come like that, all three practically abreast, their powerful strides ripping up clods that soared high in the air behind them. Their mouths hung open and their eyes stared at him as if he were the only object on the earth, yet he knew they watched each other, straining to reach him first. Raggar always won. It wasn't because they deferred to him, either; this was one time there was true competition.

Today, though, Gan saw a change that tightened his throat. He wanted to shout at them to stop. He wanted to turn back the race, turn back time itself.

Raggar was losing to Shara.

Over the winter the older dog felt the wet cold of Harbundai far more than he'd ever suffered on his drier prairies. And Shara had grown, eating like a tiger. He was within a few pounds of Raggar's weight, and fully as tall. In a few months he might even be larger. His strength was prodigious, so much so that Raggar no longer tussled in play with him for very long before snapping and snarling to reaffirm his dominance.

They were almost on Gan by then, close enough for him to see slabs of muscle bunching and stretching in broad chests, and to see the heavy winter coats rippling in the wind of their effort. They didn't slow when they reached him, but flowed past in an avalanche of exuberance that curved and bent back to him.

Gan barely heard the Baron's muttered exclamation, but he saw the hasty Two-sign. He would have laughed, but Raggar's plight overruled amusement.

The gray dog knew he'd been beaten. He accepted Gan's welcoming pat with dignity, but refused to meet his master's gaze. He looked out over the fields. Gan greeted the other dogs in turn, praising Shara in particular, and then fell to his knees beside Raggar. It brought their heads to the same height. He put his arm around Raggar's neck, speaking soft reassurance.

The Baron watched, puzzled. "Is he hurt?" he asked.

Gan shook his head. "He's never lost. He doesn't understand."

Baron Jalail made a heavy noise in his chest. "Understanding only makes it worse." He walked off, gesturing Gan to remain when he started to rise. "Console him," he said. "It's the least—and the most—any of us can ever hope for."

After lavishing attention on Raggar, Gan praised Shara and Cho again.

She lolled under his petting, enjoying the attention, her chest heaving as she regained her breath. As for Shara, Gan would have sworn the animal knew exactly what he was saying when he told him what a fine animal he was becoming. The liquid-brown eyes looked back at him with sober pride.

Walking toward his quarters, he knotted a string message for Clas and tied it to Cho's collar. He aimed her in the direction of the hand-weapon training ground and ordered her to find him.

He was just sitting down at his desk when Sylah entered. He greeted her warmly, teasing her, asking why he and Neela saw so little of them anymore. "We used to see both you and Clas in the evenings," he said, straight-faced. "Now the men say he never comes to their fires at night to join in the singing and storytelling, and he never joins in their off-duty games anymore. They wonder if he's well, if he really needs so much sleep."

She tossed her head. "My husband can answer questions as well as any man. If anyone chooses to ask him. And you might be interested to hear some of the things being said about the disappearance of another, younger, couple since a certain wedding."

He reacted as if scandalized, and then they both laughed until Sylah grew serious. "I came here from the Baron. You're leaving in two days."

"Yes, we are. Will that affect you?"

She shook her head, a bit too quickly. "No, not at all. It's just that— Clas says Noble Malten isn't to be trusted. I think he's right. I was hoping you wouldn't go at all."

He said, "You meant to deliver Neela to Harbundai because you knew she was working to help Church protect women from men like Altanar. My goals should be a help to you. There must have been people who were supposed to help you. They may be able to help us both. Who are they?" He saw the wince just as the perfect mask slid down to cover it. He wondered if his eyes were growing sharper, or if she was less practiced in her deceptions. On hearing the touch of resentment in her answer, he decided it was the latter.

"I wasn't allowed to know. They were to contact me." She told him of the roses, going on to reveal the blasted, frightening message pinned to her door. "Someone—friend, enemy?—knows we're here. There's been no other sign of them, however."

She dismissed the event too easily. Despite the seriousness of the subject, she actually seemed distracted. What else could weigh so heavily on her mind?

For no apparent reason, he thought of Jones. The image was unsteady, clear one moment, wavering the next. As quickly—and unreasonably—as it had appeared, it was replaced, and for the second time that day the bejeweled, intriguing weapon was in his mind's eye.

Speaking more roughly than he intended, he asked, "Is it possible the Moondance people have penetrated Church and knew of your mission?"

"Possible." She was a bit taken aback by his change in manner. "They're enemies to anyone who doesn't believe exactly as they do. I believe the roses were from Church, a warning that everything had gone wrong and I must be cautious."

"Sometimes boldness is the best caution." He rose swiftly, pacing the room, speaking almost to himself. "Clas has probably told you I mean to rule. I must either eliminate this king or acquire his power and let him keep his throne. I cannot tolerate a thing like Moondance, and that includes this Jones man. My mother's prophecy—" He stopped, looking at her with such pain it startled her. "I must reach out to every opportunity, Sylah. It's my fate. Even so, I'm not promised success. Achievement on one hand, oblivion on the other. I accept that. But one mistake, and I go down. Neela goes with me. How am I to think of her married off to someone as a 'kindness' to her? Can you imagine her a semislave in the lockup? I can't. I won't." He stopped to face her. "I know the idea of better status for women is the thing you hold most dear in this life. Because of Neela, I agree with your aims. If you can, help me, and I swear to help you." Without another word he was past her and out the door.

Her heart was pounding, his words rolling through her mind. "Hold most dear," he'd said. So had Lanta, at the Seeing.

Sylah will lose what she holds most dear.

Once that had been the mission, but now it was Clas. Wasn't it?

It shocked her to realize she was at least as concerned for her husband's safety as she had ever been for her goals.

She turned away, irritated by the weakness and confusion her introspection created. Not to mention the pointlessness of her concern. Clas would never be safe. Sometimes she suspected the only thing he feared was safety, as if not being in the very front of every action challenged his view of himself.

She knew he loved her. She hated his mistress, that wanton Virgin of Battles, whose excitement was ever new, ever changing. How could she compete with that?

She wanted to hold him in her arms. That very moment. Not later. Right then. She wanted to feel the unyielding strength of him, the sweet mixture of contentment and passion that welled in her when she was encircled by his arms. She never knew which of those feelings would take precedence. Sometimes the fire in her took hold, and she wanted nothing but the straining, exalting physical sensations he brought her. Other times she was cozy in a sense of quiet peace.

She shivered, freeing herself of her daydreams, instantly resentful that

right that minute, while he was probably discussing fighting and dying as
calmly as sane men discussed crops or prices or the weather—right that
minute she could have cried out for one moment of that peace and assurance.

But she waited. That was what she must do. That was their bargain. It
was never spoken of, although both understood it, down to the finest nuances. Clas na Bale was a warrior. Whatever diminished that fact diminished
his soul. How many times had she asked herself if she could live with less
than the fullness of the man as she knew him, as she loved him? Better to
worry about a love that could be snatched away than to watch it wither and
whine itself to misery. To his credit, he was as good with his understanding.
Of course, she'd never mentioned the Door—and never would—but when
her determination to do something for the women of Jalail troubled him, he
gritted his teeth and kept his silence. In fact, he'd even helped on some
occasions. There was understanding between them. She prized that above
all.

Startled, she realized she'd heard his voice, making a point. He was
coming toward her, talking to Emso. Sometimes he snapped out words just
that way in his sleep, and the sweat ran from him rank with energy. Those
were the times she truly hated the heartlessness of his first love, the bitch
mistress that drained him then discarded him to his wife's bed.

She despised sharing him. Worse, he had no need to share her. What did
she have? Church? Church was going to cast her out; she was sure of it. The
Door? She didn't know if it existed, much less where it might be. And did
she really care, now that she was married to the man she loved?

The man. That was the thought that kept her awake on certain nights.
What if she'd never met him? Could there be another man somewhere that
she might love as she loved him?

Impossible.

They were happy. Why couldn't she be satisfied with that? He lived at
the edge of life. Could she love a man who burned like green leaves, all smoke
and no heat?

The flame of her own being sparked, flared. Who else could be his woman,
his wife? Consciously, she straightened, lifted her chin. Who else could be
his match?

The meeting broke then, and as it did, he turned and saw her. The hard
line of his jaw changed, and something—not a smile, but a softening, a secret
welcoming—moved across his face. It was as indefinable as the feeling that
precedes a change in the weather, and as fulfilling to her. He came to her
with controlled step—great fool, so mindful of his dignity!—and closed her
hand in his.

Gan was returning to his hut, and she caught him looking at them, not at Clas' back, but directly into her eyes as she glanced beyond his shoulder. His gaze held her for the briefest moment, just long enough to shock her with its sudden revelation of uncertainty and a hint of dark, twisted thoughts. Instinctively, she knew that what she'd seen had nothing to do with battles or prophecies. She'd seen the naked soul of a man in love, and that was what was in Gan, but there was more there, things she'd never seen in him or any other man, and she only knew they frightened her very much.

Clas was leading her away, looking at her with raised eyebrows. She said, "We should tell him now." She didn't know why she said it, but it suddenly seemed very important.

He smiled before he spoke. "Not yet." He squeezed her hand. "It's such a good secret. It's ours. Just ours."

"I meant—"

He put his arms around her, silenced her in an embrace that almost took her breath away. "I know what you meant. It's not time. We agreed; he mustn't be distracted now." He eased his grip as she pulled against him, and he patted her stomach, grinning as if he'd split his face. "Anyhow, he'll certainly be able to guess in another few days."

"You!" She stepped back, blustering fake anger. "I don't show at all. I won't for weeks. You insult!" She stalked off toward their tent.

He laughed softly, catching up. "Did I ever tell you there's a history of twins in my clan?"

She refused to answer, trying to mimic the Abbess' look that scorned the brash boys who called at her Chosens when she took them shopping in the market. Twins! Insufferable *man*. To think she actually loved him. He was beside her then, his arm around her, his hand so casually, so surely, resting on her waist. His child. Hers.

The murdat at his side struck her hip. The blade moved against the scabbard. The coldness of the metallic sound touched her back.

She pressed both her hands over his, blended it to her growing baby.

How could love be so grand and so confusing?

They were in their quarters. She spun in his grip, facing him, and their hands were like pale flying creatures, unrestrained in their anxiety. They moved to their bed together.

CHAPTER 68

The Wolves moved through the sparsely settled farmland west of the castle with all the wariness of their namesakes. Squads on horseback acted as point and flank guard. Frequently some galloped off to investigate a place that might shield an ambush. When a detachment of the foot warriors broke away from the main body to inspect a place, they were not only much slower, but much more thorough. They were still on Baron Jalail's land, and regarded such caution as wasted effort, but Clas' linguistic torching kept them warmed to the task.

Watching a ten-man squad run ahead of the column to look over a heavy growth of bamboo, Gan had to smile at their blunt efficiency. A man on horseback could afford all the flourish he wanted; the horse did the work. The man on foot always bought his progress more dearly, and he took a sterner view of life.

The mounted Wolves hunted for trouble. The foot troopers *were* trouble. It was an interesting distinction. It had taken him a while to grasp it, being a horseman himself, but now that he understood the difference, he kept it firmly in mind.

As usual, he rode at the head of the larger column with a headquarters group that consisted of himself, Clas, and a unit of twenty horsemen. The escort was changed daily, taking their place on the scouting screen while a different twenty made up Gan's personally controlled unit. Emso stayed out with his men. Tate rode in the rear, responsible for rearguard as well as the supply wagons. Clas was in tactical command of the remainder of the column. While they were in country that featured cleared areas, he was constantly in touch with all elements of the unit through signal flags and mirror signals that were a combination of ancient Dog techniques and Tate's new codes.

The day drew to a close as they neared the limits of Baron Jalail's land. Fields became isolated small plots hacked out of the resentful forest. The houses were squat, tough-looking huts. Of themselves, they were mute testimony to the price of living far from the center of power. Only the hardiest, most independent-minded would settle here where the "others" on the far side of the invisible boundary might swoop down on them at any time. Raids and cross-border feuds were as much common currency as copper coins. The few people the Wolves saw eyed them with the wariness of the unillusioned.

Gan felt the weight of the encircling firs. He pictured them closing ranks ominously in the fading light.

They halted in completely uninhabited country. Shouted commands resonated strangely in the thick forest, seeming to come from everywhere and nowhere. Soon, all the orders were being given at an almost hushed, conversational level.

Morning came more as a weakening darkness than a growing day. The process of getting under way took place in an oppressive silence. The Wolves marched as the first pale light of the sun broke against the intermeshed branches above them. Once on the move down the narrow trail, signals were exchanged by whistles. Infrequently, a bird responded, usually one of the jet-crested sapphire jays. The chatter of a squirrel was a welcome interruption.

Gan watched how the troops reacted, and felt a bit better about himself; this was more their country than his, and they, too, kept one eye scanning the flanks at all times. The entire column squeezed in on itself as men unconsciously closed the gaps between themselves and their comrades.

All that was minor. Gan was concerned about Emso's screen. Forest cover made it very difficult for the scouting horsemen to see everything. A raiding party might escape detection and swing in behind the column to do what harm it could before running away. The prospect brought a sweat to Gan's neck and shoulders. He had to fight to avoid a sense of unseen eyes watching them pass.

Raggar hated the cautious pace, and he hated being trapped in the middle of the column. He slouched along beside his master's horse disconsolately. Gan finally called Clas to his side, saying, "I'm going to take the dogs and ride ahead to scout with Emso." Clas opened his mouth to object, and Gan talked over him. "I'll be careful. I know it's not my job. It's more for Raggar's sake than anything else. He's bored, hiking along in the middle of this herd."

Clas snorted. "That makes two of us. Keeping these so-called warriors alert and moving is like kneading bread; no matter how much I push and shove, they look just the same. Go ahead; I'll keep things moving."

"I know. Thank you, Clas." He gave a low whistle, bringing Raggar to tail-wagging life. Even his horse responded, trembling as if his energy was trying to burst through his skin. Then they were away. It occurred to Gan he hadn't been on a gallop in so long he'd forgotten the exhilaration of it, and even the confining walls of the forest lost some of their menace as he pounded down the trail. The dogs fanned out, Raggar to the left, Shara on

the right, and Cho behind. They whirled between the trees like misplaced
prairie wind-devils, scrambling up and over fallen trees, occasionally even
leaping clear across a smaller one. When they came to a stream, Raggar
veered to run in it for a few yards, snapping mouthfuls of water.

They caught up to Emso much too quickly. The dogs came to heel on
command, their disappointment clear despite their panting. Emso said nothing until Gan was finished petting them. Then he asked, "What brings you
up here? Boredom?"

"Exactly. Any sign of anything?"

"Not yet."

Gan looked at him quizzically, and Emso half smiled. "I don't want to
criticize the Baron, but when I soldiered for him, we walked into so many
unpleasant surprises that I developed a nose for them. We've found no one
on our flanks, but someone's watching. I guarantee it. Trouble's coming."

"There's no one there, but you know they *will* be? I could say that, too;
it might take a few weeks, but I'd be right eventually, wouldn't I?"

Emso grinned, but he was firm. "Something's coming our way. Might be
a scout, might be a division, but I'll bet you we strike sign of observers
within—" He paused, judging, looking to Gan exactly like an old dog sniffing
the air. He finished, "—within six hours."

"What stakes?"

Emso considered. "A sharp edge. We find sign, you sharpen my sword.
In public. We don't, I sharpen yours. And the loser has to shave with it."

"Done. I know you, Emso."

The older man shook his head. "I remember that's the way you Dogs greet
each other. You seal a bet the same way?"

After Gan nodded, Emso sobered. They were entering a forbidding place,
an area they'd scouted on one of their winter trips. A windstorm of staggering proportions had preceded them by many years. The blowdown created
a swath almost five miles wide and a good ten miles long. Its western flank
was where the road left the forest and ran through the first major fields of
Harbundai. The wind knocked over far fewer than one tree in ten through
most of its path, although in a few isolated cases it had flattened patches
many acres in extent. For all his dislike of the forest, Gan felt the downed
trees had a tragic air. Some lay with their roots on edge, aimed at the sky
like the feet of dead men. Many more were broken off high above the
ground. From a distance they all looked small, and one wasn't surprised that
they could be broken. Up close, they were so thick it took two men to reach
around some.

Emso pointed out a particularly tall, naked spire. What Gan noticed about
it was that the clear space created by the loss of its top had allowed sunlight

to penetrate to the earth, and an incredible tangle of plants struggled to survive where the light allowed life. Even the fastest growing were endangered, however, by the flanking trees that responded to this unexpected bounty of sun by growing longer branches that extended into the opening. Gan looked at it all with distaste, thinking how even the cruelty of this place generated only screams of silence.

The road continued on, with evidence of the old storm growing more frequent around every bend. In fact, most of the bends were the result of the storm, as the earliest travelers after the blowdown had taken twisting, wandering paths that led around fallen trunks. They found some stretches where bamboo created canebrakes that were impenetrable except by dint of hard sword work. Even then, the cut-off ends fought back, stiff and sharp enough to badly slash the unwary. The combination of thicket and barricading treefall forced some of the flank guard riders so close they were well within earshot of the trail. Their horses snorted and thrashed, the riders urging them on. Even Gan's dogs moved closer to him. Then, from ahead, a rider hurried toward them. The man's excitement told Gan he'd lost a bet. Emso tried to hide a sly grin.

The red-faced youth was startled to see Gan, but managed a proper salute. He said his squad had found a stand of timber that was unaffected by the storm, so they'd made good time through it, quietly. They almost stumbled across the man, he said. He was eating, and he left in such a hurry he dropped everything. He held up a piece of something that looked like cloth, but had a different texture. "Paper." Emso was certain. "Harbundai stuff. No one else makes it quite the same way." He asked the trooper, "Did you catch him?"

The boy turned even redder. "He ducked into one of these tumbles, tree trunks laid across each other like straw in a barn. We gave the horses to one man to hold and went after him, but he left us like a rabbit in the briers. We heard him head west."

Emso turned to Gan. "Should we put out a stronger screen?"

Gan stroked his jaw, his gaze locked on Raggar, as if the dog might have an answer. When he looked up at the rider, he asked, "The man was eating? Alone? You found no sign of anyone else? Was he armed?"

"He was armed and wearing light armor. He was eating. We searched the area, and the only other thing we found was his footprints."

Gan made his decision. "Pull in your flankers, Emso. Drive straight ahead until we're out of this mess. Find a good defensive position that covers the road, organize the ground, then scout around and clear anyone who looks hostile. I'll bring up the rest of the unit. We'll camp at the site you choose. And don't use your sword to cut firewood before I get there. Play fair."

Emso saluted, the suppressed grin now out of control. He was issuing orders to the rider before Gan was turned around and headed rearward.

Later, beside Clas, Gan explained his reasoning. Putting himself in an enemy's place, he weighed the possibilities of moving troops into the blowdown fast enough to intercept the Wolves on the move. It would be difficult, but possible. On the other hand, a force exiting from the forest at the edge of the blowdown would find it nearly impossible to get into battle formation because the piled, broken trees would lock them in place on the road. So, then, a good tactician would hide his forces a hundred yards or so from the point where the road left the forest and wait to surprise the Wolves as they filed out in their vulnerable column. Gan meant to be clear of the trees before anyone could move against him.

The men, unaware of any of that, knew only that they'd been ordered to hurry forward. Hundreds of feet thudding on the trail overwhelmed the brooding silence of the forest. Hundreds of heads stopped swiveling and looked straight ahead with anticipation. Gan sent word back down the line for the company war drums to establish a cadence, and the mounted drummers set to work.

The column became an arrow, slashing through the forest, seeking a target, but the men—the individuals—were the Wolves. Gan dismounted, running as they ran. His blood sang, boiling with the joy of the hunting pack.

CHAPTER 69

The head of the column reached Emso's position with plenty of daylight left. It was a good location, several hundred yards outside the blowdown area, on one of the forested round-topped knolls that dominated the immediate area. Farmers had cleared the ground all around them. The effect was of very small islands of wilderness surrounded by an unkempt sea of rough pastureland.

Gan complimented Emso on his choice, then set out to inspect it in detail.

The plant growth on the knolls was vastly different from the fir forest. The trees were of incredible variety, and instead of one smothering canopy, there was a series of levels. This was deciduous growth, and the new replenishment of spring was still spare and translucent, so the lower reaches swam with a gentle, pulsing aura. There was a warm, wet smell in the air, unashamedly fertile. Everywhere new leaves reached upward, small, green candleflame forms. Occasional rhododendrons were already in flower. From a distance their pale flowers merged into amorphous, ever-changing shapes that made Gan think of old, half-forgotten ghost stories.

He welcomed the change. This countryside in no way relieved his longing for the prairie, but at least it didn't make him feel it wanted to crush the breath out of him.

He was sitting outside his tent finishing the last of a chicken dinner with Clas when he recognized Tate at the head of a mounted patrol approaching across the open meadow to the north. He frowned. She wasn't supposed to go outside the perimeter, much less lead scouting patrols. Not that she had trouble with the men. They obeyed her without question; that was the problem, actually. She was a favorite, and he worried they'd take risks to protect her, greater risks than they normally would. A moment later he had to smile. She—and Neela and Sylah—would skin him alive for what they'd call male thinking. He couldn't help it. He couldn't accept armed combat as a practice for females, and he never would. But he hoped he'd never have to go into battle without Tate's contribution. When he thought about it, it surprised him to realize he'd forego her weapons before he'd relinquish her skill.

Which was undoubtedly what the men thought, he decided with a sigh, and abandoned the whole problem.

By that time she was inside the defensive position and riding toward him. Her pace told him she had something important to report. Clas noticed, as well, and they both rose to greet her.

She saluted, saying, "We found Noble Malten." She described the countryside ahead of them as fairly easy, rolling ground, with plenty of cover. There were some deep draws, and one large river. Malten and six other men were camped on its southern bank.

"You're sure it was Malten?"

"Certain. We saw their smoke from a distance. I sent in two scouts on foot. They got close enough to overhear him called by name. He's yelling at everyone."

"Did they hear anything important?"

"They heard him say something about a schedule being ruined."

Gan started to turn away, then made a face. "I'll bet you haven't eaten. Stay with us. I'll have your dinner brought up here." She accepted, swinging off the horse with easy grace, then pulled her wooden plate from the saddle-bag. Everyone carried one. Gan had done away with men cooking for themselves. There was a cook and helper assigned to every fifty-man unit; they had a five-horse train for carrying supplies and equipment. Everyone carried a plate and utensils, and was responsible for their cleanliness. As Tate always rode with the rear-guard unit on the march, she drew her ration from that unit's cook. Within a few minutes the trooper had gone there and was back with her stewed chicken. "We passed some farmhouses. Everything's deserted," she said as she cut her meat. She did it in the manner of the Dog People, holding a bone in the left hand and slicing the meat with a razor-edged shortknife. The slices were speared or lifted to the mouth with the blade. Anything too small or awkward for that was spooned up.

"Milk cows," Gan said, and she stopped chewing to look at him blankly. He repeated it, expanding. "Did you see any milk cows? Other livestock? Were the houses cleaned out?"

She resumed eating, looking thoughtful. "A lot of cattle, but they looked like beef animals to me. Pigs, chickens. Other stuff. The houses still had plenty of bedding and stored food. It looked like the owners moved out recently. What do you make of it?"

"They left in a hurry. They didn't intend to travel fast, and they expect to be back soon. Most stock survives pretty well, if it can forage. Milk cows have to be milked, or they sicken and die. And they don't run far or fast. How do you read it, Clas?"

He wrinkled his nose. "We haven't surprised anyone as much as we thought. We're playing with a trap." He reached up to massage the black tattoo. The gesture distracted Gan. He hadn't seen it for a long time. Clas was more disturbed than his words indicated.

Gan knew why, too. It was necessary to challenge the trap. The Wolves were too weak to march directly against the force the King had put together. Even if they established the defense Noble Malten suggested, that only served to pin them down so they could be overwhelmed. No. They had to poke at the trap, learn its workings, in order to defeat it.

"We'll talk to the Noble tonight," he said, turning to Clas. "Pick some men to go with us; no more than ten."

Tate looked up from her dinner and frowned at both of them. "You said tonight? You're going to ride up on his camp in the dark? You'll scare them half to death. You don't know what they'll do."

They grinned at each other, Clas suddenly as exuberant as Gan. She attacked her meal, taking out her exasperation on helpless vegetables. "Kids," she said huffily. "My leaders think war's a Halloween prank."

"A what?" Gan said.

She looked up quickly, hoping she hid the ice-wash of fear that ran through her at the question. She was relieved to see he was still chuckling at her behavior. "A mean prank, I said. You're not trying to frighten Noble Malten for any reason, except you think it'll be fun. You could get killed."

Clas stretched and got to his feet. He opened his mouth to say something, and froze, staring into the distance. "Who could that be?" he finally managed, dropping a hand to his murdat grip. Gan and Tate rose, following his gaze. So far away they were barely discernible, two men were setting up their own camp, building a plainly visible fire.

Apologetically, Tate said, "Emso told me about them earlier. They're Messengers." When both Gan and Clas continued to stare at her, she went on, "He said they always seem to know when something important is going to happen, and they're just there. They never explain, and no one's allowed to question them. I think he's a little bit afraid of them. I know some of the troops think they're witches, or something like that."

Clas made a noise deep in his chest. "Like the birds." It was Tate's turn to look confused. Clas said, "Haven't you noticed? The hawks, the one's we call bloodtails—see them circling? They're carrion eaters. We say they smell war, because they always seem to come before a battle. I think they've learned that a lot of people in one place usually means a fight, and they come to investigate. Same with the crows, like those perched in the trees on the other hills. I'm surprised you haven't noticed. Don't you have similar things where you come from?"

Tate answered with some asperity. "Well, I'm surprised you didn't know about the Messengers."

Gan's sarcastic drawl put an end to the subject. He said, "We don't have as much need for Messengers as these more civilized people. Especially in our fights. There aren't so many 'arrangements' to be tended to. I agree with Clas; I don't like the idea of people who follow around waiting for others to die."

Tate said, "Let's hope no one has to do that."

Clas started away. To Gan he said, "I'm going to sleep until you want to leave. You need rest, too."

Gan agreed, and, when asked, Tate promised to wake them. She made it plain she didn't want to, but they only laughed.

A few hours later Gan and Clas were positioning their ten men. The moon was a sliver that spared them barely enough light to cast a confusing shimmer over everything. The Noble and his escort were camped beside a hedgerow, sprawled carelessly around a large fire. Gan was sure the flames had destroyed their night vision, but he took no chances. Everyone remained flat, feeling their way through the pasture weeds. When Clas had positioned the men who came with them, he returned to where Gan waited with the dogs. The two men, with the dogs trailing, rose and walked toward the fire. They took several steps before anyone even suspected they were nearby, and when the first man actually saw them, he refused to believe his eyes until Gan spoke.

"I know you, Noble Malten," he said, adding volume to his normal speaking voice. "Clas na Bale came with me to greet you."

Except for the Noble, everyone scrambled upright, clutching weapons, trying to look prepared and to read the darkness in all directions at the same time. Gan examined them carefully. They seemed to be reasonably fresh, and the scraps of food lying on the ground or hissing in the fire indicated they'd eaten well enough to throw away plenty, but their clothes were torn and dirty. In fact, they were filthy, and they'd not bothered to attempt to change that situation before eating. He wondered if the horses had even been watered; they were dim figures outside the firelight where they shuffled and snorted on a picket line.

The Noble returned their greetings smoothly, complimenting them on the stealth of their advance. His eyes shifted constantly from the men to the dogs, betraying disquiet behind his surface calmness.

Gan went directly to Tate's discoveries. "My scouts report everyone's moved out of this area. Our arrival was expected. Is Baron Malten in the field with his troops? How far away are they, and how many are there? What ratio of cavalry to infantry? And what of the King and his men?"

The Noble listened to Gan's questions politely. In fact, his controlled stillness had a catlike quality, so Gan was unsurprised by the malice in his tone when he answered. "I can answer all your questions, plus one you haven't asked. I'll save that for last."

His brother had taken to the field, going north hurriedly after sending a Messenger to the King. Tomorrow—the day after, at the latest—Gan would find himself confronted by over three hundred mounted men and at least three times that number of infantry. He paused dramatically, then said, "The reason for all this activity is the answer to the question you didn't know to ask. You should have wondered *why* they're all ready. Haven't you seen my clothes? I'm practically in rags! These poor, loyal fools are the only friends I have left. Someone informed on us. My brother tried to have me killed this morning. As soon as Jalail's Messenger told him of your early move to come here, he confronted me. He knew about my visit to your baron. At least you can run back to your master. All I can do is beg you to take me with you."

Clas bristled. "Never say we have a master. Who informed?"

"I don't know. I'll worry about that later. My brother has almost as many soldiers as you. Well-trained men. It would be unwise to pursue them. Too dangerous. If you retreat, they'll follow you into Jalail. We should be preparing defenses while there's time."

Gan turned to a seething Clas. "Take two men and get back to the Wolves as fast as you can. Tell Emso we'll need scouts ready when I get back with Noble Malten."

Clas made no effort to hide his disgust at Gan's pliant acceptance of the Noble's abuse, but he moved without question. The Noble and his party looked more frightened than ever when Gan whistled into the darkness and the eight Wolves who'd been hidden materialized, leading horses.

In camp, Gan ordered a man to see to the Noble's party, ignoring them after that to draw off for a private conversation with Clas, Emso, and Tate. He called for the leader of the scout squad that had accompanied him to the Noble's camp, sitting him down in front of the group. The youngster was clearly awed to be the center of attention, but when Gan asked him what he'd discovered, he answered confidently. "The horses were calm, and just a little damp, Murdat. Not wet, mind. They covered some ground today, but not hard-driven. Grained just a while before we got there."

"How do you know they weren't ridden hard? Or what time they were fed?"

He warmed to his report. "Saddle blankets were just about dry, and it's a damp night. Grain got spilled on the ground. In daylight birds would have gotten it. At night it draws mice and such. Plenty laying around means nothing had time to get at it. Oh, and they have leather reins; they were dry, too. Soaked leather stays wet, you know."

"I understand," Gan said, cutting a hard look at Clas' choked laughter. "Did you notice anything else?"

He thought a minute. "Their clothes are a lot dirtier than their horses or their saddles. I heard that Noble tell you they had to run this morning because his brother wanted to kill him. If that's so, how come they had time to load up so much food for themselves and grain for the horses? When Emso tells us to hurry, we got no time for nothing but what we always carry. I don't picture that Noble living like that. Do you, Murdat?"

This time Clas couldn't hold back the laughter, and Gan had his own difficulty. Still, he answered as soberly as he could. "No, I don't think he lives with his gear packed the way you do. And I don't think he sees half as much in a day as you saw in the dark tonight. You did a proud job. Go get some rest. You'll need it for tomorrow."

The young scout swaggered off.

Tate, who'd only seen the Noble and his men at a distance, said, "What's this about ragged and dirty? My patrol didn't mention that."

Gan said, "Ask them."

She turned and called a name. A man trotted forward. She asked him if he'd seen how the Noble was dressed, he looked surprised. "Well, he's a noble, isn't he? Clean, clothed in the best. Fancy. Even his escort." He was even more surprised when his answer set off a round of head shaking and grim looks, and escaped gratefully when Tate dismissed him.

Gan said, "We almost caught them before they had time to get into costume. They lied about their escape. And why'd the locals abandon their homes here? Why would they think we'd fight here?"

He pointed at Emso. "Find out. Where are the King's forces? I want to know what's going on in all directions within a day's forced march of this spot."

Emso's concern scored deep lines in his grizzled features. "With a scout like that, you'll have little rested cavalry by the time we get finished, Murdat."

"I know. We don't have any choice. We're blind, and men are moving out there. Either we control them or they destroy us. Find them for me, Emso. Give me my sight."

The older man jackknifed erect, pushing with his hands on his knees to raise his torso. His smile was wryly lopsided. "I'll find them, but I don't think they're going to be satisfied to just be looked at. Before this dance is over, somebody's going to have to kiss somebody."

Clas said, "You'll pick us the prettiest partner, won't you?"

Tate said, "Wait'll I tell Sylah what you said."

Gan and Clas were laughing as Emso left. Still, for almost a full minute after the cavalryman was gone, they didn't look at each other. The crescent moon, which had been a silver axe cutting through wisping clouds, was finally darkened by a solid mass. Gan suggested they get some sleep in preparation for a very unpredictable day.

CHAPTER 70

The first of Emso's horsemen began to trickle back into camp shortly after Gan's impatience reached the boiling point. The area around his tent was noticeably free of other people by the time the first five-man team showed up. They approached down the straight lanes of a planted field, which accentuated the way they wobbled in the saddle. The horses had the loose-limbed shuffle that comes shortly before collapse. Gan bit back the order to send them a signal to hurry; it had been almost thirty-six hours since they'd slept. It was one thing to drive men and animals to the limits of their endurance. It was quite another to abuse them.

Emso questioned them only briefly before dismissing them. Gan tried to control his fidgeting while the older man mounted and trotted to report.

This team had ridden due west. They'd seen no sign of troops. Most of the farms at the far end of their patrol weren't abandoned, and there was no indication of activity. One of the men had noticed something that puzzled him, however; he said he understood they were concerned about Baron Malten's men, who'd gone north to join the King. The scout said that when the farm people saw them, their first reaction was to look south. His scouting partners said they hadn't noticed anything like that, but the man stuck to his story.

Emso stroked his jaw, the gray stubble rasping audibly. All he said was, "We've got riders out to the south. No sense in guessing; we should have an answer soon."

By then two more teams were riding in. They moved a bit more smartly than the first arrivals, Gan noted, and his eagerness increased. He told Emso to have them report.

They'd gone north, and their weariness was overlaid by a wash of excitement as they spoke of dodging Baron Malten's riders. The team leaders refused to call them scouts. "Clumsy farmers," one said scornfully. Hearing himself, he laughed shortly. "They looked like we used to."

Gan asked, "Did you see their camp?"

They nodded in unison, adding that their scouting area was as abandoned as this place. They'd seen no one except the enemy riders.

For the next two hours they listened to weary men add pieces to the puzzle, and the last two bits dropped at the very end. One patrol had found a Peddler trying to slip past them, and in order to buy his continued passage, he'd volunteered the information that the King's forces were a good two days' march north. Gan seized on it. It offered a golden opportunity to destroy Baron Malten's force before the King arrived.

He waited, more impatient than ever, for the final five exhausted riders from the south. They reported Olan units pulling back from the border.

It was the perfect scenario—the rear was now safe, and the enemy was divided and weak.

At Gan's request for privacy while he and his friends discussed their next moves, the Noble made a polite half bow and withdrew to his own tent. Gan thought he seemed very pleased by events. He called to the young Wolf in charge of the guards around the Malten group's tent, telling him to pull his men and let them get some rest. He waved casually at the Noble's smiling nod of thanks.

"Why'd you do that?" Clas scowled disapproval. "It'll be dark in a few minutes. It wouldn't surprise me to see him slip off to warn his brother."

"The Baron's already waiting for us. The Noble can't tell him anything he doesn't already know." Gan made a brushing motion, then turned to Emso. "You'll screen for us as we move north. Tate, you take care of the rear. We'll leave here at first light. Tell the cooks I want a hot mixed grain meal for the men. We're not stopping for midday."

Clas rolled slowly off the sleeping mat and pulled his clothes to him. Cat softly, he made his way past the tent flap. The stars were like tiny ice crystals. He pulled on the leather shirt and trousers, cinching the belt carrying the murdat. With the swift silence that had seen him through many sleeping enemy campsites, he moved to take a position between Noble Malten's tent and the horses on their picket line. Lying down, he drew the murdat, holding it beside him.

For over an hour he remained absolutely motionless. In his mind he was part of the night, a creature that had only one thought. He waited for something else to move.

Once he thought it had. To his left, a little bit downhill. His neck hackles rose, and he brought the murdat up by his head. He listened. There had been something there, he was sure of it. Shrew? Rat? An insect could make that much noise, a beetle toppling a balanced stick.

He concentrated on the tent again.

Time passed. The stars wheeled farther into their turns.

The tent flap quivered. A slit opened near the top, pulled wider to reveal the deeper blackness of the tent's interior. A voice whispered. A man came out, silhouetted against the lighter material. He moved away in a crouch, not headed for the horses at all.

Clas gathered his legs under him. Just as he started to break in pursuit, a hand clasped his. A bolt of energy like lightning burned through him, and then the hand was saying, *Quiet. Quiet.* He recognized Gan's touch and exhaled shakily. The man was out of sight by then, although small telltale sounds marked his westward path.

Gan signaled *Come,* and led Clas to his own tent.

Clas didn't even bother to ask Gan why he'd done this incredible thing. Gan lit a candle and turned to face him. He said, "I had to let him go, Clas. Like you, I was sure this Noble was lying."

Clas said, "You know his man's going to tell the Baron we're coming. He'll send a rider on to the King, who'll march to meet us."

"He can't make it," Gan said. "If the Peddler was right, the King's too far away. Not even a forced march will bring him to the Baron fast enough, and if he tries that, his men will be so tired we'll walk over them. But think—that man who crept away in the dark believes they have a plan so clever he's willing to risk his life to tell someone to put it in motion. We're warned. And they're not as undiscovered as they think."

Clas was unconvinced. "We should have caught him. We'd know their plan."

"And when he didn't arrive they'd know we suspected something. It's better to let them think we're unconcerned. Let them grow careless."

"We've already grown careless. Letting him go was a mistake."

"It's my decision." His need to command put ice in his tone, solidified it into a barrier between himself and his friend, and he didn't know how to call the words back. Clas—the steadfast, indomitable Clas—looked away. For a devastating moment Gan thought of Raggar, of the race with Shara. He reached for his friend. Clas was already turned, though, swooping to snuff the candle, and continuing the move so that his hurried progress through the tent flap was a whisper in the dark.

Gan settled onto his bedding slowly. He knew he'd done the right thing. His father had told him a thousand times—do what you can to make an enemy complacent. Help him underestimate you.

What he'd said to Clas was right. Clas should have understood that, even if it had been said badly.

Why hadn't his father told him what it cost to be right?

Emso joined Gan at the head of the marching units. The dogs watched him come, wagging their tails eagerly. They'd learned that his presence usually meant action, and it had been a long, uneventful morning. The sun had climbed to its noon position, and the first truly warm day of spring sat heavily on the column. Gan noted the older man was clean-shaven, his armor oiled and polished. Well-trimmed hair peeked out from under the edges of his helmet mask. Gan had to smile. The old Emso was always grubby. The new one was a bit neater, but unworried about appearances unless he expected combat. For that he believed he should be an example to his men, and on those days he liked to describe himself as neater than a wet frog.

He pointed far ahead. "You can make out Baron Malten's hill. I sent some men ahead to get a close look. They're set for a hard fight, Murdat—dug in."

Gan looked at him with increased interest. "Fortifications?"

Emso nodded. "Trees felled and lashed together. Sharpened branches aimed outward to add to the hazard. A ditch in front of the troops. Trip lines to cripple the horses. They've done a good job."

"And your other scouts?"

"Nothing."

Gan nodded. "We'll wait here for a while."

Clas and Tate were just riding up. She was frowning, but Clas' stony control revealed he was still thinking of his dismissal the previous night. Tate asked the obvious question. "Why are we waiting?"

"I don't exactly know." Gan glanced at Clas, who stared off toward Baron Malten's hill. Gan went on. "Has any of you noticed that the Noble's group has shrunk by one?"

Tate and Emso stared at one another, and Clas seemed to relax a bit at their surprise. Gan said, "Clas and I watched him leave last night. It's why I told you, Tate, to keep a close watch on all of them today. It's also why I personally ordered a couple of your scouts to do some tracking for me, Emso. And why they were ordered to report what they found to me, and me only."

In the commotion that followed, he repeated the explanations he'd given Clas. By that time, Emso was showing a bit more understanding. He said, "That explains those riders fanned out behind us. You think the Olans are coming, don't you?"

In answer, Gan drew his murdat and drew a sketch on the ground, showing how a battle with Baron Malten would pin them to one place. The deceit was immense. Baron Malten's men were bait for the Wolves. The King of Harbundai believed he and his three barons were rushing to join Baron Malten in a plot against Jalail's growing strength. The hidden plan— Noble Malten's plan—was to have the Wolves and the Harbundai troops engage each other. The Olans would then attack.

Gan was convinced the Malten forces would be ordered to join the Olans as soon as they appeared. He finished by saying, "I imagine the Noble's reward for all this is to be the new Baron, under Ola's protection."

Clas said, "It's a likely guess, but a guess."

Gan agreed. "I wish I had absolute answers, my friend. But Emso's scouts tracked our escaper to the south."

Emso said, "You intend to wait here until we hear from the patrol that's out there now?" Gan nodded, and the older man pursed his lips, shaking his head in satisfaction. "Then you can pay me what you owe me."

"I owe you?"

Emso drew his murdat, handing it and a whetstone to Gan. "The bargain. Sharp enough to shave, Murdat."

From their respectful distance the two Messengers saw the Wolves surge forward. They looked at each other, then spurred their horses forward to see the cause of the excitement. Apologetically insistent, they forced their way close enough to spy Gan diligently running the blade of a murdat across his cheek. The Wolves began to cheer, some howling wildly.

The shorter Messenger turned to the taller and brought out a coin. He said, "Whatever message this young madman sends to anyone is going to be like nothing either of us has ever heard, my friend. A privilege to carry. And a rich fee. Choose a side of the coin. When he needs us, the winner serves him."

The other never took his eyes from Gan. He said, "They're all mad. I'll take the King's side."

The shorter man flipped the coin and caught it. His companion continued to watch Gan, fascinated. The shorter man looked at the coin, saw the King's profile. He closed his fist over it. "Wrong side up, friend. Too bad."

The second man scowled. "My luck."

CHAPTER 71

The scouts raced up the road from the south a few hours afterward. Lather sprayed from mounts wall-eyed with strain. The team leader tried to yell at the relaxed Wolves to clear a path, but the words were only a harsh bawl. The men understood his urgency and intent, though, and parted before him and his team, closing behind them immediately. From where Gan waited, it looked as if the riders were fording a river. The leader reined his horse to a skidding stop in front of him. Its gusting breath was rank with the acrid smell of an animal run to its limit. The team leader saluted and delivered his report while his men and their horses drank greedily from the small stream a few yards away. He said Olan units were moving north at their best speed, not even taking time to loot the countryside. At least a thousand men, the lead units no more than two hours march behind him. He was certain the patrol had been unobserved.

Gan had arranged for Clas to hold Noble Malten and his group at a distance all day, and now he sent him a hand signal to release them. The Noble's nervousness was apparent through his bluster. He was gesticulating wildly and pointing. Clas pretended to be swayed by his arguments. What the Noble failed to see was that, immediately on allowing him to hurry to Gan, Clas ordered his followers to go along with him. Their acting skills weren't the equal of the Noble's.

When Gan repeated the scout's report, the Noble appeared stunned.

"This changes everything," he said. "I warned you we should go into defensive positions. Who could have suspected the Olans would attack now? If I don't warn my brother, they'll massacre my people. Whatever our differences, they must be protected. I'll ride to him."

Mildly, Gan said, "What if he still wants to kill you?"

"It's a chance I must take."

He blinked at Gan's laughter, then nervously joined in. He was still smiling, albeit uncertainly, as Gan spoke again. "You were willing enough to have *me* kill your people if they resisted your claim to the barony. You wanted the Olans to catch us in battle with your brother, or in a defense. When they attack us, your friends are supposed to mutiny. One of them will murder your brother. You expected to destroy us, and attack your own king beside the Olans. All so you can be a toy baron for Altanar."

As he talked, the Noble's smile altered slowly, until at the end it had become a snarl. He said, "You lie."

Gan looked away. He said, "Clas, have them tied." The Noble reached for his weapon, but Raggar was on him before his hand was halfway. The violence of the charge bowled the man backward, and the two of them tumbled several of the rest of his party. Shara and Cho reacted a hair slower, leaping forward to crouch in front of those still on their feet. Growling, ears laid flat, their glowing eyes dared anyone else to move. Raggar stood with his forepaws on Noble Malten's chest. His muzzle was inches from the quivering throat where a thick, blue vein pumped furiously.

Around them the young Wolves were like stone. It was the first time they had seen the dogs move to protect their master. Some had seen them in combat at the Bear Paw, but a man understood ferocity in combat. To see it erupt like a flame in the night was unnerving. A single astonished intake of breath rose from them. In the farther background, the unending rattle and croak of the gathering crows was ignored. Gan called to the dogs. Shara and Cho backed up slowly, the male moving to Gan's right, Cho taking position behind. Raggar inched away from the Noble, growling constantly. The reluctance of his retreat was almost as terrifying as his charge. The Noble remained rigid, fixed to the ground, while Clas detailed the men to bind him.

As soon as that was taken care of, Gan had Clas fake an attack on the Malten hill. He disliked exposing his men to a dangerous charade, but felt he must, if he was to spring this trap to his advantage. Unit war drums sounded the intricate, surging attack rhythm. The Wolves moved forward. A few Malten cavalrymen intercepted them, loosing a scatter of harmless arrows before galloping away. When the advance reached a point two hundred yards from the base of the hill, whistles shrilled and the music of the drums changed. The men fanned out left and right, forming a line of attack. More arrows soared toward them from the hillside, all falling ridiculously short. The drums stopped.

Some brave souls up the hill rose to beat on their shields and shout insults. The Wolves held where they'd stopped. While all that was in progress, Gan sent for the Messengers and had Emso send out riders to observe the Olan advance.

The Wolves continued to play at attacking the hill for another hour. The men were into the spirit of the game, dodging the infrequent arrows and slingstones from up the slope, exchanging insults with the defenders. The thought of the unseen Olans closing on him made Gan too nervous to enjoy the coarse humor of the yelling. He hoped no one was injured. One broken bone from a stone, one minor wound from an arrow, and the blood lust would break free. The play would turn deadly. He already saw growing tension; some of his men, as well as those on the hill, reacted angrily to the slurs flung at them. Worse, the Malten people were growing more confident by the minute, beginning to believe they'd frightened their enemies into inaction. The Wolves were chafing more and more under that particular taunt.

The last scouts galloped in from the south to report. As they described the size and organization of the Olan force, the first of its advance elements began to appear.

The trap was closing, the Olan jaw from the south, the King from the north. Gan decided it was time for the intended victim to escape. He wished he could stay to see the frustrated trappers snare themselves.

Whistles sounded once more. Red and yellow flags burned bright in the late afternoon sun as they whipped out their signals. Moving with precision, the Wolves fell back, forming into their units on the run. Without pausing, they wheeled into a column, flowing east, away from the battlefield and back into the protecting forest. Quiet seized the hill, a dazed sort of surprise, and then the forces on it began to cheer like victors. Gan, waiting to see the last of his men clear the area, listened with grim amusement. The Olan divisions expected the Malten forces to come over to their side and smash the Wolves—only the Wolves were scampering for home; and the traitor who was supposed to execute the change of sides was bound and gagged, kicking his heels like a hog tied up for the market. The Olan commander was going to feel very abused; when he was finished with the skimpy Malten force, he'd be anxious to tangle with the King and his units approaching from the north.

Heeling his horse into a trot, Gan searched ahead until he spied the Messengers. At his signal, one hurried forward. They rode together until they'd haggled a price for the man's service, then Gan stopped and said, "Ride north and find the King and his allies. They're hurrying this way. Tell them this: 'Gan Moondark and the Wolves send you greetings. Baron Jalail, who commands me, would have been your friend. So would I. Instead, you tried to destroy my Wolves and me. None of your barons trusts the other, none trusts you. Baron Malten is under attack from Ola. Your treachery brings you what you've earned. If you survive this day, think on this, King: You have made an enemy of your best hope to defeat the Olans."

The pudgy Messenger listened with his eyes fixed on a distant point, his head nodding in cadence with Gan's speech. When the message ended, he repeated it exactly, catching all the rhythms and the precise bite of contempt. "Is that all?" he asked then, and it seemed to Gan he was disappointed. Assuring him he was finished, Gan watched him turning to leave, then suddenly reached out to grab his horse's reins. The Messenger, secure in his inviolability, watched with arch unconcern. He seemed almost to dare Gan.

Gan said, "This is a Dog horse."

"If you say so." The Messenger pulled tentatively at the reins. When Gan held them, he looked bored.

"It has the mark of a war-horse, but it was never trained. If it had been, it would have attacked me when I reached for it. No such horses are ever sold."

The Messenger sighed hugely. "It was a fair purchase. A trader in Ola. He said he got them from one of the Mountain People."

"Them? How many?"

"I don't know—maybe eight? Ten? Who knows?"

Gan's hand was clenched so tightly to the reins he had to concentrate to release them. When he had, he flexed the fingers and told the Messenger to be on his way. The man was backing the horse to get maneuvering room, when a sound quavered into the air. It came softly at first, its source undiscoverable, as though it grew from the ground all around them. The Messenger made a hurried Two-sign, his head swiveling in all directions. A wolf pack was around them, all howling at once. A deer appeared in a break in the brush, bringing the dogs to full alert. Hardly noticing them, preoccupied with the pack's song, she slipped away with the soundless grace of wind-bent bamboo.

The Messenger happened to be looking at Gan, who cocked his head, listening more closely, then said, "I hear you, brothers. Trouble. Help me if you can."

The howl stopped on one short yip. The Messenger jerked his mount around and fled. His partner watched him come at a run, and whipped his own mount to a gallop to join him and stay alongside. He looked as irritated as curious. "Was it an interesting message?" he asked.

The shorter Messenger looked at him as if surprised to find him there. "Message? Oh. Yes, interesting." He looked over his shoulder at the empty path behind him and slowed his horse. Turning again to his friend, he said, "I never believed it, but it's true. The wolves talk to him."

"Of course they do. He's their commander."

"Not the Wolves, you fool—the wolves. Real ones. Didn't you hear them howling?"

They were at a walk now, although the short man continued to peer backward every few steps. The taller said, "Birds sing, wolves howl. So?"

"They spoke to him. He understood. He *answered* them. I saw it."

The other man looked back over his shoulder. He started to say something, but a wave of doubt washed away his disbelief. He slapped his horse's rump for more speed.

Clas was waiting with Tate at the van of the column when Gan rejoined it. He smiled broadly, saying, "The men heard the howling. They say it's because you outsmarted the King and all his barons."

Gan smiled back, hoping it would cover the foreboding gnawing at him. He responded amiably to Tate's congratulations and even managed to make some conversation about the action. They all paused at the far-off mutter of war drums and the mournful lowing of battle horns. For a moment they were still, listening, and they Gan rode forward. As he moved toward his accustomed place at the head of the marching men, he exchanged comments with them. They were still ready for a fight, but they realized their mission had accomplished far more than they set out to do. Gan knew that better than any of them, and yet . . . He tried to tell himself he was being foolish, that everything was all right.

He couldn't stop worrying about Neela. At such a time, with so many military and political considerations, she was the uppermost thing in his mind. Other men would expect him to be thinking of important matters— the fate of the King, of the barons who supported him. Or that's what he'd always thought other men would expect. Did they go into battle wondering if they'd ever hold their *her* in their arms again? They must, he reasoned; they were the same as he. He looked over his shoulder at the double column just snaking its way into the first part of the forest blowdown. The faces seemed completely at ease, wrapped in the problems of keeping their footing and the pace of the march.

No wolves had spoken to them of danger.

Neela was in Baron Jalail's castle, surrounded by stone walls and men to guard them.

Still, the nameless, insistent fear wouldn't leave.

Fear.

It was no longer worry. He accepted that he was afraid.

Signaling to Emso, he ordered a faster pace.

They smelled the disaster before anyone could see it. Gan insisted on a predawn march, to the surprise of everyone. For the first time since the Wolves were formed, there was a stiff look of discontent in every move they made. Nevertheless, they were well under way before first light, and so it was that the first harsh stink crept out of the darkness to infect their minds with worry and speculation. Instead of marching toward a dawn of warm return, the men whispered questions. Some few offered reassurance, projecting more hope than conviction. Some made grim predictions, and were threatened to silence.

They passed farmhouses. They were abandoned. Still, none was responsible for the smell.

Burned habitations have their own signature. Nothing else blends consumed cloth and wood and paint and metal and leather into such a weight of loss and pain. Nothing else smells like charred human flesh.

As they marched, the smell grew stronger. Emso's scouts rode ahead, probing for that which they knew and dreaded. When they came back, he went alone to Gan.

"The scouts say the castle was burned. They said no one knew any of the details." Under his breath, he cursed the freshly risen sun that might reveal the lie on his face. What man would tell the Murdat what the people said?

Gan took no time to ask for more. He whipped his horse ahead, the dogs streaming after.

At his first sight from the road, the castle looked little different than it had when he left. As his horse closed the distance, he tried to tell himself he was mistaken about the smell, but that deception crumbled under reality. People, forewarned by the appearance of the scouts, peered from houses as he rode by, but whenever he looked, they ducked out of sight.

Her name was in his throat, on his tongue. He would have screamed it but for the fear that she might not answer.

Clas galloped to join him when he reined up to stare at where the blackened remains of the massive castle-door timbers lay in a heap at the entry. The brave pennants hung slack, some burned away. He drove his frightened horse across the rubble. It stumbled, and he kept it upright by sheer strength and will. Triangular stains marred the walls above the castle's windows, mute testimony to gutting fire. Some stone buildings appeared untouched. Some, made of wood, were totally gone. The lockup had ceased to be; the castle wall where it had stood was cracked and chipped from the intense heat of its burning. Nearby, the battle walk around the inside of the wall—including the place where the Baron had stood to address the recruits for the Wolves—had burned through.

The House Director stepped through the door of the main building. He saluted left-handed, his right arm suspended in a sling. He walked toward Gan in a bent, crabbed manner. Stopping in front of him, he drew himself painfully erect. "They surprised us, Murdat," he said. "Ten nobles. Men the Baron never suspected. They came with Moondancers, at night. They said you and Clas and Emso and Tate were all dead. They said Noble Malten had tricked you, the Olans, the King—everybody."

Gan grabbed him by the shirt and jerked him forward, put his face almost in contact with his. The House Director gave a sharp cry, clutching at his side with this good hand. Gan said, "Where is my wife?"

The House Director looked over Gan's shoulder. Clas and the three great dogs waited. Emso and Tate were riding through the burned-out entry. When Gan shook him and practically shouted his question again, the man composed his features. Resignedly, he said, "They took her and the Rose Priestess when they heard you didn't die. They went to Ola, to ask King Altanar to protect them."

Behind them Clas made a low, moaning sound. Gan heard the sibilance of his murdat sliding from the scabbard.

The House Director reached up and lifted Gan's suddenly limp hand from his shirt. Standing free, he said, "Your wife killed one noble and at least two of the Moondancers. The Baron killed two more nobles. Many Moondancers died. Altogether, only five nobles rode away. But we failed you. They captured the women. I'm ready to die, if I must. All I ask is that you know that I fought for them."

Behind Gan, Clas' voice strained. He said, "Is she— Are they hurt?"

"No. But the Baron's dead. Four, Ops—them, too."

Gan told himself to hear, to think. He said, "How did it happen? How long have they had to get away?"

The House Director described how a rider had trailed the Wolves. He was to report their destruction, but when he saw Gan avoid the trap, he raced back with the news. Until then, the traitors had been enjoying a drunken celebration. With his news, they panicked. They'd chained Neela and Sylah and left within an hour, taking the road south toward the Bear Paw. They'd taken no other hostages, only two horses apiece, but plenty of food.

Clas, with a voice as calm as death, said, "Get us fresh horses, the best we have. Food."

Gan added, "For the dogs, as well. And something to give them a scent."

The House Director's injuries reduced him to scuttling, but he made the best time he could. Emso intercepted him. After hurried whispers, he re-mounted, leaving the injured man to lead Tate to the food storage.

Clas said to Gan, "How many men do you want?"

Gan shook his head. "None. They'd slow us."

Only the bright red spots on Clas' cheeks revealed his emotions. The one highlighted the tattoo, and a muscle twitched under it as Gan said, "There's something you have to know. There's more at stake than you think. Neela made Sylah and me promise to keep her secret until you returned from this march. She wouldn't have you distracted." He took a deep breath. "Neela carries your child."

CHAPTER 72

Tate and the House Director watched the two Dog warriors leave. Tate still wore her camouflaged battle gear. She fondled the wipe thoughtfully, contin-uing to look south long after the riders were out of sight. He seemed to expect her words when she faced him. She said, "The castle needs repairs. You and Emso know what needs done. I don't. I'm taking a patrol to follow Clas and Gan."

"You can't. They'll make you turn back."

"They won't see us. They're too busy looking ahead."

The House Director said, "Catching up to the nobles and Moondancers won't be the hard part. Getting back here will be. They'll have made contact with the Olans, and that means hard fighting. You'll need at least ten or twenty men." He swallowed hard, then went on. "You're a warrior. And a friend. But I think this is man's work. Please, tell Emso."

Tate smiled, a bit wry, a bit hurt. She said, "No. I have an obligation." She held up her hand, exposing the thin line of the blood scar that marked her kinship with Clas. "That's why I go. It's why you'll help me, and keep your mouth shut."

He saluted, breaking into a rueful grin. "Be careful. If you're hurt, none of them will forgive me."

She laughed, grateful for the break in the tension, then said, "I'm leaving in two hours. There's no sense in trying to stay on their backs. And I have questions. Was Jones among the traitors?"

He shook his head. "No, he wasn't." His composure cracked. "He knew about it! He must have. Everyone says so."

"He's still here?"

"People fear him. The Moondancers said there are more of them—'hidden believers' they called them. Shun him, Tate. He's evil."

She gestured helplessly. "He's—He's of my people. I promise you this: he'll make no more trouble here."

It was a short ride to Jones' hut. The warming spring had brought the goldfinches back from their southern wintering, and their garrulous twittering was everywhere as they swooped and fluttered among the blooming dandelions at the roadside. They were just coming into color, replacing the prim browns and grays with brilliant yellow. They looked tweedy and unprepared, as though they'd come half dressed to a party. She stopped to call her favorite llama once again. He, with his pretentious monocle, clearly disapproved of their fluttering, and he wasn't entirely sure of Tate's horse. He came to the fence anyhow. She rewarded him with a slice of dried apple, and he favored her by extending his neck over the top rail so she could scratch his head for a while.

She wished she could spend the day there. Perhaps the rest of her days. It was strange; in less than two hours she'd be riding into the teeth of an army that hated her, an army that protected slavers as one of its duties. Yet she dreaded far more the talk with Jones. She slipped His Lordship another slice of apple and rode away, sending a fortune of goldfinches sputtering across the road.

Jones' sawtoothed voice bade her come in as she was tying up her horse. He was alone, as usual, although the room had the feel of a gathering. There was nothing Tate could put a name to, but something about it spoke of communion. The dirt floor seemed harder than it should, as though wearied by the weight of more feet than belonged there. The bare walls gave off an abnormal warmth. She sought the center of the place, wanting space around her. The position blocked all but a thin shaft of the sunlight coming in the open door at her back. Instead of brightening the room, it exposed the raw ugliness of the few rough furnishings, and cast shadows that hinted at things in hiding.

He sat on a stool at a table, propped forward on his elbows. Like herself, he'd adapted the local clothing to his own taste, a loose, flowing shirt, wonderfully embroidered with lighter designs of winged creatures against a dark background. He shifted his torso to get a better view against the sun. For the first time she saw a silver disk swinging from a silver chain at his breast.

In the diffuse light the pink skin of his injury stood out like a mute accusation. Tate tried to keep her eyes away from it, leaving her no choice but to look directly into his foxlike features and their unconcealed hostility.

He said, "Come to question me about the kidnapping? The fancy blond queen and that haughty pagan witch? I thought they'd send that clod Emso, the one that always needs a shave. Why you? They afraid to torture me? They think you can coax me into confessing something?"

Tate's temper flared. "What's wrong with you? Who said anything about torture? I only came over here to—" He half straightened, backing away from her intensity. The silver disk bumped his chest and he reached for it. His lips moved in—what? Silent prayer? Curses? Suspicion and growing horror replaced Tate's anger. "You *do* know something, don't you? Don't tell me you knew before it happened. Please, don't tell me that."

"None of your bloody friends would believe it."

"You knew the ones who did it. You knew they were Gan's enemies. You knew they planned to overthrow the Baron."

Throwing back his head, he crowed, and when he stopped, he leaped to his feet, fists on the table, eyes burning. Tate's hand went to her pistol. He either didn't see or didn't care. A drop of spittle caught on his lower lip, crystal-glittering as it bobbled from the force of his words. "Of course I knew! No one had to say it, but a blind fool could see it coming. Your friends hate me. They have to be made to understand. This One in All, this One Who Is Two—it's all blasphemy! Apostasy!"

Tate stared. "What's that have to do with killing the Baron? With kidnapping two innocent women? Sylah saved your life!"

As suddenly as he was wild, he was a cartoon of calm reason. He wiped his mouth with the back of his hand. "They can't be brought back to true faith until they've tasted the fall, savored the bitterest dregs of sin. Moondance is only the first step. To be truly saved, they must become genuinely evil, evil enough to destroy the forces that misled them. Destroy themselves, if need be. I saw that right away, of course. I've tried to hint as much to you. Your association with these people has contaminated you." He leaned forward, extending a hand like a claw, twitching the fingers. The other fondled the disk. "Come stand beside me, Donnacee. Moondance is pleasure. Taste the freedoms that will bring you to the serenity of submission. We shall bring them to their bellies, groveling in shame. When the foulness is burned from their minds and bodies, when their false institutions are ashes, we shall be the ones to raise them to blessedness."

Unconsciously she stepped back and to the side. The sunbeam fell full on him, making him wince and cringe like something exposed in its hole. She said, "You can talk to me about evil? You knew the Wolves were marching into a trap. You knew they could die. You knew I could die, damn you."

"I was assured you'd be spared." He grinned slyly. "You're hard to mistake, even among your new friends, you know. They said you'd be protected."

"That rock ruined your brain. How could anyone 'protect' me in a battle?" Irresistibly, her hand was drawn to the wipe. Jones' eyes widened. He inched backward. She said, "I'm going after Neela and Sylah. I have to tell Gan and Clas what you told me. If you're here when we get back, they'll peel the skin off your living body. I'm not sure I'd stop them if I could." Her wrist ached. She glanced at it. The muscle under the blood scar throbbed and writhed. She stepped to the table and shoved Jones away. He hit the stool and continued over backward.

She was out the door when he called, a pitiful, begging cry. Squeezing her eyes shut, she tried to ignore him. He called again. Furious, she turned and stood in the doorway, unwilling to reenter his hut.

He whined. "You're rejecting me. I'm only interested in eventual, everlasting mercy. Don't do this. Please."

She hated herself for weakening. He was kneeling, elbows on the table, hands clasped as if praying. She said, "You would have had me killed. You'd do it again, wouldn't you?"

It was as though she'd burned him. He leaped upright. "See? You and *them*! Unforgiving. Beyond redemption. Very well. I curse you. All. You'll never know the peace of surrender. Go! Fight! Forever. Our evil will swarm over you, our forgiveness will ignore you!"

He was laughing as she left, too shaken to concern herself with dignity, running to leap into the saddle and gallop away. She never saw His Lordship race to the fence to watch her, not understanding how she could fail to come to him as she always had.

Lowering darkness blurred the distance between the forest's black-trunked trees. The trail ahead wavered to nothingness in the half light. The dogs were invisible. Clas reined up, and despite Gan's protests, made him do the same. He forced the younger man to look at the hoofprints of the horses they followed. He measured the length of the stride, spanning the ground carefully with his fingers. Similarly, he made him inspect the depth of the prints. The animals were clearly untired, their pace controlled. There was no sign of clods ripped up. The stride was long and sure, with no stumbling or foot dragging. Gan was forced to admit that the kidnapping party wasn't as worried about being followed as he'd expected them to be.

Clas put a hand on his shoulder, spoke directly into the stony, unchanging expression. "These men aren't afraid, Gan, and we both know they expect us. There's something waiting. Even with the dogs scouting for us, darkness is no time to be riding into ambush. I'm in as great a hurry as you." Gan tried to disagree, and Clas' voice rode over it. "The other half of our secret is that Sylah is also pregnant. I don't have any intention of losing her or my child by being thoughtless. Anger isn't enough, Gan. We all need rest."

Sylah pregnant. He never thought of it. And Clas so composed, so contained. Gan thought the shame of his own behavior would stifle him. He snapped at Clas, "So much more reason for continuing. You think I can rest?"

"You must. You will. We'll have to fight for them. You, me, the dogs. The trail tells us they expect help. We'll need all our strength."

He considered it for a moment, watching the deepening night claim the forest. Clas was right, of course. It was only embarrassment that wouldn't let him admit it aloud. He'd been dangerously careless, merely following where the tracks led. He'd been so glad there'd been no rain to obscure them, he'd forgotten all about reading what was there. His sole thought had been to rescue Neela. Clas was right; he must think more of the how of it, not so much the when. He nodded approval, whistling for the dogs before moving to hobble his horse.

He accepted saker from Clas. The first bite of the leaf-wrapped trail food released a terrible wave of nostalgia. Eagerly, he abandoned himself to a rush of memories of the men of the tribe building the fish traps, and how they gasped laughter when they dove into the cold water to place them. It sucked the breath from them then, and again when they went into it to catch the fish. He felt that, too, the startling strength of the huge, silvery shapes as they lunged to escape the grasping hands. He heard the songs of the women cleaning the fish, hanging them on sweet willow wands to smoke and dry. The rich smell of fresh, summer-hot berries was the signal for making the pulpy sake, the mix of fruit and fish, that would be formed into the individual sakers to be redried. He listened to the thudding of the huge wooden pestles in hollowed log mortars.

He saw Neela, the golden chain of her hair dancing across the collar of a sleeveless jacket, lifting the pestle, dropping it. Her arms flashed honey-tan in the sunshine, and when she looked at him, her eyes were bluer than kingfisher feathers, her teeth like the snow on the mountaintops.

Had he really seen her like that? Was he remembering or dreaming?

Raggar's hesitant approach disturbed Gan's thoughts. He was sitting with his back against a tree, legs stretched out in front of him, and when he turned his head, he found the great dog's eyes peering into his own. He looked worried, as if he understood his master's frame of mind, and he lifted one huge foreleg, pawing at Gan's shoulder. When Gan offered him a piece of the saker, he took it without enthusiasm, continuing to stare. Gan scratched his neck, and Raggar seemed to relax. Soon he was lying down, his head pinning Gan's legs to the ground.

Clas was already stretched out on the ground, and Gan asked if he was asleep. He got a muffled grunt in response. Gan said, "There's something I've been meaning to tell you. The Messenger I hired this morning was riding a Dog horse."

Clas grunted again.

"It was a young war-horse."

That brought Clas to a sitting position. "Impossible."

"Not trained, but selected. The Messenger bought it from an Olan trader. He got it from a Devil."

"That's very bad news. What do you think—"

"Another raid like the one we heard about. Not even Bay and Likat would sell war-horses. We have to get back there, Clas."

" 'Back there,' Gan? Not 'home'?"

Gan was glad the darkness would hide the color heating his face. He said, "You know what I mean. Anyhow, Dog People travel everywhere, and where they stop is home."

Clas was silent, and finally Gan said, "Are you disappointed in me, my friend? Do I want too much?"

There was an even longer silence, and then Clas said, "I hunt the men who stole our wives. For you, the world is different. More complicated. When we find Neela, all the wanting, all the concerns about missions and prophecies, will come to risk. They may end. Will you have trouble deciding what you want most?"

"You offend. I will save her or have no life."

"Good." He made a gruff, comfortable sound as he lay back down. In a voice muffled by the jacket pillowing his head, he said, "I don't understand all the changes I see. I do understand that the important things are unchanged. We'll do our best. No one in this world or the next has a right to ask for more."

Before Gan could get to sleep, an owl quavered, the little darksinger. Half aloud, Gan said, "You again, my friend? Will you read my thoughts when I sleep? Are you so anxious to see the worry, the fear I dare not show anyone else? Go away; find a safer place."

He listened a long time, but the owl never called again.

CHAPTER 73

They were two days south of the Bear Paw, well into Ola, when Raggar came loping back toward them. Gan immediately reined up, stood in his stirrups. "He's limping," he said.

Clas squinted into the distance. "It doesn't look serious."

They rode forward slowly. The dog's reappearance was a warning, and both men redoubled their caution.

Raggar was almost on them before they saw the blood at his shoulder. They exchanged glances, and Clas said, "I'll ride ahead a ways while you tend to him. That's a wound, isn't it?"

Gan nodded, dismounting. Raggar came to him wagging his tail. He looked sheepish, as though being wounded was an embarrassment. Gan inspected it. The cut was a thin, shallow slice in the skin, not at all dangerous. It was from something man-made, however, which was another story entirely. "They nicked you, did they? Either you're getting careless or there's someone up there who's very clever." From his saddlebag he produced a pot with a leather top laced tightly at its neck. A small dab of its pine-tar salve stanched the bleeding.

Walking his horse forward, Gan kept Raggar close. The trail was rank with weeds there, the ground almost obscured. It was vivid testimony to the harsh uncertainties of life in the area, Gan thought. They were close enough to Devil country for raiders to haunt it. Like the trail leading east from Baron Jalail's land, and the border territory between Malten and Jalail, it was too dangerous for peaceful pursuits.

From his hiding place behind a laurel thicket, Clas signaled Gan to get off the trail. A few feet ahead, a thin cord stretched across the trail only a few inches above the ground. Scuff marks showed where Clas had seen it and hurriedly checked his horse. Slowly, looking for secondary traps that might be positioned to protect it, Gan traced the string to its source. It was tied to a trigger. Pressure on the trip line would release a small stick. That, in turn, freed the heavy cord restraining a bent sapling as thick as Gan's wrist. It was firmly lashed to a tree, positioned to swing horizontally out at the trail. The weapon was tipped with an obsidian point almost a foot long.

Its arc was about four feet high and its striking force would be devastating. In addition, there was a whistle just behind the obsidian. Whoever planted the device wanted to know when it struck.

Working rapidly, Gan cut the whistle free, then dismantled the whole thing. He brought in Shara and Cho before he ran with it to another tree, around a bend in the trail and about fifty yards farther south. There he reassembled the device, without the whistle, but reversing its aim. The trigger slipped the first time he tried to put it back together, substantiating his judgment in removing the whistle. When he was satisfied it was properly set up, he signaled Clas to watch ahead. Then he blew a hard puff on the whistle. It gave a thin, carrying shriek.

By the time he rejoined Clas, three men were breaking cover some three hundred yards away. Raggar growled, continuing to grumble deep in his chest even after Gan patted him. Two of the men came north on foot, hurrying to see what they'd caught. The third raced away on horseback; a man on foot appeared on a distant ridge, watching him come.

The two men left behind weren't overly cautious. Gan puzzled over that, then realized there had been no scream or shouts after they heard their trap spring. They were fairly certain it had killed whatever it hit, and that no humans were there to make noise about it.

Gan and Clas watched the blade hit the lead man. The continuing sweep of the sapling threw him back to knock the second man sprawling. Gan was on him from behind, holding him down with the point of his murdat at his throat before the man knew what was happening.

"Where are they?" Gan said. The man's mouth worked jerkily. His eyes rolled in shock. Gan slapped him with his free hand, repeating the question, and the man again tried desperately to speak. A drop of blood peeked out at the point of the murdat, only to be washed away in a sudden flood of sweat. Clas knelt and put his face close to him. "Was the other man riding to tell your friends?"

The man tried to nod, earning himself another pinprick. Gan moved the blade, and the man repeated his effort. Gan said, "Where is she? Is she hurt? Where are the women?"

He managed to say, "With the others. Where the rider went." He brightened slightly, adding, "He's the one shot at your dog. I tried to stop—"

"Is she hurt?" Gan tensed.

"No!" It was a strangled plea.

Clas asked, "How many are there?"

"Five Jalail nobles. They just joined up with us—fifteen Olan infantry, we three cavalry, and an officer. A dozen or so Moondancers came with the nobles; three of them are women."

Gan brightened. "Infantry? They must have wanted all their cavalry for the battle in Harbundai. That helps."

The man was anxious to be helpful. "The Jalails were angry. They expected cavalry to escort them. They wanted to go on ahead, but the officer says they have to stay with us. With them." He swallowed, then added lamely, "Our officer said you'd be dead. The King told him. He said he doesn't care about the nobles. He wants the women."

Clas said, "They'll be expecting a signal from this pair."

The Olan soldier said, "That's right. We're supposed to wave if the trap killed or wounded you. If there was a large party, we were supposed to be sure the officer can see us ride straight to the bridge at the next river. We were to meet the others there."

When Clas asked, he freely described the route to the bridge, even estimating how long it would take the party to reach it. Only when they were taking off his helmet did he realize what they planned. The sweat popped out on him again.

Idly, Clas said, "Shall we kill him here, or make him walk off the trail first?"

Moaning, the man shook his head. He held up his hands in a Two-sign, too overwrought to speak. Gan rose. "Here," he said, and raised the murdat.

"Don't!" The soldier tried to squirm backward. "I can lead you to the bridge. I can tell you more. Don't kill me!"

"Tell me what?"

"About the other soldiers. Maybe fifty. Coming to the bridge to meet our officer."

"When?"

"Tonight. Tomorrow. I don't know. But I told you! Don't kill me."

Gan smiled at him. He didn't see Clas look at it, then frown and turn away. He said, "I don't kill the helpless. Not even scum." To Clas he said, "Please, will you tie him up? If I touch him, I'll cut his throat."

Clas nodded. He used the cord from the trap, lashing the man's wrists to his ankles. It was done in seconds, and the two of them kept to the shielding forest, leading their own horses, until they found the hiding place where the three Olans had waited for them. Clas slipped on the Olan armor and helmet. They could only hope the watchers would assume he was a survivor when he dashed out of cover, racing for the bridge rendezvous. Gan took the dogs and other horses and held to the thick cover, hurrying in parallel.

They reached the bridge in the middle of an afternoon so peaceful it made Gan's throat tighten dangerously.

They were at a river when he asked her to marry him. Surely a man didn't learn of such happiness to have it ripped away so soon?

The valley was broad there, the land quite flat. The river cut a bright slash through the crowding, dark forest, a canyon of sun and warmth. The current flowed softly, its strength spread wide. A large marsh swayed gently downstream, new-growth cattails crowding aside the spent brown of the old. Seed heads, broken and tattered, released clouds of dancing fluff as redwing blackbirds whirred from one to the other to claim nesting territory. Their metallic challenges rang out in a thousand harmonizing bells. The gabbling flocks of swimming birds were more discreet, although their antics frequently erupted into great splashing squabbles. Elegant geese in their black, white, and gray cruised regally through a lesser cast of mallards, widgeons, mergansers, and grebes. Wood ducks, so colorful they demanded the eye, whirled and glittered in their courting ritual.

Gan turned to Clas. "We'll have to hurry," he said. As the dogs loped down the trail to find the column, the two men hurriedly collected dry wood and stacked it in the middle of the bridge. The old boards and timbers caught fire easily, and in minutes a tower of flame and smoke rose above the river. Chunks of burning wood were caught in the updraft, spinning, sparking, finally falling with angry hissing into the river. It carried their spent excitement seaward, unaffected.

Satisfied that any reinforcements would now be sufficiently delayed, they rode into the forest. Drawing apart, they took time for nara. When they were finished, Gan saw Clas was still too tense, as though he'd fallen short of complete cleansing. There was no time to be concerned. They moved out, keeping a distance from the trail. Soft duff cushioned their steps. Their movement was no louder than the light breeze stirring the leaves.

Glancing at the two soldiers slightly ahead and abreast of her, Sylah saw they weren't paying any attention to her. She hoped the same was true of the pair behind her, where Neela walked. Careful to avoid giving the appearance of hurrying, she managed to acquire a few inches of slack in the chain binding her to the waist of the mounted noble ahead of her. She'd stopped hating him.

That wasn't accurate. She'd stopped thinking about how much she hated him. The flame still burned in her heart, the taste of gall still filled her mouth. Time had already convinced her it was best to avoid thinking of him. Escape was essential. Nothing else mattered.

Using the slack in the chain, she raised her hands to surreptitiously touch her stomach. How Clas loved to tease her about the coming swelling that would soon show there. How hard he struggled to avoid appearing sentimental, yet he could never stop talking about the baby.

She was glad there was no perceptible evidence of pregnancy yet, for

Neela as well as for herself. Altanar's reaction to the information could be too horrible to think about. The Moondancers worried her, as well. With mouths as cold as lizards, they spoke of slaughter and wrath. There was excitement in them, but no joy. They gave the impression that destruction was central to their progress, yet the only goals she'd heard them mention were the elimination of Church and its replacement by their own vision. She was Church; Neela was Authority. She wouldn't allow herself to dwell on what Moondancers would think of their pregnancy.

Again, she told herself it didn't show. Not even the best Healer would know. Not yet. Even if it did feel like a mountain.

It was a mountain.

The rider saw the chain hanging loose and quickened his horse's pace, drawing it tight once more.

She didn't trouble to look up. She'd touched her baby.

There, in her, was power. It was a good thing; there was more to life than personal power. At least this march had forced her to think about that. Giving birth, actually producing a child, was a marvel. More important than that was giving life, and that had nothing to do with bearing.

It meant to love.

She would do both. She would love her child. The Abbess, who had no children, loved her. Of all the people she'd known, the Abbess was the one most responsible for the life in her. She'd saved her from real death, as well as from the nonlife of those Chosens who never learned more than survival.

Who could question such power? Who could suggest it wasn't greater than swords and arrows? To take life was so easy, the freeing of a bird from a flimsy, ugly cage. To create happiness, to give meaning, to create intelligence—that was power. That was love.

She hoped Clas was beginning to understand that. She wondered if Gan ever would.

The noble yanked on the chain, almost spilling her onto her face. When she regained her balance, she hid a self-mocking smile. Hatred also lived, the child of helplessness and fear.

She would escape. She would *not* be helpless.

Turning as best she could, she looked back at Neela. The girl's blue eyes were bleaker than winter, but she smiled. It showed courage. She, too, was chained, but to a noble who rode behind her. It was a bit more comfortable. Sylah knew it made no difference to Neela. She'd never once acknowledged pain, fear, anger—anything. She smiled for Sylah. At all other times she was as cold and distant as the white head of Snowfather Mountain. Even the Moondancers kept a wary distance from her, as though they understood they had a particularly dangerous animal on their hands. They taunted her more than Sylah, and with greater malice. Sylah believed they'd poke her with sticks if they weren't afraid she'd grab one and pull them within her reach.

Sylah wondered how she'd raise her child.

It was better to think of escape. She would *not* let them see her fear.

Raggar's growl warned Gan and Clas of the nearness of their quarry. When they arrived where Shara and Cho were waiting, they heard the voices.

The Olans marched in two columns, each man almost in contact with the man next to him on the narrow trail. By striking directly from the side, Clas and Gan would only have to deal with four men—eight, at the most—before breaking out on the other side. They'd grab the women as they fought their way through.

It was a desperate chance, but the only one they had. The burned bridge would check the Olan force coming to meet the kidnappers; it wouldn't stop them. Success depended on surprise and an escape fast enough to defeat pursuit.

Easing through the undergrowth, they found a reasonably clear view and waited. The point consisted of two nervous troopers who moved well, perhaps a bit too fast. Gan and Clas exchanged glances as they noticed both men kept looking over their shoulders, as if more concerned about their rear than any threat from the front. They passed on.

The rest of the men followed after an interval. Neela and Sylah were near the middle of the group. Gan noted the four armored Olans in their square and remembered Clas' description of them as turtles. They certainly weren't moving like turtles, he thought grimly, then stiffened. Their armor was loose, indicating they were more interested in haste than protection. The behavior of the point duo should have told him; they believed they were running from a larger party. The spring-trap ruse had worked. For a moment he allowed himself to wish there were others with him. If there'd been more time to round up horses for Tate, Emso, ten or twenty Wolves . . .

There was no time. Not then, not now.

He recognized the traitorous nobles, two in front of the square, three behind. The sight of the chain, its faint jingle, enraged him.

Calming, he realized its greater significance. The nobles would fight with particular desperation. If they lost Neela or Sylah, or—the thought was fire—if either woman died, their bargaining position with Altanar was greatly damaged.

With hand language, Clas asked, "Ready?" and Gan nodded. Whipping the horses with the flat of their blades, they drove at the column, only a few yards away. The faces of the Olan troops rounded as white circles of shock, their eyes unbelieving.

Gan's horse never stumbled. Whatever tripped it took its forelegs from under it completely, and it went down instantly, giving him no time for anything except an instinctive tuck that kept him from landing on his face and snapping his neck. Shouldering his way into the soft earth, he felt himself compress as if his own weight would crush him, and then he was rolling, up on his feet, stumbling forward, the murdat miraculously still in his hand. Raggar was to his left, the other dogs hanging back slightly in counterattack attitude. Clas had struck the nobles in front, and both were already on the ground.

A soldier came at Gan, was cut down. Another appeared. His first thrust screeched off Gan's blade, driving through to open a scalp wound above his left eye. Half blinded, Gan slashed at the man, felt the solid jar of a good hit. There was a scream, and then a mounted noble was coming. Gan dodged behind a tree just as a sword whistled past his head, burying itself in the trunk. Cho leaped to savage the horse's hind leg. It screamed and bucked, shaking its rider free of his weapon. Gan thrust up at him, under the skirt of his chest armor. The rider dropped in front of him, face up, and Gan blinked in dumb amazement. It was the father of the boy he'd brought back alive from the slaver's raid.

Wiping his eye clear, he raced toward Neela, now only feet away. She raised her hands just as he realized the noble at the other end of her chains was drawing a bow. By then Neela was between them, unaware of the danger behind her. Gan pushed her down, shouting at Raggar.

The dog launched himself at the man's throat.

The arrow seemed to take forever to strike, and still the impact surprised Gan. He stumbled backward, throwing out his arms for balance. It was another surprise, this one more pleasant, to see how well his senses were working. He took it as proof that he wasn't dying. He watched Raggar bear his man to the ground, falling clear of him, then whirl to seize him by the back of the neck. Roaring, he shook him like a rat; the crack of the spine had the finality of a torch extinguished.

Too many things happened then. Gan felt a tree interrupt his retreat, and as relieved as he was to stop falling, he couldn't seem to make his legs work. Another arrow stuck in the tree over his head, the hum and thud so loud it might have been thunder. He smelled the glue of the feathers.

Neela called him.

Dimly, he saw Clas, still mounted, battling a mass of people. Sylah, her hands chained, still linked to the dead noble, struggled to join him.

A soldier rushed at him, sword flashing. He tried to lift his own murdat, but, like his legs, his arm was being very perverse. Would it behave better if he spoke to it? he wondered.

Shara flew through the air, a brown lightning bolt. The soldier went down screaming.

Neela was calling his name. And Clas'. Why would she call him? As soon as his body would cooperate, he'd get her free of her chain. Somehow.

He felt himself sliding, easing to a sitting position.

Two more soldiers appeared, and Raggar went for both of them, knocking one down with his charge, snapping at the other as they fell past him. The gleaming teeth raked the man's face, and he staggered back. Raggar was tearing at the one on the ground when the wounded man recovered. Gan screamed louder than the dog as the blade bit into his side. Cho appeared, clamping on the sword wrist. The soldier's mouth gaped in a soundless cry. Cho went for his throat. Raggar stumbled toward Gan, fell heavily against his legs, looking deep into his eyes for a brief moment before turning to drag himself between his master and their enemies again.

Then, unbelievably, terribly, there was an arrow in the dog's side. He rocked under the impact, then tore it out with his teeth, only to have another strike. Gan half moved, half fell forward, put his arms protectively around the heaving, bloody chest.

Raggar licked his hand, then pushed at it with his muzzle until it was resting on his head. He sagged, forelegs reaching out in front of him.

The enemy was falling back. Gan saw his horse, up and moving well. A glow of hope warmed him. "Be strong. Please, be strong. We'll save her. We'll get you out of here. We will. We *will.*"

The dog's great body trembled. The forelegs finally surrendered and extended flush against the ground. Raggar groaned. It wasn't a thing of pain, but the sound Gan loved most, the deep rumble of contentment he gave when he could lie down and rest, firmly in touch with his master.

Raggar closed his eyes and slept.

Tears streaming down his face, Gan lurched forward, crawling toward Neela. She was crying, too.

Voices. Confusing, all mixed together.

That one had to be the Olan officer, exhorting his remaining troops to attack. Looking past Neela, he saw them gathering in the forest off the trail. Clanging steel off to his left said Clas was still fighting there. Then the ones in the woods were coming. He took some satisfaction in their reduced numbers. Stabbing the murdat into the earth, he struggled to lever himself erect.

If he could just get his breath, everything would be fine.

He was standing.

Rising above everything else, he heard a war horn. And howling. Not his brothers, but his men. He wished there were Dog war cries. It would have been good to die in the company of his own people.

An arrow dug into the ground at his feet. He tried to kick it away, almost tripping. It made him very dizzy and he quit.

For a moment he was sure he heard Tate's voice. And Emso's.

He leaned against a tree and, using both hands, raised the murdat.

Then came the pain, breaking through his nara, claiming him. The world erupted with it; he was lifted in the air and pummeled by storms of it. The last thing he recognized before the red agony claimed him was Neela's voice. She was saying, "Thank you, Clas! Thank you! Go! Save yourself!"

CHAPTER 74

Neela.

He strained to lift his murdat.

The pain. It leaped back into his recovering consciousness, seized him and crushed him flat.

Hands joined it, helped it immobilize him. He flailed at them uselessly.

He called her name. She mustn't lose hope. He'd break through the pain, rescue her. He could. Must.

A voice said, "His mind won't let him rest."

It sounded like Clas. A friend. He was still holding off the front of the column. They'd save Neela. The child. Sylah. They'd get Raggar home, heal him.

Raggar was gone.

Neela said, "Thank you." She said, "Save yourself."

To Clas.

He strained to rise. He bit his lip, hoping that pain would offset all others. An eyetooth punctured tissue with a soft noise that echoed hollowly in his skull. Salt-sweet blood tried to choke him.

The worried voices and hands descended on him again.

He lost them in all-consuming darkness.

Tate watched the back trail, her expression twisted with helpless fury. "If we'd been just a little faster. I keep thinking—"

Clas rode directly in front of her, both arms bandaged. A red smear marked the center of a large cotton pad on his right side. He turned in his saddle. "You did all you could. Think; Gan didn't want you to come after us at all. And once they shot my horse out from under me, Gan and I were finished. If your group had been a hundred yards slower, we'd both be dead." He gestured at the horse-drawn litter directly ahead of him. Gan lay in it unmoving, Shara and Cho limping stoically beside him. Tate looked at his blue-white color then turned away.

She said, "Will he ever forgive us, Clas? Will he understand that those filthy traitors made it across the river to join the Olan reinforcements? We're twenty strong; there were at least fifty of them, plus the escapers from Harbundai. We'd never even have made the shore." She pounded her thigh with her fist. "If only the rear guard hadn't fought so well, covering their retreat. How can men be willing to die so bravely for something as foul as stealing another human being?"

Clas laughed, and the sinister bite of it jerked her head up. She stared at him, fascinated by the near-mad glitter in his eyes. The very calmness of his voice added impact to his words. "We must heal for a while, and gain strength. Then you will have many—*many*—answers to your question about how Altanar's men die."

The escort surrounding Sylah and Neela blocked whatever view they might have had of the darkened city of Ola. The clopping of the horses' hooves covered whatever sounds might have given them some reference. There were impressions: the abrupt edge of the city wall and the tunnellike gateway through it; the sense of closure when the horses were forced to crowd close in the narrow streets.

Sylah welcomed the relative smoothness of Ola's streets, thinking they might be the first such surface Neela had ever experienced. She hoped it made the young woman's steps easier. Their captors had been harsh, although the Olan soldiers were far less so than the Moondancers. No one was more surprised or pleased than she when they wakened to find them gone, disappeared in the night. She was too tired to wonder much about their reasons or destination. Even Neela, so much stronger than herself, walked with the leaden legs of exhaustion, her bruised face expressionless, the animated eyes now no more than bits of dull color trying to warn a fogged brain about potholes in the road.

They still carried the chains that had secured them to their individual captors. A search of the noble's clothing produced no keys to the massive locks, and the Olans were in too great a hurry to hack through the links. Unable to separate the chains from the bodies, they showed their contempt for their deceptive allies by separating the bodies from the chains. They gave the women a few moments to wash when they reached the river.

Entering the castle by a small side gate, Sylah and Neela were hurried

across the grounds and thrust through a doorway. Smoky oil lamps il-
luminated the fore end of a stone passageway that stretched away into
forbidding darkness. Two men dressed in pristine white waited for them.
Sylah quickly addressed them as "protectors." She hoped it warned Neela,
made her remember what she'd been told of them. One jerked her away from
Neela's side, warning both of them to say nothing more.

A few minutes later they were shoved into another room. Altanar sat in
the only chair, smiling pleasantly. He frowned at the chains, making sympathetic noises when Sylah explained why they carried them. Still, he offered
no refreshments, no chairs. When Neela remarked that they were exhausted,
he apologized profusely for the pace that had been imposed on them. He
was shocked that they'd not been provided horses.

Sylah wanted to spit out the taste of his lies. He was enjoying his game,
ignoring her, watching Neela's helpless struggle to understand what was
happening. She'd tried to tell Neela of Altanar's cunning malice, but she
apparently hadn't understood. Behind her back Sylah formed a Three-sign,
praying Neela would remember to say as little as possible about herself and
Gan.

The appearance of the Iris Abbess, puffy from being just awakened, almost
shattered Sylah's own control. The older woman was supported at either
elbow by two Chosens. At the door, she ordered them to stay outside and
painfully gathered her strength. Bent, moving with halting steps that made
her floor-length black robe twitch erratically, she behaved as though something hidden deep in her was eroding the core of her being. Nevertheless,
she planted herself between Sylah and Neela and met Altanar's smirk head-
on with a dignity that refused to crack.

He said, "I waited for you to tell Sylah she's staying in my prison."

"Ridiculous." The Abbess didn't blink. "You can't imprison one of my
abbey, especially a trained Healer."

"I can. Yes, I can." He appeared to take strength from his own assurances.
"She's to be cast out. If I don't imprison her, she'll run away."

"Where, King? Church will find her. And if you abuse her before she's
cast out, Church will exact compensation." She raised her voice. "You risk
your soul."

Altanar's tight, superior smile wavered, collapsed. "I won't abuse her. I
won't have her free, working against me. No."

The Abbess let the subject drop, changed her tack. She turned to Neela.
"You are the wife of Gan Moondark?"

Neela lifted her chin, forming the words as carefully as her battered lips
would allow. "I know you, Iris Abbess. Rose Priestess Sylah has spoken often

and warmly of you. Yes, I am Neela, wife to Gan Moondark. You know of my husband?"

Altanar interrupted smoothly. "All know of your husband. That's why you will be my guest here in my castle. Your presence here will help me convince the War Chief of the Dog People that it's in his best interest to help me contain your husband's growing power."

Neela drew herself erect. Despite the bruises and dishevelment, she glowed with pride. "If you threaten me to influence my brother, you'll make enemies of my clan and my tribe. They'll never forgive you."

His eyes widened in surprise, then softened to broad, sugary pity. "You haven't heard, then? You don't know? And to learn here, like this. How sad." He leaned forward. Sylah wanted to scream at him. When the Iris Abbess tried to speak, he barked at her to be quiet. In the same syrupy voice, he went on, "Bay Yan was killed. A hunting accident, it was said. A bear. And the three oldest brothers behind him are gone, too. That happened in a raid. The Mountain People, of course. Such terrible news."

Neela stared at him. "Likat. It was Likat."

He said, "Likat, dear? He's the War Chief. He'll be glad to see you again, won't he?"

Neela took a tentative half step backward, as if she could distance herself from the brutal shock of his news. Without further warning, she melted to the floor, the chains she carried clattering harshly on the stone. Sylah brushed past the Iris Abbess to reach her.

Altanar watched, vastly amused. "Everyone said the Dogs are unbreakable. She's no different from any other woman. Nothing but flutters and faints." He clapped his hands. The door opened and a protector stepped in. He didn't bother to look at Neela or the two women rubbing her wrists and throat. Altanar said, "Bring in the smith."

The protector came back with a short, heavily muscled man in a worn leather apron that covered him from neck to knees. It failed to hide his shaking. Altanar told him, "The Priestess goes to the cells. Knock off her chains there. The one on the floor goes to your shop." He went into a detailed description of what he'd have done to the smith if his guest was injured in any way.

Seizing the opportunity, the Iris Abbess leaned closer to Sylah. "Does he know you're both pregnant?"

Sylah started, but immediately shook her head.

The Abbess clutched Sylah's wrist. "Don't waste time, girl. I'm the Abbess, the Healer of Healers. I *know.* These old hands are weak, but my eyes aren't. Altanar must not know. If he learns, you die."

Nearly blurting the words, Sylah said, "He doesn't know. How can we tell her?"

Neela's eyelids trembled open. One of them closed slowly. She said, "I heard," and then both eyes were closed again.

The other two women were smiling at each other when Altanar shouted at them to stop talking and make way for the protectors who'd carry Neela to the smithy.

Neela watched the smith move her hands on the anvil, positioning the chisel with anxious precision. She thought how little difference the chains actually made. Altanar hadn't called her a prisoner. Still, her recollection of the way "guest" slipped from his mouth made her want to shiver. So did the unshakable image of that bloodless secret smile. It stirred undefinable dark things in hidden corners of her mind.

She thought of Likat.

She'd escaped him once.

And Gan had escaped the Olans. Every morning when she faced the sun to greet the One in All, she asked for him to heal well. She asked blessings for Clas na Bale for saving him. She closed her eyes to see it again, heard the outraged cries of the Olan troops who were so sure they had him. Looking at her arms, she exulted in the livid bruises marking the beating they gave her because she laughed. It had been unwise—they'd lost nine men, all five of the Jalail nobles, and half of the Moondancers. If one of the soldiers hadn't stopped them, she was sure they'd have killed her. As her rescuer pointed out, fighting back had been stupid, too. She didn't feel as badly about that. She was a Dog woman; they should have expected it. Pretending to faint put a temporary end to Altanar's questions and answers so she could get some needed rest and prepare for the coming ordeal. A faint wouldn't have impressed the enraged soldiers. In fact, if she'd stopped fighting—

The silver shine of the descending hammer face froze her thoughts. It struck the chisel. Steel music stung her flesh, sang in her ears. The metallic stink of hot iron and burning coal, unnoticed till then, suddenly prickled in her nose. The chain fell free. Vibrations from the anvil danced in her arm, trembled through her body.

The smith dropped his hammer to clutch her wrist. "That didn't hurt?" It was more of a plea than a question. While she rubbed her chafed skin before answering, he chewed his lower lip impatiently.

She said, "Not at all. I'll tell the King."

"Thank you. Thank you." He kissed her hand, and she pulled back. Instantly he was afraid again. He said, "No offense. Please, you'll tell him I didn't hurt you?"

Laughing, she said, "He wouldn't do what he said."

The man blanched. He looked around carefully before speaking. "I've seen his protectors do worse. You—" There was a sound behind him, and he closed his mouth like a trap, dropping to one knee at her feet. When he straightened with the ends of the severed chain in his hands, his face was perfectly neutral. Showing the cut link to the white-clad protector in his doorway, he said, "Here it is. Not a mark on her from my work."

The protector pulled Neela into the light of the door to inspect her wrists. Satisfied, he directed her outside in the peculiar, toneless voice, walking out of sight behind her, telling her which way to turn. She'd already protested that treatment on the way to the smith and been told that this was how it would be done. A quality in his monotone convinced her that further objections would be unwise. She felt demeaned and degraded by the realization. Less than a week earlier, she would have said no one could quiet her so easily.

He'd frightened her to silence. She balled her fists and admitted it.

She'd felt like a prisoner from the moment they brought her to Altanar. Being chained to the scum who'd kidnapped her hadn't accomplished that. Of course, she'd been afraid they might kill her, or rape her. Those were ordinary dangers. She understood them. Her fear of the traitors and Moon-dancers, like her fear of the soldiers who'd beaten her, was intertwined with a fierce anger that made her want to strike back.

Altanar bred panic. She'd felt her blood go thin when she talked to him. Then, when she meekly submitted to the humiliating white shadow of the protector, there was no thought of fighting. She wanted to hide, sickened by an overwhelming sense of helplessness. Altanar made her a thing. Likat had the same eyes. Altanar was worse, though, because in that secret smile was his certainty that he would have your utter obedience. Understanding of what he was created a dread she actually tasted, an acid at the back of her throat.

She looked around her as they walked from the forge back to the castle. The blatant curiosity of those who noticed her didn't bother her, but the resignation in the expressions of those going about their routine business was chilling.

The Abbess stepped around a corner and confronted Neela, looking past her at the protector. She'd changed to official dress, a ground-sweeping robe of green and blue. Above its high collar, her features had settled, gained strength. She met Neela's surprise with steady dark eyes. A touch of breeze lifted stray wisps of her gray hair. Neela noticed they seemed as fine as spider silk, and as gracefully light. The woman raised her hand to stop the protector, exposing a massive gold bracelet.

Neela said, "I know you, Iris Abbess."

The woman lowered her hand, sighing. "I came to accompany you to your audience with King Altanar. I would hear your story from your own lips."

On the way to the castle, Neela confessed being awed by the buildings. The Abbess said, "They're only ordinary things, built by ordinary men, child. Calm."

The protector droned behind them. "You know the rules, Abbess. You must speak so I can hear."

The Abbess turned and smiled at him sweetly. "I don't care if you hear, young man. What would surprise me would be if you understood." Neela's shock surfaced as an undignified giggle, but then the Abbess had her by the elbow, gesturing to some finer points of the buildings, pointing out her abbey, the castle, and identifying the huge structure that was the King's Hall. She tightened her grip as she ushered Neela into the building.

Neela gasped in wonderment at the scene. Sylah had told her of the dimensions, of the immense firepits lining the way to the throne. She'd spoken of the hostility that weighed on any woman stepping in there without a male escort. Neela had thought she knew what to expect. It was a mistake. The thick smell of the place dazed her. The space defeated her. Nothing could have prepared her for the raw contempt that seethed on the dozens of faces staring at her.

A silent voice cried out Gan's name. For one cold moment she allowed herself to think how very alone she was. Her pulse raced.

Sylah's face swam before her, a shadowy image against the smudged clouds of incense rising from the cold firepits. She remembered how Sylah's whole being changed when she spoke of her treatment by these men. Neela steeled herself to resist. She stared back. Gan would cut through them like wheat. Clas would frighten them out of their wits. Any Dog warrior was worth the whole roomful of them. So was a Dog woman.

One locked gazes with her. His neck swelled and he turned red, but it was he who looked away. The crowd saw, and was offended. A low, growling murmur moved through them, an animal warning. The skin on her arms and back crawled, but she defied it, looking for another man to challenge.

The Abbess propelled her forward. From the side of her mouth she said, "Calm, child. For my sake."

Chastened, Neela broke off further eye contact. She concentrated on the throne altar and matched the Abbess' pace.

The King was dressed in a loose, bright yellow shirt and matching baggy trousers. There was silver piping up the middle of the shirtfront and on the collar and sleeves. The trousers had similar vertical stripes on the outside of the legs. He paced impatiently as they advanced, and his bright colors against the gloom made Neela think of flame. In that instant her fear was back.

A thin band of gold encircled his head. Two-inch spikes of silver jutted from it, and a tiny bell dangled by a silver chain from each of them. When he nodded at the two women, their chiming was incredibly fine and pure. In this most inappropriate of all places, Neela heard them as the sweetness of birdsong from her home. Pain welled in her breast, threatened to force tears from her eyes.

Altanar spoke soon enough to spare her that embarrassment. "Show your wrists." She forced herself not to pull back when he handled her. "Did the smith hurt you?" he asked.

"No. He was very careful."

Chuckling, he said, "I was sure he would be. Are you well enough to talk now? Don't take my time with any more female displays. If you need food or sleep, speak up."

Neela gritted her teeth. "Thank you, King. I'm well."

He sniffed and turned his attention to the Abbess. His words were like cracks of a whip as he launched a tirade at her for what he called Neela's "troubles." For some time Neela heard only the high-pitched rasp of his insults. Then, dimly at first, but with growing awareness, she felt the crowd pressing forward behind her. By turning her head the least bit, she could see some of them from the corner of her eye. They were loving what they were hearing. This was spectacle, entertainment. It was the mighty humbled.

Neela's face burned with shame for the Abbess. She waited anxiously for her response, and was amazed at the unconcern of it. "We don't know why Sylah took Neela from her people."

Neela had to protect her friend. She said, "I asked her to take me."

He blinked, then threw a quick glance at the crowd. Neela heard their surprise. Altanar hurried to cover his mistake. "You'll explain to me in private. This will affect our alliance with your people."

Neela and the Abbess rose at his gesture. He swept out through his own exit.

They had to wait for a protector to bring Neela a pair of indoor slippers, but the King was still nowhere to be seen when they reached the room. The Abbess said, "This is where the King gave permission for Sylah to go on her mission to your people. He stood in that doorway and gave her the title of Rose Priestess. How I wish that day had never happened!" She swept around to face Neela, bending close to her. "Say nothing!" she whispered. In a normal voice, she went on, "My own thought is that living with the Mountain People through most of the winter put too much strain on her mind. I'm afraid she's not right anymore. Church will decide." Gesturing Neela to a chair, she sat down opposite her and asked innocuous questions about her childhood.

A few minutes later Altanar swept into the room. With a short glare for the Abbess, he told Neela, "Much has happened to you. It's good you were delivered to my protection. I realize you're saddened by your great losses, but you're safe with me."

Neela straightened. "No one's safe from those who count treachery their favored weapon, King. My husband will discuss it with you."

Color appeared on his cheeks, but he smiled. Neela saw past the surface of it and wished he'd cursed her. When he spoke, he practically purred. "Did I forget to mention his death earlier? I'm sorry to be the one who keeps bringing you such devastating news."

Her stomach collapsed in on itself, became a burning coal. Her eyes lost focus. She made herself concentrate on his lying, shrewd features. Summoning up her strength, she said, "He lives. He was injured and the great dog Raggar died at his side, but he lives. He was stolen away from your soldiers by Clas na Bale. My people will sing of it for all time."

"He died. I must be honest."

"No."

He shrugged, maddeningly sure.

Doubt stabbed at her. "Prove it to me," she said, telling her mind she was speaking of someone else, some stranger, an enemy. "Show me his head. Describe his scars."

Altanar wrestled for self-control. Then he calmed. "My men may have been overeager to please. I should have thought to ask them for proof, as you asked me. That was clever."

Once again he made her think of Likat.

When he asked her to tell her story and she repeated that she'd left voluntarily with Sylah, he ordered the Abbess away. Then he sat down and settled back to listen to her story. She permitted herself only two lies, the first being the omission of the part Likat and Kolee played in her decision. She told him she left for love of Gan. She reasoned that Likat would either still want her or would want to be sure his secret was safe from the tribe. She praised him fulsomely, telling Altanar how cunning and able he was— just what the Dog People needed. She simpered, hinting she might have made a mistake in leaving with Gan.

The lies were bile in her throat. She had to live, however. Gan would come.

She finished with Gan's departure for Malten, and secretly rejoiced at Altanar's bitter look on being reminded of that failure. When he rose, telling her he'd personally escort her to her quarters, she was sure she'd said nothing Gan would object to. Her confidence was high.

The walk to her room was unimaginably long, down corridors with so many turns she lost track. Her lungs yearned for fresh air as eagerly as her body craved sleep.

More troubling than either of those things, however, were the mysterious sounds that crowded in on her. The narrow, reaching halls should have been utterly quiet. She saw no one besides herself and Altanar, and they each wore the soft indoor slippers, but she kept hearing things. More than that, Altanar was obviously immune to them. To her, however, it was as if the slabs of stone and rough timbers were trying to speak. Her ears strained at whispers and sighs and mumbling that she could neither understand or locate. When Altanar showed her into her room she was barely able to avoid rushing into its sanctuary. She pushed the door shut behind her, grateful for its heavy drum that canceled the other voices.

CHAPTER 75

The gentle cough behind her brought Neela around in a defensive crouch. The sight of the small woman in the shapeless gray robe was so far from what she expected that sheer surprise held her in place long enough for her to become aware of the pounding of her own heart. Straightening, she demanded the intruder's name and purpose.

The brown-haired head remained aimed at the floor. In a soft, singsong voice, she said, "I am Tee, slave of the castle, assigned to you."

"I want no slaves. I want none working for me."

Unperturbed, Tee said, "I'm ordered to see to your feeding and clothing."

Neela wrestled with the situation for a few minutes while she inspected the room. It was a windowless box, not much better than a cave, she decided. There was an ornately carved cabinet to hold clothes and a pair of chairs. The large bed had a headboard and footboard decorated with the same complex design as the cabinet. Neela wrinkled her nose; it looked like someone's dream of a bear, or a beaver. When she sat on the sheer coverlet drawn over the feather mattress, the leather suspension straps squealed softly.

Looking up at Tee, who appeared not even to have breathed, Neela said, "I need a bath."

Tee shook her head. "The closest women's baths are in the abbey. You can't leave the castle."

Neela refused to believe there wasn't a bath she could use in such a huge building, and Tee had to argue hard to convince her. Finally Neela said, "Get me the biggest thing you can find that'll hold water, then. And have someone bring hot water. I'm filthy and sore and I want a bath."

She thought she saw a hint of a smile on Tee's face as she hurried away, but her continuing downcast manner made it impossible to say. When the small slave returned, she was followed by a man laboring under the weight of a large circular wooden tub. Three more men behind him each carried two big buckets of steaming water. They, too, wore rough gray robes and stared at the floor the whole time they were in Neela's presence. She decided the clothing must be common to the household slaves; she'd seen others. They were certainly subdued, too, but not like Tee or these men. It was unsettling to have people act as if they were afraid of your very eyes, and when the men were gone, Neela asked about it. Tee raised her chin a fraction, as if considering something, then resumed her regular pose. "We are ordered. You are particularly honored, and we must treat you so."

Neela had to laugh. She said, "Honored? I've been beaten like a drum. I'm black and blue all over, my hair's full of leaves and twigs, and my clothes look like a Peddler's throw-offs."

Tee actually smiled, although the sadness lingering at the edges of it pulled at Neela's heart. However, the expression disappeared immediately, and all she said was, "You should take your bath now, before the water cools."

It was an irresistible argument, and Neela stripped quickly, squeezing into the tub. It barely reached her waist when she sat down, and her chin practically touched her knees. She tensed with anticipation as Tee raised the first bucket, already savoring the delightful shock of hot, cleansing water.

Instead of pleasure, the first touch brought remorse. She'd been so self-centered, concerned with nothing but her own situation. She rounded on Tee, demanding information about Sylah. The slave's expression turned hollow once more; she knew nothing of Sylah. Neela persisted, ignoring her bath. Under pressure, Tee finally admitted that she knew something of the cells. For the first time she looked directly into Neela's eyes when she spoke.

"The less you know of them, the better. The Priestess won't be tortured, but the cells are very small, very dirty. It's . . . unpleasant." The small pause told Neela more than her words.

"We have to get her out!"

Tee moved; it could have been a shrug. "When Altanar decides."

"No! I mean today. Now." She struggled to stand in the tub, and Tee put a hand on her shoulder.

"You can't get her out. Understand that. Perhaps I can see that she gets better food. I'll try. You'll only make trouble for her and for yourself if you interfere." Suddenly she lowered her face to within inches of Neela's. "Patience is all you have, all you need. With it, you'll survive here. Without it, you cannot." As quickly as she'd revealed herself, she disappeared back inside her shell of subservience.

After a while Neela said, "You were in the cells a long time, weren't you?"

Tee said, "Did I tell you how they complained in the laundry room when I said I needed one of their precious tubs?" She dipped into a pocket of the robe, producing a chunk of soap and some scented oil. Turning away, she stopped to gather up Neela's clothes. Clucking her tongue, she deplored the damage, then openly admired the material and workmanship. Neela told her they were made by the wives of the Wolves of Jalail. Tee seemed to draw tight. Her free hand gestured in a swift motion that implied threat despite its feminine grace. She said, "We've heard of your husband and his Wolves. The soldiers of Ola fear them like plague. The officer who let him escape when he tried to rescue you is being punished right now. If he still lives. The King was already angry when he heard; everyone says the plan to kidnap you and the Priestess was just one part of a larger scheme to destroy the Wolves and the King of Harbundai at the same time, and it failed. Did you know Noble Malten and his brother, the baron?"

Neela heard the past tense. "They're dead?"

Tee nodded. "Baron Malten died in battle. The Noble sang at the Beach of Songs for almost two days. The King was pleased."

Neela asked exactly what she meant. Tee's answer set her to shivering as if the water Tee poured over her had ice in it. Tee said, "I'll take these clothes to the laundry and come back with a robe for you. Sleep, if you like. None will bother you. I'll be quiet."

The mention of sleep seemed to drain her. The bruises ached deeper, her eyes burned hotter. Tee wasn't out the door before she was drying herself. Her fingers were clumsy as she applied the pungent, tingling oil, paying close attention to her chafed wrists and the places where fists or boots had broken her skin. The bed absorbed her with a sigh much like her own.

The trip with Baron Jalail's murderers had taught Neela to lie still on waking. She listened, trying to locate another presence. She heard nothing. Still, she was sure she wasn't alone. She opened her eyes the merest slit. Tee was in a chair against the door. Neela tried to read what she saw in the woman's face. Once again the sadness, even in repose, struck at her. Then Tee turned, her attention drawn by some slight sound outside. The movement exposed her profile, and Neela realized she'd unwittingly exposed the telling facet of her appearance. She found herself thinking of a bird, fluttering a false broken wing, drawing attention to anything except the truth. At first look she was merely subdued and pretty. Then one saw the sadness. Under that was toughness. She wished she had a more elegant word, because it was a beautiful thing to see. The defeated behavior hid a steel core.

She pretended to wake, sitting up slowly, smiling fuzzily. Tee was many things, but not trusted. The only one for that was Sylah's friend, the Abbess.

Tee interrupted her thoughts, suggesting they get something to eat. Again, as with her mention of sleep, Tee had said a very important word. As soon as Neela acknowledged her hunger, it seized her.

Tee had found her a loose, flowing robe. It was a rich blue, thoughtfully with long sleeves to hide discolored arms. Best of all, it was clean, sun-scented. They rushed through the combing out of Neela's hair, and then they hurried to the kitchen.

Sharing those few minutes opened them both a bit more, and they chatted freely on the way. Even so, when anyone else could see them, Tee was careful to resume her servile attitude.

Neela's first impression of the kitchen was its immense size. The major firepits, massively black and forbidding, squatted in the two corners of the room that shared the outside wall. Their polished, ribbed copper hoods made Neela think of gleaming teeth. Each was large enough to roast an ox. Smaller ovens and firepits ranged the wall between them, so all hoods vented outside. A wide worktable ran up the middle of the room. A tall, thin woman, red-faced, strode among the scurrying workers. She carried a long, supple rod, with a foot-long tip of braided leather. She reached out with it to touch a small boy, calling his attention to some error. Apparently dissatisfied with his response, she swung it with more purpose. A hot, red weal leaped to life on his cheek.

Tee diverted Neela's open-mouthed indignation with a timely bump, insisting they look into the fish tanks, another marvel for Neela. The sides were made of two-inch-thick cedar planks as long as a tall man and wide enough to sleep on. Each had its own water delivery and overflow system. A school of trout swam in one, dozens of plate-sized crabs scuttled about in another. A third held clams. She clapped her hand to her mouth. "So many!" she said, pointing at the latter. "We trade for the shells, but I never saw one alive. What *is* that ugly thing sticking out?"

Tee made a choking sound. When Neela turned, however, her face was averted again. She said, "That's the neck. When they're frightened, they can pull it back in." She put a hand in the water, and a circle of clams around it retreated into their individual forts. Neela laughed unabashed amusement. The sound of it was unnaturally loud.

Looking about, she saw everyone in the kitchen was aware of her presence, and all were falling into the same head-down posture as Tee. The rawboned cook hurried toward them. In front of Neela she bobbed her head up and down, asking what she'd like to eat.

Tee suggested clam chowder and the trout. Both women ushered Neela to a seat at a small table, and then Tee moved to leave with the cook. Neela rose to go with them, and Tee shook her head. "I have to watch the food prepared."

Neela looked blank. "I want to watch, too."

The cook shook her head so hard her cropped hair bounced. "Sorry. Forbidden. Only slaves near the food making. Sorry. Forgive."

Tee said, "Only slaves work in the King's kitchen. We watch each other, because if anyone tries to poison him, we're all punished the same. You wait here, please."

Grudgingly, Neela sat alone, taking out her irritation on a green salad and a slab of bread and fresh butter.

She thought of Sylah, and the earlier guilt returned with a vengeance. This time, however, she thought of Tee's advice, and she remembered Sylah's own courage. To succeed, one first survived. To excel, one endured. She would do that. Others needed her. Her child. Sylah. Gan.

The last thought rather surprised her, and she savored it, tested it. It was true. More than she'd realized. The darker side of him was too strong for him to control alone. She'd never considered it until that moment, and the clarity of the discovery startled and troubled her.

A little girl, no more than six, broke Neela's concentration as she scurried up with a pitcher of wine and a mug for the table. Her wide-eyed distrust as she scampered off made Neela think of a chipmunk. When she called after her, wanting to reassure her, she gave a startled squeak and sprinted for the door, chubby legs churning.

More than Tee's self-distancing, more than the behavior of all the others, the child's frightened innocence carved loneliness into Neela's heart. When the meal came, she tried to show the enthusiasm for its beauty that Tee clearly expected. Two trout lay together on a bed of crisp lettuce. The aroma of hazelnuts drifted up from its accompanying creamy sauce. Beside the fish a small circle of perfect peas glistened, sharing that part of the clay platter with thin strips of carrot that smelled delicately of honey and thyme. The bowl of chowder steamed its own invitation. The cook herself arrived with a platter of bread, still hot from the oven. She stood next to Tee, quivering with concern.

Neela was in a quandary. Her stomach still craved food, and the meal was luxurious. Yet her desire to eat was gone. She kept remembering Sylah and the little girl. Smiling, hating the fakery, she ate. Each bite was tasteless, every swallow heavy in her throat.

Fooled, the cook finally backed away, using the peculiar gait she'd shown earlier. Neela was surprised to look down and see the food was gone. She asked Tee if they could walk for a while, and Tee agreed reluctantly. They couldn't go outside the inner wall of the castle.

Tee answered questions slowly, carefully, with as few words as possible. Neela had the impression she practiced the phrases in her mind several times before giving them voice. When Neela bluntly asked why she didn't want to talk, Tee affected embarrassment, begging Neela not to report her stupidity. The lie puzzled Neela. Tee was no more stupid than she was happy to be a slave.

They strolled until dusk, and again Neela was confronted by beauty that failed to please. The castle grounds were studded with small gardens and artfully arranged conversation places. Fountains splashed and sparkled. Exotic birds jeweled the trees. Yet, for her, everything was artificiality and alienness. It was so different, and she was constantly reminded of her separation from everything and everyone she loved.

It was Tee who suggested they return to the room, and Neela appreciated her thoughtfulness. Tee only grew even more silent. She was tense, as well, a mass of nervous tics and gestures. Nevertheless, Neela was telling herself how foolish she was behaving by the time they reached a familiar corner. Just around it she was certain was the hallway to her room.

Suddenly, without warning, Tee had her by the upper arms. With surprising strength, the small woman held her immobile while she looked back the way they'd come. Still silent, she peered around the corner, pulling her head back quickly, then indicating Neela should look. In the distance, beyond her room, she saw the knot of lounging white-clad protectors. Tee yanked her back, and when she met Neela's eyes, she was grim. "I can't let you go back there without telling you," she said, and coldness crept through Neela. Tee squeezed her arms until they hurt. She said, "You've seen the way we all bow to you. You must understand there's nothing you can do. He's chosen you. The protectors are there to see you can't escape. They want you to try, you understand? They hope you'll be foolish enough to enrage him, and then he'll give you to them. *Do you understand me?*" The hoarse violence of her whisper shocked Neela out of her stunned disbelief.

Neela had only one word. "Altanar?"

Tee nodded. Sympathy and grimness warred across her features. "Some women have said he has no concept of normal love, so none of lovemaking. He can only use us. He doesn't have the sense to know there's more. Close him out of your mind and he's nothing—only another unpleasantness among the many."

Neela shuddered, shook her head. "I can't." Then, fiercely, "I'll kill him. Or myself."

Tee shook her. "You won't be *allowed* to die. You can survive what he means to do tonight. He may do it again. You won't die." She took another look around the corner. "They're moving this way."

Stomach churning, Neela shrank back. She heard herself say, "No! I'm pregnant."

"*Listen!* If you want to save your child, do what you must. When he learns of the child, he'll assume it's his, and then he'll leave you alone. He'll protect you."

"Protect me?"

"He won't touch a pregnant woman, if he thinks it's his child. If he learns otherwise . . ." She shrugged, letting the silence take effect. Then she added, "If he learns I spoke to you of this, you finish me."

"I couldn't!" Neela pulled free of the grip on her arms, embraced Tee. "Never. But how can I do this? Is he there? Will they make me go to him? Can't you help me? Can't anyone? I hate him, Tee! I can't do it!"

"You can. Or Gan Moondark will never see his child. Or you."

Neela sagged against the wall. Her voice was barely audible. "He may not want to see me again."

Tee slapped her, hard. Neela reeled. Tee said, "Then let him rot, and raise your child to know his father wasn't worthy of his mother. But *live*. Give the life you can. Don't let anyone steal that from you."

Shaking her head, Neela moaned, then said, "I can't. Everything I was ever taught is against this. Give me a knife. A piece of glass. Anything." She looked at Tee. "You don't know what it means."

Rage drained Tee's face of color, transformed her into a creature of vengeance. She trembled at the inner power of conflicting emotions before a series of deep breaths calmed her. She said, "I know more than you can imagine. I know you can stand this."

Neela's hand rose to her mouth as the import sank in. Tee turned away brusquely. "Come."

Half of the protectors were almost at the near end of the hall when they rounded the corner, and Neela clamped her arm to her side, trapping Tee's supporting hand against her body as they walked past the smirking group. It gave Neela pride to meet their gaze, just as she'd met that of the nobles in the King's Hall. She remembered Sylah speaking of the trance, and she let her mind empty of everything but hatred.

She refused to flinch, looking at the protectors. Diminished by her insub-
missiveness, their smiles twisted and wrinkled like blighted leaves. She saw
the worried twitch of humiliated eyes searching the other faces, wondering
if their failure had been seen. Beside her, Tee, head down, made a sound
like keening, so high and so soft it floated in the air, softer than the light
of the oil lamps.

Then she was past them, with nowhere to go but where Altanar waited,
and she wished her heart would stop.

Tee took her hand from Neela's arm. She said nothing. Neela touched her
shoulder and thanked her. Then she opened the door and entered the room.

Altanar sat in a chair brought for him. It was large, the arms carved as
killer whales, each rolling to the side so the dorsal fin was part of the arm-rest.
He was dressed in a scarlet robe with a black pattern. She couldn't identify
the design, but every detail, every minute particle of what was taking place
hammered itself into her awareness. She smelled him, rank of sweat, incense,
and floral essences. She saw where a thread on his robe was snagged and
hanging free. She saw whiskers that the barber missed, and a stain on his
house slippers. It was as if some perverse twist in her mind was guaranteeing
that nothing about this night was ever to leave her.

Another figure sat in the corner on the floor. It was a young boy. Sightless
eyes stared past her, fixed on a point far beyond the stone walls. He looked
sad and afraid, but his hands moved with fluid grace across the strings of a
boxlike musical instrument in his lap. The music was beautiful. The obscen-
ity of the concept turned her stomach.

Altanar talked to her, senseless mouthings about the bond between peoples. Once more he tried to make her believe that Gan was dead, but never
by saying so directly. He spoke of Gan's courage, nearly breaking her heart,
then salvaged it for her with more idiocy about her ability to bind her people
to his. When he offered her wine from a jar he'd kept hidden until the proper
moment, she refused it, and amazed herself by smiling.

She thought of her child. It must live. My son, she told herself. This one
had to be a male, to grow strong, to hate as she hated, fight as his father
fought. A male, to rend and break and burn.

Her obsessive memorization of detail faded while she thought of those
things, and although she continued to listen and answer appropriately, the
rest of the conversation was lost to her.

And then he reached for her, put his hand on her breast. It was a clumsy,
lust-raddled move, and it offended her beyond all reason. She hit him with
her fist.

The musician stopped, his sudden silence heavy in the air.

Altanar's head bounced off the back of the chair. A trickle of blood ran down his chin. His eyes swam with tears until he blinked them away. When he saw the blood on the back of the hand he used to wipe his mouth, he laughed.

The strings rang discords. Frenzied, manic music filled the room.

He beat her with singleminded delight, shouting his pleasure when she struck back. When she fell, he lifted her to her feet by her hair, encouraging her to strike at him again, and when she did, he hit her some more.

Her last blurred, collapsing image was as he stripped off the robe to stand naked and triumphant over her. She spat at him. He cursed her for getting blood on him and raised both his hands over his head, one clasped in the other to form a single massive fist.

The music was a single insistent, repeated, driving chord.

At the blow, a burst of light dazzled her, and then she was tumbling over and over in a cool stream that bathed her in freedom, washed away her hurt.

CHAPTER 76

Nearly doubled over, clutching his chest, Gan leaned on Clas while the latter fumbled with the handle of the door leading to the meeting room. On the other side of the carved wood panels, indistinct voices rose and fell in passionate argument.

Standing behind the two men, Tate told herself Gan would never get through this meeting.

He turned in hesitant increments to look at her. Speaking from the corner of his mouth, he asked, "Am I pretty?"

His appearance didn't trouble her nearly as much as it did when she and her patrol came across Clas carrying him slung across his horse's rump like a sack of grain. Restraining Clas when he wanted to ride back alone was another unpleasant memory. Still, Clas was handling the problem better than Gan. The voice was as good an indicator as anything. It had never recovered any sense of liveliness. The sound was like bad steel scraping stone. She said, "You never were pretty. Even without that silly hat on." She reached to adjust it. "It hides the wound pretty good, but you've got to leave it alone, or it pulls up and everyone can see the rest of the bandages." Satisfied with her work, she stepped back and flipped a hand at the door. "Why won't you listen to us? We can delay these people for a few days."

"No." The tone forestalled argument. Pulling back from Clas, he closed his eyes, inhaling deeply. Tate couldn't believe what she was seeing. He straightened as he'd turned to face her, little by little, paling with strain. Sweat beaded on him and tendons lifted under his skin as if ready to snap. He trembled violently. But he rose. He gained his full height, lifted his chin, filled his lungs. At last he took his hand from Clas' shoulder, panting with exertion. Facial muscles relaxed, built a smile that grew more confident and natural as she watched. He took a cloth from his sleeve and wiped the sweat he could reach. Were it not for the stains remaining under his arms and on his back between his shoulders, the demonstration of will might never have happened.

He turned to Clas. His first words were hesitant, but he steadied quickly. He said, "I'll go in alone. When I signal, you come in. Tate, wait here until this is over."

With a mixture of pride and nervousness, Clas agreed, and Tate suddenly wished she could grab them both and shake some sense into them. She had no time to dwell on the pleasures of the prospect before Gan was stepping through the door. There was an expectant silence. She crowded forward. In her haste to see how the three barons reacted, she nearly propelled Clas into the room. He muttered at her to behave with some dignity.

She ignored him, shaking her head in disbelief as Gan walked almost jauntily to his chair at the head of the table. He stood behind it, hands resting on the back.

She turned her attention to the seated men. They were dressed in the custom of their individual baronies. Gan introduced himself, and she wondered about the absent ones, especially Baron Malten and his brother. Stories of their deaths probably contributed to the apprehension showing in these men, as they openly tried to assess Gan's condition.

A tiny catch in his voice alerted her to his continuing struggle. She hoped he wasn't tearing the stitches. Again, irritation scratched at her concern; if he'd let her, she'd have sewn him up with Sylah's Nion thread, but he had regained consciousness just long enough to watch her, and he insisted she use sinew. As if anyone in the barony were more deserving of the best. She'd felt as if she were tugging boot laces through his hide; it had to have hurt like fury. He insisted the Nion thread be saved for "someone who needed it." It was foolish pride; she said so then, and she knew it now.

She could tell by the way he was standing that the arrow wound was turning his lung into an open flame in his chest. Every time he stopped speaking, his shoulders twitched. That was from smothering the insistent cough. It was less than twenty-four hours since he'd stopped coughing blood. She shivered, thinking what would happen if that control failed. If these Barons got one glimpse of the way the wracking coughs left him gasping, too weak to wipe his own lips, they'd race each other to seek the best terms from Altanar.

First he had to convince them he was healthy. Then he had to convince them to join him. Sooner or later he would have to decide how far he could trust them.

There was the bearlike Galmontis from the farthest north, one-eyed, his scowl as black as his eyepatch. He wore his beard cropped square and shaved his head. A zigzag scar marked his skull from front to back. Next to him was his opposite in personality, the sly little Fin from the barony immediately north of Malten. Tate thought he looked as if he never said anything without knowing exactly how it would profit him. The one down the table from him was named Eleven West. His people were an ancient offshoot of the Mountain People, with the same peculiar names. His people were as tough as their relatives, but more civilized. Nevertheless, Gan eyed him more closely than the other two.

Addressing him as Murdat, they made a valiant effort to hide their surprise at Gan's appearance. Clas left Tate to stand behind Gan, who introduced him, then went right to the point.

"You've all come here to see if I'm dead." He swung his arms and hopped up and down. Tate held her breath. Clas looked to be in greater pain than Gan. A muscle in his cheek made the black tattoo dance.

Galmontis spoke, his stiff beard bristling like an angry dog's ruff. "Altanar's troops mauled us badly, Murdat. Thanks to your warning, we at least had time to form to meet their attack and then stage a reasonably orderly retreat. We all owe you."

Gan shrugged. "I would have helped you more, but that would have meant helping the King. He meant to see me destroyed."

Little Fin's normal speaking voice was almost a whisper. He said, "And now he's dead." His quick glance at his two companions suggested they carried the burden of their grief rather lightly.

Gan's expression hardened. "I understand he died at Malten Castle after he retreated there with your forces, Baron Fin."

Fin said, "A tragic accident. Sad, sad. He rushed to the wall, looking for our pursuers, you see? He was so excited, he leaned too far. Awful. Still, as soon as the Olans heard of his death, they were satisfied to go home. You could say he served his people to the last."

Galmontis broke in before Gan could respond. "We all agree with your claim to be Baron of Jalail and Malten. What we suggest is an alliance among the four of us. We can control all of Harbundai."

"To what purpose?"

They all paused, taken by surprise. Gan's transparent effort to appear obtuse made them suspect a trick. Warily, the baron called Eleven West stated the obvious. "If we control, we decide who trades with whom, who can use the trade routes, who owns the land with the best timber, the best mining."

"And we argue constantly," Gan said. He forgot himself and leaned over the chair. Tate hoped no one else noticed the clenched fists and slow, aching return to a more erect position. He stared at them until they were all shifting uncomfortably. He said, "I have a better plan. All of you collect a force to match the numbers of my Wolves. We—Clas, Emso, Tate, and myself—will teach them our way of fighting. We will defeat the Olan armies, and we will make one kingdom of all our peoples."

Galmontis rose. "Is it your plan to be King?"

Gan nodded, his expression challenging. "Part of my plan." He signaled Clas, who hurried to spread out the Baron's old map on the table. Gan said, "Altanar will use my wife to force the Dog People to join in his attack on Harbundai. I will stop him, but I need help. Those who join me now will be remembered well. Those who do not help me will find the future a hard place. Those who oppose me have no future; they will be forgotten." He flattened both his hands on the map, spanning from the Sea Star islands to the prairies of his own tribe. "We will make this all one place of peace. You know what we've done here. You see our prosperity, our common purpose. Your Queen Mother tried to influence your king in much the same way, I understand. Join us, and we can create something new. I offer my hand and my sword. We will win. Join us now."

Galmontis sat back down, his earlier confrontational look now confused and uncertain. As if afraid of the consequences but too forthright to hold back his feelings, he half mumbled, "You're not much more than a boy, Murdat, for all you've done here. I've got more children than you've had shaves. We have to ask ourselves how much of your success is luck."

Without turning to look, Gan put out a hand to restrain Clas, then merely smiled. It was hard, almost predatory, nothing like his old smile. These men didn't know that. He said, "My life is bound by prophecy. You've heard it. You know that I go—and those with me go—wherever it takes me." He paused to stroke his chin. "As for my shaving, I do it myself. Are you that certain about all those babies?"

When the laughter subsided, and Galmontis was no longer grumbling, Fin brought the discussion back to center. "As soon as you claimed Malten, I thought you might reach out for the rest of the kingdom. You outsmarted the Olans and the Maltens. And the King. I'll give you that. Still, why should we submit to your rule? We outnumber you greatly. What if we choose to test you?"

Clas spoke before Gan could. "We defeated five Olan divisions at the Bear Paw, more than it took to send you and your former king scurrying for home. If you attack us, we'll accommodate you, but all you do is make Altanar's task easier. Do you think he'll let you keep your baronies? We must form a union to rule together. A single man must lead, but we must be united."

Galmontis asked, "Who would you send to train the young men?"

"No one. Send them here, with their arms. Let them see I trust you, that I'm not afraid to have your armed men on my land." He sent a quick look in Tate's direction, adding, "Send some with their wives. They must learn their new roles, as well."

Eleven West objected strongly. His people's women were their property, he said, and the matter of their treatment had long been a bone of contention between his people, the late king, and the Queen Mother. He glared at all of them, saying the old ways would remain.

Smiling easily, Gan held out his hand in a placating gesture. "When your people discover yours has become the poorest barony in the kingdom because your women contribute nothing but children, who'll face the blame? Look at Jalail for yourself; see the pride, the work going on. If a man falls, I guarantee land and help for his family. Your people's needs are no different than ours in Jalail. I urge you to make the changes that have been so good for us, but I won't interfere with your barony. We must cooperate and progress."

He stepped back from the chair, and Tate almost moved to him. His shaking hands crept into his pockets. He said, "Clas na Bale and Tate will explain the details of our organization and tell you exactly how we'll train your men. You can watch the new Malten unit training now, if you wish, and visit the homes and workshops of the Wolves and their wives. We have nothing to hide. But I must know by tomorrow morning if you're with me."

Tate reached to trail her fingers across his cheek as he passed, and he tried to smile. Exhaustion and pain turned it into a grimace, but he managed to say, "Help me, Tate. Then go back and make them believe. We need every man we can get."

She caught him when he swayed, pulling him clear of the doorway. His skin was greasy to the touch, hot with fever. She led him, staggering and panting, to the bed they'd made on the floor for him. He was asleep—or unconscious—before she could loosen his jacket. The puckered wound left by the arrow was still closed, and there was no sound of liquid in his breathing. His scalp injury looked healthy enough. She covered him up with a light blanket, wishing for Sylah.

*   *   *

It was a week later when one of the house servants ran to her, breathless, with the news that the Murdat was going for a ride in the sunshine. Muttering under her breath, she hurried to intercept him. She had to concede his color was good, and he was moving with confidence. He'd not yet managed to completely repeat the flair he'd put on for the visiting barons, but he seemed reasonably comfortable. He made a rare attempt at humor when he saw her, holding up his hands in mock self-defense. She saw through to the unending anguish it barely covered, and her planned tongue-lashing melted in pity. She scolded him half-heartedly for appearance's sake. That done, she asked, "Where will you go? It can't be far, you know."

"The hill where the boys fly their kites."

She moved away as a servant helped him into the saddle. His war-horse pranced with excitement, and she flinched when he brought it to a quivering stop in front of her. The animal's liquid eyes seemed to accuse her of extending its inactivity, and when it heard the barking approach of the two dogs, it was too excited to contain itself. It tossed its head and whickered joyously.

She said, "You were there before, carried in a litter. You should be today, as well."

He touched the place where the arrow had struck. "I'm practically healed. Anyhow, what could be more soothing than watching kites fly?"

He rode away with Shara and Cho frolicking around him, knocking each other sprawling, barking delightedly. He never looked back.

The ride to the hilltop was only a matter of an hour, even at the slow walk he maintained. In truth, the jarring of any faster pace made his ribs feel as if the arrowhead were still wedged between them. He felt sorry for his horse. Its eager strength yearned to gallop off across the fields as the dogs were doing. He patted its neck and promised they'd do just that in the next few days.

The boys were waiting for him at the base of the low hill. They jostled each other to extend their kites to him. He praised them all for workmanship, or the color, or the style. The boys saw he meant it, and their eyes shone.

They had no way of knowing they were the only people he genuinely relaxed with. It hurt him to acknowledge the fact. Even Clas—he corrected himself—*especially* Clas no longer brought the warmth of friendship alive in him.

When he thought of Sylah, he suffered for both of them. It was impossible to think of her, though—or Clas—without hearing the hateful sound of Neela calling out to him.

Not to her husband. To her husband's best friend.

Her first love.

What else?

The thoughts shamed him, made him feel queasy. He loved them both. He wanted to trust them both.

Why did he let the loathsome worm in his brain continue to torture him? He'd free her. Everything would be all right then. Everything.

A boy at the edge of the group waved, broke into his thoughts. He waited for Gan's summons. At the gesture, he sprang forward, forcing his way to the stirrup. He said, "He's here, Murdat, waiting for you." The other boys melted back, faces bright with envy and expectation.

Gan looked beyond them, to the crest of the small hill. He told the boys, "Well, let's go see what we have," and reached down to give the one who'd spoken a lift up to ride behind him. His horse turned to look at him with surprise, but when Gan urged him forward, it responded as always.

The man waiting at the top saluted Gan in the traditional Jalail manner, and Gan returned it. Dismounting and helping the boy down, he said, "You finished them all?" Shara and Cho loped up to sit beside him, pretending to ignore the small hands petting them. Their guilty glances caught Gan, then quickly looked away.

The man pointed to a mounded blanket. "Under there, Murdat," he said.

Gan smiled approval. "All three? That's impressive. Thank you." The boy who'd ridden up with Gan, suddenly shy, ran to his father's side, close enough to lean against the reassuring familiarity. His father put a hand on the boy's shoulder.

"Let's see what we've got, then," Gan said, and the boys scrambled to help their friend's father. The first kite they assembled was huge, a rectangle taller than Gan, with a large open space between the two bands of tough paper that encircled the top and bottom. The cord was as thick as a finger, and as some boys hurriedly fitted its strings and sticks together, others were attaching a bulky sack to extra-thick crossbars at the bottom end of the construction. A separate cord led to it. When all was ready, everyone stood clear of the kite flier.

The contraption strained at its line, which was snubbed around a convenient tree. It needed only a lift to break free of the earth, although the dangling sack stifled its grace and made its maiden flight a stodgy struggle to gain altitude. Climb it did, however, and soon it was high in the sky, a good quarter of a mile away from the group on the hill. The kite flier said, "Now, Murdat?" and Gan nodded. The man pulled the second string, simultaneously tugging and releasing the main cord in a rapid series of movements.

The kite reacted by laying over on its side and sliding across the wind. As it did, the sack popped open. They were too far to count the rocks tumbling free, and as they fell, they spread apart from each other, becoming practically invisible. When they landed in the fields below, however, all saw them kicking up startled puffs of dirt. When some hit a small tree and ripped off branches, the boys cheered spontaneously.

Gan was unsmiling, deep in thought, as he and the boys helped the kite flier drag the monster back. As soon as it was grounded, the man readied his second model. Far smaller, it was a sturdier version of the children's diamond shaped model. It went aloft eagerly. When it was about a hundred yards out, the man produced a device that looked like a tube with flanged wheels at each end. The wheels were attached to wires that held them about two inches from the tube. When the wheels were mounted on the kite line, the tube was suspended below them. There were tiny wings glued to it. The man released the device, and it fairly raced up the string. The boys, obviously familiar with the technique, laughed happily at its progress. When the tube reached the kite, however, the shriek that split the air stopped them immediately. The man sent the kite into a series of wild maneuvers, and the whistle responded with a continuing piercing wail that rose and fell with the speed and course of the action.

The kite flier smiled at Gan's expression. "We use the messenger on the kites all the time," he said. He told his son to show Gan another of the devices, explaining, "When it hits the kite, it releases that small pin in the front. Usually we just attach a piece of paper or a leaf, so we can see it fall. Your idea was no trouble. The pin releases the cap on the whistle. You heard what happens."

"Excellent," Gan said. "And the last one?"

The man pulled a third kite out from under the cloth. It was a little larger than the second, but identical in shape. What distinguished it was the thin, two-foot-long metal blade extending from its bottom. The man held it out at arm's length. It vibrated in the breeze, twisting, making the blade glint and shine. The man frowned. "This is a little trickier to handle," he said, indicating the harness with two control lines, rather than one. "Much more control, though, once you know how." He shooed the curious boys away and let the string out as the kite sped away. As with the first, it disliked the extra weight, but it flew well. The kite flier experimented with the dual strings, getting the feel of the new design. When it was far enough away to satisfy him, he sent it into more intricate patterns. It began to make an eerie hissing noise as its speed increased. Sliding back and forth across the sky, it dramatically swooped like a falcon. The man checked it mere feet above the ground, sending it whistling across the fields. The glittering blade seemed to search for a target. At the limit of the line, he hauled back, sending it rearing a hundred or more feet in the air.

Tugging, cajoling, he held it there, its bright beauty as fragile against the sun as any butterfly. Then he twitched his hands, and in an instant it menaced again, streaking about like a thing possessed. Some distance away his son was still flying the kite with its whistle, the sound forgotten in the excitement of the knife wielder. The man glanced at it for a moment, and in a burst of speed his kite careered across the sky and the blade was through the whistler's string. The whistle screamed to declining silence as the kite fluttered down.

Gan watched as silently as the boys until it hit the ground. By that time the kite flier had his deadly toy almost in hand. Gan called for the boys' attention, then told them, "You must never speak of what you saw here today. It's a secret between all of us until we use it against our enemies. Do I have your word, all of you?"

Solemn, half afraid, they all nodded. He thanked them, then turned to the man who'd made the kites. "I'll want twenty of the larger ones, ten with whistles—see if you can make different notes—and twenty of those devils with the blades. Tell Clas na Bale what you need for payment."

On the ride back to the castle, Gan evaluated what he'd seen. Good troops would treat the kites as the galling little nuisances they were. Bad troops would afford them more respect than they deserved.

He looked over his shoulder. The boys had their own kites up now, colorful flecks dancing against towering white clouds. That was what they should be, things of harmless pleasure. Under his influence, they were to become weapons. The children who'd shared their fun with him were conspirators.

Toys. He spat in disgust.

What he *needed* was a way to free Neela.

All this—the infuriatingly slow, necessary business of healing; the hammering out of an understanding with the barons; the training of the recruits from the other baronies—none of it was receiving his best effort. Without his best effort, he knew he must fail. Clas and the others were working themselves to exhaustion, and their results were outstanding.

Why couldn't he break out of this fog?

Fin, Eleven West, and Galmontis were agreed to his leadership: Why didn't he feel like a leader anymore?

Neela.

His head spun. He had to stop his horse. The reins fell slack as he swayed, clutching the pommel. He knew what was coming, and was powerless to stop it. Before it had come in the night, never in the daylight. His eyes burned, wouldn't stay open.

The vision came, as always, a pulsing, brilliant disk of pure light. Her image was trapped within it. She pleaded for help with outstretched arms.

She cried out, and he heard nothing. Then the circle grew smaller. Neela's image diminished, grew obscure.

Every time the vision came, the circle shrank to a smaller thing.

His mother had promised him a life of great success or oblivion.

He knew—he *knew*—that if that circle of light should shrink to nothing, the mind that perceived it would welcome oblivion.

CHAPTER 77

Sylah twisted away from the flaring torch when the thick cell door squealed open. Some of its light penetrated to the back of her cell, exposing loathsome insects, darting for cover. She scrambled after them, stepping on as many as she could before they scuttled into the chinks and cracks of the stone walls. Ignoring whoever carried the torch, she searched eagerly for further victims, all the while dabbing at tears of frustration and disgust. Whoever was at the door was of minor importance, compared to the prospect of reducing the population of her cell. Only when the light persisted did she understand that it wasn't simply another meal delivery. Raising a shielding hand to her brow, she turned and peered into the dazzle. The figures were indistinct. One was the blinding white of a protector. The other was in black. Her eyes adjusted fractionally; the man's clothes were green. Dark green.

Memories of green choked her thinking. She saw crocus sprouts against snow. A laughing sea. The forest. A meadow in the sun.

When Altanar spoke, it was almost a croon of pleasure, and she doubled over with the quick instinct of a frightened animal, protecting the growing rise that was her child. Her fear made him laugh. "How like one of you," he said, sneering now. "Because of your interference, dozens of men will die who might have lived. Yet when you hear your king—when you're face to face with justice—your first thought is to protect your own brat." He muttered something and the torch was lifted higher, cascading more light into her cell. Altanar went on, "I'm not here to hurt you. In fact, I gave my word to the Abbess I'd look in on you to be sure no one tortured you."

He paused, and she felt him waiting for her to beg. It would be wrong, shameful to Church, degrading to herself.

She wanted to.

In the trance she was strong. With the crusted grime on her skin revealed, and the welts of the insect bites, there was no such thing as pride. Her own stink threatened to choke her.

Perhaps seeing her beg was all he truly wanted. She'd never thought of that. Perhaps if she humbled herself; after all, she had deceived him. It was right that she be punished. She could admit that.

She pictured herself on her knees, arms around his legs. Yes, she'd do that. Anything. Tell him he'd been right to punish her. Thank him for making her see her error. Make him believe. Tell him it would be proper to punish her even more.

Not like this, though. Not the cells. He didn't really know what it was like. No one could. Not even he would punish someone so cruelly if he understood what it was like. She'd tell him about the food. No, not the food; he must be aware of that. The filth, and the things that touched her in the dark. It was a sin for her to go uncleaned. He'd know about that.

"A bath." The words blurted out, barely comprehensible to herself. She repeated them, getting them a bit clearer.

How long since she'd spoken? A month? More. It made no difference. The cells had no days, nights, seasons; they had the time of the grave.

His face was a gleaming blur. There was a smile in his voice when he said, "I barely understood you. How odd. You used to be so glib. No matter. I'm afraid a bath's out of the question. Not until Church says I must free you."

"When? Please—*when?*"

Again the long pause before his answer.

How could he do it? When he could see how much misery he'd piled on her, how could such a simple thing as keeping her in suspense give him any more pleasure?

He said, "The Peddlers speak of bad weather to the south. Floods wrecked bridges and ferries. The delegation from the Iris Abbey won't be back until late summer. Perhaps early fall."

She would plead. Yes; beg.

When she tried to speak, her tongue was wood, the muscles in her throat stiff as leather. The sounds had no connection with words.

Altanar laughed. "Don't thank me," he said, his laughter mocking. The door slammed shut, closing out the light with its noise. She screamed, throwing herself at it. Hoarse, guttural sounds bubbled out of her mouth, nonwords that implored. Pounding on the door, she cried for him to hear, to understand, to pity. Suddenly she realized he was speaking again. She forced a fist in her mouth to quiet herself, so his words might be as clear as possible.

He said, "Your old friend Likat and his warriors are coming here soon. They're going to help me attack Harbundai and that child-king, Gan Moondark. You should be glad you're here. You won't see your husband die. I may keep Moondark alive, though. Let him see his wife bear my child. The world should know what happens to those who stand against me."

Their slippers made no sound as they left, and she could only follow their departure by watching the smear of torch flame wane from her floor. She dropped to all fours, sensitized fingers drifting along the juncture of stone and wood. For a few moments she stared at black nothingness where it had been. Waves retreated like that, carrying the sparkle of sunlight with them, back to the sea's darkness. Sometimes the wheat in the fields bent under the wind in similar change, bright to dull.

She threw herself back against the wall, chewing on a knuckle until she remembered the danger of dirt creatures in this place. The discipline that kept her from rubbing the itching insect bites would be wasted if she gnawed a raw spot on her hand. Her knotted emotions wouldn't ease without some release, however. She threw herself into the physical exercises she used to keep up her strength. It would make her sweat. The air in the cell would grow fouler yet. Hysteria tickled the edges of her thoughts—what difference did more smell make? She stifled laughter, started running in place, counting the steps that would carry her her quota of miles. She glided across the castle grounds, through the gates toward town. Clas was coming from the north. They would meet somewhere.

Her bare feet kissed the sun-warmed earth. She ran to him.

Altanar stood at the foot of the stairs leading out of the cell area. He held a small cloth bag under his nose. He gestured with it, speaking to the protector. "This rotten air has killed my flowered packet. Now it smells like everything else here. How do your people put up with it?"

Flatly, the protector said, "We must."

"Yes." Altanar nodded, pleased with the answer. He rubbed his hands together briskly. "Now, what's this about one of the cell guards becoming involved with this Moondance thing?"

In his nervousness, the protector actually allowed some concern to color his voice. He said that one of his men was known to be attending Moondance ceremonies. His wife wore the disk, although he didn't.

Altanar considered making the protector sweat. He'd reported on the criminal, true, but he was still responsible for anything his men did. He should be made to suffer a little. Altanar sighed; there was too much to do. He said, "I want you to promote him." Surprise jerked the protector's eyebrows. Altanar went on, "I want him in charge of the Priestess' cell area. Her food ration is to be cut in half." The surprise faded to confused apprehension. Altanar was prepared for it. No one understood anything without every tiny detail being explained. "She'll die. No injuries, not even a small bruise. And no poison; those hags in Church know too much about it. If she wastes away out of grief and remorse, they can't say much. And if it turns out that Church doesn't cast her out, you'll claim the Moondancer starved her because he hates Church, the way they all do. Is all that clear?"

"Yes, King."

"I hope so. How long will it take?"

The protector studied a spot on the far wall. He pushed his nose to the side with a judicious index finger. "One month. Five weeks, at the most."

"A month?" Altanar was disgusted. "Ridiculous. As soon as Harbundai falls and the Dogs are under control, I'm getting rid of Church. I don't know how yet, but I will. I'm sick of their interference. A month! For one trou- blemaker."

Gan found his only solace in watching the Inland Sea. Only then could he find a few minutes to think past Neela and the cold well that once was his heart. Even a month after arriving with the Wolves to take over Malten Castle as his own, he spent every available moment watching the water, caught by its constant movement. The mysteriousness of its shifting color and perspective intrigued him. When the light was right, the distant moun- tains of the Whale Coast were so close he could believe that the smell of snow was in the west. Other times the sky went dark with rolling clouds from the Great Sea beyond. He would stand and watch the gray mass inexorably overwhelm the entire range, then shroud the sea itself as it poured eastward.

Boats fascinated him, too. He could watch them cut across the water by the hour, and had even learned to handle one of the small boats called balance bars. Their speed and maneuverability made him think of the long- legged waterwalkers he threw stones at as a boy.

Two summers ago. He'd been a boy, caught up in no more than a boy's dreams. Now he was training an army to destroy a king and create a new kingdom.

He was caught up in a dream not his own.

Father-killer. King-killer. King.

Prisoner.

Like Neela.

From the castle he could look far down the coast into Ola. She was there. His Messengers to Altanar returned with no answer to his demands that she be returned. Two had learned that she was held in seclusion in Altanar's castle. Sylah was in something called the cells. There was no other informa- tion about her.

They'd learned that Likat was elated to discover Neela was in Altanar's hands. He was expected in Ola very soon, and he was already demanding to have her.

The news was a dagger in Gan's side. Altanar had everything to gain by turning her over to Likat.

And he had no plans to prevent it.

Daily—sometimes hourly—Clas bullied him to put together some sort of raid to free the two women. He wanted to. He tried to. He couldn't.

Jones constantly intruded on his thoughts. He remembered how a blow to the head had changed the man entirely.

The sword slash on his own head was completely healed now, nothing more than a red brand of defeat and loss. Still, he continued to drift in lethargy. He slept as little as ever, ate the same, even exercised the dogs and his horse. The only thing about him that was different was his inability to move on anything important.

The little sleep he got was riddled with dreams of freeing her. The thought of her danger paralyzed his brain.

From dark, blank nights, he heard another voice. He believed it to be his mother's. It spoke of victory or oblivion, glory or disgrace.

If he tried to rescue her and failed, the disgrace would be absolute. It would complete the prophecy. His wife and child dead or enslaved. Himself destroyed. Everything he'd touched or loved would be mocked and shamed. Neela's love would have been for nothing. His father's love—and death— would be scorned as foolish and empty. Clas. Sylah. Raggar. Baron Jalail.

If he failed.

It didn't have to end that way. The fear that it would was a snare to his thoughts. He couldn't move against it. He hated himself.

He didn't look up, even though he was well aware when Tate came to sit beside him. For a while neither spoke, simply sharing company, watching the sea and clouds. Then Tate said, "The troops from the allied baronies are coming well in their training. They'd do even better if you were to pay some attention." She hesitated long enough for him to turn to face her, and she met his eyes determinedly, going ahead. "There's some hard feeling growing because you don't supervise."

He said, "I have things on my mind." Then he rounded on her, his expression spiteful. "Do you ever hear anything from your Moondancer friend? The one who ran away when Neela was kidnapped?"

"Gan, I told you I sent him away. He had nothing to do with Neela's kidnapping."

He looked back to the south, sullen. After a long while he said, "I apologize. Why do any of you put up with me? I've lost my way."

She said, "Helplessness does that," and at his sharp glare, she merely nodded slowly. " 'Course, that's what you are. You'd have gotten her back by now, if there was a way. There hasn't been, but there will be. That's the difference between hopelessness and helplessness. Take it from an expert." She looked down where her hand was idly rubbing the stone wall and jerked it back. She'd been feeling the texture of a piece of granite. Now she saw it had once been deeply incised with Roman numerals. The edges of the carving were chipped and worn. One end of the thing was discolored, as if it had been subjected to intense heat. The numbers were barely discernible; she could make out a couple of M's and some X's.

Suddenly she was shaking with repressed fury. She wanted to grab Gan's head in both hands and push it down until his nose ground on the carved rock, wanted to scream at him that he couldn't understand the first particle of helplessness, hopelessness, or anything else. What could he know of loneliness? Her *race* was gone. Her only friends from her own world were escaped from Ola—but to where? No one knew.

His loneliness was *nothing*.

He was staring at her. Only then did she realize she was clutching the hand that felt the inscription under her arm, as if it were burned. He said, "Are you all right? I didn't mean to offend you."

"I was thinking of something else. No problem. Are you coming?"

He accompanied her without argument, and he saw she was right. The men clearly picked up their effort when he appeared. It shamed him. If they knew what a shell he was, they'd mutiny. And he wouldn't blame them.

They were responding to what had been. Not that it mattered. The important thing was that they learn. For the next hour or so they watched together, and then he felt he had to get away.

He said nothing, but he was grateful when Tate went with him. She talked of training performance and schedules while they made their way back to the viewpoint on the wall. A particularly large balance beam caught his eye. It sliced the chop like a knife, the left outrigger breaking clear of the water as the skipper drained the last bit of energy from the freshening breeze. As it approached the docks, the minute figures of the crew bustled about, positioning themselves to lower the twin sails. At the last instant everything was let go. They leaped on the fluttering cloth in a frenzy of activity while the skipper, a large man with a full black beard, aimed the boat directly at the dock. He flared her broadside just when it seemed he must crash, and his linesmen hopped onto the dock as easily as stepping across a doorsill.

Gan turned to Tate. "That's no fisherman," he said. "I'll bet you anything that's a trader, when he has something to trade, and a pirate when he hasn't."

Tate shook her head. "Not me, you don't. I wouldn't take—" She stopped, reaching for his shoulder for support. Almost as quickly she pulled the hand back, and when he asked what was wrong, she laughed nervously. "I thought I saw something, but I was wrong. It was just—" She stopped again, and this time something like a cross between a moan and a scream welled in her throat. She raised her hand to her mouth, the sound growing louder. Gan followed her gaze. "What is it? You know the man?"

She pointed, so excited she jumped up and down. "Not him, not the bearded one! The one sitting beside him! That's Conway, one of the people I was in the— One of my people! It's him!" Tears ran down her cheeks unheeded. She leaped up on the wall, holding onto Gan's shoulder for balance. "Matt!" Her voice cracked, and she shouted again. "Matt! Matt Conway!"

The figure in the boat stirred, seemed to be looking about. She called again, waving. The man stepped onto the dock, obviously trying to locate the call.

Tate drew the pistol from her holster and fired a round. Hundreds of sea gulls rose screaming from the surrounding buildings and docks. Great blue herons croaked indignation, and entire flocks of ducks and crows scrambled madly into the air, whirling past and around each other in a frenzy of caws and quacks. People shouted alarm. A flock of disoriented pigeons fluttered around Tate and Gan, so numerous and so close they blanked out the view to the dock for a full five seconds. When they cleared away, the man was looking up at them. He threw back his head and let loose a cry that rose to a high pitch and ended with an echoing *hah!*

It was Gan's turn to act surprised. "That's exactly the call we use to start the herds moving. Did he learn it from my people?"

"The other way around, my cowpoke friend—the other way around!" The remark was gibberish to Gan, but she was running like a deer as soon as it was said.

He couldn't remember the last time he'd felt so excited. He also couldn't imagine why he did. In any case, he hurried after her to be part of it all.

CHAPTER 78

Gan watched the reunion on the dock with a sense of unreality. He knew Tate as a woman of great integrity and humor; he had never seen her behave with childish abandon. Even her friend, the man she called either "Matt" or "Conway" or "Darling," seemed taken aback by the exuberance of her welcome. He kept glancing around as if waiting for someone to calm her down. As it happened, no one even tried, and it was quite some time before she stopped kissing him and telling him how glad she was to see him and thought to introduce Gan. Conway took his right hand in his own and moved it up and down. For a moment it puzzled Gan, and then he remembered that Tate and Jones had done the same thing when they first met him. They seemed to consider it some sort of bonding. Religious, probably.

By then Conway was introducing the skipper of the balance bar. His name was Wal, and he not only admitted he was a pirate, but introduced himself as one. Gesturing at Conway, Wal said, "I know you, Gan. We came as soon as we heard Baron Malten was gone. You're Baron Jalail-Malten now, is that it?"

Gan said, "I know you, Wal. I'm Gan Moondark. The baronies are mine. I don't claim any title."

Tate interrupted, moving away from Conway to stand beside Gan. She said, "He's too modest. He's going to be King of Harbundai. We're training troops from three other baronies right now. When they're ready, we're going after this Altanar clown."

"Clown?" Gan frowned. "You never used this word before."

Tate stammered, "It's from our language. He understands." She grinned mischievously. "It's not a respectful word."

Soberly, Gan said, "Then it's a good one for Altanar. Clown." He liked the sound of it. "Clown Altanar." To Wal he said, "You came for a reason. It's not polite for me to let you speak of important things on bare earth. Come, we'll go inside the castle. I ask you to accept my hospitality." He went through the phrases easily, wondering if they could sense the excitement building in him. He tried to attribute it to Tate, telling himself he was simply reacting to her joy in rejoining her friend. That was part of it, surely, but there was more. He *felt* things differently. The world was touching his senses again. Tentatively, uncertainly, he explored. Walking the wooden dock, he was aware of the sound of lapping waves and the constantly changing smells from the boats. The sky seemed warmer, more intense. He was surprised to realize how long his thoughts had been of bleakness, of loss.

The Malten Castle was almost at the water's edge, so it was a short walk to the doors that pierced the sheer walls. There were two of them, a latticework iron gate made of circular bars an inch thick in front of iron-bossed timbers that showed adze marks. Huge winches lifted both barriers vertically. Massive chains dangled from the pulleys. Gan pointed at the system as he passed with Wal. "The staff said this castle's never been breached. They say these doors have never been really tested."

Wal smiled, ruffling the thick beard. "That's one of the things we have to discuss, Murdat," he said. He was watching Gan for reaction, and he enjoyed surprising him. He went on, "Yes, I know your title. And some other things. Pirates need the very best informants."

Once they were inside the castle, Gan sent a man to get Clas and Emso. This new quickening of his blood made him want them present. He lengthened his stride toward the eating hall.

Tate, on the contrary, slowed. She wanted more time alone with Conway. They rushed their words, interrupting, exclaiming, talking over each other and falling against each other with laughter. They summarized their situations quickly. Only when Conway had to explain about Falconer, and when Tate had to relate Jones' experience, did they slow down. For a while they spoke in lowered tones, their bodies slack, in contrast to the exuberant, earlier dancing about. Still, their excitement in finding each other was such that even the tragedy of their friends couldn't dampen their enthusiasm for long. Merriment was replaced by a deeper, shared awareness that was happy without being frivolous. In Tate's case, hearing that Leclerc, Carter, Anspach, and Bernhardt were all well brought a rush of joyous tears. Conway paused for her to regain her balance, and then they were prattling again.

When she described the battle of the Bear Paw, he was complimentary about the scratched message on the helmet, but the talk of combat brought a sly glint into his eyes, and when she tried to pursue it, he only winked and told her she'd have to be patient. Then, without explanation, he grew serious. "I think of Madge Mazzoli a lot," he said. "Probably too much. Remember how sure she was we'd find a peaceful, pastoral society? I'm glad she never saw the totality of our legacy." He nodded at Gan and Clas. "They're pastoral enough. Not very peaceful."

Tate was surprised at how much resentment his remarks touched off. It was a complete failure to understand, she decided, and said, "He does what he has to. Anyhow, you told me what this Altanar's like. Shouldn't someone do something about him?"

Conway sighed. "We will," he said. "That's why we're here. We'll be talking about it. Tell me about your new home. You all moved in here a month ago?"

The animated conversation picked up again, the seriousness forgotten.

The kitchen staff was already spreading out food and beverages when Clas and Emso entered, breathing hard from hurrying. For the next few minutes everything was protocol and polite introductions. It was Clas who forced the conversation. He said, "I think you're more like us than most of these people around here, Wal, so I'll ask you plain: What do you want?"

"I'll take that as a kind remark, Clas na Bale. I think we can be friends, and I need friends. Especially those who count King Altanar an enemy."

Gan said, "I think you know he holds our wives. You've come to his worst enemies."

Wal poured half a long wildcow horn of beer down his throat, drew the back of his hand across his mouth, and calmly asked Gan to support his piracy. His plan was simplicity itself. Gan had only to provide him occasional safe harbor and he'd give Gan first price on whatever he was able to loot from Olan ships. It would make them rich while weakening Altanar.

Gan said, "Only safe harbor?" and Wal blustered. Then he said, "Well, there's the matter of an occasional raid. Altanar will know it's Whale Coasters who're picking off his boats. He'll come after us. We'd expect you to help by nipping at his heels from here when we call for help." He made a coughing sort of noise. "Not that we'll need it often, understand. We ask no one to fight our battles."

Gan felt another surge of energy. This Wal stirred his pride. He said, "I command two thousand, five hundred Wolves. We don't nip. This is what I offer you. Be one of us. I am going to crush Altanar, and then rid my tribe of the man who is destroying them. Join me. Join the new Harbundai, one nation. No more lying alliances. No more slavers. The sea will be free to all who want it, the land will be safe for all who need it."

Wal was bluntly skeptical. "You? Overthrow Altanar? You're outnumbered at least five to one. Altanar's been weakening Harbundai for years. Now he's ready for the last throw of the dice. He'll have Dog warriors with him."

Gan's growing excitement was edging into impatience. He practically leaped to his feet. "Why must I constantly argue? Listen to me! If we don't destroy him, he'll destroy us! My tribe is being used up like kindling tossed into a firepit." He spun from facing Wal to point a peremptory finger first at Clas, then Emso, and finally Tate. "I've been a fool. Because Altanar held my heart, I surrendered my soul. I've been asleep for months. We have almost no summer left. Get the word to the barons that I will winter in Ola. Tell them the Wolves hunger, and I mean to feed them." He turned to Wal again, including Conway with a swift glance. "I need you. I'll move without you, if I must. The time to speak is now. You are with me or you aren't. No maneuvering."

Wal met his gaze evenly, unflinching. They measured each other for so long the others began to move nervously, drumming the table, shifting their feet, pulling at clothes inexplicably grown tight and binding. Wal chuckled. It was a deep rumble, and Tate obviously thought it was a growl at first, because her hand went to her pistol instantly. Wal said, "You're right. We've always fought Altanar by letting him feed on the weakest of us." He shrugged, but lifted a hand in warning. "We'll help you. More than you think. And there *will* be maneuvering. The Whale Coast won't be dominated by mainlanders and river fishers."

Gan wanted to shout his relief, let them know the anticipation and new life burning in him. He resolved to make them understand by showing them what could be done. There was no need to shout. He would make them see what he'd seen.

The strength of the Dog People was their combination of speed and force. The horses carrying their riders into contact were the finest. The Dogs struck fiercely and left before an enemy could respond. The Dog warriors boasted they had no flanks and their enemies never knew where the front was.

Wal's boats gave Gan the same opportunity. They could strike anywhere on the coast. Altanar would never know where to expect them. If things were done properly, he'd never expect them at all.

Gan moved to drop a hand on Wal's broad shoulder. "We'll have no trouble with cooperation. We need each other. Before the barons arrive, there are some things I have to discuss with you."

He looked around the table. His friends. They'd trusted him, waited for him to live again. They were grinning, recognizing the new-old Gan, and he wondered how anyone could have such comrades. Unable to speak further, he hurried out of the room, leaving them buzzing behind him. He ran up the steps to the battle walk of the castle wall, pushing himself as hard as he could, exulting in the fiery pain in joints and muscles suddenly called on to perform. Standing in the sun, pulling air deep, deep into his lungs, he stood where he and Tate had been talking.

Ola was still there. It beckoned. It taunted.

He leaned out, gripping the warm stone, squeezing until his fingers cracked. He said, "Be brave. I'm coming."

*   *   *

That evening after the last meal, Tate stood beside Wal's balance bar with the blackbearded skipper and Conway. Conway helped her aboard, and the first thing he drew her attention to was the sail. "You have to see this," he said, handing her a fold of the drab blue-gray material.

Surprise lifted her eyebrows as she felt its weight. She remarked on it, and he said, "Believe it or not, it's a kind of paper. See if you can tear it." She looked to Wal, and he smiled and nodded. It wasn't like Conway to push her into a strength test, so she was reasonably sure there was a trick to the thing. Nevertheless, she tugged at a corner. It seemed to stretch a bit. With a fake glare, she dipped it in the water to weaken it. Still, it resisted her. Intrigued now, she examined it for wear, especially where the grommets were sewn. Some chafe marks revealed that it was layered; a tangled, fibrous mass sandwiched a conventionally woven fabric. The fibrous stuff actually penetrated the weave, effectively welding everything into a whole. Pointing an accusing finger at the evidence, she accused Conway of lying to her.

Sheepishly, he said, "Well, two-thirds of it's paper. Anyhow, the point is the lightness and strength of the stuff."

"I never saw anything like it. It's heavier than our ripstop, but not much. How do they do it?"

Wal burst into laughter. He said, "No one knows the entire process. The weaving of the cloth is very ordinary, but the making of the paper, and the way it's married to the material, takes several steps. According to our tribe's storytellers, a smith who was disappointed in his son's strength challenged his son to do anything to match his skill. He disowned the boy and said he was too soft to be a man. The boy made our first sailcloth, to show the father that soft isn't necessarily weak. Today, some people know one step, some know another, and so on. It has something to do with kelp and crabs and mussels." He made a face. "If you ever work a new sail in its first rain squall, you'll know there are dead sea creatures involved, I promise you."

They laughed with him at that, and he left them, explaining that he had to talk further with Gan.

Watching him until he was out of earshot, Conway turned back to Tate. He looked at her questioningly, then said, "Not everything in this world is invented for war. We've got to find a way to provide direction. We—the aliens—know where everything else leads."

She understood. Without any conscious thought, she was pouring out her story of the inscribed piece of granite. When the tears started, he put his arm around her, getting her to sit on the thwart with him. He told her of his own similar experience at his first sight of the massive diamond called the King's Badge, and his feelings when he realized it had to have been looted. For a while they shared examples of the things that triggered memories of their own world.

Tate sighed and said, "It didn't help, did it? I mean, I thought I felt better about things, during the telling, but now it's over. I know the emptiness won't ever go away. Life's not going to change for us, you know? I've gone for weeks without seeing something that reminds me of home, and then—bam!—I see a murdat with a piece of Coke bottle set in the handle like a jewel, or this castle's gate made out of concrete reinforcing rebar, and it's like a blow, Matt. It hurts."

He squeezed her shoulder. "We all get it. I think it was harder for the other women than it's been for you." He told of the Iris Abbess, taking them to the Beach of Songs to make them realize where they were. "They were able to retreat into the abbey, so they didn't see as many things as we did, but they had such a neat, structured life that when something from the past did hit them, the shock was all the greater. I told you Janet Carter nearly got us all put away; it was only because she felt so cut off from anything familiar that she started identifying with the captors. You've heard of it."

She nodded shortly. "Maybe that's what I'm doing. I've worked hard to help these people. Especially Gan and the wives of the Wolves." She looked up at him as if afraid she might be laughed at. "I'm going to do it. I'm going to make a mark. I don't know how, yet, but I figure there was some reason I lived to get here." She paused, then plunged ahead even more defiantly. "So far, I've worked for Gan, and I'm glad, because I think he's headed the right way. Maybe I stay with him, maybe I don't. But I'm going to *make that mark.*"

"Whoa," he said, drawing it out, part humor, part admonition. "The others want to help, too, Donnacee. How do you think Carter and Bernhardt and Anspach feel? They were supervising kids, but if they taught them the simplest thing about arithmetic or writing, they'd have been dragged down to the beach and flogged." He laughed quietly, and she sent him a sharp look. He told her of Leclerc and his "discovery" of black powder. "He saved our lives with it. The history of this world will put him right up there with Sir Francis Bacon, if he's ever able to make more of the stuff. And he's sick about it. For all that, if you want to talk about self-contempt, think how he and I felt, training Altanar's men to use our weapons."

"You got out with all of them, you said?"

"Absolutely."

She rose slowly, arms wrapped around herself as if the lowering sun robbed her of warmth. When Conway offered to get her a jacket, she smiled appreciation. "I'm not really cold," she said, taking his hand for the step between boat and dock. She thought she sensed a reluctance in him to let it go. It was so fleeting, she told herself she was imagining things.

He said, "I never said I was sorry for you—about what happened with the Pastor, I mean. That must have really hurt."

"It's the not knowing that's worse. These Moondance people are nuts. Fanatics. You wouldn't believe the change in him. I never talked to anyone so downright mean. He truly believes he's got to make everyone go through evil to get to good. It's scary."

Conway said, "When they run into Church, there's going to be trouble. Even Altanar's half afraid of Church. The abbesses in Ola walk a narrow line, but anyone else who challenged him would have been eliminated long ago."

She stopped. "We've got to help Jones, if we can find him. It's not right, a good man like that. He needs help."

He nodded, unspeaking. The lights were coming up in the castle, orange squares answering the lingering western glow limning the bulk of the Whale Coast range. Tufts of cloud hovering over them gleamed rose and salmon. Beside them, black water slapped playfully at the pilings. Conway said, "It's not all bad." He looked to the south. A few stars were barely glinting there. He went on, "A person could make a life. There've been some moments . . ."

When it was obvious he wasn't going on, she stepped into the gap. "Who was she, Matt?"

Startled, he looked down at her, then made a wry face. "Had to be a woman, didn't it? She introduced me to Wal, and had a hand in our escape. I don't even know if she's still alive."

"You fell in love with her?" She took his arm, started walking toward the castle again.

"I don't know. That's the trouble with us, isn't it? We're always so confused. But yes, I think I did." He took a few more steps, then, with conviction, said, "I do. I'm not confused. I'm scared. I didn't want to admit I love someone who may not be there."

They were at the gate then, and the crew began to lower it as soon as they were inside. The chains clattered horribly and the immense pulleys squealed and groaned. Tate wished she could thank the men. Had it not been for them, she would have spoken of her own loneliness. He longed for one woman. She mourned a race.

And someone. She ached for someone.

Had his hand lingered on hers? If it had, how could he do that to her, then speak so easily of loving someone else?

She shook her head, stopping when she realized he might notice. He wasn't like that. It was wrong to even think it.

It was wrong to be so grindingly, achingly lonesome. It was wrong to be looking ahead into a life that had nothing else to offer.

CHAPTER 79

The summer had started with the loss that made Gan's life a numbed progression from unwanted day to unwanted day. Now, with life back in his blood, the season seemed determined to race away from him. Every sunrise brought new reports of growing Olan strength. He watched the increasing capability of the Wolves with pride and hope that soared one day only to fall in depression the next. Three of the five-hundred-man packs—the proper term was "division," but the men ignored it steadfastly—were fully equipped with proper arms and equipment, but even though the smithies were at full production day and night, the late arrivals from the last two barons were just beginning to be properly turned out. Nevertheless, by the time the blackberries were ripening, he had the satisfaction of knowing that every pack had been involved in at least one skirmish with Olan border troops or slavers.

Gan had more than raw recruits and ripening crops to remind him of the passage of time, however. Every pregnant woman, every infant he saw, graphically underscored it. He found the sight of them wondrous and frightening. He took to going out of his way to avoid them.

At least Clas was by his side again. In his despondency, Gan had failed to see the depth of his friend's suffering. Clas afforded himself none of Gan's self-inflicted debilitation. He acknowledged helplessness and waited. His hope never flagged, and he bore his pain silently. He urged Gan to act, but never once criticized. It humbled Gan. He was determined to make Clas' self-restraint up to him.

Now Clas was a storm of activity, driving, inspiring, explaining—whatever was necessary to bring the Wolves to a high pitch of efficiency. Even during Gan's incapacitation, he'd taken the particularly valuable step of assuring that the men identified as Olan spies were "able" to see the Wolves in training and "stole" full details of their housing, the women's weaving and papermaking facilities, and the pottery works. The resistance movement provided Gan with another outlet for spreading disaffection. Two reported an ever-increasing spiral of unrest and repression.

Angry young men from Ola came north to join the Wolves. Wal's numbers benefited, as well. His ships found eager volunteers waiting to join him every time they hauled into some quiet bay on business. It wasn't unusual for a man to come to a clandestine market to sell a bale of furs or shell beads or bird skins and leave as a new crewman along with his merchandise.

The protectors were responsible for seeing that the tribes provided the manpower Altanar demanded. Reports of their effectiveness were disturbing. Army units under protector command ranged from the border only a few miles distant all the way to the banks of the Mother River in the south, and from the Enemy Mountains in the east to the sands of the Whale Coast. Altanar's strength was immense, and growing daily.

All of this was on Gan's mind as he stood on the dock with Shara and Cho, watching Wal guide a large balance bar into position. It was one of a pair, the heavy earners in his smuggling work. In addition to those two, he had ten smaller vessels that poked and prodded the coast for commerce or the odd bit of loot as far north as the country of the people called Skan.

Wal scampered to the dock on the top of one of the frames that held the outrigged balance bar in place. It was a remarkable feat, as the arched wooden member was a bare four inches square and at least ten feet long.

Once he was on the dock and coming toward him, Gan lost interest in his agility and hardly noticed Conway's quick greeting as he hurried past. Wal was very disturbed; not even the bushy beard could hide that. Apprehension pulled at Gan's back muscles.

Coming up to Gan, Wal said, "It's as I expected, Murdat. Almost every Olan boat is north of us, waiting for Harbundai fishermen and merchants to run from their army. I had to dodge them all the way to my base, after our last meeting. We made a run to the capital in this monster to sell whale meat—and talk to our friends. Altanar started moving troops toward the border two days after we docked. People say your boast that you'd winter in Ola reached him. I think you might have frightened him a little. I know you angered him a lot."

"Good, on both counts. Anything that muddies his thoughts works for us. What other news?"

Wal's manner eased a little. "Your wife's handling her situation well. We have someone in the castle, so the report is true. We even got word to her that you're coming after her."

Gan reached out, almost touched the other man. "This person spoke to her, saw her? Is she well? Is she comfortable?"

Smiling sympathetically, Wal held up a hand. "Our person can't say any more than I've told you. There always seem to be more ears and mouths than there are people. The person in the castle is my responsibility."

"Of course. I'm sorry." Gan sent him a lopsided grin that disappeared instantly under an embarrassed frown. "I didn't ask about Sylah. What word?"

The heavy brow drew together. "Nothing good. She's still in the cells. There's no decision from Mother Church. We can't learn any more. The fact that Altanar has stopped berating her in public . . ." The sentence dropped away to silence.

They went directly to Clas. He thanked Wal calmly. The words were as flat and emotionless as his crystalline stare. Wal, offended by the cold rudeness of it, stepped back. His hand edged toward his sword. The dogs tensed, and Shara moved a step closer to Gan. Only then did the men realize Clas saw neither of them. His eyes were on something far from that place. Suddenly, however, he blinked. He seemed puzzled by Wal's changed position, but made no reference to it. He turned to Gan, moving with a peculiar stiffness. He said, "There's a pack coming in from a training run. I should be there to meet them. I'll join you for evening meal."

Gan agreed quickly, speaking to Wal with a heartiness he didn't feel. "I'd like to see your boat. There are things I have to discuss with you."

Once aboard, Wal introduced Gan to his crew. They were an impressive group, seemingly drawn to Wal from every tribe touching the Inland Sea and many farther inland. A few still wore the traditional garb of their people, but some had obviously worn out their original clothes. The replacement items tended toward a uniform, a coarse blue cloth made into loose trousers and shirts. To a man they wore beards and long hair, some in braids, some coiled and held with ribbons. None wore it loose, and Wal explained that loose hair sometimes got caught in the lines. He pointed at one man, who laughingly displayed a naked, scarred scalp. "Snatched him bald one morning," Wal said, slapping him on the back. "If he'd a tougher hide, we'd have run him up top the mast. Flown him like a pennant. Would have scared the land rabbits to death, likely." The rest of the crew enjoyed what was clearly an old, familiar joke, and Gan was impressed by their closeness as well as their toughness.

Wal went on to explain how the great double sails were controlled, and how, in emergency, they could be swung clear around, turning the bow of the vessel into the stern instantly. "Impossible to steer until we run the rudder to what we call the hasty post at the other end," Wal said, "but it's handy when we have to make a quick departure. We overstay our welcome sometimes. And that reminds me; this one Conway and his friend Leclerc said I'm to give you a package. Leclerc made it." He disappeared down a ladder into the hold and returned in a few moments, carrying a paper-wrapped package. A string that looked like a rat's tail dangled from one corner. Gan looked at Wal, who smiled benignly. "Ugly lump, isn't it?" he said. Gan moved to jerk the string away, and Wal stopped him. "You're to leave it the way you found it until everyone's together for the evening meal. Conway wants to talk to you about it."

Gan made a face. "It's not polite to give presents with instructions. They come from a backward society, these strangers. Why didn't the one named Leclerc come with you?"

"The women wanted him to stay with them." Wal tugged at his beard. "If you think these ones are odd, you should meet them. Raccoons—all bright eyes and pesky fingers and scrinchy noses into everything. Make more mischief than there is time in the day. But you have to like them. Do anything for you, and twice as much for the women. Always thinking, too. Funny—none of them are warriors. This Tate of yours, she's a tiger."

Gan's sharp laugh drew the attention of the closer crewmen. He said, "You have her name right, but don't let her hear you call her 'my' Tate. Not unless you want to learn about the front end of that lightning weapon. A very independent woman."

Wal nodded glumly. "They've got that in common."

For an instant Gan saw Tate with Neela. Fair and dark, laughing so brightly. He drew a hand across his eyes to drag the image from his mind.

Almost as mere courtesy, he asked about the carrying capacity of the balance bar, and as soon as the words were spoken, an idea that had been trying to assert itself for days began to take solid form. Half musing, he wondered aloud if there was a place in Ola—somewhere between the border and the capital city—where a signal fire could be seen at sea. What if, he went on, a ship at sea wanted to relay the signal to Malten Castle? Could that be done?

Wal perceived the thrust of the questions immediately. He slapped the rough mast in his enthusiasm. "I know the exact place for your signal, the quickest way to get there. Any small balance bar will do to pass the signal along. The idea will work. Better than you dared to dream."

The last was a cryptic statement. Gan peered quizzically at this new friend and saw only bland innocence. He decided to let the man clarify his meaning in his own time. Squinting into the setting sun, he said, "The day's gotten away from us. Bring your assistants. My friends and I eat with a different group of Wolf officers every night. Your men should be with us for this occasion."

Wal sent a man to let his people know of the invitation. Then, with a broad grin, he grubbed in a large sea chest for a minute and produced another surprise. "Drawings of the castle and grounds," he said, flourishing rolls of paper. "Thought you'd be interested."

Gan murmured thanks, greedily inspecting the pictures. He ran his fingers across the inked lines and sensed Neela's presence. He thought back on the inconsolable Gan of a few short weeks ago and despised him.

As they arrived at the dining hall, Gan was saying, "We've missed you since your last visit. Everyone enjoys your lies. Or are they true stories?"

Unembarrassed, Wal said, "True stories, told with the slightest touch of necessary artistry; nothing more."

Gan grunted. "Lies, then. Now, can you remain here for two days?" Wal thought for a moment, glancing shrewdly at Gan before nodding. Gan accepted his answer without comment. Taking his guest's arm, he introduced him to the others.

Because of the increased number to be fed, there was some delay. Beer was brought and consumed. A festive air soon reigned, and the meal was eaten amidst the laughter of the Wolf leaders and Wal's officers. Soon, however, that was replaced by an aura of expectancy. Slowly, the crowd quieted.

Shara and Cho settled on opposite sides of the empty hearth behind Gan, chins on forepaws. They scanned the gathering constantly.

Eventually Gan had to acknowledge the pressure. He got to his feet. Servants hurried in with great clay pitchers of beer. Guards at the doors waited for them to finish that chore, then left, closing off the room behind them. Looking around the table, Gan brought it to silence. When the sound of breathing was all that could be heard, he drained a tankard of beer and said, "We move against Ola in forty-eight hours. All packs will leave for full field training the morning of the day after tomorrow. They will not be told of the planned attack. That night, we go to Ola. We must have surprise. Anyone responsible for breaking security will be executed on the spot, his body left unburned, his name taken from the list of Wolves as if he were never born." Gan pointed to Tate. "You remain here with fifty of the Jalail pack and Wal's balance bar. Clas and I, with the remainder of the Jalail pack, will circle east around the Olans massing on our border. All other packs, except the last two to arrive here for training, will attack the Olan force. The newest arrivals will remain behind as reserve. Emso, you're in command when Clas and I leave. Trade space for time; retreat, maneuver, defend— anything, but keep the main Olan force busy. Once Clas and I are behind the main Olan force, we'll light a signal fire. Wal will have a balance bar offshore to relay a torch message to the castle here. Tate, when you see that, you and your fifty leave for Ola on Wal's large balance bar. You come ashore as close to the castle as possible. You strike from the sea, we attack from the land. That's the general plan. Tomorrow morning we attend to details."

He turned his back and walked to the hearth, ignoring the murmur of uncertainty behind him. Inside the cold fireplace, as requested, he had Wal and Conway's gift. It couldn't weigh more than a pound, he thought. What a storyteller Wal was, claiming the ugly thing would answer everyone's questions about getting into Altanar's castle. And Conway, nodding agreement to every lying word, smug as a Peddler.

He disapproved of magic, more out of skepticism than Church-induced requirement, but he'd agreed to go along with their request for a demonstration. Lighting a smoldering taper from the coals in a firepot, he felt like a complete fool. The thing was probably mushrooms that gave off vision-producing smoke, he told himself glumly. A lot of good that would do when the arrows and slingstones were in the air.

He turned to face the commanders again. Everyone was enjoying the beer. Strange, the way it made him rock-solid but made them all look fuzzy. Tate sat with Wal and Conway at the far end of the table. Now they all looked smug. Waiting to see him tricked, he thought.

Wal shouted at him to move the dogs. It was a good idea. No sense in having them sniffing picture-smoke and throwing up all over. He ordered them to the opposite end of the room.

He pictured himself standing there with the smoking taper. He must look demented. The room was decidely warmer. He had another drink of beer, then held up the gift. He said, "We have a way to break into Altanar's castle. This ug— This holds something Conway's friend has sent us. Wal says if I touch a taper to the end of this string, we will all be pleased and surprised. So."

For several seconds it seemed nothing at all was going to happen. Some pretty sparks sizzled and jumped from the string, but that was all. Then, unexpectedly, the end was being eaten by lots of sparks that hissed and crackled. They moved with rather disconcerting speed toward the package. Quite pretty, he thought.

"Toss it into the fireplace!" Wal shouted. "Get back!"

His alarm offended Gan. Dog warriors didn't get into a flutter over sparks. He glared at the impertinence, then placed the package on the floor of the fireplace with a dignity intended to remind Wal of his manners. Then he condescended to step a few feet away before turning to watch the hallucination-inducing smoke.

Later, as they lifted Gan from the table where he lay stretched out among the remaining roast meats and boiled vegetables, everyone shouted at each other about the effective demonstration. They remarked how the sudden light not only lifted Gan several feet to deposit him in the leftovers, but the noise set off bells in everyone's head that refused to stop ringing. Some blamed that effect on the clouds of soot still billowing from the chimney. Others inferred the beer was not of the best. The man from Eleven West's barony shouted repetitiously that it smelled exactly like the last time The Destroyer exploded. No one paid any attention to him; the fact that he was wearing the noodles from the soup degraded his prestige.

Gan's first thought was the dogs, and he sat up to see Shara and Cho, black as coal, looking up at him with an air of sad reproach. He scraped bits of meat from his clothing and threw it to them, which they sniffed carefully and ignored. Cho kept looking about as if trying to locate something. Gan assumed she must hear the same gentle ringing as the rest of them.

Wal helped him down from the table, deftly plucking a half-eaten pork chop from between two buttons of his shirt as he steadied him. He said, "There's forty pounds of that stuff in the hold of my boat. Imagine what that'll do." Rapping the bone on the table to dislodge some ashes, he took a bite.

Gan was too busy trying to coordinate his knees to consider forty pounds of anything. His head began to clear as soon as he sat down in his chair, which was good, except that it made him aware of the gravy soaked into his trousers. It had grown distressingly cool.

When Tate and Conway approached, it took him two tries, but he eventually managed to ask, "I suppose this is another of your lightning weapons? Loud. Dirty."

Instead of answering right away, they exchanged glances. Conway said, "I see what you mean about indestructible. He probably could walk through the castle door without it. This way's faster, though."

He realized Conway was being complimentary, but it was silly. He got to his feet again. He said, "Everyone wait here until I get back."

The walk to his room was longer than he remembered it. The second time he bounced off a wall, he realized he was drunk. That had never happened before. Childish giggling pulled his head around; he might be drunk, but he was still Gan Moondark. It was unwise to laugh at him.

A moment later he realized it was himself.

It embarrassed him. He hung his head and hurried to his room, where he opened a cabinet and rummaged around until he found the short sword. Even with the beer twisting his vision, it was still a thing of incredible beauty. Too beautiful to keep hidden.

Too beautiful to be forever a traitor's weapon.

It deserved a better reputation. It should be known as the treasure of a man of honor, of skill, a warrior who would use it to bring it the glory it deserved.

He replaced the blade in its scabbard and clasped it to his chest under his shirt. By the time he reached the dining hall he was much steadier and much thirstier. He drank some more beer and pounded on the table. When he had their attention, he told them how he came to own the blade. Then he told them how he'd meant to keep it, never even showing it to anyone. Lastly, he drew it clear for all to see. "I give it away," he said, waving it. "The man who is to men as this is to all other steel. Clas—you will bring each other honor."

The room echoed with the cheers. Gan smiled at them. For the first time the beauty of the weapon appealed to him without claiming him. By giving it away, he freed himself of it. It was a rich feeling.

The men demanded a speech, and poor Clas tried. He managed to express his thanks. When he was done, Wal's second-in-command, a man named Talmarin, came to where the skipper was having one last drink with Gan. Clas watched them, half smiling. Talmarin apologized for leaving early, but explained he wasn't feeling well. He seemed more sober than everyone except Clas, and he certainly looked uncomfortable enough. Wal excused him with a wave and advice to get a good night's sleep.

As Talmarin walked out the door, Gan took Wal's arm, moving that way. "Let's go outside ourselves," he said. "Get some air, watch the sea."

It was a sentiment Wal could respond to. Clas joined them, and the three walked outside arm in arm. Wisely, Clas took the middle, where he could provide some stability. They rolled in unison.

They were almost to the dock when Wal stopped abruptly. "That's odd," he said, swaying forward. "The sail's are rising. What's he doing?" He launched himself into an uncertain trot. It steadied as he moved, but it was movement without grace. Gan and Clas ran beside him. The dogs lumbered along behind. When they reached the boat, the first thing they saw was several men with swords and torches obviously directing other crewmen about the tasks necessary to get under way. Spreading his feet, hands on hips, Wal roared orders to get his sails back down and for somebody to get Talmarin on deck.

The second-in-command appeared, grinning across the balance bar frame at them. At his order, two of the armed men leaped to the mooring lines, ready to cut them. Talmarin laughed. "I'll be in Ola by morning, Wal," he said. "Sorry to do this to you, but you can't match Altanar's generosity." He turned his attention to Gan. "Your plans will be worth much gold."

He raised his hand to signal the men at the mooring lines, and then suddenly his other arm was coming up. He said, "Your life's worth more yet." He held a small, steel-handled axe. It arced upward in his hand. Then, so swift it was a gleaming blur, something struck his stomach. He doubled over, staggering back until the sail boom stopped him. Throwing out his free hand, he held himself upright. The axe fell, striking a chiming note on the wooden deck.

While he struggled to straighten up, his hand clasped on the sword handle, the crewmen turned on their stunned captors. Wal recklessly dashed across a frame, throwing himself into the melee. Gan and Clas were close behind him. It was over in seconds, the erstwhile mutineers either surrendering at the sight of their leader finished so dramatically or overpowered by the loyal crew.

Gan's mind was turmoil. He moved in a daze.

Talmarin dropped to his knees as they approached him. He managed to get a grip on the axe handle. He strained to raise it, never taking his eyes from Gan's until he toppled over. Clas reclaimed his sword, going to the side to wash it clean.

Wal, watching him, said, "You said he and the blade would honor each other. That was enough for any man or weapon." He nudged Talmarin with his foot.

Clas overheard. He turned from the rail. "Gan is destined. He has a mission. And more; no one else can save his wife. Or mine."

Gan felt his pulse leap. There it was! Neela's name first. And the "mission." The accursed, inescapable mission.

In the dream, the man used the same axe, but the scene was a room, not a boat. The blackness that he'd seen in the dream was here, though—the waiting sea.

Nothing was exactly as it should be, yet all happened as the dream promised.

Including the unreasoning hatred.

Once more Clas had saved his life. Once more Clas was the better man.

CHAPTER 80

The panoply of five Wolf packs marching to war was a scene of savage beauty. Each had its own signal pennants, proud colors raised on long poles. The Jalail pack claimed Gan's own family red and yellow. The Eleven West's were a green background with a white wedge. The Maltens favored solid red, the Galmontis men solid blue, and Fin's people used yellow with black stripes. They snapped in the breeze, their eager crackling seeming to respond to the mile-eating step of the Wolves. They marched in column while they had a good road, and the tread of their feet was the mumbling thunder of a distant storm. At their front, his war-horse practically dancing with excitement, Clas led the foot column. On this their second day in the field, they were on the move to contact Olan forces.

Clas waved an arm in signal. The drums of Jalail pack struck a marching cadence.

The dogs padded along beside horse and next to Gan, oblivious to the need for drums or pennants. Their tongues flopped wetly. It would have been easy to look at their relaxed, almost slouching, gait and decide they were tired. In fact, they were loafing. They'd long since learned there was nothing for them to do while in formation. They conserved their energy and waited. Every so often Shara, in particular, would glance up to assure himself there was no need for greater attention. Cho was her normal, businesslike self.

Gan swiveled to scan the sky. Tomorrow night they'd need the wind ruffling those pennants. If Tate's fifty men couldn't make it down the coast, the raid on Altanar's castle would be seriously endangered.

That was a bad thought. He'd tried to cleanse himself through nara and failed. The morning after the incident on Wal's boat he'd had a vicious headache and a grinding sense of guilt. The former was the beer. The latter was reaction to his feelings toward Clas. On this second day, resentment at the memory of the jeweled sword flashing through the air was still a weight in his stomach. He knew it was wrong, that he should feel gratitude. The confusing thing was that he *was* grateful.

Half of him continued to love his friend.

Half of him hated.

There was no sense to it.

The Jalail pack stopped drumming. The Malten pack, immediately behind them, started a pattern of its own. The louder sound and its different line intruded on Gan's thoughts. The drums pleased him. There were several different sizes, so the inventiveness of the drummers provided something like melody. It entertained the ear and picked up the feet of the heavily laden troops. More than that, though, the instruments were another unifying element. Each pack was proud of its musicians and bragged of them, but the drums were standard, forcing all of them to perform within the same framework. They exchanged ideas and techniques, a thing that was virtually unheard of in the old Harbundai.

He watched the men again, seeing a cohesive unit, men from traditionally untrusting baronies, ready to fight with and for each other.

At least, that was the theory. They'd know by this time tomorrow.

Conway particularly liked to point out it would be even better if they were able to work together in peace. He seemed to think the idea was original. Another strange man. Moody.

Col had been like that sometimes. Usually when something reminded him of Murmillanh. Perhaps Conway thought of a woman. He hoped Col and Murmillanh were watching, looking into his thoughts.

The prophecy. He wanted to fulfill it. He wished he could be rid of it. It was as treacherous as his feelings for Clas.

Perhaps he was mad. Would he fall from his saddle and start eating dirt? Would he ride into this battle screaming for death? Would he run, shaking and crying, his manhood lost?

Perversely, the thoughts calmed him. Those things weren't in him. Battle seemed to be the one place where his doubts and confusions wouldn't follow.

A disturbance ahead demanded his attention. A squad of Eleven West cavalrymen were riding in from the forward screen, and they were escorting a rider. For a moment Gan puzzled at their pace, and then realized the man in the middle of their box formation was riding a donkey. He said, "Bilsten."

A few minutes later he was looking at the Peddler.

Bilsten stood up in his stirrups and saluted, Jalail fashion, as soon as he saw Gan. One of the scouts aimed a quick backhand at him for the presumption of it, and Bilsten dodged it with the skill of long practice. Before the youngster could wind up for another blow, they were close enough for Gan to shout at him to stop. Without looking at the surprised trooper, Bilsten rode confidently out of the box. When the donkey's pace quickened, the choppy step bounced him until his whiskery face was a blur. He said, "I know you, Gan Moondark."

Gan answered and saluted with equal formality. He hid a smile as the man confidently maneuvered his donkey into place beside him. Looking down at his new companion, Gan said, "What are you doing around here? You must have heard we're going to fight Altanar. You're not one of those human coyotes that picks over the bodies on a battlefield, and there's no trade around here now, so what could interest you?"

The bright, grass-green eyes danced. "Peddlers always find a way to profit, young Murdat. Even in war things are bought and sold, don't you know."

Gan's face hardened into unforgiving planes. "Slaves?"

"Never. No real Peddler does that. Nor robs the dead. Many are called Peddlers who aren't. Because a man buys and sells and lives from hand to mouth doesn't mean he's one of us. We have our rules."

Again Gan turned away to hide a smile. He wasn't quite fast enough. Bilsten said, "Don't be too quick to underestimate those who'd befriend you.

I'll give you a sample of what I might sell to one who would be King." He chuckled hugely at Gan's surprise, then went on, "If your cavalry's worth a moth-eaten rabbitskin, they'll be riding up from the south in about an hour, all lathered up about finding a big Olan camp drawn up straight across your advance."

"You saw them? They know we're coming?"

"Yes and yes. Their cavalry will have run into yours by now. By the time you reach them, your surprise will have flown." He grew serious, tugging at his beard. "They outnumber you at least three to one. And Likat will be here with another five hundred of your people by sunset."

"So many? He left the main camp undermanned. That's dangerous. And I hear we've had casualties." He related the Messenger's story of the war-horse.

Bilsten said, "It's worse than you've heard. Likat abuses the best qualities of the warriors. Any who show reluctance to fight for him are accused of cowardice. He has bullies who challenge any who disagree with him. The fights are never fair, but you know how proud your men are. Clan distrusts clan; his bullies set one against another, and then he comes around as the peacemaker. Most of the tribe would like to get rid of him, but there again he has them by the throat. He's the *leader,* don't you know. The Devils have done them so much damage, the good men are afraid to split the tribe even more by opposing him openly. If one man was to step forward, he'd have to know he had support from somewhere else." The last was delivered with significant emphasis, and once it was said, Bilsten was silent.

When Gan turned to look down at him, bright green eyes met his gaze with blunt challenge. Gan believed he saw something else there, too. He thought at first it was hope, but what reason could Bilsten have for hoping he'd help the Dog People? Still, he felt compelled to reassure the bearded man. More than that, he found himself wanting to confide in him. Virtually forcing words past an outraged sense of propriety, he explained his battle plan to him, finishing by revealing his intention to organize the two king-doms and the Dog People into one entity. Bilsten asked about the Mountain People, and Gan made a brushing gesture. "Either they join us and act like men or they'll be driven out. Imagine it, Bilsten; from the Whale Coast to the land of the Buffalo Eaters, from the Sea Stars all the way to the Mother River—people living without fear."

Long seconds stretched into long minutes before either spoke again. Again, as he'd felt a need to talk to Bilsten, now Gan felt obliged to wait for him to respond to all he'd told him. Rather than an answer, however, he received a question. "Is there anything more important to you than this ambition, young Murdat? Think carefully. Be sure of your own mind."

Gan felt his neck grow hot. He tried to keep the anger from his voice. "My wife. If I fail to free her, let the tribes find their own fate."

"Ah." The sound was barely audible over the drums, yet it had the savor of satisfaction. Without looking at Gan, Bilsten asked, "Once more, I ask you to search your soul for an answer. Only utter truth can help us here. Is there anything you would hold more precious than that?"

"Nothing." Gan snapped the word. He stared ahead at the cracking pennons. The heavy silence between them echoed with unspoken thoughts. Gan coughed. "I spoke in haste," he said, apology and pride clashing. "Honor is more important. Not just to me; to her, as well. We couldn't live dishonorably."

Bilsten said, "I believe you. Perhaps your mother was right." He laughed, the bright amusement surprising after so much seriousness. "My, won't that make some angry."

Gan demanded an explanation of the remark, and in response Bilsten dug in a saddlebag. Holding out two cupped hands so only Gan could see what he held, he said, "You've heard of this."

Sylah had shown them her smaller version of the Iris Abbess' bracelet, and Gan recognized this one immediately. The dragonfly was there, the amethysts. Before he could collect his wits to ask questions, Bilsten spoke. "Hear a tale, Murdat. Forget your little war for a few minutes and learn exactly where you are in the storm that tosses all of us. In the time when living men still remembered where the sacred cities had stood, when radeath still struck down the unwary and the godkills were certain death, Church was born of woman. She created Healers, then War Healers. She established rules for life, ceremonies for death. Last, she created Teachers. Everyone knows what happened after that, but one of Church's secrets has been the existence of survivors. Church saw the Teachers were doomed. Some were men."

Gan jerked away from Bilsten, who continued to ride straight ahead, unperturbed. He said, "Teachers who aren't allowed to teach are rather like Dog warriors who've lost their honor, don't you know. But they decided to find another function. We, who are of their blood, have worked with Church all these centuries, exploring, organizing, preparing the way for the missionaries, providing whatever small service we can." He turned the sparkling eyes on Gan, and there was such pride in them Gan was moved despite his near overwhelming astonishment at what he'd heard.

Stupidly, Gan could only find one word. "Peddlers?"

"The same. Despised, outcast, alone. How else could we continue to serve Church? And there are others. An even smaller number left the home of the Teachers as smiths. Many perished, burned by radeath, taken by disease, ambushed and killed before their abilities were known to their killers.

Enough survived to spread various capabilities. Some were called Siahs. Not all smiths are descended from them, of course, but there are some who trace their line back that far. One is Saband Guyd."

"Ha!" Gan pointed at him. "Now I know you lie. Saband? Church? He barely acknowledges the One in All at sunrise."

Dryly, Bilsten asked, "Would you have him sing hymns and wear a cross?"

Gan nearly fell out of his saddle, whirling around to make sure no one overheard. Shara whined anxiously, unable to determine the reason for his master's concern. Gan whispered hoarsely, "Don't mention such things in front of me! What if I told someone?"

Bilsten shrugged. "My life's already in your hands."

"I don't want it!"

"Ah, but I want yours. You've been discussed, Gan Moondark, and chosen." He hesitated, then plunged on. "A man who drifts at the whim of a prophecy disturbs many. Still, I'm ordered to share certain knowledge with you—as I have done—and provide certain services. In return for these things, you swear on your honor to maintain our secrets."

Gan's head throbbed. He said, "The roses on Sylah's door. You did that."

He nodded. "I had to frighten her. Everything had gone wrong. And I sought you out in your camp to help you over the mountains. I was lucky to find you."

"What do you want of me?"

"Now? Nothing. On the contrary, I'm here to help you more. Saband Guyd is with Likat. If you promise to help Church in future, whenever called on, I will ride to him with your promise to march directly to the Dog camp after you've broken Altanar's army. I can guarantee he'll lead the bulk of the Dog warriors out of the battle."

A tight smile failed to reach Gan's eyes. "My first mission is to free Neela and Sylah. I may fail. I may free them and fail to destroy Altanar. And I have no idea what Church will ask of me."

Bilsten said, "We believe you'll succeed here. As for Church's request, you must trust her. As I have trusted you."

They were into an area that had enjoyed much less rainfall than others. The fields were parched, and the road was thick with a fine, floury dust. There was no escaping it. The drums were silent, as though sulking. The dry cloud settled on everything, including Gan's lips. He tasted it, hot, almost crisp in its dryness. There was a ripe flavor to it, a hint of the good things that grew from it.

He said, "My destiny is to bring glory to the people. My parents said so. Tell Saband if I live, I will come. We will crush Likat."

Bilsten said, "Now I will tell you what I was required to hold back until you agreed. The Devils are gathering for a final raid on the Dog camp. Saband and his men will come on them by surprise. Your people will be saved. Likat will fall in due course."

Pale, shaking, Gan said, "You would have let my people be massacred?"

Coldly, Bilsten said, "Your prophecy has two roads. You must ever choose. We have decided to walk beside you, so long as we benefit each other."

"You tempt me, Peddler. No one—not even Church—plays with me. Another time I would cut you in half. Now . . ." He took a deep breath. "Warn Saband." Gan called a messenger and ordered him to take Bilsten to the cavalry relief mounts, gruffly adding he wanted him moving at better than donkey speed.

In the distance two horsemen flew toward Clas, leaving coiling whirls of dust behind. Gan looked at the position of the sun. His conversation with Bilsten had lasted almost exactly an hour.

He closed his eyes, closed the issue from his thoughts. There was a battle to be fought.

I'm coming. He held his breath, imagined the words flying to her. In his imagination he saw them, tiny, precise, iridescent as hummingbirds. They hovered by her ear. She heard the throaty buzz of the near-invisible wings and understood. She smiled.

Clas signaled, "Enemy four miles ahead."

Gan threw back his head and howled. The men stared at him. One cheered. Then they all joined him. The chorus swept the column, end to end, repeating. It rose and fell, confident, challenging, riding on the booming approval of the drums.

CHAPTER 81

Leaning against a tree, alone with Shara and Cho, Gan watched the fifty handpicked men of the Jalail pack conducting a last-minute equipment check. A thin sliver of new moon provided barely enough light. They grumbled about it, as soldiers grumble about everything, but they all knew that within the hour that same minimal light would be their best hope of being undiscovered.

If there were any hope at all.

The arrival of the Dog warriors had jeopardized the entire scheme.

The opposing armies were drawn up on opposite sides of a large, flat area, cultivated for table crops. During the last hours of daylight they sparred with each other. Dashes of cavalry collided between the poised forces. Their war cries and shouts eddied over the fields in the confused, passionate clamor of combat. The foot soldiers, required to hold place, reacted like tethered animals. Fear and blood lust touched each one, even as they counseled each other against the dangers of both. Occasionally a potential hero would break from the masses of foot soldiers, racing out ahead of his friends, beating his shield, singing a war chant or screaming challenges. Sometimes an opposing soldier would respond in kind. A great, feverish surge would move both armies. Beastlike, the formations would strain toward each other. That brought the officers galloping forward to restore order. They hauled on their reins. Horses bowed their necks and pranced with exaggerated ardor. The overwrought champions trotted back to their respective units. Their friends praised them and whooped.

As darkness fell, a line of fires grew across the front of each army. Silhouettes of men, batlike in their rush and flurry, dodged past the flames on their way to outpost positions. Most hid, cautious as mice, happy to look and listen. The best of them prowled aggressively. They were the stalkers, men whom other men—even their squadmates—spoke of in the careful mix of pride and fear that men afford those who prey on other men.

Earlier, during daylight, the Wolf commanders had looked out over the fields unhappily. Only an occasional house or small grove of fruit trees broke the monotony of the plain. Level ground without cover favored the largest numbers, and the Wolves were sorely in the minority. In addition, the Olan commander had chosen his ground well. Aware of the Wolves' ability to maneuver in combat, he'd stretched his line between a scrub thicket on his left and an old-growth forest on his right. Emso's scouts reported the scrub forest was regenerating after a large burn. It was a mix of young trees, bamboo, and briers, virtually impenetrable save for narrow, aimless game trails.

Initially, Gan and Clas congratulated each other on one piece of good luck. The old forest might interfere with troop movement during a battle, but it was an excellent avenue for their planned night move around the Olans.

Then the Dog warriors came. They took position on that flank. Again Emso's scouts did outstanding work, determining that the Dogs had positioned Nightwatchers in the forest.

It was still possible to get around them, but only by riding farther east before turning south. And time was already a precious commodity.

That thought was uppermost in Gan's mind as he moved to inspect the horses tied to picket lines behind him. They, too, seemed to understand that something unique was taking place. They munched their grain with much tossing of heads. The moon gleamed from their eyes.

The raiding party wouldn't actually mount and ride until daybreak, when they'd be well beyond Olan lines. They would lead the animals in two columns on a route Emso's best scouts were marking.

Darkness and speed were their allies. Gan hoped to gain them another—terror.

He made his way to where the kite fliers waited for his orders. The men were ebullient. The wind was almost perfect, their confidence in their equipment unquestioning. Gan wished he were half so optimistic.

They were organized in five-man teams, one launcher to four fliers. At his orders they dispersed, spreading out to cover most of the front. Gan took a place next to a flier and watched the launcher move toward the Olan lines until he disappeared in the darkness. After an impatient wait, the flier jerked to sudden action. He leaned back, unconsciously lifting his chin, exactly as if watching the kite swinging up into its accustomed sunny sky. A moment later he turned to Gan, white grin gleaming against the blur of his features. "She's up, Murdat. You can see her, if you look close—black against the stars."

Gan twisted his head and peered. He never actually saw anything, but an invisible presence blinded stars and moved on. It gave him an uncomfortable feeling in the pit of his stomach.

Clas had the raiders organized in their twin columns when he returned. In an hour the whistles would be wheeling up the kite strings. Without speaking, Clas reached to grasp Gan's shoulder. Gan did the same. For a long second they remained in contact, and then they moved to head the columns.

Gan kept the dogs close as they walked. Emso's men had used small strips of white cloth to mark an excellent trail that permitted a rapid pace. The even breeze that lifted the kite so nicely was an asset now, too, as it murmured through the treetops. The noise of the columns, never loud, would be masked. Hopefully, the Nightwatchers and their dogs would hear nothing. If they did, there was the hope that their lack of experience in this place would convince them it was only the wind.

By the time they had made the turn south, Gan was ready to believe there would be no problems.

Then they heard the warning bark from downwind.

Hackles rose on his neck. He stopped to listen, murdat in hand. The dogs trembled, cocking their heads, ears flicking rapidly. They'd heard a Night-watcher's whistle.

Slowly, Gan resumed the march for two hundred yards before he saw the figure. When it moved, there was more disturbance near it, as if the darkness itself wavered.

Gan caught his breath. He was looking at a Nightwatcher and his dogs. Reaching for Clas' hand, he signaled that he was going forward. Clas grabbed at him. Gan eluded him.

Shara and Cho were against his legs, growling steadily, a bass heaviness, a thing he felt in his bones rather than heard. He touched them to stop their noise.

The figure remained immobile. Suddenly, it crouched, and Gan prepared to charge.

A young man's voice, so strained it threatened to crack, said, "Speak your name!"

"I'm Gan Moondark." He cast his voice low, and still it sounded like a war drum. "I don't know you."

"I know you, Gan. I'm Darbannen Vayar, son of Gonmall. Saband Guyd sent me."

"I know you, Darbannen." The formality in these circumstances sent laughter racing up Gan's throat. He managed to choke it back. They were close enough to speak directly by then. Behind each of them, dogs strained against ingrained discipline. Clas came up beside Gan and more introductions were exchanged. The Nightwatcher said, "Saband Guyd said I should look for scouts marking a trail. I watched them pass south. I was hoping it was you when I called out."

Gan asked, "What word from Saband?"

"All Nightwatchers and almost all Dog warriors will leave in the night with him. He thanks you for warning him of the Devils. We'll welcome them."

Just as he finished, a blood-curdling screech ripped the dark sky to the west. Shock pitched Darbannen's voice upward, as scratchy as the sound of his murdat scraping free of the scabbard. "What's that?"

"Something we prepared for Altanar's army," Gan said. The screaming noise was joined by another. Vaguely, they heard shouts. "Go back to Saband. Tell him I said Darbannen Vayar is as brave as any Dog warrior ever born, and tell him I'll join my people soon."

Darbannen stammered. "I can't say that, Murdat. You embarrass."

Gan said, "Would you embarrass me? Am I to be disobeyed? Go."

The Nightwatcher's dogs growled at the sharpness of the command, but the youngster snapped orders at them, and they melted into the forest with him.

Clas said, "The luck is with you. Pray we keep it."

They led the column forward with a quickened pace.

In the silvering light of dawn, the general of the Olan forces received the shocking information that his right flank was now manned by a mere fifty-eight Dog warriors. When he went to sleep, there were hundreds of them. Worse, his officers were slinking into his tent from every unit to report massive numbers of men missing, fled from the terrible spirit-shrieking above them. Officious protectors sneered as they described how many captured deserters they'd turned over to their units. The general ached to point out that they, too, were able to escape the worst of the noise by chasing them, but he didn't. He reminded himself that no man lived to his age by debating with protectors. Anyhow, even with the losses, the Wolves were massively outnumbered.

He took up his position in the observation tower he'd had constructed for himself. What he saw reaffirmed his battle plan.

The Wolves were drawn up in a very conventional formation, prepared to defend. It was what he expected, what he would have done.

First, he'd send the heavy cavalry to break through the position, then lighter cavalry, including the remnants of the Dog savages—Altanar had been very specific that they must take heavy losses. They would penetrate, then wheel and attack from the rear. Finally, he would throw the infantry at them to finish the job.

If it was unimaginative, it was certainly solid. It had always succeeded in the past. Nevertheless, the efficiency of the Wolf units in matching his new dispositions disturbed him. He massed his cavalry; they bowed their line so his men would have to run a gauntlet. He moved archers forward to fire into the formations and disrupt them; Wolves moved forward and attacked, forcing them to defend themselves and muffling their effectiveness.

The accursed signal flags never seemed to stop flitting, keeping him checked. It was irritating. However, the cavalry were almost in position, apparently recovered from the fear of the previous darkness, eager to charge. He gave the signal to advance.

Then a strange thing happened. Men carrying large, colored boxes ran out from the Wolf positions. More amazing yet, they turned their backs on his lines and stood there, holding the silly boxes off the ground. When they lifted, he cursed bitterly.

The screaming in the night! Of course, kites. Anger burned his face. They'd made a fool of him once, and now they thought they could do it again. He watched the cavalry's pace speed up and smiled grim satisfaction. In a few minutes the real games would begin.

The archers expended their arrows and fell back. The long, glinting lances of the cavalry reached forward.

The general had dismissed the silent, lumbering kites. When one of his personal slaves at the foot of the tower pointed overhead and shouted "Look!" he thought the man had gone mad. Then he saw the rocks falling. They seemed so slow. For a moment he dared hope they'd come down behind the unsuspecting cavalry.

It was not to be. Horses and riders dropped in writhing, screaming heaps as the missiles crushed armor, bone, flesh. Clouds of arrows flew from the Wolf lines, striking down more riders. The confusion grew worse. More kites sloped across the sky to drop their loads on the collapsing cavalry charge.

Men looked overhead, dropped their lances and retreated.

The attack was faltering. In the cries of the wounded and dying, the general heard his future at Altanar's hands. He shouted for an all-out attack. The protectors, stationed behind the units, broke out their whips and repeated the demand. The army sluggishly rolled forward. Halfway to the Wolves, it received its baptism from the kites. True to Gan's analysis, they took their losses and pressed ahead. Those who saw their friends die were in a different mood now. Shields came up higher. Swords were drawn in anticipation.

The smaller kites rose and darted toward them, their knife blades hanging like wasp stings. The Olans were ready by then. The new threat did little damage, as the marching men watched them eagerly, like foxes waiting for chickens. Each time a kite dove to slash at them, they slashed back. In minutes there were no more kites in the sky. When the last one dropped, the great war horns signaled the charge. Arrows from both armies whirred through the air like conflicting flocks of murderous birds. Cheering, the Olans ran to the assault. Howling, the Wolves rose to meet them.

Wolf signal pennants danced in the air. The blast of whistles came to the general as faint calls. Drumbeats changed. The general gripped the rail of his tower, exultant. The entire Wolf line was falling back. Then he noted that their cavalry was protecting their flanks very well, even managing an occasional flurry against his own. And the large kites were being pulled in. Some were already on the ground, far to the rear of the lines. It seemed they were being readied to fly again.

Some Dog warriors pulled their horses around in wild circles and rode from the field. They shouted and gestured at him. He couldn't discern their words, but when a squad of protectors ran up to them, whips in one hand, swords in the other, the Dogs calmly arrowed them before they could even turn and escape. Other Dogs joined in the departure.

It occurred to the general that, if Altanar lost this battle, his kingdom was finished. The possibility had never crossed his mind before.

Gan Moondark's reputation as an accommodating victor was well known.

The general reached inside his mask helmet to rub his suddenly aching temples.

Chapter 82

Gan looked out to sea at Wal's balance bar. A white feather of wake marked her passage, but it was a frail thing, nothing like the boiling swirl that trailed her when she first appeared. Then, water had flung away from her bow, fierce and slashing. Now it coiled off in small waves that lapped back into the sea almost as soon as they were born. He said to Clas, "They're still falling behind."

"I know." The voice was grim. "It's going to be a hard fight without Tate's fifty and Conway's extra weapons. There's plenty of wind here. Why not there?"

Gan ignored the unanswerable. "At least there's no sign of pursuit yet. We'll make the best time we can and hope they arrive in time to help."

The plan called for the seizure of Olan boats to use in their escape. Without Wal's men to supervise Wolf crewmen, there was no hope for success in that direction. Worse, the mounted raiding party's horses needed replacement. After such a sustained effort, they couldn't last if pursued. It wouldn't be enough to free the women; without fresh mounts, escape would end when chase began.

Realizing that time was slipping away from them once again, Gan pressed the pace. As the miles disappeared under the steady beat of hooves, he remembered the night, so long ago, when they sought the strangers who were under attack by the Devils. He'd felt part of the darkness then, invisible and invincible. This was different. He concentrated on the road, but faceless, formless monsters of defeat roamed his imagination, threatened him, threatened Neela. He acknowledged the fear, then looked beyond it.

He thought of Neela and how her life was support to another life. Her mind and beliefs are yours, a voice said; nothing is worse than life without secure honor. Yet another voice whispered as urgently. It was quieter, contained. It said: You can never compare your honor with hers. Neela must protect her child. You think of kingdoms, while your wife thinks of sun and stars and all below them. Would you buy a kingdom at the price of your child? Would you buy it at the price of Clas'? If not those children, which ones? Men are dying for your ideas now. More will die. For peace? For your people? *For Gan?*

The voices nagged at him, arguing. The words of his mother's prophecy were brands that flared in his thoughts.

He wanted Neela. He wanted his child.

He looked at the stranger shaking his arm, and recoiled, ready to defend himself. It was a matter of an instant, and in that time he recognized Clas, saw his concern. He pulled free. "I'm all right," he said. "I was thinking."

Clas raised an eyebrow but made no comment. Instead he pointed through the edge of the forest. "The town," he said. "We go around or through."

"Through." Gan didn't hesitate. "Wal's pictures showed that the town will hide us until we're within two hundred yards of the castle wall." He halted the column while still in cover and rode down its length, personally thanking everyone. Neela was his wife, no kin of theirs, he said. He could only appreciate what they were about to do. "The men guarding the castle are Altanar's animals," he said. "They're the torturers, the cell masters, the bulk of the protectors. They know what their lives are worth if the people get their hands on them. This will be a vicious fight. We will win it."

They broke out of the forest at a gallop, flying at the north gate, storming through while the guards were still fumbling with the winch to lower it. Once inside they simply cut down anyone who offered resistance, and then they were pounding down the streets. At first the scattering townspeople cursed and shouted, but as soon as they realized this was an attack on the castle, many poured back outside to shout encouragement. The noise roused the castle guards. They barely had time to drop the gate before the Wolves were dividing in two separate columns, each racing parallel to the wall, firing arrows at the increasing numbers manning the embattlements above.

At Clas' command three men raced directly at the thick wooden door. Other Wolves concentrated their arrows on the small towers flanking it. In seconds the black powder was emplaced, the fuse lit, and the trio were retreating.

The engineers who built the walls had anticipated attempts to burn it. In the silence that followed the placing of the explosives, a new sound carried to Gan, a high-pitched, regular squeaking. Suddenly, a stream of water flew from an arrow port in each of the twin towers, spraying the gate. The fuse was extinguished immediately.

The defenders were much encouraged by the failure. They cheered loudly.

Red-faced, Clas snatched the taper from the man holding it and galloped forward, ignoring Gan's shouts. When it was apparent Clas wouldn't be deterred, the unit rushed forward as one, unleashing a blizzard of arrows to protect him. Hunched against the continuing torrent, protecting the taper with his body, Clas leaped from his horse and pulled his waterproof shelter from his saddlebag. He ran the last few yards, then crouched over the jars and relit the fuse under the protective cloth.

Again the Olans jeered and laughed when they saw their enemy scurrying off. Water and arrows continued to spew from the towers, one of the latter dealing Clas' mount a glancing blow as he remounted. Its pained leap nearly unseated him, but then they were both cleanly away.

The Wolves fastened all eyes on the mounded blanket. No smoke was visible. Clas kneaded his tattoo while mouthing silent exhortation.

At the sound of the explosion, the gate seemed to move back from its fittings and hang in the air, suspended by sound and bright orange-yellow light. Then, as if it had absorbed all the force of the powder into itself and couldn't hold it, it flew apart. Shattered timbers whirred like hunter's throwing sticks. Smoke and dust rolled from the broken portal in a mix of white and brown that melded and blended in billowing softness. One tower fell backward into the castle grounds. The other leaned drunkenly. Howling Wolves were pouring through while pieces of gate were still falling. Once inside, the warriors abandoned their mounts to fight on foot.

Most of the castle's defenders had had time to put on their whitened armor. If anything, Gan discovered quickly, he'd underestimated their desperation. They fought with the frenzy of men who know they must win or die. Individual battles whirled across the grounds, in and out of buildings. What had started as a raid was now a maelstrom of individual duels.

From the balcony off his summer quarters on the west side of the castle, Altanar and Likat were admiring the view toward the Whale Coast when the messenger arrived to tell of the battle under way at the Harbundai border. The news pleased Altanar. He confessed mild surprise at the boldness of Gan's maneuver, but dismissed it with a flick of his hand. "They achieved no great tactical advantage," he said, "and we have them vastly outnumbered. My men wear far more armor. I hope the Wolves fight well. The more that die today, the fewer to deal with later."

He paused at that point. The growing malevolence in his expression drew a speculative frown to Likat's features. Altanar, unaware of his guest's heightened interest, continued his remarks, staring out to sea. He spoke softly, the words clearly for his own benefit. "I want the strangers alive. All of them, even the black bitch and the religious. But especially the ones who betrayed me. I gave them everything, treated them as honored guests. They shared nothing. Took all, gave nothing. Shamed me. Oh, yes—I want them to live.

For me. So I may learn what they know. They will tell me as I show them all my little secrets. Slowly. Lovingly."

Uncertainty clouded Likat's face, and Altanar brought out a comradely smile to reassure his ally. "And you shall have anything else, my brave friend. Neela, of course. Gan, Clas—if they survive. And a generous share of loot."

Abandoning the attempt to draw Likat into conversation, he sent for his armor and dressing slaves, before ordering breakfast. Likat refused to have any. The continuing surliness troubled Altanar. He'd assumed the Neela woman was simply a hostage until Likat arrived the previous night with his escort in tow. It had been a nasty shock to discover the gaudy-clean savage coveted her for his own. There was a certain amusement in such self-deception, though. What woman could be attracted to such a strutting fool? The half-shaved, half-braided head alone would make her laugh. He almost smiled, remembering the Dog woman's spirit. (What was her name? Neela. Easily forgotten.) It was unfortunate she'd conceived so quickly. She'd been stimulating.

Now it was necessary to keep Likat away from her for just a little longer. He was proud of the persuasion he'd used until then. Reasoning with an animal took skill.

The start of the battle was a blessing, in that regard; it offered the perfect excuse for getting him out of the castle.

Until later. He'd see his prospective bride. Under the proper circumstances. An amusement to complete the destruction of Gan Moondark and all the Dogs.

He continued to talk as the slaves put on his armor, taking pleasure from Likat's increasing irritation. Fools are always so full of their own intense selves, he thought; they have no sense of others' feelings.

The King was ever obliged to present an appearance and know he was admired and feared. He inspected himself in the several mirrors held by the slaves, brushing dust from the gold-and-silver-decorated steel armor. The helmet was wondrously formed in the likeness of a shark's mouth. He peered out through the steel teeth that formed a cage to protect his face. A razor-edged dorsal fin jutted from his backplate. Smaller fins at each shoulder were to deflect blows at his neck. They would also slash anyone if he threw himself at them. He took the steel-handled mace offered him. The shark theme was repeated in the iron teeth of its head and upper handle. He swung it in a whistling arc, scattering the slaves. He toyed with the idea of using it. It felt cold, dangerous.

Sneaking a glance at Likat, he felt almost sorry for the man. He was so primitive. His mask helmet was clumsily made, if sturdy, and decorated with bear claws, of all things. It was hanging open now, a bear face when the two halves were swung together and joined. He sighed. It was so primitive.

He was taking a sweating mug of grape juice from a slave's tray when the first sounds of Gan's attack came to them. Likat frowned uneasily. Altanar pretended not to see it, saying, "Some fools from the city must have heard of the battle and come to annoy the guards on the walls. They'll be taken care of in a few minutes."

Likat frowned. "I want to see Neela, then we ride north. I dislike having my people in a fight without my presence."

The noise increased. There were louder shouts inside the walls as the protectors mustered their men.

Altanar smiled for his guest. He hefted the mace and clapped a hand on the hilt of his sword. "First let's test our weapons on those making the noise." He was sure once the savage tasted blood, he'd forget everything else.

The vibrations of the explosion reached them an instant before the sound. They swayed, paralyzed for a moment, making them study each other with goggling, senseless fish eyes. Likat recovered first. "Lightning weapon!" he shouted, shoving Altanar out of the way, rushing for the door. He called for his men.

Gan and Clas fought side by side, cutting their way to Altanar's part of the castle with workmanlike determination. Shara and Cho lunged and retreated, harrying, mad with excitement. When Clas dodged a flying spear and tripped, it was Cho who placed herself squarely in front of him, defying the three swordsmen who rushed to finish him. When Clas rose, she already had one of them by the sword arm, spinning him away from his companions. In seconds all three were finished and Cho was back at Shara's side, working with Gan.

They entered the castle through the main door of the King's Hall, barely managing to catch it before it shut. Inside, they found protectors pouring in through the door at the far end. Gan hurriedly called for help. Those Wolves able to break away came running.

The fight took on a nightmare quality. The white protectors loomed in the half light, and every sound echoed ominously. Wounded men screamed; the walls repeated it over and over. Sound became a weapon, striking at the heart of attacker and defender indiscriminately. Soon, however, the Wolves had the protectors retreating.

Altanar, Likat, and the six Dog warriors ran into the room through the door leading to Altanar's quarters. At the sight of them, both Gan and Clas roared war cries. Two Dog warriors froze in alarm. They looked to Likat briefly, then sheathed their murdats and disappeared back the way they'd come. Altanar shouted at the protectors. The words were swallowed in the tumult, but four men abandoned the struggle and ran to him. They all disappeared through the door.

Gan forced his way past the last men between him and the escaping group. Clas was close behind. They hurried down the hall, kicking doors open as they went. Beyond one they discovered a huddle of slaves waiting to be slaughtered, but no sign of Neela. At one empty room, however, Cho whined and balked. Gan reached for her collar, then he, too, stopped. Shara charged into the room, barking. Finding no one, he circled rapidly before stopping in front of a closed wooden cabinet. Gan yanked it open. Neela's blouse and skirt hung there, mocking him with tantalizing familiarity.

Almost before Gan could finish the command to seek, they were past him, hurtling down the hallway, scrabbling sideways on the smooth stone as they turned the corner. Gan and Clas ran as hard as they could to keep up. Clas shouted, "I saw nothing of Sylah's."

Gan nodded. He didn't want to think of the implications. The dogs were just ahead now, clawing at a door. The men threw themselves at it, with no appreciable effect. Again and again they battered it with their heels, finally shattering the jamb. Bursting in, they found only an old woman, struggling to get to her feet. The side of her face was swollen and the petal-fine skin was already an ugly blue-gray. Her hair was awry. She reached for something to pull herself erect, and Gan noticed her hands were almost doubled into fists. He rushed to help her to a chair. She said, "They came with Neela. Took Sylah. I found out, you see. Made them let me nurse her. Myself. She's the one. I know. Always knew."

"She's babbling," Gan muttered, reaching to touch her shoulder, and the old woman froze him with a look. Just as suddenly, she was sly, bent forward confidentially. Gan stepped back. She went on, pointing a crippled hand at the far wall, "Over there. A passage. It leads to a warehouse. They'll try to bargain with your wives. Hurry! Catch them."

The wall was solid stone. Gan and Clas exchanged meaningful glances. The dogs, however, were already attacking it as fiercely as they'd attacked the door to the room, rearing on their hind legs, scratching and barking. One of them touched the right spot. A section of the wall creaked open. Both men lunged into the gap. Gan held Shara's collar. There was no light, no sound but their own progress. The rock sweated a stink of long-trapped moisture and decay. Still, the dogs led with eager whines.

After what seemed an eternity of bumping through the slimy passageway, they were aware that the air took on a fresher quality. Once they thought they heard voices, and stopped, listening, holding their breath. A few yards farther it happened again, and they knew the chase was coming to an end. In the dark neither could see the other heft the murdat in his hand, check the accessibility of his shortknife, and make a quick Three-sign.

The tunnel exit was still open, a door into a warehouse larger than Gan had ever seen. Trade goods were stacked higher than a man's head for at least fifty yards in front of them and half that distance on both sides. Alleyways separated stacks. At the far end Altanar and Likat were almost to the door to the outside.

"Stop!" Gan shouted, leaping from the tunnel. The group turned. The women, bundled in blankets, were each carried by two protectors at the wrists and ankles. At the sight of their pursuit, the protectors dropped them and drew their weapons.

Altanar moved quickly to stand over Neela, his sword at her throat. "One step," he said. The smugness of the words was intensified by the resonating mask. Gan heard Clas mutter something that might have been a prayer. Altanar added, "One step and she dies."

Neela tossed and moaned, flinging out a hand. Gan was almost overcome with relief. He knew she lived. He lowered his weapon, breathed deeply to steady his voice. "Give us the women and go free. Harm our wives and you die."

"Wives?" Likat brushed past Altanar. "You said wives." It was an accusation.

Neela lay on her side. Gan pointed with his murdat. "That's my child she carries, Likat."

Likat leaned over to glare down at the unconscious form. When he straightened, he turned on Altanar, so enraged he seemed to have forgotten everything else. "You said nothing of pregnancy. You had her bundled up so I couldn't see."

Altanar said, "He lies! It's forbidden for me to touch a pregnant woman. My clan—a bargain with Church." He looked ill. "It's my child. It must be."

Gan flinched at Clas' restraining touch. He knew he must be calm, hold himself back. His heart raced, and it felt as though his throat were closing. Nevertheless, he heard himself flatly, unemotionally claiming his child. He taunted Altanar, telling him that his palace guard was destroyed, adding that he had reinforcements on the way. He finished by pointing out that no matter what happened to their armies, Altanar couldn't leave this place alive without his permission.

Likat suddenly began to shout, raging, unintelligible. He drew his murdat and raised it over Neela's form.

"No!" Gan screamed the word, racing forward. "Don't, Likat!"

One of the protectors moved to save his own life. He grappled with Likat, spinning him around so the murdat swished harmlessly past Neela, striking sparks from the stones of the floor. The other men, confused, milled uncertainly before facing the two men and the dogs. Likat continued to struggle, but the protector had him from behind in a chokehold. Likat was visibly weakening.

Altanar read the scene quickly, and with equal speed put the point of his sword to Likat's throat. Likat's eyes bulged and he went limp. The Dog warriors shuffled indecisively, their eyes darting from him to Gan and Clas, and back to Altanar's equally confused protectors.

Altanar removed his helmet to reveal a fixed smile slashed across waxen features. Sweat poured down his face. His hands shook. There was a pleading whine in his voice when he spoke, and Gan remembered a dog that wagged its tail and wiggled welcome before snapping at his throat. Altanar said, "You made an offer. I accept. I have your word you won't kill me if I turn over the women to you?"

Clas growled. Gan nodded. "You have."

"And a boat from the docks for me and my men?"

"No more." Gan's legs were trying to cramp. His eyes burned. He couldn't tear them from Neela.

"Fair enough." Without a glance in Likat's direction, he leaned into the sword. Likat gasped, a pitiable sound for so treacherous a wound. Altanar moved away just as the stunned protector let go. Likat clutched at his throat, unbelieving, tottering. He took one step toward the light before sprawling on his back.

Altanar wiped his blade on a goods sack. He was sheathing it as he said, "You may have that," pointing with his chin, "as a sign of good faith. He'd have been as much my enemy as yours, so I've done us both a favor. Now, I depend on you to keep your men away while we leave."

Gan hardly noticed Clas slip past him to Sylah. He was concentrating on Altanar's steady, gliding steps toward the door. Only one of the protectors moved to go with him. The man stared constantly at Sylah. Gan realized something was terribly wrong. He said, "Wait. No farther." He put his hand on Clas' shoulder. "Is she—" He couldn't finish it.

Clas was shaking. "She lives," he said. "The baby is gone." He rose slowly, like a force growing from the earth. He took a half step toward Altanar. "My child. You killed my child. I made no promise, King."

Altanar held up his hands. "I tried to help her. You saw—she was with the Iris Abbess. I had her taken there." The protector in front of him twisted to stare in disbelief, quickly looking back at Clas. Terror replaced his original expression. He reached for his sword, opening his mouth to speak. But the shark-toothed mace whispered cruelly just before it struck. There was a metallic crushing sound, and the protector pitched forward. Amazingly, he kept his feet. His face went slack, then bunched in pain. He fell forward.

Altanar dropped the mace. It rang, bell-like, echoing in the warehouse. "There," he said. He shook his hand as though to dislodge something, before going on, "That's the man who failed to feed your wife properly. I accept blame, but not responsibility. He's a Moondancer, an unbelieving fanatic. I stopped him as soon as I could, and I've executed him for his crime. And your king gave me his word for my safety."

Gan looked at Clas, and his friend's misery tore at him. He gestured helplessly. "I didn't know, Clas. I thought only of saving them. Forgive me. Please."

Without answering, Clas once again sank down beside Sylah, kneeling by her. He stroked her hair before scooping her up in his arms. Gan picked up Neela the same way, and they walked out into the sunshine, following the wary Altanar.

The Dog warriors and Altanar's protectors retreated as well, a frightened buffer between the King and the two Dog warriors. Anxious to maintain their now-neutral status, they all sheathed their weapons. Just outside the door, Likat's warriors moved to be together. When the first one slumped to a sitting position, the others hurried to emulate him. They sat with their heads lowered onto crossed forearms that rested on raised knees. Their faces were hidden.

The protectors watched them closely, exchanging looks. As if rehearsed, they moved to join the Dogs. Altanar stood alone. His face flamed and his eyes looked ready to explode from his head. He said nothing, however, but turned and ran toward a small balance bar bobbing some distance down the dock.

Out on the Inland Sea, finally making some way, Wal's vessel approached.

Altanar clambered aboard his escape vessel. As he bent to handle the sail lines, both women stirred. Gan and Clas lowered them. Gan barked an order to the Dog warriors to fashion a white cloth of surrender and go find Healers. They responded instantly, hurried by Shara's growling disappointment at seeing them go.

Neela opened her eyes. For one moment there was surprise, and then she smiled. He kissed her, quickly, gently, and when he pulled away, the smile returned, a thing of confirmed belief as well as happiness. He murmured foolish, wordless things. When he thought to tell her he loved her, the smile tried to form words, and then she was unconscious again.

He barely heard Cho's warning bark, and never saw Clas' sudden move. He only knew that something threw him over backward. He continued the motion, tumbling, springing upright as part of it, murdat in hand.

He was just in time to see the sun-golden blur of the ching's disk before it crunched through Clas' armor. The impact made Clas stumble awkwardly and drop to one knee. In the boat, Altanar was recovering his balance from his throw. The balance bar's sails were already up, straining against the stern line. He hacked it in two. The boat leaped free. Gan could only watch helplessly as it heeled over and whisked away. Altanar's laughter drifted back like a black curse.

Clas was clutching his chest, coughing hard. Blood streamed from under the armor and stained the spittle spraying the dock in front of him. His breath whistled shrilly.

Gan moved to get the ching free. He was able to grasp it by its dull handhold, and he wrapped the tag end of his shirt around the other hand to avoid the sharp edge. Then he pulled. Clas made a sharp, grunting sound and rolled over onto his side before Gan could catch him.

As he stripped off the armor and clothes to expose the sucking chest wound, pictures flashed across his mind, pictures of himself hating Clas na Bale, distrusting his own wife. A few moments later, when the Dog warriors raced up with two War Healers, they all assumed he sat with his wife's head in his lap, crying unashamedly, because he was relieved that his wife and friends lived and was concerned that they were all injured. It never occurred to them that Gan Moondark was ashamed.

CHAPTER 83

Sylah woke to green and gold. Silver points and lines pierced that soft fog, shooting through it to touch her eyes with a pain both wonderful and exciting. Her thoughts were equally inchoate; something in her longed a loss too precious to be borne, while in another sense she felt an unimaginable elation.

No. It wasn't unimaginable.

There had been another time like that.

She tumbled out of the basket with the other children in a knot of cramped arms and legs. She had sores from the rough slats, and her eyes burned from long-exhausted tears and rubbing and lack of sleep. She stood up, and the hard white face inside its nightlike cowl said, "You are Chosen."

Then, as now, she didn't understand what was happening to her. She knew, however, that although a life she loved was finished, she was meant to live.

Again. It was happening again.

Sounds filtered into her growing consciousness. Warbling song, above her. It was the little brown bird with purple-red markings, the one called the wine finch. She remembered. Such a small feat, yet she felt it had a grave importance. She concentrated to see if there were other sounds. There—a bee. Again, somewhere overhead. It moved slowly, left to right. They always moved more slowly when they were cool. Shade, then. Yes, she was outdoors, under trees. A smell of damp earth, the green-acid tinge of crushed cherry leaves on the air.

And then she heard Clas.

She would see. She *would*.

It hurt. Oh, how it hurt. Her head thundered with it. Without meaning to, she made harsh, rasping noises in her throat.

He touched her cheek. A hard hand, the first two fingers thick with calluses from the murdat, from the bow string. The little finger not as supple as the others, the product of a long-ago break. So strong, so gentle.

He said, "Abbess! Look, tears!"

The odd, inconstant light grew dark directly over her face. Of course; she was lying down. Was she injured? Headache. There was dull pain everywhere, but nothing specific. She couldn't be ill, or they'd never let him near her.

Why couldn't she remember?

She forced her mind to her eyes, willed them to focus. The dark center of her vision took form. It was him. She made out the line where dark hair ended, the lighter color of his face. She saw the blackness of the tattoo, told her vision where to find the planes and curves of jaw and nose and lips.

She said, "Clas," and he was kissing her, no heavier than a sigh.

Somewhere—a few feet away? a hundred miles away?—the Iris Abbess was talking. She said, "When the fever went down, I thought we could hope. Now I'm sure. She'll recover. She's been given back to us."

There was strength in the words. She closed her eyes, telling herself that even if she couldn't remember the details, she should accept that a cruel, mind-numbing journey was ended. It was safe to sleep now.

Chosen.

A week later she was sitting up in bed in her room in the healing house, combing out her hair, one eye on the door where he would enter. When he did, it twisted her heart in her chest to see how he favored his left side. She'd only learned of the wound when the Iris Abbess described how she and Neela had been rescued. Meanwhile, he'd brought her up to date on all the things that had happened in the ten days she'd drifted in the empty land between this world and the next.

There had been so much! It was as though she'd been gone for years, not days. She'd especially enjoyed hearing Tate tell of turning Wal's balance bar around and sailing north to disembark behind the Olan lines. Tate got so excited, describing their charge, fifty howling warriors, Conway, and herself, against an army of thousands. Even the Wolves didn't believe it when the lightning weapons started firing and the Olan general surrendered so readily.

And Neela. After all she'd been through, talking so matter-of-factly about telling Gan he owed it to her and to all the Dog people to ride to Saband Guyd's aid. Rescued from Altanar by her husband one day and sending him back into battle on the next. But the weight of the Wolf cavalry had crushed the surprised Devils. The entire tribe was in a headlong retreat north, abandoning everything they couldn't carry. Gan joked about her being his best general. She was more. She was a queen.

A wave of self-pity reared when Sylah thought of Neela. What Altanar had done to her made her cringe inside, but Neela had her child.

Clas had been stoic when she told him how hard she fought for theirs. She didn't tell him how she begged for food, nor of the frustrated, raging, agonized tears. He'd seen the cells for himself, so she never mentioned the darkness that only ended when a torch-bearing protector opened the door to throw in whatever one got to eat. She was sure he'd seen the little bloodsucking insects. It was possible he missed the things that crept from between the rocks to try to share the food, because they always slithered away at the first hint of light. When a wounded soldier passing her room peeked in and told her Clas had ordered the cells walled off forever, she was proud. The rumors that came to her afterward, whispering that he'd found three of the protectors who'd been her guards and put them in the cells before walling up the area, troubled her. Asking him if it was true had been useless. With the look that could still frighten her a bit, he said, "Some people will say anything. Exactly who told you that?" She'd decided it was best to forget.

But when she had to talk, to try to make someone understand what it was like to be alone in unending darkness, to feel the life you'd die for slip away like the frailest leaf in autumn, he listened. He held her in his arms and rocked her, kept her closed away from the things that wanted to crawl back into her brain. He dried her tears and praised her courage and told her he loved her. He helped her see that she deserved to live. He comforted her.

When she made him show her the ugly gash in his chest left by Altanar's ching, she realized how it must have tortured him to hold her as he had. She berated him for letting her hurt him. He grinned.

He was as infuriating as ever.

Right now he filled her door almost as fully as he filled her life. He said,

"The Abbess says I can take you for a longer walk today. All the way to the bluff, so you can see the sea. Just as you asked."

"You bullied her."

Indignantly, he straightened. "I did not. It was her idea."

"I'm glad. I am stronger, you know."

"Patience." Concern furrowed his brow. "She also said you'd try to do too much."

She turned her head, looked at him from the corner of her eye. "What do you think, husband? When should I try to do too much?"

He knew exactly what she meant. It was mean to tease him so, but such fun. His thoughts ran across his features the way wind rippled wheat. And, in his abashed way, he enjoyed the teasing as much as she did.

She resolved to eat more, exercise more. Strength couldn't come too quickly.

When they reached the bluff, they were surprised to find Gan there alone. The dogs lay nearby, while, unaware of their approach, Gan threw stones out over the edge, watching them arc and plunge to the driftwood piles on the beach below. Sylah was surprised at Shara; he seemed to have grown larger, and his coat was so rich it almost glowed. Cho favored them with a quick wag of her tail, then shifted closer to Shara, making deep contented sounds.

Gan saw them when he bent for another stone. He smiled to see Sylah, and for a while they talked about her recovery and steady improvement. It was apparent, though, that he was troubled. Indicating to Clas that she wanted to sit down, Sylah bluntly asked him what was on his mind.

For a moment he stumbled about, not actually denying a problem, but unwilling to address it directly. Finally he threw up his hands. "If I can't talk to you two about it, I can't talk to anyone," he said. "It's the tribe. This thing with Likat has affected them more than you can imagine. They're not the same, Clas. You know how it is if you let a young dog go at a bear before he understands exactly what a bear is, or if he's sent into a battle when he's not properly trained. You damage him, take the heart out of him."

Clas bristled. "You're saying our men have lost their courage."

"No. It's more like the whole tribe is embarrassed, as if they've lost confidence in their ability to lead themselves. I would never have believed it could happen so fast. A warrior told me just this morning that the big argument splitting them now is over who's responsible for letting Kolee slip away. Everyone knows she was the force behind Likat, but who cares about her? She's helpless now. They have other things to worry about."

"You say that as if you have something in mind."

Gan frowned. "I hope no one else sees through me so easily. Saband Guyd says the Buffalo Eaters are pressing onto our hunting grounds to the east.

Both the horse and cattle herds there are much smaller than he thinks they should be."

"They steal our animals?"

"Perhaps." Gan shrugged. "When you're stronger, I'd like you to visit and see what you think."

He changed the subject then, and Sylah was glad of it. The thought that Clas would go over the mountains sent a surprising shudder through her. She sensed no physical danger to him, but as soon as the words were said, the image of the circled tents and the dominating curve of Earth Heart gave form to her ever-present feeling that he harbored a rival in his heart.

She had always seen combat as the danger, and it shocked her to realize how shallow her thinking had been. Combat affirmed him in his own eyes and the eyes of his people. Now, however, she saw the tribe as the mother and father of that attitude.

In a sense, his love for Gan was her own lifeline. When he fought for Gan, he fought for Gan's vision. So long as Clas stood beside Gan, she shared him with a solitary man, a solitary goal. It was far short of perfection, but it was definable, acceptable.

What if he went back to the tribe as War Chief? Everyone would have their claim on him. He would risk his life for any.

Clas misinterpreted her withdrawal as weariness and insisted he take her back to her room. On the way she asked—as nonchalantly as possible—how he might help the tribe. She held her breath, waiting for his answer.

He rejected the idea out of hand. Saband Guyd wasn't a War Chief, true, but he was a good man. He'd hold the tribe steady until a War Chief made his appearance. One always had, always would.

Meanwhile, Gan's troubles were obvious. He'd mentioned the Buffao Eaters' new aggressiveness, but he hadn't spoken of the talk of an alliance between the defeated and dispossessed Devils and the Salmon River people in the far north. Gan needed time and help to consolidate the kingdom, and the Dog People would have to help, not hinder. Clas' hand worried at the tattoo incessantly as he talked.

She settled onto her bed gladly, suddenly extremely tired.

Clas na Bale would never lead a peaceful life, but at least he wasn't a War Chief, taking bones, constantly expected to display his valor and prowess.

Her eyelids closed of their own weight, but not before she noticed he was running his fingers across the tattoo again.

It was just his habit, she thought; she mustn't read things into every little nervous gesture.

* * *

Conway stood in the middle of the market alleyway, oblivious to the knocks and bumps of the passing crowd. His face was long. He said, "She's not here anymore, Donnacee; that's the last of it."

"She must be." Tate's wide swing of the arm almost knocked a heaped tray of string beans out of a man's hand, and she hurriedly apologized before continuing. "Look at this place. There're hundreds of people here. She could be living with any of them. All the other freed slaves said she never mentioned going back to her people."

"And you know why. That's why I have to find her. I love her. She doesn't believe that. She doesn't believe anyone can love her, after what she went through. She thinks it made her 'unacceptable.'" He spat the word. "Now she's crawled off by herself, hiding out."

Tate hid a sympathetic smile, wishing she could point out the illogicality of arguing with one breath that she'd left the city and with the next that she'd hidden herself in the immediate area. She supposed love had its own reasons for everything.

It had never happened to her. Attractions, yes. Relationships, yes. Love? Someday. Maybe.

Conway was saying, "Let's try this aisle. We haven't been through here yet, have we?"

Shaking her head no, Tate followed him, shifting the wipe to a more comfortable position. Even now, she mused, with the countryside under one rule, life was a tricky proposition in this world. People were evening a lot of old scores, and support for Altanar hadn't evaporated with his disappearance. Many of the old nobles made no secret of their preference for the old days. They were especially clear about it when she was present. Black and female seemed to be twin stigmata that survived the test of centuries. So much for "give it time."

Snapping her chin up, she moved away from those thoughts. What was important was the woman called Tee. She had only Conway's star-struck description to go by, so she found herself scrutinizing every woman a head shorter than herself. Any who had honey-colored hair got a double scrutiny; a pair of blue eyes warranted a tap on his shoulder and a discreet point. So far the best she'd earned in return was a disappointed grunt.

They were outside the food vendor's area then, among the leatherworkers. The redolence of oils, waxes, and hides coiled around them, and she savored it in deep breaths. She slowed to examine a vest that looked just about her size, a piece of exquisitely creamy antelope skin. It was decorated with iridescent fringe at the shoulders, green as emerald. On close examination, she saw it was small pieces of material, cunningly glued to leather strips. The seller cheerfully told her each piece represented a small bee called a wasp killer. She held the piece at arm's length to inspect it more closely, and there, on the far side of the next market alley, she saw the woman who had to be Tee.

The blue eyes bored through the crowd, through the racks of dangling merchandise, through the occasional flaps of cloth hanging down from the overhead fly. Only her head moved, turning to follow Conway.

Tate was afraid to move. Then she realized she had to; the woman could turn and disappear in an instant. She threw down the vest and ran for Conway, heedless of anyone in her way. As soon she could, she shouted directions at him. He turned, puzzled, then looked where she said. On the instant of recognition he vaulted tables of merchandise, scattering belts, purses, and wallets. She could only follow. Behind them, vendors screamed curses that were guaranteed to blight entire family trees.

Tee fled.

Having seen her, Conway wouldn't lose her again. She was quick and nimble, slipping through the crowd like a rabbit racing through a thicket. Conway was more like a runaway boulder plunging downhill. What he couldn't easily go around, he went over. If need be, through. He caught her just as they exploded out the end of the market into a relatively uncrowded street.

Tate slowed, then stopped. Conway had obviously forgotten her. Around her, stall keepers and offended citizens yelled insults at him and Tee. Some were ugly enough to be a little worrisome, even if the two people they were threatening were oblivious.

Tate turned to face the crowd, glad for the solid heft of the wipe. Holding up her hands in a peacemaking gesture, she explained what they were seeing. They looked past her, where Conway and Tee were walking away, still too involved with each other to realize anything else existed. Tate jollied them, offered to pay for damaged merchandise, apologized for bruises to body or ego.

It didn't take her long to soothe them. One by one, then in numbers, they calmed down. Most even refused payment, caught in the romance of what had happened. Soon, Tate was alone. When she looked, Conway and Tee were out of sight.

The others—Janet Carter, Sue Anspach, and Kate Bernhardt—were with Louis Leclerc at the abbey. The old Abbess was working on some scheme that involved them, but she'd been too busy with merging the remnants of the Olan army into the Wolf structure to pay any attention. For that matter, they weren't all that anxious to include her in whatever they were up to. She headed back toward the castle. Maybe Gan would want to ride out and watch training. Or something. She wished Falconer were alive.

Conway didn't even know Tate was gone. All he wanted was Tee, and now he had her. When he was close enough to grip her arm, she stopped, offering no resistance. In fact, he was sure he saw relief in her expression. It seemed to him they stood without speaking for ages, and then he asked, simply, "Why?"

Of course, she knew exactly what he was asking. She didn't answer at first, but half turned, still making no effort to be free of his grasp. She walked and he followed, holding her much more tenderly. She said, "I didn't want to see you again."

He made a noise, inarticulate, and she glanced at him before continuing. Her chin rose, her voice bold. She said, "I don't love you. Why do you bother with me? I don't even know who I am. There are other women; prettier, wealthier, smarter. Find one who loves you."

He said, "I don't want another woman. I love you. I want you."

She shook her head, not answering. When he tried to go on, she held up a hand. "Not now. I have to think."

He said, "You've had months to think."

"That's why I didn't want you to find me. I didn't want to have to try to explain. Now I must, so let me put my words together."

They made their way to one of the rooftop squares. Because it was a market day, the plazalike expanse was almost deserted, with only a few children playing and an old man enjoying the sun on one of the benches. She led the way to one that looked over the city toward the castle, then sat down. He settled on the brick surface in front of her. Staring past him, eyes fixed on the angularities of the distant wall, its towers, and the blunt shapes of the buildings behind it, she told him how her tribe supplied the King a young bride every other year. The King returned her with his child. It was a bond from generations before, when children were the prime necessity of the tribe, and when a strong King was necessary to bind the tribes together.

He interrupted. "I know all that. It's the past, it has nothing to do with us. Gan's canceled all those old tribute laws."

She turned a piercing gaze on him. "It has everything to do with us. I lived through it." Suddenly, she thrust herself so close he instinctively rocked backward. She continued, "No one fought for me, for any of us. From the time I was old enough to understand what was happening until I was in my fifteenth summer, I saw our women inspected like livestock, then saw the 'lucky' one 'accepted' by the protectors and taken away. If the young man who loved her objected, our own people silenced him."

Calming herself, she leaned back, looking to the castle again. She told him how she'd challenged the women of the tribe, swearing that if she was ever picked to be the King's bride, she'd never bear his child. The women who believed it was her duty were so frightened by such defiance they didn't dare mention it. Those who believed defiance was her duty offered her encouragement and tears, the only support they could manage.

By that time she was shivering as if the roof were exposed to winter, rather than summer's sun. He reached to embrace her, and she jerked away violently. Awkwardly, he settled back. She continued, telling him of the torment of her trip from the Whale Coast to Ola. The protectors told her—graphically—what she must do to please the King.

She smiled at Conway, and he turned away from it. Merciless, she said, "I knew what was done. I'd never heard of such variety. Or cruelty. They enjoyed lecturing. Some of the things—"

She bit her lower lip. When she spoke again, it was much softer. "I'm sorry," she said, "but what you saw is what I've become. Because I failed to bear his child, I was given to the protectors. After a time, even the most determined person can be convinced to act a part rather than live in pain. I was never able to hide my hate, though, so they usually sought warmer company. Still, this is my twenty-fifth summer. Ten years of what you might call ready availability. You see why I think another woman would be best for you?"

He stared at the bricks between his feet as if he expected some magical answer to appear there. Finally he said, "I didn't know. I suspected. I knew it had been . . . difficult for you. I'm talking about the world we can make for ourselves."

She leaned over gracefully, extending a hand to brush his hair from his temple. One finger traced the curve of his lip, and when he kissed the tip of it, she shuddered, but made no move to pull it away. She said, "I can't love anyone now, Matt Conway. You have to understand that. I want to love you. I wish I did. I can't. There's nothing good where my heart was. The past still exists there, and it would destroy you. That would destroy me." He tried to interrupt, and she pivoted her hand, covering his mouth. "No. Listen. Live your life. Let me try to find mine. If it's meant to be, we'll meet again. Perhaps things will be different. Perhaps I will."

When she rose, he made no effort to stop her. He got up slowly, and she reached for him with both hands, watching him tower over her. She put her arms around his waist and said, "Kiss me, Matt Conway. Kiss me once, for the girl who should have been. I want to kiss the man who should have been hers."

He didn't open his eyes when she drew apart from him. He let his hands fall to his sides, straining his other senses for her. He heard her steps recede; that took only seconds. Her warmth where she'd pressed against him, the feel of her arms around him—those things lasted a bit longer, perhaps the best part of a minute. Her scent lingered longest, a mix of flowers and sun-touched hair. He cherished them almost desperately, savoring until they were gone, trying to tell himself they still remained when he knew better.

When he opened his eyes, a small boy was watching him curiously. Conway nodded, finding a partial smile he hoped was reassuring. Then he sat on the bench and looked where Tee had looked, to the darkening bulk of the castle.

CHAPTER 84

For Gan the fall and winter months were a time of continuous trial. He had expected contention from his barons and chiefs and was prepared for it, but the pettiness and irascibility of the entire population came as a shock. The Harbundai barons demanded the Olan slavers be handed over to them. The Olan clans steadfastly reported them missing. The Olans were furious because both the Whale Coast people and Harbundai charged Olan ships extra taxes whenever they docked at either place for business. It seemed that absolutely no one, family, clan, tribe, or barony, was satisfied with any particular about boundaries, grazing rights, timber rights, water rights, or anything else. Gan appointed courts and judges by the score. The few written records that existed were sketchy; in most cases, illegible. In a world that distrusted learning and forbade education, the simple act of scratching squiggles on paper was considered toying with dark forces. Those who could read pronounced it acceptable; those who couldn't took their word. These matters, for all their tumult and shouting, however, paled beside the violence of those who found themselves unchained, able to strike back at oppressors. The barons of Harbundai reported little of that activity, but Ola was rife with it. The protectors, in particular, were hunted like animals, run down and eliminated on the spot. Many of the Olan tribal leaders who'd supported Altanar died in the battle that overthrew their king. Many others disappeared, waiting for better times to reappear. The bulk of the nobles, however, those mid-level privileged who'd carried out the orders of their leaders, were suddenly no longer inviolate. It was a time of vengeance, a bloody time. Detachments of Wolves were marched back and forth across the country continually, maintaining order. Gan was surprised at the way Conway threw himself into that function. He volunteered for any mission that took him out of the city, and he proved to be amazingly effective at resolving differences. At first Gan assumed it was the roaring efficiency of the lightning weapon that allowed him to create harmony from discord, but he soon learned that Conway was considerate and adept at bargaining. He managed compromise.

A major problem was the condition of the Dog People. Gan organized pack trains to supply them with dried salmon and other foodstuffs to tide them over to the spring. Clas supervised the long columns, providing Gan with reliable information on the tribe's status. It was tenuous, especially when winter shut down the passes with masses of snow. One train actually made it through during that season, with men on snowshoes pulling loaded sleds. It was a dangerous undertaking, and mutters about Gan's favoritism toward his own people were circulated happily by his enemies. The Moondancers, in particular, did everything they could to irritate that sore spot. Not everyone in Gan's lands had the energy or initiative to improve their lot in a normal manner. Moondancers sought sparks of envy and resentment, carefully fanning them into flames with promises of better times for those willing simply to take what was rightfully theirs.

The thing about the movement that troubled Gan even more than its secrecy or its appeal to the unstable was the shadowy figure of John Jones. He stalked the countryside, preying on minds, conducting ceremonies people shuddered to speak of. More to the point, he preached rebellion. Not an immediate storming of the strongholds of power, but a quiet, shrouded infiltration that destroyed from within. Gan could never hear of one of Jones' unannounced appearances at a Moondance meeting without remembering his intense conviction that the strangers at the mercy of the Devil warriors were to be pivotal in his life. Without Leclerc's invention that battered down the gate to Altanar's castle, there would have been no hope of rescuing Neela and Sylah. Without Tate and Conway's decisive attack on the Olan army's rear, that battle might easily have been a disastrous loss.

That was why he had such a bad feeling about Jones. All the efforts of the strangers had been powerful influences on everything he accomplished. He had to wonder if the one who opposed him might not have an equally adverse affect.

All of that was forgotten for a few brief days in the middle of winter. Clas barely made it over the pass to meet the Dog People and turn over the sleds to them then return between storms. He arrived the day Neela gave birth to a bawling, red-faced son.

Gan declared the first day of spring would be his son's naming day. Ola would stage a fair, a celebration, a gathering of all the people. He promised a new code of laws, and proposed that every barony and every tribe send

representatives to Ola at that time to create an alliance acceptable to all. The
naming day of his son would be the occasion for the formation of a government that acted as a coordinating power, not a dominating one.

The same autumn that saw Gan starting his struggle to unite his disparate
peoples saw Sue Anspach, Kate Bernhardt, and Janet Carter in the Iris
Abbey, resuming their relationship with the Chosens. None of them would
admit it openly, but the children had become central in their lives. They
missed them and wanted to help them. In fact, the children were the lever
of change that allowed Anspach and Bernhardt to accept Carter as one of
their own once again. Forgiveness came easily; they continued to share life
in a place where everything they did carried overtones of deceit and felt her
vulnerability as their own. After a short period of stiff discomfort, the
memory of her collapse gave way to the need for cooperative effort. For
Anspach and Bernhardt, the children provided expression. Janet Carter
found that, and rehabilitation, as well.

A sense of change was in all of them as they debarked from one of Wal's
balance bars. The reunion with the Abbess in her quarters was a joyous event.
At first they were a bit uncomfortable when they discovered the other
woman present was the famous Rose Priestess Sylah. She herself was non-
plused to be called inspiring. However, they established a bond quickly, and
the conversation was warm and friendly. Fall's sharp touch made the crackling fire in the Abbess' receiving room doubly pleasant. A spray of autumn
colors decorated the mantle; crimson and gold maple leaves, hard green
holly, and the softer verdance of fir. Sprigs of blue spruce accentuated the
quiet gray of the stone background. Rich tapestries covered one wall, and
handsome quilts tastefully decorated the others. Colorful, as well as practical,
they held off the chill of the walls.

The Abbess kept to her chair, swaddled in the heavy, jet-black robe of a
War Healer. Hers was decorated at the left breast with the iris symbol. The
cowl, sleeves, and skirt hem were heavily embroidered with a running pattern
of the same flowers in gold, green, and blue. No one remarked upon the
ubiquitous dragonflies.

The Abbess listened patiently to their plans for the Chosens while she
supervised a serving girl's preparations for osh. She'd often wished she could
think of a polite way to ask how they knew what osh was, when they
persistently denied any previous contact with the Nion culture. Everyone
knew the Nions were the sole source of the herb. It was one of the many
vagaries in the stranger's background. Still, this was neither the time nor
place to be concerned with that, she warned herself, and paid more attention
to what her guests were saying. When they finally slowed down so she could

make a comment, she told them frankly she was unready to plunge headlong into their programs. They were so disappointed, she hurriedly explained, warning that the common people were well conditioned to their way of life. Change, no matter how benevolent, had to come at an acceptable pace.

Carter disagreed. "The changes are necessary. Remember, Abbess, it was you who showed us a woman being punished for learning to do arithmetic. She risked horrible punishment to *learn.* The want still lives, and no one will torture the learners."

The Abbess took the kettle from the serving girl, pouring the boiling water over the osh herself. The act allowed her to retreat from the argument and appreciate the slender coils of fragrant steam. They soothed aching knuckles as well as delighting the senses. Reluctantly, she returned to the matter at hand. She said, "And you've forgotten the spectators. They weren't there simply to revel in someone else's pain, Janet. They believed the woman deserved punishment. They hated her for subjecting her husband to the same thing, and they despised his weakness for letting her do it. You won't eliminate those attitudes by simply declaring them no longer fashionable. Your goals are correct, but we must approach them with caution."

Kate Bernhardt, straightforward as always, said, "We have to do some-thing, Abbess. We were told Gan's authority extends over the largest united area known to Church. We have to seize the opportunity to work with him, to work for him. It's the chance you've always wanted to establish equality for us. You can't be saying we have to wait."

"Indeed I'm not." She wished she could reveal the plans she'd had once, how her dreams had soared far beyond any borders they could imagine. Now it was too late. However, Gan had provided a climate for gain here, and as Bernhardt said, something must be done with it. "I have a plan." She caught the servant's eye and indicated the door with a look. The girl hurried out. The Abbess looked back to the foursome. "Neela will have her child this winter. Gan will probably delay the naming ceremony until spring, but we have plenty of time, in either case. We must enlist his support before then. You will teach the youngest Chosens—all of them—to read and write before the child is born."

Sylah paled. "So many? So young? Only Healers are allowed— Are you sure, Abbess?" She looked around the room, incapable of voicing her next words without first searching for listeners. She said, "It sounds like what I've heard of the Teachers."

The word hit the Abbess harder than she thought it would. She'd expected it, but the effect was much greater than she'd anticipated. Perhaps if it had come from someone else, she thought, and then chided herself for a truly worrisome tendency to wander off the subject. She stirred her osh as she spoke, watching how the delicate swirls caught up to each other, merged, separated, and finally disappeared. She said, "The Teachers are a thing of the past, more legend than truth. You know that. We must forget such stories and look forward. Whatever went before is finished."

The other women sipped and nodded sagely, and for a second Sylah hated them. Couldn't they see the loss in those honest, aged features? What was wrong with their ears, that they couldn't hear the resignation in her words? Had they no understanding of defeat?

On the other hand, they hadn't grown up under the Abbess' guidance or cloaked in her love. She smiled to herself then; the Abbess had tricked people far more suspicious and distrusting than these three. Nevertheless, for one with a Healer's eye and training, the Abbess was more concerned with a loss—one she clearly refused to express—than with this immense opportunity to advance both Church and women.

Sylah wondered what could be so powerful. The freedom to bring reading and writing to the people was unimaginable when she'd ridden east on her mission to the warrior tribes. Now it was here, and the Abbess could almost dismiss it in her sorrow. At a time of such triumph, what was tearing at her so?

CHAPTER 85

South and east of Ola a mountain reared over a narrow valley. What made it unique, in a country known for mountains, was an odd accident at its base, where a cataclysmic earthquake had shaken free a wedge of granite over two hundred feet long and fully sixty feet high. The resulting notch in the mountain looked much as if an immense axe had bitten a chunk out of the living rock. As the ground continued to shake, the wedge broke in pieces and slid down a long slope, where it dammed a creek to create a small lake and waterfall.

A squat fort lurked inside the cavity now. From a distance it could have been part of the landscape. Its rough stones were protected from the snows of winter and were the same gray as the mountain. With the decline of the sun, the change in light created a sinister quality. Brooding, massive, the notch became a black maw poised at the head of the valley's deceptively gentle whiteness.

A single trail led to it, a dark rut in the deep snow, although the smaller ruts leading from it up onto the high ground warned that hidden observers watched the main route at all times.

To Altanar, riding up the trail, the pathways suggested an artery and veins, with the building the heart that pumped life into them. He enjoyed the image, seeing himself inside, the mind that stirred the heart. Let Gan Moondark dream his dreams in Ola, he thought. Spring brings new life. Someday this ugly pile of stone will be a shrine. People will come to see where the rightful King plotted his return.

He thought about that for a minute, listening to the huffing of his horse, watching the jets of steam shoot from its nostrils. "Plotted" wasn't the word; "planned" had a more dignified ring to it. ". . . the rightful King *planned* . . ." Much better.

Far away, tons of snow rumbled into another valley. The horse's ears pricked at the sound, but lopped forward again when it realized there was no cause for concern. Altanar peered up at the walling mountains. It would be tragically ironic to end up under an avalanche now. Everything was falling into place so nicely. A nudge here, a suggestion there—they thought he was beaten, but they'd learn how wrong they were.

The muffled thud of the horse's hoofs lulled him the last hundred yards to the entrance. The snow around it was walked flat, soiled with horse turds, mud, ashes, and other less identifiable detritus. Chickens scratched at it, vacant-eyed, as if aware of the pointlessness of hunting insects in the snow and embarrassed to be caught at it. Altanar thought of his manicured grounds and the strutting pheasants at Ola and spat, muttering Gan's name under his breath. A young trooper scampered from inside the fort to take his reins as he dismounted, and he cuffed him for not being outside waiting for his approach. The act made him feel a bit better.

The rest of the fort's defenders kept their distance, watching him enter and go directly to the fire. As soon as he sat in one of the bulky leather chairs before the hearth, slaves ran to strip off his heavy outer clothes and boots, replacing the latter with the soft indoor slippers. The floors here were so coarse they scuffed them terribly, but he refused to wear ordinary boots indoors.

Not that anyone here had any sense of quality. The baron who offered it as a hiding place made it clear he would forever deny any awareness that Altanar was using it. He was a Moondancer, a hater of Gan Moondark, and a loyal supporter of his king, but he had no intention of dying for that king, should Gan find him. It was a prudent attitude. One had to protect oneself. He smiled, wondering if the baron would be equally understanding when he learned the price of attaching conditions to his loyalty. No man withheld anything from the King. Why couldn't they ever understand that?

He left the comfort of the chair to poke at the fire, sending a spray of sparks up the chimney. He enjoyed their madness, identified with it. A touch of wildness, of unpredictability, was called for in this situation. That was the sort of clever thinking that brought him to the answer. Not cold logic. Oh, no. Mad, searing hate. *There* was the way. He'd always known the weak link had to be broken, but only today become certain of the technique and the opportunity.

He jabbed with the poker again, knocking a log off the pile and releasing a veritable storm of sparks. Something burst inside it, releasing heated gas that hissed and burned blue. The flame flicked like a snake's tongue, and where it touched, the dead, blackened wood glowed red with life again.

That was what he'd do. He'd breathe life into his subjects. Pain would set them to dancing again, just as before. There were so many accounts to settle. In a way, losing the kingdom to Gan would have benefits. Now that a return to the throne was more than a dream, the prospect of revenge was no longer mere solace. It was a weapon, a thing to be smoothed and polished mirror bright. People also responded to fear. They would know fear as no others ever had. His return would be such a lesson to them, they'd sacrifice anything to avoid a repetition of his embarrassment. He would make them see that he must be kept pleased and proud at any cost.

Until then, he would have to be patient.

That was the hardest thing, the waiting. Especially here, with a total of three people to talk to. One was the commander of the defending troops. His entire intellectual scope and physical awareness seemed to be confined to the geography between his navel and his knees. When he wasn't in one storage bin or another, grunting delights and frolics with one of the servant girls, he was sitting at the table in the troops' quarters talking about similar events between belches. Not a conversationalist.

The other two were brighter, far more articulate, and, as far as Altanar was concerned, rabid. Still, they were going to restore him to his throne.

The man Jones swayed hundreds, perhaps thousands, of simpleminded fanatics—such as the baron who offered him protection at risk of his life— and entertained a wondrous hatred for Gan Moondark. However, even Jones' emotional peaks were minor humps compared to those of their other shelter mate. The mere mention of Gan could turn Kolee into a slobbering blob of venom.

A combination made to order for his purposes. Altanar recognized that fact the very night he'd come slinking into the fort, dazed from uncounted hours of sleepless riding, half starved, shivering. Even then, when the momentarily nonrutting commander of the guard told him who else was sharing the fort with him, a flash of inspiration told him that these two maniacs were integral to destroying Gan Moondark. No other two people hated him so passionately. They would never have met, nor would Jones have taken her under his wing and brought her to the fort, if fate hadn't decreed that they should be used to his purposes. He refused to consider any other argument. Jones might think he had other things to live for, but that was simply another of his delusions. Kolee knew she had only one purpose, and that was to avenge her son.

Likat. Altanar jabbed the poker into the coals, stabbing again and again. What a waste that savage had been! So tenderly recruited, so lavishly paid— and for what? Treachery.

He threw down the poker and dropped back into the chair, squirming at the pain-pleasure of hot cloth pressed against his skin. Just as the contact eased, a movement caught his eye and he looked up to see Jones entering. He took it as an omen that Jones entered the room alone. Altanar was pleased to note he wore the headdress that covered the ugly scar on his head. It made him think of an empty eye socket. The thing he wore to cover it was as ridiculous as the wound was disturbing. He called it his turban. It looked like a cloth mushroom.

Faking as much joviality as he could muster, Altanar waved at a chair, inviting him to sit. Perversely, Jones stepped to the fireplace, warming his backside and blocking most of the warmth. Altanar swallowed his anger.

"I've spoken to you before about my intention to regain my throne," he said.

Before he could continue, Jones said, "Too often. I have no use for thrones or other trappings."

Gritting his teeth, Altanar continued. "I'm aware of your goals. I've always believed we could support each other. Today I discovered how it can be done."

Jones smiled unpleasantly. "I despise all kings, all kingdoms, save one. I travel the land, and I see all leaders in league with the apostate shame they call Church. My course is clear. The people must be brought to their knees, debased, *forced* to seek the true salvation. What use have I for your notion of power?"

It was exactly the response Altanar expected. He could have mouthed it along with him. He was too shrewd for that, however. Let the fool think he was thinking.

Calmly, slowly, he confessed his disillusionment with Church. Had it not been for Church, his grip on the population would have been too firm to be broken. Church accepted his friendship, then worked behind his back to organize the people against him.

He played that theme for a while, then changed to another, saying how he'd always known that power demanded fear. Without fear, without the certain knowledge that someone stronger than yourself was aware of your every move, no ruler could hope to control masses of people.

Love didn't come after fear. Love came *through* fear.

And Jones understood that. That was why he was organizing the secret Moondance groups he called "choirs" throughout the land.

Here Altanar put on his foxiest expression. "I could be your greatest supporter," he said. "I understand leadership, organization. Of all people, I understand the depth of your wisdom, because I came so close to understanding, and fell short. Never again. Especially if I have the benefit of your guidance, and if the people have the benefit of your experience."

Jones pretended to watch the fire, but Altanar saw the light score the sudden uncertainty in his expression. Without turning, Jones said, "You're a defeated king. My Moondancers grow stronger every day. When we're ready, we'll strike from our darkness, silent, final. Why should we share our achievement with you?"

Altanar wanted to shout his joy. The question was an admission. Jones knew he couldn't rule. In his heart he knew his sole accomplishment was destruction. Yet he realized he had to have control before he could put his plans into effect. He wanted to be assured that it was possible.

Standing, moving next to Jones, Altanar said, "Getting rid of Gan Moondark isn't enough, nor is it enough to get rid of his most powerful supporters. You want to overturn the entire structure, and when we do, you need someone to provide you freedom to create the society you seek. Church will strike back. Other rulers will covet your population, simply because people are wealth, and wealth means strength. Without someone like me to make a kingdom and an army out of our true believers, Church will find allies to crush us."

Jones drew himself erect. "I shall be a martyr."

"And Church will have defeated you." He put a hand on Jones' shoulder, ready to retreat at any sign of offense. There was none. He said, "You need me, and I need you. Church is our mutual enemy. And Gan Moondark strengthens Church every day."

"That savage." Jones stepped out from under Altanar's touch to pace, and Altanar rubbed his hands together gleefully.

Softly, almost whispering, Altanar described Gan's dependence on Sylah, the Rose Priestess. He sympathized for the terribly clumsy job she'd done on his injury, saying he'd seen hundreds similar, and none so terribly botched. When he finished, Jones was still pacing, but one hand kept rising to touch the side of his head.

Taking a deep breath, Altanar tried to secure the arrangement. "You see," he said, "even without your teaching, I had an awareness of driving the people to their knees, making them understand that their strength was nothing to mine. With your guidance, we can create the debasement you seek." He moved in front of Jones, forcing Jones to look him in the eye. "We'll tear the souls out of them, make them so miserable they understand their only hope is the one true faith, the faith you bring. After they're broken, you'll raise them in your name to worship in your way. I'll administer the kingdom in your name. But first we must have control. We never can while Gan Moondark lives."

Jones turned to the fire again, and Altanar returned to his chair, giving the man the illusion of solitude. With the ruddy light silhouetting him, Altanar had a bad moment, remembering that some of his followers swore he could breathe fire. Jones said, "Thou shalt not kill."

Altanar shrugged. "So Church says. If you're willing to agree with it, thou shalt not succeed."

Jones suddenly giggled, a reedy trickle of sound. It lifted the hair on the back of Altanar's neck. The gangly man sat across from him, bony elbows jutting out of his robe, resting on his knees. His hands were clasped under his chin, prayerlike. "How do we do it?" he asked.

CHAPTER 86

Gan pushed the door open, letting thin clouds of steam boil into the room. On contact with the colder air, they recoiled, then whisked away to the ceiling, where they painted a glistening sheen on the cedar timbers. He bowed to Neela, who held a wide-eyed, excited Coldar against her brown-and-yellow floor-length robe. The baby was wrapped in a scarlet-and-gold blanket, a gift of the wives of the Jalail Wolves. Gan wore only a large blue drying cloth that wrapped around his waist and tied securely with a black drawstring. He said, "My first contribution to the castle of Ola—our own soak. Come, look."

Coldar crowed happily when Neela moved forward, as if approving the idea. The sudden heat when she entered the room was a different matter entirely. His face wrinkled uncertainly, but when she spoke to him and smoothed his fine, golden hair, he decided to hold his tears. He kept his frown, however, lest they forget he was reserving judgment.

"It's bigger than the ones at the camp," Gan said, hurrying to stand beside the cedar soak, "and there's a shower, so we can bathe and step right into it." He pointed at the opposite wall. "Those doors open onto a balcony. When it's warmer, we can open them and let the daylight in. We're facing the sea; from up here you can see every mountain on the Whale Coast and the boats and the eagles. It's beautiful. And those closets hold extra robes and drying cloths and all the bath scents and oils. Did I forget anything?".

She laughed at his enthusiasm, then the amusement trailed off to tender concern, and she ran her fingertips across his face. "I love it, Gan; it's perfect. Promise me you'll use it often—at least once a day. You've been working so hard. I'm worried about you."

He nodded, unsmiling. "I'm tired. No matter what I do, the problems multiply." He reached out, took Coldar from her, looking down into the small face. "Even when I do something right for one of the tribes of Ola or Harbundai, I keep thinking about our own people. They're still suffering."

"A good spring for the herds will make a big difference. And being able to trade with the people here has helped a lot. Everyone wants Dog blankets and material for clothes."

"There's trouble, though. Some are already saying things were better under Likat. They say he was a strong leader. They forget everything else."

She flared. "He was no leader, he was a bully, a murderer. Saband Guyd should—"

He cut her off, smiling. "Easy, you'll frighten Coldar. Saband's a fine man. He's not the man to rebuild their confidence, though. Our leaders have to be able to embrace the lightning from all the factions and hammer out one decision. Then, most important, they must *lead*. Saband wants everyone to like him."

"Send Clas." She lifted her chin defiantly, ready for a blast of disapproval.

His solemn response surprised her. "The main reason I haven't is because he wants to be here with me. I owe him more than I can ever repay, Neela; I've told you why. I'm afraid to do anything that might hurt his pride."

She sat on the edge of the soak, letting a hand fall back to dabble the water's surface. Watching it, avoiding looking at him, she said, "I've wanted to say this for a long time. I don't care about your mother's prophecy. Not one bit. I did, at first, but too many things have happened, and it was you who met every problem, not her. You made choices. You inspired others. You led. Clas himself was the one who told Col, 'Prophecies don't throw lances.' I started thinking then, because I knew you'd blame yourself for his death. And another thing—Murmillanh said you'd 'raise your people to glory,' or something like that, right? Well, *these* are your people, too. Not just the Dogs. You were supposed to exceed your father. You've done it. If you want to walk out of here right now and go back to our tribe, I'll be beside you. No matter what you do, I'll be there. But I don't want to hear any more about fate or prophecies or anything else. Gan Moondark's enough for me, and if the world says its not enough for them, it'll have to fight both of us." When he reached for her, she spun away, and he saw the brittle light of tears in her eyes. Her voice was strained but determined even as she avoided him. "Now get in this soak," she said, "so I can rub some of the tightness out of you. You make me furious; you look like an old man. Give me Coldar; I'll make a place for him to lie down. There's no need for you to bathe first, so go on, get in the water."

Unsure whether to smile or argue, Gan elected for discretion and did neither, unfastening the drying cloth and stepping into the soak, settling onto the submerged seat. When he looked, Neela had already made a nest of drying clothes and extra robes for Coldar and was on her way to him with a wooden tray of jars and a bar of soap. She leaned on the end of the soak and started kneading his shoulders. His attempt to talk earned him a swift ducking.

Like the almost unobservably slow drain of a water clock, the tension flowed from him. His eyes closed and he leaned back against the slender strength of her forearms, abandoning himself to the delicious languor. His mind raced across the myriad things that had happened since that first morning on the windswept prairie when the dogs had warned him of Sylah's presence. In the redolence of herb-scented water he found the sage and mint of that day. He remembered the duel in Earth Heart, and an unidentified acrid tang reminded him of the animal stink of the warriors waiting for blood. There was the pine of the forests, and something with a nose-tingling bite that called to mind the peculiar crackle in the air following the avalanche Tate triggered to save them.

There was stone and wood, the smell of Altanar's castle.

A spasm twisted his body, jerked him so hard the top of his head hit Neela's chin. It was a painless contact, and he tried to explain it away as one of those starts that precedes sleep. She was too perceptive for that, however, and demanded to know what he was thinking of. He told her. "Your capture. Of all the things that have happened, that's the one I can never forgive myself for. When I think of you suffering because of me—" He shook his head, unable to finish the thought.

She said, "It was no fault of yours. Men like Altanar are the same as sickness. They take any victim they can find, they kill because that's what they do."

He felt the wearying tug of muscle reacting to stress coming back. So did

Neela, and she dug her fingers into his flesh, forcing it to surrender. He said, "He escaped. I let him go. It eats at me every day, every hour. I dream of finding him once more."

"You mustn't blame yourself." She stopped rolling his biceps to ask, "Why haven't you ever asked me what it was like?"

He twisted to look at her, astonished. "I know enough. You told me what happened."

She turned his head to the front with a finger. "What happened; not what it was like." Her hands resumed their work. "What he did—" He felt the shudder wrack her body, but when he tried to turn, she was ready and stopped him. After a deep breath, she started from the beginning. "What he did was cruel. Awful. At first I tried to tell myself it was my duty to die. There was Coldar, though, so I couldn't. And there was you. I told myself you needed me. So I left. When he came into my sight, I went away. The things he did, the things he said—" Her breath caught, an almost infinitesimal pause. Gan almost reacted, but some deeper instinct told him to hold, that her speech was more important than all his sympathy. She went on. "The woman who stayed behind had no feelings, no senses. She had no concept of time or place. But I did. I flew, Gan. I went to the mountains, to the clouds. I hid until he left. I never learned how to return, though. I always fell coming back, and hurt myself, sometimes so much I'd be sick for days. I had to go, though, and I always knew that one day I'd come back from my secret flight and my husband would be there and he'd catch me, and I wouldn't hurt anymore. I wouldn't have to fly away or hide ever again. The other woman could leave, too. Now I pray for her to find a place like mine, where she can be as happy as I am."

He caught her hands so she couldn't stop his turning, and never even noticed that she made no effort to try. He stood, taking her in his arms, both of them trying to ignore the wall of the soak separating them until he decided to tolerate it no longer. When he moved his hands to span her waist, she smiled anticipation and put her hands on his shoulders, helping him lift her until she stood on the edge of the soak. Gently he untied the drawstring at the throat of the robe and, fumbling, released the toggle buttons that ran to the waist. Still smiling softly, looking into his eyes, she shrugged it off her shoulders, let it sigh to her feet. Free of it, she raised a hand to draw the comb restraining her hair, letting the sunlight brightness cascade down her back, onto her shoulders and breasts. He lifted her again, bringing her into the soak with him. Brushing aside the veiling hair, he kissed each nipple, hearing her sigh as a soft breeze. Together, deliberately, savoring every contact, each prolonging second, they found their way onto the board seat. She straddled his thighs, and when she leaned back, raising her breasts to the surface, he traced the rich softness of them with a tender eagerness that was as wondering as wonderful. She reached for him under the water, and when he rumbled with pleasure deep in his chest, she opened her eyes to study him with such burning intensity it was as if she might never see him again. Then, satisfied with what she saw, she closed her eyes again, stroking, fondling, until he pulled her to him with a need that exploded simultaneously within her.

A while later they lay side by side on his drying cloth. He slept on his side, an arm for a pillow. She watched his chest rise and fall, traced the faint pulse of a vein in his throat with a fingertip. Coldar moved, and she looked to him, then back to Gan.

"We already have the world, my husband," she said. "If you want more, we'll get it, but get it for yourself, not to answer for someone else's dream. Never for me, either. You can never know all the things I want to accomplish, even if I think you would understand why I must try to achieve them myself. If everything fails, though, I can live without what I want. I have what I need."

She lay down between them to sleep with them.

The fields outside the northern city wall were transformed into a fairground. Brilliant flies and awnings of every color created streets facing a piece of ground specially leveled for the event, and on this, the morning of Coldar Moondark's formal naming day, the population of Ola's capital city was at least tripled. Even the Nion ship in port, with its high stern and odd, slatted sails, had elected to stay for the ceremony. Her crew, with their cropped heads and exotic appearance, mingled with Dog warriors, the hawk-visaged mountaineers of Eleven West, and the short-sleeved whale hunters of the Whale Coast, the latter seemingly impervious to the chill in the air. For the first two days of the celebration, Wolves had patrolled the new cloth city in teams of four, anticipating the brawls between tribesmen thrown into contact for the first time, and they'd been kept busy. Constraint and fairness seemed to be winning, however; in his morning report to Gan, Emso reported no major casualties for the previous twenty-four hours.

Gan, seated in Altanar's old working quarters, treated himself to the luxury of a second tiny cup of osh, smiling inwardly at how quickly he accustomed himself to these little benefits of his position. He acknowledged a twinge at the self-indulgence, but took consolation in the fact that he still trained daily with the warriors. Clas had found good men to officer the remains of the Olan army; they'd make fine Wolf units when properly trained.

A real problem was the delegation from the Dog People. They showed a solid front to everyone else, but in his chambers their uncertainty and division surfaced like a foul-smelling bubble in a pond. Too proud to ask for help, he saw the way their faces tightened when he led them to a table heaped with food. They ate with dignified restraint, and only by extending the conversation for hours was he able to keep them at it. In the end they left nothing but well-gnawed bones and pits from dried cherries and prunes.

He was determined to do something about it.

When Clas came in, Shara and Cho rose to greet him, tails wagging. He scratched their ears, waiting to see why Gan had called for him.

"I need your help," Gan said. "More than that, I need your understanding."

Clas grinned, pulling up a chair. "That's a pretty frightening combination. What sort of trouble are we in this time?"

"Not us. Our people." Gan refused to respond to the humor, somber as he rose from the chair and strode to the open window. "I'm king in everything but name; everyone knows that. My heart is a Dog warrior's heart, a Nightwatcher's. You saw the men who came here for Coldar's naming." He shifted his feet, moved his shoulders, trying to physically generate the words his mind wanted to say and couldn't find. Dismissing subtlety with an explosive sound of disgust, he turned back to Clas. "I want you to go back to them. Be their leader. They need you."

"They want you. They told me so."

Gan shook his head. "They forget who trained me, who advised me, who saved my life when I failed. I've thought about it until my head throbs, and you're the only man who can bring them back to what they should be, raise them higher than they ever were. We know I have to stay here. Remember, I was supposed to take the Honor Journey and didn't. My return would revive the tensions between North and South clans. You're South Clan, yet you own the loyalty of every North man. The tribe needs you. I need you with me, but I need you there even more. Once again I'm coming to you for help."

Clas spoke to the dogs, as if he needed the reassurance of their calm attention. "It insults if I say you need me beside you, yet it's where I want to be. Still, I miss our people, the land, the freedom." He looked up at Gan, his face a mask of released emotion. "These walls, all this stone, all this flat, ugly *brick* is killing me. I would never speak of these things, but now you open the way. I long for my home. Yes, I will go. Only because you ask, but with a gladness I can't speak."

Softly, Gan said, "And Sylah?"

"I have a duty. She understands those things."

*   *   *

The Iris Abbess sat in a chair in the sunshine, watching thousands of geese vee across the cloudless sky, and wondered how she came to be there.

Initially, it was a puzzlement, nothing more, and her eyes wandered from the gabbling, honking flocks in their variegated lines, looking down to the neat geometry of the docks and their counterpoint of rush and bustle. So like the geese, she thought, everyone rushing to catch the new season at its earliest.

But where was she?

With the growing realization that she simply didn't know, fear sunk its teeth in her. Her heart pounded, hurting her ribs, and she struggled to lift her arms outside the blanket. Suddenly, terrifyingly, hands seized her shoulders, pinning her to the chair. She pulled back, almost upsetting it.

A controlled, patient voice said, "Abbess? Are you all right?" She knew the voice was familiar, but couldn't place it. Straining, she turned her head as far as the grinding bones in her neck would allow, and swift embarrassment swept away all the fear.

Sylah let go of her hands as she circled around from behind. She was worried. The Abbess mumbled something lame about drifting off to sleep, and then spoiled any chance the lie might have had by trying to grasp Sylah's hand through the heavy material and asking, "How long have we been here? Why did we come?" Then, worse yet, she felt the all-too-familiar flutter of her left eyelid. This time there was an accompanying tic in her cheek on that side. Fortunately, Sylah was on her right. She kept her face straight ahead as the younger woman knelt beside her; welcome warmth, reassuring pressure.

Sylah said, "Don't try to avoid me. I saw the tremors in your face. We're just outside the Sungold Gate, so you can get some sun. We've been here almost an hour, talking about organizing the Olan women the way we did in Jalail and Malten. Do you remember now?"

"Yes." It was coming back to her. Feeling her face warm, she asked, "How long was I—"

"Only a moment. A few heartbeats, no more."

"It's very frightening. I'm used to the pain in my joints. They make me feel old, but we're friends. This thing tells me my way is growing short. It's no friend." She chuckled, a surprisingly warm amusement. She said, "Maybe I misjudge it. It'll certainly make my joints stop hurting, won't it?"

Sylah said, "Don't make bad jokes. These lapses—they never happened before Likat struck you, did they?"

The Abbess shook her head. "That's true. I'd thought of it." She worked a hand free, touched her temple. "Sometimes I feel something, way deep inside here. Not a pain, but pressure." She reminisced for a while, recalling in perfect detail cases from before Sylah's arrival, trying to use one of them to give her a sense of what was happening inside her own head.

It was almost funny, actually. So many lives had gone under her hands, each of them teaching her something about the wonderful complexity of the human body. Now she had no answers for her own situation. Oh, she had an idea; it was probably one of the blood vessels, pinched by a piece of bone, or weakened by the blow. Perhaps a small clot, trying to close the thing down. At her age it made little difference. If the problem didn't get her, the solution almost surely would.

Taking Sylah's hand, she leaned back in the chair again. Her heart was still beating too quickly, and she closed her eyes, invoking the trance to relax. Instead, she thought of the young woman beside her.

There were so many things about herself Sylah didn't know. She could never know of her family, whether any of them lived or not, or even where she came from. Nor could she know of the times she'd been "helped" to achieve trance state. What would Sylah say if she discovered how much of her life was her own ideas, and how much of it was suggested to her when she couldn't help herself? Did she ever think of the Door anymore? Did she think of the old Abbess, lying in her bed, babbling secrets while she wandered the land between this world and the next? If she knew the truth, could she ever forgive her abbess for pretending to babble? Would it have been better to simply mold the child by direct pressure?

From the corner of a slitted eye, she studied Sylah. The young, austerely beautiful face was turned to the geese. She looked pensive, and the Abbess' heart gave a leap.

What if she truly was supposed to search for the Door? Could it be possible that she'd been seducing the girl into something she was meant to do all along? What a delicious irony! It could very well be. She'd wanted to believe that, at the start. After all, she'd selected her because she showed the courage, the perseverance, the toughness. She didn't flinch at plain hard work. She proved that in Jalail, if nowhere else, with her two friends. What they did was the envy of every other woman.

That life was surely best for her. Now that she had a husband, there was no place for a dangerous trip of unknown length to find something that might or might not be discoverable. Yet it was wrong to let her go on living with the belief that all the things in her mind about the Door were honestly come by.

The more the Abbess thought about it, the surer she became. Sylah had a right to all the information possible about herself, the better to know herself. Lies told in a good cause are lies, no matter, she scolded herself. It's time to speak the truth, and let the woman judge for herself the quality of what was done and why.

Pangs of doubt assailed her immediately. There was a good chance Sylah would be too angry about being used to ever forgive her. So be it, she decided. If that's to be my punishment, I'll take it as bravely as I can. No one can say it's not well earned.

"I have some things to tell you," the Abbess said, and Sylah turned full blue, innocently curious eyes on her. The Abbess looked away, in order to continue.

The dry, diffident voice scourged Sylah. At each new revelation of deceit, she felt as if she were being flayed. Then, strangely, as the tale rapidly approached the time when they actually petitioned the King, she began to get excited all over again, just as she had then.

It still called her. More, she found herself drawn back to the tired, pained old woman who'd tried so hard to create in her a unique person. What dream could she have had if the Abbess hadn't created one for her? Her lies sprang from fear, not lack of love. How could she know that her Sylah would have fought tigers for the opportunity to search for the Door? And if nothing had come of it, whose fault was that? Not everything turned out as planned.

An out-of-place sound broke her thought pattern, and she looked back at the Abbess to see the tears streaming, uninterrupted, down her cheeks. Sylah rushed to dry them with a pocket cloth from the Abbess' robe. As she dabbed at them, she said, "I know what you meant, my Abbess, and I love you for it. You took a frightened little girl to yourself and gave her a dream. I still have it. I always will. It's not important to *achieve* all of your dreams, it's important to *have* them, and never let them go. All my life I'll picture myself seeking that mysterious thing we call the Door. What is it? Where is it? Why is it important? I'll always wonder. And dream of knowing." She looked around, noting that the Abbess was watching, and then she asked, "Would you like to know my secret? My own secret about the Door?"

Half afraid, the Abbess nodded without speaking. Her eyes darted about, as well, before she looked to Sylah.

"I wanted the power," she said. "I was going to find the Door and claim whatever power is there for myself. Then I was going to destroy Altanar with it, and everyone like him. I told myself that if Church was so afraid of it, it was made to order for me." She laughed easily, bending forward to kiss the almost transparently delicate skin of the Abbess' cheek. "You see, not even you can predict the course a dream will take."

The Abbess sighed, nodding silent agreement. It was true. Even so, what a joy it would have been to see that strong, resilient stride moving toward a goal of such import.

A second, more resigned sigh settled her deeper into her robe. At least she'd done no harm.

Or had she?

How long, she wondered, does it take for a failed dream to wizen into bitter brooding about what might have been?

CHAPTER 87

The throng crowded as close to the raised stand as the sweating double row of Wolves would allow them. The warriors stood with arms locked, leaning into the cheering mass. When they weren't shouting at their fellow citizens to stand back, they were turning their own heads to steal a glance up at the gathering on the platform and yell themselves hoarse. Resplendent in a robe of his clan colors, Coldar ignored the proceedings, studying his mother's face with what appeared to be scholarly dignity.

As a concession to the festivity of the event, Gan and Clas wore their best buckskin, decorated with clan color sashes. Neela dressed in a white woolen robe, bordered at hem, sleeves, and cowl with wide bands of embroidered flowers. Every hue of the rainbow was represented, in the hope, as she told Gan, that anyone looking for clan or tribe representation would be satisfied. Clas wore the bejeweled shortsword given him by Gan, and his steel trophy collar. The small bones glowed softly in the bright sun. Sylah, beside him in her finest black robe, pointedly avoided looking at it. In fact, Gan remarked to Neela while they waited for the Iris Abbess to start the ceremony, Sylah seemed preoccupied. Neela almost snapped at him, reminding him of the child she'd lost. He blushed; in his joy, he'd forgotten.

The actual giving of the name was brief, the Iris Abbess sprinkling the baby with the Water of Holiness as Gan and Neela held him between them. Those close enough to distinguish expressions laughed at the way Coldar frowned and fussed, and then everyone grew silent as the frail old Abbess gave out the full name, rolling the words formally. "Coldar na Bale Moondark," she said, and the stunned surprise on Clas na Bale's face created as much delight as the presence of the child himself. Once again everyone cheered, and the Wolves, both those in ranks and those off duty in the crowd, added howls of approval.

When the Abbess stepped back, indicating the religious part of the ceremony was over, a great murmur of anticipation moved through the crowd, a sound of storm winds high in the trees. No one knew what to expect. The Murdat was an unknown quality to most of them, and the naming day of the King's first son was a time of portentous announcements during the dynasty of Altanar's clan. There had been rumors of new taxes, and of recruitment for the new Wolf units. Some faces in the audience showed fear.

Gan and Neela stepped to the edge of the platform. For a moment neither spoke. Then Gan took the child and raised him even with his own head. In a voice that carried across the entire gathering, he said, "This is my child, no different than any other, a boy his mother and father hope to see grow to be a man, a man who must prove himself, war or peace, to be worthy of his neighbors. Neela and I wish you and your children all blessings. We ask yours for our son." He raised him as high as he could, brandishing him. "Coldar na Bale Moondark!"

At the roar that followed, young Coldar na Bale Moondark jerked like a hooked fish. His chin jutted. He balled his fists. And then, without warning, he punched at the air and laughed. Turning his head from side to side as if welcoming all his friends, he continued to whoop back at them as merrily as they cheered him.

Gan lowered him, handing him back to Neela. She was flushed, excited. Out the corner of his mouth Gan said, "Did you see what he did? He'll think he's king before he's old enough to walk."

She sniffed, never forgetting to keep smiling, and said, "It must be something he inherited. What do we do now?"

"Go look at the fair, meet the people." At the foot of the steps two squads of Jalail Wolves trotted from behind the stand to form a protective wall around the group. Clas and Sylah helped the Iris Abbess down, and two more soldiers appeared with a chair on carrying poles for her. The crowd parted reluctantly, and the party inside their human box seemed to progress through a forest of waving, wiggling, reaching hands.

Toward the back of the mass, standing on a crowded logging wagon brought to the fair to provide a perch for spectators, Kolee muttered to herself as she watched them come toward her. She'd chosen her position carefully. The bright tents and stalls immediately in front of her featured the finest craftsmen in the land. It was one part of the fair the party was sure to visit, probably the only place where they might actually stop and linger. She was on the edge of the wagon, too; no one could get in front of her.

She leaned on a staff with several crossbars, each of the latter hung with garlands of flowers—violets, pansies, fuchsias, and azaleas. Their numbers suggested she'd had no luck selling any, and one look at the red, angry face, its lips puffing in and out in silent diatribe, explained why. Even in such a crowd, there was a bit of space on both sides of her.

Her mind was moving, however. She had instructions to remember, memories to fondle. Jones had told her, and he was nearly always right, that her thoughts would be clearer if she kept telling herself why she must do this thing. "Hate makes us strong," he'd said. It was true. All she had to do was look at them, all of them, so proud, so vain. So *alive*.

Likat was dead. They killed him. Altanar was there, and he saw it all. Everyone said *he* killed Likat, but that was lies, spread by people who favored Gan. They wanted to keep her away from him. They knew she'd avenge her Likat. They feared her.

They should.

Altanar said the people feared and hated Gan. It certainly didn't look that way, and if he'd lied about that—

She turned to hiss a warning at someone who bumped her. The crowd was getting more excited. The official party was coming her way. She almost smiled anticipation. She'd known they would. Jones promised.

Altanar. She was thinking about Altanar. What was it? How poor Likat was murdered? It must have been. Nothing else mattered.

Gan Moondark struck him down from behind. Coward. Ran away from the Honor Journey. Backstabber. No warning. No reason.

That wasn't right, either. There was a reason. Jones said so. It was so hard to remember everything. Didn't he say there was a reason? As if anything could explain such a terrible thing.

There must have been.

And what did Altanar say about the crossbar? They were getting closer all the time. Yes. Caps. That's what he called them. The caps had to come off.

She fumbled with the near end of one of the bars, working at a wooden cup fitted over the end. With the butt of the vertical pole on the logging wagon deck, that particular crossbar came just to Kolee's mouth. She tilted the display forward to rotate it. There was another wooden cup on the other end of the bar. She twisted and tugged until it popped free. The crossbar was hollow. Frowning in concentration, she patted her robes until she finally found what she was looking for.

This was the dangerous part. Jones and Altanar had argued that she should carry the dart already hidden in the tube, but they had no business telling her about that sort of thing. The poison lost effectiveness every minute, once it was exposed to the air. The thing had to be done right.

Her hands shook so badly she feared she'd drop it as she reached inside a voluminous fold to draw out a long object with a tuft of cotton on one end. Cautiously, shielding the act with her body, she unwrapped the other end, revealing the needle point smeared with a black, gummy mess. Peering about, she raised her hand, and, pretending to arrange a garland, slipped the dart into the tube, shoving the cotton ball out of sight with her little finger. Loosely replacing the cap hid it completely.

Once more she looked around at the crowd. They didn't even know she existed.

The people she hated were only about fifty yards away now.

They had to be very close.

Jones said hatred would steady her aim. He knew about those things. Why did he say Gan killed Likat? He was a bit wild, but such a loving child. A son. It was a sin to kill someone's son.

Of course! That was what Jones said. He and Altanar knew Church the same way she did. That was it. Jones and Altanar hated Church, and so did Likat, because they'd treated her so badly. And Gan was under the influence of that witch who called herself a Priestess. Sylah, that was her name. If she hadn't made a fool of Gan, he'd never have been Likat's enemy. He'd have served Likat, as all the Dog People had, and made him rich and powerful. If it wasn't for Gan, she'd be surrounded by respect and love. It would be Likat's son being named, and she'd be the one giving names to his child.

It wasn't just Gan, though. Nothing was as simple as it looked, no matter what Jones and Altanar said. Whatever Likat had seen in that nasty little Neela, she'd hurt him very much. Made him unhappy. That's what caused the fights with Bay Yan, too; they were never as friendly after she ran away with Gan and that Sylah.

Her again.

Gan killed Likat; Altanar saw it. What Altanar didn't understand was that they were warriors, and they were supposed to kill. She smiled to herself. What did they know about boys? Full of fire, they were. Especially Dog boys. What was important was knowing who influenced him, because they were all such children, really, so anxious to please. Someone had to guide them.

And every time she thought she saw a person behind Gan, it was *her*.

They'd made a bad person of Gan. It started with his father. Everyone knew. A cheat. Fool.

The first of the soldiers surrouding the party were just a few feet away. She could see the runnels of sweat on their faces, the way their eyes jerked as they scanned the crowd.

She uncapped the tube, and suddenly realized they were going to pass *under* her. Jones. Altanar. So clever. *Do as we say, Kolee. Don't argue, Kolee. Kill Gan, the one who killed Likat, and you destroy his straw kingdom, the one that supports the Church that wronged you so terribly. Your vengeance is total. We've thought it all out for you.* And now the weapon that was to gain the revenge she so richly deserved was useless. If she depressed it far enough to aim at them, she couldn't reach it with her mouth. They were too close.

Their weapon. *Their* plan.

Panic clutched at her. She dropped the butt of the staff off the edge of the wagon, tilting it. Looking past the garlands at the group, she watched them come.

A few more feet.

Clas na Bale. A mindless fool.

Neela, who spurned Likat, changed his entire life. She had no right to be happy.

Sylah. Schemer. Spy. Destroyer of lives. She twisted Gan, made him Church's weapon. Arrogant.

Gan. Murderer. Ambitious. Coward. Smiling at Sylah, smiling at the witch Abbess. Smug. Sharing secrets.

The baby. The baby. Of course. Why shouldn't Gan and Neela suffer as she suffered? Let them feel grief crumble their brains, let them know unending loss.

She put her mouth to the tube and inhaled. To launch the dart, one brought the air from the lungs, almost a cough.

Garlands slipping off the bars caught her eye, broke her concentration. She looked back at the group.

The flash of decision made her blink. Pictures flashed across her mind, lightning bolts so quick she hardly saw one before another was there. Murmillanh, babbling of Old Church and her son's "destiny." Col Moondark, so noble and good, forcing the tribe to accept his heir. Sylah, twisting and perverting both Gan and Neela with her false concern and sophisticated lies. They all used Gan, made him the man who killed Likat.

And they, in turn, were controlled without ever realizing what evil led them.

One knew. Kolee knew.

A puff of air sped the dart into the Iris Abbess' neck just above the collar of her formal robe. She exclaimed at the sting, raising a hand too crippled by arthritis to properly pull it free. Sylah was there instantly, yanking it out, sucking at the wound. Gan and Clas shouted at the troops to push back the crowd, and Neela dropped in a huddle, completely enfolding Coldar in the curve of her body. Gan crouched in front of her, seeking, while Clas held Sylah behind him with one hand while the other pointed the shortsword. Shara and Cho snarled indiscriminately at anyone who appeared to move toward the group.

For the first time since she'd heard of Likat's death, Kolee felt the warmth of happiness. Amid the screams of the dissipating crowd and the curses of the Wolves driving away the morbidly curious, she heard the laughter of the student Healers who found her so comical, and the artificial patience of the bored Priestesses at the abbey. There was the source of all manipulation, the single tap root of the conspiracy that sought power over everyone.

Jones and Altanar would be disappointed, at first. She would make them see her wisdom. Moondance would lead the way: "Through darkness into a new light," Jones said.

The old light was now challenged.

A boy on the ground under the still-positioned blowpipe held one of the garlands. He appeared to be frozen, eyes wide in question, the hand holding the flowers partially extended upward toward her. She glared down at him, wishing he'd just take the flowers and leave her to her thoughts. The useless blossoms had served their purpose, and it was time she started the long ride back to the fort.

A Wolf pushed the boy. He resisted, and the man looked at him, annoyed. The boy said something, holding up the flowers, gesturing at Kolee. The man bent over him, and then the boy puffed out his cheeks. He pointed up at her, then to where the Iris Abbess was lying on a pile of blankets hurriedly stripped from a fair stall.

Kolee turned to run. Others had seen the boy, however, and understood. A man twisted the display pole from her hand. When he looked through the tube, he backhanded her across the mouth with such force she literally flew off the edge of the wagon. She barely had time to think he must be another of Church's mindless dupes before she hit the ground. The crowd surged around her in a maelstrom of fists, knives—anything that would injure. In seconds it was over. They edged back, ringing the messy heap that had been the woman who killed the Iris Abbess.

The sounds coming from that direction didn't even distract Sylah. She continued to work on the wound. The Abbess reached to push her away, saying, "I can feel it, my child. You didn't swallow, did you? You were careful?" At Sylah's nod, she said, "Clas, get her some water please. She really must rinse. Who knows what was on that nasty thing?" He ran, just as the Wolf from the logging wagon hurried up to report to Gan. The Abbess shook her head. "How foolish. I wouldn't have lasted many more weeks, in any case."

Sylah cried out, taking the old woman in her arms. The Abbess shushed her, patting her back. "Straighten up now," she said, "and listen to me." A spasm shook her, making her mouth and eyes fly open in a silent scream. When it passed, the breath rattled in her lungs. She said, "You taught me something very important. Remember? You said, 'It's not important to achieve all your dreams; it's important to have them.'" Another convulsion, shorter and more violent than the last, twisted her on her makeshift bed. She clutched Sylah's hand, her face desperate for time. "You gave me ease to accept myself. I love you—for so many reasons, my Sylah. I love you."

"And I love you." She barely got the words out before her control snapped. Clas rushed up with the water just in time to take her in his arms.

They hovered over her as the Abbess closed her eyes. She shivered, the clear brow forming tiny creases of a frown. Neela quickly put another blanket over her. Her features relaxed. She sighed.

CHAPTER 88

"**I** am going." Sylah pronounced each word emphatically.

Clas said, "We've argued for days, and you've never given me a reason." She turned swiftly, angrily, and he held up a hand. "You say it's something you've wanted all your life, it's something the Abbess wanted. Those aren't reasons, Sylah. You don't know what you're looking for, if it's good or evil, where it is, or if it even exists. If it were anything less farfetched, I'd go with you without—"

"I've told you before; it's not necessary for you to go with me."

"And I told you it is. I'm your husband."

How could she explain to him that she deserved to be allowed to fight her own battle the best way she knew how? How could she not tell him how much it hurt to leave him or how greatly she feared this decision? She got to her feet, walking away, hoping he'd follow. He did.

They were at the Beach of Songs, a few yards south of where Altanar's racks used to stand before Gan had them burned. The sky was an irregular mass of clouds, a meld of grays that hung lifeless over a sullen green sea. Hundreds of dark birds rode the uneasy swells, keeping far offshore. Sylah wondered if they were avoiding the troubled humans.

Sand and gravel crunched underfoot, and the strong smell of the sea's darker depths rose from the neat tide row of seaweed between them and the wide expanse of beach bared by a low tide. Gulls and crows made their pompous, strutting way across the flats, searching out food, squabbling mightily.

Sylah broke the silence. "I know you want to be with me, and I wish you could be. You have a duty to your people. I understand that. Please, I'm asking you one last time, try to understand that I feel I have a duty, too. My search is not a whim, Clas. My need is not a fancy."

"Can you touch either, search or need? My people are real. Your Door's a rumor from hundreds of years ago. You can't compare them."

"I can. You can't." She stopped to face him, put a hand on his arm. He looked into her eyes, then out to sea. She said, "You left the tribe because you believed in Gan's mission, in Murmillanh's prophecy. Is that so much different? It didn't work the way you thought it would. It's you, not Gan, who's returning to the tribe to build its strength."

He walked out from under her hand, and this time it was she who had to go along. He said, "No prophecy can be absolutely exact. He's built a peace that will allow our people to grow ever stronger. It's the same thing."

"That's not what I meant, and you know it. I'm saying I have a dream to pursue, to support, just as you did. I started it once, and now I'm going to finish it."

"Give me a year—two years—to settle things. I'll go with you. Anywhere. For as long as you want."

"I won't wait." Another lie. How could she tell him she dared not wait, that every day it became more difficult to do this thing? Why wouldn't he agree, before more lies came? She went on, "Why is it that your obligation requires that mine wait?"

Stubborn now, his jaw jutted, his mouth curved downward. He said, "A wife's place is with her husband."

"I agree." He turned back from searching the sea, suspicious. She said, "I'll come back. No matter what. I love you, Clas. Nothing changes that. And I sing in my heart because I know you love me. I hope you love me enough to understand and forgive."

"I do, too." The words were near-shattering, but the look in his eyes and the tone of his voice were tender. He went on. "I'll never understand. I know you believe your arguments. I can't. Nor can I stop you from doing what you will. But forgive you? There's nothing to forgive. Go. You say it's your fate. So be it."

She had hoped for something less grudging. Her mind told her he was being more generous than any man she'd ever heard of, yet her heart yearned for more, for the smallest shred of understanding that would have taken some of the pain out of her decision.

He took her hand, and her knees were suddenly weak, her mind afire with doubts and fears. She stumbled, and his quick strength caught her immediately. Almost inaudibly, she thanked him.

She would stumble again. Often. He wouldn't be there.
She pulled back her shoulders, raised her chin.
She would catch herself. She would succeed.

Gan and Neela were entertaining. The large room off the dining hall was filled with guests from Harbundai and Ola as well as ten senior officers from the Wolves. The food wasn't yet on the table, so they filled the room with a buzz of light conversation while they waited. It wasn't the sort of gathering that attracted many Church people, and Gan was surprised when the servant came with the message that four Priestesses asked permission to speak to him. He was even more surprised when he learned they were the three strangers, plus Sylah. He told the servant to bring them in right away.

She looked as he expected. The fiery arrogance of old was subdued now, and he thought of how Saband Guyd used to bank the fires of his forge at night. It had been a favorite game to pluck a straw and set it on the apparently cool mound and watch it suddenly twitch, then curl, and finally char away to ash. He had the feeling that anything that disturbed or startled Sylah now might very well release that same unsuspected heat. Still, she smiled when she saw the two of them, and it was as bright as ever.

The three others—Carter, Anspach, and Bernhardt—were nervous. Gan nudged Neela. "They want something," he said. "You don't think they want to leave with her?"

Neela looked superior. "That's not it," she said, and he knew there was a plot afoot. And that it would unfold before he learned any more.

Sylah wasted no time. She said, "The Abbess had a project she wanted you to support. It meant very much to her, and she believed it would help you administer your lands."

He couldn't understand why Neela kept smiling. He said, "How can I help you?"

Sylah glanced at Carter, who swallowed before asking, "Are you willing to pit your officers against an equal number of our ten-year-old girls in a game, Murdat? Just for a few minutes. No one'll be hurt." A number of people couldn't help but overhear, and they laughed at the choice of words. Carter quickly stammered an amendment. "I mean embarrassed. Not hurt."

One of the officers caught Gan's eye. He said, "For the Priestesses, we'll chance injury, if you want, Murdat."

"When would this contest take place?" Gan asked.

Sylah said, "Now."

He raised his eyebrows. By then the rest of his guests were paying attention. Cries of "Yes" and "Play the game" went up. He nodded. Bernhardt hurried to the door, opening it for fifteen little girls to file in. They didn't

know if they should be frightened or not, but they were determined to be
serious about their business. In their black, floor-length robes, they seemed
to glide into place along the wall opposite Gan.

Bernhardt defined the rules: An equal number of the Wolf officers were
to line up on their side of the room, as the girls had on their side. Gan was
to issue an order for battle, a complicated one. He would tell it to one officer
and one girl. The message would be passed down the two lines. Whichever
team came closest to repeating the message exactly was the winner.

Bets were made immediately, even before Gan had started thinking. The
odds favored the girls heavily, to the disgust of the Wolves, although they
admitted freely they suspected Church had come up with some sort of trick
memory technique. When Gan was ready, he whispered to the first officer,
who happened to be Tate. She was already talking to the next officer before
he reached the little girl.

The child listened intently, totally involved in every word. She asked him
to repeat it. Then she nodded and turned her back. So did all the others,
leaving him staring at a line of bowed shoulders. He made a face, getting
a laugh from the adults, and returned to Neela's side.

The last officer called, "We have it, Murdat," just as the girls turned in
unison. The last one in line piped, "So do we," in the way of all little girls,
and for a moment it appeared the game might end in the ensuing laughter.
Then Gan asked for the message. The officer looked a little less confident.
"It doesn't sound like something you'd normally say, Murdat. 'Emso takes
the four cavalries too late to assist eleven Wolves on the west flank. Cavalry
sleeps in the rear.' "

Again, more laughter stormed the room. Even the girls smiled, although
theirs was a trifle cocksure.

Gan turned to them. The little one on the end held up a small piece of
paper in front of her. She said, "Emso takes the cavalry forward to Tate to
assist the Eleven West Wolves attack the west flank. Cavalry sweeps the
rear." Her friends applauded wildly. The adults were stone silent until
someone said, "She's *reading.*" A low, worried buzz followed.

Gan walked toward the line of children. He stopped in front of one near
the middle. "Can you tell me what was written on the paper?"

She nodded. "Yes, Murdat."

"You can? You remember it?"

"No, Murdat."

He looked stern. "Then how can you tell me?"

She dodged between him and the girl next to her, running to the end of
the line, where she grabbed the paper and ran back. She handed it to Gan.
"It says what Priestess Sylah told us, Murdat. The other Priestesses made

us know how, and Priestess Sylah says if we can do this, we can tell people far away what we want them to know. Like you, if it was a real battle."

Someone in the crowd said, "One has to have permission to learn reading. It's the way."

Gan turned, deliberately avoiding looking in the direction the voice had come from. "Not any longer," he said. "Mistakes like that could cause my Wolves injury or death. We have the Messengers when we need them. We should have writing when we need it. All who wish to do these things in the future will be allowed." He pointed at the three stranger Priestesses. "All Chosens will be required. You are responsible."

Their smiles showed how readily they accepted their charge. They ushered the girls out, but Gan called to Sylah to join him and Neela. Drawing away from the crowd that was still bubbling about the game and its result, he said, "I've spoken to Clas. He told me of your decision concerning this thing you call the Door. I know nothing of that, I know nothing of any understanding between you and the Iris Abbess. I know my friend. I know you. Is there anything I can say or do—"

"No." Neela's voice cut his words off abruptly. "There's nothing." She took Sylah's hand between hers. "Our love and hope will go with you. Go when you choose. Come back to us as soon as you can."

Sylah kissed them both quickly, then hurried from the room.

Tate watched Conway's departing back from where he'd left her at her door. She called, "Wait a minute," and when he turned, she gestured him back. He came, mildly puzzled. She pointed at his face. "That's what's driving me nuts," she said, scowling. "You ought to at least look confused, or mystified, or seriously curious. *Something.* There's more life in these stone walls than you."

He shrugged. "I know. I'm sorry."

"That's no help, partner." Swiftly changing, she was sympathetic. "You can't mope forever, man. The lady will get better in her own time, her own way. You've got to live until then. Don't give up on me."

Defensively, he said, "I know I'm not much fun, but I'm not hurting anyone."

"That's not true. Everyone who knows you hurts with you, Matt. Why do you think Leclerc's moved back out to that old horse farm of Altanar's? He could do the same work here, but it tore him up to see you so down."

He leaned against the wall across the narrow hall from her. "I never thought anything like that could happen to me again. I was married before, you know. Had a child."

"I know." He looked up. She said, "I told you I was supposed to keep an eye on Falconer, remember? You were assigned to the same command group—if things went according to plan—and I had to read a personal synopsis on all of you."

"You never mentioned that." His expression soured.

"Different world. No point now. Except it brings us to what I wanted to talk to you about."

He was still irritated. It was several seconds before he said, "What's on your mind?"

"Sylah."

"Her? What about her? She's going off to hunt for Never-Never Land, or something, isn't she?"

"She's leaving here. From what I hear, Church claims there was a place called the Door, somewhere south of here. There was an organization called Teachers mixed up with it, somehow."

He cocked his head to the side. "You want to go with her."

"I want to look for something, Matt. Anything. I told you some of these women can stop conception through mind control, and about Clas stopping his own bleeding. What else is out there for us to discover? I mean, do we spend the rest of our lives refighting historical battles? What if this Door thing's another crèche? What if somebody else made it like we did, and they just stayed where they were? We could tell them what's happening here. Maybe we could even bring Teachers back here, something like that. If we go, we're *alive*. We're *doing* something."

"What about Louis? The other women?"

"I talked to them already. They've got work that pleases them. I'm not satisfied. Sylah doesn't know it yet, but I'm going with her." She straightened against the wall, daring him to contradict her.

He shook his head dubiously. "I don't know," he said. He seemed to be studying his boots. "It's a lot of maybes and what ifs. We already know how dangerous it is to travel. I don't think it's a smart idea. Not at all."

He walked away without looking back, eyes still on his boots. Their steady rhythm echoed back to her long after he disappeared from the patch of light thrown by the lamp next to her door. She listened carefully, telling herself there was a change in the rhythm, that his step had picked up a new firmness. But she wasn't certain.

Sylah stood with Clas on the balcony of their quarters. Arms around each others' waists, they looked up at a sky that had cleared since their talk on the beach. Stars glittered and sparkled against a moonless, cottony darkness.

There had been no conversation for a long time, nothing but a sort of communion as they shared the night and the knowledge that this was the last time it would happen for a long while.

Neither had yet been willing to suggest that it might be the last time. Sylah thought of the words as a knife, and the two of them were circling, waiting to see if the other would reach for it.

Clas said, "I had to tell Gan I was leaving. I think I have some courage, but I can't stand being near you, knowing you're leaving, any longer." A wry tone slipped into his voice. She pictured his crooked, deprecatory smile. He said, "Now I'm the one asking for understanding."

She tried to sound light. "And you have it. Women are better at this sort of thing."

He said, "And anything else. You think."

He was joking, making peace between them the only way he knew how. Her whole body trembled with love for him, the kindness, the strength, the tenderness.

She said, "Remember me, Clas. Please. Every minute, every day, think one small thought of me, and we'll be together, because you'll never be out of my mind or my heart. I'll be back. You'll be proud of me."

He turned her to face him. Above him a red-orange star gleamed torchfire. He said, "I could never be anything else. We're cursed, Sylah, you and I, and we're blessed. We've created a king and won his kingdom; now we're driven different ways. We belong to each other. We will win again. We will be together again. I love you, and I promise you it will be so."

She stepped inside his arms, melted into the support of them, blended her body to the hammering beat of his heart, felt herself lifted and cherished.

Loved.